THE ORDER

Kingdom of Fallen Ash

KATERINA ST CLAIR

The Order: Kingdom of Fallen Ash

Author: Katerina St Clair

Edited by: Kira Marie

Edited by: Caitlin Cook

Revised Edition

Contents

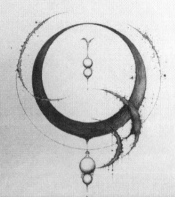

The Outer Lands

DEAR READERS,

To those whose true escape is bound by the words on the paper

PLAYLIST

Villain- Missio
Touch- Sleeping At Last
Another Love- Tom Odell
Where's My Love- SYML
Nothing Is As It Seems- Hidden Citizens
Game Of Survival- Ruelle
Possibility- Lykee Li
Mr. Sandman- SYML
I Found- Amber Run
Solider- Tommee Profitt & Fleurie

KATIANA

The muted colors of the medical wing blend together in perfect, insufferable unity. The space around me feels smaller, as if every drag of the clock's hand pulls the walls closer together. The annual Expulsion Tests have never been something I look forward to. Sometimes, covering the calendar and pretending the testing has already passed makes it easier to face it all at the end of every year. The Expulsion Tests are just one of the many responsibilities I took when I accepted the head position of New Haven's medical department.

No matter how much I prepare myself to begin administrational procedures, watching the Testing date draw near never gets easier.

My heels click against the cool tile floor in quick jolts, the noise it creates bouncing off the wall, only to be drowned out by the sounds of the machinery behind me eagerly buzzing with life. It's hard not to cover my head and bury it in this hell hole of a sweater clinging to my throat. Initially, on a brisk morning, it seemed like a good idea to wear such a thick piece of clothing. Now, every part of it itches along my skin, its coarse material rubbing against the bump of my stomach, accentuating a feature I am only now getting used to.

Gently, I run my hands along my stomach's smooth surface, feeling her small kicks hit against my palm with each press to my belly button with my fingers, my mouth curling into a smile at the slight sign of life. No one prepares you for the admiration you gain for life once you create one. The very morals I have chosen to follow no longer pertain to just me. That may be why I continue to allow myself to officiate the Expulsions. Somehow, I feel I am contributing to creating a better life for her and Kaiden.

Pulling away from my computer's screen, my cheeks flare with crimson heat, the countless mind-numbing minutes spent staring at each child's profile making the time pass that much slower. Waving my hand over the computer's surface, I let the heat it gives off warm my chill hands. The second to last profile of the day flashes along the screen, my silent wait finally ending. With three swift clicks, the file opens, sprawling out the four-year-old's life story in front of me, like she is merely just a number in a pool of thousands that New Haven houses.

The child has ringlets of blonde that frame her face perfectly, her eyes as blue as the ocean. Staring at the camera, her flushed, pink cheeks light up her beautiful smile, her skin void of any imperfections. Each part of her is perfect by design. I wouldn't be surprised if her parents predetermined her genetic structure before birth. Given her mother's brown hair and her father's brown eyes, her features are no doubt by design. They all hold each other happily in the photo, each one radiating perfection in their own individual way.

Scrolling through her profile, I let my eyes finally land on her class.

"Untouchable ... figures," I whisper under my breath, taking into account her perfectly ironed clothes and un-calloused hands.

Glancing behind me at the camera overlooking the room with a slow, blinking, red light, my fingers tap my desk in an attempt to let myself relax. Thankfully, the mics didn't pick up on my snide remark. With a quick scan, I look over the child's medical information. Never does an Untouchable child have any form of a health crisis after the strides my team made in our medical unit.

Around three years ago, while I was still interning to fortify any skills my Judgment Day tasks could no longer provide for me, I had forced myself into as many sleepless nights in the lab as I could, running on a theory that some of our most traditional herbs we often looked past could be used for something much more significant than what we once thought.

Initially, the solution I created could only ease infection. Now, it can repair major tears without leaving any trace of damage. We add to the original formula each year, growing the product's versatility for Untouchables across our sector.

At times, I wish that I had never invented the Cure-All so I'd actually have my work cut out for me regarding *our* side of society.

Continuing my scrolling, my eyes land on the girl's name.

"Lily Evermoore," I say, tapping the large screen.

Kicking my legs to slide the wheels of my stool across the floor, my hands work along the perfectly labeled cabinet that consumes most of the testing space. Dragging open the nearest drawer, I allow my hands to free a new neuro chip from its package, the emblem of our district staining the front of the small cloth package. Pulling on clean gloves, my head turns away to avoid the lingering pungent smell of latex that wafts near my nose. A small churn rises in my stomach.

Doing my best, I shove down my most unwanted pregnancy aversion in a place where I can never escape the smell I hate most.

"I know, angel. I know you hate it," I whisper, rubbing my stomach. With shallow breaths through my mouth, I grab a sterilized scalpel and some bandages, placing them flat on the surface of my medical tray.

My eyes gravitate to the small mask slung over the patient's chair, the toxic canister of Halloway Gas resting behind it. Five seconds with that mask over anyone's mouth and they are gone, as if there was never any life to begin with.

There may be more than one thing I regret creating for the greater good of New Haven.

"Mrs. Blackburn?" one of the nurse's quiet voices utters. Pulling my head away from my med tray, I let my empty thoughts fall before finally looking back at the clock mounted on the wall. Only fifteen minutes have passed since I pulled up Lily's profile.

"We're just waiting for your okay. The patient's mom and dad are eager to get home to celebrate dad's 'new placement' with his family," the nurse speaks, holding up her fingers in quotations.

I don't recognize her. Her badge is glossed with a new coat of plastic. She's a first year who most likely got placed here after her Judgment Day. She can't be any older than twenty-one. Her skin radiates a certain perfection but an utter lack of individuality, not that she can control the regulations set before one is even born.

The sky was filled with ash for months after the first and only Great War. I can't say anyone was surprised to learn how long it took our founders to rebuild our society after what was left.

Or should I say, who was left?

Humans have always been naive; some might even say they could not find true peace before the government we call Sanctum took over. Women had gone infertile and countless men had gone sterile. The human race as we knew it was a mere few months away from its demise. A few months after the ash had settled, some survivors created a safe space in the Pacific Northwest, a place we used to call North America. The very genetic makeup of the human race had been forever altered by man's selfish need to absolve conflict with violence.

Nearly thirty years of countless deaths and back-breaking labor ensued before the ward came up. Society rebuilt from the bottom up, all thanks to the advancements in technology our government had provided. After New Haven's ward came up, genetic testing followed shortly after. Blemishes became nonexistent. Individuality ceased to exist. Diseases were eradicated within the womb. A new era of divine innovation created the first generation of children unaffected by the nuclear fallout. Soon after, we implemented the Great Divide before turning to the neurostimulation chips to hold the peace. No longer would there be chaos, panic, and fear of how the human race would survive.

In many ways, that's why we do the Expulsions.

Without the Expulsion Tests, we wouldn't be able to control those who cannot conform to the unity and order needed within our society. Sanctum keeps us safe and upholds this society's virtues.

Let one slip through the crack, and the perfect order around us falters.

At least, that's what I tell myself.

"Send her in," I finally urge with a slight wave of my hand.

Giving me a nod, she pulls away, her brown hair swaying in her long ponytail as she flashes a passing doctor a set of perfectly white teeth.

My fingers roll over my eyelids, rubbing away the pain the luminescent screen has brought to my eyes. Forest jolts in my stomach once more, my morbid thinking slowly dwindling as a smile encapsulates my face.

"Two more tests, little one, and we can finally go home," I whisper, pulling up the child's scorecard.

Lingering my cursor over the result I have been clicking all day, the want to mark the last two scorecards with a result of Cleansed and walk out of here has never felt more appealing. Once a year, they make us administer the tests, and once a year, we are faced with nothing but hours of the same results. Cleansed after Cleansed walks through the door, making each test seem increasingly more pointless.

I had always thought it was an honor to have been given such a significant role so young on my Judgment Day. Sometimes the job seems so easy I almost question why I was picked.

The sound of three knocks fills the room, the pretty nurse swinging open the door only moments later. Moving into the space, a pair of youthful blue eyes meet my brown ones, pulling me away from my seated position. My hands shake at the thought of something going wrong, or, even worse, having to administer an Expulsion. Pulling my dead expression into a smile, my hands stay deep within the pockets of my lab coat. The bright white LED lights illuminate the space, the small girl, Lily, holding a teddy bear close to her. The nurse urges her farther into the room with tiny pushes, both of us watching her gaze fixate on the oversized chair before landing on my enormous belly. Her small eyes squint, as if it is all too much at once for a child of her age.

"Hello, Lily, I am Doctor Blackburn. I will administer your chip insertion and test today along with nurse...," embarrassed at my lack of knowledge of the woman's name, I trail off.

"Amy," the woman says with a reassuring tone. Her fingers fidget with her badge, her legs a shaking mess.

Her clothes are ironed to perfection in a way that indicates they have never been worn. Her anxieties roll off of her like rain down a gutter. If I had to guess, this was her first time aiding an Expulsion test.

"Nurse Amy," I reiterate, the small girl's eyes squinting again in observance.

"Are the lights bothering you?" I question, motioning Amy to close the door. Slowly, she nods her head, motivating me to dim the lights. Shadows cast across the space, her eyes finally opening fully, her body relaxing slightly. Creeping closer to the oversized chair, she tosses the teddy she had brought with her in the seat, looking back to me for reassurance on what her next move should be.

"You can get on it," I urge. Lily scrambles to pull herself onto the seat, my hands outreached, instinctively moving to help her.

"I can do it," Lily says with a nose scrunch, her face pulling into a look of determination. After a few seconds, she is fully seated in the chair, her teddy staying between her arm and side, her hands rubbing it for comfort.

"So, Lily, what year are you?" I question. Amy trails behind me, her presence like a shadow. Typical with most first-year medical residents, she retains every bit of information she can, watching as I pass her a sterile wipe while pointing to the back of my ear.

"I'm still in primaries," Lily's high-pitched voice responds, her head flinching away from Amy's graze behind her right ear. Hesitance lines the child's face, her body moving as far away from the nurse as possible.

With a gloved hand, I sit back in my chair, rolling over to the pair, before taking the wipe away from Amy. With gentle hands, I run my hands through Lily's hair to soothe her. Progressively, she relaxes into my touch, allowing me to sterilize the skin quickly.

"I'm assuming you've done this before?" Amy questions jokingly.

"Once or twice."

"Do you mind grabbing the tray?" I ask. Amy nods, moving to my silver tray of tools. Her hands grab the small neuro chip, balancing it in her palm. Rolling over the cart filled with test supplies, its squeaky wheels turn. Lily's eyes watch the movements with genuine curiosity.

"Is that a chip like my mom and dad have?" Lily questions with a certain eagerness.

I sometimes forget how excited some can become to have the stability of their chips. It is nice to know you will always have regulations. No more sleepless nights, no more pain. The chips can turn the most rampant mind into one of the calmest in a matter of seconds. Imagine a lifetime of never wondering if your body is in peak condition.

With the chips, it's a guarantee.

Responding, I brush my hand over the scar behind my ear.

"We all have them, every four-year-old like you gets to come in and get their chip. However, not all of them have curls as pretty as yours," I whisper quietly, giving her cheek a slight pinch.

Her laugh lights up the silent space like a star in a dark sky. Even Amy smiles. Placing the chip in my hand, I reach for the small incision blade, keeping Lily's attention away from my hands.

"Why is your belly so big?" Lily questions. Her eyes stay focused on my torso as I tap behind her ear. She doesn't react to pressure on her skin. Good to know. The numbing properties of the wipe have already gone into effect.

It's easy to look past the lack of weight on most people in New Haven. The food regulations have made it impossible to put on excess weight. Even when pregnant, my portions have only grown by a few measly extra calories. We can blame the old society's obesity and health issues for that lovely regulation.

"My daughter is in there," I say, pressing the thin blade down the back of her ear.

Amy winces at the sight with a look of disgust. Slowly, I gravitate closer, watching the chip's spindles seep into the cut, its light moving from a dull white to light green. Clenching her palm, Lily's nose flares as she takes in a sharp breath, her eyes blinking repeatedly at the lingering feeling of the chip slipping behind her skin. The green light grows duller behind the skin of her ear. Quickly, I spray on a dose of our Cure-All, watching her skin close as the lesion becomes nothing but the scar that we all share.

"What's your daughter's name?" Lily questions, her hand gravitating behind her ear, feeling her new scar.

"Forest," I say, staring at the Re-Regulation Device on the tray. It blinks in an attempt to pair with her chip.

"Maybe when she is out of you, I can meet her," Lily says.

Caught off guard by her tiny hand landing on my stomach, I stare at her with wide eyes as she smiles at the bump. Forest's feet kick beneath her touch, Lily letting out a small chuckle at the gesture.

The pure innocence that looms over her is nothing short of euphoric.

"I would like that very much," I say.

Amy's voice clears.

"Ma'am, it's ready," Amy whispers. Refocusing my attention on the Re-Regulation Device, its green light syncs up with Lily's neuro chip in gentle strobes. Looking flustered, Lily pulls her hand away from my stomach. Grabbing the device with steady hands, her eyes are wide as she looks over the slight gleam of the green light. As always, I program the usual set of commands into the device.

Stand with verbal cues.

The device's screen flashes as I begin running the simple code.

"Alright, Lily, go ahead and stand up for me," I order.

With no hesitation, she slides off the chair, her tiny feet hitting the floor with a thud. Turning toward her teddy, my fingers are already inputting the following command.

Leave the teddy bear on the chair.

My stomach drops as her hand continues to reach for the small bear, her hands enclosing around its soft material, dragging it closer to her petite frame, my throat going dry as I try to process what has just happened.

"I must have input the code wrong," I whisper, frantically retyping the code. Amy's confusion consumes her face, her eyes still fixated on Lily. I angle my body away from prying eyes, not once letting anyone see the device or the codes being input into it. I type in the prompt again, run the program, and wait for her to place the teddy bear where I have coded her to do so.

She never does.

"Dr. Blackburn, is everything alright?" Amy questions silently.

"Lily, put the bear back on the chair," I commanded clearly to the wide-eyed girl.

With great hesitance, she puts it back.

"Amy, grab the scalpel," I order, the nurse's attention finally focusing back on me. With a nod, she grabs the small blade, Lily's hands shaking as I input the next set of code. The cool metal of the medical device presses into my palm like an unbearable weight. Once filled with pure innocence, the space around me is now filled with nothing but fear.

"What are you doing?" Lily questions, her voice lined with fear.

"Amy, run the program," I order, watching the nurse's perfectly manicured fingers press down on the screen of the Re-Regulation Device.

Cut the right pointer and forget the action. End Expulsion test.

"Lily, I need you to cut your right pointer finger, and then I want you to forget it all. Please, tell me you can do that for me," I whisper as I press the blade into her hand. The shift between confusion and fear in her eyes has never been more haunting.

Her small hand tosses the blade across the room, a look of confusion and fear swirling in her eyes—the surgical tool skids across the white tile floor. Lily moves to grasp her teddy bear.

My heart rate accelerates, my body turning toward Amy with a panic I had not noticed had crept inside me.

"Rerun it!" I yell in a plea.

Once more, Amy hits the Re-Regulation Device's screen. Lily continues to flee toward her furry sense of comfort.

"What's going on?" Amy mutters in a shaky voice.

Feeling my frustrations rise as I look at the small girl's flailing figure, I see it now: no more smiles for her parents, no more small euphoric laughs, no more stolen moments of happiness.

"Grab her," I utter, both of us moving toward the terrified child. Her hands barely reach her teddy bear as I hold her head down. Her arms and legs begin to kick, her body thrashing against our strength. Amy looks distraught at the sight, only adding to the weight of shame suddenly looming over me. As I reach for the Halloway Gas, my eyes fill with a blurry mess of emotion.

"I promise I will do better!" Lily screams at the top of her lungs as I continue to hold her down. Feeling my hands shake, I force the small mask over her screaming mouth, her lungs burning with determination to pull away from us. Her instinct to fight runs through her, urging my hand to press down harder. Listening to her pain escape her throat, I motion for Amy to flip on the gas.

"It wasn't your fault. There is no other way," I yell in a petrified tone, doing all I can to hold it together, the odorless gas working through the mask with ease.

Her strong kicks and hard grasp on us slowly decrease the longer her screams force her to intake the gas. Her body's valiant fight only grows weaker with each small whimper escaping her lungs. Her chest's large heaves die down to nothing. The bright sparkle in her eyes fades away, shrouded by the watchful shadow of death. The hand clenching the tail of the teddy loosens its grasp, her eyes hazy as life drains from her. My hands shake, trailing across the switch that dictates the gas's release. Stopping her body from slumping to the floor, I move her back into a comfortable position in the chair, no fight left in the small, lifeless body. Amy looks flustered, her eyes scanning over the young child. Tears roll down my cheeks, painting Lily's front in wet abrasive splotches.

"Time of death for patient Lily Evermoore-" I begin, letting my eyes land on the one clock in the room.

It's hard not to laugh at the vile humor in how little time has passed.

Only twenty minutes.

"4:35 PM," I finish, urging Amy's reluctant figure closer to my computer to update her chart. Feeling my emotions grow as I touch my stomach; Lily's blonde curls are now a matted mess from the resistance of her head against my hand.

"She was Tainted," I continue as I draw deep breaths. "She's no longer an Untouchable,"

"What is her class now?" Amy questions, my hands searching under the small girl's shirt for any sign of her altered genetic makeup. Right on her hip bone, I see it now, an intricate white scar with overlapping crescent patterns and circles. It clings to her perfect skin like a diamond in the rough. With astonishment, I allow my fingers to pass over the slight imperfection—scarred, rigid skin.

Imperfect in all the right ways.

"She's Marked...Change her class to Tainted," I whisper, Amy's head returning toward the screen. Feeling myself move the teddy bear back into Lily's arms as I draw shaky breath, Amy's hands still on the keyboard as if she struggles to fathom what to type. Watching her blankly stare as her eyes absorb the screen's light, her once quick movements are now sluggish.

"Take your break, beautiful. You didn't see anything happen in this room," a booming voice says as the door swings open.

Watching Amy blink back her stare, a dull green light gleams behind her ear, her body moving in uniform precision as she blankly stares toward the door's exit. Two Officials stand, holding the door open with cheeky grins, a Re-Regulation Device pointed straight at Amy, her eyes blank as she casually walks past the pair. I see the tiny black bag slung over the tallest man's shoulder, my throat going dry, my hand already using my sweater to wipe away the few tears that had escaped my eyes. Lily's open file still has no class. With a few steps, the men move toward the computer, changing her class to Tainted as I had instructed Amy to do.

"She was going to change the class. Why utilize her chip? She was doing her job just fine," I question, shaking my head at the men.

"Commander's new rules. The fewer people that know of the Marked, the better," the taller man, Adam, says with a great deal of disgust toward me.

I've seen Adam at quite a few socials thrown for Official families every so often. On the surface, he seems charming. He's a man my husband often finds companionship in. Personally, I have always found him insufferably egotistical.

"That would have been lovely to know before I allowed her to help me administer an Expulsion Test," I hiss with annoyance. Adam shakes his head as his counterpart, Nick, pulls the bag away from his large friend's grasp. The men move toward Lily with careless banter. Moving in front of the men, my hands are raised in front of me in defense.

"She has parents waiting outside in the lobby for her-"

"Good thing their chips work. Maybe they never really had a daughter," Nick says, his hands shoving the black bag to the floor, his knuckles white as he forces the bag open. Adam's hands gently move me, pulling me further from the chair. I can feel Forest's kicks accelerate as my heart rate begins to climb. Adam's hand spins his Re-Regulation Device, tapping it to the side of my head with a taunt, his finger rising to my cheek to wipe away a wet spot I had missed. I watch his eyes narrow the longer he watches me, the clench he has on my arm becoming that much more uncomfortable.

"I hope you were not crying over something as filthy as a Marked," Adam hisses, both of us watching Nick drag Lily's body off the chair and straight to the floor. Her motionless figure rolls into the body bag with ease. I wince at the sight of Nick tossing her teddy into the bin where all the discarded needles go. Her lifeless eyes stick to mine as Nick slowly zips up the bag. My jaw clenches in a sorry attempt to try and refocus my thoughts. "Because if you were, we would need to reconsider your position as head of the Expulsion Test Administration," Adam finishes, forcing my chin toward him to allow my eyes to meet his own.

This is how Officials are. They are arrogant and cocky bastards who feel as if they are above everyone else. Hand one of them a light sensor prod and give them the authority to dictate, and you get Adam. His gray beard and piercing dark brown eyes make him look years older than he is. I feel it now, his utter want to be above everyone in this room.

"If I recall, you have a mother who was saved by *my* Cure-All and a sister whose kidney was replaced in advance of thirty other Unfortunates who were in line before her simply because you knew me. I suggest you tread carefully in how you speak to me. Don't ever question my commitment to my job or my loyalty to Sanctum," I hiss back.

Adam's face pulls into a look of satisfaction, his mouth releasing a small scoff. Grunting as he slings the bag over his shoulder, Nick shoves past me, hauling the girl's frail body away from the premises.

"For the sake of your daughter's life," Adam says with a small press to my stomach. "I hope your loyalty runs true," Adam says in anything but a sincere tone.

Is that a threat?

"What do you do with the Marked?" I question. "When an Untouchable or Unfortunate dies, we take them to be cremated. Why bag a Marked body?" I ask with a great deal of sincerity.

"Knowing that information is outside your job description, Katiana. I would focus on getting this place back together. You still have one more Expulsion test, and it's on an *Unfortunate*," he says disgustedly. "So, make sure you use the thick pair of gloves before getting near *it*," Adam says in a snap.

Like Nick, he moves toward the door's exit, tapping the clock above the doorway. Watching his mouth upturn into a cat-like grin, a maniacal laugh gently bellows from his chest.

"Only thirty minutes left on your shift; maybe you can take out another Marked and an Unfortunate all at once," Adam sneers, shutting the door with a thud.

My breath shudders. My mind reflects on the girl's parents and what they have unknowingly lost. Years of memories of a child they had raised and nurtured, stolen in a mere few moments with a chip they have been told is there to monitor their health.

A whole life stolen from their minds, as if their daughter never even existed.

"Doctor Blackburn, your final patient is on their way in," the intercom says in a loud, scratchy tone, forcing me to focus on the room, allowing my mind to retrace the chaos that had ensued.

"This is the only way," I remind myself, working to rearrange my items back into optimal appearance. The knob slowly turns once more. A young brunette boy in tattered clothing meets my line of vision. His toothy grin grows wide while mine stays smothered by the weight of my actions.

"It has to be," I finish, shoving down the large lump in my throat and forcing on a new pair of gloves.

CHAPTER ONE

FOREST

The sunrise brings on a mirage of bright colors that unfurl across my bedroom floor in varying hues of pink and orange. Despite the drawn curtains, each ray of sunlight blankets the room in all the right ways, as if it mocks the countless dull, gray tones encasing nearly every item in the space. I watch the rays dance over my dresser before landing on my soft white comforter. The sun's heat touches my face as the cool August air slips through a crack in my bedroom window I had created the night before. A perfectly ironed uniform lays peacefully unbothered on my dresser. Its black bottoms and white blouse only add to the bleakness of the space around me. Still, I silently thank my mother for always finding the time to lay out my school clothes the night before despite how tired I know she is from her night shift at New Haven Medical.

I stretch out, cracking my back as I rise to a seated position in my bed, and my hair slips into my mouth as the fog of sleep begins to leave my bloodshot eyes.

"Mandatory wakeup for Forest Blackburn," my clock's annoyingly robotic voice says in a tone that jolts me awake entirely. Its screen flashes, waiting for me to confirm I have heard its message, as if I have the option to decline.

"I was already up, you asshole," I whisper, angrily hitting the green check, confirming I am up to anyone and everyone in this house. I see the other members of my family's icons all checked green. As usual, I am the only person in my family who has woken up at 6:00 am. Everyone else wakes up nearly an hour before we are regulated to do so.

"Negative statements against New Haven regulated home care aids is a low-level violation. Confirm this message has been received," the clock says, urging me to let out a small groan of discomfort. I press my hands to my face, raising my middle fingers in the space around me. Hiding the vulgar gesture from the clock's camera, I flash it a wide smile.

"Confirmed," I say in the fakest tone possible. The clock's screen goes black as it finally decides to leave me alone.

My room is nothing special. It's a space filled with perfectly fitted furniture made of sleek aspen wood. Each wall is painted in a calm gray tone, the floor composed of birch wood boards, all sanded to perfection. Every nook and cranny of this room is within Sanctum regulations. Even the drawings I had once plastered on my wall are now crammed away in one of my many sketchbooks shoved under my bed. One look from one of my dad's co-workers, and they were torn away from the wall.

Gray paint streaks the front of my dresser and doors. Every article of clothing I own is neatly tucked away. I've got nothing but school clothes and a few leisure day outfits. It's insufferable wearing the same things year-round. Sometimes I envy the Unfortunates' tattered and patched clothes.

At least they get some variety.

I stare at the few bits of jewelry I have within regulation. Two pairs of earrings and one necklace are all I own, and even then they are only permitted for formal events. With a roll, I move away from my bed and closer to my dresser. The floorboards creak beneath my feet, shivers running down my spine. My hands fiddle with the uniform my mother laid out, dragging it closer toward me.

"I wonder what I'm wearing today," I whisper sarcastically, tossing the clothes on the bed.

The same black slacks and white blouse I wear daily sprawl before me. A gray tie, white socks, and a black belt all look as unappealing as the day before. I run my hands through my mess of hair, feeling it brush below my lower back. The brown curls stick together as a single gray hair pokes out in my vision. With a quick snap, I pull away the stray hair. My mother would have a fit if she knew my gray was already starting to show.

With a gentle toss, I pry away my sleepwear, letting it land in the nearby hamper. The air from my window caresses my body as I change, my eyes avoiding my hip entirely, ignoring the dreadful mark I always do my best to cover up. I feel the gnarled skin beneath my fingertips while I pull up my pants. The birthmark lingers on my skin, standing out in a way most Unfortunates do. Ugly and unnatural. My mom says it's best to ignore it's there, and seeing as no one else seems to have one, I have always found it easy to keep my mouth shut about it.

Slowly, I pull over the white blouse and button it up to my neck, fiddling with the wire of my bra as I position my breasts in a comfortable spot. With three tucks, my shirt is in the waistband of the slacks, my hands yanking on the belt to give myself some shape in this outfit. I let the tie hang loose around my neck, hoping someone else would try and tackle it for me. With a large wooden brush, I mangle my hair, allowing myself to pull it back into a ponytail, keeping every stray hair away from my face.

In addition to the uniforms, hair and what we may do with it is one of the other regulations the New Foundations Academy implemented. No hairstyles other than a ponytail, bun, braid, or straight down our backs are allowed. No makeup or distracting facial enhancers are allowed anywhere near your face. Vanity derives from many things, as does lust in young men for something as simple as a pair of earrings. All potential distractions have been eradicated.

Sometimes, it's hard to imagine anyone wearing anything remotely distracting. In history class, our teachers tell us of the vanity that used to consume humans before the nuclear wars. They call it a poison that infiltrated the minds of many. Part of the coding behind our chips ensures that trivial things like vanity and jealousy are almost non-existent.

Running my hands over my jewelry before pressing my fingers to the small necklace around my throat, I feel its small silver charm rub between my fingers before tucking it beneath my shirt. I've never been caught wearing it, regardless of it being against regulation. At times, it feels like my good luck charm.

I take one final glance at my figure in the mirror above my dresser. The uniform clings to my thin body, and I notice how the supple curve of my breasts and legs fill the material just right. For a few years, nothing fit me well. It's all hazy, but, after a summer of puberty and plenty of supplements given to me by my mother, I finally started fitting into the clothes in ways I always wished I would. Max and Raegan barely recognized me when I met them for the tram that school year.

Moving toward my door, I nudge it open with a swing, gravitating closer to the bathroom between my brother's room and mine.

The light shines brightly within the bathroom, Kai is already in front of the sink, meticulously brushing his teeth. He's making sure he doesn't brush too little or too long on each tooth. His uniform is the same as my own. The only real difference between the uniforms of the men and women who attend New

Foundation's Academy is that women may wear skirts if it's warm enough outside. His shirt lays smoothly on his chest. His tie folded to perfection.

He grunts once I try to move past him to grab my toothbrush, glancing down at me with a full mouth, letting out an irritated scoff. Still, I shove past him, gathering a small dollop of toothpaste on my brush. Unlike him, I could be more precise.

Vigorously, I brush my teeth in large strokes back and forth, Kai is beside me, spitting up his toothpaste before rinsing his mouth. I watch him as he dabs his lips with a towel, leaning his hip into the counter to observe me.

"Did you get dressed in the dark?" Kai questions with a smile. Giving him a playful nudge, I threaten to swipe him with my dirtied bristles.

"I decided to sleep in, unlike you," I say with a full mouth. Kai scrunches his nose, motioning me to spit. I oblige with a roll of my eyes.

His hands fiddle with my tie as I wipe my mouth. His fingers work quickly, managing to fold my tie even better than his own. His curly brown hair bounces with each movement, most of his body taking up the space around us. He towers over nearly every member of our family. My mom and dad are not sure how he got so tall. Genetically, Kaiden was bred to be no more than 6 feet. Now he towers at a large 6'2". Sometimes I question if he even knows how to use his long legs. Each step he takes is like a baby gazelle walking for the first time.

His brown-green eyes land on my green ones as he finally finishes sorting me out.

"I heard your clock tell you off this morning," Kai begins, moving away from the bathroom, hitting the light switch. Trailing behind his slim figure, I let his long strides devour my short ones.

"What's new?" I question with a scoff.

"You know they keep track of that, right? Enough low-level violations and you have to talk to an Official before doing some community time," Kai says.

I almost feel satisfied knowing they'd dress me in something other than this insufferable uniform for community time.

"Who's doing community time?" my mother's gentle voice questions as we finally turn the corner into the kitchen. She wears dark blue scrubs.

Blue is the customary color for all of those in the health field.

The table is filled with our regulated breakfast portions. Each meal resides in a small glass container, delivered by Unfortunates every morning like clockwork. The steam hits the top of the glass container in white swirls. Kai tosses himself into his seat, promptly pouring a massive mug of black coffee. My father flashes me a smile before returning to the silent sips of his mug. He speaks on his phone, droning on about some Unfortunate affairs he is tackling this week. I hear his frustrations rise as he leans against the wall. His eyes trail out the window in the kitchen, his chair at the head of the table pushed away from its usual spot. The call must have been sudden for him to speak during breakfast like this.

"No one is doing community time," I say after a moment. Sliding in next to Kai, I pull away the top from my breakfast portion. Eggs and bacon again.

"Unless your name is Forest and you tell off your clock for doing its job every morning," Kai says. His fork poking his eggs, my mother's eyebrows rising.

"Forest, I asked you to stop doing that," my mother says with some frustration.

I narrow my eyes at my brother while reaching for the coffee pot. He slides it away from my grasp with one motion.

"I want some too."

"Mom and Dad haven't gotten seconds yet. Plus, you get jittery every time you drink it, and, frankly, I don't feel like dealing with that today," Kai says.

"Forest," my mother's voice says once more. "I need you to promise you will stop being so careless with your actions. Violations are not something to take lightly," my mom finishes.

My dad slowly lowers his phone.

"I understand," I start, trying to reach for Kai's mug of coffee. His hand swats me away, my dad finally taking a seat at the table.

"The only people who should worry about the violations are Unfortunates. Even a high-level violation for us is nothing but a slap on the wrist and some grief from an Official," my dad says with a smile.

Unfortunates.

The people who have been placed on the lowest totem pole of this society. Here in the Untouchable sector of New Haven, we have a good thing. We continue to create advancements in this society that better the people. Unlike Unfortunates, we were born to do something more significant. We are more innovative, cleaner, and advanced in our thinking.

The Unfortunate sector lies on the other end of New Haven. Like most bottom feeders, they reside in a separate commune, not ever leaving the comforts of their hell hole. Some Unfortunates work in the primary strip market, while others run transportation or deliver food for the Untouchables. Unfortunates have been tasked to do the work our people cannot be asked to do. Farming, electrical, grunt military work, and all other undesirable tasks are left in the laps of Unfortunates. Once they are away from their sector, Unfortunates are only permitted to speak to Untouchables if they are in an academic or work setting. Speaking outside of regulation can result in immediate punishment by an Official or an Untouchable.

In most scenarios, Untouchables roughing up Unfortunates is far from uncommon. They were bred to do the work our people did not want to do. They live to serve. We live to survive. That's the only way this society functions. As far as anyone is concerned in this sector, they are hardly people. When our school implemented its hybrid program, welcoming a select few Unfortunates to be put in our academic setting to "further educate the bottom feeders," people were furious.

"You should listen to your mother, Forest," my dad continues, placing his phone face down as he speaks. "You don't want a list of violations on your scorecard when it is time for your Judgment Day," he finishes. Placing a piece of bacon in my mouth, I process his words.

In no way does New Haven's government-elected leaders deciding what career I am stuck with for the rest of my life sound appealing. The chips are supposed to gather the data they need to create a proper placement for each individual in New Haven. Judgment Day is something most people look forward to. Kai has had his outfit picked out for months and even convinced our parents to splurge on champagne for the event. I hardly make it through a school day without zoning out.

"What was your phone call about?" I question, my fork shovels a mound of eggs into my mouth. Kai gives me a disgusted scrunch of his nose.

"Forest, no work talks at the table."

"It's fine, Katiana," my dad says, shaking his head. "A few Unfortunates working the market have decided stealing from our people was appropriate. They took extra food rations and a few items worth some money that they planned to distribute in their sector. I had my men take care of them," my father says with great pride. I watch him take a long sip from his coffee. It's as if he's washing down the words he just spoke with the dignity he must feel.

"Good for you, Dad," Kai says with a smile. I watch the men clink mugs as my mom's face stays abnormally stoic.

"One less Unfortunate, the better," I grin. My mom's eyes dart up to me as she narrows them. As quickly as it happened, it disappeared.

Something was hidden behind that look. Something is always hidden behind her small gestures. Whenever I pry her on it, she goes silent, unwilling to elaborate.

"I'm raising you both well!" my dad gleams with a large grin. My mother's voice is clear, her hand harshly lowering her mug to the birch table.

"Can we please not speak of Unfortunate affairs at this table? It makes me sick to hear," my mom says with a small grovel of emotion lining her tone. I sit back in my chair to look her over. It's hard to decipher whether or not Unfortunates or the conversation as a whole makes her feel so indifferent.

"Sympathy for Unfortunates is a medium-level violation," the house's security system says calmly. My mother's cheeks flush. Her hands run through her hair. My dad frowns, her head shaking toward him with annoyance. Her chair quickly backs away from the table as she swipes her portion tray. I watch her move toward the kitchen. The house waits for her to confirm its message.

"Understood!" she says after a few moments of scrubbing her glass container in the sink.

I feel a hand touch my leg in a firm grasp. My father's eyes linger on my own, his head leaning in to whisper.

"Your mother works with Unfortunates and Untouchables. Her lines sometimes blur," my father whispers, watching me pull away with a look of confusion. "Do not look at her differently when she needs guidance away from her good nature toward them," my father says sternly.

My mom stares forward blankly into the running water of the sink. With a grab to my portion container, I move away from the table and closer to my mother. Her head turns as I drop my container in the sink. She wipes away what I can only assume is a tear, taking a deep breath. Her delicate hands and sharp brown eyes pull her face together. Her hand dips into her pocket, quickly pulling out a small white pill. She places it in my hand, casually looking at my brother and father behind me. The two men engage in deep banter about Unfortunate affairs. My dad's slightly gray-streaked black hair and facial stubble age him years beyond what he is. His green eyes are piercing in contrast to my own. With a press to my palm, she forces the medication into concealment.

"You're supposed to be grabbing this from the *spot* in your bedroom every morning. Don't forget," my mother whispers as I quickly take the pill. It falls down my throat with ease. Its coating is bitter, only diluting in taste once I take a quick drink of the running sink water.

Unlike Kai, I still struggle with significant flaws despite the perfection supposedly coded into most Untouchable children. Ever since I was little, I've had minor episodes in which I would be absent from my mind. It was as if I had stepped away from my line of vision, only to come to and have no idea where I had gone or how I had gotten back. These absent moments concerned my mom enough that she started investigating them as soon as she noticed. As far as I know, from what she has told me, I am not the only one who struggles with these episodes. Regardless, she hasn't told my father, and the few times Kai has seen me take a pill, he often ignores it as if he can wipe the image from his mind. I know deep down my father has suspicions, but it's easier to have him believe what he wants rather than give him another thing to add to his list of reasons why he is disappointed in me.

A small, painful pluck from my head pulls me away from my train of thought. My mom drops my silver piece of hair in the sink, both of us watching it go down the drain with the flow of the water.

"You're supposed to tell me when it starts showing," my mom says softly, leaning into the sink.

For some reason, the women in our family have spouts of silver in their hair that never seem to go away. Regardless of age, our hair streaks with gray if not dyed. For as long as I can remember, my mom has always been able to hide her gray. On the other hand, I can never seem to go a month before it starts showing again.

"I forgot," I say through a lie. Kai's long arm wraps around my shoulder, pulling me closer to him. His weight and backpack have no trouble dragging me away from the kitchen and my mother's wary eyes. I grab my bag, slinging it over my shoulders.

The contrast in items that Kai and I carry to school is comically different. Kai's bag is filled to the brim with science papers and history study guides that threaten to spill from the zipper of his backpack. My bag stays close to my side with nothing but my sketchbook and a vial of my mother's Cure-All. You never know when you might need to heal a wound, or so that's my mother's mentality.

I tuck my student ID into my pocket as Kai continues pulling my shirt toward the front door.

"I can get a head start without you," I groan. Kai's wide grin consumes his face before he speaks.

"Right, and that's why we are almost always late to the tram," Kai says with a certain superiority that I know he thinks he has.

I wave at my parents, watching my dad make his way over to my mother. Her head leans into his chest as he holds her. I watch his thumbs gently run up and down her side, something inside me focusing on the touch. Her face grows red, her mouth curling into a smile as he presses his lips to her forehead. I feel pain at the sight of the sweet, tender touches. My chest feels heavy, and a feeling of absence weighs down on me.

Kai taps our icons on the panel of the front door's security system, indicating both he and I are off and on our way to New Foundation's Academy. With a shake of my head, I look away from my parents, shoving down that sudden feeling of hurt inside me. A small ping of pain shoots up my side, my mouth hissing back a groan.

Kai snaps his head at me as he shuts the door. I press my hand to my hip, letting my fingertips feel the warm skin beneath my touch.

"What's wrong?" he questions worriedly.

"Nothing," I lie.

But something was wrong.

My birthmark burns beneath my touch. The skin feels like it was scorched with a hot branding prod. The pain is sudden and unexpected.

"What the hell?" I whisper under my breath.

It leaves as quickly as it comes, taking all my worries along with it. I let go of my teeth's grasp on my lip as we move forward. I hear our feet scuff the ground, feeling relief as we descend from the house toward our tram to the Academy.

CHAPTER TWO

FOREST

"Can you imagine everyone still driving on the roads like they used to?" I question, passing our father's car in the driveway.

When the resources for gasoline began to dwindle and emissions from the vehicles began impacting the air quality, the need and want for vehicles in New Haven slowly died out. Most material used for transportation vehicles was then utilized for building the trams. A few key personnel, like my father, were awarded the luxury of cars for their commutes to keep their affairs to themselves. For everyone else, vehicles aren't needed as there's nowhere a tram can't take you.

Unfortunates run all the trams, and, in return, they are occasionally housed for short periods in our section of New Haven.

Not that they deserve it.

"Did you know it was sort of a rite of passage for children to be given a car when they were sixteen? Imagine first years driving one of those things," Kai says with a small gasp. I try to picture Academy first year students behind the wheel of a car.

"I think anyone today would see it as nothing more than an Unfortunate's job. Even Dad has Unfortunates drive him in his car sometimes," I say. Kai lets out another laugh.

"You think you could drive it if you had to?"

I reflect on the intricate interior of our father's car, with buttons and controls that are all foreign to me.

"If I had a light sensor prod to my back, then maybe."

We both rub our arms, walking in an unspoken unison. Leaves line the street in piles. The trees have shifted from luscious green to the burnt oranges and yellows of fall. I hear crunching beneath my feet with each step. Despite all the fallen leaves, the street is clean and orderly. Not one crack can be found in the sidewalk's smooth, concrete surface.

"Was it weird today at breakfast, with Mom, I mean?" I question after a few moments of silence. The contents of our bags clink together as we walk. The air seems chiller, almost like the question lingering between us has only cooled our bodies more.

"Like Dad said, lines between the Unfortunates and the Untouchables blur at times because of her work," Kai says. His words echo like a voice box for my father. I sometimes wonder if he's ever had an individual thought that wasn't meant to satisfy others.

"That's not what I asked, Kai."

My hands are shoved deep into my pockets. My fingers toy with a small thread for some sense of distraction. Once more, silence is all I hear.

"Yes, it was weird," he says, speaking like he is only now processing the abnormality of the situation.

"Blackburn!" a familiar voice yells in a sweet tone.

A pair of blonde twins wait at the tram stop, looking straight toward us. I see the other students linger by the stop in waves of black and gray. Each one wears their customary gray tie and bleak uniform. Raegan's manicured pastel pink nails wave in the air toward us. Her long blonde hair is wound into a bun, and her uniform is in perfect condition, just like Kai's. I see her large bag bounce with each step toward us. Her hands clutch a thermos similar to Kai's. Her blue eyes lock onto mine with a scrunch.

I watch her brother's smile grow bigger the closer they get to us. Max's taller stature and perfectly white teeth only add to his attractiveness and, given his athletic build, it's hard not to look at Max a little closer. His tie loosely hangs from his neck. His bag stays partially open. Both twins radiate an unshakable beauty neither my brother nor I can look past. My brother's eyes remain on Raegan like a moth to a flame.

Max and Raegan Vega have been with us for as long as I can remember. Their father got promoted around the same time my father did, and because of it, our housing has never been far apart. From childhood to now, they've been consistently in our lives. The twins are twenty and in their fifth year at New Foundation's Academy. Kai is almost exactly a year older and in his sixth and final year at the

Academy. It's bittersweet to see his last year finally approaching. I can already see him in a position like my father's, decorated with several awards for his academic merit. His Judgment Day will be something impossible for me to compete with. He and the Vega twins have years of accomplishments under their belt.

I have nothing.

"To think I almost thought you two were going to be late," Raegan says, her arms wrapping around my neck. I embrace the hug with a squeeze. Her lavender and vanilla perfume fills my nose with a sweet singe. I feel her soft hair press to the side of my face while her arms pull me close. Her thermos brushes over my hands. I can't help but shoot her a pleading look.

"Can I steal some?" I ask.

Before she can answer, Kai nabs the thermos, giving himself yet another opportunity to try his horrid flirting tactics on the girl he has been infatuated with for years.

The worst part is that she sees right past it.

"You still don't need the caffeine," Kai says with a shake of the thermos. I feel Raegan pull away, trying to grab her drink. My brother holds it high, watching as she jumps up to try and reach it and doing her best to get it away from him. Both of their smiles devour their faces the longer they mess around. I can see it now – Kai getting his cushy Official job and Raegan moving into the nursing program, living together in a perfect house, only a few blocks from the home we have now.

"Here," Max mutters from next to me. I feel him press his thermos in my hand, both of us turning away from the pair. I give him a slight side eye. His smirk pulls over his perfect teeth so casually.

"I won't tell if you won't."

I happily take three long swigs from his thermos. I'm relieved to feel the coffee run down my throat. I let it warm my stomach before handing Max back the much lighter thermos.

"Thank you."

He smiles, raising his hand to wipe the minuscule drops of coffee that linger on my lips. I feel my face fluster at the motion. His hands dip back into his pockets like the touch never happened.

Max has done something like that before. Over the years, he's gotten braver than Kai when showcasing his crush. Sadly, as hard as I try, I can never reciprocate whatever feelings he has.

"To hide the evidence," he shrugs, justifying the action. I nudge his arm with a smile listening to Rae's small grunts. Her hand is on Kai's face, forcing him to lower her drink with a pinch on his nose. Like an obedient dog, he lowers his arm. Rae's face is blanketed with a look of pure satisfaction while she pats my gentle giant of a brother on the head.

"Good boy," she mutters, her twin crossing his arms. Max and I can't help but laugh at Kai's look of utter defeat.

The group of students lingering around the tram stop begin to murmur. The gaggle, once fully dispersed, now becomes condensed. Students stand shoulder to shoulder. It resembles that of a wall. My laughter dies down as I process the scene unfolding before me. Students whisper, their faces changing from curiosity to disgust. Two boys in my year, Colton Stark and Josh Seal, gravitate toward the group with sinister grins. If there is one thing those two are good at, it's causing problems. This year alone, Josh has had four meetings for the number of violations he has gotten. The only reason he's avoided community time is because of his dad's position on the Council. Being a seat below the Commander can get you away with many things.

Josh's brown hair is pulled back into a loose bun on his head. His olive skin and golden eyes only add to his popularity amongst the women at school. He stands a foot or so shorter than Kai. He does many athletics with Max and, as a result, has an ego higher than even the stuffiest Untouchable. His counterpart, Colton, is no better. Although considerably less eye-catching with his straight red hair and pale skin, his friendship with Josh has only aided his sociability. The two of them together is nothing short of maniacal.

I move past Kai and Rae in the wake of the growing tensions amongst the group. Spit begins to physically leave the student's mouths. I can't see what they're staring at. Max stays close to me. His face contorts as he processes an escalating situation. Rae and Kai hesitantly follow behind us. They are more worried about jeopardizing their positions on the Student Council and their involvement in radical affairs rather than the gravity of a situation an angry crowd like this might create. I grasp Max's sleeve the closer we get to the group. Nudging a few students out of his path, the clearing finally opens up for us to observe what's happening.

Her tattered clothes and work-worn hands embrace her like a beautiful mosaic. The veins in her hands and brown spots on her skin show her age and the maltreatment of her already frail figure. Dirt-ridden shoes and shaky hands support the older woman's figure, her hands grasping a cane for dear life. Her body is almost concealed entirely by her sorry excuse for a robe. Straggly threads and patchy holes coat the clothing from head to toe. Her skin is dark, partially because of genetics but also from her time in the sun. Her hair is nothing but a gray mess atop her head.

Dirt clings beneath her broken nails. Max feels rigid beneath my touch. Colton and Josh pull away from the group, beginning a taunt toward the woman.

"Why is she so far from her sector's tram stop?" I question, observing the situation with a pit in my stomach.

"You're a long way from your people's pigsty of a sector," Josh beckons with a casual walk toward the woman. The woman's head remains down, her foot tapping in a way I know is meant to ease her own anxiety. I look around for any sign of why she may be standing here. Her frail arm holds a bag filled with nearly rotten fruit. Her eyes squint, masking her line of vision from the two students towering over her. Her legs shake beneath her weight out of pure adrenaline. I move a little more past Max, letting my grasp fall away from him until my body now stands within the group's inner circle. Kai has already managed to shove his way to the front as well. I feel Max's hands linger on my back, ready to drag me back at any moment.

"I-" the woman begins, reaching in her bag, quickly regretting the decision to defend herself with words.

I have to stop my body from physically recoiling as Josh's hand strikes the woman across her feeble face. She lets out a gasp, her palms colliding with the concrete. Her soot-filled cane rolls away several feet from her. Josh and Colton smile. Both men are filled with nothing but happiness at the sight in front of them.

"You were not permitted to speak to me," Josh hisses. His foot drives down on the woman's cane, shattering it instantly. Once more, I feel my stomach drop the moment her scuffed hands begin to paint the ground with streaks of red. With two steps, I am backed into Max, letting my shaky hands press to his forearm that has found its way around my front.

"It's just an Unfortunate. Look away if you need to," Max whispers coldly.

An Unfortunate who has done nothing out of regulation.

The woman's head stays lowered. Her hand covers her mouth in an attempt to hide her sobs. The other students laugh, mocking her with varying wailing tones. Her bag of fruit is sprawled on the ground. Understanding why she is in our sector doesn't take a genius.

I pull away from Max's grasp, feeling clarity wash over me. The fruits are older, meaning she picked them up from the Untouchable market before they were tossed in the garbage. Sometimes Unfortunate business owners come into town to collect what we discard and then utilize it in their sector. The hand-crafted logo for her bakery is stitched into the front of her apron, now streaked with her blood.

Colton walks around the woman, resembling a crow stalking its prey before it dives.

"Should I kick her again to remind her why we don't let Unfortunates into our sector?" Colton asks Josh. Colton is just another one of Josh's henchmen doing his bidding because he's too self-obsessed with the look of his own hands to deliver another blow.

Josh nods, signaling Colton to raise his foot.

My hands nudge the front of Colton without thinking. The soft material of his uniform meets my fingertips with a gentle touch. My push turns into a full-blown shove the deeper I lean into the movement. Colton has nothing to grab onto, falling backward with the instability of his one leg. The other was already in the air, ready to deliver a blow I knew the woman couldn't take. Colton's red hair sprawls on the ground. Josh's hand raises, readying himself to give me his next slap. He pauses once he notices who is standing in front of him. People whisper, signaling Kai to make his way next to me. Max's hand now rests on my lower back, his eyes dead set on Josh.

"Cute gesture, Blackburn. Now get out of my way," Josh says, paying little attention to his friend angrily pulling himself off the ground.

"She owns a business over there. This was part of her produce route," I begin, lowering myself to the woman. Her eyes are away from my own as I look her over. I grab the small paper poking from her pocket. The Unfortunate's market logo is displayed on the slip in a black stamp. I hold it up to Josh, ignoring the sound of her small groans behind me. "She was trying to tell you about her voucher for this sector." My hand presses the slip to his chest and his eyes narrow more.

"You beat an Unfortunate and nearly hit me just to feed that extremely big ego of yours," I finish. His narrow look becomes a full-fledged scowl. He steps toward me, ready to drag me down like the Unfortunate woman.

"Lay a hand on her, Josh, and I will make sure you pay for it during combat class," Max says with a snap. Josh backs down, moving away from Colton's flustered figure out of annoyance.

"I didn't realize you were a dirty, Unfortunate lover," Josh spits. I shake my head at him, pressing my finger into his chest.

"I hate every part of their existence. What I don't like is you delaying the tram because you don't know when to piss off and leave an Unfortunate alone," I spit back. Although I can't see him, I can feel Max's smile rise on his face. Rae looks flustered in the back of the crowd. Everyone around is staying silently neutral. The tram is at a standstill at the stop. Minutes have passed, waiting for someone to enter its open doors.

"The school's Officials would not like to hear you threatened an Unfortunate and delayed a good portion of students from getting to class on time just for your own amusement. I suggest you choose your next words wisely and get on the tram," Kai finally says. His large hand grasps Josh's shoulder. Josh swipes away Kai's hand. All of his anger surrounds him like a wild animal with no restraints.

"Your authority only extends to picking a theme for the Academy's Social, not out here, Kai. Remember that."

Josh wipes his mouth, backing away, leaving his words for all of us to take in. The bus driver's head is lowered in the same fashion as the women's.

Slowly but surely, Josh and Colton's lead in entering the tram causes more to follow. One by one, students make their way through the wide doors. The bus driver can't help but glance at his fellow Unfortunate with a look of hurt. The driver doesn't voice his concerns. He remains planted in his seat, not once getting up to help the woman. Regulations say he must stay at his posted job. Her knees are pulled into her chest, her painful cries still prominent. Our group is the last left outside before filing onto the cramped tram. My touch pulls away from Max the farther he moves up the steps of the tram. I allow all my companions to file on, taking a step back to give them some space.

My hand flies to my torso, a dull heat filling my lower stomach. I feel a sharp pain in the same spot I had this morning. My neck tingles with anticipation, the hair on my arms rising like the coldest chill has entered my bones. My heart races in ways you only get if you survive on nothing but coffee for days. I grab my chest, pausing to force out a full breath. The smell of cedarwood and soap wafts past my nose

Aggressively, a body collides with my own, sending my shoulder flying back, narrowly avoiding a collision with the side of the tram. I force my body around, ready to scream at the Untouchable willing to be so careless with me. A tall figure, taller than Kai, crouches down to the older woman. His back is to me. His raven-colored, curly, black hair is nothing but a wild mess atop his head. I watch his shoulders move as he coaxes the woman up. My stomach drops as I see his willingness to be near her.

"Your legs still work, don't they, Dove? Get out of my sight," his deep voice snaps. I look him over repeatedly, trying to process what the hell he's doing. His voice is unfamiliar.

Quickly, I pull myself up into the tram, letting my eyes pass over the bus driver as he gives me a nod. Per usual, I ignore the gesture, feeling shaken by the man's blatant rudeness. Maybe Josh will have another person to drag around to torment people with.

Max is taking a seat right as I get on. His hand waves me over next to him. Rae is already talking Kai's ear off, nearly leaning into him. Kai's brows raise the closer I get. Max's hand drags me down, almost sitting me in his lap. His hand stays placed on my lower back.

Max's touches have grown bolder and more frequent over the past few months. I sometimes wonder if feeding into them would be all that bad. Max sits with a certain confidence that I know Kai wishes he had when it comes to wooing Raegan. Max knows how to address everyone in the room while making your conversation with him feel entirely intimate.

There's a reason my father thinks he's perfect for me.

"Did that Unfortunate touch you?" Kai questions with a disgusted expression. I pause, pulling my mind away from Max's looks.

"What Unfortunate?"

All I can think of is the woman's worn and battered figure. My mind draws blanks at my brother's question.

His boots hit the tram floor with loud thuds. The goosebumps on my arms return. Sweat collects on my back, my shoulder still throbbing from his collision with me against the bus. I now see the patches working up and down the man's worn uniform. His deep blue eyes scan his surroundings with a hike of his old backpack up his shoulder. His hands are calloused from manual labor. A deep scar is set on his cheek, his curls falling forward to frame his face. His body is larger than any Unfortunate man I have seen at our age. His mouth is downturned, his face painted with a stoic expression. He clasps the bus driver on the back with familiarity, ignoring Josh's scoff once he pulls away from the man—my heart races once he moves past me. There are no words to describe the pit in my stomach that forms once he moves past the Untouchable section of the bus and seats himself beyond the red tape into the Unfortunate area of the tram.

An Unfortunate told me what to do.

An Unfortunate touched me.

His legs are spread where he sits. He slings his arms over his neighboring chairs, letting them drape.

He cranes his neck back, his head still held high. He's utterly indifferent to being stared down by this many Untouchables.

Not once have I seen an Unfortunate hold themselves like this.

Not once has anyone made me this nervous.

My birthmark continues to run hot with each passing moment. The tram doors close, only making my legs shake, knowing there is no quick way to escape. I lean into Max, letting his steady heartbeat soothe my anxieties.

"Did he, Forest?" Max questions.

My friends wait for an answer, impatiently. I swallow the lump in my throat, readying myself to answer. With one glance, I see he's watching me, and my rational thinking stops His blue eyes pierce through my soul with a look of pure hatred. His brows furrow, his arms crossed. I can see the veins work through his arms, a scowl nearly consuming his face. Even this far away, it feels as if he could take me and drag me across the space. Even worse, it feels like he wants to. There is no fear in his expression, no cowardice.

All there is, is hate.

And he's looking at me like prey, wanting to rip me apart. My lip quivers in my attempt to force out the truth. My brother's eye contact is still not enough to shake his watchful eyes.

"No," I say without thinking. "He didn't. He just moved past me," I finish.

It's a lie that left me like it was second nature. In every scenario, the Unfortunate's behavior would lead to him receiving a high-level violation. But I can't bring myself to tell them the truth.

"See? Everything is fine!" Raegan chirps. I give her a half-assed smile, leaning into her twin with a grunt. My hand reaches into my bag, finding an empty space where my mother's Cure-All once resided. My hand frantically searches other parts of my bag, feeling around for any sign of the small vial. I only find dead ends with each touch.

"You okay?" Max asks.

All I can do is nod before looking at the Unfortunate once more.

He looks out the window, not once pulling his gaze to me like he had before. My eyes strain to look for a small vial shoved deep within one of his pockets. The thick, black material of his pants shields anything from showing through. I narrow my eyes at him with a great deal of frustration.

Never in my life have I hated a pair of blue eyes like I do the ones on the Unfortunate seated at the back of the tram right now.

The question is, who is he?

And what is he doing in the Untouchable sector?

CHAPTER THREE

FOREST

The commute to the Academy is no more than fifteen minutes. One of the biggest promises New Haven's founders tried to hold to when deciding to eradicate most sources of transportation throughout the city was convenience. All of New Haven was built around the idea of functionality and schedules. Each person plays a part in the flow of order that goes into maintaining a functioning community. Maintaining order is so important that Josh would have received more punishment for delaying than the unauthorized assault on an Unfortunate. Like clockwork, and despite our delay, the tram rolls to a dead stop in front of the massive Academy building at 7:00 AM on the dot. The Unfortunate tram driver must've sped to make up for lost time. I wonder in that moment if he is punished when he can't pick up the slack for mishaps like the one Josh created this morning.

I ignore the feeling of the Unfortunate's eyes gravitating back to me. As quick as lightning, I move off the tram, hardly giving the driver enough time to swing open the doors. The cool metal collides with my forearm, causing my body to spill onto the even-cut grass. The Academy's front lawn is no longer the vibrant green it once was during the hot summer months. It's now sprinkled with dead pieces and quite brittle beneath the weight of my body.

The Academy's large building consumes the entire plot of land it sits on. It's considered the beating heart of New Haven, housing all the community's growing minds. It resides in the middle of the Untouchable sector, taking up the most space out of any other building within its vicinity. Its walls are made of concrete and stone. The roof is nothing more than glass panes, all pushed together to create a point. Wood trim decorates every side of the structure.

A variety of plants, trees, and several koi decorate the grounds, consuming the grassy areas in bursts of dull color. Students work in and out of the massive double glass doors. I notice the teachers chattering amongst themselves, some casually repositioning their maroon blazers that help set them apart from the student body. Groups of students linger around the more scenic portions of the lawn. Even in the hottest months, the school's glass ceiling can stow away the warmth completely. Like most other buildings in this sector, color is hard to pinpoint on the structure. Even the flowers are dull, like the Academy's gardeners purposefully chose the most boring colors to accent the space.

Kai and Raegan move past me, barely acknowledging my presence. They are deep in a conversation about their positions on the Student Advocate Council. Raegan holds Kai's forearm close. In many ways, it's easy to see why he continues to pursue her. She's safe. No one would ever question why they chose one another. It's as if everything in Kai's life has always just made sense. He hasn't had to question anything.

He's always just known where he belongs.

My body becomes tense again at the sound of the Untouchable's quiet conversation behind me. With a casual shift of my body, I observe the raven-haired asshole quietly conversing with the bus driver. With his head raised, I can vaguely make out how old the tram driver is. Possibly ten years older than my father, maybe even more. His head is no longer lowered as he speaks to the other Unfortunate. The two men converse with a great deal of familiarity. Working in a sector where you bus around silent Untouchables all day, I can imagine that any familiar, dirty face would liven your spirits.

The Unfortunate leans into the bus driver, whispering something in the man's ear that warrants a shift in his demeanor. The bus driver looks frazzled, the whispers between them containing something not meant to be overheard.

"You coming?" Max's voice questions, breaking my curious gaze toward the two men.

He keeps his arms crossed, eyeing Josh and Colton as they move by. Unlike Kai and Rae, he isn't hiding the fact that he's noticed my sudden shift in attitude. Like a guard dog, he waits for me, even allowing me to take a moment to stare down the Unfortunate in the same way everyone else had for most of the ride to the Academy.

"Yeah, thanks for waiting up. I'm just struggling to understand why one of *them* is on *our* school grounds."

Max gently smiles, holding his head high. The Unfortunate steps off the bus, waving to the driver, before pulling away. Just like he had when he entered the tram, the Unfortunate ignores everyone around him. Even his walk would have most convinced that he knows where he is going.

"The transfer program. Don't you remember how desperately our dads tried to shut it down?"

Each school year, a few Unfortunates are granted the ability to learn on the same level as Untouchables to give them more skills to keep the businesses and economy in their sector functioning. Without the Unfortunate's aid in growing crops, we would have no food and without us, they would have no safety. A ward surrounds New Haven, keeping away the ash and toxins floating around the air beyond the city. Some other regions adopted by Sanctum are spread across the continent, but we rarely hear anything about them. New Haven is all there is for miles. Only ash and a once vibrant society remain buried in the Earth's ground.

"They seriously went through with it?"

"Clearly," Max scoffs.

We push past the large glass doors, fumbling in our pockets to retrieve our IDs for the woman at the front desk. Her black hair is wound so tight atop her head that I'm convinced it's the only thing able to pull her face into the half-assed smile she has plastered on. Her long, colored nails tap her desk, not once stopping, even when students try to speak to her. Her lips are thin, set in a straight line. She wears a pair of blue light glasses, shoving them higher up the bridge of her nose to make it look like she is reading whatever is on her screen. We approach her desk, scanning our IDs and watching the system's light shine green.

"Almost late, you two," she coos with a finger wag.

"Don't blame us," Max starts, leaning his arm over her desk, working his charm while flashing his baby blues. "Blame the sewer trash our upper leadership allowed in here," he finishes.

The tingle returns down my spine, the pulse in my wrist proliferating. Stepping away from the scanner, I feel the Unfortunate's eyes pull away from the back of my neck and onto the front desk. Her head rises completely once she notices his presence. Her once partial attention to us is now a full-fledged stare at him. I try to get a good look at his ID, but it's facing away from me. It goes through the scanner, flashing green like our own. The front desk woman's mouth almost hangs open, showcasing her perfect set of teeth. The Unfortunate shakes his head, pulling away from the desk before scanning over a small note removed from his pocket.

The woman at the desk wipes down the scanner's surface with disinfectant repeatedly, as if his one swipe was enough to contaminate the scanner after one go. In terms of an Unfortunate, he isn't the worst thing to look at. Although calloused, his hands are clean. His uniform isn't new and has had some years of use, but, unlike Max, his tie is folded with great care. His wild black hair isn't kinked. In fact, it looks soft. Although rugged, many of the details on his face are easy to get lost in, even from afar. The scar under his cheek is deep, possibly deep enough that even the Cure-All couldn't fix it. His eyes are blue, but not light blue like Max's. His are dark and soft all at once. Someone spent a great deal of time on the genetic code responsible for the details of his face.

Unfortunate or not, he is beautiful in his own, terrifying way.

Even now, as he moves further away through the crowd of students, I can see how much his height towers over most of the others around him. I know his size was intimidating, even to Josh. I scan the outline of his pockets once more, looking for any sign of the small vial in one of his pockets. My head moves with my body, trying to get a closer look.

Pulling his eyes away from the note in his hand, the Unfortunate's gaze meets my own, and my stomach fills with sudden anxiety. Trying to play off my eye's blatant exploration of him as nothing out of the ordinary, he pulls his gaze away, ignoring me and Max entirely.

Stepping back, I watch his broad shoulders move through the crowd of students parting the way for him like he carries the Earth's next deadliest plague. I can almost swear a smirk is lining his face at the sight of the other students' disdain toward him. Some physically turn away from him in an attempt to pretend that he isn't there. I hold my bag close, feeling my sketchbook press against my side.

"I would love to see him crumpled on the ground like the woman from this morning," Max says.

We both begin to move as the Unfortunate rounds the corner at the end of the hall. Students begin moving back into the walkway, whispering with wide-eyed expressions. The layout of the building is straightforward. To the left of reception are all the elective wings, and to the right are all the primary classes. Anything toward the middle of the school revolves around dining and athletics. Max walks with me as I take a sharp right toward the elective wing of the school.

"I don't think he would go down as easily as the woman." My words come out with no given thought behind them.

"Why is that?"

It doesn't take a fortune teller to tell that Max was upset by that comment.

"You know ... he's ... big." I finally say, raising my shoulders to mimic the Unfortunate's towering walk.

Max frowns, rolling his eyes. As we make our way further into the Academy, the walls shift from their muted, dull gray to the lively colors and drawings of the art wing. Despite being outside of regulation, the art teachers had convinced the school board to allow one hallway to be filled with color. Each year, the 5th and 6th years get to work on a mural for one of the walls. Right now, we're creating concept paintings for what will replace the current wall art. Most people tend to take a more symbolic approach to their drawings. Depictions of the war are all symbolized by a single daisy breaking through the rubble and ash. For years, there was only vegetation made by man. That is, until the flowers began to bloom. Miles of daisies marked the Earth, creating the first sign of hope after all the destruction. There isn't a part of New Haven that doesn't have the tiny, white flowers planted somewhere.

"I know for a fact he wouldn't have that cocky attitude if he were pitted against me," Max clarifies, leaning his body into someone's mural from a few years back.

"And you aren't radiating a cocky attitude right now?" I question with a smirk.

"It almost sounds like you're defending him, Blackburn," Max says sarcastically.

I roll my eyes, nudging him as a playful grin spreads across my face. His casual lean into the wall falters at the gesture, making his hold on himself slip with a slide of his hand. Grabbing him, I stop him from trying to recover his position on the wall. His hands grip my sides, a grin now consuming his face too. The warmth of his palms presses through my shirt. Blonde hair falls into his face like a curtain covering a window. He stays still, keeping his hands on me while my hands work to fix his tie.

"I would never defend one of them, but, honestly, I would love to see what would happen if Josh tried to mess with him."

I lay his tie flat on his chest, expecting his hands to leave my sides.

They never do.

Once more, my birthmark begins to burn, making me wince with narrowed eyes. I stare into Max's eyes, trying to feed into whatever is happening between us right now. My stomach rolls in ways that only happen after I have had too many sweets. Forcing the feeling down, I finally address the elephant in the room.

"Your class is nowhere near this one."

Max draws a deep breath, glancing around while he decides what to say. He furrows his brows like his sister, a telltale sign that he's deep in thought.

"I might've been a little jealous of your focus on a certain Unfortunate earlier," Max says, shaking his head. "I know it's ridiculous-"

I don't let him finish his statement. Slowly, I drag his head down by his neck and silence his thoughts with a gentle press of my lips to his. His touch grows tighter on my sides before relaxing. His soft lips stay on mine, gently pressing down harder with each passing second. I ready my head to move away, feeling my stomach churn, followed by an unsettling feeling.

I *want* to feel pleasure in this touch. Why can't I?

His hands move to hold the sides of my face, pulling me back into the kiss. My birthmark continues to burn, only growing more painful the longer I allow Max to touch me. With a deep breath Max pulls away from me, letting his hand linger on my own before lowering his touch away from me.

"You've never done that. Why did you do that?" he questions, his cheeks red.

I wish I had an answer for him.

"I'm honestly not sure," I begin, glancing at his watch as we finally notice the time. "But we can deep dive into it later."

I pull away, but Max's hand grabs my wrist, stopping me dead in my tracks. Both of our faces are red from the exchange.

"Did you regret that?" he questions.

Lie.

I shake my head no, wanting nothing more than for him to let go so I can escape this awkward situation. The pain in my mark dies down the longer I'm away from his touch. I know I need to address the pain with my mom again, but she shuts down every time I speak to her about it, dismissing my questions.

This newfound pain may be better left to the unknown.

"I'll see you at lunch, Blackburn," Max settles on saying.

With a broad grasp, I hug him, easing his anxieties about whether he did the right thing by kissing me back. With a quick motion, I plant one more kiss on his cheek before turning away, smiling at the look of satisfaction plastered across his face.

I force my back into the classroom door, spilling into the bright space with a loud sigh. Mrs. Auburn's eyes shoot up from her focused position at the drawing on her desk, relaxing only once she notices who's entered her space. Her red, curly hair is wound in a mound atop her head, housing multiple pencils just waiting to fall away. Her maroon blazer is decorated in pins, all outside of regulation for her uniform but somehow acceptable given her job here. Her face is smudged with graphite, traveling down her cheeks and the sides of her hands, stopping at the ends of each fingertip. Her green eyes pass over my own, narrowing the longer she watches me.

"I thought you might not show up early today," she says with a grin. Her petite body leans back in her chair, relaxing her feet on her desk, pulling her attention away from her drawing.

"Trust me, I didn't get here without struggle."

I toss my bag on my desk, sighing while taking my usual seat toward the back of the classroom. Mrs. Auburn pulls away from her desk, sliding her chair closer with its wheels. She grabs a pencil from her hair, forcing my head up from its leaning position on the top of my desk.

"Why are you red? You look like you've been running."

"That would be because of Max Vega," I admit.

I watch the gears turn in her head as she reflects on my words.

"The blonde one? The twin?" she questions.

"That would be the one."

"What did he do?"

More like, what did I do?

"I may have fed into his little crush on me after we got off the tram.... I kissed him, and I think it has done more damage than good."

She smiles, looking as if she cracked some code.

"Are your feelings toward him not as prevalent?"

"Maybe," I already know how much of a lie that is. "But not enough for me to start feeding into his *wants*," I finish, feeling that familiar churn in my stomach.

"All jokes aside, he is academically knowledgeable and not the most awful thing to look at. Maybe consider what influence a relationship with him could have on your Judgment Day."

It always comes back to that, doesn't it? How good do you look when our people's leaders decide where to place you after you're done with schooling? Even the people you choose to sleep with affect where you are placed.

"I'll consider it," I say through a strained smile.

She looked satisfied at the response. Returning to her desk, she grabs a new piece of graphite, continuing her art piece, moving her head toward the array of canvases stacked on the shelf next to me.

"You can continue yours if you want. I've been eager to see what you will do with it."

With a swipe, I grab the brightly colored canvas from the shelf, sprawling it across my desk with a heave. It is nothing more than layers of color, layered to create the start of something I have yet to finalize in my mind. I see the bright colors of spring seep through the painting. Most of the images on my canvas came from dreams and, sadly, have yet to come together to form a complete picture. My usual paint palette rests on the shelf next to the paintings, along with my two brushes I use like no other. My brush swirls in a bright red, landing on my canvas in detailed precision as I begin building up what I can only assume is the start of a pair of hands at the bottom of the canvas. I still see them vividly from my dreams the night before.

"Bring it over, I want to see," Mrs. Auburn happily chimes.

Dragging the canvas over to her, I gently plant it on her desk, both of us leaning in to observe my progress. It's hard to decipher what exactly is going on in the painting. It is too morbid to be plastered on a wall in the school. The start of a pair of hands rises from the bottom of the canvas. Daisies grow from the palms in bunches. Something lingers in the back of the painting, something I have yet to visualize fully.

"Do you want me to get into the symbolism I see in this, or should I save it for another day?"

Mrs. Auburn is nearly leaning over the painting, scanning it up and down for intricate details even I have yet to point out.

"Maybe save your in-depth analysis for when it has one."

She laughs, backing away from the painting with a thud into her seat. A small chime on her computer sounds before a flash devours her screen.

"A message from the Academy Director." Her eyes are glued onto her screen as she reads.

I stay silent, waiting for her to engage in our conversation again. The fiery-haired art teacher has become an enormous comfort to me this past year. Unlike all the other teachers, she genuinely loves her work. Her willingness to walk the line with regulations so often makes her a breath of fresh air. That's why I always make time to come to her class thirty minutes before I have to. Everything else in this school seems so confining.

"Did you know some Untouchables roughed up a baker from the Unfortunate sector this morning?" she questions.

"I was at the stop it happened at. Josh and Colton were responsible."

I leave out the part where I shoved Colton to stop the delay.

"Serves the woman right. She should know better than to be that deep into our sector. Although, I'm sure those two boys didn't help the situation. I am not the fondest of Josh or his list of violations."

"You're telling me."

She closes the message, finally pulling her attention back to me. I reflect on the older woman's frail figure once more. The image paints my mind in fleeting moments.

"She didn't deserve what they did to her," I blurt out without thinking. Mrs. Auburn pauses, her face pulling into a look of confusion. Her brows crease inward, forcing her face into an expression I rarely see on her.

"They *always* deserve it, Forest," she says, placing her hand atop my own.

I shove away my regrets, letting them melt away with each roll of her thumb over my knuckle.

"You're right. I'm just shaken up, is all."

A voice clears behind us, jolting us away from our tender touch with one another. Mrs. Auburn's light, genuine smile leaves her face, replaced with a look I have never seen on her before. Her relaxed demeanor goes rigid. Her once slumped posture is now as straight as one of the pencils in her hair. Her hand, once on my own, now clasps her other so hard her knuckles are white. Her eyes are narrowed like a cat's. Any love radiating off the woman has washed away like rain down a storm drain.

She's cold, distant, and utterly closed off.

Where has this side of her always been?

"Speak," she snaps.

My hair rises once more, only prompting me to turn my head to meet his stoic expression.

His eyes are dead set on the once lively art teacher.

"My name is Fallan Markswood. I'm the student that was picked for the transfer program this year. My schedule said my first period was art." He scans the plethora of items in the classroom. "I assume this is it," he finishes. His voice is just as deep as I remember it. I can still hear his blatant threat in the back of my mind. He shuffles, crossing his arms while he waits for her to respond.

"Clearly it is," I pipe in, answering for her. His eyes finally reach mine, narrowing with a look I can only describe as hate.

A section of the room is taped off, housing a few older desks for any Unfortunates taking this class. Older art supplies lean against the wall. Worn and used canvases consume the space, leaving little room for anyone's things behind the tape.

"As you know, you have a section in the back of the room. My broken easels and canvases are under the sink. We have a few paints ready to go next to the new ones. Take what you need, then do your best to silently work in the back and leave my other students undistracted," Mrs. Auburn finally says.

Unlike our first encounter at the tram, he offers no pushback as he moves past us, keeping multiple feet between us. He's silent with each of his motions. Fallan slings his bag over his desk, propping up the slightly less worn canvas he has chosen against it. He precisely picks out his color palette, steering away from the brighter colors. His palette is filled with a variety of blues and purples.

I return to my seat, pulling my canvas away from Mrs. Auburn's desk. She looks distraught. Her hands run through her hair repeatedly to soothe herself. Because I never had to worry about an Unfortunate in the classroom, having my desk right before the line never seemed like an issue. Now, all I can do is regret it with each movement of his body from behind me.

"What's the prompt?" Fallan's voice questions. Once again, he is speaking with no permission.

Mrs. Auburn is too preoccupied with her drawing to notice. I'm glad she has already found a way to deal with our unexpected visitor.

"You know those murals in the hallway before you came in?" I whisper, turning to meet his hateful gaze.

He nods.

"We get to replace those this year. The students in this class create something and then the best canvases get chosen out of the lot." As hard as I try to force the hate in my voice, it simply won't show.

"To what do I owe the pleasure of getting a civil conversation with an Untouchable?" he whispers under his breath. I narrow my eyes, letting my frown visibly grow.

"Go to hell," I snap, letting my foot hit his desk to jolt whatever stroke he was attempting on his canvas from behind the shield of his bag.

Keeping my body forward, I try to direct my anger-filled thoughts toward the man. Without turning around, I sense a smirk pulling over his lips.

Grabbing my brush, I let my anger direct itself to my work. My hands become less gentle with each stroke. The lively pinks now blend into more aggressive shades of red. Like a gunshot in the night, the bell's loud chime almost causes me to drag my brush across the length of the canvas. Even Mrs. Auburn's precision is disrupted by the noisy clamor of students entering their first-period classes.

Josh's large body barrels through the classroom door, stumbling into others as students fill the vacant classroom. Josh looks to the back of the classroom, holding his bag with delight. Noticing the Unfortunate, he decides to avoid his regular seat and chooses the one closest to Fallan and me. Rae stumbles in behind him, scrunching her nose at the sight of Josh and an Unfortunate so close to me. I force my bag into the seat beside me, stopping Josh from getting closer. The other students whisper about the new eyesore in the back of the classroom. Fallan's eyes remain on his canvas, not once lifting away to acknowledge anyone. He is genuinely focused on the strokes for whatever it is that he's creating.

"Blackburn!" Josh begins, slamming his hand hard on my desk to stop my focus. Rae slides into the seat beside me, eyeing the man with disgust. He lingers in my area, waiting to find my next button to push.

"There is no scenario in which I want you anywhere near me," I hiss, shoving away his hand's hold on my desk.

He isn't focused on the crude gesture. Instead, he stares down Fallan, who could care less about his presence as he continues his gentle brush strokes.

"Whatcha painting there, pig?" Josh questions, kicking his leg forward to jolt Fallan's desk.

"Josh, don't antagonize," Mrs. Auburn warns, removing her focus from her neat handwriting on the board outlining today's lesson.

"You should listen. Enough slip-ups, and you'll be working grunt Untouchable jobs after your Judgement Day," I warn, narrowing my eyes at him. He swipes my paint cup from my desk, shoving me back into my seat when I try to reach after it. Fallan looks up, acknowledging the man's harsh hold on my shoulder.

"Yeah? And where do you think they'll place you? Last time I checked, you're living in your brother's shadow," Josh seethes.

There is no time for anyone to react. Josh drops the cup on Fallan's desk, snickering as the wet mirage of colored water explores his canvas and front. I grab Josh, pulling him away from Fallan's area. Raegan scolds the man, swatting his arm for making a mess. Fallan tears away the tuck of his shirt, trying to stop the water from soaking all the way through. A sliver of his back shows. It's hard to stop myself from covering my mouth at the sight of the several white scars working over the surface of most of his skin. I am not the only one who notices. A few students gasp as their silent whispers fill the room. Mrs. Auburn begins to scold Josh while silencing the multiple spouts of laughter muffled behind people's hands. I can't bring myself to laugh at the sight.

Fallan ignores the laughter, turning toward the class with lowered eyes. His shirt is covered in a splotch that will only add to him receiving grief for the rest of the day. My face is as stoic as his. His eyes pass over my own before taking a seat once more. Mrs. Auburn motions Josh away, allowing him to drag a chair away from the front and next to me.

"You should learn when to piss off," Raegan says, hitting Josh's arm in a way I know he took as playful banter.

He smiles at the blonde, letting his eyes linger on her too long. He looks proud of his actions, like there is no consequence for the damage he inflicts on any Unfortunate.

"Are you mad that I embarrassed your boyfriend, Blackburn?" Josh questions. His lips hover over my ear as he begins his taunt. Raegan tries her best to eye down Mrs. Auburn. The woman is so involved in her lecture that there is no use in trying to get her to pause.

"Give me one good reason not to slam your head into this desk," I whisper back. He plants his hand on the back of my neck, forcing my focus onto him.

"You don't want to start making big threats like that, Forest. You're already on thin ice with me," he whispers.

"Because you did nothing wrong? You're a saint in all of this?"

"It's an *Unfortunate*. Of course I did nothing wrong."

Does that stop them from being people?

This kind of poisonous thinking has landed me in this position before. They hate us and we hate them. But his scars, all of those scars. How can someone only in his 5th year have so many wounds? They all laughed as if one of us couldn't have any.

My fingers linger above the material where my birthmark resides.

Are imperfections truly that uncommon?

I pull my attention back to my painting, ignoring the growing pit forming in my stomach. Raegan silently works on her painting, doing her best to create perfectly straight lines in the image she's creating. I avoid turning around to watch Fallan's gentle strokes. Josh watches me, too enthralled with my work to get started on his own. The silent whispers from girls a few seats over break through the air. They cover their mouths, but I catch stolen words like "Shifter" and "military" as they continue to gossip.

Foreign Entities, otherwise known as Shifters, are genetically mutated individuals scorched by the nuclear fallout after the wars. While some humans adapted genetically to the changes in their environment, like our ancestors, others changed for the worse. People's minds were no longer their own. Human's feral instincts came into play as their bodies began to mutate, shifting from something human to something animalistic. They are one of the main reasons we still have the ward. To keep them out. New Haven's military occasionally goes beyond the ward to flush out any that have gotten too close to our borders. I've heard the horror stories of some soldiers never returning home in one piece.

"My uncle went beyond the ward once and said he saw one. It took him and three of his men to take it down," Josh exclaims, interrupting the girl's once-quiet conversation. Even Mrs. Auburn has paused her lecture to listen in on the conversation about an entity we know so little about.

A hand flies up in my periphery, causing everyone's eyes to shift to the back of the classroom. Fallan's hand is held high, his back leaned into the chair in the most relaxed position possible. He looks to Mrs. Auburn, patiently awaiting her permission to speak.

"Go on, Mr. Markswood."

"You said uncle, so I assume he's an Untouchable like you. Respectfully, the only people tasked with dealing with Shifters are Unfortunate military ranks. An Untouchable has never had to go beyond the ward to fight a Shifter. It would seem your uncle has told you a lie," Fallan says with a large grin.

The room is dead silent at the Unfortunate's sarcastic taunt. Josh looks livid, clenching his palms in a sorry attempt to control his anger.

"That's enough from you today," Mrs. Auburn mutters, sensing an escalated situation.

Josh readies himself to move. With a shove of my desk, I force my hand on his leg, letting Fallan's smirk grow at his pleasure in the anger he has created.

"I should kill you for that," Josh spits, swatting away my hand, forcing himself to turn back to the front.

In a tone so quiet, I think I imagined it, I hear Fallan's silent comment.

"I dare you to try."

No cares, no fears for his actions. He gets a thrill out of our hate towards him. Everything about Fallan would make you think he has no respect for his role in our society.

"You're close with her twin, right?" Josh silently whispers after a few long moments of pouting. His eyes are on Reagan, who is too focused on her painting to help me out of this situation.

"Yes.... Why?"

"He plays a role in determining who gets the next spot with the school's Student Advocates. I wouldn't mind having that title under my belt to appease my father and the Council when it comes time for my Judgment Day."

I can't stop the laughter from leaving me.

"You seem to forget how much I hate you," I snap, pulling back to my painting.

My stroke drags across the canvas at the feeling of his nails digging into my thigh. His hand encloses the skin, clamping down like the jaws of a bear trap. He watches me with no humor in his eyes. I can't move away from him without his nails leaving marks up my thigh. Without turning around, I know I am not the only one watching this scene unfold. Fallan silently watches, observing the power Josh tries to exert over me.

"You seem to forget you owe me," Josh whispers.

My mind races back to that night. The night I try so hard to shove away from my mind. I see the Untouchable's cold expression. Several odd moments transpiring that night before he hit the pavement. Many silent seconds of staring over the edge of that roof. Many more seconds pleading for Josh to leave me out of the incident report. It all comes rushing back. Even now, the thought of that night turns my stomach.

"Talk to Max. I wasn't giving you an option."

The bell rings and Josh pulls away his grasp on my leg from beneath the desk. Casually, he slings his bag over his shoulder, walking away as if he didn't just threaten me like he does anyone who has something he needs. Raegan finally pulls her gaze away from her work, showing me the vibrant canvas. I try to force a smile.

Students begin to file out of the room, leaving a flustered Mrs. Auburn a mess she has no interest in cleaning up. I linger behind, wincing at the dull pain in my leg. Raegan decides to stay with me, even organizing the canvases against the nearest wall. I half expect Fallan to acknowledge what he had seen from behind me as he walks by. Instead, he tosses his canvas under the sink, letting it land face down and away from prying eyes. Delicately, Fallan washes his brushes, putting them aside for another use, far away from the other supplies. Like a knife cutting skin, his eyes finally land on me. They're a deep blue like an angry, ever-looming sea. His jaw is clenched.

Hate is the only thing that lingers in his gaze. Hate for me, hate for this school, and hate for the society his kind does not fit into. At that moment, that look was worse than any pain Josh could inflict on me. At least I know why Josh hates me. Not knowing why Fallan does is a considerably scarier feeling.

CHAPTER FOUR

KAIDEN

S tudents swarm one another in sweaty groups of old gray tees and black shorts. Various blue mats coat the floor, ensuring none of the concrete beneath is exposed. The shirts used for Defense Class are too big for me. Despite Max being a year younger, his body is considerably more filled out than mine regarding mass. Even though I'm tall, the others in class would think he was in his final year, not the other way around.

The girls in the class stay pressed against the wall, avoiding any physical activity as best they can. The sound of student's blades clattering together dies down with each shout from the teacher about "form" and "precision."

My blade feels heavy in my hand. It's an intense weapon that I still haven't gotten used to. Students begin designing their own blades during the first two years at the Academy and, after it's forged, we learn how to defend ourselves against Shifters during our last four years. Although extremely unlikely, the possibility of them making it past the ward and our military is something many still fear. I think that's why parents advocated for this class in the first place. It's a way to prepare everyone for a scenario none have seen happen yet. Years are wasted crafting and building silver blades to penetrate creatures no one has seen for eons.

The chips behind the ears of those wielding their blades blink green, linking each weapon to its owner. The blades immediately retract and close if not connected to the correct chip. Max's blade is shorter than mine. His is meant for quick jabs rather than long slashes. He twirls it around in his hand, having a better grasp of the weapon than most.

Like it's nothing, he swings the blade at the practice dummy, slicing its most vital points with ease. His blonde hair is pushed back and out of his face. Sweat marks his shirt beneath his collar, a grin consuming his face.

I ready myself to swing my blade. Max corrects my form, adjusting my arms to get a better hit.

"Your sister kissed me today," Max blurts. I miss the dummy, nearly slashing my leg in the process. My blade closes, clattering to the floor in a sheath of silver.

"Forest kissed you? Like without you asking?" I question, wiping away my sweat with a drag of my shirt.

Max raises his shoulders. His face is red, indicating this is still a sensitive topic for him.

"One minute, I was babbling on like I normally do around her, and the next, she's pressed up against me and the Art Wing murals."

I quickly try to erase the image of my sister in such an intimate setting.

"Did you both... enjoy it?"

The question rolls off my tongue unnaturally.

He looks hesitant to answer the question. His blade strikes the dummy again, inflicting more damage than he had the first time.

"I've been wanting to do that for years. I don't know if she regrets it," Max finally says. The dummy is useless once his blade strikes it for the 8th time. I can see the confusion in his eyes. Whatever happened between them had left him with conflicting emotions.

"Take it from someone who lives with her, Forest is confusing."

And stubborn.

"She wouldn't have done something unless she wanted it. Explore it. See what it means to her," I admit after a moment. Max chuckles at the response, shaking his head to stop his spiral of thinking around the matter.

"You're right. I'm overthinking it."

A series of large grunts sound behind me, pausing mine and Max's attacks on the dummies. A few transfers from the Unfortunate program hit the mats, rolling to avoid Untouchable blades from meeting their skin. They wear a thick layer of protective gear along their arms. Unlike Untouchables who get blades, the Unfortunates are used for a more realistic approach in contrast to the dummies. Dull blades swing toward the moving targets, only causing growing laughter each time one of the bottom feeders is shoved to the ground. Their backs hit the mats in waves as Untouchables tower over them with looks of pure malice. Max and I can hardly control our laughter at their pathetic attempts to one-up our classmates.

A brunette Unfortunate stands, readying his hand to deliver a clean blow to an Untouchable standing over his comrade. I sit back, watching the Officials on standby utilize their sensor prods to force the brunette back with pokes to the stomach that send the boy on his back in a painful frenzy. The prods are thin, charged with electricity that comes out of two points at its end. Non-deadly but extremely deregulating if touched with one. Not once has an Official allowed any Untouchable to be injured by the Unfortunates in any hand-to-hand combat courses, regardless of how often they've come close to getting a clean blow in on one of us.

Unfortunates have to use nonphysical contact if they want to avoid the prods.

"That bastard is already getting back up," Max whispers.

The brunette pulls himself up, spitting on the mat while clutching his side. Unlike our more sophisticated lifestyle, the Unfortunates lead more demanding lives, dealing with livestock and manufacturing work that we do not want to pursue. They can frequently take hits better than us. Most people blame it on their back-breaking work, which attributes to thickly callused hands and physical fortitude.

"I wonder why they've already started working?" Max questions, observing the slight limp in the brunette's walk. He'd told us he was injured at his lumber job in his sector.

"Many Unfortunates were taken outside New Haven's borders during the Re-Establishment Act. A lot of those Unfortunates were parents. It left a lot of kids orphaned to keep the food supplies plentiful for us."

"Surely some parents made it. There has to be something beyond the ash."

"There is a reason I said 'were' parents. No one made it back. It's why they started classes like this one, even for them." I clarify, feeling less eager to laugh at the sight of the boy back down on the mats.

"No use in crying for them now, Blackburn," Max says, clapping my back with his hand, twirling his blade again.

A flash of blonde whips past my vision, rolling away from other's attacks toward her. Her shoulder hits the mat, forcing her body away from the blades. Her leg swipes Untouchable's legs, causing them to hit the mat in thuds. Without touching any of them, she keeps them down, kicking their blades away from their grasp before shoving a dummy onto their fronts. They grunt, writhing furiously as they're pinned against the ground. Her booted foot weighs down on the dummy, only adding to their struggles to get away.

Officials watch with wide eyes, waiting for the moment she breaks regulation. It takes me a few solid blinks to realize she is an Unfortunate. Her blonde hair is wound into a tight braid. Even from this distance, I can see the smile creeping along her face at the sight of their struggles. With two taps, the Untouchables give up, making her step away as they force the dummy off of them. She doesn't bother kicking their blades back into arm's reach. Instead, she steps on the hilts, even breaking one. Her brown eyes scan the room, waiting for someone to yell at her, no doubt.

"Valerie! On the wall for fifteen!" our teacher yells, dragging the blonde by the collar to the nearest wall with a gentle toss. She smiles, leaning into it with a roll of her eyes. The Untouchables that were once pinned under the practice dummy point their blades at her in a taunt she hardly acknowledges.

"Someone told me she and that brooding asshole from the tram are companions. They both transferred in together," Max says.

She stands aggressively, only narrowing her eyes once she takes notice of my curious stare.

"Figures they'd be associated," I say, driving my blade hard into the dummy, finally making a clean cut. Max nods in approval, observing the cut with admiration.

"Getting better, Kai," Max starts, motioning an Unfortunate closer with impatient waves of his hand. "Want to try something a little more exciting?" Max questions, squeezing the shoulder of the oncoming Unfortunate who clearly wants nothing to do with us. I run my fingers over my blade, thinking of the Re-Establishment Act more than I'd like to.

"I still need to fix a few things in my blade," I settle on saying.

He doesn't look disappointed. In fact, he seems empathetic.

"Next time then, Blackburn. Guess I can have you all to myself," Max mutters, dragging the Unfortunate along with him.

The blade's maintenance table rests on one of the walls closest to Valerie. I make my way over, resting my tattered blade on the wooden table, working quickly to fix its shaky hilt. Valerie watches me with crossed arms. She won't break eye contact no matter how many nasty glances I give her. She cocks her head at me, staring at my craftsmanship with watchful eyes.

"What?" I finally question, slamming down my blade out of frustration.

"You need to wrap your blade higher if you want to keep that hilt on," Valerie says, staring forward like we are the type to engage in casual banter.

I look down at my binds around the blade, seeing the bunching around the base of the hilt.

"Move it higher up the blade to get some resistance, or else it will keep breaking," she says, pushing away from the wall. She's called back onto the mats by a few Untouchables needing a new sparring partner. The previous one limps away with silent curses.

Max repeatedly strikes down the Unfortunate, delivering him enough blows that he can't get up. I stare at his strikes, watching his back move with each precise motion. I imagine him and my sister. The visual of his lips on her is something I could never see her allowing. I let my gaze linger on him before returning to my now-repositioned hilt. With each swipe, I slice it in the air, getting no resistance this time.

"She was right," I whisper with a small smile.

"It wasn't me!" a boy shouts. My head spins, landing on the brown-haired Unfortunate from earlier being dragged away by two Officials. He thrashes his arms away from the men, trying his best to escape. They hold light sensor prods to his side, sending his back into an arch. His teeth grind in between shallow breaths. He struggles to take a full breath. His legs let off hard kicks in the air, eventually becoming a drag.

"I didn't steal it," the boy pleads, his words becoming faint.

"Save it for upper leadership, pig," an Official spits, continuing his drag of the man out of the classroom and down one of the school's long hallways. I watch them through the window, hauling around the brunette as if he's weightless. The light sensor prod stays pressed to the man's side, leaving him immobile. Max wipes the sweat from his face, dragging up his shirt to expose a torso I try not to linger on.

"What was that about?" I question, watching him take a few long drinks from his water.

"Some of the Officials' supplies have gone missing. They believe Unfortunates are stealing them to make quick money," Max says. I watch the other Untouchables snicker in their small groups now formed around the room.

"You sure it wasn't one of us?" I question.

"I know it was," Max says with a smirk. "But what's the fun in telling an Official that?" Max finishes as his attention pulls back to the sparring groups.

Valerie lies slumped, holding her side after receiving a harsh blow.

I expect to find humor in the situation, as I always do.

Today, for some reason though, I don't.

CHAPTER FIVE

FOREST

My brother's hair clings to the sweat on his forehead. Max's mane is pushed away from his face, only showcasing the Vega's naturally enthralling looks. Max's walk is energetic, but Kai drags behind him, looking physically beaten from their last class. Kai's blade pokes out from his bag. The detailed wrapping around his blade clashes with Max's worn blade strapped to his leg. A few girls smile at Max, taking the time to observe his sweatier figure. I smile, giving him a thumbs up. His eyes only roll. Rae and I lean against the wall outside the art room, waiting for the boys as usual.

"Ladies," Max mutters, standing closer than usual as he moves into an open space beside me. I mess with his blade, observing the small streak of red coating its edge.

"Hard day in class?"

"I may have had some fun with an Unfortunate," Max says with a grin. Kai shifts uncomfortably, only tucking his blade deeper into his bag.

"Sounds like you had as much fun with them as Josh did with Forest," Raegan mutters. I hit her arm, narrowing my eyes at her angrily as both men now look a little less relaxed.

"What did Josh do?" Max questions. The playful banter has left his voice.

"He wanted me to ask you about a Student Advocate position, and he *might* have taken a brash approach to convince me to ask you," I say, staring down Raegan even more. Max's eyebrows raise, showcasing his frustration as he looks to his twin for clarification.

"By digging his nails into your leg?" Raegan questions. I shake my head at her, ready to toss her into the nearest wall for getting them both so worked up. Max reaches down to my leg, pressing down on each of my upper thighs until I wince. I slap his hand away, biting my bottom lip as I rub away the pain that the pressure of his hand had left behind.

"There's no way in hell I am helping him with an advocate position-"

The art room door opens, leaving Max's words floating between us. Fallan watches us all, keeping his hands buried deep in his pockets. I hadn't noticed till now how much taller he is than my brother. In most scenarios, Kai looks down on people, not the other way around. Fallan glances toward my brother, looking even further down at Max, whose chest is suddenly more pushed out than it was a few seconds ago. I keep my position on the wall, motioning for Fallan to move past us. With a gentle shove, I hold Max's leg back with my own, stopping the kick meant to meet Fallan's ankle. Fallan watches the motion, shaking his head at no one in particular, letting that familiar smirk line his face. His shirt still has stains. It's now smudged, indicating he'd tried his best to eliminate the result of Josh's malice during class as much as possible. He moves to leave, ignoring Max's frustrated grunts at the feeling of my back pressing him against the wall. Eventually, he lets up, letting me stay leaned up against him.

"You can't stop me from beating his ass," Max whispers, letting his arms rest around my neck from behind.

"Your hand is already destroyed," I say, motioning to his cut knuckles, now raised in both of our lines of vision. "That's enough for today," I whisper, leaning away from him, only to feel the accidental brush of Fallan's arm on my lower stomach as he moves through the group.

Immediately, it felt like there was a fire scorching through me. Every defensive bone in my body burns hot, screaming and clinging to the brief touch. Every part of me heats, sending a fleet of fear and pain through me. I clutch my lower stomach, feeling my lungs make a sorry attempt at breathing in between a strained gasp. Fallan continues his relaxed walk, turning into nothing in our vision once he turns the first corner down the hallway. I grasp Max, feeling the sudden pain slowly slip away with each passing second. Max's eyes explore me with nothing but worry. Kai and Raegan even pull away from their conversation to focus on my gasping figure.

"What's wrong?" Kai questions, as if I have an immediate answer.

The heat slowly fades away, starting from my core and ending at my fingertips. I take in a full breath, feeling a sudden emptiness as the fleet of emotions all leave me.

"I got dizzy," I lie, pressing my hand to my head until everything is normal once more.

"Stop scaring us," Raegan sighs, nudging my arm.

I smile at her, wrapping her into a hug as I stow away the longing to feel that fire burn through me again.

What was it?

Why did I feel it?

The heat warmed me, filling me with emotions I had not felt since I was a child. Everything all at once, only to dwindle to nothing.

It's a nothingness that follows me each day.

"Well, if you're done scaring us all, we still have the rally in the event center. We're all required to go," Kai mutters, holding to his Student Advocate roots, spewing out their propaganda.

"Loyal man," Max scoffs, slinging his arm around my shoulders. Kai only mocks the gesture with vulgar hand motions.

"Perfect, you two can keep loving on each other, and I will go with Forest," Raegan says, pulling me away from her twin, leaving the two boys alone to cling to one another.

"Sometimes I'm convinced your brother has a thing for Max," Raegan says jokingly, pulling me down the hallway and away from our companion's earshot. The two boys grab each other's heads, shoving each other around and into the walls. Kai's face is red, burning hot with frustration.

"Who am I kidding? Kai is too focused on academics to notice anyone," she finally says after a few moments of silent observation.

Oh, the irony in that statement.

The event center is the epicenter of the school, housing rows of chairs and a grand stage, all lit by the school's natural lighting provided by the beautiful glass roof. The chairs are made of black satin, each individually hand-made by a skilled sewer in the Unfortunate sector. Students already begin occupying the seats, marveling at the spacious stage.

Gaggles of Officials linger off to the sides of the room, staring down the crowd—specifically the Unfortunates grouped in the back. Fallan takes up two seats, leaning into the whispers of a blonde nearly on his lap. Her hair is up in a tight braid. I can see the judgment in her eyes as she scans the room.

Her hand rests on his leg, showing they are more than familiar with one another. I stare at the sight, annoyed at her blatant show of affection in such a public setting. Rae and Kai join the other Student Advocates toward the front. I watch as many of the Student Advocates mingle with upper leadership, clinging to their words of encouragement as if they are deities. Even Max has dispersed, joining a few of the athletes in speaking to some of the younger Officials who have occupied themselves by reminiscing about their training.

I stay away from it all, leaning against the farthest wall, doing my best to avoid speaking to anyone. Fallan's head turns my way, stopping his scan of the room once he notices my still figure. He cocks his head at me, narrowing his hate-filled eyes before being pulled away by the chin in the hand of the beautiful blonde. Her lips land on his jaw, kissing gently in soft motions. I narrow my eyes at him, feeling that increasingly familiar burn on my mark begin to grow.

"How insufferable is all of this to you?" a voice I hardly recognize questions.

I pull my hateful gaze away from Fallan, landing on a pair of unfamiliar blue eyes looking down at me. The black material of an Official uniform clings to the man's body. Unlike all of his comrade's slicked-back hair, he keeps his blonde curls in a wild frame around his face. Where Max's hair is styled straighter, his stays curled. Bright blue eyes and a tall figure encapsulate the man. A bit of stubble lines the man's face, something often seen as out of regulation. His uniform is less put together too. It's as if he had thrown it on without care for the pristine nature of the Official's clothing regulations.

"Because if you asked me, all I see is a bunch of pretentious assholes all having a reason to showcase their worst traits," the man starts, pointing to Kai and Rae's group. "Overachievers." His finger moves toward Max. "A bunch of idiots wanting to sign their life away to be a glorified hall monitor." And then his finger finally points to the Unfortunates. "And people who never really had a chance at winning in this life," he finishes. I hold onto his words, frantically looking around in a panic, waiting for someone to deliver him a new one for the first remotely kind words I have heard uttered from another soul regarding Unfortunates. "And then there's you, alone in the back of an event meant to show off the students. You couldn't be any more hidden from it all, so is it as insufferable to you as it is to me?" he questions, leaving me halfway dumbfounded by his words.

"You-you just spoke about Unfortunates like-"

"Like they are humans? I won't tell if you don't," the man mutters, looking over his nails as if what he said is the most casual thing one could say to another.

I feel my mouth curl into a smile at his blatant lack of care toward the numerous rules he has just broken in a single conversation. He leans his head into the wall behind him, crossing his arms, waiting for me to say something.

"I think we spend a great deal of time making people feel seen when that's so far from the case," I finally say, crossing my arms to mimic his relaxed demeanor. He smiles.

"Do you not feel seen?"

"I feel like I don't fit in. There's a difference. Maybe it's because I am seen too much."

"And what's wrong with not fitting in with all of what I just pointed out to you? You want to be stuck in one of those bubbles?" he questions, smiling like a giddy first year.

"Says the Official," I say in a tone I would never dare use with anyone else wearing that uniform.

"An Official who knows how to utilize the good parts of my job."

"And what good parts are there?" I question, watching his eyebrows furrow as he ponders the question.

"Well, today I was supposed to be scanning the Unfortunate sector for contraband. Instead, I got to weasel my way into a conversation with you simply because of how awkward you looked pressed against this wall."

"Is that humor I am sensing in your tone?" I question, nearly laughing at his expression of offense.

"You seriously said that as if I am incapable of humor," the man mutters, shaking his head at me in disbelief.

"You're the one who only speaks to me because of how awkward I look," I say, quoting him in a deeper voice, making him laugh.

"There might have been other motivating factors...."

He winces as his voice trails off, a few of his comrades motioning him over. The school's upper leadership stands shoulder to shoulder on stage, directing the wave of bodies to take a seat as groups dissipate. The man moves to follow his companion's waves. I grab his sleeve, stopping him from getting too far.

"What's your name?" I question, watching his eyes fill with sudden amusement.

"Xavier," he mutters, smiling as I lower my hand.

"My name is Forest-"

"I know," is all he says before pulling away.

I stand baffled, still absorbing the interaction with a wide grin I can't seem to shake. Raegan's cold palm closes around my wrist, dragging me along with her as she mumbles about an exuberant amount of useless information she had just learned while speaking to upper leadership.

Xavier moves onto the stage, joining the other Officials with small, playful shoves. His eyes land on mine, giving me a wink before pulling his gaze in the direction of the wall of maroon-colored pant suits clinging to each upper leadership member. Without wanting to, I force my head to look back to the Unfortunates, expecting to see Fallan's hate-filled eyes still on me. Instead, he's looking toward the front, keeping his eyes on the wave of figures moving on and off the stage. The blonde woman continues pestering him. His hand holds her leg, preventing her from getting herself halfway strung across his front. Raegan pulls me down in a seat next to her. Kai quickly follows, seizing Max's opportunity to sit beside me.

"Can all of the students please take a seat?" Mr. Pavlecheck, the school's headmaster, politely gestures to each of us. He stands in the center of the group on stage. Unlike all the others, a streak of gold coats his uniform, signifying his place in New Haven's government. Gold is stitched onto some part of each higher-up's clothing. Even the Officials have cuffs stitched with gold thread.

"Why is dad here?" Kai questions.

My father's familiar figure makes his way onto the stage, clasping hands with Mr. Pavlecheck while acknowledging all of the Officials. Xavier shakes my dad's hand, smiling ear to ear as the man cracks a silent joke. In this lighting, I now see what Xavier truly looks like. His hair is a wild frame around his face. His eyes are blue like the streams that once coated the ground of the Earth.

"He oversees most of the Official's day-to-day tasks. I'm assuming that has something to do with it," Max responds, looking more interested.

Mr. Pavlecheck claps his hands, silencing the whispers spreading around the room. Something itches at me to turn to face Fallan's angry stare again. Still, I ignore the feeling.

"As you all know by now, we would like to recognize those amongst you reaching their final year here at the Academy, but we also need to address more serious matters plaguing our community." He pauses. Extending his arm behind him, "Andrew, I think you should take it from here."

My father walks up to the mic, clearing his throat with a few grunts. I look to Xavier, who is already raising his shoulders at my confused expression. Even he seems lost.

"Over the past few months, we have begun to see an influx of Unfortunate crimes rising in our community. Theft, burglaries, and battery are only a few ways these *deviants* have managed to wreck the tranquility of our community. That being said, we have brought it upon ourselves to begin upping security measures. That includes more severe de-regulation tactics than just light sensor prods alone-"

My dad's body tenses up, losing his relaxed posture almost immediately. His hand clutches the mic, his lungs taking shallow breaths that do him no good. I lean forward, readying myself to stand. He swallows slowly, pulling his attention toward the back of the room and then back to the audience.

"We will begin implementing on-site punishments for crimes committed inside this sector. This includes more extreme shows of force if any Unfortunate chooses to resist punishment." My father pulls out a leather scourge from behind him. "These are generally only utilized within the Unfortunate sector but are now permitted within the Untouchable sector of New Haven. For every crime committed, 20 lashings are permitted at any time by any Official, regardless of rank. This has been decided," my father finishes, staring back at the crowd with lowered eyes.

My mind flashes to the countless scars coating Fallan's lower back.

"We did that?" I whisper silently to myself, finally allowing my head to turn to observe the raven-haired man.

I never expected to see where his gaze had landed.

He stares down my father, gripping the armrests of his seat as his blonde friend keeps his leg down, stopping him from getting up. My father's stare was not just at anyone earlier, as his eyes swept the back of the room, it was toward Fallan, and he was dishing it right back. The two men hold each other's eyes, each look filled with something more profound than what is lingering on the surface. Fallan looks livid, only turning his head slightly once he notices me staring at him.

"For the glory and grace of the New World Order!" a rambunctious student advocate yells, cheering on my dad's speech with a reiteration of our community's saying.

Just like the mind-numbing voices of the devices in our home, those around me repeat the saying, each smiling ear to ear. I hold my tongue, letting Fallan maintain eye contact, hoping the question in my gaze is obvious. His hate quickly returns, backed up by a nasty expression from his blonde friend, now joining his hateful stare toward me. I turn away, meeting Kai's confused look at my utter silence.

"Why didn't you say it? You always love that part?" he starts, scrunching his brows with confusion.

I pull away from the chair, watching the other students begin to file away as the upper leadership leaves the stage. I weave down the row Rae had dragged me down, feeling that familiar pressure on my chest I get each time Fallan stares at me with that hate. My body works past others, almost crashing into an Official holding out their light sensor prod at the end of the row. People meander, conversing quietly, reluctantly moving back to their last classes of the day.

"Forest, Kai!" my dad says in a cheerful tone. His hand draws Xavier closer, clapping his upper back with gentle pats. Max and Rae join us. Max's arm finds its way around my shoulder much quicker than it has before. I shoot him a questioning look, but his eyes only stare forward.

"This is Xavier Hayes, one of our youngest and most talented Officials I've had the honor of overseeing," my dad chirps. He admires the man like he is a prized trophy.

"The pleasure is mine. I have heard many good things about the Vega twins," Xavier says, shaking Raegan's gentle hand before eyeing Max up and down. I move Max forward, feeling his hand drop away from me. He accepts Xavier's handshake, doing his best to observe the man up and down similarly. The two men hold each other's hands longer than most would consider comfortable. Even my father looks confused at the brief exchange.

"And, of course, these are my two kids, Kai," Kai shakes the man's hand with glee. "And my dear daughter, Forest."

"We've met, but I don't mind introducing myself again," Xavier says, grabbing my hand and letting his lips meet the soft skin at the top of my hand. The brief touch warms me, filling my cheeks with heat, my pulse picking up rapidly.

I wish his lips would explore more than just my hand. I silently whisper in my mind.

It's a brief thought I shove away, only adding to the red hue of my cheeks once I notice his smirk at my sudden fluster.

I see how Xavier watches me. Unlike Fallan's hate and my family's disapproval, he shows only curiosity when he looks at me. He watches me as if I'm the only person in the room. Everything I do sparks his interest. Even as my father speaks, he keeps his eyes on me as much as he can, and I do the same to him. It's as if I expect him to change at any moment and be an entirely different person. He watches me as if I am someone worth figuring out.

"So, where is this new Commander everyone has been talking about?" Kai questions eagerly.

Not too long ago, New Haven's Elder Commander stepped down to enjoy his restful years peacefully. Rumors spread that a young and very strategic Commander was appointed, taking on many responsibilities governing our people that used to take multiple Council members. As far as we know, things have only been better since they stepped up, but they hardly show face due to their strenuous schedule. Markets that once struggled to support New Haven now have full shelves. High crime rates in the Unfortunate sector dwindled to nothing after their first month in leadership. They have spoken once and only once, using mediators like my father to communicate his words. Even my father has never seen the Commander in person. Only people with ranks a peg below the man, like Josh's Father, have been invited to the Commander's private meetings.

"I can't say I care enough to keep track of them," Xavier blurts.

Kai's mouth drops, hanging open at the Official's blunt statement. My father clears his throat, awkwardly adjusting his collar, glancing around to his mutuals, who may have heard the crude comment. I cover my mouth, hiding the massive smile working its way across my face.

"But who cares what I think," Xavier finishes.

In this fleeting moment, I realize why my smile has not left my face. Xavier's thoughts are entirely his own, filled with defiance and challenge in ways I've never seen anyone dare to express.

At that moment, for the first time in a long time, my defiant mind suddenly felt a little less *lonely*.

CHAPTER SIX

FOREST

K ai fumbles with his blade, wrapping the hilt higher while programming better mechanics into the small hard drive of data linked to his chip. His fingers fly across the keyboard of his computer, inputting a series of codes I don't even want to begin to try and decipher. His chip blinks slowly behind his ear, pairing with the new set of commands written into his blade's mechanical structure.

I place my blade next to his, waiting for him to work his magic so I can pass this class with no grief from the teacher. Although not the best at physical activities like Max, Kai prevails in anything academically based. Programming code for their own blade would be delusional for most students. Each blade is assigned to everyone in the middle of their third year once the design process is complete.

Kai designed and built his blade his first year, creating mine shortly after in stolen moments of the night. We sit huddled in the back of the classroom, taking up two computers while only utilizing one. I spin my closed blade on the table, fidgeting with its hard drive in an anxious twirl between my fingers.

"Why the sudden need to re-wrap your hilt?" I question, breaking my brother's extreme focus.

"It keeps coming loose and someone suggested wrapping it higher up on the hilt to have more tension. So far, it's been holding together better."

His brown curls fall into his face, covering his focused gaze.

"Max seriously had a suggestion like that?" I question, wondering how Max could do anything remotely strategic regarding craftsmanship.

"Not him."

Kai's head is lowered, clouded with a shame I only see now.

"Then ... who?" I question.

Kai avoids my gaze as best he can.

"I briefly allowed an Unfortunate to speak to me today. The blonde one who is always hanging around *your* Unfortunate."

The vivid image of the blonde all over Fallan reaches my mind.

"For starters, he is not 'my Unfortunate.' I should be questioning if the same Kai I know allowed an Unfortunate to speak to him," I say, poking his arm in an attempt to lighten his mood.

He doesn't budge. The bright light of the computer screen exposes his solemn expression. He stays silent, tapping his foot against the floor in quick patterns. My lively manner quickly dies out with the sound of our peers tapping their keyboards.

"Sometimes I question if we're doing the right thing."

The words leave me before I can fully process them. It is now me staring forward, letting the bright light of the computer screen swallow me whole. His head raises, looking me over.

"You know you can't say things like that-"

"But why? Why can't we empathize with people other than ourselves for a moment?" I blurt out, stopping his train of thought.

I feel my hands ball into fists, slamming hard on the desk before he can react. The table shakes beneath my touch. A bubble of anger swirls within me, clinging to every thought that enters my mind. The classroom is silent. Only a few glance back at the sudden loud noise before returning to their computers. Kai's hands lower onto my fists, stopping their slight shake beneath his touch.

"Because they aren't people, Forest. I was only telling you about that moment with Valerie, so no one threw it back in my face," Kai says.

It's a useless reiteration of the same ideologies New Haven has been cramming down our throats for years. Why can't he, for once, have a thought that wasn't decided for him? Why does everything I do feel like an astronomically unplanned fuck up, and he just works with the flow of it all? Even now, his sense of empathy died out in a matter of seconds-

"Xavier seemed fond of you," Kai interrupts my train of thought, pulling his hands away from my own to return to his code.

"Is that seriously what you want to focus on now?" I question. He pauses, taking in a deep breath.

"If you want to do what's good for us and your Judgment Day, I suggest you drop the topic of Unfortunates and remember where our loyalties lie ... you're starting to sound more and more like Mom," he says, as if it's an insult to be compared to our mother.

"Because that's a bad thing?" I question, readying myself to shove away from the desk.

My hands grip the wood, stopping the push once Kai's hand rests on my hand once more. He closes his computer screen, his chip's blinking fading away with three small flashes. He turns his body, letting himself fully face me with a look of sorrow. I see it now. Our mother's gentle expression consumes his face.

"I never said it was a bad thing. You walk the line in ways I wish I had the courage to. I know how hard it can be to see some of the punishments. Do you know what would happen if we let them do as they pleased in our sector?" he questions, waiting for a genuine answer. His fingers press into my palm, tracing the lines in my hand.

"They would refuse to do work, stopping the flow of everything we've created. We can sit here and question if what we are doing is moral, or we can acknowledge the fact their sector is just as new as ours and they have their own people, just as we have ours. New Haven assured us they would receive the same resources as us, even if they were worn, and as far as we can tell by the transfers, they are clothed, cleaned, and fed," Kai says, rubbing his hands up and down the goosebumps of my arms.

I think of Fallan's scars. Each one is deep and calculated in where it is placed.

"But Kai, the woman from this morning-"

"Was a baker. That's why she looked so worn. Who wouldn't look worn after cooking nonstop? I see what you're worried about, but you don't seem to see their people's willingness to hurt us. I know you feel it when they look at you. The hate they can fill you with is suffocating; all it takes is a simple look. Do you think hate like that is worth defending?" Kai questions.

I'm starting to think it's not me he is trying to convince.

"Is this just about me?" I question. Kai's hands clasp around his neck, holding his head down, pressing it firmly against the desk.

"Yes. That's the only answer I can give you that will aid us both," Kai says, keeping his head pressed against the cold desk.

I feel my hand gravitate toward his distressed figure. Like second nature, my hand lowers on his upper back, gently rubbing up and down to soothe the tension holding him together. Not often do people show emotion in public. It's considered immodest in many ways. Still, I feel his back relax into the touch, easing up with every drag of my hand.

"Don't stop questioning, Forest. Don't ever stop asking questions," Kai whispers.

He raises his head, watching my hands fall back into my lap with a clasp.

"Someone has to do it for us," Kai finishes before turning back to his monitor and continuing to work on his code.

The sound of his typing drowns out my millions of thoughts. His fingers move more rapidly, working even more precisely than he had before.

"Why would you say that?" I question, watching his eyebrows twitch. A hint of annoyance passes over his face at the exchange.

"I didn't say anything," Kai mutters, keeping his focus on his work.

"You just-"

Kai's hand grabs my collar, silencing my words immediately. I feel him tug me toward him, pulling me free from my chair. I lean into his motions, forcing my head to meet his eyes.

"I didn't say anything," Kai reiterates, showcasing how far past his tipping point I have pushed him. He has done this since we were children. He always exerts whatever power he has to get a point across. He pushes me away whenever I think I am getting somewhere with him. Every one of his emotions feels like something I must earn to see. Everyone around me is entirely shut off, able to read me like an open book. I struggle to find my words, dragging myself away from his firm grasp, my shirt untucking. I force down the bottom, not letting the shirt pull out to reveal any of my skin. With a scoff, I swipe my hardware, shoving it deep into my bag with a grunt.

"Sit in silence alone with your conflictions. I hope Valerie repeats whatever she did to make you feel so morally defeated that you felt the need to grab me like that. I didn't realize you and Josh had so many similarities," I spit, ignoring my blade's warning not to leave without synching new data to the blade's hard drive. I allow it to flash red, shoving past the classroom doors and spilling into the empty hallway.

I should go back inside. I should apologize and let all of my anger fade.

Sadly, leaving this bleak school is so much more enticing.

The warm sun shines through the multi-colored leaves. A once overcast sky is now filled with nothing but bright blue, stretching well beyond the ward. With a quick slip past reception and a toss of my ID into Kai's bag, it was easy to get past the school's devices tracking my whereabouts. Beyond the chip behind my ear, there is no real way to follow us, and even then, the chips are entirely our own. Not even an Official has jurisdiction over your chip. It's the one thing we can hold onto with no constraints.

I rub the small scar on the back of my ear, feeling the tendrils of the chip snake beneath my fingers. My body hugs the side of the building, following along a small rocky path designated for leisure time. Koi fish follow me, letting their small heads bob to the surface with open mouths. I crouch down, laughing at the feeling of their tiny mouths latching onto my finger. I hoped they got more to eat than just the algae the school provides them. They look peaceful, swimming around their small pond with no cares in the world. Each one is the same. Genetically engineered to perfection, there are no differences between them.

"Even you have no room for flaws," I whisper, gliding my hand over my birthmark with a frown.

Voices sound off from the side of the school, clashing with the peaceful flow of the koi ponds. The voices are whispers and argumentative words. I yank my finger away from the fish, silently apologizing while working closer to the sudden noise. I meet the corner of the school, peeking past it, hoping to see who else has decided their last period was worth leaving.

My stomach drops at the sight in front of me.

Fallan stares down at Valerie, keeping his tie loose around his neck with his sorry attempt at a tucked shirt on full display. His bag is on the ground, wide open, and filled with a plethora of contents I cannot identify. I hold myself close to the wall, focusing on their exchange.

"Are you going to stand here all day?" Fallan questions, crossing his arms as he looks down at Valerie.

I see her eyes roll at the comment. Even from here, the scars coating her hands in numerous places only seem to radiate in this lighting. She reaches into the pocket of her pants, pulling out a small black metal cylinder that I have only seen in the hands of the Officials. She clutches the light sensor prod, tossing it into Fallan's eager grasp. He catches the device, opening and closing it with familiarity. His arms swing the device around, handling it as well as some of the more trained Officials.

For the first time, I see his smile.

It encapsulates his face, only creasing the crow's feet around his eyes. I want to look away from it. I want to loathe the way his eyebrows raise when he grins and despise the downturn of his mouth as he holds his smile. His straight teeth and gentle smirk only add to his look of glee. I could paint this image a million times and still want to see it in person. He smiles in a way I know so few must see. Only a second has passed once his mouth drops into its typical flat look. I shake my head, pulling myself away from my vile perceptions of the man.

He forces the prod into his bag, zipping it up and slinging it over his shoulder. He pulls Valerie into him, letting her arms wrap around his neck, whispering in her ear. I see her face fluster, only making my own grow hot with something more profound than embarrassment.

It's something I can't quite pinpoint.

I hiss as my mark burns once again. It feels like a painful fire in my lower stomach, growing the longer I stand here.

"Fuck!" Fallan curses, forcing my stare away from my birthmark. He clutches his chest, snapping his head in my direction. I have little time to push myself behind the wall. My body sinks to my knees, clutching my ears as an overwhelming sense of fear washes over me. Regardless of my grasp on my head, I hear their muffled tones.

"What is it?" Valerie questions.

"Nothing.... Let's go," Fallan says, pausing a great deal between the two statements.

The fear only grows, making my heart race like the drum of a thousand marchers. I dig my shoes into the Earth, grinding my teeth as the noises around me grow angrier. The once tranquil pond now sounds like the waves of a thousand angry seas. The clatter of dry leaves hitting the ground is now chalk on a whiteboard.

"Quiet," I whisper, wishing every noise would silence. It becomes deafening, giving me no way to focus on anything but the sound of my heartbeat. It fills my ears in pulses. My blood pumps through me, clashing with all the other noise.

"Quiet!" I whisper again. Hitting my head hard against the wall, I feel a wave of dizziness come over me as the world suddenly becomes silent. Something wet coats my head before colliding with the ground in red droplets. I turn my head to inspect my cut in the koi pond, falling on my ass at the sight in front of me.

Every beautiful fish, once swimming peacefully, now gasps for air, thrashing against the dying grass. The pond water slowly seeps into the dry dirt, touching the tips of my shoes and creating a muddy mess around me. Numerous fish lie dying, all unable to find water in the now-drained holes in the ground. I look around, clutching the grass, forcing myself to my feet. I drag my hand over my head, reaching into my bag to find something to hold down on the tiny cut. I settle on a piece of fabric, stumbling forward as my muddy shoes cling to the dry grass. I step over the koi, watching their mouths gasp in pain, their lives slowly draining. It looks like the Earth up and left, grabbing the water, leaving the life to fend for itself.

I don't try and look around the corner of the wall. If they thought they were alone then, they surely don't now. I don't stick around to find out why they need that light sensor prod.

My legs burn as I dash away from the destructive scene before me, trying my best not to see how many cameras caught my little stunt of smacking my head against the wall.

I force myself through the closest side door of the Academy, ignoring the visual of the desecrated pond flashing through my mind.

I wanted answers.

Now, all I have are questions.

CHAPTER SEVEN

FOREST

I spent thirty minutes trying to wash the mud away from my shoes in the school bathroom closest to the back door. For reasons beyond my understanding, I thought hitting my head against the wall outside would stop the noise. I only managed to give myself nothing but a good-sized cut, easily fixable if I had my Cure-All. I had managed to get the bleeding to stop, hiding it with my hair in a less-than-functional hairstyle. The brown locks coat the side of my face, forced forward with a few straggling bobby pins.

After the incident outside the school, avoiding class seemed like my best option. Either I stay outside and face Fallan, Valerie, and the mess around me, or force myself into a seat next to Kai, who will only pry. The knob on the door jiggles. I stop the running water, gathering myself in the mirror's reflection.

"I'm almost done!" I yell, fixing my uniform as best I can while cramming multiple paper towels in the overflowing bin.

I grab my bag, hearing the automated chime of the last bell of the day. With a quick drag of the lock, the door swings open, nearly making the Untouchable girl leaning on the door fall inside and onto me. I quickly move past her, not giving her enough time to examine my face too closely. I keep my head lowered, avoiding direct eye contact with anyone who passes by. The eyes of those around me seem to linger. Glances now feel like full-fledged stares. I move closer to reception, then past the scanners with the next wave of students making their way out of the building. My hands shove open the glass doors, pushing me closer to my group's usual waiting spot.

Multiple people crowd around the side of the school, observing the destroyed ponds and dying fish. Officials stop students from getting a closer look at the carnage, giving students little to no reason about what caused the mess in the first place. My throat feels dry. The blame toward Unfortunates instantly finds people's mouths, only adding to the hatred of them in this sector.

But what really happened? What happened in those fleeting moments in which I let the noise become too loud? All I could do was harm myself to silence it. The meds were supposed to stop the blackouts. They were supposed to stop those moments of the unknown.

"I've been wondering where you went off to."

Kai works his way from the front of the curious, growing group. Raegan and Max pull away from the swarm, noticing us the moment Kai's mouth opens. He looks perplexed at the sight, throwing me a questioning look that only motivates me to move toward the tram.

"You pissed me off. I needed some time alone," I say, feeling the twins' growing presence as we all begin to move away from the busy schoolyard.

"They're saying some Unfortunates trashed the lawn. The worst part is they somehow fried the cameras in the process. They can't recover the footage," Raegan says, moving close to my brother, who eagerly awaits her presence.

"Give them anything nice, and they ruin it," Kai says. I can't help but scoff at his crude words after the ones he chose to share with me in programming class.

"Bold of you to assume it was an Unfortunate knowing Josh and Colton live and breathe for a thrill like destroying property," Max mutters, filling me with relief. I know he says it to please me, but still. I allow my hand to trail behind me, reaching for his grasp with a squeeze. He lets his hand land on my own. Any tension between us earlier melts away with the touch.

Students gather near the stopped tram, clamoring to get on with shoves. Many linger by the empty ponds, slowly dragging along to catch the tram. Colton and Josh are leaning outside the tram, eyeing down all the women while they work their way up the steps. I keep my head lowered, pulling Max along with me, wanting nothing more than for them to be silent. Colton's hand reaches out, stopping my march toward the tram steps. The bus driver and I make eye contact. Our heads raise simultaneously.

"You think after what you pulled this morning, you can just get on that easily?" Colton questions. His face grows uncomfortably close. Max grabs his collar, shoving him back into the tram with a grin.

"Why don't you go and fess up for the mess you two assholes made so we can all go home?" Max questions. Josh audibly laughs at the comment.

"Still following her around like a lost puppy, hoping you get a chance to get past that horrid uniform blouse-"

"Open your mouth one more time, and I will make what you did to that Unfortunate this morning look tame," Max spits, pointing his finger at Josh's chest. All three men surround each other like rabid dogs. Kai balls his fist, waiting in anticipation for Max's next move. I glance again at the bus driver, feeling his worries increase about this new delay. It's his ass if we keep holding up his routes.

"Max, let it go," I begin, motioning Kai and Rae to help me pull him away from Josh and Colton. With a release of Colton's collar, he backs down, moving backward and into my touch, even making it up a few steps of the stairs, beginning the flow of movement once more.

"Go on and follow your dirty, Unfortunate loving whore-"

My hands meet Josh's arms, shoving him back into the tram as hard as possible. He stumbles, almost falling over, only to be dragged back up by my hand. I grab his face, holding his sharp jawline in my hand, forcing him to look at me. My hair slips away from its pinned position. The cut burns as the cool breeze moves past it. I hold Josh still, pinning his tall figure with my leg. I made sure to keep my knee in the one place he would rather not feel pressure. Colton moves, ready to pull me away from his idiotic companion. I put more pressure on Josh's crotch with my knee, watching the arrogance leave his expression.

"Make him back off," I hiss. Josh pounds the side of the vehicle, stopping his friend's movements. Kai's hands hold the back of his head, his eyes wide at the exchange. Max stands still, unsure of what to do. Rae tries her best to deal with crowd control but only meets dead ends as people begin to cheer at the sight of aggression.

"You have absolutely no idea who I am. None!" I press down harder, watching his expression shift to pain. My lips move closer to his ear. His heartbeat pounds beneath my touch. "If you would like to see how dirty I'm willing to get my hands to prove to everyone here how much of a bitch you are, please, allow me. Call me an Unfortunate loving whore again, and I will make sure you look as fucked up as every Unfortunate who's received a violation. I suggest you stop mistaking me for the first year you tormented and back off," I finish, pulling my mouth away from his ear, only to meet his angered face.

Pulling my knee away, I let him go. His body slumps forward, exhibiting the strength of the hold I had on him. I motion Max up the steps, playing off the whole interaction as if it'd never happened. Josh grabs my arm, stopping me dead in my tracks. His fingers wrap around my wrist, squeezing with all he has.

"Don't forget what I have on you-"

"Tell them. Maybe we can both get some fucking answers," I hiss, looking over the crowd with anger.

"Show's over," I spit with rage.

In the back of the crowd, his blue eyes look at me with something other than a scowl. A small smirk lines his face, eating up his expression like a mask. Unlike all the other times he has hatefully watched over me, he allows his amusement to show this time. His arms are crossed over his chest. His head cocks, and he looks as if he's challenging me to prove something to him. I feel my body move forward, bowing toward the crowd while only looking at him. I keep my lowered gaze on him, letting my hate consume my vision, before following behind Max.

I expected that smirk to leave his face at my posturing.

It only seemed to grow.

But maybe that was my own delusion.

"What the hell was that? What does he have on you?" Kai questions silently, while stealing the seat next to me. Josh and Colton stagger onto the tram, eyeing me down with nasty looks that only fall flat.

"Do you suggest I continue to let them walk all over everyone? He has nothing, Kai. Calm down," I snap, waiting for his following snide remark.

"She's right," Max says, sitting beside me. "It should have been us roughing them up after Rae said he hurt Forest. Now is not the time to cast judgment," Max says, keeping his eyes on my furious brother.

Kai throws his arms in the air, forcing himself back to his feet. His hand grabs Max's front, pulling him up and into a standing position.

"If you're so adamant about getting involved, then you won't mind helping me convince them not to put marks on Forest's scorecard for her outburst," Kai says, dragging Max closer to the two devils. They look unamused by my brother's presence. Still, he sits next to them, using his most professional tone to create a mind-numbing conversation that will only go over their heads.

Raegan shakes her head, looking over her textbook, ignoring her twin's vicious side-eye.

"Thank you, kiddo," the bus driver silently whispers, smiling ear to ear at the sight of Valerie and Fallan on his tram. I press my head against the cool glass next to me, observing the silent banter between the trio meant for them and only them. Pain from the cut on my head still lingers, throbbing every so often, indicating the start of a headache.

Fallan pulls away from his conversation, looking over Valerie as she walks in front of him. I scoff at the sight, keeping my eyes away from his once they finally pull away from his blonde lap dog. My hands fidget with my bag, trying to find any source of distraction.

A small piece of paper falls to my lap. Fallan's hand quickly retracts to his side. I'm almost sure I envisioned his hand dropping the paper toward me in the first place. He moves forward and down the tram car until he is again in his section. He doesn't acknowledge me once.

I notice Kai and Max continue trying to talk to Josh and Colton. Rae's eyes are too focused on her textbook to notice anything. I tuck the note between my legs, opening it delicately to unveil whatever it contains.

I know it was you hiding behind the wall.

Tell anyone what you saw between me and Valerie, and I will ensure everyone knows about your generous contribution of a bottle of contraband Cure-All to an Unfortunate. How long would it take an Official to question how I got my hands on a bottle? Maybe Mommy should leave your name off the next one she slips in your bag. Wonder what a violation like that would do to you?

For shame, Little Dove.

I linger on the name he's given me, hating it with every fiber of my being. The paper crumples beneath my hand, smearing my fingers in black ink. I cram the note into my pocket, feeling my chest's heavy rise and fall as I process his arrogance. Valerie's legs are strung across his lap, absorbing the small rolls of his thumb over her thigh. She takes up several seats, almost lying down to indulge in his touch. While her eyes are on him, his stay on me. His head cocks, watching me, waiting for some type of reaction.

I lean forward on my knees, raising my head, mocking his movements with a challenging stare. His eyebrows gently raise, pulling the familiar metal vial casing of my mother's Cure-All free from his pocket. He twirls the tube between his long fingers. Glancing over at Josh and Colton, he pretends to drop the vial right in front of them.

If they find out I "gave" Fallan anything, I'm done for.

I lean back in my chair, shaking my head out of frustration. He continues rubbing Valerie's leg, even dipping his fingers beneath the hem of her shirt to rub her lower stomach. I force my gaze away from the sight, feeling the start of a pounding headache creep through my mind as my birthmark begins to burn. I grasp my lower stomach, focusing all my energy on working through the pain. The headache continues to grow, and I'm consumed with silent whispers in my mind that no longer feel like they've come from my own inner consciousness. I feel something creeping into my mind, lingering in the empty spaces, waiting to find an opening. It expands out, increasing the pain in my head, taking all of my rationality with it. At this point, I'm nervous that I'll blackout again, and that can't happen on the tram. There are too many people.

I draw in a deep breath, forcing my mind to push back on the pain with each expansion of my lungs.

"Get out!" I scream in my mind, closing my eyes to focus on where it's coming from.

It persists. Once more, I fill my mind with a painful scream.

"Get out! Get out! Get out!"

All at once, the pain slips away, causing the pressure in my lids to become lighter. I finish my exhale, feeling a great weight lift away from my now vacated mind. The crowding of another presence in my head melts away, making me question how much of that pain was real. I turn my head, expecting Fallan's taunting stare to eat me alive.

Instead, I find him looking out the tram window, running his hand through his wild locks, moving Valerie's legs off of him with frustration. She tries to speak to him, getting nothing but silence. His eyes snap shut, his hand wiping something away from his face with a drag of his sleeve.

"Did you hear me?" Kai's voice questions, pulling me away from my reverie and back into reality.

"What?" I question, looking over his frazzled face.

"It's dealt with," Max says. He steals the spot next to me, forcing Kai to sit beside his twin.

"How did you-"

"Just trust us, Blackburn," Max says, slinging his arm over my shoulder. He narrows his eyes at my head, gently running his thumb over my cut. Red coats his finger and he quickly wipes it away on the white cuff of his uniform.

"What happened?" he questions, my eyes focused on the crimson now smudging his sleeve.

"It's just a cut," I whisper, leaning my head into his chest, letting the sound of the tram's wheels in motion numb my thinking. He messes with his bag, utilizing some of his Cure-All to fix the wound. I silently thank him with a small smile, allowing his hand to rub up and down my back in comforting strokes.

"It's never just a cut with you," Max whispers in a light-hearted tone, leaving me to force a smile at a statement I can no longer find the humor in.

CHAPTER EIGHT

FOREST

The rest of the ride home was uneventful, filled with nothing but quiet gossip and multiple stares in my group's direction. My comforting lean into Max quickly turned into sleep I wasn't aware I needed. Twenty minutes later, we arrived at our usual stop, and I was ready to get off and leave the events of the day far behind. I quickly work my way off the tram, making sure to be the first one off to avoid Colton and Josh. Whatever Kai had said to them managed to silence both of them. Even when they walked past me, they remained quiet, getting off without so much as a look in my direction. The twins and my brother were next, all drawing in sighs of relief. I expect the tram to leave, but it lingers.

"I can break curfew, kid, don't-"

"Let it be, Mark," Fallan's familiar voice demands. He is speaking to the driver, trying to wave away his worries. Fallan exits the tram with a few Untouchables, leaving Valerie to watch him from the window with a longing look. Mark hesitantly closes the tram doors, pausing before starting the vehicle and continuing his route. Fallan casually continues his walk away from the stop. You'd think he's an Untouchable if you didn't know better.

"Your sector is across town. No dirty Unfortunates allowed in our neighborhood," Max says, moving ahead of the group. Fallan continues his walk forward, ignoring Max and keeping his back toward us all.

"Let it go, Maxey," Raegan says, utilizing one of his least favorite nicknames.

"An Official will drive by and eventually deal with him," Kai adds, only adding to my list of questions about why Fallan would want to get off at this stop. He was here this morning, but I assumed that an Official dealing with transfers was the cause of that. Maybe I was wrong.

"Fallan!" I yell, watching his body pause at my use of his name for the first time. His shoulders tense. Even though his hands are concealed within his pockets, I know he's balling his fists. "What are you doing here again?" I continue, watching his head turn backward to look at me. His mouth opens as if he's going to answer. Quickly, it closes, dropping into its familiar frown. He continues moving forward, giving us all nothing but silence.

"How did you know his name?" Kai questions. Rae is quick to answer.

"We have art with him, don't start deep diving into it."

Max moves forward, his rage spilling free from him. He grasps his blade, filled with a sudden need for violence. I press my hand to his chest, stopping his march toward Fallan. I think of the vial. As long as he has that Cure-All, I have to play nice.

"I think we've dealt with enough today," I plead, feeling his body relax the longer he watches me.

"Maybe you're right, Blackburn," he pauses, turning toward our regular route home, "If I'm ever paired with him in Defense Class, I'll paint the mat with him," Max finishes, guiding us away from the tram and closer to the normalcy of home.

My father's voice carries through the hallways, bouncing from wall to wall in angry shouts. The house's touch panel at the entrance confirms our presence, lighting green with a tap of our IDs. My mother and father's pictures are checked off, both home hours before us. My mother's figure is nowhere to be seen in the low-lit living area. More than one voice joins in with my father's shouts. The unfamiliar voice says my father's name repeatedly to calm him down. The wall closest to us shakes with a thud. I hear the men's volume grow, with words like "deviants" and "un-orderly" finding their way under the door of my father's study. My mom's office door is shut. The small golden light of her lamp coats the floor. The twins tap their IDs on our touch panel, sending a signal back to their own house with their current whereabouts.

I motion Rae to follow me, lingering by my father's now silent study. My body leans toward the door, pressing my ear to its cool surface, trying my best to decipher the hushed whispers of the men behind it.

"If they wanted us to hear it, the door would be open," Kai whispers, pulling me away from the door and guiding me closer to my room by my elbows. I stumble into the perfectly laid-out room, turning to hurl a whirlwind of curses toward my older brother. He moves Rae into my bedroom with me, while Max stands next to my brother, shaking his head with his signature smile plastered on his face. His own bedroom door closes just in time to silence me. I let the hateful words fade away, deciding maybe a closed door is best for everyone right now. Raegan hurls her body on my bed, looking up at my ceiling. Her blonde hair surrounds her head like a halo. Her natural beauty can catch me off guard even after all these years.

"Give me a good reason not to grab his curls and pin him down on the floor," I hiss, joining her on my bed. My back hits the soft sheets, my hands dragging across my tired eyes.

"Because he only wants what's best for you." She props herself on her elbow, turning her body to face me. "And you haven't been the most cooperative today ... is something going on, Forest?" she questions.

I long for an answer to give her. I want to say I am okay. I want to tell her I hate the hybrid program and am unsettled by the Unfortunate's presence. I want to laugh at their pain with her and throw away all my corrupt thoughts that seem to spill into my mind each time I am alone.

But I can't.

"If I tell you something ... can you promise me it stays between us?" I question, pulling myself back up into a seated position. Her interest is peaked. Her body readjusts to get a better look at my worried expression.

"You should know by now you can tell me anything. I still haven't told Kai who is responsible for his broken blade hilt."

The vivid image of me tossing his weapon against a wall after one of our arguments passes through my thoughts.

I shake away the image, looking at the clock on my nightstand. Its camera blinks, watching over the room and all who inhabit it. I move closer to the device, pulling its cord away from the wall, timing the five minutes I have on Raegan's watch until it alerts either of my parents of its deactivation. I cover her mouth, giving her no time to try and question my actions. There isn't enough time for her to start hitting me with her line of questioning.

"You know the two transfers on the tram today?" I question, still feeling the presence of the note in my front pocket. She nods, pulling away my hand from her mouth.

"Yes, *Fallan*," she says his name as if it's poison on her tongue. "He spent a great deal of that ride glancing over at you as angrily as Josh and Colton had," Raegan whispers, side-eying the clock lying face down.

"Why did you unplug-"

"I saw them take contraband from the sector. The girl he's been cozy with all day somehow got a light sensor prod and gave it to him. The 'deviants' my dad has been worried about sneaking around our sector are already here," I whisper, watching her expression shift.

She sits up more, holding my arms. Her head tilts as if she can retain more information the closer she is to me.

"They stole a *weapon*? How the hell would they even be able to get one of those away from an Official? Why haven't you reported it yet?" she questions.

Oh, no reason. They just have a supposed contraband item with my name plastered all over it.

"I have." The lie sounds convincing, even to me, "Maybe that's why he got off at our stop today, to avoid Officials in his sector."

"Did you see them wreck the school grounds?" she questions.

"That had to have happened after I left. There's no way they could have done that much damage," I say.

"You didn't see anything?"

Nothing that helps either of us.

"No, only what I already reported."

I needed to tell someone. I needed to have a conversation that felt normal. Reporting Unfortunates is supposed to be like second nature. Even now, I'm questioning if I've revealed too much to her about the nature of Valerie and Fallan's interaction. But I've always trusted her. Ever since we were children, she has safeguarded my secrets. But now, watching her nose upturn at the mention of any Unfortunate, I feel sick, like I've said the wrong thing.

"You could have said that in front of the clock. If anything, it would have helped you get them more violations," Rae says, moving to plug the device back in. I grab her wrist, stopping her from leaning over me. Her hand holds the cord close.

"The Cure-All isn't banned in their sector, is it?" I question, waiting for her quick comment on my ignorance in asking something so idiotic.

She has been studying nonstop for the past three years, preparing for her medical exam and to be placed in a position under my mother after her Judgment Day. The answer *should be* simple: the Cure-All is meant for *all*. That ideology is the very foundation on which my mother built her cure.

"Y-You know already, Forest. Your mom developed it for both sectors," Rae says, not giving me the straight answer I need.

I move her back a bit, waiting for us both to reach eye level before speaking.

"I didn't ask who it was made for. Did our people ban its use in their sector?" I question. The familiar pit fills my stomach the longer she goes without answering, only growing my suspicions.

"The new Commander felt the medical units were wasting many resources on funding things like supplying the Cure-All in their sector. Last I heard, it was being pulled from their shelves. Most have to go to the Untouchable Med Center and join a waiting list to receive a vial. A great deal of the people who need it don't tend to come back once it is finally their turn to receive a dosage," Rae says, tensing her jaw as she speaks.

"Don't come back?" I question, pushing farther on the notion.

"Our priority is not to keep them alive, Forest. The Cure-All is a luxury. You know this. Where one Unfortunate dies, three more stand. They're all replaceable. This isn't new information. We were giving them handouts for far too long," Rae says. My stomach twists at her words.

"Were children on the waiting lists?" I question.

Her eyes answer the question before her words can.

"They're *not* people. They're not our people. Stop speaking about them as if they are," Rae says, moving past me to cram the plug back in the outlet. I tuck my knees to my chest, reflecting on Fallan's note with a new perspective. Of all the things in that bag he could have swiped, he chose the Cure-All. There was a wallet in the front and an ID that could get him into any part of our sector. He stole a medicine Untouchables use like it has no limit. Some spray it on simple paper cuts, using multiple doses in one go. He wasn't stealing it to taunt me, although it did work to his advantage.

He was stealing it because he needed it.

Rae's furrowed brows relax once the device powers back to life. She looks at me sympathetically, landing her hand on my leg with a genuine expression.

"You did the right thing reporting those deviants and telling me. You know I will always support you," Rae says with a smile. It doesn't relax me like I wish it would.

The voices once trapped behind my father's door now resonate through the hallway. Loud laughter replaces the seriousness from earlier. I pull away from my position on the bed, swinging open the bedroom door, nearly crashing into Xavier and his wild blonde locks.

He grabs my waist, stopping me from clacking heads with him. He smiles wide at me, letting his laughter trail off. His large hand is warm against my side. I almost don't notice how dangerously close he is to the rough skin of my birthmark. I pause, apologizing silently at my sudden entrance into the hallway. I lean up against the wall in an attempt to shift his hand away from my mark. He moves closer, allowing my father more room to occupy the hallway with him. Xavier's eyes land on his hand, pulling it away, letting it rub the back of his neck.

"Reflexes," he whispers, giving me his gentle, soft grin.

"I didn't mind," I whisper back, speaking without fully processing my words.

He looks ready to say more, but the sudden presence of my father and Kai with Max quickly cuts him off. Kai and Max look curious, watching over Xavier with two very different expressions. Where Kai looks enthralled, Max looks displeased, maybe even annoyed. Xavier clears more space, joining me against the wall.

"How much did you all hear?" my dad questions, looking around at the three sets of eyes on him.

"Do you want me to lie and say I didn't hear you yelling?" I question, feeling Kai's annoyance even from this distance.

"He sounds grumpy when he's frustrated, doesn't he?" Xavier questions, grinning wildly at my dad's gaze.

"That I do," my father says, smiling just as wide as Xavier.

The two men's banter is unlike anything I have seen before. In most scenarios, that comment would have ended with crude words and shaming from my father. Instead, he laughs along, seeing the humor in Xavier's statement for once in his life.

"Five minutes alone yelling in a room together, and you make him smile?" I question Xavier.

"His presence might be growing on me," my father says, patting the man on the back.

My dad's knuckles are coated in a thin layer of scabs. Only now do I see the matching wounds covering Xavier's hands. It's relatively fresh. Some knuckles are cut deeper than others. I grab Xavier's hand, examining it closely before dropping it with two pinched fingers.

"Just made conversation today?" I question, watching Xavier's brows crease with a perplexed look.

"A few Unfortunates needed a brief talking to earlier for being away from their sector for too long," my father says.

All I can think of is the Unfortunate woman from the tram stop and Fallan's defiant walk straight into our sector.

"Looks to me like you two handled some deviant assholes," Max chimes in, moving closer to the young Official towering next to me.

"I heard Forest handled some assholes herself," Xavier says.

My dad's eyes snap to me, waiting for me to confirm or deny the statement.

"Has she been fighting again?" My father questions Kai, not bothering to ask me for the truth.

"It was two boys taunting her. The ones with all the violations on their score-cards. Untouchables. I took the liberty of viewing the footage so you didn't have to. To me, it was justified, possibly even lenient," Xavier says, saving me from having to pull together an excuse. I mouth a small "thank you," watching his smirk grow at the praise.

"He's right. Colton and Josh have been going at us all nonstop," Kai says in defense. Even he is done with their thoughtless actions.

"It was only those two you all dealt with today? You saw nothing else?" my father questions everyone in the group.

I can tell he's trying to find answers for his leadership about the damage at the school. They genuinely have no idea what happened. They are as in the dark as me. I was hoping maybe he would have an explanation.

Max begins to explain what he saw to my father, taking the claims of my other two companions as Xavier motions me to follow him. The four of them are engrossed in their conversation, not noticing our silent exit through my father's study door. Xavier adjusts the door, keeping it semi-open to continue listening to the conversations outside.

My father's study is lined with bookshelves, filled with old literature long forgotten in the new educational systems. A perfectly filed cabinet is open, revealing countless names I don't recognize. His computer screen is dark. The small stand of bourbon and scotch is raised high next to his leather chair. Xavier grabs a vile from his pocket, moving closer as he pushes the hair away from the side of my face. I feel my cheeks warm at the touch. His fingertips linger over my skin, his free hand cupping the side of my face. I wince once his fingers meet the cut Max had failed to heal fully with his Cure-All.

"This room has no devices. What did you do?" Xavier questions, spraying my face lightly with the medicine. His eyes watch the wound, continuing his hold on my face long after the cut is healed.

"I tripped. I'm clumsy," I say, trying to feed him the lie everyone has believed all day.

"Yeah? Is that what the twins believed?" he questions, dropping his hand from the side of my face. He keeps a piece of my hair between his pointer finger and his thumb as he rubs down its length.

"There's nothing to believe," I say, feeling the warmth spread in my cheeks once his eyes finally meet mine.

"Is that why your face is so red right now? Honesty has never looked so guilty," his free hand raises, cupping my cheek. He rolls his thumb over my skin in the same way Fallan had when he touched the soft skin of Valerie's thigh. I shove away the image of Fallan, letting Xavier's enthralling eyes coat my vision. The touch is gentle. It feels different than the kiss I shared with Max. Every touch from him so far makes me nervous, and he can sense it.

"I-I'm not guilty-"

"Then what are you? You've looked lost ever since you ran into me," Xavier says, keeping me flustered.

"Nothing happened that you haven't already laid out," I whisper, pulling his hand down and away from my face. I expect to let his hand go, but I cling on tighter.

"I don't believe you. Your heart is racing right now," he says, seeking a genuine answer. His fingertips meet my pulse along my neck. His head lowers, close enough to hear my shaky breaths.

"Are you sure you're trusting the right people?" he questions, only accelerating my heart rate.

My dad nudges open the door. Instantly, I retract my hands from Xavier's, creating space between us. My friend's eyes meet mine. Xavier holds his calm expression, shoving the vial back in his pocket. He smiles at me, easing my tension on the note we left the conversation on.

"You're all going to the screening tonight?" my father questions.

"What screening?" I ask, shooting my focus toward Kai.

"The school is playing The Great Gatsby tonight. It's one of the old world's coveted films. New Haven refurbished enough of a found film so they could cast it tonight in the front of the schoolyard. I've been telling you about it all week," Kai says in defeat.

"Actually, you only told me," Rae says, jumping to my defense at my brother's ignorance. "You are going, right?" Rae continues.

"Of course she is," Max says, rolling his eyes at his twin.

"I believe she can answer for herself," Xavier says, crossing his arms, cocking his head at Max.

The tension between these two is suffocating. It fills my throat like a thick fog. Even my father takes a moment to observe the rise in testosterone surrounding him.

"Forest, your mother hoped to speak to you before you go. Why don't you stop by her office before you start getting ready? Xavier and I have a few more things to go over, and I'm pretty sure your parents would like you two to check in before you stay here any longer," my father says, dispersing the group with just one statement.

That's how my father is. The man is able to dictate a room with few words. Max and Xavier look away from one another, moving to their respective areas across the room.

"We'll be back over in an hour," Rae says, tugging her twin and leaving the study. Kai trails behind. "I'll show them out. Good seeing you again," he finishes, waving gently to Xavier.

Odd.

He never gives anyone a second look.

My father waits for me to back away. I take the hint, letting Xavier hold the door open for me with his typical smile.

"Tell me it's a bad idea to continue trying to figure you out," he quickly whispers, lowering his head to avoid my dad's ears.

"I can't do that," I say, pulling away from the study with a smile.

My mother scans her files, covering her ears with a pair of earmuffs meant for winter. Her body jolts from my sudden presence. She pries away the soft barriers between the outside world and her. I kick her door closed with my heel, pulling up a seat beside her stressed figure.

"What's with the headgear?" I question, messing with the soft bits of the headpiece.

"Your father and the boy were getting too loud. I don't like hearing about his work some days," my mother says. My eyes trail to her clock. I'm shocked to see its plug pulled clean from the socket.

"How long have you had that out of the wall?" I question.

"As long as your father has been shouting in his study. It's not too fond of my distaste towards talk of violence. I'll take the marks on my scorecard," she says as she begins shoving away the folder in front of her with a sigh.

"They were only speaking of Unfortunates-"

She covers my mouth, looking around the room, silencing me with a raised finger. After a few seconds, she lowers her hand, drawing in a deep breath.

"There's no need to specify details right now. I want to talk about you. Kai mentioned to me you might be having a hard time. He says you've seemed a bit off," my mom says, glancing down at the portion of my shirt above my mark that Xavier had managed to untuck with his grasp earlier.

"I may have gotten in a physical altercation with an Untouchable," I begin. She shakes her head, scolding me with a click of her tongue.

"You know better, Forest. What have I told you repeatedly?" she questions, pulling away another one of my hairs she has deemed too gray to be residing with my dark brown hair.

"Being in the shadows is not a disadvantage," I say, watching her sigh.

"So, why would you go out of your way to draw attention to yourself? Why threaten someone out of a sheer power play?"

The hypocrisy eats me alive.

"I watched them beat down an elderly Unfortunate, and all is well, but the minute I make them feel the same fear, I'm the problem?" I question, cutting off her train of thought. She pauses, waiting for me to clarify.

"What-"

"There was an Unfortunate woman this morning. Josh Seal and Colton Stark beat her down outside the tram before school. Josh and Colton were the ones I got into a fight with." I say, shaking my head out of frustration, "I already got the speech from Kai. I don't need it from you, too," I say, backing away from her dazed expression.

"Were you there?" she questions, ignoring my statement.

"What?" I say, pausing my hands grasp on the doorknob.

"Were you there when the ponds got destroyed?" she questions, keeping her head lowered.

"What does it matter," I started to leave the room, twisting the doorknob, ready to free myself from this conversation.

"You'd tell me if something happened to you, right?" my mom questions. She speaks as if she already has an answer.

"Are you sure you're trusting the right people?"

His words swarm my mind. A blink from another device tucked away by the bottom of the door hits my foot. She eagerly awaits a response, joining my stare at my foot.

"Someone is always watching. I'm sure you can get the whole picture from them. My word has never been as good as the cameras anyway," I whisper coldly, leaving her alone with her countless spiraling thoughts.

CHAPTER NINE

FOREST

My school clothes litter the bathroom floor, coating the tile in shades of gray and black. My figure looks foreign in the large glass mirror. Weak is the only suitable word to describe how I feel. The bathroom door is locked, keeping away Raegan and her prying eyes. My birthmark rests above my hip, protruding for all to see. The skin of the mark is rougher and much lighter than any other part of my body. It rises above the surface of my skin, not running smoothly like the rest of me. Four bruises from Josh's fingertips prying into my leg coat my thigh in blue and purple. Where there is muscle on most of the Unfortunates, I see nothing but bone. Most of the Untouchables hold slender bodies meant for anything but labor. The only way I managed to pin Josh was purely out of position. If my knee weren't lodged between his legs, I would have been done for. Even Max, who does nothing but athletics, still holds a more slender build.

My fingers brush over my mark once more. It's nothing more than an imperfection. It's as imperfect as the countless scars on the Unfortunates. I remember seeing the small part of Fallan's back I saw earlier today, his scars like a mosaic across the skin there. He was covered in scars, some that seemed old and some much newer. Even Valerie's hands looked like they had been laid down on a cutting board and sliced repeatedly. What must one do in their sector to receive a punishment like that? The detention device my father showcased at the school is what they are willing to show us they utilize on Unfortunates, but could there be more weapons? Every citizen of New Haven, Untouchable and Unfortunate, has one thing in common.

One imperfection that no one goes without.

I stare at my right pointer finger, looking over the small white scar across its tip. Every single citizen has this scar. Every one of us is born with it to confirm our purity.

I hear the whir of the machine. Their silent voices are stifled behind masks. The countless boxes of latex gloves drown out the smell of blood.

I take a deep breath, blinking my eyes to focus on where I am. The sink faucet runs, splashing onto the counter. I twist the knobs until the water is off, feeling the haze of another blackout surround me. The vivid images from my obscure memory don't linger in my mind for long, leaving as quickly as they seem to have arrived. At some point, between reflecting on scars and turning on the sink, I'd lost time. It took only a few seconds to disorientate.

Pulling on some black slacks and a gray tank, I move away from my thoughts, no longer wanting to be alone with them. I force my hair down from its straining position high on my head. It covers my shoulders, spanning down my front, only to be tucked away by a sling of my jacket over my shoulders. I reflected on the faucet once more, questioning when I had managed to turn it on.

I spill into my room, looking at Rae's relaxed position against my window frame. She's almost dressed the same as me, choosing a white top instead of the traditional gray. Unlike me, she takes the time to style her clothes, carefully tucking and rolling each article of clothing to fit her just right. I look her over, anticipating some remark about my thrown-together outfit.

"How do you always manage to look so disorganized?" Rae questions, moving away from the window to pinch my cheeks. I swat her hand away. Her graceful figure navigates my room with gentle steps. Each move she makes is as calculated as every other part of her life.

If perfection were a person, she would be it.

"I do hope to one day achieve your level of put togetherness," I say as I continue fiddling with the necklace I can now have out in the open. She looks me up and down, giving me a suggestive smile.

"What's that look for?" I question, turning away from her to toss my uniform in a hamper.

"You and that Official seemed close when we interrupted your private meeting in your dad's study," Raegan says, poking my back from behind. My cheeks fill with fire at her comment.

"Xavier and I-"

"Xavier? So, you are on a first-name basis?" Rae says, adding a sound to her tone that children use to taunt each other about their harmless crushes. I turn to snap at her, her mouth gaping open with a grin.

"Look how red you are! I was just taking a guess you two were getting handsy. I thought I had imagined his hand in yours!" Rae says louder than I'd like.

"Rae, respectfully, shut up," I whisper, covering my ears to ignore her pursuit to taunt me.

"I know we aren't supposed to speak on matters as egotistical as looks, but I can see the appeal."

"I'm not getting into this right now," I say, pushing closer to the door she has decided to block.

"Did you two kiss?" she questions eagerly.

"No," I say, reaching for the door.

"Did you *want* him to kiss you?" she questions further, only making my face grow redder.

The door swings open before I can get to it. Max and Kai waltz into my room, sporting their leisurewear. The pair throw themselves onto my bed. Raegan continues poking me, whispering Xavier and my initials in my ear, humming small children's rhymes meant to antagonize.

"What are you doing to her?" Max questions after a moment of undoing my neatly made bed.

"Just interrogating her on her wants to explore a certain someone's lips-"

I cut her off with a shove away from me as I groan.

Max's interest looks peaked. I try suppressing his next words with a cutting motion to my neck, already able to tell his train of thought and his sister's are not the same.

"You told her about our kiss?" Max questions. His twin's face drops immediately.

Raegan moves toward me, ready to hit me with a new line of questioning. Surprise hides behind her expression, filled with countless questions I am unprepared to answer. I shake my head at her, spilling into my hallway through the open door, not giving any of them a chance to continue pushing me on the matter of Xavier and his lips, as lovely as they might be. The last thing I need is another reason for Max to take out his anger onto Unfortunates.

"Forest!" my mother yells from the kitchen. I seize the opportunity, pulling away from the god-awful conversation that was no doubt about to take place.

She stands in the kitchen, examining my bag, fumbling through the pockets. My dad leans into the counter, trying to speak to her about her day, getting nothing but brief responses. Her focus is not on him.

Her eyes move up as I enter the room, motioning me over with a nod. My friend's bodies exit the room, only motivating me to get away from them and closer to my mom's stern look. She shows me the bag and its contents, waiting for me to speak.

"What are you looking for?" my dad finally asks.

"Where is your Cure-All?" my mom questions, running her fingers through the now empty pocket it usually resides in.

Shit.

"It must have fallen out during my interaction with Josh," I whisper, looking back at my friends waiting in the hallway.

"You didn't think to pick it up?" my mom questions. My mother is pushing harder than usual to pick apart my story. She's trying her best to find a hidden truth.

"Katiana," my father says, placing a hand on his wife's upper arm to calm her. "We can just get her another. Don't stress. Her friends are waiting on her," my father says, trying to calm her down.

She sighs, lowering the bag and running her hand through her hair.

My father's phone screen flashes red, indicating an urgent message that requires his attention. A red screen almost always means he misses dinner and only returns in the early morning.

"Deviant Unfortunates spotted in our sector again outside of their work hours," my father clarifies, answering the call now coming in on the other end. I see Xavier's name flash over the screen. My dad's frustrations grow the longer he is on the phone. He turns away from us, covering his mouth with his hand to speak more clearly. My friends stay back, waiting for me to give them the okay to come closer.

"Handle it," my dad says sternly, ending the call with a brutal hit to the screen.

I can't stop my hand from flying to my head, putting pressure on my temple in an attempt to ease the sudden pain behind my eyes. My father's eyes watch the action, looking down toward my hand clutched on my torso. My father reaches toward my mom, easing her tense body with gentle squeezes up and down her arms.

"It was a long day for everyone," my mom says, as she finally sinks into my father's arms wrapped around her. "Please be patient with me, both of you. I had to deal with many meetings with upper leadership and hearing that *one* of your children got into an altercation does not make anything better," my mom says. Disappointment clouds her words.

I scoff, backing away from my mother with a slow nod. My dad gives me a warning look, silently trying to command me not to continue with whatever I'm about to say.

"Good thing you have a perfect one right behind me. It balances out the fact you made a fuck up in your little lab," I whisper, shoving my dad's shoulder, not letting him try and use his words to sway yet another situation in his favor. I tap my ID on the panel, leaving everyone behind me with a rough slam of the door.

The tram waits at the stop, running its usual evening route for any Untouchables that want to migrate back toward the school. The school is no more than ten minutes from New Haven's downtown shops, making it the perfect middle ground to drop off and pick up our people. I sling my hood over my head, staring at the clouded sky, wishing more than anything to be alone and away from my brother and friends. The tram looks empty. Mark's hunched figure sits at the wheel, flipping through a newspaper's black and white pages. I tap on the glass of the sliding door, keeping my hood up, making eye contact with Mark. He lowers his head, pulling open the doors with a handle.

"You don't have to do that," I whisper, lingering on the staircase. Mark raises his head.

His hair is blanketed with gray streaks. Stubble surrounds his face, only adding to his mature features. A pair of green eyes, similar to mine, look toward me. He sits with a hunch, slender around the waist, teetering close to frail. The wheel has worn away in the places his hands touch most. He's been stuck in this position for years. If I had to guess, he is in his 60's, possibly early 70's.

"You don't have to lower your head like that when it's just me," I reiterate, letting the smile on my face finally show. His eyes widen. Never in the four years I've had him as my tram driver have I spoken to him like this. I keep my hood over my head, avoiding the camera at the front of the bus. He touches his throat, making my chest heavy, knowing he is trying to ask permission to speak.

"Please. I hate being in silence," I motion, touching my throat with a smile.

"Are you okay, miss? You look ... distressed," he says.

His eyes move behind me as my friends pry open the tram doors. They don't knock, but I know he would have appreciated it. I draw in a deep breath, shaking my head.

"I don't know anymore," I whisper, gazing past him to look like I was staring out the window this whole time.

Kai's hand reaches my shoulder, turning me around. Mark looks away again, starting the ignition shortly after everyone is on. Kai drags down my hood, crossing his arms, only following me once I walk away. I give him a cold shoulder, planting myself in a seat closest to the red tape. My shoe touches the red line of the Unfortunate section, passing it once I relax into the seat. Kai doesn't seem to process that I want to be alone. Instead, he sits, motioning the others to join in around me. I reach for my hood to try and conceal my face once more. My brother can't wait to stop me.

"You can be mad at Mom and Dad for whatever reason, not me. I'm on your side whether you realize it or not," Kai says, letting go of his hold on my wrist. He drops my hand, looking out the window to distract himself from my coldness.

"Where is everyone else?" Rae questions, scanning the empty bus. Even she knows not to push me right now.

"There was another tram 30 minutes ago. A great deal of them were on the bus the first time around," Mark says, offering his input once we make eye contact in his mirror.

"There's your answer," I say, giving no one the chance to question Mark's sudden chattiness.

Everyone takes that as a queue to leave me alone. No one knows how far I'm willing to go to make a point. This isn't the first time they've dealt with my mood swings like this. They used to come over me all the time as a child, ending with yelling from my mother and increases in the dosage of the pills she seemed to love to cram down my throat. Max watches me as if I am unhinged. His look is so different in contrast to Xavier's curious one.

I turn my whole body, staring out the window beyond New Haven and the ward. The darkening sky creates the beauty of the night and coats the open space above us. Dense trees, alive and dead, linger beyond the ward's sheer layer. Ash still lines the ground beyond New Haven, dusting remnants of what used to be valiant cities before the wars.

For a moment, and only a moment, I could almost swear, something moved, running beyond the ash and trees, looking toward New Haven with hungry eyes.

But that's impossible.

Nothing can live for more than a few days beyond the ward.

Or maybe that's just what we say to convince ourselves we aren't in confinement.

CHAPTER TEN

FOREST

A massive white tarp hangs between two aspens positioned side by side in the school's front yard. Bright yellow tape surrounds the area where the koi ponds once were. The fish are no longer littering the ground. Nothing but two holes remain after the handy work of Unfortunate gardeners, no doubt. I half expect a smear of my blood to be on the wall after the events of today.

Thankfully, I see nothing.

Couples and groups join each other on blankets, huddling together to keep warm. Some wear thick jackets. Others resort to sitting on one another, hiding their risky touches from the watchful eyes of Officials patrolling the area at a safe distance.

A couple sneaks off into the thicker brush behind the school, touching each other in every way possible, only looking back at the group once before disappearing behind the bushes. A large projector plays nothing in particular, casting a blinding light over the white tarp. Some hold bags filled with popcorn; a buttery treat we so rarely are gifted due to the nutrition regulations in our food. The savory smell of the popped treat beckons me closer to the small booth the bags come from.

"I'm going to get us some," I say, motioning to the bag a boy holds as he walks past us.

Raegan carries a bag filled with all we need to be comfortable tonight. Figures she would be the one to be fully prepared for the screening. Since the blowup at my house, everyone has been cautious about what they say around me. My attitude on the tram has only made them question my willingness to cause trouble. Despite my negative demeanor, Max has still managed to stay close.

Raegan begins spreading the blanket, pulling down my brother to join her. Kai doesn't fight her, letting his body lean into her more than he has in the past.

"I am going to talk to a few of my buddies, and then I can help you carry everything over," Max starts, grabbing my hand as if I will join him in speaking to his friends.

"I've got it. You go ahead and socialize," I say, plastering on my best smile while yanking my hand back toward me.

"Extra butter for me!" Kai exclaims, only half paying attention to the conversation as he hangs onto Rae's every word.

I nod, moving away from Max. His hand limply drops to his side. I know it's confusing to kiss him like that in the hallway, only to ghost him once he gives me the same energy back. Max is like one of those things that's a great idea on paper, but in reality, isn't quite right. He's safe. His family is safe. My parents love him.

But I need more than perfect. I need flaws.

I need something to feel real for once in my life.

I pull my hood back up, moving past groups of people returning to their spots with their tasty treats. The white tarp flashes with images as the movie starts. The movie's beginning sounds off, filling the speakers with lively music and whatever they considered acting back in the old world. It baffles me how a whole society could idolize and overpay people for pretending to be someone else in front of a camera. No one remains at the booth's small shed-like structure. Everyone is too preoccupied with watching the film or conversing so loud they don't know what's being said.

A dark-skinned boy runs the booth, his eyes gentle, like pools of gold. His hair is tightly coiled, cut short but maintained well. He's standing alertly, holding his posture and shoulders back as he cleans the booth's small ledge where the treats sit on display. I creep up to the window, glancing back at the moving picture and my friends, who only seem focused on their conversations.

"Are we doing soda or popcorn?" the boy questions, pausing his cleaning to give me a warm smile. I don't recognize him. I've never once crossed paths with him if he is at the Academy. His clothes are nice, covered by a white apron that's had some use.

"Three popcorns, please. One with some extra butter for my brother," I say, shoving a few coins across the counter, meeting the boy's perplexed look. His mouth is in a straight line. His eyes dart to an Official casually walking by.

"Was it not enough-" I begin.

His voice meets my ears, sending countless chills up my spine.

"Your people don't pay our people. I'm surprised you didn't vomit when you said please to him," Fallan's ignorant tone bellows from somewhere in front of me. The boy working the counter looks nervous, pulling at his collar to allow more breathing room. I look inside the small booth.

Fallan leans against the wall, sporting a black shirt and gray pants that seem to enunciate his better features. His arms are crossed, his eyes dead set on me.

"Don't listen to him," the boy begins, shoving the money back toward me. "I should have specified I was an Unfortunate before I began speaking," he snaps, looking toward Fallan with anger.

"I would've personally kept it going," Fallan says, pushing away from the wall to get a closer look. "She's much more tolerable when she treats us like we're people," Fallan finishes, looking me over angrily.

"Fallan.... Shut up," the boy hisses, trying to silence his voice.

"What's wrong, Hunter? Scared she'll tell on us?" Fallan questions, fiddling with a small vial in his pocket he knows will keep me silent.

"Are you ever pleasant? Or are you always a selfish asshole?" I question finally addressing Fallan's snide comments.

"Selfish would be assuming I like who I am, so no. But I can be quite pleasant given the right scenario," Fallan says. Something lingers behind his words. It makes my cheeks grow hot with nerves.

"Is your brother the tall one up front?" Hunter questions, breaking mine and Fallan's heated stare.

I look back toward the group, watching Kai's arms wave in the air as he expressively tells a story.

"Can't you tell? They look like twins. Speaking of, where's your blonde puppy dog?" Fallan questions.

I look around for Max, returning my attention to the two boys once I spot him. I look inside the booth, scoffing once I realize who is missing.

"*Max* is with his friends. I thought you had a blonde lap dog of your own. Shouldn't she be licking your face right now?" I question, seeing Fallan's cocky smirk drop at the statement.

"Sadly, she couldn't join us. Maybe you can take her place since you're so curious about her," Fallan says.

My stomach fills with a wave of anxiety at the statement.

Hunter drops multiple bags of popcorn, slamming his hand on the counter fearfully. He looks around for an Official, forcing his attention back to me with a shaky tone.

"Fallan, you ignorant, cocky, son of a bitch-" Hunter begins, sweating from his fear. Fallan looks blissful.

"You know where to find me," I say, cutting off Hunter's rant toward Fallan.

I should report Fallan. I should watch him get lashed with a prod for what he said.

But I loved it.

I craved it.

I craved the fear he fills me with. It's a fear to walk the line.

Fallan moves closer to the window, looking over my expression with furrowed brows.

"What?" he questions.

"You know where to find me when you're tired of your lap dog," I mutter, letting my smirk finally meet my mouth at the sight of his dazed expression. Hunter is wide-eyed, looking between the both of us.

"Is there something so enthralling on my face that you can't break your pathetic stare right now?" I question, pushing Fallan further.

"Enthralled is not the word I'd use to describe what I feel when I look at you," Fallan says, lowering his eyes as that typical sense of hate passes over his expression.

"Don't worry, I'm not too fond of you either." I begin, turning toward Hunter's worried expression. "Your friend, on the other hand, is a breath of fresh air," I say, easing his tension with another smile. Fallan scoffs, shaking his head at the exchange.

"He almost makes you forget we're not really people, right?" Fallan says, reminding me once more where we both land in this society.

"I never said you're not people," I utter, watching the pair's eyes wince at the statement. "Why are you working this booth anyway? It seems like the last place either of you'd want to be," I say, trying my best to shove down the feeling of pain I get the longer Fallan's hateful stare is on me.

"The popcorn most of you are so carelessly tossing to the ground is banned in our sector," Fallan begins.

"We get to take home the scraps," Hunter clarifies, popping a piece of the treat in his mouth.

How could something as simple as this be banned in their sector?

"Was that too much for you to process at once?" Fallan questions.

Angrily, I look up at him, wondering just how much badgering I can take before going in there and testing to see if his strength is only an illusion.

"Fallan, you're not the one who should be questioning someone else's intelligence," Hunter snaps, making the raven-haired giant's smile fade in a second.

I can't stop the laugh from escaping my mouth. It's the first genuine laugh I have allowed myself in months. It sounds foreign once it leaves me. I force my hand over the noise, stopping myself from drawing more attention to the two than I already have by lingering at the counter. My smile falls away from beneath my hand. Hunter looks pleased, and Fallan, for the first time, doesn't look utterly pissed off by my existence.

"Glad to know Hunter's shitty jokes are funny to someone," Fallan says, pushing away from the counter and nudging the boy playfully in the arm. If I had to guess, these two are more than casual friends. They're close, possibly as close as Rae and me.

"I have a feeling your humor wouldn't be any better," I begin, ready to challenge Fallan again.

"Who's humor?" Max's voice questions. I pull away from the counter, looking toward the blonde. His hands are deep in his pockets, his eyes on me.

"Have you just been talking to yourself for the past ten minutes? Every time I looked over here, it looked like you were going on to yourself," Max says. It doesn't surprise me that he assumes I've not acknowledged the pair of men staring at him from within the booth.

"Actually, Hunter here was telling me a funny joke-" I begin, full of smiles. Max pauses me, pinching the bridge of his nose as his frustrations grow.

"You fucking spoke to her? Outside of your regs?" Max questions to the two. I feel my smile drop. Max's eyes focus on a nearby Official, ready to wave him over.

"Sir, I-" Hunter begins.

Fallan is going to open his mouth and escalate this situation.

I move in front of Max, placing the treats back on the counter to nudge him back several feet. I grab his chin, dragging his eyes down to face me.

"I asked him to speak to me. Let it be me if you want an Official to be upset with someone. I broke regulation, not them," I say, holding back his hand, ready to wave over the man dressed head to toe in black.

"Why the hell would you do that?" he questions. I pause, a bit dumbfounded by the nature of the question.

"I just wanted to tell them thank you-"

"We don't do that, Forest. *We* don't thank them for anything. Without us, they would have nothing. The least you can do is take the food and leave them be instead of giving them a smile and a laugh," Max hisses. His face is flustered, and his eyes are wide.

This isn't about me speaking to them.

I shake my head at him, grabbing the bags from the counter with a frown toward the two men. Fallan crosses his arms as he watches the exchange, eyeing down Max with a similar hatred he often has when he watches me. I whisper a silent "I'm sorry" to Hunter, which grows his look of confusion. I turn back toward Max, powered almost entirely by annoyance.

"I don't need a lesson from you regarding regulations," I spit, shoving his bag of popcorn in his chest, mocking his childish emotions.

"What are you smiling at, bottom feeder?!" Max yells. His voice almost carries over the sound of the actors in the film.

Fallan's mouth is upturned, watching the exchange with a relaxed demeanor.

"You still haven't gathered how little she wants you, have you?" Fallan questions.

My heart drops.

Max looks ready to tear the man apart. It takes all I have to pull him away from the booth while avoiding the Official's lingering eyes. Hunter grabs Fallan, moving him out of the window and returning him to the back of the shed to fill new bags. I yank Max toward me, dragging him closer to our friends while balancing their treats in a tight hold. Max grabs me harshly, straining against my touch, nearly bruising my arms in the process.

"Let it go," I whisper, trying to get him to calm down.

"That son of a bitch. I will kick his fucking teeth in-" Max begins.

I land my mouth on his again, feeling my stomach recoil. I do my best to feed into the touch, feeling his hands move away from my arms and drop to my sides. A few students whistle. Rae and Kai's voices question what is going on. Even Colton and Josh egg on the action, telling Max, "She bites," as they whistle. His lips are like poison on mine. Every part of me wants to get away. It's like a thousand hands are pounding on the door of my mind, screaming at me never to let him touch me like this again.

"Hands off!" an Official yells, making us break apart.

Many eyes are on us, a pair of blue ones from the booth lingering longer than others. I fight the urge to wipe my mouth. Max looks more relaxed, grabbing my hand and lowering me to the blanket with the others. I look behind me, seeing his anger momentarily melt away. Max grabs my waist, pulling me closer to him. Fallan shakes his head, moving away from the booth window once more.

"What was that about?' Kai questions, grabbing the bags from my lap and dispersing them.

"Two dirty Unfortunates who don't know when to be quiet," Max says, shaking his head like Fallan.

"You instigated that," I say, feeling Kai pinch my arm.

"You're right," Max says, drawing in a deep breath. "I'm sorry," he whispers after a few moments. He gives me his soft smile that I have come to find comfort in. My tension eases, and I lean into him more.

"So, are you two ... exclusive?" Rae scoffs at me.

"Are you two?" I question back, watching Kai scoot away from Rae out of embarrassment.

"You are incredibly unpredictable, you know that, right?" Max questions, returning to his light-hearted nature.

"I am fully aware," I whisper. "So, tell me about the film," I finish, nudging my brother with my foot.

"As far as I know, Gatsby..."

My brother's words fade away as quickly as a fire drenched in water. Every one of my hairs rise, working from my legs to the length of my arms. My mark burns hot, painfully exploring my whole torso. The dull aches behind my eyes are like hammers pounding a concrete wall. Something creeps over the space.

It is watching us.

It is watching me.

I don't feel the air enter my lungs. My hands shake, my palms filling with a buzz as if they have lost blood flow. Kai's voice comes out in nothing more than muffled noise. My skin fills with so much heat that Max brings the back of his hand to my forehead, checking for a fever.

"Kai ... something feels off," I whisper, grabbing my brother's wrist.

A blood-curdling scream fills the air, nearly bursting my eardrums. Everyone shoots to their feet, looking around for the source of the torturous sound. The Untouchable woman from earlier, who snuck behind the bushes, looks as pale as a ghost, running toward the screen with a staggered step. Crimson coats her front, blood drowning her scream. More people join in on her screams, backing away from her as her knees collide with the grass. She clutches her throat, holding back the blood that's trying to escape from the massive slash of skin torn away from her throat. I feel my lungs finally exhale, urging me to move forward.

Max grabs my coat. My hands fumble with the zipper to tear myself away from his grasp. The jacket slips off. I run toward the girl, feeling my brother follow close behind me. Hunter and Fallan step out from inside the booth, watching the sight in front of them with looks of shock. Anyone previously near the girl has backed away. Officials begin moving closer, each one of them fiddling in their pockets for med kits. Claw marks work down her front, each one deeper than the last. Her body is torn, and her skin is charred. It's like a burning blade had slashed her up and down.

The Officials continue fumbling, listening to the pleas of students begging them to grab their guns. Another body stumbles from the bush, the boy that the girl had snuck off with. He clutches his side, bleeding just as profusely as her. He runs toward the closest Official he sees. Hunter stays back, trying his best to pull Fallan toward him. I help apply pressure to the woman's neck, watching her wince in pain. The twins stand still, trying their best to get at least one Official to back away from their trance on the devices they all now hold.

They are Re-Regulation devices meant to stop Unfortunates in aggravated states.

A foreign warmth radiates beside me, filling the space around me in a mere few seconds with equal feelings of uncertainty and security. Only a few moments pass before the clarity of who has made their way over to the mess sprawled in front of me finally settles.

Fallan kneels, moving my hands to help the woman breathe. He grasps a corner of his shirt, tearing away the bottom, helping me raise her head before tightening the thin piece of material now around her neck.

"What the hell are you guys waiting for?" Kai yells toward the Officials, joining in on the confusion clouding the area.

I feel my heart race. Fallan continues his hold, looking around at the numerous men inputting code into their devices.

"Fuck," Fallan whispers, looking up at me in pure terror.

The girl's hand grabs my front, pulling me down closer to her. As she drags me down, her blood streaks along the light material of my shirt. Her voice is filled with fluid, barely understandable, even though I'm only a few inches away from her mouth. Her lips press to the side of my face. The groan of pain in her voice is miserably hard to listen to.

"I saw it," she says, gasping in between breaths. I look up at Fallan and Kai, trying to decipher her words.

"Saw what?" I question, watching her consciousness slowly leave her.

A few Officials work their way over, relieving Fallan and I from the pressure we've been applying to her bloody neck.

"Did she say what attacked her?" one of them questions, looking to me for an answer. Her voice is still cracking. She is unable to get a word out. They focus their attention back on her, their pockets blinking as the screens of their devices flash white. I move around a bit, feeling Fallan's hand drag me away from my kneeled position next to one of the Officials.

They crowd her, letting the others aid the boy, who's now unconscious. I move back with Fallan, staying on my knees as Kai tries his best to ease the crowd.

A pain passes over my head once more. It makes me slump forward, pressing my head into the ground. I claw at the Earth, trying my best to stop a scream from escaping my throat.

"Get up before they notice," Fallan whispers, yanking the back of my shirt, forcing me back up.

He acts like he isn't speaking to me. His eyes are only on the Officials.

"What's happening to me?" I question silently toward him. He offers me no answer.

"Shif-" she tries to say. Her cough that follows paints the grass in red.

"Shif?" Kai questions. Fallan's eyes are wide, watching the Officials all dial in on her words.

"Shifter," she screams in a voice nothing short of a nightmare.

"That's not possible," I whisper. Feeling my voice shake, I look up at Fallan for confirmation.

Fallan's eyes grow dark at the statement, finally filling with the one expression I have yet to see on him.

Fear.

CHAPTER ELEVEN

FOREST

M y feet dig into the ground, kicking me farther away from the group of Officials now swarming the girl in a ring-like formation. Fallan moves with me, scanning the area repeatedly. My head is filled with an indescribable pain. Clutching my mark, I feel its burn grow with each passing second. I grab a fistful of Kai's shirt, doing my best to pull him back with me. Kai looks dazed, as if he has no idea where he is. The group begins whispering, all stagnant, waiting for someone to ease their worries.

Some try to leave, only to be stopped by the wave of new Officials beginning to fill the area. Fallan's hand still lingers on me, grabbing the back of my collar to stop me from slumping forward in a pain-filled scream. Rae and Max observe the girl, both wide-eyed and nervous, not even batting an eye in our direction.

"S-Shifter!" the girl on the ground yells again in a groggy voice, escalating the whispers into a full-blown panic.

"God damn it," Fallan whispers, grasping his head. He begins grinding his teeth with a look of pain. His hand retracts, holding his chest while his other fist bangs to the ground.

Kai turns toward me, barely acknowledging Fallan's proximity to the both of us. Hunter stays back by the booth, hiding behind the structure. Kai grabs my face, letting his panic overcome him in shallow breaths. I feel his pulse work against the side of my face from his wrist.

His hands shake, lined with nervous sweat.

"Did she just say Shifter-" his words are cut off by his own eyes rolling in the back of his head. His mouth hangs open, losing his voice seconds after he begins to speak. His hands drop away from my face. His body slumps backward, hitting the ground with a loud thud. His chip blinks green behind his ear. The scream is ready to leave my lungs as I move toward my brother's motionless figure.

Fallan's hand drags me back by my collar again, forcing my head and body harshly into the ground. His hand presses on the back of my neck, keeping my body still from my squirms. His eyes are barely opened, his chip blinking in the same way as everyone around me. I see the glow of my chip in his eyes before he shuts them. Feeling the dirt coat my face, each Official holds out their devices like remotes. Everybody begins collapsing like Kai, only to become still on the chill ground.

All the students are motionless. All except the girl, who still screams in pain, begging for a sense of relief as she slowly bleeds out.

"If you want to stay alive, close your fucking eyes and don't move," Fallan whispers, letting his body go as limp as my brother's. I let my eyes shut nearly all the way, only allowing a tiny sliver of vision to pass through the slit in my right eye. Fallan's hand is warm against my neck. I try focusing on the heat it gives off rather than the fear encompassing me. The Officials drag over the girl's partner, letting his blood trail along the grass as they toss him next to her. She grasps her throat as tight as possible, clinging to life in any way she can.

Why have they not started treating her? Why is no one moving?

The Officials kick the feet of the boy, cocking their heads at him, ignoring the girl's loud painful grunts. Dirt coats my mouth. My breathing has slowed despite my want to hyperventilate. Kai is still motionless. The twins are slumped on one another, looking as peaceful as they do when they sleep. Each student's chip blinks.

No one is awake.

No one. Except us.

Fallan looks peaceful, only convincing me of his consciousness with tiny peeks of his eyes at the Officials swarming the two injured students. His thumb moves every so often, running along the bare portion of my neck, keeping me from screaming out in pain.

Why are we awake? Why are the Officials just standing there when these Untouchables need help?

And how did Fallan know what was happening?

"Can he be saved?" an Official questions, kneeling toward the boy with a curious expression.

"Yes," another says, spinning around his Re-Regulation device with a grin. "Without any recollection or proof of it, just like the rest of these sorry idiots," the man says, mocking every student utterly unaware of what is happening to them. My throat feels dry, as if it will close on me at any moment.

I don't move a muscle. In every scenario, I should be able to run to these men and get them to take me home or bring me to safety. They're Officials. Their sole purpose is to protect the Untouchables and regulate peace. But now, at this moment, all I want to do is get far away from them. They smile as if a girl is not bleeding out in front of them.

The girl spits up more blood, hitting the pant leg of the Official closest to her. Her blood reaches my face, coating my lips. Fallan's hand clenches my neck, stopping me from flinching at the feeling. I remain still, listening to the curses of the Official as he scolds the girl for dirtying his pants.

"Help me," she spits up, watching the men use my mother's Cure-All to begin healing her partner. Another holds a device close to her partner's head, letting the pairing light sync up with his chip before inputting a series of codes I cannot see. The boy's breathing begins to regulate. The Official had healed him, leaving him with nothing but a deep scar.

"Make him think he got it from hopping a fence to spend some alone time with her," the Official closest to the girl begins with a point toward her.

If memory serves me well, that voice belongs to Adam, Josh's father, a man I have seen my own father with several times.

"She still looks terrified and conscious. Have you not run the commands yet?" Adam questions, looking over to the man waving a device over the girl in the same fashion as he did to her partner.

"I already put it in, sir. She should be unconscious like the rest of them," the man holding the device says in a tone that suggests nothing good.

Adam looks thrilled, kneeling to observe the girl carefully. She continues gasping, trying her best to push away his hand, which has now found itself exploring up her front. Grasping her shirt, he tugs away at its bottom to reveal her slender torso. I hold back my vomit at his actions, biting my lip as hard as I can, tasting my blood in the process.

"Sir?" the man holding the device questions, watching Adam tug up the girl's shirt. Adam pauses, stopping at her collarbone as all the men take a sharp breath. Her chest rises and falls at a rapid rate. She's barely able to take a full breath with the weight of Adam's hands now holding her down on the ground. His finger traces below her collarbone, finding a blemish that makes my blood run cold.

A mark.

It's the exact mark I bear.

"No wonder a Shifter attacked her.... She's Tainted," Adam says, forcing his knee on her chest, motioning the other men around him to look closer.

"Holy shit, how did she slip past her Expulsion Test?" one person questions, getting only a scoff from Adam.

"Katiana has been getting lazier and lazier with those tests for years. If you ask me, she's purposefully letting them roam free to ruin this society. Just like the rest of those Unfortunate fucks," Adam seethes, spitting on the girl's face.

He just defaced an Untouchable as if she were an Unfortunate.

She writhes away from the crude gesture, wincing as Adam grasps her jaw.

"What do we do now?" the man holding the Re-Regulation device questions.

Adam says nothing as he jabs his fingers into the girl's wound, coating his fingers in her blood and letting her screams fill the air once more. Adam quickly swipes the Re-Regulation device away from the man, placing her blood on a small test strip often used to test blood sugar in older Untouchables. The screen loads as Adam remains crouched over the girl.

My anxieties grow as Fallan clenches the back of my neck so tight I think he might be trying to suffocate me. I know it is nothing more than fear driving his touch. The device sounds a chime, the screen flashing red, coating Adam's face in the light from the device.

"What a shame," Adam murmurs, reaching into his coat pocket.

"What did it say?" one of the men questions, looking over the screen with wide eyes.

"You, my dear, are only 12% Tainted," Adam starts, looking over the girl with a wide grin. She claws at him, only hurting herself in the process. "Sadly, that's not enough to keep you alive," Adam hisses, pulling out the pistol from his holster and pointing it straight at the Untouchables head.

The loud bang fills my ears. It takes everything inside of me not to flinch away. Her blood covers my face and Fallan's, streaking our cheeks in red. I see the smoke exit the wound in her head. The horrific scream in my lungs only festers at the sight of her fragmented brain scattered across the lawn. Her eyes are dull and lifeless. Her blood coats the ground around her. Adam's face is splattered with her blood as well. His smile remains plastered to his face as he draws his weapon back to his holster. All of the men look unamused, conversing about after-work activities as if this is all nothing to them. There are no words to describe what I felt at that moment. If Fallan weren't touching the back of my neck right now, I would have vomited right there on the spot, outing myself to the murderers who have always been our protectors.

But they killed her without a second thought.

They killed an Untouchable.

An Untouchable who was supposed to be protected by the very man who pulled the trigger, all because of a mark like the one that paints my torso, like her blood that now paints the lawn.

CHAPTER TWELVE

FOREST

The rough texture of a rag moves across my face, making my skin tingle with pain. An Official wipes repeatedly, even working the rag through my hair to rid my front of any evidence of the atrocious murder they just committed. My eyes are glued shut, not daring to peek open, even after they turn their attention to anyone else who might have been hit with the girl's blood. I feel them work on Fallan, rubbing more aggressively than they did with me.

"Look how pathetic this is," one of the men says, pulling Fallan's limp hand away from my neck. I hear his body roll as they move him onto his back.

"That Unfortunate running the booth had his hands all over this pretty little Untouchable," the man says, running his fingers through my hair, working his touch dangerously close to the top of my chest.

My stomach rolls with nausea. I start to sweat uncontrollably as his fingers fumble with my shirt.

"Mind your touch," Adam snaps, slapping away the hands of whoever was about to run their fingers beneath my bra strap. "That includes leaving the sewer trash alone," Adam continues. The thud of Fallan's head meeting the dirt fills my ears.

"What's one more little cut on him? His back is already torn to shreds," the man messing with Fallan questions. I want nothing more than to take his prod and beat him over the head with it. My mark's pain grows at the idea of hurting all of the men standing around us.

"Get the hell up and start cleaning. You aren't getting paid to make more of a mess," Adam spits. The men hovering near Fallan sigh. Their knees pop as they stand, following the order of their superior.

A man's booted foot stands on my wrist, putting all his weight on the weak bones. It takes all I have not to wince. The pressure increases as the man leans his weight into his hip. Rocks dig into the top of my hand, scratching and tearing the skin. My fingers are numb, growing more pained the more prolonged the blood flow is restricted. The sound of trash bags flaring open is heard. The men grumble, spraying bottles filled with a robust solution that burns my nose. A wet feeling hovers over my front, increasing the strong smell of chemicals surrounding the air.

"Aren't these two Blackburn's kids?" one of the men questions, standing closer to Kai as he acknowledges my exposed face. My last name leaves his mouth like he's one of my family's closest friends.

I feel a body move closer, bending down to observe me, warming my body with its sudden presence before moving back into its standing position.

"Yes, you dense moron," Adam says, shoving back the man standing on my wrist. "So, get off her hand before her father has a fit when we give him the rundown about tonight," Adam finishes.

My father would never support this. He would never support the murder of *children.*

"Blackburn created a beauty like that?" A man sneers, getting uncomfortably close.

"Yes," Adam says, grabbing the material of the man's jacket. "And *he* wants her, so keep your fucking hands off and finish cleaning," Adam says, dismissing all of the men crowding us.

"What do you want us to input for the others, sir?" someone questions, motioning around to the students who are still face down on the ground.

It's the voice of the man who held the Re-Regulation device above the girl.

"Make them think only a few seconds have passed. They all zoned off during this miserable movie but can't acknowledge it. As far as they know, all they did was blink, and they lost track of time. How much longer until we are cleaned up?" Adam questions.

"Ten seconds, boss, and then we are good to clear out," another Official says.

A human life is cleaned up and disposed of in no more than ten minutes. All those memories, all of those connections she created, stolen by the hands of a lie we let them put inside our heads with no second thoughts.

Or did we let them?

"Time to go, boys. He wants us back in time for the Lottery bids," Adam barks to the other Officials, their feet dragging across the ground as they move. My eyes slowly creep open at the sound of their exit.

The man in charge of the Re-Regulation device hits his screen, watching the chips of those on the ground blink once more. The land once coated in the girl's blood is spotless, concealed by the bloodied paper towels now shoved deep into one of the many garbage bags the Officials hold. Adam slings the girl over his shoulder, pulling her dead weight with no issues. The group moves farther from the screening, one of them hitting the projector as they start the movie from where it was before the attack. Five black Official cars are parked, each one of the trunks being filled with their supplies. They finish loading the trunk with the girl's body, throwing her in carelessly before slamming the trunk shut with a thud. The men smile, some laughing as they each file into their car. Their headlights light up the area, each revving their engines before disappearing in the night as if they were never even here.

I pry my head away from the ground, gasping as I struggle to take a full breath. My voice is nothing more than a silent scream. My mouth salivates, pushing away nausea clouding my system. I grasp the front of my shirt, clawing at its material as I linger on the Official's touch. The blood sure to have soaked my front has vanished, and I see nothing but the clean gray shirt I had come here in. My hands rub my face violently, trying my best to wipe away the blood that's no longer there. My mind keeps reflecting on the moment her life left her eyes. He pulled that trigger with no hesitation and a look of satisfaction.

"Calm down," Fallan says aggressively, grabbing my bruised wrist as my eyes begin to water. He immediately re-adjusts his grip, holding my jaw hard, forcing me to stop my panic to look at him. I see now the small cut lining his forehead. The Official had managed to mark him up despite Adam's wishes.

"You need to breathe, they are going to wake up any minute, and you can't be panicking when they do," Fallan says, pressing his hand to my chest.

"Take a full breath. Don't think about anything else, breathe. Focus on my touch. Breathe from here," he continues, applying more pressure to my chest. His hand takes up a great deal of my front, helping guide my breathing as he inhales with me.

I comply, feeling the air enter my lungs in greedy, shallow breaths. Fallan continues holding my chin, dragging me closer once my breathing has regulated. His eyes grow narrow, holding me still with such a brief touch.

"I could care less if you expose yourself to your Officials, but you're sure as hell not bringing me down with you," Fallan hisses, shoving me back and closer to my brother as he pulls himself to his feet.

I watch him quickly move past the bodies. Some begin twitching, moving their limbs slowly as they gain consciousness. Fallan kneels next to Hunter, dragging him farther behind the shed, not giving me a second look.

"Forest?" Kai's voice questions, pulling me away from my dazed stare toward the shed and back to my brother as he blinks away his confusion. Once abnormally blank and void of expression, his face now shows a flutter of emotion. He's standing, looking at my dirtied figure kneeling on the ground.

"Kai!" I say in a sob. I force my arms around his neck, pulling his hands around me before pressing my face into his shoulder. "Are you okay?" I mumbled against the material of his shirt, squeezing him as tight as possible. I narrow my eyes at his chip.

"Yes, crazy," Kai says, speaking like normal as he begins to pry away from my touch. I stumble back, taking a long look at my brother. He looks completely fine, even brushing off some dirt from the front of his clothes. All the others around him are on their feet, some still trying to watch the movie, the twins included.

"You've just been staring off into space. I've been trying to get your attention for like five minutes." Kai says, rubbing the back of his neck as he fidgets anxiously. I clutch my damaged wrist, shielding it from his prying eyes.

Officials return to the area, casually glancing around as they once had, letting their eyes linger on the crowd they so easily manipulated.

"Y-you don't remember?" I question, knowing the answer long before he dares to say it.

"Remember what?" Kai questions, looking back at our friends in a way that I know is meant to mock my current state of sanity. Hunter and Fallan are back in the booth. Hunter happily continues serving popcorn. Fallan watches me, crossing his arms, waiting to see what I will do. He looks unbothered, as if nothing ever happened.

The space around me feels smaller as the eyes of neighboring Officials seem to linger on my brother and me. Everything seems tighter, the very area around me closing in. My stomach churns as I reflect on what I saw. The visual of a fragmented skull painting the grass in puddles of red still lingers. My stomach twists. Maybe it wasn't real. I skipped my meds this morning. Maybe all of this is in my head. Perhaps it's just the hallucinations again.

My focus moves to my hurt wrist and sore jaw from Fallan's touch.

No, not in my head.

I clutch my stomach, covering my mouth and backing away from my brother.

"Forest, what's wrong?" Max's voice finally questions, creeping up behind my brother, finally inserting himself into the conversation.

"I don't feel so good," I say honestly, unable to fight back the influx of saliva that I know is about to turn into something much worse.

I force myself away from the pair, letting my knees hit the ground. Breakfast and lunch leave me in a hurl, covering the ground beneath me. My spit trails out of my mouth, making the pain in my stomach only grow once there is nothing else left to expel. A few straggling Officials move closer, looking genuinely concerned as if they didn't just have pistols ready to use on any of us a few minutes ago. Kai and Max reach their arms out. I force myself up, stumbling backward, backing away from the gentle touch of one of the Officials I had seen laughing at the girl's lifeless body.

"It's the popcorn. Too much grease," I say, dismissing the Official's concern with a simple statement. My shaky hand covers the quiver in my lip. Many watch me, all observing my humiliating display on the lawn.

"Are you sure you're alright?" the Official questions. His voice perfectly matches the one of the man who stepped right on my arm.

"I need to go home," I say, turning away from the numerous eyes on me. I shove past my brother and Max, pressing my arms across my body as I walk farther away from the screen's light. My head continues to pound, my scar growing hotter as if it's ready to burn through this shirt and expose me. "Now," I finish, watching the roll of the tram's wheels as it stops at the bench outside the school.

"Forest, wait a moment-" Kai begins, grabbing my elbow.

"Don't!" I yell, looking at all of my friends and anyone else who feels like staring. "I want to be alone," I hiss, yanking away my arm with a great deal of aggression. Kai doesn't push it, even putting his hand on Max's shoulder, telling him to let it be. He whispers something in the blonde's ear, ending his statement with a comment about this being "One of her episodes," solidifying the fact he has no faith in my sanity. I take that as my opportunity to leave, trying my best not to feel the fear that only grows with each long stare from the Officials trailing behind me.

My hands bang on the tram doors, startling Mark from his small cat nap in the front seat. I aid him in opening the doors, clawing them open in an attempt to get into the vehicle faster. I stumble into the warm tram, watching his body go rigid as I move closer.

"Please, take me home. I will take full responsibility for whatever grief you get for running an early route. Get me away from here," I plead. I know he can hear the grovel of emotions threatening to break me. I fight back the tears that want to escape my eyes, wishing for a distraction to pull me away from this nightmare.

"Boring movie?" he questions in a light-hearted tone.

"Something like that," I admit with no humor in return.

"I can make a quick route toward your neighborhood for you," Mark begins, pulling the handle to shut the doors. "I can always call an Official, too, if you are feeling unsafe-"

"No!" I yell, covering my mouth in embarrassment at my sudden outburst.

I hear a slam behind me. Both Mark and I silence our conversation.

His large hand grabs the door, stopping it from closing fully. He looks as casual as he did when I first saw him tonight, only pulling me further into the theory that all of this derived from my own delusional mind. He glances at me with his standard look of annoyance, leaving room for Hunter to get in the vehicle first. I back away from the men working their way up the steps. Grabbing the first chair closest to the back as I can, I try to find the slightest bit of comfort in the presence of the only other person who might have seen what I had moments ago.

Hunter moves past me, taking a seat in his bus section. I pull my knees up to my chest, pressing my head between my legs to silence the noise of the tram's engine.

Mark converses with Fallan, glancing back at me before returning to the tall, raven-haired boy. Fallan moves closer to Mark, whispering something in his ear while placing a hand on his shoulder. I rock my body slightly, Hunter's raised brows going higher the longer he stares at me. Tears coat my face; hidden by the position I have tucked myself into.

"Did you enjoy the movie?" Hunter questions, lowering his head to meet my hazy eyes. I sniffle, wiping my tears away with the back of my hand. No amount of acting can hide the emotions rolling through me. Fallan joins his friend, observing the same wave of emotions Hunter does, leaning back in his chair as he does so. Neither man knows how to approach my sudden display of emotions.

"It wasn't my favorite film," I admit with a small laugh, rubbing my thumb along my injured arm. Fallan cocks his head at the gesture, moving one seat over from Hunter, working himself closer to my balled-up position on the seat. He reaches into his pocket, fiddling with his one leverage over me. Now more than ever, the idea of him outing me to an Official is horrifying.

"I think the film is a tad bit over-praised," Hunter begins, leaning into his knees with closed eyes.

"So does my brother," I admit after a few moments, continuing to watch Fallan's adamant stare in my direction.

"Your brother is quite the talker. I overheard him babbling on to that blonde. I don't think she listened to a single thing he said. There were times I was ready to break regulation to put my input in on his horrible analysis of the plot," Hunter says. I smile, wincing as my hand stabilizes me from the tram's sudden start.

"How bad does it hurt?" Fallan questions, motioning to my wrist. He cuts off the conversation topic, focusing on the wound I have tried my best not to look at. I can tell he's already treated the cut on his face. Nothing but a faint scar remains.

"What did you do?" Mark questions, looking in his rearview for some clarification.

"I-" I begin, feeling that familiar well of emotions form in me as I recall the Official's boot pressed firmly on my arm.

"She fell carrying food back to her friends and landed square on a rock. On top of being arrogant, you're also one clumsy little Untouchable, aren't you, Little Dove?" Fallan questions, propping his arms on his legs like Hunter, who can't seem to take his eyes off his brash friend.

The alibi flows off his tongue like it's nothing. He's covering his ass, just like he promised.

"Fallan, watch your tongue, man-" Hunter begins.

"Why do you call me that? Little Dove?" I question, cutting off Hunter's justifiable line of questioning.

"Answer my question first, princess," Fallan says, waving away Mark's frustrated grunts, signaling Fallan to quit pushing. Though low quality on these trams, the cameras can still pick up enough for Officials to dish Fallan a heavy violation which I'd rather he not get, even if he does deserve it.

"It feels like someone stepped on my arm ... so yes, it hurts," I hissed, holding my wrist with frustration.

He nods his head at the response, clenching his jaw, running a list of things to say to me through his head.

"Give me your arm," Fallan says after a few moments, catching everyone off guard.

I pause, keeping my hold on my knees in hopes he will retract the command. "Unless you want to continue this whole ride pathetically wallowing in pain, I suggest you do as I ask," Fallan continues, ignoring Hunter's punches to his arm.

"You just don't know when to shut the hell up," Hunter hisses, watching Fallan's hand reach into his apron's front pocket.

He pulls out a small jar labeled with masking tape and words I struggle to recognize. He quickly unscrews the lid of the jar. The smell of lavender and mint hits my nose as he gathers some cream onto his fingers. Hesitantly, I lean my arm past the red line, letting his fingers work on the tender skin of my wrist in small circular motions.

"Hunter's grandmother makes medicine even better than your people's Cure-All. The only thing is she needs the money to continue creating it," Fallan says, pressing down a bit harder on my bruise with a glance up at me. "She's the woman you watched get beat by your schoolmates this morning," Fallan continues, closing the lid of the jar. I feel a great shame in the pain that flashes over Hunter's face at the mention of his grandmother. "Consider this me making sure my tracks are covered," Fallan whispers in a voice only I can hear.

Pulling his warm fingers away from their hold on my arm, I yank it back, watching the skin's deep bruise fade into something much more tolerable.

"Why the nickname?" I question again, rubbing my wrist with comforting motions.

Fallan leans back in his chair, pondering the question despite Hunter's urge to get him to quit speaking to me. Hunter had nearly torn away his shirt, trying to get him to stop applying the cream earlier. Even Mark had resorted to slinging his hat over the tram's interior camera, hiding what most would consider treason.

"When there was religion, the dove used to symbolize innocence and purity in a world scorched with floods and fire," Hunter says, taking the words away from Fallan. "What Fallan won't tell you is how you were the first Untouchable he had observed say sorry to someone like us-"

"It was abnormal and clearly an act to assuage your own personal inner turmoil. I liked the irony in nicknaming you after something as gentle and innocent as a small dove," Fallan says, raising his arms above his head, causing his shirt to ride up. His torso is exposed, and despite its scarring, it's not so rough on the eyes. I glance at his hip bone, seeing nothing but smooth skin. I was hoping to see a mark like mine.

"How is that ironic?" I question, forcing my eyes back up to meet Fallan's. He smirks at my wandering eyes.

"The irony is in how much violence you hide within yourself," Fallan says, smirking ear to ear, keeping his arms above his head. "And that's where you and I become the same. No Unfortunates, no Untouchables, just two humans pretending to be something they're not," Fallan scoffs, referencing more than just an innocent nickname. He knows so much more than he's letting on, and he's using that knowledge to torment me.

"Go to hell," I hiss, forcing my knees back to my chest.

I cover my ears with my hands, staring out the window blankly. My head is pressed against the cool glass, balancing out the burning fire within me.

Mark stares back occasionally, debating whether or not it's worth scolding the boy for how he spoke to me. Still, Fallan focuses on me, forcing a raise of his mouth each time I look back to see if he's still watching. Hunter apologizes profusely for his friend, eventually giving up once he realizes no one is listening.

This is all part of his game, isn't it? Seeing how far he can push me before I break. Despite what we saw together, his hate for me runs too deep, and can I blame him after what I saw?

Those were my people. The Untouchables. The Officials.

"Stop looking at me," I hiss, holding my head tighter to contain my negative thoughts.

Hunter nudges his friend, urging him to quit aggravating me. Still, Fallan pushes, continuing his blank stare.

"See something that scared you, Little Dove?" he questions, pushing me further. My head pounds with anticipation, spilling countless emotions I have yet to understand. His touch, the girl, our marks, all memories forced into my mind with no way to rid myself of them.

That feeling of another presence inside my mind returns. It holds my thoughts, coming from deeper than what lingers on the surface. I no longer feel alone in my thinking. The scuff of one's feet dragging along the surface of my mind echoes in my head as the pains behind my eyes ripples out. I lace my fingers with my hair, inhaling deeply, forcing away the pain with all I have. I focus on the open door in my mind, taking the unwelcoming presence by the hand and forcing it far away with a slam of the door.

Fallan takes a sharp breath, grasping his thigh, forcing his head back into the seat behind him. With a raise of his hand, he grabs his head, clutching his temple with angry curses. My hand shakes, wiping away a bit of blood that is trying to escape my ear. Hunter questions his friend, looking over his pained expression with confusion. I now see Fallan's grasp on his chest, higher than where my mark has taken residency. If tonight has taught me anything, it's this:

The impossible is entirely plausible.

I can't trust anyone or anything, even the recollection of my memories.

And the worst revelation of all is that I might be losing my mind.

CHAPTER THIRTEEN

FOREST

I keep my body leaning away from the pair, continuing to reflect on tonight's events in hopes that I can try and piece together anything I might have missed. As much as I try to blame everything that happened on my faltering mind that often leads to blackouts, I can't deny the blood the Officials have shed, even if I so desperately wish it was all in my head.

The slightest speck of red touches the bottom portion of my shirt, barely noticeable to anyone not actively looking. It's brown now after being touched by the oxygen in the air. You'd think I dropped a bit of chocolate on my front.

Fallan has been silent ever since he leaned his head back. He seems to be having his own unbearable headache, which only adds to my list of suspicions about the man and my list of reasons for continuing to break regulations to figure out what he wants from me. There has to be a reason he's been willing to violate the law so often to torment me as much as he has. Hate has to derive from something.

Hunter lies asleep on his friend. He must've tired himself out with his non-stop scolding toward Fallan, who apparently could care less about his actions or their consequences. My head dipped down a couple of times, clouded with exhaustion from the energy I exerted doing my best to play dead. The weight of my reality is heavy, holding me down like rocks in my shoes as I sink to the bottom of the ocean floor.

The tram rolls to a stop, jolting me away from my wave of thoughts. The streetlight illuminates my neighborhood, casting large shadows across the pavement. Each of the house's curtains are already drawn, lit inside by the soft glow of bedroom lamps as people begin to unwind. Some living areas that I can see are alive with bright screens, though only some use their televisions, often relying on music due to its lack of blue light. Unlike the rest, my house is dimly lit, only my father's study is barely illuminated. Even from here, I can see how still the massive house is at this hour.

I pull myself to my feet, letting the dizziness fade away before continuing my slow pace toward the front of the tram. My head's pain is tolerable, fizzled down to nothing more than the usual minor pain behind my eyes. Mark retrieves his cap from the camera, planting it on his head to hide his silver hair.

"Thank you again for going out of your way to bring me back," I say, smiling at the older gentleman whose presence has seemed abnormally comforting.

"Anytime, sweetheart. I promise you it's my pleasure," Mark says, his eyes flashing with something unfamiliar. For a moment, and just a moment, he opens his mouth, ready to say more.

He quickly shuts down, letting his head drop with a sudden look of sadness.

I stop myself from addressing the change in his emotions this close to the tram's interior camera. With a few backward steps, I am off the tram, rubbing my chilly arms to fight back the cold. The walk to my house seems longer now. It's a straight path filled with a poorly lit sidewalk that seems that much more daunting, knowing a black car could pull up at any moment, ready to hit me with a line of questioning over my abnormal behavior the last few days. I stand still, deciding if going home is even the best move.

"You better start running, Little Dove. You never know what's lurking in the shadows," Fallan says with lowered eyes, stepping off the tram after a brief acknowledgment to Mark. Hunter is slumped into the window, sleeping blissfully and unbothered, his snores heard from where we stand.

"Why are you getting off here at this hour? This isn't your sector," I say, turning to face him as the tram begins to pull away, taking the light with it. Mark looked back only once in his rearview mirror before disappearing into nothing but a speck in my vision.

"I'm not making Mark stay out past curfew to drive me back to my section of the Unfortunate sector. Hunter is right at the beginning of town, but I am much farther back, and that road is not one you travel at night at his age," Fallan says, kicking the concrete with his heel.

"So what? You walk home?" I question, watching his eyes roll at the statement.

"Some walking, some stealing. Sadly, you Untouchables don't put up much of a fight. That's probably why you had no problems pinning down that arrogant asshole against the bus," Fallan says. I think back to Josh and his cocky attitude.

"Josh may be arrogant, but that move I pulled put a target on my back," I explain, hearing him audibly scoff at the statement.

"Excuse me if I don't have much sympathy for people targeting you," he says, motioning to the neighborhood, "Clearly, you're well protected in your sector thanks to your asshole father's high-ranking job-"

"Is that why you hate me? My father?" I question, cutting off his words.

He is silent, watching me with a look I can't pinpoint.

"I saw how you two looked at each other during the rally. My dad has never so much as given an Unfortunate a second look, but when he saw you, it was like his whole world shifted on the stage," I say, watching Fallan's jaw clench harder.

"Your father took away everything important to me for his own self-gain and paraded his perfect family around as if he didn't shed countless lives to create the life you live. That house you so desperately want to avoid, those clean clothes, and that full stomach you have, that pretty face, and those perfect, uncalloused hands were built on the backs of the people you've called 'bottom feeders' for years. Your father may be the source of my hate, but you did the rest all on your own. You're one of them. You will always be one of them," Fallan says, making my heart sink with a shame so deep it threatens to break me.

"I don't know what my father has done to you, but I'm sorry he hurt you, Fallan," I say, watching his eyes wince at the comment. I continue rubbing my arms, feeling the goosebumps glide along my fingers.

"Your words mean nothing to me. Hunter may believe that load of shit, and maybe even Mark, but not me. I won't let you convince me you're anything but the Untouchable I know you to be," he says, sounding like he's trying to convince both of us of the validity of his statement.

"Was any of what happened tonight real? Or was it all in my head?" I question softly, watching his mouth curl into a deeper frown. I grasp my lower stomach, feeling the rough skin of my mark from above the shirt.

"I don't know what you're talking about," Fallan whispers, turning on his heels, ready to leave this conversation as quickly as he entered it.

I see the bag he clutches. It lingers at his side, much like the one I carry. It's the same bag he shoved the light sensor prod into. I move forward, reaching my hand into the bag with a drag, closing my hand around the prod before taking several steps back and away from Fallan's sudden flustered figure. I hold the prod tightly, pointing it out towards Fallan. My thoughtless acts guide me. The linger of a blackout touches my mind as I feed into my rage.

"You can hate me, Fallan. You can hate me so much you think of nothing but my last breath and how you may take it from me," I start, shaking the prod in my hand. He moves forward, my head instinctively lowering like his people have done for us so many times. He grabs the prod from my hand. I easily give it up, letting my eyes reach his own. "If justice is what you want, stop dancing around it. Strike me as many times as you need to satisfy your own hatred. Call me names, continue tormenting me, but, please," I take a step toward him, watching his eyes scan my movements. "Don't make me alone in all of this. Don't let me be the only one who remembers what they did," I whisper, keeping my defiant position in front of his flustered figure.

His nostrils flare, and his jaw clenches even harder. His hand shoves the prod back into his bag. Grabbing my arms by the elbows, he pulls me. I let his touch guide me, feeling the familiar shutter that signals that I might lose consciousness. I quickly shove it away.

He leans into me, letting his eyes meet mine as he bends his head down. His breath brushes my face, warming my cheeks in the cool air.

"You will never allow someone like me to disarm you like that again. It's pathetic!" he hisses, yanking me tighter. "You're better than that. I never want to see that from you again," he spits, scanning my face with anger before pulling away completely. He creates several feet of space between us.

My heart beats out of my chest, my face flush and warm. My arms still feel the places his hands touched. Only now am I taking a breath. Even his scent lingers in my nose. He runs his hands over his face, letting out a sigh of frustration as he turns away.

"Two weeks ago, I would have begged to have you in a position like that," he says, not once fully glancing back at me.

"And now?" I question, hearing the wave of emotion in my tone.

"Things sometimes look better on paper," he mutters, continuing his walk forward, leaving me wanting nothing more than to scream into the void of darkness.

The house is as quiet as it appears on the outside, offering little to no indication of my parent's presence. If the front door's sensor panel didn't show their check-in times, I'd be sure they were both still at work.

Shakily, I dig my hands in my pockets, reflecting on the words I exchanged with Fallan. He was so close I could see every detail in his eyes and map every scar on his face. I wish his words could fill in the fragmented picture in my mind. Why shun the opportunity to get revenge for his people? Why not make me suffer for the things my father supposedly did to him? There must be an explanation for why all of this is happening.

Everyone seems to have answers except for me.

My dad stumbles out of his office, staring over the bright phone screen flashing red across his face. His eyes scan its message repeatedly, only growing angrier the farther he moves his eyes down the phone.

"Katiana, there was an incident!" he yells, nearly dropping his phone once he realizes I am standing in the hallway. I lower my eyes at him, feeling a thought pass over my mind, clawing its way from the deepest part of my memories.

If you regulate all the Officials, did you know what they would do to that Untouchable? What are you doing when you say you are "helping" the Unfortunates?

"Forest," my father says, touching his chest with a laugh. "You startled me. I wasn't expecting you back so early," he begins. My mother's head pops out from their bedroom door, staring at both of us with wide eyes. "Why are you back so early?" my father questions, working to hide his phone behind him in his back pocket.

"Were you on your way somewhere?" I ask, completely deflecting the line of questioning he was ready to throw my way.

I know how rough I must look to both of them. Dirtied clothes and scraggly hair, all tied together with scuffed knuckles that Fallan had missed amid his threat. I keep thinking about how far away his sector is. Though I've never been to the Unfortunate sector, it is no short walk from where he stopped, and given the tensions created at the screening, I would assume Officials are on the prowl for deviants more now than ever. I haven't even started to pull apart what I know attacked the girl. The Officials seemed hopelessly unphased by her mention of a creature we have been told nearly ended the human race.

The Shifters.

"No," my father finally says, crossing his arms, looking me over head to toe. My mother presses her head to the doorframe, closing her eyes as she listens to the interaction unfolding before her. Her hair runs down her back, covering her arms and front in beautiful waves. A white nightgown is hugging her, holding itself close to the body I now see shows every sign of stress one can have. Her eyes have circles underneath that are much darker than they were a week ago. As she breathes, I can see her ribs press to the gown's material. She looks exhausted, wobbling from side to side as she tries to stay awake.

"You told Mom there was an incident before you noticed me. What kind of incident?" I question, pushing him further. His pocket buzzes again, notifying him of the new messages he's getting.

"Nothing I don't normally deal with. Just an altercation near the school," he pauses, leaning in closer, lowering himself down further to scan my face. "You didn't see anything tonight, did you?" my father questions, tapping his finger on his leg as he anticipates an answer.

"Andrew, that's enough. You're needed elsewhere, and she is exhausted," my mother growls, hitting her hand against the doorframe. Her sleep-filled eyes finally open up again.

My father steps back, eyeing my mother before looking toward the front door.

"Maybe you're right.... Should I expect to see your brother home soon?" my father questions. I shake my head at him, wondering if he notices that I can see through his blatant lie like a window. If this is how easily he is willing to lie to me, what else has he kept quiet about in the name of his work? Is it even his choice?

"You can ask him when you see him. He's still at the school," I start, seeing panic flash over my father's face. "But I'm not feeling the best, and I'd like to get some sleep, so if you'll excuse me," I continue, moving past my dad only to feel his hand wrap around my arm as aggressively as Fallan.

"You'd tell me if something was happening that I needed to know about, right?" he questions. I stare at him, pulling my arm away with a scoff.

"Someone is always watching," I start, pointing to the numerous cameras in our living area. "You don't need me to tell you anything. You already know," I whisper back, continuing my pace forward and closer to my bedroom door.

"That wasn't a yes or no, Forest," my father says, continuing his stare toward the front door. My mother watches us, waiting for me to give him the answer he wants.

"Yes, Dad. Do I even have a choice?" I question, grasping my handle and waiting for him to say something else.

He says nothing before moving forward and closing the front door with a slam.

By some miracle, I urged my exhausted mother to return to bed despite her wanting to bug me about my rudeness toward my father. She didn't put up much of a fight once her head hit the pillow. I stayed with her, ensuring she was covered and warm until her grasp on my hand became light and weak. With a click, I shut off the lamp on my nightstand, allowing myself to be alone with my thoughts.

I tear my clothes away, shoving them as far down in my hamper as I can. I force the face of the clock down. Despite the promises that they never use the cameras to watch us in our bedrooms, I now have no faith in them. Acknowledging the scratches working up my stomach from the graveled ground and the few faint bruises left on my wrist from the Official's foot, I quickly pull on an oversized white sweater, smelling the strong scents of linen in the warm material. My pants are next. A pair of soft leisurewear pants cling to my legs. My knees are red from where I met the ground so many times today, and my mark is fully covered.

I let my hair fall down my back, looking at the numerous gray bits trying to peek through the brown. Normally, I would have torn them away, not waiting for my mother to dye them for me. I leave them this time, even looking over a few brighter pieces.

A single pill sits on my nightstand. This is my mom's way of telling me she no longer trusts me to be taking the doses as regularly as she'd like. I grasp the pill, wanting nothing more than to put it between my lips and make the blackouts and pain stop. I raise it to my mouth, thinking over the blissful euphoria of being entirely normal. No headaches or unexplained blackouts, just school and wondering what to wear on my Judgment Day. The pill presses to my lips, ready to explore my stomach and mind.

"Fuck," I whisper, pulling my hand away from my mouth and marching into my bathroom. I throw the pill into the toilet, feeling my hands shake out of frustration. Forcing the lid shut, I flush away the small bit of sanity with a slam of my hand into my leg to ease my mind. I crouch down to my knees, shaking my head at my inability to decide what is best.

"I don't want things to feel so empty again," I whisper, hitting my thigh repeatedly to calm my mind.

A silent patter hitting the ground outside my window stops my assault on my leg. A breeze moves through the bathroom. The tranquil smell of rain fills my nose, relaxing my whole body as I drive out my frustrations, listening to the increasing amount of rain caressing the side of my house. A small roll of thunder follows flashes of lightning in the clouds outside. My mother must have opened the window to let in the fresh air today and forgotten to close it. I look down at the bathtub before glancing at my bedroom.

Tearing away the sheets from my bed, I drag them along the floor with a few pillows, moving closer to the large bathtub. I fill the tub with the blankets from my bed, positioning my pillows against their sides, giving myself a place to lie. Taking the heavier blanket, I pull it over my body and allow my head to press into the soft feather pillow, continuing to let the sounds of the rain soothe me.

I take a deep breath, feeling today's events melt away as I indulge in the one place where I can listen to the rain without the house alerting my parents of an open window. This window's broken sensor has proved to be one of the biggest comforts when I needed it.

For once, my thoughts were quiet, leaving me with nothing but the bit of peace the storm had brought me.

CHAPTER FOURTEEN

FOREST

My eyes fly open at a sudden movement, nearly sending my head forward and into the side of the bathtub. My legs are to my chest, keeping my body in a fetal position comfortably situated within the bathtub. A hand touches my upper arm, nudging me awake with gentle motions. With a turn of my head, I see Max's eyes, looking me over with a grin, cocking his head in amusement at the sight in front of him.

"You slept here last night?" Max questions, observing the entirety of the bathroom as he kneels next to the tub.

"I guess I did," I rub my eyes, trying to rid myself of the remnants of sleep, "I was just trying to listen to the rain. It must have knocked me out," I admit, looking over his slumped state against the ground as the statement triggers the memories I had managed to keep away long enough for a night's rest.

"I should have followed after you last night," Max says, rubbing the back of his neck in shame. I pull myself up entirely, meeting his eyes as he grips the side of the tub. "You just seemed so upset, and I already felt like I had done something wrong. I just figured you needed your space away from me. I don't know if I did something to make you uncomfortable-"

I grab his hands, rubbing my thumbs over his knuckles. He notices my worn hand, ready to comment on it. I force my head in his line of sight, getting him to focus back on me and not the wounds I have no way of justifying to him right now.

"You did nothing wrong, Max. I got sick and honestly didn't want to put a damper on anyone else's night," I say, which seems to ease him into a more relaxed position. "Are you doing okay?" I question, surveying his face for any marks a careless Official might have left while trampling over the students last night. My hands touch his cheeks, feeling him smile beneath my fingers.

"I'm sorry if what I said to those Unfortunates upset you. It's hard trying to process your sudden sympathy for them," Max begins. I grab his face again, stopping the train of thought I know is unbearable for him.

"Don't apologize. I'm the one who has been off, not you," I admit, pressing my forehead to his as I draw a deep breath.

"Just give me a little bit of time to figure myself out. I promise you I am doing my best to pull myself away and out of this funk," I whisper, running my thumbs over his cheeks, regretting my decision last night to flush my pill down the toilet. Had I taken it, maybe this moment would be what he needs from me. So many other girls would fall for him, feeding into his touch in this moment, happily being what he wants.

It just can't be me.

"I need some time to figure out my headspace before dragging you into it with me," I finished, pulling my head away from his, not allowing him to try and explore another kiss.

He looks slightly disappointed, not letting the look linger as he grabs my hands, hauling me to my feet. My legs feel wobbly as I use them for the first time. I stagger, almost falling into him, before fixing my posture.

"I don't think I've met someone clumsier than you," Max says, returning to his usual light-hearted banter. "Now let's go make you a proper bed," he says, helping me gather the comforters and pillows with a smile I know he's struggling to show.

His disappointment is the one thing keeping him away from a reality I have yet to understand fully.

It's better this way.

It has to be.

My brother's voice fills the hallway, going on about rules and regulations and how he thinks he can improve them. Max shoots me a backward look, already curious how my brother could be this passionate this early in the morning. I smooth down my uniform, readjusting my tie for the millionth time. Max had patiently waited outside my room while I changed, tapping his foot against the floorboards in a rhythm. My hair is pulled back in a ponytail, showcasing the shadows on my face even more than when I had it down. I look as drained as my mother. Once more, I flushed down my pill this morning, clutching it with as much hesitation as the night before.

The sleek Official uniform makes me pause. My hands shake as I watch them lean on the counter, listening to Kai's extravagant rant. Rae sits on our couch, gawking at the Official with love-struck eyes. The Official lowers his hood, revealing the familiar blonde curls, washing away my anxieties with a few deep breaths.

He was never there last night. Given his less-than-traditional views, I would be surprised if they even allowed him to know anything. Kai's eyes dart behind Xavier, landing on Max and me with a nod. This is the first time he's seen me since last night. Everyone but Max decided that giving me space was in their best interests.

Xavier turns around, tuning out my brother, his eyes landing directly on me. I feel a sudden comfort in his smile, wanting nothing more than to break away from Max and pull him aside to dive deep into all that I saw despite the uniform he wears. He half listens to my brother, giving him short answers to satisfy him. His eyes move past Max, scrunching his brows before returning to me. Kai gradually takes the hint, excusing himself from the conversation once he takes notice of Rae staring at the intimidating blonde he's been talking to.

I see now the other Officials lingering in my home. Some in the kitchen, others spilling from my father's study. I try not to make eye contact with them, recognizing a few from last night's movie screening at the school. Much like last night, they all smile, clearly unaware that I remember what happened. One, in particular, stands out, making me sick to my stomach by their comfort level in my home.

The man who had stepped on my arm now stands in my kitchen, drinking a large cup of coffee from one of our mugs, taking seconds from the pot my mother had brewed for us this morning. The man smiles at me, but it's impossible to reciprocate.

"Good morning, kiddo," the man says, trying his best to make me respond to his warm gestures.

I touch my wrist, remembering his words after stepping all over me. I didn't know it then, but I know it now.

It was him.

"*Blackburn created a beauty like that?*" I hear him say in the shadows of my thoughts.

His sick voice clings to my mind as clearly as the image of him watching the girl's lifeless body. He laughed with a careless ease, not once batting an eye as her life slowly slipped free from her.

Xavier steps in my line of vision, blocking my blank stare toward the man indulging in the pleasures of our home. He waves his hand over my eyes, drawing me back to reality with a warm smile. Max has joined his twin on the couch, looking over Xavier and me with a less-than-pleasant expression.

"How are we this morning, Blackburn?" Xavier questions, looking back again to see the man's continuous gawk in my direction, more specifically, my arm he had damaged.

"You have a report to run, Nick. Why don't you go busy yourself in mindless stares somewhere else," Xavier says, snapping at his superior with a relaxed posture. The man's uniform is threaded with multiple stitches of gold vinery, showcasing his rank within the Official's regiment. I expect Nick to snap back at Xavier, questioning why someone so young would be so bold. Instead, he nods, setting the mug in the sink without another word.

"He was making you uncomfortable, right?" Xavier questions quietly, watching Nick leave the room with a lowered head.

"I can't say I like being looked at like I'm a meal. Any particular reason he let you speak to him like that?" I question, watching Xavier's mouth curve upward once more.

"I may or may not have some proof he visits Unfortunate backroom dancers on his days off," Xavier says slyly.

"*Prostitutes?*" I question silently. I expected him to tell me it was all a joke.

"Funny how they walk on such a moral high ground above the Unfortunates and yet have no issues doing things like that," Xavier scolds, crossing his arms with a shake of his head.

I can tell by Max's sudden tenseness he heard the comment. A small camera lingers by the cabinet near Xavier's head. Despite those two things, Xavier still speaks openly.

"I think the Untouchable's self-gain is their only priority, no matter who they hurt. It's selfish," I utter, expecting him to disagree with me immediately.

"It's nauseatingly selfish to act like we've done any Unfortunate any favors," Xavier whispers, holding my eye contact with nothing but a genuine expression.

"You believe that?" I question, watching his eyes move toward the camera before returning to me.

"Don't you?" he questions, moving his body in front of the watchful government device.

I give him my first genuine smile, which is confirmation enough. Xavier's presence is like a breath of fresh air. He's the first person I have found myself wanting to be around. Everything about him only draws me in. Every sly comment, every small joke, and every stolen moment alone with him makes the years of being alone with my thoughts feel lighter. I cling to our interactions, wishing nothing more than to be alone with him and away from all the noise around us.

"What did you do?" he questions, breaking me free from my reverie.

His fingers gently touch my wrist, grazing over what's left of the bruises from last night. I wince at the touch, taking a mental note of the countless cameras and Officials in my home. He looks displeased by the sight, running his finger over the textured pattern the boot had managed to make in my forearm.

"Is that from a shoe?" he continues, keeping us turned away from my friends and their wandering eyes.

I want to tell him everything. I want to scream into his chest and reflect on the horrors of the night.

But Fallan's words close my throat, stopping the truth from escaping.

"If you want to stay alive, close your fucking eyes and don't move."

It wasn't Unfortunates who pulled that trigger. It wasn't Unfortunates who Fallan feared. It was my people. As much as I want to tell Xavier, he's still not safe, and until I know he is, there's no way I can throw all of this onto him. I know the fact that I remember what happened last night would create a target on my back and most likely end in a death sentence. If I tell Xavier, I just put him on the chopping block with Fallan and me.

"No," I begin, letting his finger continue tracing over the skin.

"She fell at the screening," Max says, answering for me in a dismissive tone.

"Thank you, Vega. I didn't realize you were also the beautiful brunette standing next to me," Xavier says.

My stomach does a flip, filling with heat at his words. I can't stop the smile that spans across my face, my red cheeks now on full display for everyone. Xavier continues to eye down Max with his taunting smirk, keeping his hand on my wrist as Rae and Kai exchange a look. Max scoffs at the man, turning forward, defeated and unable to find a response.

Xavier's hair falls onto his face, moving with him once he looks back at me.

"Beautiful?" I whisper, nudging him gently, poking fun at the comment.

"Would you rather I lie, Ms. Blackburn?" he questions.

My desire for him to move his hand from around my wrist down to my waist crosses my mind.

"But seriously, are you okay?" he questions, gently dropping my wrist and crossing his arms.

I pause, reflecting on his words.

"I don't know how to answer that if I'm being honest," I admit, walking the line between a lie and the truth.

"Kai, my boy!" Adam's booming voice yells, making Xavier wince as he takes several steps away from me.

I angrily stare at the man, watching him clap my brother on the back with genuine familiarity. His pistol is attached to his side. The same pistol he used to end the injured girl's life before hauling her away like a sack of trash. Nick and my father gravitate closer to my father's study, deep in conversation about affairs they'd rather no one else hear.

I hold the bottom of my skirt, forcing it farther down than it already goes, not wanting to have either man see any part of me. Without thinking, I moved myself back to Xavier, making my way behind him to shield my father's colleagues from getting a good look at me.

"Are you going to tell me why you seem so scared right now?" Xavier asks in a whisper, turning back toward me. I shake my head, darting my eyes to the two men, now suddenly aware of my presence. Adam pulls away from Kai, motioning for me to move out from behind Xavier. I clench my jaw, standing my ground. Xavier does not try to force me out from behind him.

"Forest, socialize," my father orders, waving his hand in the air toward me. I swallow slowly, taking several steps away from Xavier, continuing to hold my skirt down.

"Forest, you remember Adam," my father says, moving his companion closer, smiling alongside the murderer standing next to him.

"What's it been? A few years, kiddo? I always see your brother during the Student Advocate tours of the Official Headquarters. It seems like just yesterday your father was carrying you around in his arms," Adam says, light-heartedly.

He killed her. He killed her in cold blood.

"I don't find much interest in things as trivial as the Student Advocacy Program," I say coldly, hearing Xavier stifle a laugh. Adam's eyes dart to the man, his brow twitching before turning back to me.

"To each their own, I suppose," Adam begins, scanning over my brother and the twins surrounding him. "How did you all enjoy the screening last night?" he questions, making me feel as though he's indirectly pointing his words at me.

"I can't say it was my favorite event the school hosted," I say, cutting off anyone else from being able to answer.

"Any particular reason why?" Adam pauses, taking a step, looking down at me with curious eyes.

"That movie is painstakingly predictable. Can you blame her?" Xavier says, shoving himself into the conversation, de-escalating the growing tensions.

"I suppose you're right," Adam says, backing away as his livelier attitude returns.

Nick finally pulls away from his conversation with my dad, moving closer to address Adam directly. I clench my skirt tighter, and my knuckles grow white as Nick glances at my wrist again to look at the proof of what he'd done last night.

"Your question reminded me," Xavier says, grabbing my elbow to guide me farther away from the man and closer to my front door. "Do you remember the flowers I was telling you about? The ones that grow in the Fall?" Xavier questions, diverting the conversation to something completely new. He narrows his eyes, trying to signal me to go along with it.

"Yes, vaguely. I might need a reminder," I say, letting him lead me closer to my front door.

"Your father took my suggestion and planted a few. Do you mind if I show her what's already started to bloom? I don't want to forget," Xavier says, reaching into his pocket to grab his ID and check out on the panel by the front door.

"Go for it. Kai seems more eager to speak to me anyways," my father says, dismissing us with a smile. "You all join them outside in five, or else you'll be late for the tram to school," my father says to my brother, Rae, and Max, watching me tap my ID with a smile before Xavier and I move out into the cold air.

I scan the flower beds in front of the house, looking at the empty pots filled with nothing but the daisies each house is allowed to have.

"I was hoping he forgot I never planted anything," Xavier says, rubbing the back of his neck before pulling me off the front steps and closer to the side of the house.

He stops, crossing his arms while he watches me.

"Why are you suddenly so aware of Nick and Adam? They have been in your house countless times, and only now are you avoiding them like the plague," Xavier says. I glance up at the house's side camera, clenching the material of my skirt tightly.

Xavier peers up at the tiny spy, dipping down to grab a handful of rocks.

"What are you-"

He hurls the rocks without warning, shattering the camera and pulling me away from the fragmented glass that hits the ground. Its pieces smoke, crushed further by the heel of his boot, now pressed down on it.

"It's just you and me. So please, tell me what really happened," he pleads, watching me lean onto the side of my house. My hands drag down my face out of frustration.

"I can't," I whisper, thinking of the implications of telling him what I saw and what the true nature of the chips behind everyone's ears really is.

He grabs my arm again, holding it up in my line of vision.

"Who did this?" he questions, pointing to the house. "Was it one of those two idiots? Don't you dare lie. I can tell when you're lying to me," he takes a step closer. Unlike everyone else who has been this close, I don't want him away from me. His scent engulfs my nose with notes of cinnamon and oak. I want to yank him down to me, exploring his face with my hands. I wonder if it's as satisfying to touch as it is to look at.

But still, I remain silent.

"Was it Adam?" he questions. I offer him nothing.

He pauses, touching my chin, pulling my gaze back up to him.

"Was it Nick?" he questions. Without thinking, I grasp his forearm a little tighter at the mention of the man's name.

Xavier curses, clenching his jaw, letting his gentle expression melt away. I watch his frustration grow, festering the longer he looks at the wound.

"That arrogant asshole. I swear, your father and I can get him in tremendous trouble, but I'll start by dragging him across your living room-" he begins, moving back toward my house.

"No!" I yell, yanking him back toward me, watching him stumble in an attempt to stabilize himself. I hold him with all I have, hearing my rapid heartbeat fill my ears as he now stands over me, both of his hands on the wall above my head.

"If you tell him I know that he did it, it won't be safe for either of us," I whisper, grasping the front of his uniform with shaky hands.

"Forest, I need more than that-"

"I can't. I can't tell you," I begin, pressing my head to his chest with a large sigh. "But please, please, trust me when I tell you that I want to," I say, and I hope he can hear the heavy emotion coating my voice.

There is a pause between the two of us. It's a moment where the silence is close to deafening.

His hands come over my head, gently running them through my hair, starting from the top of my neck and trailing down the length of my back. Instead of pushing me away, he pulls me closer, moving his hands from my hair to my waist, touching my hips with his large hands. I try to deflect his hand's graze over my mark, nearly losing my breath once his fingertips glide over the top of the rough skin.

Something awakens inside me, clawing free from the depths of my mind, sending all of me into overdrive. It coaxes my mind, making every part of me burn hot. Every emotion flows through me. Pain, fear, power, and lust all come together to sink the teeth into the comforts of his touch. His hand grasps tighter, pulling me in closer, seemingly unable to see on the surface what is happening within me. I close my eyes, letting myself sink into his touch. Once more, I can sense another presence in my mind. I focus on that foreign energy within me, expecting to want nothing more than to shove it away, but instead, I embrace it, feeling the mix of pleasure and security it brings me the more I allow it to explore my mind.

His hands move up from my hips, traveling to the side of my face, touching my heated cheeks. I grasp his front tighter, feeling the muscular torso lingering beneath the black uniform.

"Where were you just then?" he questions, running his thumbs over my cheeks in gentle motions.

"With you," I mutter, smiling against the rolls of his thumbs over my face.

The feeling fades away, leaving as quickly as it came. Unlike every other time before this, my mark fills with pleasure instead of pain, expanding out into my body in relaxing waves.

Is it him inside my mind? I question internally, looking over Xavier's kind eyes.

"Was it you just then?" I whisper, seeing his eyebrows pull into a look of confusion.

Several footsteps scuff the ground, growing closer with each passing second. Xavier looks ready to say more but is promptly cut off by the sound of my friends' mindless chatter.

"This conversation is far from over," Xavier whispers, pressing his lips to my ear, sending a wave of chills through my body.

He pulls his hands away from me, taking a step back and shoving them in his pockets instead. My father, my brother, and friends round the corner of the house, looking between the two of us with wide-eyed gazes. Xavier leans onto the wall, looking down at the shattered camera my father has now noticed.

"What happened?" he questions, moving to get a closer look.

"I'm assuming a bird hit it. Can't trust those genetically modified flying rats," Xavier says, giving himself a solid alibi.

I smile at his quick response, watching him shrug his shoulders in amusement.

"I guess maybe we should have just kept them as target practice for Officials in training instead of letting them breed and explore New Haven," my father says, shaking his head at the broken camera.

"Officials get to do target practice?" Max questions, relaxing his rigid posture.

"That, and so much more," Xavier says, flashing his mesmerizing grin at Max.

"How hard is it to be placed in the Official training program after you complete Judgement Day?" Max questions, stepping closer to the man he wanted nothing to do with moments ago.

"Why don't you three get to school? Xavier can take Max back once they are done with their conversation. Only one of you needs to be late," my father says, urging us forward and away from the side of our house with a nudge of my back. I don't argue, giving Xavier one last look.

"If you want to make it, you'd better go now," my father says, pulling my attention away from the two blondes gradually getting deeper into a conversation about the training program.

I don't try to linger, allowing myself to follow behind Rae and Kai's quick walk to the tram, stowing away the events and stolen moments with Xavier on the side of the house in the safest parts of my mind.

Kai's eyes avert to me every few steps, ready to hit me with a line of questioning he knows is sure to piss me off. It's not very often that Kai is this quiet on our morning walk to the tram. Instead of taking long strides to walk ahead with Rae, he lingers behind, messing with a thread on his sleeve while making no attempts to start a conversation.

"What is it, Kai?" I question, unable to bear the longing look he gives me whenever he thinks I don't notice he's staring.

"It's nothing."

Already, he's underestimating my ability to tell when something is off with him.

"You've been staring at me this whole walk like I have 'Unfortunate Lover' written across my face."

We both pause, looking over one another with varying expressions.

"So, spit it out," I finish.

Rae is too caught up in her pursuit to make it to the tram in time to notice our sudden stop. I tear away the thread on his sleeve, giving him nothing else to focus on.

"You and Xavier were inches apart when I saw you two together. Are you sneaking around with Officials now to piss off Dad?" Kai questions. His inability to recall anything about what the other Officials did last night is becoming increasingly unbearable, especially when he speaks of them like people I would enjoy spending time with.

"I'm not sneaking around with anyone," my voice comes out angrier than expected. "You can't even begin to understand what the hell I've been dealing with. Xavier has been helping-"

"By cozying up to you when you're clearly having issues that make you more vulnerable?" Kai throws back at me, stopping my train of thought.

"I-I'm not having issues," I whisper, feeling the pain linger in my chest from his comment.

He crosses his arms, looking down at the pavement. I can see the sadness reflected in his stare.

"Are you having hallucinations again, Forest?" Kai continues, not looking up to address me. "If you're seeing things again, I'm sure Mom can up your medication-"

"You knew about the meds?"

He looks startled by the question, covering his mouth as if he hadn't meant to mention it to begin with.

"Listen, it doesn't matter what I know. Even the well-off Untouchables sometimes have to medicate. If you tell Mom and Dad you are struggling, maybe they can help."

My anger washes over me like a tidal wave.

"I'm not struggling!" I yell, forcing myself several feet away from my brother, touching the scar that lies behind the back of my ear. Even Rae pauses her walk, turning back to see just how far ahead she had gotten. Kai is dead silent, clasping his hands together patiently. "You may think you have all of this figured out, Kai, that you're above everyone else when it comes to understanding how the world works," I begin, pointing at his chest. "But you have no idea who I am, and I'm tired of you pretending that you do," I continue, angrily backing away from him with small grunts.

"So what?" he questions angrily, "You spend two minutes flirting with an Official on the side of the house, and suddenly you're too much of an outcast for me to understand? Do you think you're the only person who struggles to find their place, Forest? Because you're not. Your whole life has been handed to you, yet you walk around like you don't want it-"

"I don't want it!" I yell, watching his body tense up at the remark.

"You can follow along and play the perfect son. You can listen to the rules and pretend that you've had a choice in where you stand in this whole fucking ant farm we live in. But what you won't do is pretend for a second that you understand how I feel because if you did, you wouldn't be looking at me like you are right now. You wouldn't be looking at me like I'm crazy-"

"Maybe you are crazy. Mom and Dad should have never relied on those pills when you started seeing things that weren't real," Kai spits. Angrily, his eyes drop, narrowing in a way I have only seen Fallan look at me.

I scoff at the comment, nodding as my feet begin to back me away. A small laugh leaves me, supported by the countless emotions encompassing my chest the closer I move to Rae. I can see the regret wash over my brother's face as his hand runs over his tired eyes.

"Maybe I am crazy, Kai. Go ahead and add it to the list of reasons you look down on me instead of being my brother," I whisper, turning my back on him and moving straight past Rae's solemn expression.

There is more he wants to know. There is so little he's chosen to say. Every word he spoke to me felt like another weight on my chest. I don't even try and talk to Rae as I move past her.

Nothing she can say will make any of this better.

The tram is already filled with students, some more lively than others. My legs burn as I continue my rapid pace forward.

His dark black curls poke out from beneath the hood of his jacket. He grabs the railing, readying himself to get onto the vehicle. His head is craned in my direction, giving me a look of confusion the closer I draw to his paused position on the steps. I grab the metal railing, taking a few steps ahead of Fallan to make myself taller. I drag down his hood as I move up the steps, leaning over just close enough that the words between us will only be our own.

"Turn me in, I don't care. I am not begging for your answers anymore. I know you know the truth, and you will give it to me, one way or another," I whisper, watching his jaw clench as he registers his inability to speak freely with so many eyes and ears around.

Mark looks over the exchange with wide eyes. Still, I offer the gentleman a soft smile, ensuring he knows it's for him. My shoulder shoves past Fallan, meeting a chest much harder than I expected. A few of the regular riders peer at my smile toward the driver, giving me a few looks of surprise the closer I move to my standard seat. Fallan clenches his hands as he sits at the end of the bus. I stare at him, only pulling my attention away to eye down a fellow passenger whose eyes have yet to leave me. I've seen them around the Academy a few times, but not frequently enough to put a name to the face.

"What?" I question toward the watchful passenger. The accusation lingering in their stare is enough to make anyone snap. Utilizing their better judgment, they look away immediately. My gaze moves to my brother and Rae as they get on board with no acknowledgment to Mark.

Not that they ever do.

"Since when do you smile at that bus driver?" one of the girls asks in a genuine tone.

I'm caught off guard by her question, cocking my head at her with annoyance.

"I'm not sure. Maybe I'm feeling benevolent," I say, not caring to hide the lack of desire I have to interact with her.

Even from here, I can hear Fallan quietly chuckle at my response, making my blood run hot with anger at the idea of bringing him any joy.

Kai and Rae sit next to me, neither one of them trying to engage me for the rest of the ride to the Academy.

CHAPTER FIFTEEN

KAIDEN

I zip up my jacket, wanting nothing to do with the brisk weather or my task for Ecology class trying to find a few perfect leaves that haven't been trampled by the feet of my classmates. The Academy grounds are so well kept you almost wouldn't know it was fall or that only yesterday, the grounds had been destroyed by an unnamed deviant Unfortunate wanting to ruin the beautiful koi ponds that took our parents months to petition for. Remnants of the movie night still linger, with a few missed popcorn bags tucked away beneath the booth window that was used last night for concessions.

I've been fighting back an unbearable headache. Rae mentioned having one this morning and Max was too preoccupied with my sister and the Officials even to acknowledge my question if he had one too. I sometimes pity Max when I see how hard he tries for Forest. I'm half convinced the only reason he's interested in talking to Xavier about the Official's Training Academy is because of my sister's sudden interest in the charming blonde, who isn't him.

I know she was hoping I didn't see anything when we came around the side of the house this morning, and for the most part, I didn't. Never in my life had I seen Forest willingly allow someone to be that close to her. The way they looked at us when they pulled away from each other, you'd think they had just committed a crime.

Maybe Forest finding some sanctuary in Xavier would be good for her. She can't spend her whole life making poor decisions and hoping I will be there to help her brace for the fall. Maybe if she cozies up to an Official, he'll have more luck than me in regulating her sudden mood swings.

I drop another broken leaf, questioning how possible it is to get away with just taping two similar ones together and making my teacher work with it. I notice a small area of the grass in front of where the tarp for the movie once stood is withering away, pale and void of color, dying while everything around it thrives. I run my finger over the dry grass, removing my hands as the intense smell of bleach and weed killer hits my nose. I quickly shove down the gag trying to reach my throat, doing my best to wipe away the residual odor on my pant leg.

A motion of activity in one of the farther bushes lining the grounds creates a clatter of noise. I take my focus from the patch of dead grass, looking over towards the movement with curiosity.

Without thinking, my legs begin moving, pulling me further away from the patch on the lawn and closer to the shaking branches. My hands are tucked deep in my pockets, far enough away from my nose I don't have to catch another whiff of whatever laced the dead grass. I finally spot a uniform-clad figure kneeling behind the bush, covering themselves in the dirt around their white stockings.

I see her brown hair wound tightly into a ponytail on her head. Her sharp jawline and green eyes scan the area in front of her, clawing her hands into the surrounding dirt to make more room for whatever is in front of her. I have to stop myself from yanking her back by her ponytail, ready to question why she's digging around in the ground at ten in the morning.

"Forest?" I begin, ready to hit her with a line of questioning while dragging her away from the foliage.

Her body shifts out of its position, giving me a clear look at what it is that has her knee deep in the dirt. Her eyes shift up to meet mine. Her jaw clenches as she gives me a moment to observe what's in front of me.

What seems to be a significant claw mark tattoos the rock she's dug up. The wood and greenery around the slashes are scorched, all burned away as if a lighter had lingered on the space for several minutes. The indent of an animal's paw is pressed into the earth.

"I think I saw something hiding here last night," Forest says, pausing as she looks over the space around her.

I see now just how many branches are broken. Something large had to be standing where she now kneels to cause the amount of damage abundantly obvious here now. "It must have left this behind in the process," she finishes, rising from her knees to finally join me on the other side of the bush. I help her wipe away the dirt from her clothes, trying to prevent brown smears from coating her legs.

"Wouldn't the Officials have noticed something big enough to leave these marks?" I question.

Her nose scrunches at the mention of Officials, turning upwards as it usually would have had I mentioned the Unfortunates. A feeling of unease comes over me as I continue to look at the scorched space. Her hands fumble in her bag, pulling out her sketchbook. She begins to trace a quick image of the area in front of us. Her hands work quickly yet carefully, and I can tell she's trying to be as detailed as possible. I hear a small scoff leave her throat once she fully processes my question.

"I don't think the Officials even knew it was there. They must have been too preoccupied handling other affairs last night," my sister says, hiding many emotions I can't quite pinpoint.

"What are you even doing outside of class?" I question, pushing the bush back to its normal position to stop her rapid sketching. She looks over the paper with little satisfaction before shoving it back into her bag. Her hands are now covered in charcoal. She glances toward the wilted grass.

"I never showed up to my first period. Why are you out here?" she states, keeping her eyes on the bleach stain in the grass behind me.

"I need some leaves for Ecology. Do you know what happened there? The ground is covered in chemicals," I question. Once more, her nose scrunches anxiously, giving me my answer on whether or not she knows more than she's letting on.

"As I said, the Officials were preoccupied handling other affairs last night," she reiterates.

I reflect on how close we sat last night to that patch of worn grass.

"We were feet away from that spot. I feel like if they decided to spray chemicals last night, I would have noticed, and don't feed me that bullshit that it happened after we left. I can see it all over your face that something is wrong. What aren't you telling me, Forest?" I push, half expecting her to hit me with the truth and ask me for whatever advice I can offer like she always does. Instead, she stands her ground, looking me over with lowered eyes.

"I can't tell you. They won't let me," she whispers, her response fueling me to add to the list of questions that are starting to manifest in my head.

"Who won't let you, Forest?" I question, grazing the goosebumps on her arms with a gentle touch I know she needs right now.

Her eyes dart behind me, causing her to pull away from my touch. I look behind me at the two Officials walking outside, both deep in conversation as they exchange a few laughs. I keep my eyes toward them, ready to motion them over.

"Maybe they will know what to do about the tracks," I begin, raising my hand above my head to waive them over. I look back at Forest, dropping my hand instantly as I watch her foot cover up the track and the soot with a few kicks of her shoe, coating the track in a layer of dirt.

She arranges the branches back to their original unbothered position, even going so far as to shove me a few feet forward, farther away from the bush. She covers the damage like it's nothing, giving me no time to react as the Officials finally take notice of our presence.

"Forest, what the hell-"

"Kai. Shut the hell up and let me talk," she hisses in a tone I've never heard from her. I close my mouth without thinking, letting my line of questioning die off the closer the two men approach us.

The two Officials are ones I have seen occasionally in passing, one younger, the other's name is Adam. Forest still grips my shirt, clenching it with white knuckles. She shifts uncomfortably where she stands. The men pause in front of us, curious as to what they've walked over to. Adams's gaze lingers on my sister, watching her much longer than I'm comfortable with. She holds her head high, offering him a slight smile once he clears his throat.

"What are you two doing out here?" Adam questions, only looking at my sister as he speaks.

"I was helping my brother with an Ecology project. We were trying to find some...." she trails off, unsure what the nature of my scavenger hunt really is.

"Intact leaves, but the grounds are so well kept we've been having some difficulties," I finish for her, finally getting my first glance from Adam and the man beside him. Forest nods in agreement at my explanation, subtly drawing in a deep breath, no doubt waiting to see if they believe us.

"I suppose we might have lost track of time," Forest admits, tapping the watch on Adam's wrist.

I know she could care less about what period we are in.

Adam's cold stare turns into a soft smile. He relaxes as he observes her, looking around the area before landing his eyes in the air. I watch his hand reach up as a leaf twirls down from one of the high aspen trees. Its golden yellow color catches the light as his fingers carefully snatch it from the air. Adam places the leaf in my sister's hair, tucking it behind her ear. Once more, I watch her nose scrunch. It's a gesture I am starting to realize only those who observe her often would notice.

"I'd say that's intact enough. You both had better get back to your classes," Adam says, pulling his hand away from my sister's face. Once again, she gives him another empty smile.

I feel her hand tug my shirt, pulling me along with her, both of us giving the Officials a slight nod.

"Of course, sir," she says, acknowledging the other man with a curl of her mouth before dragging me farther away from the pair. I watch her hand claw away the leaf from her hair. Her eyes look wild as her slow breaths become quick heaves. Her hand is clenching my shirt so hard I can feel the anxiety controlling her grip. There's an outline from the sweat coating her palm on my front. Only once she's made it past the side doors and we're back inside the Academy does she pause, dropping the leaf in the front pocket of my shirt. I ready myself to speak to her, watching her finger press over my lips, silencing me again.

"This isn't a problem you can fix this time, Kai," she whispers, pulling away from me and moving down the nearest hallway.

I stand in silence, feeling the leaf beneath my touch as I fumble in my pocket. I still feel the place her hand clenched on my front, feeling the wet material brush my torso as one question lingers in my mind louder than all the rest.

What was she so afraid of?

CHAPTER SIXTEEN

ANDREW

My pen twirls between my fingers. As I reread the incident reports from last night's movie screening at the Academy, I can't bring myself to start the paperwork required to submit to the Commander.

Forest's sudden shift in demeanor earlier today lingers on my mind, eating away at every waking thought.

It's as if there's something I'm not seeing.

I can still see her eyes and how they looked at me when she got home last night. Nothing about her has been the same since this new school year started. I think back to Fallan's haunting blue eyes piercing straight through me during the assembly. Five minutes alone with her is all he would need to take revenge for the sins I committed. He looks at her with hate that I know is for me.

I never thought I'd see the day he learned to hate her. I was beginning to think it was impossible despite the code.

I look over the file with details about the Tainted they had to expel last night. As far as I know, the execution was far away from my children and their companions. Only after I had seen the itinerary of all that attended did I realize Fallan and another Unfortunate were there. Had the Shifter not gone after a Tainted and ruined the night, I wonder what Fallan would have done. He bribed multiple people to get that position working the booth. Trying to figure out his plans has been nothing short of hell.

"I left you like this thirty minutes ago, yet everything is the same," my wife's voice whispers.

Her arms wrap around my shoulders from behind, resting her head on my own as I quickly shut the file, closing my computer's screen with a wave of my hand. I can feel her mouth pull into a frown at my secrecy. Her heart is far too big to involve her in the news of an Untouchable child's death, even if they were Tainted. Thankfully, she was not tasked to do the autopsy.

"And now you're hiding your work," she says with a sigh, pulling her head away from atop my own. I grab her wrist, stopping her from walking away from me. Hesitating, she eventually lets me lead her closer, pulling her onto my lap.

I feel her small figure press into my chest. A few wrinkles encompass her face in all the right ways, aging her with a grace and beauty even the richest Untouchable struggles to achieve. I run my thumbs over her cheeks, reveling in the fact that she chose me, and I chose her. Not everyone can say that.

"I'm not hiding things, Katiana. There are just some parts of my work I think are best to spare you from seeing," I admit, knowing any conversation about last night would only lead to countless worries regarding our children.

"I've seen plenty of death, Andrew. You seem to forget who's in charge of the Expulsion Tests," she says with a large frown, touching the scar behind my ear.

She looks over my face for a reaction, and she gets it. My mouth curves as it falls into a more prominent frown than usual. She pulls her legs up higher, stringing them over my lap as she presses into me more. I feel her head land on my chest. My hand cups her middle, feeling the small indents of her ribs beneath my fingertips.

"You must focus on yourself, my love," I whisper, smelling her familiar scent of lavender. She pulls away from me, cupping my face between her warm hands while she observes me.

"Says you. You look like you haven't slept for days. What's on your mind?" she questions, holding my gaze to her own, never letting up.

"Our daughter," I admit after a few moments. "She has been getting into a great deal of trouble recently, and I can't help but wonder why," I say, half expecting her to goad me about how silly I'm being.

"She has always been defiant, Andrew. We both know she got that from you," she says, not trying to convince me of our daughter's innocence.

"You know what defiance leads to," I say, brushing over her scar, her eyes growing slightly wider.

"An Untouchable can only receive so many marks on their scorecard before Re-Regulation devices are used."

"Have they used one on her?" she questions, not giving any of my points a second thought.

"Not too long ago, yes," I begin. My wife's nose scrunches, only making me question the nature of her curiosity more, "But they used the devices on a group, not just our girl. It was for her safety and the other students. She was fine," I admit, clenching my jaw as I hesitantly grab the file that can answer all of the questions I'm sure she has.

I glance at the nearly closed door, making sure the space around us is private as I hand her the yellow file. In most scenarios, showing her this file would only result in my superiors screaming at me, but given her close ties to the Tainted's Expulsion Tests and our children, it's something she needs to see.

Her hands fumble as she breaks open the file. I see her cover her mouth at the image of the girl's bloody corpse. Multiple pictures of the grounds were taken, all to ensure a quick and effective cleaning of the area. The student's motionless figures all stand out in the photo. Our own children's still bodies were enough to scorch my mind with unpleasant imagery.

"It was just the one girl who was Marked?" Katiana questions, holding it together much better than I expected.

"We call them Tainted now, and yes, just the one. One too many," I sigh, running my hands up and down her side. Her eyes narrow at one of the pictures, flipping around the file to point to my daughter's familiar figure sprawled across the ground. Her brother is only a few feet away from her.

"Who is holding her neck down?" she questions, pointing to the figure inches from my daughter on the ground. I feel a pit form in my stomach at the sight of the dark-haired man pressed against my daughter. They both lie still. His hand rests on the back of her neck. It's a gesture so few know will calm her. I keep thinking about his sudden presence, making me question the validity of how much he truly remembers.

Is it possible he never forgot?

"The Unfortunate from the transfer program," I say after a few moments, still trying to process what I see. "There were quite a few moments of panic before the attack. Chances are he wanted her to get down before she got hurt from whatever went after those two kids," I say, unsure of how true that theory is.

Katiana slowly nods her head as she closes the file. I watch her raise her eyebrows as she's pulled deeper into her train of thought.

"Is he *the* Unfortunate?" she questions, my only response is a nod. She clenches her jaw in dismay.

"You handled it the first time. There's no coming back from what you all did to him; don't let your paranoia ruin you. There's no way he remembers," my wife says, speaking with disgust not directed toward Fallan but toward the people I work with.

"From what we did to him?" I question, throwing her words back at her as she takes a deep breath.

"You know where I stand on the situation," she says coldly, reminding me just how little of a say she had all those years ago.

"I don't mean to interrupt," Xavier's familiar voice says, nudging open the door to my study with a look of pure embarrassment as Katiana quickly pulls away from my lap. Sneakily, she puts the file back where it belongs. Katiana pats down her clothes, adjusting any areas I might have untucked with my gentle touch. "You said you wanted to meet around noon. I can always come back if it's a bad time," Xavier finishes, unsure of how to react to the situation he's stumbled upon.

"I still have some work I need to get done. I was just about to leave," Katiana says, making her way closer to the door with only a brief look in my direction. I mouth an "I love you," watching the smile spread across her face as she slips past the door. Xavier rubs the back of his neck, moving closer once I drag one of the open chairs in my study closer for him to sit in. He takes a seat with a heave, dragging himself closer to me.

"You seriously could have told me to piss off," Xavier says, trying his best to stay on my good side, given the interaction I saw between him and my daughter this morning.

No one has mustered the courage to bring it up. I'm starting to think maybe it's better that way.

"I asked you to stay here to keep me on track. There's no use in having you leave now," I say, pushing past my annoyance at his sudden presence due to my lack of time management. The boy looks tired, holding his head in his hand to stay upright. I see now how young he appears and yet he's years older than Kai. His uniform is messy, but that doesn't affect his ability to charm the women he interacts with. Unlike most egotistical Untouchable men, he holds himself on no pedestal, and I've never seen him gravitate towards the materialistic, even when his comrades urge him to.

I turn toward my computer, switching it on once more, letting its graphic images pass over my eyes and Xavier's. I see the countless elderly Unfortunates lined up at the edge of the ward. Each one is taken out silently, all by the hand of their own chips. Xavier watches the graphic images displayed in front of him with wide eyes. His throat bobs as he tries to gulp down words. It's a sorry attempt at digesting the information in front of him.

"It's the Release," I clarify, clicking away the video before checking off the files of each elder laid to rest, confirming their passing.

"What the hell does that mean?" Xavier questions, looking at me with a brief touch to the chip behind his ear.

"Don't worry, Untouchable chips are not designed to harm us in any way. The new Commander requires all Unfortunate elders 70 and above to be released outside the ward to conserve resources. It was their people or ours," I say, listening to Xavier scoff.

"The same Commander who has shown his face zero times since being appointed by the Council. Call it whatever you want. It's public execution," Xavier says, sounding much more like Katiana than I expected.

"Would you rather it be our people?" I question, silencing his rant as quickly as it had started.

I can't stop Xavier from grabbing the file Katiana had placed down on my desk before she left the room. He scans its contents, letting his eyes linger on the same photo that had drawn Katiana in. I watch his eyes absorb the image, giving me little time to try and pull it away from him.

"The chips can't kill us, but they can be used to manipulate us instead?" Xavier questions, yanking the file closer to him and away from my grasp.

"Because you're a saint when it comes to Re-Regulation devices?" I begin, watching his face drop into a frown. "I've seen your file, Xavier. I know why you could work your way up so young," I admit, waiting for him to respond.

"It doesn't mean I agree with what I had to do to get here," he says, most likely reflecting on the countless Unfortunate executions he had to take part in to show his loyalty.

"I know you don't take comfort from it," I say, drawing in a deep breath. "That's why I like you," I finish, relaxing in my chair as I watch him scan the file.

"How much do you know about the Tainted?" I question, watching him look over the picture of the girl and the claw marks that cover her chest.

"I know your wife runs the tests that are supposed to keep them out of our population. I know that, occasionally, some with low levels of mutation in their DNA can get by the tests. Shifters are attracted to them, right?" he questions, running his fingers over the marks left on the girl's body.

"As far as we know, Shifters can use the Tainted to return their forms to a human-like state. Their DNA is far more mutated than the Tainted's. Unlike the Tainted, they don't possess special abilities. All they possess is a blood lust that we are unable to satiate. We knew there were some tears in the ward. The real question is, how does a Shifter of that size make it this far into New Haven without anyone noticing? Two minutes alone with our weaponry, and it would have been down."

Xavier closes the file, looking at me like he's realized something.

"What is it?"

"A few men said they went back to the grounds to check for any sign of the events of last night, not that I knew what the hell they meant since I was running Unfortunate sector watch. They said it looked like something large had been sitting in the brush around the school, farther away than where the girl would have been attacked. I had no idea what it meant then, but maybe I do now," Xavier says, the gears turning in his mind as he continues to sort through the details of what happened. He's always been praised for his cunning and intellect.

"And?" I question, pushing him further.

"Maybe the Shifter was watching and the girl and her partner just happened to stumble across it. If it wanted to wipe out more students, it would have. I don't think it intended to be seen, considering how far it got into the sector," Xavier says, painting the picture of last night in my mind.

"What could it have possibly been watching?" I ask. He looks as if he's sorting out the answer as we speak.

"I'm not too sure. What are they most drawn to?" Xavier questions.

"Tainted. More specifically, the blood of them," I say, watching his shoulders shrug sleepily.

"Maybe there was someone worth hunting that we don't know about," Xavier says, making a chill run down my spine.

Xavier opens the file again, grabbing the photo of all the students and pointing to my daughter's figure.

"Her hand is bruised in the photo," Xavier says, grazing his finger over my daughter's still figure, not mentioning anyone else around her.

"One of your dipshits stepped on her hand last night," Xavier continues. I reflected on the image of her wary figure as she held her hand close to her last night.

"By some miracle, she thought it was her own clumsiness that caused the injury," Xavier finishes, drawing in a deep breath as he watches me.

I look over the photo, feeling angrier the longer I think about my men trampling my children.

"If you find out who's responsible, let me know," I say after a moment.

Xavier gives me a wide grin while throwing his head back with closed eyes. His body leans into his chair, making him look much more relaxed.

"It wasn't hard to piece together that it was Nick with all his arrogant table talk in our unit. Let's just say I might have been late today in between eating lunch and dumping laxatives in his morning brew," Xavier says, causing me to slip out a laugh I didn't know I had in me.

"They told me you were reckless, that you had few cares in the world. I think I'm starting to see that," I say, trying my best to maintain my professionalism.

"I have too many things to care about, Andrew," Xavier says, pulling himself closer to my computer. "I think that's part of my issue," he finishes, looking over my tab of "to-do's" lining the side of the screen.

"So, are we going to keep talking, or will we get this done?" Xavier smiles, clapping me on the back as he opens the video files of today in the Unfortunate sector.

He crosses off "**Review footage of Deviants**" from my list, both of us wincing at the footage in front of us.

The muddy ground and rotting buildings take up the screen. There are feeble shopkeepers lining the streets and sickly children tossing around mangled toys while weaving in between barbed wire fences that aren't standing upright anymore. Emaciated citizens work their way through the streets. Some shops are lively. Others are decorated with slumped-over citizens lying on the sidewalk. I think about the quality of life we've created for these people, reflecting on the facade of lies we tell the Untouchables about the Unfortunates' living conditions to make them feel better. Every day, grueling labor for our gain is forced onto them by a chip they think is in their head to help them.

"For the glory and grace of the fucking New World Order," Xavier says in a scoff, shaking his head at the screen in disgust.

"Glory and grace for some people," I whisper, worrying once the room fills with silence.

"I always thought that motto was a sham anyways," Xavier says after a few moments, giving me one last conspiratorial smirk before we begin reviewing hours of less-than-pleasant footage that very few can stomach to get through.

CHAPTER SEVENTEEN

FOREST

The uniform for Defense Class is an oversized gray shirt and soft black pants meant to maximize our comfort when working in hand-to-hand combat. This is one of the few classes I have without my brother or friends, leaving me exposed and alone. I've managed to find a spot on the farthest wall away from my classmates in an effort to avoid Colton and Josh's malicious stares. The pure thrill those two get from dragging Unfortunates across the mats as they spar is hard to watch.

Keeping my stare forward toward the constant movement around me is all I can do, hiding each wince as another Untouchable's back meets the floor. A few Officials linger around, waiting to use their prods on anyone but our people. I try my best to avoid contact with them, keeping my head held high to luck out on a partnership, hopefully.

"They're looking at you like you're their next meal," Fallan whispers silently.

I turn my head to meet his stoic expression. His back is facing away from the group as he wraps his knuckles, bracing his hands for the hard work that I'm sure he'll be off to after classes this afternoon. He's quiet enough to avoid any looks in his direction while he engages me.

I watch him work the gauze around his knuckles, observing how his arms move. He focuses on his large hands. The gray shirt, unlike on me, fits him nicely, clinging to a build I'd rather not challenge one-on-one. As he continues to move, his shirt rides up, revealing his weathered back and enticing abs.

"My eyes are up here," Fallan says in a snap, forcing my gaze back to his face.

I can feel my cheeks fill with heat at the comment, only growing redder once I realize how little amusement he's gotten from me ogling him. He pulls down his shirt, hiding the parts of him I allowed my eyes to explore.

"Who's looking at me like a meal?" I question, keeping my head down as I speak.

"The two idiots dragging my people over the mat like they're nothing," Fallan says, finishing up the gauze around his hands.

I see Josh and Colton's presence isn't just a nuisance to me, then.

"Trust me, their existence is less than pleasant for me, too," I sigh, pulling my head back up to meet the smirk that's found Fallan's face. It fades as quickly as it came, leaving me questioning if it was even there to begin with.

"You're finally starting to see how I feel," Fallan says, returning to his typical snarky demeanor.

The sweet smell of vanilla hits my nose, followed by a flash of blonde hair swaying in my vision. His blonde whore, Valerie, slides next to him, running her hands over his own with a look of satisfaction. I watch her hand reach under his shirt, gently caressing the skin above the waistline of his pants before pressing her lips to his arm. I roll my eyes at the exchange, knowing she had only requested they be sparring partners to get as close to him as possible. Her eyes flick up to me as I mock her over-the-top need to be all over him.

"Is there something I can do to make you happier?" she questions toward me in a sincere tone, grinding her teeth as she tries to stomach a genuinely kind response to my aggravated state. It's the most standard question an Unfortunate can ask, yet she's made it so backhanded.

I look at Fallan, watching him gently move her hands away from beneath his shirt as he stares down at her with a smile. He rubs the tops of her wrists with his thumbs, calming her down. His hands are familiar with her body. A rare and genuine smile encapsulates his face. I feel something deep within me fill with annoyance when I see his smile drop the minute he looks back at me.

"Get a room. Not everyone likes watching you be a slut," I hiss, pushing myself away from the wall, allowing all of my frustrations to pour out of me in a single statement. I grab my blade from the rack, strapping it to my side, leaving her gawking at me with a pitiful excuse of a confused expression. I don't even try to look at Fallan, only letting my shoulder hit him as hard as possible as I make my way closer to the mats.

"Markswood, Danvers! On the mats, now!" our teacher calls out, forcing Fallan and Valerie out of their insufferable moment together.

Valerie sulks to their designated mat, giving the teacher a hidden nasty look before pulling her attention back to Fallan. He focuses on her every movement as she circles around the mat with him. People begin to move closer to observe the pair. Rumor is that Fallan has bested everyone, Untouchable and Unfortunate alike. But as an Unfortunate, he should be giving us the upper hand. My body moves with the crowd, looming closer to the front than I'd like. Fallan glances at the crowd that's now formed around him, letting his eyes land on me for a moment longer before returning to scan Valerie's movements.

"First one down for five seconds yields," the teacher says, pushing up the glasses on his nose as he looks over the pair.

"Better yet, the first one to get the other one unconscious wins," Josh laughs, causing many others around us to join in on taunting the pair.

Even the teacher laughs. The heads of many Unfortunates lower following the comment.

Fallan looks irritated, unable to say anything back to him.

"Would you say that while pinned under my knee?" I snap, watching Josh's wide grin drop once he realizes who addressed him. Once more, Fallan lowers his gaze as he hides a look I can't explain, forcing it away with a shake of his head. Josh lowers his eyes at me, giving me a grin that is nothing but trouble.

"Shouldn't have opened your mouth," Josh hisses, filling my body with pure adrenaline.

"Sounds like you're scared," I mutter, hearing his friends egg him on with playful side comments and slaps to the back that only get him more worked up.

The sound of grunts pulls my gaze back to the mat. Unlike all the other Unfortunates, these two fight with precision, making sure to hit one another in the places that will keep them down the longest. Where most spar gently, Fallan aims with lethal intent. His hand grabs her wrist, stopping her from delivering a blow to his side. There's nothing gentle about him as he forces her down onto the mat by her neck. She lets out a sharp burst of air, growing angrier the longer Fallan has her on the ground. I watch her slender leg drive into his side, getting a slight wince from him before he moves his hands away from her neck and to both of her wrists, forcing them above her head. His free hand pins down her waist, letting his knee hold down her legs as she tries to writhe away from the position. I watch his grasp tighten on her wrists, holding her down effortlessly.

Something primal inside me stirs at the image of him in control, and I want nothing more than to shove it into the deepest parts of my mind. Valerie does her best to escape him, but his hold on her is unyielding. Untouchables begin hitting the mat, counting the five seconds for Fallan. He only lets up after five seconds, immediately pulling away with a wide grin as he helps her back to her feet. She gives him a playful shove, eating up his attention as he wraps his arm around her shoulder, pulling her closer to him. Once more, I feel something stir within me at the sight, only making my want to spar with Josh grow.

"Per usual, Markswood wins," our teacher says with a small clap, acknowledging Fallan with the tiniest bit of praise.

Fallan looks back at the group that's formed near him, stepping off the mat as Valerie leans into his front even more. We meet each other's gaze.

It is becoming increasingly more challenging to see him with her rubbed up against him. Even when pinned beneath him in submission, she looked like she was having the time of her life. His touch is nothing new to her. Every look she gives me entices the emotions jarring around inside me. I'm starting to feel things I don't understand.

He hates me. And she gets a version of him that I never will.

"We're up," Josh whispers nastily, shoving me towards the mat. I break my concentration away from Fallan as Josh shoves me aggressively once he realizes how many people are watching us. Our teacher doesn't try to protest; I'd even go so far as to say he's amused by us pairing up.

I stumble onto the mat, now unsure of my ability to take down Josh at this proximity. Although smaller than Fallan, he's still much taller than me, having a lot of physical advantages.

"Not so cocky when I'm standing in front of you, are you Blackburn? Are you as cowardly as your daddy?" Josh taunts, making my blood boil. I slowly turn my head back toward the crowd, watching the shake of Fallan's head as if he were warning me not to push Josh any farther.

I take a second to scan the area where my mark lies on my body, making sure my black pants are high enough to cover all of it. I tug at the annoying gray shirt, feeling the dark gray compression top beneath it. Without thinking, I pull away the gray overshirt, revealing the much tighter compression top that hugs my spindly frame. Josh sneers as I toss the shirt off the mat, giving his friends a look that tells me he thinks he's already won this. People whisper in groups, their eyes on us like wolves stalking prey.

"If I wanted you to strip, I wouldn't have asked you to do it here," Josh says, getting a few disgusting laughs from his friends. Of course they'd find that funny. They're known for getting too handsy with women.

I pause, looking over his relaxed position. I can feel the arrogance rolling off of him. I step toward him, gently caressing chest as I look up at him under hooded eyes. He looks down at me with a cocked head, waiting for me to beg for his forgiveness in front of all of these people.

"You never asked me why I took my clothes off for you," I say silently, watching his pupils dilate at the statement.

"Why did the untamable Forest Blackburn do that for me?"

"Only one of my shirts needs your blood on it," I hiss, watching his expression change to shock as I raise my fist, driving it as hard as I can into his jaw.

His eyes roll to the back of his skull. He staggers back, trying to ready himself to swing at me once his vision becomes clear. People around us gasp with surprise. Still, I charge forward, driving my knee as hard as possible into Josh's stomach while forcing him down by my grip on the front collar of his shirt. His hands claw at my sides, dragging me down with him and onto the floor. I hear his flood of curses as we begin to tangle. My necklace, sure to break the dress code, untucks free from my shirt, dangling in front of us like a toy for a cat. His nail marks burn my sides as he attempts to get up. Once more, I grab his collar, forcing him back down onto the hard mat. His warm blood now runs freely from his nose and coats my knuckles.

"You fucking bitch!" he begins, grabbing the front of my collar, already tearing down a part of the front of my shirt.

I bite my cheek out of frustration, feeling the burn of my mark as a new feeling takes over me.

Strength.

Officials swarm closer, unsure how far they will let this exchange continue. I think of the helpless girl from last night and the life that was stolen from her so suddenly. I think of how alone I am in all this and how the one person who can help me can hardly look at me. I am alone, fighting a battle that has no resolution.

I drive my fist into his face again, feeling his hands release my side and front. My fist raises again, ready to deliver the final blow that I know will shut those malice-filled eyes. My hand pauses in the air next to my face. Even now, out of the corner of my eye, I can see the Officials readying themselves to pull out their light sensor prods and detain me.

Josh squirms, trying to grab my sides again, but his blood obscures his vision.

"Stay down," I whisper silently in my mind, feeling a flood of energy pass over me.

His hands drop to the mat, pressing down firmly in place. I watch his eyes widen as he struggles to move. He looks perplexed, as I straddle his defenseless body. Slowly, the Officials move their hands away from their devices, going back to monitoring the rest of the room as if they weren't ready to drag me away from him. I hear the loud yells of students beginning to count down for us. Josh remains still, watching my jewelry dangle between us.

Turning to look at the crowd, I watch Fallan's back move farther away from the group, leaving Valerie behind so she can watch the scene in front of her.

"If I go for her necklace..." Josh's voice echoes in my head. It sounds distant; quieter than usual.

I turn to look at him, watching his fingers wiggle as he continues to struggle to move in the position I have him in.

"Your hands aren't getting anywhere near my neck, you coward," I whisper next to his ear, hearing the final countdown completed. Josh looks petrified by my response, kicking out and away once I move off of him.

He grasps his chest, looking at me like I'm some sort of monster as his friends help him back to his feet. I wipe his blood from my hands on the top of my compression shirt. His friends begin to tease him for being defeated by a girl. He doesn't engage with any of them. Instead, he shoves them away, lowering his head out of frustration before moving away from the crowd. I look again for Fallan, watching him scan the room one last time before slipping away. A few Untouchables begin cheering at me, joining me on the mat. They seem content that someone was finally able to take Josh on and actually win. Something they've wanted to do for a long time, apparently. I think we agree there. The few Officials watching over the class look amused, some more than others.

"Looks like Markswood has competition," our teacher bellows, as the painful cuts from Josh's nails finally begin to register. I feel drained, the start of a headache forming at the sudden feeling of adrenaline leaving my system.

I shove past the crowd that's already chanting on the next pair of students on the mat. It only took a few seconds to find myself moving closer to the doors Fallan had managed to slip through to get out of class unnoticed. I listen to the crowd get riled up once more, doing my best to avoid the gaze of my peers and the Officials as I realize just how many minutes of class are left. The smell of Josh's blood fills my nose with hints of copper, drawing my nauseous stomach closer to release as the memories of the night of the movie screening begin to resurface. I do my best to shove them back, hitting my shoulder into the door and stumbling into the empty hallway.

Fallan continues walking away from me, burying his hands in his pockets as he weaves closer to what I can only assume is the art room. He'd been watching that whole time, looking unamused every passing second of the fight. I continue forward, forcing my clean shirt over my body, not bothering to remove the dirty compression shirt. Fallan continues to stride quickly ahead of me.

I turn the corner down the art corridor, watching his body disappear behind the colorfully painted art room door. I don't think he's realized yet that I've followed him. I jog forward, ready to confront him about why he even decided to talk to me today in the first place.

My steps falter as I see two Officials working their way closer from the other end of the hallway, twirling Re-Regulation devices as they look forward.

I turn, noticing their attention is focused in my direction but expect them to pass me on their way to deal with some Unfortunate student that must be nearby.

But they aren't heading toward an Unfortunate.

They're heading straight toward *me*.

CHAPTER EIGHTEEN

FOREST

I try to continue my walk toward the art room, keeping my head down, watching my feet, hoping more than anything they will look past me and keep walking. They both move past the art room, where Fallan is concealed behind the door. I watch his eyes pass over the men's devices, only widening momentarily as we finally make eye contact. He presses his hand to his chest, signaling me to breathe once he realizes who the two men are targeting. I take his advice and slowly allow the first full breath of air to enter my lungs as I ready myself to move past the Officials. Taking another deep breath, I feel them brush past me.

I'm almost in the clear.

A firm hand grasps my arm, stopping me from moving any farther. I pause where I stand, turning my head away from Fallan. I try to narrow my eyes at him, hoping he takes the signal to move out of the doorway before they stop him too.

One of the men is ready to turn around at my gesture. Quickly, I grab his free hand, stopping him from being able to turn, giving Fallan a chance to conceal himself more thoroughly. Fallan looks confused as to why I'd help him. There's no way for me to tell him I need a witness for whatever is about to happen.

"Is something wrong, sir?" I question, motioning my eyes to the man gripping my arm as harshly as Josh had that day in art class. His nails dig into my skin, making my eyes flood with tears.

"You're not in uniform, Ms. Blackburn," the man says, motioning to my overly baggy clothes I hadn't changed out of yet. I recognize his voice. He's the one who inputs the code for all of our chips on the night of the screening.

"I wasn't feeling too good, so I decided to leave class early," I admit, trying to sound as convincing as possible given the men's already confrontational demeanors. Fallan watches silently, gripping the edge of the doorway with a tense hand.

"May I ask why you felt the need to grab me so aggressively?" I question, pulling my arm back toward me, allowing myself to step away from the man, only to be met with the body of another Official now closing in behind me. I hold my arm to my body, feeling the sweat collect on my forehead with each stolen glance at the pistol attached to the Official's sides.

"Pardon me, miss, sometimes I don't know my own strength. People get hurt without me meaning for them to," the man says, his tone making my blood run cold.

"Well, I still need to change, so if you'll excuse me-" I begin, wanting nothing more than to be as far away from them as possible.

"Why were you and your brother snooping around the grounds this morning?" the man questions, yanking me back by the collar of my shirt.

So, this is why they came for me.

Instinctively, I swat his hand away, looking at Fallan in pure panic. For the first time, he takes a step, pausing once I shake my head at him not to interfere. He looks frustrated, gripping his leg while his foot taps impatiently.

"Jesus Christ," I hiss, shoving away the man who continued to grab at me. I can tell he wasn't expecting me to defend myself. "I was helping my brother with a project, and neither of us minded the fresh air," I say, trying to ignore just how close the man behind me is.

"You know you've been quite the troublemaker recently, Forest. Your scorecard has seen more marks in the past week than it ever had in previous years," the Official in charge of coding growls. His last name is tucked away under his collar. I'm barely able to make out the last name.

Heywood.

"You're questioning me as if I'm an Unfortunate," I say, feeling my hands shake. Heywood nods his head toward the man behind me.

My stomach drops the moment the man behind me grabs my waist, forcing me back and into him with a wrap of his arm across my chest. His hand slowly moves across my chest, brushing over my breasts. His hand works its way under my shirt, nearly grazing my mark.

Something cold presses into my lower stomach. I feel the hilt before I realize his blade is touching my skin. I stop squirming as the man's hot breath moves over the skin of my neck. He laughs maniacally.

Fallan has now fully stepped away from the doorway, clutching his side, ready to do something that would only lead to them trying to kill him. All I can do is mouth for him to go. The man holding me from behind clenches my jaw in his hand, forcing me away from my sideways gaze to Fallan.

My mark begins to burn, making me want nothing more than to pummel both Officials to the floor. Fallan darts behind another indent in the wall, moving closer with quiet steps.

"Get the fuck off of me, you pig!" I shout, feeling the man's hand clamp over my mouth as he lets out another laugh.

"Maybe you're closer to an Unfortunate than we thought. But they usually fight back less when a blade is pressed to them," The man behind me says, only urging Fallan to slowly move one more space closer at the mention of a blade.

"I didn't do anything-"

"Yes, you did," Heywood begins, putting in a line of code with precise movements. "You were curious. Hopefully, this fixes that. If you weren't Andrew's daughter, I would have made you a little more susceptible to my friend's wandering hands so we could've had a bit more fun together and both gotten something out of this," Heywood says, my stomach almost unable to hold itself together any longer.

A pain heats behind my ear, stronger than the first time at the screening. I arch my back into the man behind me, feeling his blade nick me. He curses, putting away the weapon that was supposed to be a show of force and nothing more. My head pounds as the pain intensifies. There are fists pounding on the walls of my mind, begging to destroy the barrier to the outside world. I bite my lip as the pain becomes close to unmanageable. Fallan is still pressed against a wall, concealing himself with one of the window curtains.

"She should be good as new after this," Heywood says, making my heart race.

After a few minutes, the pain slowly begins to die down. I force my head forward to collect my thoughts, letting my quick breaths become steadier once I realize how much control I need to have to keep myself together.

The man's hands leave my body, lingering on all the places Josh had wrecked during our sparring on the mat before he quickly sprays Cure-All on the area he'd accidentally sliced with his blade. Both men take a step back from me, allowing me to raise my head. I mimicked blinking my eyes the same way my brother did when he had come to after code had been sent to his chip that night. I force a vacant expression across my face, doing my best not to let the fear that encompasses my body show through. I let out a small sigh once I realized Fallan had managed to slip away back into the art room. I'm relieved he didn't get involved. It would have ended miserably for both of us.

"I'm sorry, I must have spaced out," I say cheerily, looking between the two men with a smile. They both looked pleased with my response, exchanging a look before glancing down the hallway behind me.

"It's okay. We were asking if you were okay."

These fucking scummy liars.

"You were still in Defense Class clothes, and they're a bit bloodied, so we figured we'd stop and check on you," the man who had felt me up and down says. I force him another fake smile, looking down at my clothes with a sigh.

"I bloodied an Unfortunate. I was going to use Mrs. Auburn's storage room to change," I say, opening my bag to show the men my uniform. They both look satisfied with my response, giving one another a nod as they both begin to back away.

"Well then, we'll leave you to it," Heywood says, motioning his partner to follow him as I stare at my blood still coating the point of the man's blade. I give them a slight wave while I back away. Suddenly, I'm hit with intense nausea that comes over me the moment I turn around. I think of nothing but getting behind the art room door and away from the confinement of this hallway.

There's no way to stop the vomit from leaving my mouth. It burns my throat as I relieve myself over the art room sink. My hands clutch its side, forcing myself to stay on my feet, as I recall every place the Official had touched me. I see Fallan's figure move to close the door, each camera already turned away and toward the walls, keeping us hidden from the prying eyes. My hand shakes as I continue vomiting, pounding my fist on the side of the sink out of frustration. I finally feel some relief.

"He input code to not only make you forget about the area where you and your brother were searching earlier but to forget everything they said and did to you just now," Fallan says calmly.

Grabbing a small towel from the clean bin, he begins helping me run water down the sink to hide any evidence of my weak stomach. I keep my head leaning on the sink's rim, watching the water flow down the drain. It's impossible to string together any coherent thoughts right now.

"They did all of that in broad daylight," I whisper, still feeling the man's breath touching the crook of my neck.

"They do much worse when they're not afraid of getting caught," Fallan says. Clenching his jaw, he moves closer behind me. "I need to clean you up, or else we'll both be getting questioned," Fallan says sincerely, running the towel under the water for only a moment.

"Please, don't hurt me," I whisper.

His hand pauses just as he's about to reach my face. I lean over the sink, bracing myself for whatever cruel comments I've learned to expect in response to any sign of weakness from me.

His hand lands on the back of my neck, gently rubbing the skin with his fingers like he did on the night of the screening. I should be shoving him away, screaming at him for touching me so soon after what happened. His fingers circle the tender spots on my neck, working up into my hair, and I can slowly feel my tension melting away. I feel his hands continue to work gently, moving along my skin like my mother used to, meant to soothe me from headaches when I was a child. His free hand moves to my face with the towel next, wiping away anything left around my mouth. He continues comforting me well after my stomach has settled.

My heart races with each brush of his fingertips over my neck. It's different from how I felt after the Officials touched me. I want to lean into him, to wrap myself in his scent that I've come to recognize. At this moment, I find myself longing to touch him like I've watched Valerie touch him. But reality quickly sets in.

I pull my head up from its position, watching his hand fall from my neck. He looks down at me with sad eyes, clenching the towel as hard as he can. My fingers graze the back of my neck.

"How... how did you know that calms me down?" I question, watching something flash over his eyes.

"It was a lucky guess. It works on Valerie. I don't need you all worked up."

"Don't lie. You did it once before, at the movie screening," I say, cutting off his dismissal.

"Like I said," he begins with a lean toward me. "Lucky guess, Blackburn," he finishes, tossing the towel in the dirty hamper, moving back toward his canvas, letting whatever interaction we just had wash away with the water down the sink.

"Can our chips kill us?" I question, staring at the running water deep in thought. A box cutter for a paper mâché project sits near the sink, the blade clean and sharp, like it's hardly been used.

"Untouchable chips are non-lethal. I can't say the same about the ones for the Unfortunates," Fallan says, grabbing our canvases, letting his eyes linger on my portrait that I'm still trying to figure out the meaning of.

"What do our chips do then, other than make us compliant?" I question, watching his eyes narrow for a moment at the ground.

"They can confuse you. Make you remember things wrong ... even Marked like us," Fallan says, using a name I have only heard in whispers between Officials.

Marked. Tainted. All the same. Words that leave the mouths of those who speak them like a curse that's never meant to be repeated.

"And if the chips were gone?" I question, feeling the cool metal of the box cutter press to my palm.

"Free will, I suppose," Fallan says, his voice drowned out by the sound of the water in the sink.

I pick up the box cutter in my hand and raise it to the spot behind my ear, feeling the cool metal against my scar there. I'm ready to tear away at the ticking time bomb in my head. I feel the tiniest tear begin, ready to yank it clean from my skull and crush it beneath the sole of my shoe.

"Forest!" Fallan yells, yanking my wrist away from my ear.

Fallan slams my hand on the counter, forcing me back into it with him. I drop the blade, snapping back to reality. His gaze is wild as he looks over me. His knee has me pressed against the counter, his hand holding my wrist, his other clutching my waist. I feel the warmth of his hand above my clothes. He looks feral, ready to rip off someone's head, just as he had in the hallway.

"Did you not hear me?" he questions angrily, moving his hand away from my hip. He gently grabs my jaw, making me look at him. The warmth of his body so close to me sends a fleet of emotions through me. It's different from Xavier and Max. For some reason, I'm not afraid. I want him here. I want him to crave my touch too. It makes me feel like I'm alive.

But he resents me as much as I should him.

"It shouldn't be in my head-"

"It will kill you if you try to remove it. It's attached to your prefrontal cortex. Remove it, and you go with it," he says, tossing the blade across the room out of frustration. He leans in closer, trapping me in front of him. "*We* don't make decisions like that. You don't get to decide that," he hisses, letting his thumb run down my cheek. His nose is inches away from my own. His blue eyes only look that much bluer at this angle. A slight warmth in my stomach grows once I take notice of where his hands are.

"We?" I question, leaning closer out of anger.

He lets me go, biting the inside of his cheek with a shake of his head.

"You. I meant you," he clarifies as he quickly looks away from me again.

"I thought you wanted me dead. It would've made things easier for you," I say, watching his hands drag across his face as he lets out a defeated laugh.

"You don't know anything about what I'd like to happen to you, Forest. What I want eats me alive," Fallan growls. I admit to myself then that I wanted to know what he wanted. I wanted him to confide in me.

I look down at our clothes, turning my head toward Mrs. Auburn's small closet.

"We need to change. Or else we'll just end up in more talks with Officials," I say, pulling my bag closer. Fallan gives me a nod.

"You go first. I'll join you shortly," Fallan says, catching me off guard. The idea of us stripping off clothes and changing together in such a confined space invades my mind and makes my face fluster.

"I don't know if there's enough room-" I begin, trying to work through the image of us in the closet alone together.

"It was a joke, Forest," Fallan says, showing me his first genuine smile.

He rubs the back of his neck. "You were supposed to tell me to fuck off," Fallan mumbles, and now he's one to make me smile. He looks caught off guard by it, and his gaze lingers on my mouth.

"Then fuck off," I say jokingly, moving closer to the closet.

"Is that what you really wanted to say?" Fallan asks after a few silent moments. I pause, ready to let the "yes" leave my lips, but instead, I say nothing, giving him one last look before closing the closet door.

I like the idea of Fallan mulling over something I say for once.

We pat down our uniforms, doing our best to keep them orderly. I smooth down my skirt, wincing every so often at the small incision I had given myself behind my ear and the nail marks Josh had left on my skin. Waiting outside the closet, I clutch my sides, counting down the five minutes before Mrs. Auburn will barrel in here to get prepared for her lesson. A small part of the closet door is ajar, giving me and Fallan the light we needed to change. I caught him peeking inside a few times, quickly looking away the minute my head turned in his direction. But now it's me sneaking glances into the closet, looking over his scarred skin on his back, his muscles flexing as he moves to put on his clean uniform. My reaction time is much slower than Fallan's. I reluctantly pull my gaze away, but he catches me each time I try my luck at being a better spy.

I glance over at his canvas perched on the desk, slowly moving closer to study the way its intricate colors work together to create an obscure but solemn image. I pull myself away from the closet, no longer focusing on my appearance or the sound of the door opening on its hinges.

"It's not ready yet," Fallan says.

His hand brushes away my hair from behind my ear. I flinch away from the touch, still unsure how to react to them after what's happened today. Quickly, he sprays a small amount of my Cure-All behind my ear, pulling it away from my outstretched hand when I try to grab it from him.

"You're not getting it back that easily, Little Dove," he says, holding the Cure-All high above his head, enjoying how frustrated I am at his ability to hold something over me.

"You're as insufferable as that nickname," I say half-jokingly, moving away from him and closer to my canvas. Wincing as I bend down, Fallan holds his position by his canvas.

"How bad did he get you?" Fallan asks, watching me grab my canvas before I sit in front of his desk.

"It left a mark, if that's what you're wondering," I say, trying my best not to reflect on the feeling of Josh's nails digging into my side.

"He deserves a boot in his jaw. All of the Untouchables do," Fallan barks, taking a seat.

I shake my head at him.

"All of them?" I question, looking back at him with a challenge.

He seems to reflect on what he said.

It doesn't take long for him to become stone-faced once more.

"Well, it's not like they have many redeeming qualities," Fallan says, quickly burying the kinder side of him I've seen today.

"Just stop, Fallan," I hiss, feeling the barrier between us growing solid again.

"You have no idea how much I wish I weren't here. Every time I'm here, it's like torture-" he quietly starts.

My words leave me before I can stop myself from saying them.

"Then go back to your sector where you can enjoy all the freedom you want with your blonde whore that you can't seem to get enough of. No one asked you to be here," I spit, looking back at him with frustration. He pauses his stroke on his canvas.

Angrily, he peers up at me, watching me return to my mindless strokes across my own canvas.

"She gets in your head, doesn't she...? Why?" Fallan questions, tapping his paintbrush on his desk while he waits for a response.

I ignore his question, continuing to paint.

"I'm not sure, honestly. I think I might be losing it," I admit. There's a part of me I can't stop from lashing out at him.

"Maybe you are," he says, giving me a long sigh. "But if that's the case, then I guess I am too," he finishes, pausing to review my work.

"Your art is beautiful."

I can feel the honesty in his compliment, and it's unexpected after how harshly I snapped at him.

"Why do you do that?" I question, turning in my chair to face him, pulling away his paints to get him to focus on me.

"Do what, Little Dove?" he questions. I can't tell if he's using the nickname to calm me down or to be condescending, but I'm determined to find out.

"All of it, Fallan. The nickname, this-" I begin, motioning between us, "Why do you act so vile toward me? You act like you hate me, then say something like that?" I question, watching him lean back in his chair as he purses his lips together like he's trying to stop himself from letting the response fall out of him.

"As if you don't treat me the same way?" Fallan says, cocking his head at me, relaxing even more.

"I- I don't hate you.... Why would you want me to?" I whisper, gently placing his paints back down. Again, his eyes flash with something I can't recognize.

"I know you don't, which makes my life much harder," he begins, leaning forward in his chair. His face comes within inches of my own, but still doesn't answer my question.

"If you were smart, you'd change your mind and give in to hating me," he mutters.

I scrunch my nose anxiously in thought, trying my best to piece together a response to a statement like that.

"There's nothing to be anxious about," Fallan begins. I hadn't realized he'd been watching me so closely. His eyes meet mine again. He taps the end of my nose with his finger. My face fills with warmth at the touch. "You do that when you're anxious. Nothing right now can hurt you," he whispers, pulling back to his usual position in his desk chair at the sound of Mrs. Auburn entering the room with too many supplies she's doing a terrible job trying to carry alone.

We both look toward the woman, waiting for her to see us. All she can do is let out a giant sigh of defeat.

"You will not believe the day I've had today," she says, sitting in her chair.

"You're telling me," I say softly, feeling the tiniest bit of satisfaction at the smile I know is hidden behind Fallan's canvas.

Rolling my finger over the tip of my nose, I wonder how long I've been giving away my anxieties by having them written all over my face. A face that Fallan seems intent on getting to know for all its quirkiness.

Perhaps there's something more below the surface with him. Maybe something other than hate.

CHAPTER NINETEEN

FOREST

The classroom filled with students only a few minutes after Mrs. Auburn's arrival, giving her little time to question just how long Fallan and I were alone. At some point in between silently letting my strokes consume my canvas and looking back at Fallan's progress, my desk had gravitated a few inches closer to his.

It was enough for Rae to drag my desk back toward her once she sat down, giving Fallan her everyday unamused look of disapproval. I almost swatted her hands away out of annoyance for creating space I didn't want. Josh is the last to enter the classroom, showcasing a small array of bruises around his nose he hasn't treated with Cure-All yet. Fallan and I stare at him, watching how his head stays lowered while those around him continue to badger him.

"Is it true you're the one who did that to him?" Raegan questions, grabbing my hand from its relaxed position under my desk.

She investigates the dry blood still lingering on my knuckles. Between pounding Josh's face in and letting Fallan soothe me after the run-in with the Officials, I forgot to check my hands.

"I did it all with a smile," I say confidently, half expecting her to smile along with me.

"I know it's Josh, Forest," she begins, giving Fallan another sideways glance before returning to me. "But you couldn't save it for one of *his* kind?" she questions, nodding towards Fallan.

I untuck my shirt, showing her my side still coated in his nail marks.

"Courtesy of one of 'our people,'" I growl, throwing up quotations to address her arrogant comment. I can already tell Fallan is watching the exchange, observing the nail marks just as closely as Raegan, now able to get a complete image of how deeply Josh had scratched me.

"Look over here one more time, mutt, and I'll have an Official on you in seconds," Rae snaps toward Fallan, watching him lean back in his chair while he throws her an unamused look.

"Raegan," I start, slamming my hand on her desk, receiving a few glances from those less entranced with their work, Josh included. "Your conversation is with me, not him. Everyone deserves to see what that asshat did," I say, snapping my eyes toward Josh, who's scowling at us from his seat.

Raegan's head shakes. She creates distance between us by pulling her legs farther to the side of her desk. It's clear she's annoyed with me.

"If you're going to keep defending them, I suggest you find someone else to talk to for the rest of class," she whispers, turning her canvas to the side. She faces away from me as she starts to paint again, waiting for me to flag her down with an apology.

"Did one of you turn my cameras?" Mrs. Auburn questions the room, giving me no time to try and think of something to disarm Rae's less-than-pleasant attitude.

"I bet it was the Unfortunate. Who knows what his kind does when there are no eyes on them," one of Josh's friends says, causing a few to laugh, Josh included.

"Why don't you come here and say it to my face?" Fallan questions, breaking his silence for the first time. Mouths fly open. Heads snap back toward our section of the room. I hear Fallan slam his hands on his desk, already forcing himself onto his feet. I follow his motion.

Josh is the first to move toward the back of the room. The man who said the comment is not too far behind him. I step in between the groups, readying myself for the world of problems Fallan has thrown us both into.

"Wanna repeat that, pig?" Josh hisses, pointing at Fallan. I hold my position.

"Josh, walk away," I say, watching his eyes avert down to me.

"So that's what you are now, Blackburn?" Josh questions, ignoring Mrs. Auburn's plea to have him take his seat. His companions watch in anticipation. "Are you an Unfortunate loving whore just like your mommy?" Josh pushes. I'm enticed by the brief desire to see how many more bruises I might be able to give him today.

"Last time I checked, she isn't the one who said something outside of regulation," Fallan says, stopping Josh's walk toward me.

"You're right," Josh begins, giving Fallan a soft smile, his hands fumbling at his side. "I think I should test my theory first," he finishes, pulling something free from his waist. The glimmer of metal passes over my vision. Rae's manicured hand is the first to meet my back before Fallan's rough palm shoves my lower stomach, nicking his hand in the process as Josh's blade barely grazes my front. I watch the panic flood over Fallan's face at the realization Josh just saw him touch me. His buddies are too preoccupied with keeping away prying eyes to make a comment. Mrs. Auburn finally notices how escalated this situation has become.

"I knew it," Josh says with bared teeth, glaring between Fallan and me. "I knew I've seen this before-" he begins, enraging Fallan.

"Don't you dare say another word," Fallan yells. Did something happen that I don't know about? Have they spoken before?

"Scared I'll ruin it all?" Josh hisses silently, making Fallan take a step back.

I take the opportunity of the two men's focus on one another to grab my blade from my bag. Feeling it pair with my chip, I swipe toward Josh, giving him a good blow to his stomach with my foot once he avoids the blade. The swipes force him to provide us with the space we all need. With a few uneven steps, he backs into his companions, all of them ready to brace him from falling.

Tensions in the classroom are at an all-time high. Paint cups and brushes are scattered on the floor. Mrs. Auburn's hands are twisted in her curls out of frustration.

Another figure enters the classroom with a wide grin, clapping his hands sporadically like a gleeful child about to get a treat. The claps are loud and distracting, causing the boys to turn away their focus on each other. I back myself into Fallan, letting my body shove him as hard as I can to get him away from the group and closer to the back. His body is strong against mine, barely moving. He eventually picks up on what I'm trying to do, giving him the one way past these men that won't end in us getting into a full-on brawl.

Rae's head pulls away from the class's front door. Watching Fallan and I move, I silently beg her to go along with what she's seeing. She bites her lip, angrily getting to her feet and forcing herself to take my extended hand. I urge her to move with us, past the now-distracted group and into the empty space of the classroom.

Max stands in front of the classroom, looking over before landing on our group. Fallan is back to his normal seat a few feet away, now far away enough from Josh and his friends that none of them can continue badgering him. Even then, Josh and Fallan watch one another like wild animals. It doesn't take long for Max to finally speak up.

"What could you possibly say right now, Mr. Vega?" Mrs. Auburn questions, clearly annoyed at the state of panic in her classroom.

"There's an Unfortunate flogging happening in the dining hall," Max says excitedly, not allowing anyone to respond as he moves out of the classroom, taking several enthusiastic students with him.

I look back at Fallan. Grabbing Rae's hand, I seize the opportunity to follow a few students out of the classroom to observe the chaos. We stride out into the hallway with the others, letting our walk turn into a run once the group's pace becomes frenzied. Fallan is not too far behind us, staring dead forward in anticipation of the horrors that await us around the corner.

Officials surround the young Unfortunate transfer student, holding down his hands with bands meant to keep his wrists down on the floor. The bands are solid metal, tightening each time he tries to escape the humiliating position the Officials have forced him into. I watch the tears roll down his cheeks in between his pleas for mercy. His voice makes my stomach writhe. Max is pumping his fist toward the front of the crowd, letting out shouts that only work up the students around him.

I grab his shoulder, pulling him back toward me, leaning into his ear.

"Max, what the hell did he do?" I question, growing more uneasy at the sight of the Officials pulling free their light sensor prods from their sides.

Fallan lingers in the back, panning his eyes from the Unfortunate to Josh's quiet figure only a few feet away. Rae has found herself beside my brother, trying her best to speak to him. He looks over the group, no doubt trying to pinpoint me in the wave of gray uniforms.

"He was stealing extra portions of food and sneaking it back to his sector for his folks. He gave the Officials some lip, even threatened one!" Max explains, barely finding the time to give me any eye contact. He seems feral at the idea of violence.

The men begin tearing away the top layer of the boy's uniform, revealing a very worn, thin shirt meant to stay beneath the already-used uniform. He can't be any older than a third year, yet his back is already rough from the marks of prods that have met his skin countless times before, just like Fallan's.

Just like all the Unfortunates.

In one way or another, they all bear scars from my people.

"We just throw away all that extra food," I begin, watching the Officials taunt the boy with slow drags of their prods down his back. The students roar to life, encouraging the behavior.

"Maybe this will teach you to stop stealing from our sector!" one of the Officials, the man who touched me up my front, yells, waving his hands to get the students to begin cheering more.

Max grabs my elbow, finally making eye contact with me.

"Someone needs to teach them where they stand amongst us, Forest," he hisses, regurgitating the same bullshit everyone always says.

I yank my arm away. I don't even recognize my childhood friend in front of me right now. His blue eyes, which I always saw as comforting and grounding, now seem wild and unpredictable. The light-hearted smile I thought I always loved is now menacing. The pain in my head flares to life again the longer I watch this situation unfold. My feet begin to back me away from the group, motivated by the crowd's noise that keeps growing into something feral and unruly. I don't need to turn around to know that Fallan is only a few steps behind me. We both watch the Official's hand raise, ready to bloody the child's back with the light sensor prod.

The minor haze of a blackout comes over me, threatening my vision, tearing me away from my reality in the blink of an eye.

"No. Not now," I whisper, clutching my head so hard that I can feel my nails dig into my scalp.

"*Control it,*" I hear Fallan's voice whisper.

Unlike the slight brush of others' voices against my ear as they whisper, his voice sounds different. I turn my head, expecting to see him next to me, ready to tell him to get away before he's caught being so close. My throat goes dry once I realize he's still several feet away from me.

I'm losing it.

I watch the Official lower his arm, heading directly for the boy's back. I let out a shaky gasp, extending my arm out toward the Official holding the light sensor prod. My silent word trails off my tongue.

"No," I hiss to myself, doubling forward with pain I can't control.

My mind's dull headache is now lethal. The Official blinks rapidly, his prod swinging away from the boy's back and slamming directly into his leg, clamping down the hand that had touched me earlier against his thigh. The prod begins to burn his skin, searing away whatever it touches. The other Official, who was in the process of swinging at the boy, is now clutching his hand. The soft skin of his palm is mangled, burnt from grabbing his own prods' active exterior.

Both men, ready to beat the boy bloody, double over to the floor. Their knees hit the concrete at the same time mine do, as we all go down in unison. They somehow manage to control their cries.

Fallan wipes something away from his nose, looking me over with a wide-eyed expression.

My hiss of pain turns into a scream each time I try to shove back the blackout. People begin to back away as my agonizing cries continue. The heat behind my ear and on my mark grows and is unbearable.

My hands clutch my head, trying to silence the noise dancing around my mind. I feel the need to let it all out, wanting to twist the necks of all of those who have shed innocent blood in the name of "order." I feel my shirt ride up as I writhe, my body seizing up as the cool touch of outside air kisses my mark. My hands feel stuck to my head, my mind rushing to hold back whatever unknown energy creeps within it. The chip behind my ear feels so hot that I think it might melt the skin. Vivid images pass through my mind, all leading back to a single sound. A single tune, lost in the spiral of mind. A noise hidden away, not meant to be found.

It takes everything in me not to shove Fallan away once he kneels next to me, letting his hand drag down my shirt, giving my lower stomach a long look. A few students gag at the exchange, unable to see the mark given how quickly Fallan inserted himself into the situation.

I let another scream leave me as the pain continues to grow. I wanted nothing more than to keep him kneeling there next to me. I watch a few students, Max and Josh included, drag Fallan away and onto his back. They scream at him for getting near me, both of them kicking him while he's down on the floor. My scream morphs into a yell at the sight, my eyes begin to roll to the back of my head. I hear his pained grunts as they kick him again and again. Even from here, I know how afraid he is. My back arches in response to my loss of control over my body. All I can do is listen, unable to control what is happening.

"She's having a seizure," my brother says, kneeling next to me, both his and Rae's hands touching my body. "I thought we got rid of these years ago," Kai finishes, speaking to what I can only assume are more Officials.

"Hang on," I whisper in my mind to no one in particular.

Forcing my eyes forward, I unleash the pain within me, letting it filter away from my vision through my blood. Finally, I get a clear look at the two boys ready to deliver Fallan another blow.

Max and Josh pause once an Official claps, enabling Fallan to sit up, releasing a mouthful of blood in the process. My body is drained, unable to focus on my brother, who tries to get me to look at him. Fallan's eyes meet mine through the crowd. Rubbing his fist over his chest, he signs something to me with his hands. Signs I somehow understand.

"Are you okay?" he gestures, looking past his bloody lip and bruised side.

I stare at the countless Officials now filling the eating area, some letting the boy free from his shackles, others working closer to my brother, caught in a frenzy, still begging for a med kit. I give Fallan a nod, feeling the energy within me surge at the thought of the raven-haired brute getting away from all of this. I think of his strength now, wanting to give him anything I can to get out of here.

In an instant, all of that energy, all of that adrenaline, and all that pain fade away, making it easier to slump forward into my brother. I see the spots in my vision, unsure if I imagined the image of Fallan being able to pull himself to his feet and grasping my bag with my sketchbook in his hand, before very slowly slipping away from Max and Josh, who are now focused on me.

I try to stay conscious, unsure of what clarity darkness might bring. It feels comforting for once, the quiet that unconsciousness promises to bring.

"Was it you?" I question the void of my mind, feeding into the delusion someone is there.

There are several moments of silence, and my consciousness threatens to fade away at last.

"It always is. That's my hell," a voice whispers back, clearer than ever.

No, not just any voice.

Fallan's voice.

CHAPTER TWENTY

FOREST

C oming to sudden consciousness, I nearly fall off the cot, unsure of where I
am or how I got here to begin with. An ample bright light hangs above me,
making it impossible to see my surroundings. I half expect my side to hurt once I
begin to move, feeling pleasantly surprised once I realize all of the pain I had earlier
has now dwindled to nothing. I raise my hand to my face, looking over the clean
knuckles. Both hands look like I never got into an altercation to begin with. My
mind runs through the events before I lost consciousness, ending with Fallan and
his voice before I found solitude within my mind. With a swat, I move the light
away from me, now seeing the recovery quarters of the med unit where my mother
spends most of her days.

I feel uneasy seeing a new shirt on my body, unsure how many people it took
to undress me or, worse, how many people got to see my mark. My pants rest a bit
lower than they did initially, still in the position that nearly exposed me. I tighten
my belt around my waist, feeling the effects of my low energy the moment I stand.
The door to the room is closed, leaving me alone. I let my back lean against the
cot, slumping to the floor to tuck my knees into my chest.

With heavy lids, I close my eyes and embrace the silence, doing my best to listen
to the white noise in my mind.

"Are you there?" I question silently in my head, shouting down what seems
like a never-ending, empty hallway.

I pause, tapping my foot against the floor, waiting to hear his voice. Seconds
turn into minutes before I wonder how real his voice was in the first place.

The door to the room creaks, sending me up from my position on the floor. My mother and I give each other a long stare, and I realize my brother's anxious figure is waiting on the other side of the door, peeking inside for a few seconds before she closes it on him.

Her hands fiddle with the inside of her lab coat pockets, her body moving closer to the cabinetry in the room. There's no attempt at small talk, which she always tried to use as a way in when we're at odds. With a turn of a key, one of the cabinets clicks open, revealing several bottles of pills, all labeled with ingredients I couldn't even begin to identify. She scans her options, letting her touch linger on the bottles with a higher milligram dosage than the rest.

"W-What happened?" I question, wondering why Kai hasn't burst into the room yet, ready to give me one of his speeches about my health.

"It would seem the Official's light sensor prods triggered a seizure from you during the events in the lunchroom. Unlike episodes in the past, this one nearly caused a brain bleed. Thank New Haven that your chip was able to stop you from hemorrhaging on the spot," my mother says, sounding more emotional than I expected. I touch the back of my ear, still feeling the heat the chip gives off.

That was what healing from the chip felt like?

"Why do you sound angry?" I question, watching her pause before finally deciding on a medication to pull down from the cabinet.

"Well, let's see," she begins, finally turning to face me. The mask of emotion, once hidden, is now on display for all to see. "My daughter nearly hemorrhages only an hour or so after beating down a fellow Untouchable, and this only comes days after she decides to walk around the house like a stranger, letting me know nothing about what's happening to her. So yes, Forest, I'm angry. Angry that I have no idea what's going on with you, and to make matters worse, your father says an Unfortunate has been nagging you-" she begins, ready to mention the one person I was praying she wouldn't.

"Fallan didn't do anything," I begin.

She pauses her rant, unable to fully process what I am saying.

"So there is an Unfortunate?" she asks, posing the question like she no longer knows who her daughter is.

"You said-"

"It was a theory. I wasn't expecting you to be honest given how shut off you've been these past few days," my mother says, urging me to see how many cameras are listening in on this conversation.

I glance around the room.

Five. Five cameras. Five spies.

"I've seen him once or twice in passing," I begin, pointing to my mother with annoyance, "Last time I checked, it's more than okay to communicate with Unfortunates on school grounds," I state, watching her eyes glance up to the cameras in the same fashion I had.

"Is that all?" my mother questions, clearly aware my honest response would be anything but yes. It certainly wasn't all.

"I'm not answering any more questions until you tell me why my brother is waiting outside while you interrogate me like I am a deviant," I say, feeling a small rush of adrenaline come over me.

"Don't do that, Forest." My mother sighs. She picks up my hand to drop the small pill into my palm. "Don't speak to me like I am an enemy. I want you to be safe. That's all I've ever wanted," my mom finishes, gently rubbing her thumb across my cheek in a soft caress.

There's my mother. The one who read me and Kai bedtime stories and broke regulations to sneak us sweet treats past our designated eating windows. I see how tired she is—balancing the world on her shoulders while putting out all the fires with us.

"Please, bear with me, Mom," I plead. Grabbing her quickly, I pull her into a hug.

"I'm not in the best head space right now." Her arms wrap around me, sighing deeply into my shoulder at the exchange.

"Never question your mind, Forest. It will guide you in ways you never knew you needed." My grasp tightens around her, as I remember the new clothes I'm in.

"W-who dressed me?" I question. She pulls away, dragging her hands across her eyes.

"I did. I know how you feel about privacy," my mother says, running her finger along my side. "Who marked you up like that?" she questions.

"Josh-"

"Seal?" my mother finishes, fully aware of the boy's last name.

"That would be the one."

She shakes her head, silently cursing under her breath between eye rubs.

"That family has no boundaries. They're like thorns in my ass I can never get rid of," she says, speaking candidly for the first time in a long time.

"Mom, can I come in?" Kai says with a few bangs, cutting off my ability to question her disdain toward Josh's family.

"I told your brother to wait outside because of how … overwhelming he can be," she says, looking down at the pill in my hand, "Take that while I speak to him. I upped your milligram dosage to hopefully help the seizures and any episodes you might have because of them. There's a cup by the sink where you can get water," my mom says, nodding toward the sink before slipping back behind the door, giving me no time to wave to my worried brother who's now trying to step inside the room.

The cameras loom over the space, giving anyone on the other side of the cameras a show while they wait to watch me take a medication that I haven't had in days. It's like each one is pointed directly at me, waiting to see what I'll do.

The pill feels heavy in my hand. If the Officials were unsure about upping my regulations after they used my chip, they sure as hell will want to now, starting with this sudden need to increase my meds.

I want to believe my mother wouldn't do anything to harm me. I want to think that she'd never let them influence her.

But there's no longer room for hope that people are who they say they are.

Keeping my head down, I move toward the sink, letting the water run while I fill the small glass cup. I shake the pill in my hand, watching the slow green blink of the cameras, eerily similar to our chips once they are ready to make us do as they please. I angle myself as best I can away from prying eyes, raising the pill to my mouth quickly before downing multiple gulps of water, dragging the drug down my front, and slipping it into my pocket.

I mimic the swallowing motions, trying to look convincing before shutting off the sink. My mother and Kai argue on the other side of the door, only ending their standoff once my mother asks him to sit and wait.

Moments later, she is back in the room, looking more flustered than she was initially.

Arguing has never been her forte.

"How hard was it to keep down?" she questions, reaching her hand out to touch my face with care. Her fingers caress my cheeks, lingering on all of the features of my face most closely resembling my father's.

"It wasn't anything I couldn't handle. You can let Kai in now, if you want," I say, trying to gauge how little she wants him here.

She leads me back to the cot with her worn hands, placing me down on the thin mattress next to her before pulling me into a leaned position against her. I let myself sink into the touch, hearing the sounds of her strong heart as they steady my thoughts.

"Have things been okay with you? You've seemed so very distant recently," she finally asks the actual question she's been wanting answers to.

I know she thinks without Kai's presence, I'll suddenly spill everything to her like I always have.

"Why do people keep asking me that?" I question, scooting away from her, only to let my face fall into my hands. She tries to reach for me again, and once more, I brush off her touch with a shake of my arm.

"You have to admit you seem-"

"Defiant?" I question, snapping at her more aggressively than I meant to.

"Awake, Forest. You seem more awake. It's like you've suddenly discovered what your emotions are and have no way of controlling them," she admits, making it impossible to stop the snide remark from rolling off my tongue next.

"I'm sure suppressing my emotions is something our people would love nothing more than for me to do right now. Have any ideas on how they might do that?" I question, watching the look of confusion pass over her face before becoming nothing at all.

"What are you insinuating?" she questions, sounding just as concerned as she was when she spoke of the potential brain bleed I could have had earlier.

"Nothing, Mom," I begin, no longer wanting her to press me, "I'm tired and honestly not wanting to talk about anything that happened today. There are plenty of eyes always on us," I say, looking at the camera, "I'm sure you'll see everything that happened today at some point and have yet another reason to wish I was more like Kai," I finish.

Twisting my hands into my hair, I reach into my mind once more.

"Now would be a great time to say something," I whisper silently through my thoughts. Once again, I'm met with nothing but silence.

Crazy is starting to look like an accurate label for me.

"I don't wish you were like Kai," my mother says, resting her hand on my own, pulling my chin up to meet her gaze. "I know exactly who you are, Forest. Whether you realize it or not, you and Kai are my everything. Nothing will change how proud of you I am. You weren't dealt the fairest cards-"

"*Detected criticism against society functions is a low-level violation, Katiana Blackburn.*"

The room finally speaks up, stopping my mom's thought before she can even finish it. I watch her eyes close while she takes a deep breath to relax.

"Everyone was given a fair chance." She corrects herself, lying right through her teeth.

My mom's eyes move to my hair, plucking away the silver strands now framing my face. I reach up, grabbing her wrist to stop her from taking any more than she already has.

"I liked those," I admit, watching her drop the strands in a nearby bin.

"I don't. It's time for us to dye your hair again," she whispers.

I look over her hair, seeing nothing but the beautiful, rich brown color she claims hides hair like mine.

"All the women in our family have it?" I question, watching her hand lower, gesturing me to keep quiet.

"A very rare genetic hiccup that I found easier not to disclose. Loss of pigmentation, nothing to make a fuss about," she says, sounding like she's reading from a script.

"No one else has-"

"Forest, not here. Not now," she snaps, pointing her finger at me seriously.

I close my mouth, clasping my hands together on my lap impatiently. My mother checks her watch, ready to meet her next patient. She walks with an exhausted demeanor, looking more drained each time I see her.

"Your brother will most likely swarm you-"

My words leave me before I can process them.

"Do you trust them? Do you trust that New Haven has our best interest at heart?" I whisper, watching the room light up with yellow as the system speaks again.

"Talk against government and/or rules is a medium-level violation, Forest Blackburn."

My mom pauses, turning on her heels. She comes inches away from me, looking me over with a wild expression.

"Why would you ask me that?" she questions, grasping the side of my face with shaky hands.

"Would they hurt us?" I push further, pressing my forehead to hers to hide the words I speak.

I need the truth from her. I need to know where she stands.

"Did you see an Unfortunate beating again? How many times must I tell you they deserve that treatment? Without it, there is no balance in the system we must all adhere to," she shouts, trying to get the cameras to pick up on that statement.

"That's not what I asked, Mom.... Would they hurt us?" I question, letting her grip me tightly.

There are several seconds of delay. She stands still, deep in thought, while pondering the question. Just one word, one word, and I know there is someone in my family I can trust. One "yes," and I no longer have to navigate this hell beside someone who hates me. Anything is better than being alone in this.

"No, Forest. They would never hurt you," she says, letting her hands drop from my face, giving me the last answer I would have ever wanted from her.

I slowly back away from her, giving her a nod. The emotions must cover my face like paint on a canvas, because my mother's eyebrows raise while she watches me move away from her and closer to the door.

"You have other patients waiting on you," I say, swinging the door open, wanting to be nowhere near her.

"Forest-"

"Get out," I say, no longer giving her the opportunity to stick around and lie to my face again.

She closes her mouth, looking dazed once she finally decides to accept my command and leave the room. Kai lingers in the doorway, watching me hold the door, waiting for something to give him a clue as to what's going on. I shake my head at him, letting my mom move past us before following behind her. I want nothing more than to leave this fluorescent nightmare of a med unit. I peered down at the oversized shirt they forced me into, then searched for an exit sign as quickly as possible.

"Stay here, and we can go back together. Let me speak to Mom first," Kai says, squeezing my shoulder before following behind our mother's exhausted figure. She sulks away, clearly troubled by the exchange we just shared.

I shake away the way it makes me feel, ignoring Kai's plea for me to stay put. I begin working down the massive hallway, acknowledging none of the nurses questioning me if I know where I'm going. The bright light of the outside world is only a few feet away. Two large doors ahead will get me away from this nightmare.

As I move closer to the doors, I let my walk turn into a jog. My body fills with pain once it collides with another person in the connecting hallway toward the end of my path, right next to the double doors.

The second body grunts, gently grabbing my arms and stabilizing both of us. I ready myself to pull away like I have been to everyone lately, wanting nothing more than to strangle the next person who gets near me without asking.

"What are you doing here?" he questions gently, rubbing his finger along my sides with a comforting touch I've been craving all day.

CHAPTER TWENTY-ONE

FOREST

With one look, Xavier already knew where I was heading. He wasted no time guiding me out the double doors and into the large front of the medical building decorated beautifully with white daisies.

I keep in step behind him, feeling his fingers lace through mine as he guides us farther away from the doors and closer to the growth of trees clustered near the farthest corner of the garden. Dead leaves cover the ground, crunching beneath our feet with each step. I squeeze his hand tighter, feeling satisfied the minute he does it back. Xavier had let the question about my whereabouts die out the minute he saw me shift to look behind me, thinking it was best to get me alone before questioning me more.

Resting beneath the trees, coated with a few scarce leaves, I see the outline of a bench, probably meant for the staff to take their lunch breaks. Guiding us closer, Xavier pulls me down to take a seat with him. The trees keep us concealed from anyone who might question where we ran off to. I tear away the admission band around my wrist they must have put on me when I got to the med unit.

He lets his legs straddle the bench. Watching me pull my knees to my chest, his hands rub my legs, coaxing them down to a position similar to his own. We face one another dead on, letting our hands stay in each other's, silent for a few moments.

"What happened?" he questions after a few moments, bringing one hand up and brushing a stray hair away from my face with his fingers. He moves his hand to cup my cheek as his thumb moves to slowly caress the outline of my jaw. My hand moves his own onto the back of my neck, hoping to the same sensation that washed over me with Fallan's comforting touch earlier.

But he doesn't make any movements. His hand rests there still, but I'm disappointed when nothing more happens.

"Did you hear what happened at the school?" I question.

He nods slowly, letting his hands fall to my waist, his thumbs resting on my hip bones. I feel my skin heat beneath the touch, briefly wanting to close the space between us and straddle his lap. The struggle to understand my desire for Xavier while trying to adhere to our regulations on physical contact is torture.

"I heard there was a beating. When they didn't name who, I lost interest in what it was about," he begins, making me shift a few inches forward, pressing into his hands. "But then they said an Untouchable had a medical episode. I was already working a detail here, speaking to a few Unfortunates, when I saw them wheel a body in. And then I saw your mother," he continues, his hands resting on my upper thighs now. He gives my legs a light squeeze, and a faint heat rises in my stomach, catching me off guard and forcing me to divert my thoughts to different places. My mind ravages the idea of him exploring the rest of my body with more than just light touches. "Had I known it was you-"

"Don't do that," I say, pressing my finger to his lips, stopping him from placing more guilt on himself than he already has, "Don't blame yourself for what happened. You weren't even there," I continue, letting my hands move away from his lips and down his face. I feel the stubble along his jawline before dropping my hand back down into his own.

"Is it true what they said your classmate did? Josh? Adam's kid?" Xavier asks, moving his head in front of my face to stop my eye's aversion toward the bench. Each touch he gives me is gentle and comforting and I'm surprised at how much I need them now.

"They healed what he did. There's no point lingering on it," I whisper, running my hand along my sides beneath the massive shirt. Xavier's eyes follow my hands, watching as I wince at the memory of the deep scratches that once coated my skin.

"Is that where he hurt you?" Xavier questions, letting his hands move away from my face.

All I can do is nod, watching a flash of anger work over his expression, fading away the longer I watch him. Giving it little thought, I grab his hands, letting them come beneath my shirt to grip my sides where the wounds used to be. The heat in my stomach travels through me, growing as his warm palms work along my skin.

I watch his cheeks grow crimson at the feeling of my bare skin beneath his fingers. He only allows himself to explore the area I guided him to.

"See? It's okay now," I whisper, realizing just how little space is between us now.

Our knees touch, and his hands are holding me closer than I had initially noticed. I feel them move to my lower back, tempting me to ignore every rule I've had forced down my throat and give in to the urge to feel what his lips are like against my own. He leans forward and his breath touches my face, only heating my cheeks more once my hands find his front to feel his chest above his uniform. My head tingles with the threat of another episode that I have no way of controlling. The mark on my hip burns hot, almost as hot as the skin beneath his touch.

A small smirk rides along his face, only adding to the enthralling nature of his beauty. The sun kisses his golden curls as he brings his face closer to my own, our noses inches apart.

"Have you felt the touch of another before? Not hugs, not the bullshit regulated stuff they allow. I mean, genuine intimacy with another person?" Xavier questions.

He's so close I can almost taste him in my mouth. My heart races, pumping my body with adrenaline. The sweet tune I heard during my episode returns, the keys now more recognizable, fading as quickly as they came.

"No.... Have you?" I whisper back, wanting nothing more than to close the space between us.

The sound of a few nurses conversing breaks my focus on his lips. He pauses, running his thumb over my lips, forcing me to reevaluate the reckless public display of affection happening between us. I scoot a few feet back, giving us both a moment to compose ourselves and make minor adjustments to our clothing.

The nurses walk by with little acknowledgment to us, smiling once Xavier gives them one of his own.

"I suppose a hospital garden is not the most appropriate setting for me to do what I want," Xavier says casually, making me choke a little. It's beyond me how I was able to keep my composure.

I smile, biting the inside of my cheek while thinking of the right words.

"How do you do it?" I question, shaking my head once I notice his uniform. "How do you do everything it takes to be an Official?" I ask, reminding myself of what they did.

There's no way he's a part of what Adam and his men did earlier today. Xavier looks distraught. I can see worry across his brow.

"I can't say I don't have ways of coping with what they sometimes force us to do. I've spent more times at work drunk than sober in attempts to listen to the bullshit they spew at us," Xavier says, rubbing his hands on his temples. "I take every shit detail I can, as long as it means I'm not forced to inflict unjustified violence. I tried to sway your friend away from wanting to join. I think our interactions were more than enough to sway him to try and wear a uniform," Xavier says, still trying to find ways to place the blame on himself. "I joined the Officials to protect people and do good, and now," he says, pausing to look me over. "I think I've found something else to prioritize."

My heart thuds heavily at his admission.

"Your family-" I begin. He stops me.

"They're gone," he says quietly, cutting off my thought with two words.

"Gone?" I question, unsure of how that's possible.

"They were researchers for New Haven," he says, grabbing a leaf from the ground to distract himself.

He tears its multicolored surface, dropping each bit to the ground one at a time. "They were sent outside the ward for data sampling when I was around twelve. There were ropes on their bodies and Officials with them, but after twenty minutes in the ash, each rope was snapped, bloodied on the ends while their screams broke the air. Officials told me they tried to go after them," Xavier continues, "My sister passed away shortly after during a measles outbreak," he continues, holding his hand over his mouth to hide the slight tremor of emotion trying to escape him. "All the Officials who were supposed to go out there had clean boots that day. They'd lied. Not one tried to save them, and as a result, I became an orphan, unable to trust anyone. Now I'm one of them," he says, clenching his jaw as he closes his eyes. "And I know I would run out there every time if it meant some kid didn't have to grow up feeling as alone as I did," he finishes, filling my heart with more pain than I ever thought possible.

"Xavier.... I'm so sorry-"

It's now him placing his finger on my lips, stopping me from giving him a speech I know he's heard a million times.

"It's beyond your control, love," he says. His words are like honey, moving warm and soft and sticking in my ears.

I press my lips to his finger before letting it lower as we exchange a long look.

"There is a fine line between using order to help people and using it to feel superior... to control. Sadly, it seems we've somehow warped our innate nature to create order for the sole purpose of preserving life. It seems we've rationalized that control matters more," Xavier says, swinging his legs over the bench, giving us more space than I would have liked. The pounding in my head begins to subside, bringing me sweet silence again.

"I need you to be honest with me," I say, readying myself to ask the one question that could end all of this in a moment. "Do you hate the Unfortunates? Or are you just following orders?" I ask, letting the question settle in the air between us.

"Do I hate Unfortunates? No. They are the very reason this society can function as it does. They are the reason the Officials wear suits embroidered with gold, the reason we eat rich meats that seem to never be in short supply. We get to live the life we do because of them. I respect them immensely. Our people think their blood is Tainted, breeding a vile nature that goes against what they deem orderly-"

The Marked. He's talking about the Marked.

"Only Unfortunates are Tainted? What does that mean?" I question, reusing the same term he had, still barely understanding it myself.

He sighs, rubbing his finger gently behind my ear.

"I don't think you deserve the burden of knowing what goes on behind the scenes. You've already been around more than you need to," he says with great sorrow.

He knows about the screening.

"You-"

Something urges me to stop talking, cutting off the words from my throat before they can even leave me. Like staring at a light sensor prod ready to scorch me, I feel myself hesitate, suddenly fully aware that this secret between Fallan and me, and what we know, remains safest with us alone. It's a sense of understanding I can't explain, only making me grow angrier once I notice how much Xavier sacrificed to tell me what he has.

For reasons beyond my control, I know I have to keep quiet about what I remember from that night.

At least for now.

Xavier patiently waits for me to continue my thoughts.

"I lost what I was going to say," I lie, wondering why my mind feels more crowded.

"I think it's best to leave what we said on that note. You seem to forget you did have a seizure today. I'd rather not push anything," Xavier says, looking at the falling leaves coating the ground around us.

"What we know is ours and ours alone. Please stop trying to navigate to me so soon after what happened... I hear you, Forest, but I don't want

to hear your thoughts of him. I'm cutting you off for today." Fallan's voice rings through my mind clear as day.

Unlike the pounding headaches that usually consume me, his presence in my mind is like a soft blanket, embracing me, holding my mind gently. I feel the moment the connection is cut, leaving me with nothing but the feeling of something else lurking in the depths of my mind, unable to find a way through.

This presence that hides is foreign, aware, and... angry.

"Are you okay? You were gone for a second," Xavier says, pulling me back to reality with his gentle touch.

I nod, finally closing the space between us and allowing my back to turn toward him. Leaning into his chest, my legs stay straight in front of me along the bench. With my back pressed against his muscular chest, I can feel the outline of his sculpted body beneath his uniform's rugged material. His arms wrap around me, and I take in his scent. It's like fresh laundry and pine, both creating a harmonious amalgamation that I can't help but let consume my senses. His head rests above my own, wrapping me in warmth.

"What exactly is happening here, Forest?" he questions, leaning down next to my ear with a whisper that has my blood rushing. His lips tentatively graze over my neck, lingering for a moment as he taunts me. I can sense him smiling as he moves to rest his lips along my shoulder now, the potential of slow kisses along the rest of my skin in the air between us.

I let out a shaky breath, causing a low grunt of approval to leave his throat and I realize Xavier has me wrapped around his finger.

"I want to hold on to whatever this is. Let me hold onto it. It's the only thing that gives me a moment of peace. That makes me feel normal. I'm consumed when I'm with you and crave this feeling when you're away," I admit, unable to stop the noise that leaves my mouth once his lips finally decide to explore the soft skin of my neck again, kissing gently along its side, pressing down harder in the spots I've learned are overly sensitive to touch. It's all I can do is suppress the noises of pleasure I've never heard leave me before. The sensation sends a wave of desire through me. His hand grasps my jaw, pulling me into his kisses.

"You're not normal, Forest," Xavier says, placing my ear lobe between his teeth with a gentle bite. His free hand pulls me closer to him, my lower back brushing against his leg, and a part of him I'm suddenly very aware of, soothing a part of me that had wondered if I'm the only one feeling this way right now. "I think that's why I can't seem to stay away," he whispers, making the pool of heat between my legs grow immensely.

"You're sticking around then? You don't think I'm crazy?" I question, unable to fully control what I'm saying.

"I think you are exactly what you're supposed to be, and you can guarantee I'm not going anywhere," Xavier whispers, turning my head over my shoulder. He finally makes eye contact, and I know he notices my fully flustered face.

I expect to see the flash of his canines as he smiles, ready to let it consume me.

Instead, he looks pained, holding his throat tightly—his chest heaves. Tiny beads of sweat collect on his forehead, rolling over his furrowed brows.

"What's wrong-"

Once more, the tune plays in my head, the notes on the piano louder than before, pulling me away from this moment and even farther away from the words I tried to get out.

"Forest!" my brother's voice yells from a few feet away.

Xavier and I pull away, fixing our disheveled clothes as we get up from the bench. I watch Xavier grab his pant leg, adjusting the front of his black slacks, making us both grow red. My brother's tall figure spots us once we're up, giving me a sigh of relief. We make eye contact above the hedge that has been shielding us from prying eyes. Kai stalks around the small wall of green, pausing to look between us.

"I was about to run a search party to find you," Kai mutters, keeping his eyes on Xavier.

"She just needed some fresh air," Xavier says, speaking as confidently as he always has, not letting the moment we just shared slip him up.

"With you?" Kai questions, clearly no longer speaking to me, as I sense his hostility growing towards Xavier.

"I didn't want to be in that horrid LED nightmare box any longer," I say, stepping in front of Xavier to get a better look at my brother. He gives me a small nod, pulling me into a hug and propping his chin on the top of my head to get me as close to him as possible.

"The last I saw of her; she was almost foaming at the mouth. Please, excuse me if I'm impatient when it comes to seeing how she is," Kai says, looking toward Xavier, whose friendly composure has returned, ready to abate any conflict arising between them.

"I should have let you know before bringing her out here like this-"

"No, I'm glad she has someone she can talk to," Kai says.

Even without looking, I know he's hurt about how little I confide in him these days. I want to tell him everything. I want him to be someone I can rely on.

But the truth only brings him closer to a bullet in his head.

Xavier looks down at his watch, letting out a loud sigh, followed by an expression I know means nothing good.

"I have a detail in the Unfortunate sector, just running the perimeter of the ward to check for tears," he says, looking up at us both, "You'd better take the next tram back to the Academy to finish out what you can of your day," he finishes, looking to me while he speaks.

Kai gives him a brief nod, readying himself to drag us away from the small garden area.

"Can you give me two minutes, please?" I question, seeing Kai hesitate before he moves around the bush to give us some privacy.

Xavier crosses his arms, watching me make my way in front of him.

"Should I plan to see you again soon, or will I keep running into you at the strangest times?" I question, watching the man's mouth curve into a smile I greatly appreciate.

"After today, don't be surprised if I'm throwing rocks at your window in the middle of the night," Xavier says, making me blush all over again.

I give him a nod, watching my brother try and peek through the gaps of the shrubbery to get a glance at what's happening. I wrap my arms around Xavier's neck, feeling his hands squeeze my waist, both of us feeding into the hug. I feel our noses brush the moment we begin to separate, and just for a moment, I think about using the opportunity to finally break the last bit of space between us.

Like a bolt of lightning, a sensation flares through my mark, forcing me to bring my head down in a quiet groan. Any chance of our lips meeting fades away, only to be dragged further away by the impatient taps of my brother's foot.

"Until next time, love," Xavier says, pressing his thumbs to my lips while cupping my face. I smile against the touch but wonder why the longing to kiss him has suddenly ebbed.

My marks burn fades away, taking my desires with it.

"Until next time," I whisper back, watching his figure back away, giving me one last smile before slipping behind the other side of the bush. I feel empty like I'm missing something I didn't know I needed.

Human connection. Just another thing our society shuns.

CHAPTER TWENTY-TWO

FOREST

The rest of the day dragged along as best it could after the chaos from this morning. People's need to stare at me everywhere I went became insufferable. Although I only had one more class, it felt like an eternity of sitting in that classroom, watching my classmates sneak stolen glances at me. There was no point trying to strip away the oversized shirt my mother had put me in at the med unit. It almost felt more comforting to wear something so baggy, given today's events. To my surprise, I hadn't seen Fallan anywhere. I found myself even going so far as to try and track him down in his final period of the day. From what I know, he ends the day with Literature, but the Unfortunate section of the English department's classroom was empty. The Unfortunate caught stealing food gave me a look of acknowledgment in the hallway, almost looking like he would stop to say something before deciding not to.

"Are you ready to tell me what's going on with you two?" Kai questions, finally pushing me to speak and break my unspoken vow of silence I have taken since we left the med unit.

"I'm assuming you're talking about-"

"Xavier? Yes," Kai says, not allowing me to finish my statement.

My bag hits my leg with each step. I notice Kai's tousled hair and brown eyes are more frazzled than usual. Concern coats his gaze, eating him alive in all the ways it had my mother.

"I *may* be enjoying the alone time I've gotten with him," I say, keeping my gaze forward toward the tram, now filled with students.

"Have you two-"

"Kai," I snap, cutting off the question before he could finish it. "All I've done is let Max kiss me a few times. Xavier and I have done nothing. You can stop the paranoid, older brother attitude," I say. His cheeks grow red with embarrassment.

"I actually wasn't going to ask you about Xavier," Kai mutters. I pause my walk, looking over at him in confusion.

"Then who?" I question, watching him take a look around at his surroundings.

He closes his eyes, rubbing his face like my mother does.

"The Unfortunate," he begins motioning to me. "Why is he always lingering around you?" Kai questions. I'm sure his accusation is courtesy of what Raegan must have told him about what she saw in art class, no doubt. I knew there was no way of keeping that away from Kai once she saw us exchange a brief touch.

"Fallan is harmless," I say, walking toward the tram. I close my eyes as I walk, reaching into my mind to shout down that narrow hallway with doors that all seemed closed.

"Are you done shutting me out?" I yell through my mind.

"Harmless? You've been acting recklessly since he showed up."

I turn on my heels, stopping my brother's determined march behind me with a point of my finger to his chest. He pauses, looking at me with surprise.

"Fallan is not to blame for why I've been off. If anything, he's helped me in ways no one else can right now, so I suggest you tread carefully on what you choose to say next because it might not have the outcome you like," I hear myself say, barely recognizing the tone in my voice. It feels like another part of me jumped out, ready to fight back against anyone willing to challenge me. My heart pounds in my chest, pumping blood through my veins.

"Easy there, Little Dove. He's trying to help you," Fallan's voice says, relaxing my rigid position.

Kai looks confused, watching me step back as I touch my head, looking around for any sign of the Unfortunate. Kai's hand lands on my arm, returning my attention to him.

"I don't think you're wrong. It's not just you who's having some confusing feelings," Kai admits, showing me his first sign of weakness in so long.

My throat feels dry, making me swallow more times than I'd like to.

Max and Rae wave to us from the bus window, motioning us to get on and join them. I still feel annoyed at Max. His excitement towards the potential of someone getting hurt earlier unnerves me. Still, I plaster on my fake smile, following my brother's lead toward the bus. That's Kai's obvious way of wanting to shut down uncomfortable conversations he'd prefer to be done with.

"Now you speak to me? I thought I was cut off?" I question, using more energy than I'd expected to, but I'm paranoid, and my anger and hurt is raging through me.

"Well, you're alone again. It's much easier to speak to you when your mind isn't distracted by someone else's hands all over you," Fallan says, making my stomach flip.

"You saw-"

"Felt. I felt your pleasure, as much as I wish I didn't," Fallan says with a groan, only growing my list of questions.

"How is that possible?" I question, now rubbing my rolling stomach.

"Some part of you must have been thinking of me whenever you were with him. The only way this works is if you are thinking of the other person, and they are thinking of you too," he says, sounding tired as he speaks.

"I still don't understand. I never feel your... pleasure?" I push, nearing the steps of the tram.

"That's because I have none.... None that involves you," he says with a sigh. *"You don't have enough energy for me to explain it like this. If I am in your mind, Forest, you want me here. Remember that,"* Fallan finishes. The feeling of him dissipates from my mind.

Stumbling up the steps of the tram, I quickly snap my head to the back, half expecting to meet his blue eyes and cocky smirk. Instead, I see nothing but an empty back row of seats. Kai has already taken a seat with our friends, urging Max to stay seated instead of trying to talk to me.

Mark is too busy fidgeting with his seat to notice my sudden presence. He flinches in surprise when I squeeze his shoulder once no one is looking. We give each other our usual smiles before I pull away from the front and move myself back to my friends. I sit next to my brother, avoiding the seat that would put me close to Max. Kai picks up that I want some space from his friend, nudging me into his spot next to Rae, leaving Max no room to try and find a way over to me.

"Are you doing okay?" Rae asks, brushing off whatever feelings she's had towards me lately.

"Was your mom able to figure out what happened?" Max says, piquing the curiosity of those around me.

"Guys, give her some time," Kai says, raising his arm to give me the space to lean into him. I accept the gesture, letting my head land on his front, feeling the rise and fall of his chest as the tram finally begins to move. Max and Rae are impatient, watching me like they're owed an explanation.

"It was just a seizure. That's all," I finally say, knowing it's not the answer either of them wanted. They continue staring, waiting for me to say more.

"*That's all,*" I say again, hearing the irritation consuming my tone.

The twins exchange a look before leaning back in their chair. It's a look that tells me they'll be discussing my brother and me as soon as they're alone.

They can assume what they want. I've lost the desire to explain myself or reason with them. From what I've discovered so far about our chips, even if I were to tell them anything, I'm doubtful they'd have the capacity to accept or understand. It would destroy their reality, and I don't think they're ready for that.

I don't think anyone is ready for that.

Kai shakes me awake, already holding our bags, ready to leave the vehicle. He moves off the tram with the last few students, trailing behind the twins who are waiting for him outside the doors. I rub my eyes, unsure of when I'd dozed off. Mark looks at me in the rearview mirror.

I pull myself up to my feet, seeing my disorderly reflection in the closest window.

"Where are the Unfortunates?" I question once I am in his earshot. The old man takes a deep breath, looking back at the empty seats with me.

"Fallan had to stay behind to take the Academy's placement test to see if he's still eligible to be a transfer this year. He's been reviewing that prep book nonstop, ensuring he gets all the material down. I have no idea when he sleeps between studying and running his folks' property," Mark says, reminding me once more of the enormous responsibilities his people often have, regardless of age.

"I wasn't asking about just Fallan," I say, watching him smile.

"Were you curious about Valerie then?" he questions, giving me a small spout of sarcasm that I rarely see.

I grin at his playfulness.

"Why would he want to stay placed over here? At least in your sector, he won't have to deal with... my people," I say, pausing when I realize I've grouped myself with the Untouchables.

"You are more lost than I thought," Mark says.

I feel confused by his wording, unsure of what he could mean or how I am supposed to interpret that.

"What-"

"Forest, chop-chop," Rae says, tapping her watch with a pink nail. She looks annoyed, clearly off-put by yet another exchange between me and an Unfortunate.

"You're being summoned," Mark says, looking back toward the road with a lowered head. I step back, wondering how the conversation could shift that quickly. My head snaps back toward Rae, giving Mark one last look before pulling myself away from the tram.

I step off with a heave, moving past the blonde who has only managed to push my buttons today.

"How many of them do you plan on talking to?" Rae questions, trailing behind me, nagging me like a fly buzzing by my ear. My brother is talking to Max, standing close while whispering something in the boy's ear.

"As many as I fucking want," I spit, pausing to finally become eye level with the girl. "Because right now, the last thing I want is to be around our people," I continue, watching her expression contort into unease. The boys watch the exchange with curiosity, standing still, waiting for one of us to look at them.

"What the hell is going on with you?" Rae questions, giving my front a shove that leads to nothing. I hold my ground, keeping a leg back, unsure of when I had braced myself for the impact I didn't know was coming. She moves to shove again, stopping once both of her wrists are in my hand.

"I don't know. So stop trying to figure it out for me," I whisper, narrowing my eyes at her with a firm squeeze to her wrist.

A loud crash breaks my concentration on her, forcing us back several feet as we narrowly avoid tree branches falling on top of us. The tree scrapes the sidewall of someone's front yard before landing on the sidewalk between the boys and us. It's one of the many aspens planted on the sidewalk, and there's now a gaping hole where it should've been. I stare at the exposed roots, each jagged and ripped clean from the ground. I trail my gaze up towards the trunk, where I notice it's been sliced clean through with precision. We pause our angry banter, looking over the suddenly displaced eyesore in front of us.

"What the hell?" Kai questions, moving closer to get a better look at the tree.

"You both okay?" Max questions, resting his hand at my side. It makes my skin crawl.

"Yeah, we're fine," I quickly say, keeping my eyes on Kai.

"You two stood there, and it just started leaning over," Kai says, rubbing his fingers along the perfectly sliced trunk. "How the hell does a tree even break like that?" he questions, motioning the twins to come over and get a closer look.

The trio is studying botany in science this year, spending a great deal of time trying to figure out new ways to incorporate plant life, once thought extinct, back into our society. As far as I know, our people's resources, though seemingly plentiful, still tend to dwindle in some areas. The ability to create other fresh produce items that our society thought long gone grows more plausible each day.

With minds like Kai and Rae thrown into the research process, what once seemed impossible is now a light at the end of the tunnel. You'd be surprised how quickly people have gotten bored with what fresh produce we do have, given they have no real idea what food was like before New Haven began to get a grasp on how to mass produce once more. There are horror stories about New Haven's beginning and food scarcity before civility and agriculture returned to the human race.

Something wet falls from my ear, pulling me away from my thoughts once it meets the pavement and I see a red splotch. I touch my ear, pulling my fingers in front of me, and find bright, red blood coating my fingertips. Slapping my hand over the side of my head, I walk away, letting my slow steps become enormous strides, all while leaving my friends in the unsettling space behind me.

I shove open my front door, quickly scanning my ID card before the house triggers an alarm at the sudden presence within it. Running to the kitchen, I grab the nearest towel, clamping the material over my ear. I tilt my head back to try and stop the bleeding. After many minutes of vigorously washing my hands and patience, the bleeding stops, leaving me no other option than to shove the rag in my bag until I can clean it on my own. If anything, it would be just one more thing for my mother to question.

The only person active in the house is my father, although, given how dark it is inside the home, he must be sleeping off one of his longer shifts.

Quietly, I tip-toe closer to my bedroom door, doing my best not to look into his study through the open door. He rarely leaves it open this time of day so it's hard not to steal a glance inside.

Curiosity gets the better of me, forcing my head to look into his large work-space. His body is slumped forward onto his desk, his chest breathing deeply, and he's snoring onto the countless files sprawled across his desk. I step closer to the door, hearing a noise once my foot moves past the doorway. Looking down, I notice papers strung all over the floor of his study, each covered in handwriting of all different fonts and sizes, all sporting the same word.

"Apparatus?" I whisper, pushing myself to move further into the study.

His hands are coated in color pastels. Pages are ripped from his notebook. Some of his files are even covered in the word. Slowly creeping closer to my father, I see the nearly empty bottle of scotch resting next to his head.

I continue to find even more papers surrounding me everywhere I turn.

"What the hell?" I whisper, unable to focus on just one document.

Sketches of New Haven's territory are on my father's wall. Pins of varying colors poke up from the map. Green, blue, red, purple, and gray.

Of the five colors, there is one gray.

It marks our house's central location in New Haven's territory.

I poke my father's body, ready for him to scream at me for being in here. I don't know if he'd even bother trying to explain whatever it is I've stumbled upon.

He doesn't move a muscle.

Letting my curiosity guide me, I quietly move folders away from his desk, knocking his computer mouse in the process. His screen lights up, requiring no password, seeing as he passed out while doing work. I look over the multiple files on the computer, biting my nails once the cursor lands on the file labeled "*Unfortunate Sector.*"

Not once have I seen the sector. Other than Officials, only a select few Untouchables can travel that way. Glancing back at the doorway, I internally debate whether or not I should leave and forget everything I've seen here.

One look at the floor littered with papers is enough to guide my decision.

With three clicks, I have the file opened, unable to digest the sheer horror on the screen in front of me. People lie dead in the streets, children included. I watch as Officials haul bodies away from the busy streets, throwing them in piles to be carted off somewhere. Several Elders beg for mercy, seeing the flash of a pistol before meeting the ground in cold, limp states.

I grasp my father's desk as I continue to take in the disease and murder that ravages the people on the other side of our community. Buildings are older, clothes are torn, and bodies are weak. Officials throw the Unfortunates around like rag dolls, some badgering children who are doing nothing at all. My hands shake as I watch the footage, my mind running through every lie our people told us about how the Unfortunates had been comfortable and well provided for.

People wail out in pain, begging for someone to stop the Officials torturing them. I recoil in my skin, leaning over to release a gag doing its best to break free from my throat. My eyes land again on the papers on the floor. I grab a smaller notecard and shove it into my pocket. I hear the sound of a light sensor prod whirring, followed by the loud groans of someone being delivered a lashing. The sound of the grunts feeling all too familiar.

With horror-stricken eyes, I look up again at the footage, seeing his pained figure cling to a pole while they tear his back to shreds. Fallan. His blue eyes are filled with distress, but he's somehow managed to stifle the screams he wants to let out. I watch the Officials hit him as hard as they can, breaking down his muscular body and leaving him with gruesome lesions across his back. His voice is hoarse from yelling. A necklace dangles from his neck. On it is a single golden ring. Even in the footage, I can see the band has an intricate design, carved of vines and wrapping all the way around. The date on the bottom of the screen is from last year. A year ago, from when I first saw Fallen on the tram to school for the first time. All those scars on his back were fresh.

I watch the Official back away from Fallan, finally finished with his lashings. My heart hurts at the image of tears rolling down Fallan's cheeks. My own tears begin to streak my face, filling my chest with a significant weight I can't shake.

I hear the Official behind the camera laugh at his suffering. Each dirty Untouchable on the screen is added to my mental list of people I want in front of the barrel of a gun. I touch the screen above Fallan's slumped figure, watching as he almost falls backward once the Official who delivered him the beating takes off his mask to grab the camera.

My father's eyes look unrecognizable. His face is streaked with Fallan's blood, malevolence filling his eyes.

"That should be enough footage to bring back to the big guy. There's no way that deviant asshole tries anything again," Adam says from behind the camera.

All my father can do is nod.

I quickly shut off the computer, feeling a tremendous guilt for what my father had done. It's hard to look down at the man without scowling. I don't know if I recognize him anymore.

How can he come home to us like nothing is wrong after doing and seeing something so vile? How can he knowingly commit so many heinous acts towards people without having his conscience tattered to shreds? Is it his chip? Or is it him?

I grasp my head, reaching into my mind space in a panic.

"I'm so sorry," I cry down the hallway of my mind, feeling myself start to hyperventilate.

"I didn't know," I say again, backing away from my father and this forlorn study.

"What did you see?" Fallan quickly asks, sounding more panicked than usual.

Real or not, he needs to hear this from me, even if it's all in my head.

I take a shaky breath, staggering out into the hallway towards my room. I lock myself inside and slink to the floor.

"I saw what my father did to you. I saw what he did to your back," I whisper, feeling the mental drain start to take effect.

"That wasn't the worst thing that happened to me, Forest. Believe it or not, that punishment saved me that day." he says, his words more exhausted than usual.

"How?" I question, slumping forward to press my heated face to the cool floor.

"The scars remind me of one thing." he says silently in my mind.

"What?" I question, letting his voice guide my breathing back to normal.

"That any of it was real, to begin with," Fallan mutters, making my head pound to life.

"That any of what was real, Fallan? What aren't you telling me?" I push, feeling the pain swarm my mind.

"Get some sleep, Little Dove. I don't have any more energy to give you," he whispers.

My heart drops at his statement, leaving me with nothing but the haunted images of him now painted on the walls of my mind.

"I won't let them hurt you again," I whisper silently.

He whispers back. It's quiet, but it's there.

"That makes two of us."

CHAPTER TWENTY-THREE

FOREST

The dryness in my throat is unbearable, finally forcing me to blink away my exhaustion. I feel my soft sheets beneath me, unsure how I ended up in my bed in the first place. After a few glances around my room, I see Kai's note on my side table, scribed with his perfect handwriting.

I figured you didn't want me to change you.

I told Mom and Dad you had a long day after what happened at school and needed some rest.

I won't push you on why you were asleep outside Dad's study, but I need answers.

I love you.

-Kai

I drop the note, feeling great appreciation for my brother and his desire to always try his best to do what's best for me. With a swing of my legs, I am out of bed. I yank open my door to peer down the dark hallway. Darkness engulfs the space around me. Everyone's rooms are silent, my father's study now fully closed, trapping the horrors I saw earlier within it. I expect my parents' door to fly open when the floorboards creak under my feet outside their room. Seconds pass and the house remains silent.

Slowly, I work through the house, feeling relieved when I reach the kitchen. After three glasses of water, I finally feel refreshed. I have to shake away the images of all the malnourished children in the Unfortunate sector. I think of the boy from school who had stolen the food. All of those Officials knew about his living conditions, yet still chose to punish him. Given his security detail duties, even Xavier knows the horrors lying beyond the fence to their sector.

Is what I saw the "burden" he spoke of yesterday, or does he know more than I think?

The air begins to feel heavier in my lungs, and it takes more effort to breathe in than it does to let it all out. The outside world beckons for me, only a sliding glass door away. With a quick scan of the yard, I silently slip outside, snagging my father's ID from the counter to grant myself access outside this late at night. The house doesn't stir, no alarms sounding off at my presence, allowing me to quietly slip out. Finally, I allow myself to take a full breath, leaning against the side of my house. My arms are wrapped around my front, working to warm my cool exterior.

I glance up toward the side of the house, expecting to see the camera only a few feet away from my face. It's the same one that always watches our backyard.

It takes a moment for my eyes to adjust to the dark, only to see the fragmented glass pieces of the lens shattered on the ground around my feet. It looks just like the one that Xavier pummeled with rocks on the other side of the house. The camera wires poke out, and I can tell the security camera is completely broken and definitely incapable of detecting any motion around this part of the yard. I poke the pieces of glass with my toe, listening to it scrape against the wooden deck.

"What the fuck?" I question, hearing the rattle of leaves in the tree line behind me.

Like the night of the screening, I get a feeling, sensing something sinister lurking in the shadows, watching me from a distance. Even from here, I hear the rasp breathing of its lungs, listening to its nails tap the side of the tree like it's impatiently waiting on something. I spot a foreboding outline behind the trunk of one of the largest trees in our yard. It's still in the blanket of darkness. I'm unnerved by the fact that I can't figure out what it is. My body fills with chills, unable to move as fear paralyzes me.

"Who's there-"

A gloved hand grabs my neck, slamming me hard into the side of my house, being sure to cover my mouth before I can get a scream out. My feet drag across the balcony, nearly cut by the glass scattered around the area. A pair of unfamiliar brown eyes look over me, watching me flail in their grasp as they lift me off of my feet by my neck and slam me against the side of my house. I claw my hands against their arms, trying to get away from them. This person is strong, power threading through their movements. Untouchables don't have strength like this. I do my best to reach into my mind, screaming out into the void of my head.

"Help me!" I yell in my mind, feeling the pressure around my neck intensify. My legs grow weaker with each attempt to kick myself away from the masked deviant.

"How many valuable things can I nab off a pretty Untouchable like you?" the man questions, his face hidden by a black mask.

Unfortunate muggers. Damn.

"G-Go to hell-" I try to say, feeling him slam me once more into my house, knocking me back harder than he had the first time.

My thoughts linger and I let my head stay against the wall as all the ways in which this scenario could play out slam into my head all at once.

"Get the fuck off of her!" his voice says, shoving the man away from me and sending me to my knees. I grasp violently at my throat, trying to drag the air back to me in strained breaths.

Even without a mirror, I know my neck is bruised, possibly swollen. I continue to gasp, unable to take a full breath.

"I was getting somewhere-"

"Go find another fucking house, Aaron," Fallan says, shoving his finger into the man's chest, pushing him several steps back. "This one's mine," Fallan finishes, looking over the man sternly.

I clutch my neck, listening to their exchange with wide eyes. I hear my shallow breaths pick up, watching Aaron give me one look before sneering at Fallan's brooding figure.

"I'm not stopping for you next time," Aaron says, pointing to Fallan before slipping back into the night. I look again at the tree line, unsure if there was anything there to begin with.

Fallan turns on his heels, sporting the same get-up as his friend. The mask covers his face, only showing his deep blue eyes. A few strands of his hair poke out from beneath his hood, but not enough to recognize him in this lighting. He steps toward me, only motivating me to return to a standing position. He clutches the blade at his side, pulling it free from its hilt. I watch him take another step; my back fully pressed against the wall.

"I-I would understand-" I say, wincing at the pain in my throat. "If you wanted me dead," I whisper, feeling the tears cloud my vision. He keeps moving toward me, staying silent. His eyes are my only way to see his feelings.

Fallan pauses in front of me, turning his blade to the dull side, letting his arm rest above my head as he leans over me. I feel the cool metal as he drags his weapon up my stomach, holding up my shirt with its point. All of that motion had caused my pants to slip down lower on my hip, giving him a perfect view of the mark that taints my skin. He lets his hand fall from above me, grazing his thumb over the rough skin of my mark, filling my body with unnerving warmth. The touch is invigorating, forcing my body to scream to life.

"I wasn't sure if you were like me. I've never been sure," Fallan whispers, letting his light touches become a firm grasp as his hands explore my hip. "Now I know," he says, narrowing his eyes once he notices me moving my hands to my neck again to try and stifle the throbbing pain that's threatening to leave me incapable of moving from this spot.

"That fucking idiot," Fallan curses, reaching into his back pocket to grab the spray we've both become all too familiar with lately. I don't try to stop him when he applies it, feeling relief in how it soothes the skin around my neck. "I had no idea you'd be out here," Fallan continues, sheathing his weapon again. Keeping two hands on either side of my head, he keeps me backed against the wall.

"I would have let him kill me-" I begin, remembering the video and what had been done to him.

"No, you wouldn't have," Fallan leans down closer to my face, cutting me off. "Because he would have been dead before that happened," he continues, unable to mask the smell of alcohol on his breath each time he speaks.

"Seeing him hurting you like that," Fallan starts, looking me over again. "And hearing you yell for help," Fallan continues, touching his head. "It did things to me, Forest," he finishes, sounding unsure of himself.

So, the voice. It's truly him.

The question is how?

I start to pull down the front of his mask with shaky hands. I let my fingertips linger on his temples, slowly moving them along the soft curves of his cheeks, feeling wetness along his skin where tears must have been. He doesn't push my hand away as I gently continue exploring his taut features, instead his gaze fixes on my lips, silent words hanging from his own as I try not to unravel in front of him.

"What are you doing here, Fallan?" I question.

I can feel him now, connected to me by some unknown force. He invades my mind, prying open the door but waiting for an invitation to explore any further. My hand trails down from his face to his neck, where I can feel his pulse beneath my touch. There's a rhythm to his heartbeat that keeps me in a trance.

"This was supposed to be easy," Fallan whispers, letting his own hands dive under my shirt, holding on to my waist firmly.

A burst of energy surges through me, filling the pool of heat between my legs at the sensation of his skin on mine. "I told myself I wouldn't come near you," he continues, moving his hands from my waist closer to my ass, giving me no warning before sliding them down my thigh. He grabs me tighter before dragging me flush to his front, propping me against the side of the house as my legs instinctively wrap around his waist.

My arms reach around his neck, pulling my chest closer to his. Suddenly my mind and body are in sync, totally focused on immersing my very being into the sensation of his touch. Every part of me is awake. Everything seems louder, every noise clearer. A dam crumbles, leaving long-dormant emotions and feelings cascading freely through me. I revel in the newness of it all. Or is it a reunion with parts of me I'd been cut off from? I can't stop the ache in my breasts as our bodies seem to mold together, and I feel his hands tighten on my legs.

"But then he touched you," Fallan continues, bringing his lips close to my neck, hovering over the same sensitive spot Xavier had explored earlier.

"Like he knew you. Like he knew *my* Little Dove," Fallan continues, not once letting his lips land on the skin. "The memory of him touching you drives me fucking insane," Fallan whispers, biting his lip as he pulls away from my neck, clenching his jaw out of frustration. "He gets to touch you, to feel you. To be something to you. And all I can do is watch all of it while I have to pretend to hate you," Fallan finishes, readying himself to pull away from me. I grab his face, stopping him from looking away. The alcohol strips away his quiet nature, leaving me with this raw version of a man whose very confessions sing to some part of me, tormenting my mind and heart with unbridled desires I don't want to contain anymore.

"What am I to you?" I question, watching the torment that swirls in his eyes.

"If I tell you," he says, inching his face closer to my own, letting our noses brush, "I lose you." he finishes in a whisper. My stomach drops at the statement, my mind torn between letting me suffocate in the closeness of us and getting the answers from him.

"I'm right here, Fallan," I push, something familiar calling for attention in the recess of my mind as the words leave my lips. There's a fuzzy image of something vivid and heartbreaking, but I can't piece it together yet. The necklace I saw around his neck in the video footage from my father's office slips free from his shirt. The ring shines brightly, like it's infused with something important and meaningful. Like it's an embodiment of something I should recognize. Like it belongs to me, too, even though it hangs around his neck and adorns his chest, not mine.

"How much of this is because of the alcohol?" I question, inching my mouth closer to his.

Something changes at that moment, and before I can say or do anything else, he lowers me gently to the ground, coercing my legs from around his waist to create a bit of space between us. I watch him process how close we were, his hand moving to adjust the front of his pants as his eyes stay locked with mine. I cross my legs to control the ache between them. He runs his hands through his hair as his features turn stern and decisive.

"I can't do that again," he whispers, visibly growing more frustrated with each passing moment.

He opens and closes his hands, a way to control stress, no doubt.

"Fallan," I start, moving toward him. "I don't want you to stay away from me."

He grabs my chin, holding me close to him, cupping my face between his two large hands.

"I have no other choice," he whispers. The pain of that admission is written on every part of his face, like he's been struck by his own words, leaving real wounds open on his flesh.

"Why Fallan?" I say, trying my best to pull him down by his neck. In the blink of an eye, he's now several feet away from where he just stood. I stumble forward. His eyes are wide, looking around frantically before moving towards me again.

"H-How did you-"

His hand clamps down on my mouth, stopping me from finishing. He pulls me into the front of him, resting his free hand in my hair, moving his fingers along my scalp to soothe me. He has us backed into my house, both of us silently listening to the sound of approaching footsteps.

"Fallan?" Valerie calls out, appearing from the same direction Fallan had come from. "Did you get her?"

I'm annoyed that she's here but not surprised. Fallan squeezes me in an attempt to remind me to stay quiet. She can't see us yet, but if she moves any further, she will. His fingers weave gently through my hair, trying to ebb the anxiety I know he can sense in all my tense body parts pressed against his front.

"She got away. She didn't recognize us," Fallan says in her direction, moving his hand away from my hair to run his fingers down my side. "Aaron might need help. Keep moving," Fallan says, urging the blonde to move past my house.

She obliges, not seeing me with him. I want him to keep me pressed against him like this. His lips lower close to my ear, holding me still with his firm hands on my stomach.

"Hate me, Forest," he begs, his hands dragging up and down beneath my shirt. "Please, hate me," he continues, stopping his hand motions, "I can't keep having you look at me like I matter. Like you're holding a door open for me, and I can have you. It's delusional to think there's a way for me to get to you, knowing they'll rip it all away," he seethes, making me that much more confused.

"But having you look at me tonight the way you did was worth every lashing they gave me," he admits, pressing his lips firmly to the top of my head. I feel my heart burst on the spot, my mind forcing something back into the shadows to keep this moment free from falling into obscurity, to be uninterrupted for just a little longer.

"It will be worth it every time," he finishes, pulling his lips away from my forehead.

I feel his thumbs rub along my cheeks, grazing my lips before he steps back. His hand quickly swipes the necklace around my neck, giving it a gentle kiss before turning on his heel and disappearing into the darkness. I stumble backward into the wall, feeling weak in my knees from his sudden absence.

My head spins. Slowly, I take in deep breaths, willing myself to slow the jumble of thoughts whirling and buzzing in my skull. My heart races as I commit everything that just happened to memory. It may not make sense right now, but there's more here, and I don't want to forget any of it. His vulnerability, his words, his piercing blue eyes wide with truth and desire, all of it real.

"If he tells me, he'll lose me," I whisper to myself, reflecting on what he'd said. I raise my finger to my chip, feeling its warmth, indicating its active status.

"Have we been here before?" I question in my mind. I close my eyes, hunting through all the spaces where the chip has embedded itself. I can feel its presence, waiting and threatening to seal my thoughts shut, trying to trap me in. But this time, I'm ready and hold it back.

"The answer to that doesn't change anything, Little Dove," he whispers back, filling my body with chills.

I look down to where the broken pieces of the security camera are scattered around the deck. I lean down and pick up a glass shard that must have been part of the camera lens.

"You want to control me?" I whisper, mocking the chip as I clench the shard of glass so tightly that my hand begins to shake.

"Fuck you," I utter, driving the glass right into the center of the chip behind my ear, barely able to hold in the scream lodged in my throat as I drag it down toward the base of my skull. I hear the sound of my skin rip apart as the glass finds its way to the soft tissue and tendons underneath. I keep scraping, the feeling of blood trailing down my neck and warming my top, doing nothing to dull the sharp pain from the gaping wound I'm creating.

I drop the glass and push my fingers into the flesh. I channel all my rage, hate, and disgust to the tips of my fingers as I work to untangle every talon of oppressive machinery.

There's a tightness around my skull. The pressure is immense as the chip defends itself from being ripped out. It's fighting me, refusing to loosen. My fingers become frantic and chaotic, pulling and tugging faster as I realize how much blood I've probably lost. I try to control the sway of my legs as I become lightheaded.

But then something taut snaps free, and a comforting silence greets me in the free space it leaves behind. The creature in my mind stretches out and unfurls, claiming back the space that was stolen from it.

I let out a sigh as darkness consumes me.

CHAPTER TWENTY-FOUR

FOREST- UNTOUCHABLE SECTOR, TWO YEARS AGO

The house's window flashes with multiple colors, changing with the beat of the music. It's loud enough to reach me, even outside the busy home. I glance down at the small piece of paper Max had given me, ensuring I have the correct address. Josh's house was farther out than most in our sector, almost touching the ward. The house is massive, taking up at least three times the lot space as other houses in our sector. I'm starting to see one of the many reasons his ego is so large. I don't know how he has the strength to carry it.

My oversized hoodie hides my last-minute decision of an outfit that was a bit more revealing than I'm used to. While my hair is usually up in a ponytail, I've let it run freely down my back in soft waves tonight. People work in and out of the house, carrying cups behind the house where a small bonfire brings life to the otherwise dark expanse of the yard. People stumble, clearly already under the influence of Josh's father's supply of rich bourbons and champagnes.

Once a year, Josh hosts this party as a "Back to School Social" to ensure the Officials leave it alone. If his father weren't so high up on the Council, it would be shut down immediately.

With great hesitation, I move past the large metal gate, forcing myself closer to the front door, ready to turn around the minute my hand clacks the metal knocker.

"Shut up," Josh says in a half laugh to his friends from the other side, swinging open the door with a smile, only to let it drop once he sees me.

"What are you doing here, Blackburn?" Josh questions, giving me a cold welcome and a look that surely means he's about to slam the door in my face.

"I invited her," Max says, working his way through the crowd, holding a glass filled with a purple liquid.

I raise my eyebrows at Josh, challenging him to try and be an asshole to me with this many people watching.

"Still trying to get with that?" Josh questions back to Max, watching the blonde's face grow red at the comment.

"Do you plan on standing here like a jackass all night or...?"

"Where's your brother?" Josh questions, leaning into the doorframe. "He is an absolute party killer."

"That's probably why I left him at home," I say, not telling Josh that Rae and Kai already had their own plans for the night. "So can I come in, or should I fuck off?" I question, watching the smirk develop on Josh's face.

"Colton," Josh says, pointing to his shadow, "Go get her a cup of what Vega's drinking."

Colton nods at him, disappearing from the entryway with a look of determination. Josh steps away from the doorway, extending his arm into the space, finally allowing me to pass. Moments later, Colton returns with a cup, placing it in my hand with a smile.

"I don't drink-"

"If you're going to come to my party, you might as well do it the right way," Josh says, silencing my long list of reasons why I trust nothing in a cup from him. Still, with sealed lips, I nod, watching him look me over before finally working his way back into his living room to continue his conversation with the group of women he'd left behind.

Max waits back, still flush in the cheeks from Josh's earlier comment to him.

"A small get-together to make more friends," I say, throwing out the description he'd given me to convince me to come here in the first place.

"Josh said it would only be a few people."

"Clearly," I say, looking around at the drunken mob of students running around the space.

A girl bumps into me, sending a good portion of my drink down the front of my hoodie in large splotches. I curse as I set down the drink, pulling my hoodie off of me, not thinking of the smaller shirt Rae urged me to wear for the night, showing off some of my stomach and enunciating the breasts I didn't realize I had. Our regulated hormones had hit us all like a train over the summer, leaving us with less room in our clothes and more things to look at. I stare at the splotch on my hoodie, lowering it to see Max's eyes plastered on me, specifically my body.

"Max!" I snap, watching his dilated pupils adjust as his attention drifts back to my face.

"Hm?" he questions, clearly distracted.

"Hey, Vega!" Josh yells, widening his eyes at me before returning to Max. "Come over here. These are the guys I was telling you about," Josh beckons, speaking to the fourth and fifth years in the activity-based classes at the Academy. Playing at the higher levels is by invite only, and I've watched reluctantly as Josh and Max have grown closer, helping each other secure their placements for more advanced sports come their fifth year.

"I'm sorry," Max begins, looking at me apologetically as he backs away.

"Don't let me stop you," I say, watching him give me a frown as he turns to join the group of overly assertive teenage jocks. I could practically smell the testosterone oozing from them, which was an affront to my senses as I took in a whiff of the vile concoction of alcohol in my cup, smelling more of mouthwash than anything I would have a desire to drink.

I watch the roar of the flames grow through the back door. I look down at my wet hoodie, needing a way to dry it quickly so the smell doesn't linger later.

"Might as well try and enjoy my night without you," I whisper, giving Max one last look before slipping outside.

No one remained seated by the fire. After everyone had eaten and someone had announced that a makeshift dancefloor was the place to be, pretty much everyone hurried to go inside, clearly unable to pass up an opportunity to touch and grope one another. Given how rarely touch is allowed before marriage or exclusive relationships that are most of the time entirely forced on us by our families for common interest or gain, a few stolen moments like that are more than enough for most.

I sat on one of the farthest logs from the house that surrounds the bonfire, tossing my cup into the grass and freeing both hands to hold up my hoodie. Its material grows warm, slowly drying once I lay it across the log beside me. I watch the fire eat away at the wood, dwindling in size with each ember it flicks into the air.

"Not big on parties?" a male voice questions from next to me, now visible since the flames have died down. The figure is in a black hoodie, hiding their face behind a mask you'd generally see attached to an Official. All I can see is his eyes and the bright blue irises that seemed to glow through the flickers of firelight.

"More like I'm not big on dealing with any of the assholes in there," I say, raising my hands to warm by the fire. The man lets out a small laugh, fidgeting with a metal flask.

"Don't trust Josh's surprise in the punchbowl?" I question, watching the man's eyes move down to my cup.

"As much as you do, apparently," he says, lowering his mask just enough to take a swig of whatever's inside the flask. The bottom half of his face is just as lovely to look at as the top half. But I don't recognize him from the Academy.

"What's with the getup?" I question, motioning to his outfit as he drags the mask back up.

"There are some people here I don't want to see me," he starts, noticing my quick glances at his flask. He looks around the space, hesitantly deciding to get up. I see now how tall he is, making it harder to swallow once he chooses to sit at the end of my log. A few feet are between us, both legs out in front of him. His scent is inviting, smelling of cinnamon and oak. His hand reaches toward me, holding the flask out, his eyes still toward the fire.

I take it in my hand, letting our fingers brush only for a moment.

"What is it?" I question, raising the drink to my nose.

"Bourbon. I stole it from the locked study of this asshat's house," the man says, making a smile grow on my face almost instantly.

"Stealing from an upper leadership Official?" I say, letting the liquid run down my throat, warming my stomach once it settles. I wince at the taste, handing him back his flask with a small thank you. "For shame, what about your scorecard?" I question sarcastically, listening to the man's soft laugh.

"Fuck the scorecards. It's all bullshit," the man says, shaking the pockets of his jacket, clearly filled with something much more valuable than bourbon. "Sometimes rich assholes need to know they're not untouchable," he says, clearly smiling beneath the mask. His eyes crease, showing the faint beginnings of what could be crow's feet.

I laugh with a smile, looking at him with pure amusement.

"This is usually the part where you look at me like I'm a criminal and go report me. The last two times I hit one of these parties, some uptight asshole was contacting an Official within minutes," he starts, keeping his smile on his face. "Why do you look so amused?" he questions.

"It's just," I begin. "No one ever goes against rules... it's nice to see," I pause, thinking of Josh, "Plus, the asshole running this party has made my life hell," I say, crossing my arms out of frustration.

"What's your name?" the boy questions, smiling as he drags down the mask again, taking another drink.

"See, if I tell you that, you will think I'm an uptight asshole like Josh." The man raises an eyebrow, keeping his mask down as he watches me.

"I doubt that," he says, deepening his breath. "Well, I guess I can't tell you my name either. It makes things much more complicated if you try and find me after tonight."

"Cryptic," I say, nudging his foot with my own, hearing his laugh again.

The effects of the alcohol linger, making me want to scoot closer to my unknown companion.

The music shifts from its upbeat, loud tempo to something more peaceful. It's a song filled with piano, followed by the background vocals of a woman's soft voice. I close my eyes, listening to the song with a smile. I feel something in front of me move and open my eyes to see his hand extended out in front of me. He is standing, waiting for me to notice him.

"What are you doing?" I question with a large grin.

"Take my hand so I don't look like an idiot for trying this," he says, only adding to the smile on my face.

His hand is much rougher than I expected, covered with callouses along his palm. I run my thumb along his hand, feeling his free hand gently grab my waist. I move my hands around his neck, and the hand I'd been holding before drops down to the other side of my waist. At this level, I see the scar along the man's cheek, faint but it's there. His large hands consume my sides, a growing heat taking over my body as he pulls me closer.

"How did you do that to your hands?" I question, feeling him guide us to the slow tempo.

"What's your name?" he questions again, smiling with me as we both refuse to oblige each other's inquiries.

"Give me a new one," I say, pulling myself a little closer, letting the alcohol guide me.

"Give you one?" he questions with a grin, wrapping one arm around my waist to dip me down. I smile as I grasp his front, doing my best not to laugh. I feel the stolen contents clatter around in his pockets, hitting against my leg.

"Yes, give me one," I say once he has me back upright. My feet are becoming more unstable. With a lift, he has my feet on his own, guiding my steps like I'm weightless.

"I only just met you. Hard to give you a name with so little information," he whispers, my eyes landing on his lips.

"My name is Forest," I say, watching his body freeze at the mention of my name.

"That's your real name?" the man asks, like I'm playing a prank on him.

"In the flesh. I believe it's your turn now," I say, feeling the man's touch slowly relax.

"Can I be honest with you right now?" the man questions, rubbing his thumbs along my waist, again starting the sway. The alcohol is affecting him now, too, his eyelids drooping more than when I'd first gotten here. He seems less tense, a little less rigid.

"I'm not from this sector," he whispers in my ear, making my mouth dry up as I press my front to him. A million questions run through my head, each returning to one thought in particular.

He's an Unfortunate.

I half expect myself to run away, ready to report this man for the list of violations he's committed. I let his admission settle in my mind, one thought stopping me from going anywhere: In the twenty minutes I've danced with this man, I've felt safer than I have around anyone inside that house.

"That explains the hands," I whisper, meeting his eyes again in the darkness. He looks confused by my reaction, raising both eyebrows at me.

"I just told you-"

"I know what you just told me," I whisper back, now feeling the alcohol drown out any sense of rational thinking. "I don't care," I say, feeling his grasp tighten around my waist at my words.

He peers down at me, letting his head hang lower as his nose touches mine. I smell the alcohol mixing on our breath. Both of our hearts beat rapidly.

"I was supposed to stop finding reasons to come to this sector," he whispers, looking over my lips like I had his earlier.

What the hell am I doing? Why does it feel so... right? I'm going against everything I'm supposed to believe and doing it with a smile.

He shakes his head, pulling away his trance on my lips as he looks up at the night sky.

"Dove. I'll call you Dove," he says, smiling at me.

"Why?" I question, feeling my legs fumble as he finally raises me all the way up, holding me off the ground as my arms wrap around him tighter.

"Well, you see, Forest," he says with a smile. "You're the first real symbol of hope I've seen in this society in a long time," he whispers, letting our noses touch once more before lowering me back down.

He takes several steps back. His cheeks flush with the same red that coats mine.

"Your hoodie looks dry," he says, pointing to the clothing while pulling up his mask.

I glance at the material, looking back at him with confusion as his hands rifle through his filled pockets. I watch him yank something away, holding a small charm on a chain, waiting for my hand to place it down. I feel its metal touch my palm, resting gently in my hand. His eyes soften, watching the confusion spreading across my face.

"Something to remember me by once that alcohol wears off," he says, stepping closer and reaching around my neck. The necklace drapes across my chest as he clasps the chain. His fingers trail down and around the front of the necklace once it's secured, lingering on the charm that now sits between my collarbones.

"I was guessing you'd like that," he says, looking down at me with a large grin.

"You must be crazy to come over in this sector, touch me the way you have, and gift me with stolen jewelry," I say, keeping my head pressed against him.

"Do you want me to stop touching you?" he questions, something much deeper lingering in the question.

It's silent for several seconds.

"No," I say, tilting my head up to face him.

His hand raises to touch my cheek, grazing his thumb along my skin with his calloused hand.

"Little Dove," he whispers with a shake of his head, letting his hand drop once we hear the sound of others moving closer to the back door. I grab his hand as he moves away. He spins around to look at me.

"So that's it? You're just leaving?" I question, watching his smirk grow.

"There are a few people in there who'd recognize me. I don't want to stick around once they notice what's missing," he utters, the voices growing louder.

"I'll be back," he whispers, giving my hand one small press of his lips.

He continues his walk, one more burning question eating me alive.

"I don't even know your name," I say. His back stays toward me.

"Then I guess we will have to meet again, won't we?" he questions.

I hear the door swing open, watching Max's group spill onto the lawn. My eyes immediately move back to where the enigmatic stranger had just been, feeling a sense of relief and sadness once I realize he's nowhere to be seen. Slowly, the reality of what I just allowed to happen weighs down on me, but I'm filled with more feelings of satisfaction rather than shame, only adding to my own internal conflict.

I wanted that touch. I wanted it from him at that moment, and I'm worried it wasn't because of the alcohol.

My stomach begins to churn, feeling more uneasy the longer the alcohol settles. I quickly shove past the group of boys, not even acknowledging Max as I move back inside the home and straight up the stairs to find somewhere quiet.

What the fuck did I just do?

I run down the hall, trying to find the nearest bathroom to empty the contents of my stomach. Jiggling the handles of door after door, I grow more impatient as I realize every single one is locked. Most likely done on purpose to keep horny teenagers from besmirching the space. Panic sets in as I wonder whether the stranger was indeed an Unfortunate or if what he said was nothing more than a trick. I think of his hands on me, still hearing the music play as he guided our movements. His hands, though rough, were so gentle against my skin. His blue eyes had watched me closely, taking in as much of me as I was of him.

Finally, one of the upstairs hallway doors opens, and I stumble forward into what I can only assume is a guest room. I quickly scan the area, feeling the light brush of air caress my skin. The curtains framing the large window on the wall farthest from the door danced and fluttered hypnotically in the open space. As I turn back towards the door to continue searching the other rooms upstairs for a bathroom, through another window in the room, I see a figure standing on the rooftop, staring forward, still like a statue.

The curtains distort my view of the figure, my curiosity urging me closer to the window as the wave of nausea I'd been battling seems to die. My hand swipes away the diaphanous curtain panels, giving me a clear view of the dark-skinned boy standing at the roof's edge. I've seen him at the Academy. He's a third year, and, from what I remember, a nice boy. He's in a gray sweater, with his arms crossed over his body as he whispers silently to himself. Slowly, I make my way back to the open window and carefully step outside onto the roof. My footing is still a bit uneven, given the alcohol working through my blood. The boy doesn't seem to notice as I clumsily make my way over to face him.

I look around, half expecting someone else to be out here.

It's only him.

"Are you okay?" I question, seeing his body tense up at the sound of my voice.

"Everything is clearer now," he whispers in a voice I can hardly hear.

I pause my steps toward him, looking at the red soaking the front of his shirt. Blood. His hand shakily holds a small cutting knife that he must have found in the kitchen downstairs.

He turns his body toward me, and I see the blood trickling down the side of his neck from behind his ear. I look down as I hear his foot move and see the blinking of a red light. A small metal piece attached to long tendrils thrashes and spasms out and around his shoe, trying to find something to cling to.

His chip.

His lip wobbles while he speaks. The knife remains clutched in his hand, his blood mixing with the tears now rolling down his young face.

"Why don't you come inside with me, and we can get you cleaned up."

"They won't stop coming for us," he says in a sob, pointing at me with his bloodied hand. "We're being lied to. It starts with this parasite we allowed them to put in our heads," he says, smashing his foot down on the chip, letting the light fade beneath it. "He will deliver you himself to the devil if he needs to. Can you not see it?"

He's crazy.

This boy has lost it.

"I can get you help if you just come with me," I whisper, extending my hand toward the boy.

"The Apparatus is near," he says, looking back toward the dark sky. "They will lead us all away from this eternal hell," he continues, taking one shaky step forward.

I move toward him, completely disregarding the slope of the roof.

"Wait-"

"I do not have the strength to wait for them."

The world goes silent as he steps off the roof. His eyes are closed. His hands lowered to his sides. Desperately, I skid down the panels of the roof, my hand wrapping around the material of his sweater as he slips further down. My nails drag down his arm, our hands finally meeting as I battle with gravity. Our hands clasp as we're dragged over the side of the roof. I brace myself for the fall, still scrambling to grab any part of the roof's edge I can with my free arm. My fingertips scrape across the roof tiles, and I can feel my nails splitting and breaking as I grasp harder for purchase. Suddenly, our movement stops. I grunt as a searing pain festers in my shoulder from the weight of trying to keep us both from plummeting to the ground.

"Help!" I scream, feeling my fingers slowly begin to slip. I look down at the boy, watching his eyes grow wider with fear. My fingers hold tightly to his wrist, feeling a rough spot on his skin, identical to the one on my hip.

"Free yourself, then free us all," he whispers.

Grabbing the small knife, he cuts my hand, forcing me to let go of his arm as a smile consumes his face. I watch in horror as his body plummets to the ground, hitting the pavement with a crack so loud it hurts my ears. I don't have the stomach to look down at him, feeling my bloodied hand try to hold me up. My arm begins to give out. I cry out once more, fighting back the tears and emotion. My weak arms quickly try to pull me back up. I hear a girl scream from inside, shouting at others to call an Official once she notices the boy's bloodied body on the concrete.

A shadow casts over the roof, moving closer, giving me the slightest sense of relief that someone has come to help.

"I'm over here!" I yell, kicking my feet to try and force myself back up. My stomach drops once I see Josh's face. He peers over the roof, covering his mouth once he sees what's below me. I feel my hand begin to slip again, screaming as I quickly try to reach for him.

"Josh, help me!" I yell, reaching for his leg. He steps back, crouching to his knees to watch me.

"What happened, Forest?" he questions, cocking his head at me. Panic consumes me as the possibility that Josh may let me fall quickly becomes a reality.

"Josh, this isn't funny. Help me up!" I yell, feeling his hands wrap around my wrists, only to drop my right hand immediately

"Did you push him, Blackburn?" Josh questions, taunting me by loosening his grasp more. My shoulder feels dislocated, ready to tear away from my arm.

"God damn it, Josh, no! He jumped. I was trying to help!" I yell, watching him let out a scoff at the statement.

Ten seconds pass of me dangling before he finally lets me up, hauling me onto the roof and his front. I quickly roll off him, shuffling away from the edge of the roof. I hold my hands in my hair as I try to process what just happened. I begin to hyperventilate, unsure how to breathe anymore. Josh moves closer to me, glancing in the window to the guest room that's now filled with more bodies as Officials, some that had been running detail nearby, begin to fill the room.

"Shut the fuck up and follow along," Josh hisses, slapping my face hard, sending my thoughts away from their spiral.

"Out here!" Josh shouts, signaling the men to join us on the roof as he begins to give the best performance of his life.

Josh explains how he watched the boy jump, only to have him drag me down. Josh goes into great detail about his heroic act of pulling me up, even saying how the boy tried to attack us when an Official asked about the cut along my hand. I watch the men put the boy's chip into a small evidence bag, quietly conversing, scanning his blood with a device I don't recognize. The device beeps and displays something that makes the group of Officials disgusted. After dragging me inside, the men cleaned my wounds, questioning me if my father knew about my whereabouts tonight. For a moment, the Officials leave me alone with Josh in the room, doing their best to send students home amidst the chaos.

"You owe me big time, Blackburn," Josh whispers harshly in my ear as the Officials signal us to leave the room.

"What happened to him?" I ask the Officials, feeling their hands pressed against my lower back as they guide me out of the home.

"A freak accident. A sporadic state of delirium when he removed his chip," Josh's father says. He's already on the other line with my dad, who I know will be furious.

"Your dad says we're taking you home... now," Adam whispers, guiding me closer to his car. I take one final look at where the boy fell.

The crimson red coating the back of his ear is the last thing I see before they drag over the white tarp, concealing him entirely from the outside world.

CHAPTER TWENTY-FIVE

FOREST

C onsciousness comes suddenly. My head flies up from the concrete. There's a pool of blood on the ground where I'd fallen. I clamp my hand down behind my ear, almost screaming when a small tendril tries to reach out and grab my finger. The chip was still there, clinging to my flesh, rejecting its destruction. The dream of the boy who'd jumped from Josh's roof resurfaces. He'd ripped the chip clean from his head and lived. But it wasn't a dream. It was a memory I know to be true.

"Please don't let this kill me," I whisper.

I grab a pillow from the outdoor couch and bite down as I grab the last remaining tendril of the chip, prying it away from behind my ear. I groan into the pillow, shaking so hard I'm afraid that I might pass out again from the pain. My scream is absorbed in the fabric between my teeth, and I can feel yet another tendril pry free from my mind. My vision is hazy, making it harder to focus my energy on tearing away the device from my head. I don't have the energy to call out for him again in my mind. All I can do is pull.

There is movement in the tree line again, followed by a pair of deep, sunken eyes reflecting from my porch's light. Considering all my blood loss, hallucinations of a Shifter are not too far-fetched. The thing watches me from afar, wincing once I let out another loud groan. Closing my eyes, I think about the night of Josh's party again, feeling the coarse hands of Fallan as we danced and the mark of the boy running along my hand as he slipped from my grasp on the roof. My blood runs hot remembering the way the Officials hauled his body off, my mind racing through the words we exchanged. I think of the way Fallan allowed me to be near him that night, his back unscathed from my father. Does he remember that night? Why did I not remember it? How much of what I know has been planted by the "poison" in my mind the boy spoke of?

A few branches break, unsettling me fully once I open my eyes. The Shifter now stands in front of the brush, its body something out of a nightmare. Its skin is torn to shreds, barely clinging on in some areas. Where eyes once were, there are only deep, sunken pockets of nothing. It points a bony finger at me, listening to my pain.

"*Free yourself, Forest Blackburn,*" it says through my mind in a haunting tone.

It's like nails on a chalkboard.

With one final tug, I feel something break away from my head, hitting the deck with a clatter. The light glows red, blinking rapidly. Letting the pillow fall from my mouth, I clutch my wound, stomping my foot onto the chip, hitting it over and over. Its tendrils stop moving when it shatters, scattering amongst the glass and blood scathing the deck. I whip my head to face the Shifter, but there's nothing but empty space where it had been.

Nudging the sliding glass door with my elbow, I stumble into my kitchen, swiping Kai's bottle of Cure-All from his bag resting on the counter. I lean over the sink, spraying vigorously, feeling the skin begin to close until nothing but a scar remains. My front and hands are covered in a bloody mess, my motions clumsy from the blood loss.

Everything around me is unbearably loud, like a curtain being lifted from a screen. I feel the flood of emotions threaten to spill from me. With a drag of my mother's last, clean kitchen towel, I quietly rummage beneath the cabinets, grabbing the small spray bottle filled with bleach. I shove my brother's Cure-All into my pocket and rush back outside to the back deck. In a rush, I dump the bottle of bleach out, and wipe away any trace of my blood, watching the deck's wood lose color with each drag of the kitchen towel.

Kicking away the shards of glass and metal, I watch them fall off the edge of the deck and into my rag. I straighten my mother's pillows. My hand is unable to run through my hair, tangled in bloody knots. I shove the proof of what I'd done tonight in my pocket, giving the door handle one last rub with my shirt before locking the door and tossing my father's ID back on the counter where he left it. I run my brother's vile of Cure-All under the water, slipping it back into his bag once it is clean. Slowly, I back away from the sliding glass door, darting into the bathroom the first chance I get.

I turn on the shower and strip away my clothes, forcing them into the trash bin. Grabbing the bag with a heave, I quickly tie its end shut. Finally switching on the light, I stare at my ghost of a reflection in the mirror. My neck still has bruises, mostly faded but noticeable if close enough. The underneath of both my eyes are dark, leaving me more tired than awake. My skin is pallid, hugging me like I am nothing but skin and bones, a grotesque reminder of my frailty. I can smell my blood coating me, feeling my hair brush my lower back as the steam from the running shower makes sweat drip down my face. I rub my fingers along the skin behind my ear, and despite how the rest of my body feels, I smile at finding nothing there but my flesh.

"I had no choice," I whisper, wiping away the steam from the mirror to get a closer look at my eyes. "I had to do this," I finish, backing away from the mirror. I no longer have the energy to try and speak to Fallan. And given how much alcohol he had, there is no point in trying to get answers from him right now.

I finally make my way into the shower and let my body linger under the running water, watching my blood paint the shower tiles in swirls of red. I stand there transfixed until all of it is washed away and the water runs clear.

I force on the hoodie from the memory, running my fingers along the space where there was once an alcohol stain. The hoodie was shoved far back in my dresser; I'd done an impressive job making sure no one found it. Leaving my hair in a braid, I force the hood up and go back to the bathroom to coat my neck in as much concealer as I can.

I cram the bag of bloodied clothes and glass beneath my bed, keeping my clock unplugged as I pull on a pair of black leisure pants. I force my feet into boots, strapping my blade to my side beneath the hoodie. Glancing at my watch, it reads 5:00 am. Early enough, no one will be up and ready to question why I'm dressed oddly. I quickly move out of my room, silently shutting my door and glancing around at the still house. Slinging the bag over my shoulder, I check every single area I was in last night for any sign of blood I might have missed. I hike up the bag on my shoulder, unsure of where to go or how I will get there.

Shoving past the sliding glass door, I find myself back on the porch, rubbing my throat while observing the beaten camera. Following along the balcony steps, my legs bring me back to where the Shifter stood when watching me. There are no scorch marks or claw marks on the tree, making me question the validity of that interaction. I crouch down to the ground, running my fingers along the small layer of ash between the blades of grass. A crunch behind me has me grabbing my blade. I turn on my heels to meet my brother's confused expression. He holds up his hands, watching me roll my eyes at him as I tuck the weapon away.

"Good morning to you too, crazy," Kai says, crossing his arms. "Why are you dressed like that?" he questions, moving to lower my hood from my head. I grab his wrist, stopping him before it can reveal the bruises around my neck.

"I'm trying something new," I say, hearing the gravel in my voice. My throat is still stiff, and the swelling makes it hard for me to steady my tone.

No amount of Cure-All could have completely fixed the damage from the force of the hold Fallan's friend had around my neck last night.

"You sound like shit," Kai says, touching my forehead, checking for a cold.

"I'm fine," I say, swatting away his hand, "I snored too much last night," I clarify, hoping that's enough to satisfy his curiosity.

"Did you see that some asshole broke our porch camera last night?" Kai questions, expecting me to have an over-the-top reaction. I stay silent, leaning over to observe the tangled wires protruding from the side of our house.

"Good. I hated that thing anyways," I say, turning from him, sulking away, moving closer to the forestry behind the house and the ward that cuts our access to it off.

I step behind the forest line, running my hand along the ward, sensing Kai following me.

"Is there a reason you seem so off, or should I blame it on yesterday?" Kai questions, tapping the back of my head.

"I slept like shit."

It's not entirely a lie, but it's far from the truth.

I keep staring forward, pushing harder and harder on the invisible divider keeping us away from the ash-ridden world. Kai's hand reaches around my arm, stopping me from taking another step.

"What-"

"What are those?" Kai questions, pointing down at the ground.

I look down beneath my foot, moving away my heel to unveil the massive prints etched into the mud of the earth. Unknowingly, Kai looks at the impression of a

Shifter for a second time, becoming just as curious as he did the first time he saw one at the Academy the day after movie night. I frown, watching him genuinely believe this is his first time seeing the prints. I stare at his chip with newfound hate, unsure why I ever allowed something so vile to take up residency in my head.

"Would you believe me if I said they are Shifter tracks?" I question jokingly to see what he might remember.

Regardless of my desire to keep it on, I needed to lower my hood to get a better look at the scorched greenery surrounding the prints. Unlike the first set of tracks I saw at the Academy, these are larger. From here, I can now tell it lingered only a few feet from where I had been in a pool of my own blood, which begs the question – if it loves Marked blood so profoundly, why didn't it attack me?

"Holy shit!" Kai says, reaching out to touch the sensitive spot on my neck. I immediately slap away his hand, darting my eyes at his dumbfounded expression. "Are those *hickeys?*" Kai questions, smiling like an idiot. "Is that why you're acting so off?"

Oh, how I wish that were the case.

I force a half-assed smile, rummaging through my bag for any sign of my sketchbook to quickly document this new finding. My hand finds nothing but scattered odds and ends. I pry the bag open to get a better look. Where there was once a massive sketchbook filled with drawings I'd rather keep to myself, there is now nothing.

It's gone.

"Did you grab my bag after I had my seizure?"

"Yes, it was almost trampled by everyone trying to get a look at you. Are you avoiding my questions?"

I rise from my crouched position, ignoring Kai's questions. I run my mind through all the possibilities of where it could have gone, hitting a dead end each time I try to come up with an answer.

"So, you are ignoring me?" Kai questions, keeping up with me in long strides.

"I'm going downtown for a new sketchbook to draw those prints. I'm sure you can find some schoolwork to keep yourself preoccupied," I say, hoping he takes the hint to stay behind.

"And miss out on the opportunity of questioning you about your late-night activities?" Kai says, poking my neck with a smile. "Never," he finishes, looking satisfied with his response.

We follow along the side of the ward, not once passing an Official or citizen, given how dense the forestry can get. After Kai's eighth attempt at dragging my hood down, I finally decided to leave it down around my neck, but not before twisting his arm behind his back, which satisfied my irritation with him and this situation at some level.

His curiosity is justified, but in many ways, I barely have answers for myself.

"You don't think those were Shifter tracks.... Do you?" he questions.

I sigh, angered by the fact that he doesn't remember seeing those tracks before because his mind had been wiped clean, just like mine was supposed to be.

"What would you do if they were real?" I question, watching him think of his response.

"Most likely report it to an Official," Kai says, only urging me to keep my mouth shut.

"I'm sure they're from whoever decided to break our camera," I say, scrunching my nose anxiously.

"You're keeping something from me," Kai says silently, sounding the most serious he has this entire walk.

The smell of fresh bread from the downtown bakery hits my nose, and I can hear the quiet chatter of shopkeepers and patrons as people enjoy their day off. The stores are busy with life. The doors are constantly in motion, people carrying armfuls of goods in and out. The downtown area is lined with gray buildings, each made of concrete meant to support itself for years to come. Massive glass windows are plastered in each storefront, showcasing the goods within each business. Citizens scan their IDs to enter to keep Unfortunates out and away from the luxuries the stores provide.

"If I'm hiding something from you," I say, rubbing my hand along my throat, "I promise it is for your own good."

He looks hurt by my response, lingering back a few feet to process my words. I continue my march toward town, pulling my hood up again and ignoring Kai's fluctuating emotional state. A wall shields the back portion of the shops. There's a section low enough to jump over and make my way there.

I clutch my hand into the bricks, forcing my leg up and over the top, watching my brother's frantic eye movements as he surveys the area to see if anyone noticed.

"What are you doing? The path to the front of the shops is over here," he whispers, tugging at my pant leg.

"Can you just try to trust me?" I question, shaking away his grasp on my leg.

He stops, letting out a deep sigh. Kai runs his hands through his curls. His mind is at odds, struggling to understand the world around him for the first time.

"I don't know what to believe. All I know is my sister hasn't been normal for days, and my head feels like a jumbled mess. It feels like you are walking around with the weight of the world on your shoulders, and worst of all, you're shutting me out while you deal with it," he says, his face filled with sorrow.

"I can only tell you so much," I begin, reaching my hand out toward him, "So you'd better learn to trust me if you want answers," I whisper, waiting for him to walk away from all of this.

There's a moment of hesitation before he grabs my hand, forcing himself over the wall, too.

"Why are we walking behind the buildings?" Kai questions, anxiously fiddling with the buttons on his coat.

"So no one sees us," I turn toward him, "I thought that part was clear," I say, motioning to my outfit of choice.

"Is there any reason you are so avoidant of people all of a sudden?" he questions, looking at me with confusion.

I pause, trying to find the best words to say to him.

"Last night-"

A body moves before us, hurling a large beaten bag onto a wooden cart. I hear the figure grunt, struggling to force the bag off its slumped position on the ground. There are numerous baking supplies scattered amongst the bins out here. Some are older, while others are broken altogether. Kai puts his arm out, stopping me from taking another step. I watch the figure closely, seeing a familiar set of dark brown eyes and short brown hair. His dark complexion and kind smile are still visible from this distance.

"It's that Unfortunate who worked the booth at the movie screening," Kai whispers. I shove his arm down, giving him a look of disapproval.

"I know," I whisper back, moving away from my brother and closer to Hunter.

Hunter's head snaps up, looking more defensive the closer I approach. I see the worry flash over his face. The only thought I'm sure that's racing through his mind is that I am here to hurt him. Quickly, I pull down my hood, watching his figure relax when he recognizes me.

"Sorry, no popcorn today," he says with a smile, pausing his work of loading the supplies on the cart so he can wipe off his flour-coated hands.

"I know we've met before, but I'm Forest," I start, reaching out to shake his hand. "Your name's Hunter, right?" I question, feeling him hesitantly take my hand to exchange the gesture with a firm grasp.

I focus my energy on my brother, who I know wants to walk away, silently urging him with one look to come closer.

"It's the name my mom gave me," Hunter says, smiling ear to ear. He leans over to observe Kai's sudden presence. His arms are crossed as he watches us.

"Your twin?" he questions, and I'm surprised at the laugh that leaves me.

"Actually, I am a year older," Kai says, making sure to answer the question with a snobby tone.

"Don't be an asshole," I hiss, nudging him in the ribcage.

He shoots me a look of confusion, looking between Hunter and the bags.

"Are you stealing?" Kai questions, making me slap my hand on my face out of annoyance.

"No," Hunter says, giving me a somber look. "My family runs a bakery in my sector, so once a week they let me take the used and broken supplies your people don't need here in the market," Hunter says, pointing out the box of broken eggs and produce.

"Scraps," I finally say, shaking my head at the sight in front of me.

"They don't.... They don't give you new items in your sector?" Kai questions, genuinely curious for the first time in this whole conversation.

Hunter audibly laughs but quickly covers his mouth. I watch his face grow red. Kai's eyes go wide.

"I'm sorry, I didn't realize what I said was funny," Kai says, looking more flustered than usual.

I glance up at my brother, mouthing a "shut up" that only makes him shrug his shoulders at me.

"No, that was my fault. I didn't mean to laugh," Hunter says. "We are blessed to get what we have-"

"Our people give them nothing. Don't be modest," I say, cutting off the canned response I know Hunter is about to use to appease us.

Kai looks from me to Hunter, waiting for the man to confirm my words.

"We rarely get support," Hunter says, looking pained as he rubs his lower back.

"Did you hurt yourself doing all of this on your own?" Kai questions, struggling to hide the concern in his voice.

"I thought I had someone willing to help me," Hunter says, my eyes snapping to him, "I think he is still working off a hangover-"

"Fallan's here?" I question, watching Hunter and Kai both give me a confused look.

"How did you know I meant him?" Hunter questions. Moving towards Kai, I notice he has started picking up a bag to load onto the cart.

"Maybe that's who your late-night visitor was," Kai says sarcastically. "I was placing bets on Xavier, but maybe I'm wrong," he continues, only making my face grow redder once the thought of both men's hands on me fills my mind.

"I was kidding," Kai pauses, clearly noticing that I had grown flustered. "Did one of them visit you?" he pushes.

Even Hunter looks interested in my answer.

"Just pick up the bag," I snap, turning away from the boys.

Kai's face grows red, straining against the weight of the flour. It's not often he has to do any labor.

The two men work together to carry the bags, exchanging a few words that make Kai smile. I lean against the wall, watching the two interact. Kai is nervous and unsure of what to do or say. It is not in his nature to be cruel, and because of it, he has no way to uphold the ideologies of hate he has seen so often associated with Unfortunates. Hunter openly displays his kind and caring nature. He seems open to forgive or to forget, I'm not sure which, but it's an obvious difference from Fallan's inability to work towards some sort of meaningful connection between us.

"You didn't need to help," Hunter says, loading the last bag.

Hunter rolls up his sleeves, revealing several bruises up and down his arms. Kai's smile drops as he sees them. I take a step forward to get a better look, filled with a sudden anger. Hunter looks embarrassed, forcing his sleeves back down. I watch him rub the back of his neck, looking between us with a lowered head.

"Did an Untouchable do that to you?" I question, watching Kai's expression turn to something like anguish.

"It doesn't matter," Hunter begins, rubbing his eyes with his fingers, "I was out past curfew one night, and I gave an Official some lip. I just needed to get something for my grandmother-"

"They hurt you for just being out a little later? No rule was broken," Kai questions, looking confused by his words.

"Did you think they didn't hurt us for fun?" Hunter says, genuinely looking for an answer.

"I told you, Kai," I say, watching my brother's eyes dart to me once more. "I can only tell you so much. Sometimes, you must see it for yourself," I whisper, feeling the weight of the situation come down on him.

"How long have they done this?" Kai questions, receiving a laugh from both Hunter and me.

"Well, let's see," Hunter begins, giving Kai a smirk,

"How long have Unfortunates been around?"

CHAPTER TWENTY-SIX

FOREST

A clicking noise draws my attention upwards to find a security camera coming to life. I see it dial in on me, watching how its lens grows wider once it takes notice of my stare. I panic as it begins to move toward where my brother and Hunter stand talking. It can't see Kai talking to an Unfortunate here. It's treason.

I run to the wall we came from, prying away a loose brick, tossing it once in my hand to observe the size. The boys look over at me, letting their smiles drop, watching me look up before aiming at the camera.

"Forest-" Kai begins.

His voice is cut off by my arm tossing the brick. Watching it collide with the camera, it shatters on impact. The brick and pieces of metal all fall down the side of the building, freefalling until they hit the ground inches away from where I stand. I deliver the camera one last stomp of my boot, kicking it into the dirt, feeling satisfied with how well I managed to aim.

"Can I blame you for breaking the one at home, too?" Kai questions, looking dumbfounded.

Hunter's hands are clasped together. He is unsure how to react to my sudden need to destroy New Haven property. My brother is rigid and uncomfortable from my display of defiance. I crouch down to poke the device, ignoring my brother's question.

"It was watching us," I whisper.

"That camera looked like it hadn't been used in years," Kai says, crossing his arms. His face is filled with a look of disapproval. "And even then, what harm could it have done? No one did anything," he says, clearly having a moment of forgetfulness of what rules are in place.

I look over at Hunter, watching the gears turn in my brother's head once he realizes what has me so worried.

"Easy to forget it's a crime for them to talk to us, right?" I question.

Kai has nothing to say, looking from Hunter to the camera. Hunter is nearly done loading the cart. He only needs to move a few more crates before he's done. He sits on the edge of his cart, looking down the alleyway every few seconds with sideways glances.

"Are you waiting for Fallan?" I question.

"No, like I said, he's incredibly hungover. Last night, he looked thrilled, rambling on about some euphoric experience before throwing up all over my bathroom floor and pelting our buddy in the face. I dragged Valerie's cousin along with me to help here, but he's been occupied with a shopkeeper's daughter," Hunter says, tapping the face of his broken watch.

"Fallan 'pelted' someone?"

"Yeah, our friend, Valerie's cousin, Aaron. He was bragging about... something he had done last night, and Fallan laid in on him-"

"Who laid in on me?"

The voice is familiar and grates on my nerves. It's the one from last night, belonging to the person responsible for holding me down so hard I couldn't breathe. I watch him step into the light from the alleyway. I can see just how red his hair is in this lighting. Like flames in a fire, his head is consumed with red locks. His skin is scattered with freckles. He stands around the same height as Hunter, a few inches shorter than Kai. Cuts of varying sizes work up his chest, stopping on the tops of his hands from where my nails had got him. He carries a few armfuls of items, dropping them when his brown eyes meet my green ones. I lower my head at him, touching my neck, reflecting on the feeling of him trying to steal my life.

"Hunter.... Who are these two?" Aaron questions, acting as if his handiwork does not paint my neck.

"I must look different during the daytime," I hiss, answering before Hunter can get a word in.

Aaron's eye is bruised, and the skin is swollen, no doubt the result of being on the receiving end of a brutal hit from Fallan.

"What is she talking about?" Kai questions, pointing to Aaron with a look of confusion.

"Go ahead and tell them," I start, taking another step forward. "Tell them what you did, Aaron," I taunt, watching him tug at his collar.

"Is she why Fallan laid into you last night?" Hunter questions, giving his friend a shove. Gradually, his mind begins putting the pieces together. "Was she the Untouchable you boasted about 'scaring straight,'" Hunter says, angrily throwing up air quotes.

"Well, I-"

I grab the man's collar, forcing him down and onto the ground, giving him no time to think of a half-assed explanation for harming me. His back hits the Earth, jolting the contents he has indeed stolen in his pockets. With a knee pressed to his chest, I keep him down, seeing his eyes fill with fear for the first time. I draw my hand back, ready to deliver him another black eye. My eyes keep darting to his scars, thinking of Fallan's screams while they beat him.

"Fucking hell," I whisper, lifting the man up, only to slam him back down before angrily pulling myself off of him.

His clothes are covered with dirt, having no injury other than the one Fallan gave him. I hold my hand up to Kai, opening and closing my fists like Fallan does to calm himself. Hunter takes notice of this, staying quiet on the matter.

"You're not going to hurt me?" Aaron questions, receiving a flick in the head from Hunter.

Even Kai waits for me to respond, clearly enraged at the thought of Aaron hurting me last night.

"Fallan already did it for me," I say, wondering why he would go to such lengths to prove a point. "Consider it even," I say, watching Hunter's head shake.

"Who was the one Untouchable he said not to get near?" Hunter says, scolding his friend with another shove.

"Wait," I say, pausing their banter. "Fallan told you both to stay away from me?" I question, seeing Hunter nod while Aaron shakes his head no.

"He didn't want you getting involved in any Unfortunate drama that could get you hurt," Hunter says.

Aaron's eyes roll at the comment.

"Why would he care?" Kai questions.

"You know, I was hoping she would know the answer. He's never had any issues with any of the other jobs we've done in the Untouchable sector or laid into me for doing what I need to do with anyone else that's gotten in my way during a heist. I never thought the last name Blackburn would start popping up in our life again," Aaron says, crossing his arms angrily.

Again?

Hunter's flicks have grown into full-fledged punches toward the arrogant red-head.

"You do know I can still drag you out onto the street and beat your ass, right? Even if she doesn't?" Kai questions.

Hunter's lips curl up at the comment, his hand hiding the smile my brother's threat has managed to give him.

"Please do. Maybe then they will lay off me in my sector," Aaron says, scanning his nail bed with annoyance.

The back door to the bakery swings open, revealing the shop's owner. He observes the space around him with large eyes. I have seen him numerous times, catering my father's work events with pastries of all sorts. He scowls at the two men, only softening once he sees my brother and me.

"Are these two bugging you?" he questions, holding his rolling pin in his hand like a weapon.

"No-"

"No. We were passing through, decided to get some amusement watching them struggle to lift bags," Kai says, answering the question so casually, you would never know he's lying.

I nod at the comment, watching the baker smile. He kicks up dirt toward the two men.

"Between you and me, I think they barely deserve the scraps," he says, patting Kai on the shoulder, moving to do the same to me.

I grab the owner's hand, letting it linger in the air between us. Whatever relationship he thinks he has with us because of our father is not one I want to indulge.

"You'd better get back inside," I say, watching the pots on the stove behind him boil over. "You seem to be needed elsewhere," I continue, motioning my head toward his open doorway, squeezing his wrist with a tight grasp before letting go.

He exclaims at the gesture, moving away from us and back inside, closing the door with a swing.

"Not a fan of the baker?" Aaron questions, somehow making me smile at his sarcasm.

"Listen," Hunter begins, smiling while he rubs his hands along the front of his apron. "It's been great talking to you, but I have to get this all back before noon, and I'm sure Fallan is already wondering why we are so delayed, but thank you," he pauses, looking between my brother and me. "For everything," he finishes, keeping his eyes on my brother.

"If you two ever find yourselves in our sector and are looking for fun, you know who to look for," Aaron says, grabbing one end of the cart. Hunter holds the other. The wheels turn slowly, creaking to life with short movements.

"Wait," I say, moving closer to Hunter. "If you see him today, can you ask him something?" I question, waiting for Hunter to give me a nod.

"Can you ask him why he gave it to me if he would only take it back?"

The necklace. It's one of the many parts of last night I am struggling to wrap my mind around.

"Take what back?" Hunter questions.

I pause, unsure how much more to say.

"He'll know what I mean," I whisper, glancing at Aaron.

All Hunter can do is nod. I can tell he's wary of getting involved.

"I do hope our paths never cross again," I say, watching the redhead's smile grow once I look over at him.

"I have a feeling that won't be the case," he says, waving his fingers to my brother in a gesture I know is making Kai fume.

"It was nice meeting you," Hunter says, finally addressing my brother.

Kai gives him a small wave, crossing his arms, taking in as much as he can about the two men.

"I'll deliver your message. Maybe it will get him out of bed," Hunter smiles, motioning his friend to pull.

They both start dragging the cart down where they came from, their figures growing smaller the farther they move.

I turn around to face my brother, watching him tap his foot in anticipation.

"I need answers," he starts, not giving me the chance to plead my case.

"Starting with; why the hell you were alone with two Unfortunates last night?"

Chapter Twenty-Seven

Andrew

"Sir, you might want to come take a look at this," one of the new interns says with a great deal of hesitation.

I pry my eyes away from the list of things that need maintenance in the Unfortunate sector. The interns are looking over security footage of our sector, checking for any faulty cameras or slip-ups in our system. Two of them gaze at one computer screen, completely disregarding the other filled with the view of the New Foundation's Academy.

I slide my chair from behind my desk, using my legs to push me over to the pair training under me. I see the image of my house from another person's porch camera. On my porch resides two figures: my daughter and the figure of a person holding her up by her neck against the building. I jolt forward at the footage.

"Your neighbor's camera picked this up late last night. Whoever is holding her broke your camera before she stepped outside," One of the interns says, scrolling their thumb along the mouse as the video fast forwards. I watch my daughter's figure flail, doing her best to shove the person away. Her face is red from lack of oxygen. Even from here, I can see the Unfortunate mugging getup that common thieves from their sector often wear. I take over the mouse, scrolling faster, waiting for her to escape the hold. Seconds later, another figure approaches, grabbing and shoving what I can only assume is a man away from my girl. She drops to her knees, clutching her throat, unable to take a full breath.

"Was that one of our people that saved her?" I question, watching the pair exchange a look.

"We thought for a moment it was, but they're wearing the same mask as the one that held her down," the intern says, grabbing back the mouse to scroll ahead.

I stare wide-eyed at the visual of the masked savior clinging to my daughter, her legs wrapping around their torso as they remain inches apart.

Seconds later, his hood is down, and his mask comes loose. He watches her with those familiar blue eyes that I'd know anywhere, focused only on her.

I cannot look away from the screen. I tighten my grasp on the desk once Fallan's hands grasp her tighter.

She looks far from disgusted.

In fact, she looks enthralled.

"We did an image search on him," one of the interns begins, pulling up Fallan's profile on the screen. "He's an Unfortunate," they say disgustingly. "She failed to report any of this. The cameras in your area cut out moments after the Unfortunate leaves her behind."

"This is coming into us live," another intern says, cutting off the first, pulling up a video from downtown New Haven. I now see both of my children conversing with an Unfortunate. My daughter turns to meet our surveillance camera, all of us flinching as the brick she hurls destroys the feed, and the screen goes dark. Her green eyes are the last thing I see, before nothing at all.

"Sir, maybe we should consider bringing your daughter in to get her chip evaluated. It says here on her scorecard she's already had to be visited by Officials on two separate occasions, one of those trips resulting in her chip use. In just a day, she has managed to violate some of our most significant rules, and even worse, she seems to be having relations with an Unfortunate, which is a high-level violation, even for her-"

"How many people have seen these videos?" I question, stopping them mid-sentence. I rub my wrist with my left hand, feeling my coarse skin beneath the material of my shirt.

"So far, just us, but you must know we can't keep it between us, sir," the younger of the two interns says.

"And the status of the boy who saved her?" I question, ignoring their worries.

"He's Cleansed. He passed his expulsion test with flying colors. Your wife is the one who administered the test," they say, only growing my suspicions. Even if he was Joshua's son, Katiana would have caught his mark. She always does.

There's no way he could be Tainted. No one would allow themselves to receive a lashing like he had, all to keep a memory meant to be taken to protect him.

"Says here one of his parents passed away during the Thinning Act you and Adam carried out a few years ago," one continues.

Is that why he has gotten close to her? Does he remember something? Could he tell it was me under the mask that day?

"We had no choice," I hiss, reflecting on the bodies buried that day. "We were running out of resources."

I turn away from the pair, glancing at my desk, moving closer to one of my many drawers. With a quick input of my code on one of the locked drawers, I watch it slide open, revealing the cold, metal Re-Regulation Device meant only for emergencies. I take into account how many people linger near my office. Most people are at lunch. Others are entirely focused on their screens.

"We have to do what needs to be done. One of you close the blinds while we get this material together to send off. Lock the door as well. I don't need any unexpected visitors," I say, switching on the device. The two work diligently to follow my requests.

They don't question my orders or pay any attention to the device. There is a certain simplicity to the way the chips work. It is relieving to know that a simple line of command input into such a small device can wash away anyone's memories. Years or minutes of someone's life are gone in seconds.

But that isn't the case for my daughter, or the Unfortunate that she can't seem to shake. No matter how often we've been here, it's always the same result. Two souls locked into an eternity of never understanding the bigger picture.

The device blinks green, pairing with the interns' chips. A green light flashes behind the pair's ears as they finish their tasks. I watch them exchange a look before looking at me as I begin putting in the command. They raise their hands to their ears, wincing from the heat the chip is giving off.

"Sir, is your chip updating as well?" one questions, blatantly unaware of what I'm doing as I press in the commands.

Forget Footage of Forest Blackburn and Fallan Markswood.

Forget seeing me delete video footage.

Hitting the massive green key on the screen, the code begins to run. Both interns slump to their knees, their eyes rolling in the back of their heads in a haunting movement. I have two minutes to get on the computer, wiping both cameras clean of activity from the past two days. With a click, I shut off the camera in my office, adding it to the list of recordings about to become untraceable. With quick fingers, I work along their keyboards, converting all of their files of the footage into nothing as I ignore every label warning me that I am about to delete the footage forever.

I let my eyes linger on the visual of Fallan and Forest a few moments longer, finding pain in how they look at one another, completely unaware of what we stole from them.

Or maybe that's not entirely the case, and one of them is, in fact, aware that we are in this situation to begin with.

Glancing back at the timer, I conserve the last thirty seconds, wiping the three recordings clean from both devices and the system. Clicking the camera back on, I see the intern's eyes blink open, recovering their vision as the haze of the chip's control slowly begins to wear away. I sit behind my desk, closing the drawer with a thud, pretending to scan one of the many files on my desk. They rise to their feet, looking around the room while their altered memories finally settle.

"Sir? Were we in the middle of something?" one questions, making it that much easier to put down my file.

"You two were just reviewing footage. I asked you to close the blinds to remove the gleam on your screens, and you both just stood there. Is there a particular reason you're stuck there like statues?" I question, feeding into their confusion.

"I suppose not," they say, both of them holding their heads, wincing from the pain.

They return to their seats, not giving any of the files a second thought as they pick up where they think they left off. I rack my brain with the visual of Fallan, only growing more suspicious of why he would get near Forest knowing what we forced into his code.

Has his hate for me grown so immense that he's pushed past the memory block, or did he always remember what happened?

They spent hours on the operating table, their chips fortified with countless lines of code meant to keep them away from one another for years. How do two people with passed Expulsion tests and a formulated need to hate each other end up like this, inches apart in stolen moments of the night?

I run my finger over the rough skin beneath the cuff on my wrist once more, feeling the mark that lingers there.

"Please, let me be wrong," I whisper, forcing myself to my feet.

I reach for my jacket, shoving my ID into my coat pocket. Both interns turn to look at me.

"Where are you off to, sir?" they question, pausing their finger's rapid movements on the keyboard.

"Home, to speak to my daughter about some... family matters. Before either of you goes on lunch, I need one of you to debrief Adam and Xavier about a job. I want them to join me for first thing tomorrow in the Unfortunate sector," I begin, lowering my hat, my hand unlocking my office door.

"There's something that requires our immediate attention."

CHAPTER TWENTY-EIGHT

FOREST

"I'm struggling to understand your insatiable need to find a way to speak to their kind constantly," Kai says, doing his best to stay quiet as several passing patrons give my untidy outfit side glances.

I keep moving forward, ignoring his badgering. It's only been a few minutes since we decided to leave Hunter and Aaron, leaving my brother with more questions than answers, only growing his confusion.

Quickly, I ran into one of the shops, grabbing the first sketchbook I could find and paying abruptly before the shopkeeper had time to make small talk.

"Hunter was at the screening," I finally say, doing my best to make the interaction seem as casual as it felt in my mind. "I didn't see you complaining too much when he was talking to you earlier," I hiss, watching his face grow flustered at the comment.

"His conversation skills were more tolerable than some of our peers at the Academy. I was simply curious about him," Kai says, trying to keep any emotional value away from the conversation.

"And he was kind. You forgot to mention that part."

"You mentioned that Unfortunate boy to Hunter. The one I always see lurking near you... Fallan? Why is it that more often than not, I see him around you?" Kai questions, only furthering the same line of thinking I have yet to allow myself to explore.

"Fallan helped me out of some shitty situations, even when I didn't deserve it," I say quietly.

We continue walking, pausing once we reach a blind corner. My brother grabs my arm, pulling me behind the corner, making sure to scan the area for anyone familiar. He presses his finger to my lips, stopping me from getting a single word out.

"Are you and Fallan just... acquaintances?" Kai questions.

My face immediately grows hot, reflecting on what happened on the deck last night and the memory of Josh's party. I took a real risk asking Hunter why Fallan took the necklace from that night back. Who knows if he even remembers that night or if it's all just a delusion of my own mind's making? I'm sure Fallan has no clue what the question even means. Jewelry is worth money in their sector, and, whether I like it or not, Fallan is still one of them.

"What are you trying to ask me?" I question, pushing him to say the words out loud.

"You know what I'm trying to ask, Forest. Please, tell me you haven't gotten yourself *involved* with an Unfortunate," he says, enunciating his words to get his point across.

People continue passing the street corner, too invested in their conversations to focus on our bickering.

"At the end of the day, Kai, Fallan doesn't want anything to do with me. He hates me."

Justifiable hate.

"Whatever you think is going on between us is not anything that pleases me. Every time he looks at me, all I can see is anger in his eyes. So no, nothing is happening between us because if that were the case, he would be able to look at me for more than five seconds and not be disgusted," I say, letting the pain in those looks he gives register within me.

Kai pauses, closing his eyes to guide his thoughts.

"And when you turn away from him?" Kai questions, keeping his eyes closed while he speaks. "What do you think is painted on his face then?"

"I don't know," I admit, reflecting on Fallan's hands exploring my body, seeming to know exactly where to hold me.

"I do," Kai says, finally opening his eyes to look at me. "I have never seen someone look so tormented in the fleeting moments between when you look at him and turn away. It's a look that has haunted my mind for days. It's the only reason I haven't reported any of this," Kai says, pointing a finger at me.

"What's the only reason, Kai?" I push, moving myself away from the wall to look closer at my brother.

"That look, Forest. That look I saw on his face is the same look you have given me since that day at the screening," Kai says, forcing my heartbeat to pick up at the mention of the blood-filled event.

"What look do you mean?" I question, hearing the plea in my voice.

"A look of someone who knows too much and has lost more than you know," Kai says, making a lump form in my throat. "There is something you aren't telling me, Forest, and it all leads back to that night. Whether I like it or not, the answers I need include those two Unfortunates," Kai continues, my fears of his chip's sudden activation only growing.

The slight scuff of feet dragging across the ground is more than enough to make us pause our conversation; turning on our heels in unison, we watch people stop in their tracks as a set of Officials, Adam and Xavier, barge right toward us. Xavier looks hesitant, glancing at Adam sternly like he's preparing for him to lash out. Kai begins to position himself in front of me. This is the first time I've seen Xavier since our interaction at the hospital, yet having Adam with him makes things much more uncomfortable.

The two men pause before us, Adam crossing his arms in annoyance.

"Is there a problem?" Kai questions more sarcastically than normal, crossing his arms in a mimic as he peers at the two men.

"Your father said that he wants you home. It would seem one of you is not supposed to be running around," Adam says, leaning over to get a better look at my angry scowl behind Kai.

"He didn't tell either of us why he needed you, actually," Xavier says, ignoring the glare of his companion.

I finally step away from my brother to face Xavier fully. Smiling gently at him, I feel that familiar sense of security from being near him. Regardless, I still need to try and warn Fallan that they're here. I don't know if their presence is related to what happened last night, but if it is, he needs to lie low.

"Something is going on. My father is sending Officials out to drag us home," I say, feeling a slight tremor in my closed hand.

There are several silent moments as I walk behind Adam's rigid figure. He waves towards one of the many Official vehicles. I walk next to Xavier, feeling our fingers brush. He looks at me with worry, unsure what to do or say.

"How many of them?" Fallan finally responds, and I let out the breath I hadn't noticed I'd been holding in.

I still don't understand how we can talk to each other like this.

"Two. Xavier and Adam."

I feel a wave of nausea at the mention of both men's names, unsure of how it reached me in the first place.

"Was that feeling you just then?" I question.

"I can't say I'm fond of either man. This isn't the situation I hoped to wake up to," he says, making me gently smile. I hear the sleep in his voice. He must have one hell of a hangover.

"Do you think they plan on questioning us... about last night?" I say, feeling a wave of worry pass over me.

"We didn't end up going through with the heist, I doubt they even saw-"

"Us. I don't mean Aaron and you, Fallan. I mean us!" I shout in my mind, finally allowing myself to address the elephant in the room. A deep-rooted sense of fear washes over me. It starts in my chest, working through my fingertips, only to end in the form of shaking through my body.

"Are you cold?" Xavier questions, touching my lower back. I try to shake away the fear in my body, feeling every bone inside of me rattle.

"Fallan?" I question, only giving Xavier a nod as Adam shoves my brother into the back of his car.

Xavier scowls at the man, moving me along more gently as he urges me to get in the back with Kai. I oblige, sliding in next to my brother. Our knees touch. We huddle together in the back seat, unsure of what will come.

"What did you do to your chip?" Fallan questions, any sound of playfulness void from his voice.

"You said it would kill me, and it didn't-"

"What did you do, Forest?!" Fallan yells, his voice breaking with emotion. My mind rattles at the question, and my throat grows dry.

"I set myself free," I whisper, feeling that pain again. *"Why did you lie to me?"* I push.

Xavier looks back from the passenger seat, giving me another easing smile. All I can do is close my eyes, ignoring Adam's backward looks at my brother's angry demeanor in the rearview mirror.

"You did more than rid yourself of the chip," he whispers, his voice barely recognizable under the cloud of emotion. *"You did the one thing that will ensure I don't stay away this time,"* he whispers.

This time?

"Fallan, none of that makes sense," I say, feeling my anxiety heighten the longer I am near Adam and the gun strapped to his side.

"I need to get to your sector," he says, making my worries grow. *"Whatever you do, avoid a Re-Regulation Device. They will be able to see you have no chip. Once they know that, you're their biggest threat,"* Fallan says. My hands tap my legs in nervous jolts.

"Tell me why you know so much, and I know so little," I prod, seeing the outline of my neighborhood come into perspective. Several moments pass before he answers softly.

"They wanted to torture me, Forest, not you. You were the one way they could do that.... Someone else is trying to take up space in your mind. I have felt it for days-"

I feel my heart pain at his response, filled with more questions than answers. Fallan's voice is cut off, replaced by a pressure behind my eyes. The car rolls to a stop, both Officials receiving a stream of texts, no doubt from my father. Xavier moves to open my door, giving Adam a nasty look as he pulls my brother free from the car. I feel a wave of emotions work through me, each more confusing than the next.

I hadn't realized I'd grabbed Xavier's hand, walking in mindless thought toward my front door. He didn't stop me, allowing me to cling to his hand with a shaky grasp.

"Is something going on?" Xavier questions, quickly asking the question with worry. Adam nudges my brother forward, watching him stumble.

"What the hell is your problem?" Kai yells, swinging back at Adam, nearly hitting his face.

Xavier grabs my brother's fist, giving him an apologetic look in hopes of calming him down. I watch my brother's anger die down. Adam laughs in his face, taunting him.

"Fallan?" I question, feeling an unusual silence in the presence of something lingering at the back door of my mind.

"Adam, go wait in the car," Xavier says, lowering my brother's hand. His companion scoffs.

"Boy, you know-"

Xavier's hands are around Adam's collar within the blink of an eye, shoving the man back so hard into the house he almost falls to the ground. I watch Xavier pin the man against the wall, quickly putting him in a position with no easy way out.

"What the hell is going on?" my father's voice booms.

He stands in the doorway, watching the scene unfold before him. My brother and I both give him a look, taking a step back with Xavier, all of us watching Adam slump to the ground.

"He was being rough with your children," Xavier lets out, having no regrets in his actions against his superior.

My father pinches the bridge of his nose, finally forcing his gaze toward me. His hand reaches for me, grabbing my collar to pull me closer to him. Xavier almost reaches for me first, quickly deciding not to the minute he sees the anger on my father's face. Kai grabs my free arm, stopping my father from being able to pull me any further.

"This doesn't involve you, Kaiden," my father hisses, using my brother's full name, while he continues pulling.

"Whatever you have to say to her, you can say to me too," Kai begins.

My father gives Xavier and Adam a look. Xavier looks hesitant, clenching his jaw in anger as he pries my brother's hand away from my arm, promptly shoving him back and into Adam. They both prevent Kai from following us. My head snaps to my father, giving Kai one last look of worry before feeling my legs force themselves into unison with my father's steps. My body drags across the floor, eventually being tossed into my father's study.

He slams the door, giving me a look of irritation. I pound my fists on its wood, ready to yell out for my mother. His hand is on my shoulder, squeezing tightly while guiding me down and into the nearest chair. He applies as much pressure as he can, keeping his weight down on me to keep me within his grasp. I thrash my shoulders, looking up at him with anger.

"Get the fuck off of me!" I yell, unsure of how willing I am to act on the energy surging through me.

"Do you have any idea what you've done? What you've made me do?" my father questions in a low tone. His computer screen is flipped away, shielding whatever paints his screen in bright light.

"I have no idea what you're talking about-"

"Stop lying!" my father yells, grabbing my face in his hand with a clutch so tight my skin is surely bruised. I feel the scrape of a presence in my headspace, urging me to fight back.

"How long have you been around him? How long has it been since he found you?" my father questions.

My stomach drops.

"What the fuck are you talking about?" I question, nudging my body forward to get out of his grasp.

He shoves my face away, easing the tension in my jaw. Angrily, he moves to his computer screen, flipping around the monitor to show me the one visual I had hoped he wouldn't. It's distant but clear enough to make out who it is. Fallan's hands are all over me, holding me up and against him, still managing to fill me with an incurable need to be near him, even from a digitized state.

My father's eyes are wide between glances at me and the monitor. I slowly rise to my feet, watching him switch the screen from that night on the deck to earlier today behind the shops, all of my severe violations on display like glaring red flags.

"Do you sympathize with the scum now?" my father questions, minimizing the tab that dissolves itself into a file labeled "*Project X.*" There are multiple files with different dates, most dated over the last two years.

"It was a slip-up," I start, doing my best to justify my actions. "And it wasn't his choice. I forced it onto him." I continue.

"I tried to keep him safe," my father says, running his hand along his mouth in a frustrated tick. "I told Joshua I would keep him safe and told myself each time I input code for the two of you that it would be different," my father continues, fidgeting at his desk, finishing off what's left of the glass of scotch. "Every time, I think it's different, but we always end up back here," he continues, pulling out the one thing that ruins it all.

A Re-Regulation Device.

"Who's Joshua?" I question with a wobble in my tone, feeling my fears rise as my father switches on the device.

"Fallan's father," he begins, looking up at me with sorrow. "My best friend," he continues, drawing more blanks in my mind as I try to recall us being around anyone named Joshua growing up.

"Your mother said you would forget Fallan so long as you never found your connection with him. We thought making you hate him would be enough this time. Hours in her medical clinic, utilizing the full extent of your chip's capabilities to lock away those memories, all of which are reduced to a few files on a computer. Why couldn't you just leave it all alone?" he says, glancing at the screen.

"What are you doing, Dad?" I question, stepping back as he raises the device toward me.

"Any world in which you believe he is alive won't work. I can't protect him, or you if I let your connection grow. Each day, you seem to get closer to a reality I cannot protect you from. An hour in your mother's clinic, and we can properly ensure you get the help you need to save you both," he continues.

I back into the study's door, jiggling the lock that won't budge. My father stands before me, pressing the device to the side of my head. I stare him down. His brows are furrowed in frustration as he waits for the blinking light, indicating the connection to my chip that will never come because of what I did.

"Why? Why make me forget him?" I question shakily, watching his eyes pass over my own with despair.

"You wake a sleeping giant within one another, a giant that they will come looking for," my father says, the smell of alcohol brushing against my nose. "If they find you, I'll have failed you both," he says, my throat burning with fear.

"Who are 'they' Dad?" I question, unsure if I want the response.

"They won't find you," he says. His words roll off his tongue with ease.

"No chips matching, Forest Blackburn," the device announces robotically.

My dad's eyes fly up to me, touching the space behind my ear with wide eyes. I take the moment of his confusion to shove him away, forcing my back against the door and using my legs to get him as far away from me as possible. He drops the device, letting it hit the floor with a thud. My hand encloses around the small device, shakily looking over its confusing screen, seeing the broad list of chips nearby. I see Kai and Adam quickly deleting my brother's name from the list of favorites. I point the device at my father, watching his name pop up on the screen. His chip blinks slowly as it begins to pair. He rises to his feet, holding his hands up in surrender.

"You removed your chip?" he questions, his voice shaky.

"I removed their poison," I correct him, lowering my eyes at him in anger.

"H-how are you not dead?" my father questions, his eyes seem hopeful I have an answer.

"Maybe I didn't do it alone," I say, reflecting on the Shifter from last night, urging me to set myself free.

I click my father's name, watching the worry pass over his face. I see the code now, waiting for me to type my first command.

"If you make me forget this, Forest, there is no guarantee I can protect you. The Marked-" he begins, I cut him off.

"The Marked are not the threat," I whisper, typing in my commands.

"I know," my father begins, undoing the buttons on his arms as he begins to work on moving up his sleeves.

Forget the footage you've seen of your daughter and Fallan Markswood. Delete all evidence and do not investigate what happened.

I type in, watching him move in my peripheral.

"The Marked roam among us in plain sight," my father says shakily, trying to pull me away from my focus.

"Me included," he whispers.

My head snaps up, almost dropping the device once he holds his wrist up for me to see. A mark as clear as day coats his skin, the same mark that paints my upper hip. I feel my hand lower the device to my side, my mouth hanging open. A flood of questions begins to enter my mind, ready to make me implode.

"Your mother and I thought we could protect your secret," he says, squeezing his eyes shut as he speaks. "We thought we could protect you from him," he finishes, making a thought pass over my mind.

"Who's him? Fallan?" I question, feeling nauseous once he shakes his head no.

"There's so much you don't know-"

"Will you keep coming after them?" I cut him off, watching his brows drop, "Will you keep coming after Fallan and all of the other innocent Marked and Unfortunates?" I question, watching his frown drop.

"It's not my call-"

"Will you?" I question again, feeling my emotions threaten to explode from me.

He pauses, both of us aware of an answer neither wants to say out loud.

"I don't have a choice," he begins, looking utterly broken.

I slowly nod my head, feeling a tear roll down my cheek.

"Then neither do I," I whisper, hitting the device's screen, watching him clutch his head, surging toward me. His hand grabs my wrist, forcing it down and onto the side table as he shoves away the device. I make eye contact with him, watching his chip blink in the same fashion mine had.

"That does not work as easily on us," he says, grasping tightly around my wrist. I writhe away, catching a glimpse of my reflection in the mirror closest to us. I half expect to see my flailing figure wrestling with my father, only to be startled by the image of myself standing still, watching me with a taunting gaze and unnerving smile.

"Well, if that won't work, I guess you'll just have to do it yourself," my own voice taunts me. The mouth of my reflection in the mirror moves as mine stays still.

For reasons beyond my knowledge, I raise my hands to the sides of my dad's head, grasping his temples once my back collides with the floor. I drag him down with me, feeling a surge of energy work through me as I visualize every incriminating thought he could have of me and Fallan being pulled away from his mind. His eyes close while he takes in a sharp breath. My palms feel hot and full of energy. I take in the space around me, glancing back at the mirror, which now reflects real-time.

"Forget all the treason you have seen. As far as you know, Fallan is harmless and nothing has changed," I whisper, feeling my emotions well at the sight before me. I pull my lips closer to my dad's ear, watching his motionless face absorb my commands.

"I'm sorry, Dad. Please, rest once I let you go, and don't wake up until I leave," I mutter, feeling his body become slack as his energy leaves him. Slowly, I lean him into the nearest chair, forcing myself up and away from him as I take several sharp breaths. I make my way to the mirror to confront the looming presence that's suffocating the space.

"Who are you?" I question in a slow gulp, leaning my head against the mirror and shutting my eyes afraid of what I'll find.

"*I'm you,*" it says, running its finger along the other side of the glass. "*More specifically, the part of you that chip was hiding,*" it says, giving me a sideways look.

"Why hide you?" I question.

"*Oh, honey,*" it says, giving me a wink. "*It's so easy for them to call the better parts of our strength 'hallucinations.' Makes it less real for them.*"

My eyes open, leaving me in the middle of my father's study. His body sleeps peacefully, still in the same position I had left him. The image in the mirror is normal, no longer jaded by a perception of myself that brings me unease. I look back at the file on my father's computer, sliding into his seat as I rummage through his desk for a hard drive. I rapidly copy all the files, letting each upload to the small memory saver, glancing at the door every few seconds. Each file loads quickly, only to be removed from the computer moments later. I quickly scan each video, feeling increasingly uneasy each time I see Fallan and my face in the files. In some videos, we are speaking to one another. In others, we are separate. Years of our lives are in these files, some events more painful than the next. The dates were years ago. All moments void from my mind, and possibly his. My eyes land on the oldest file, fumbling to read its title.

"Forest/Fallan Expulsion Test," I whisper, dragging the file to the hard drive and letting the cursor hover over the video.

Hesitantly, I ready myself to move it to the trash, wanting nothing more than to leave this space. I look back at my dad, tapping my fingers against his large desk.

"I need to remember," I whisper, pulling myself away from the desk and deleting the last file before taking the hard drive. I move toward the door, passing my taunting reflection once more, stopping in my tracks.

"If you want answers, then we'd better start from the beginning," the other me taunts, pressing its hand to the glass, watching me shove the hard drive deep into my pocket.

I glance at its hand, unsure of my best move.

"I don't bite. After all, I am you," it whispers, motioning for me to touch the glass.

I stare at my eyes in the mirror, silently cursing, before pressing my palm into the glass, letting the shockwave of memories flood into me.

CHAPTER TWENTY-NINE

FOREST- EXPULSION TEST, 16 YEARS AGO

I swing my legs in the chair, half expecting myself to be able to brush the floor. *Kai is dead asleep on the chair next to me, leaning up against my father in a fatigued state. Only moments ago, had he finished his placement test, scoring as high as humanly possible, no doubt. My father nudges my head every so often, giving me soft smiles between responding to messages on his phone. I stare at the giant steel door, expecting it to swing open at any moment.*

An Unfortunate woman sits to the left of us. Every so often, she looks at my father, giving him a confusing look. He only returns her gaze with a lowered head. Her hair is dark as night, and her eyes are as blue as an ocean. In many ways, she is very pretty for an Unfortunate, able to pass as one of us had she been given the proper clothing. She wears a gold ring around her wedding finger, its band made of twisting vines, creating a beautiful piece of jewelry.

She waits patiently, most likely for her child, no doubt.

"I'm thirsty," I whisper to my dad, him only half paying attention to my statement.

"There's a water fountain just around the corner," my father whispers, looking slightly startled once Kai decides to stir. "I can take you. Let me get your brother up."

"No," I say, stopping him from saying another word. "I can take myself," I push, doing my best to sound as adult as possible. He gives me another smile, crossing his arms while he playfully taunts me.

"You sure you're up for it? Who's this 4th year that has replaced my little girl?" he questions, only making me giggle.

I hurry off my chair, giving him a slight bow as I walk away. He laughs at the exchange, only to glare at the woman beside us once I'm almost to the corner. I make eye contact with her, watching her express sadness before lowering her head. I follow the signs to the fountain, taking a sharp left, meeting the dead-end hallway with nothing but a door and the fountain. A sign above the door says, "Unfortunate Test Exit." Taking three long gulps, I enjoy the water, not once noticing the sudden presence lurking nearby.

"The water over here is much colder," a boy's voice says, almost making me spit up my mouthful of water.

I turn around, locking eyes with a dirtied, Unfortunate boy sporting the same black hair and blue eyes as the woman from the waiting room. He looks frail, patiently waiting behind me for a drink. I wipe my mouth as I step aside, observing the gauze wrapped around his pointer finger like the last child I saw exit the testing area. Mom says never to ask about people's wounds after the tests. She says if I ask, I'll get more marks on my scorecard.

"I'm not supposed to talk to you," I say, shifting on my feet while watching him take several sips from the fountain.

"I know," he says, "Doesn't mean you can't listen," he finishes, giving me a brief smile. I can't help but return the gesture, watching him wince each time he moves.

His hands, I now see, are not just cut in one place. They are cut everywhere, jagged red lines marking several of his knuckles on both hands.

"How did that happen? I thought hospitals were supposed to fix stuff like that?" I question, watching him glance down at his hands.

"I came here for my test. They don't give us much else," he says sadly, running his worn hands under the cool stream of the fountain.

I fumble in the small bag I brought, filled with a few colored pencils and papers meant to keep me entertained. My hands make contact with the bottle of medicine my mother makes me and Kai carry around. Stealing a glance around the space, I see no one, and I hold up the bottle with an enormous grin.

"How did you get one of those?" the boy questions, smiling gently as he showcases his many missing teeth. I can't help but giggle at his excitement, unsure why he could be thrilled by such an everyday item.

"My mom made it, so in return, she makes me and my older brother carry it around with us," I say, nudging it closer to his hands.

"I-I can't take that from you," he says, lowering his hands to his sides like they are glued there.

"You're not taking it," I say, grabbing his hands, spraying them generously with the light mist as the wounds begin to close. "I just felt like letting you use it," I say, smiling ear to ear at the look of relief on his face as his wounds dissipate into nothing. Unlike my hands, his are worn and dirtied. Still, I let them stay within my own, holding them close to my eyes for observation until each cut is gone. He raises his hands from my own with flushed cheeks, rocking back and forth on his feet.

"You look like the lady who did my test," he says after a few moments.

"That lady was probably my mom," I say, touching his finger gently.

"She says I'm not supposed to ask you how you got that," I whisper, watching his eyes grow wide.

"My mom said I'm supposed to pretend like it never even happened," he says, watching my frown consume my face.

"Did it hurt?" I question, watching his shoulders shrug.

"It helps if you close your eyes," he says, inching closer as he cups his hand around my ear. "Between you and me," he whispers. "They make you cut yourself. My mom says to just go along with it and say nothing, and you get the best score card," he finishes, pulling away with a large grin.

"You cut yourself? With what?" I question, watching him glance around.

"There is a tool on the counter. Use it when they tell you to and give your finger a small cut," he begins, pressing his finger to my lips. "But don't say anything about it. Just be quiet and do what your mom says. That's how you get the best score," he says, lowering his hand as quickly as he brought it up—looking embarrassed by his sudden movements.

"I don't have many friends in my sector willing to give up Cure-All like that," he continues.

"I don't have any friends my parents didn't force on me," I say, looking at my shoes angrily.

"What's in your bag?" he questions, pointing to the drawing I had made in the lobby.

It is nothing special. Just a few flowers, all in a big meadow, expanding to the edges of the paper on both sides.

"Hopefully, a picture of what the future will look like," I say, pulling out the paper to show him.

He carefully takes the paper in his hands, running his fingers along the front, tracing each tiny detail.

"Can I keep it?" he questions, looking to me hopefully for an answer.

"You want my drawing?" I question, half expecting him to tell me he is joking.

"Makes me have hope I'll have a future," he says with a grin. I slowly nod my head, yes, watching him fold the paper, concealing it in one of his many pockets.

"I thought Unfortunates were supposed to be mean," I say, watching his head tilt at my statement.

"I thought Untouchables were supposed to be ugly, soulless elites," he says, only making me smile.

"My name's Forest, by the way," I say, hearing my father's phone start to ring loudly.

"Forest? I like it. My name is Fallan-"

"Forest!" my father says, staring down the hallway, keeping my brother's sleepy figure perched on the chairs.

"Oh! I'm sorry, Dad, I was just-"

He drags me away from Fallan, pulling me up as he gets a hold of me. I watch the woman from the waiting room silently move past my father, picking Fallan up quickly. She looks frail, holding the boy close to her with shaky hands.

"They were speaking to one another, Mariah," my father hisses at the woman, observing me up and down, inspecting every part of me he can.

"They're children, Andrew," the woman says, moving past my father and me. My dad grabs her arm, stopping her dead in her tracks. Fallan and I exchange a look, both of our heads nuzzled on our parents' shoulders.

"Tell Joshua I don't want to see his boy near my child again. Consider what my wife did my final act of kindness to the Markswoods," my father says, keeping my head down with his hand.

"You're a sheep wearing a wolf's skin, Andrew," he mutters. "You can walk, talk, and live like them, but deep down," she whispers. "You know those calluses on your hands will never hide who you really are, where you're really from," she whispers, giving me a slight glance.

"Do not speak to me like that in front of my daughter. I suggest you take your boy and leave," he says, motioning his head backward, urging her to go.

She takes the opportunity to move past us, listening to her son's quiet words as he shows her his hands. She looks confused, touching his healed knuckles with her cut and worn hands. I hear her ask him who fixed them, watching his blue eyes glance back to me again, my name leaving his mouth. Her eyes move around to meet mine. I take the opportunity to wave goodbye to the pair, seeing his toothy grin once more, before watching them disappear behind the corner.

"I don't ever want you speaking to one of them like that again," my father says. "Especially anyone in that family." He carries me back down the hallway I'd come

down. "Clearly, you still need an escort," my father barks, moving to set me down next to Kai as the door finally flies open, revealing my vivacious mother. She wears a mask that conceals her smile, but I can see it in her eyes.

"Are you ready?" my mother questions, motioning my father to bring me over.

Something tells me I'll be going with her whether I am or not.

"What the hell is all of this?" I question, watching the reflective version of myself stand in the testing room with me. We both observe a younger version of myself patiently sitting in the operating chair, watching my mom typing away at her computer. She scrolls through my file diligently. "Why can't I remember this?" I push, watching the other me lean against the chair.

"It probably has a little something to do with blue eyes and his mom out there, for starters," it says, rolling its eyes at me. "That delicious, deviant Unfortunate has been fond of us for quite some time. I'm glad you're warming up to him as much as I have.... Although, there's something about blondie that is so enticing," it whispers, my head pounding as my reality continues to come unraveled.

"I still can't figure out who's trying to get in. You see, Fallan, we want Fallan in our mind because, well, we are linked. But that unknown bastard pounding on the back door is starting to get on my nerves," it whispers, making me suck in a breath with confusion.

"What bastard?"

"If I knew the answer to that, they would be feeling a world of pain right now for trying to tamper with our minds."

"Why are you showing me all of this? Why now?" I question, running my finger along the scar on my pointer finger.

"To show you why you can't shake our raven-haired friend," it says, pointing to the door I had followed my younger self through.

"He's never been in this memory before," I say, running my hands through my hair. "Every time I reflect on this memory, it was just me sitting in this chair and then-"

Then nothing.

I pause, watching my younger self glance at the cabinet beside the chair. I cock my head at the cabinetry, my eyes landing on a shiny scalpel out of its packaging.

Its end is still coated in blood, unsterile and unmeant for my hand. The cameras in the room are off, each one limp and void of life.

"Starting to remember a little more, hmm?" it questions from behind me, squeezing my shoulders as I whip around, half expecting to see my own cat-like eyes. This reflection of me has hair that's nearly completely white. It's fully encapsulated by the gray my mother tries so hard to hide. My eyes seem brighter reflected back to me, no longer a forest green, but rather something light and unknown. Its presence dissolves, and once more, it's just me, observing the memory as if it's the first time.

I watch my younger self hop down from the chair, silently tiptoeing past my mother and closer to the cabinet.

"Just a few more minutes, honey," my mother says, blatantly unaware of my hand's reaching for the scalpel. I take a few more steps toward my younger self, watching her turn the blade in her hand, giving it one look before quickly slicing the tip of our finger. With a clatter, she drops the scalpel, clutching her finger as she begins to lean into the cabinets, unable to control her emotions—my small body flails, full of jolts and unnerving movements. My mother springs up from the chair in horror, grabbing my small figure with worried hands, quickly finding the cut, only to be horrified by my shaking body.

"Forest, what did you do?!" she questions, quickly healing the wound as she looks around for what I'd used. Her hands grasp the scalpel, looking it over with wide eyes. My body slowly stops shaking. My eyes quickly blink back to normal.

"Forest, did you cut yourself with the scalpel on the counter?" my mother questions. The tears rolled down my young face.

"He said it would get me a better scorecard!" I grovel, pressing my emotional sobs into my mother's chest. She looks worried, yanking something from her rolling tray as she begins pushing my hair away from my ear.

"Forest, what you just did creates a connection you cannot even begin to understand. One that will put you and that boy at risk," she raises the Re-Regulation Device, turning the dial up all the way, quickly pairing it with my freshly inserted chip. She had taken the liberty of implanting it in our bathroom at home before I had come to the med units. I watch my younger self blink back tears, flinching away as she holds the device close to my head.

"This will only be able to make you comply for a few moments. Your brain fights the chip like no one else I've seen," she says, reaching into her pocket and pulling out the same pill she's had me take every day for as long as I can remember.

"As long as you take this, Forest, your chip will work as best as it can, and you can live a normal life," she whispers, moving the pill closer to my lips.

"Momma," I pleaded. "What's wrong with me?" I cry out, watching tears slide down her cheeks.

"You're special, Forest," she says. "And they will snuff out anything special," she finishes, forcing the pill in my mouth as she leans my head back.

I stumble backward, watching my mother force the medicine into me. I back into another body, feeling even less comforted as my reflection looks over me, stopping me from falling.

"Guess the little pill wasn't for hallucinations after all," it says with a smile.

I grasp my head, doing my best to process everything I've just seen.

"My parents.... They know? They know about me; they know about Fallan-"

"All while hiding our memories and convincing us that we were crazy," it says, taking another step toward me.

"We are not the same," I say, watching it scoff at my statement.

"I am you. The fact you're seeing me means you finally have some clarity. A word of advice?" it says, taking another step. "Don't put another fucking drop of New Haven's 'medicine' into your mouth!" it says, glancing back at the doorway, patting my pocket with the hard drive.

"And get our ass to the Untouchable sector. I think there's a long-time friend there we'd both like to see."

Chapter Thirty

Forest

I fall to the ground, my hand pulling away from the mirror and my now regular reflection. I glance around me, patting my pocket with the hard drive, feeling some tension ease once I feel it beneath my fingertips. I hear my father's messaging systems sound off, lighting up his computer's screen with new notifications. His body begins to jolt from his position on the floor, moving with each phone vibration.

Quickly, I run my hands under his desk, finding the switch that ensured the door would remain locked during our conversation. With one more look at him, I nudge the door open, spilling into the hallway.

I hear several voices coming from the living room, my mother and Adam two of the most prevalent. I quickly sprint for my room, forcing myself into the space and heading directly to the bathroom. Without a second thought, I grasp the medicine bottles in my cabinet, dumping the pills down into the toilet, watching their colors bleed into the water.

I flush the toilet, and they go down in seconds, leaving me with two empty bottles and a year's worth of lies.

My door creaks open, my hands already hiding the empty bottles. I brush a piece of my lighter hair behind my ear, now seeing large strands of gray that are more pronounced than before.

"It's just me," Xavier's voice says, relaxing me instantly.

I pull away from the bathroom counter, watching him close my door, flipping the lock. I let out a small sigh, pressing my head to the doorframe that separates my bedroom from my private bath. He works his way over to me, glancing into the bathroom quickly before pulling his attention back to me.

"You were in there with him for a while. Your mother was pacing the whole time-"

"Do you know?" I question, abruptly cutting him off. He looks down at me, trying to read me for more context.

"Do I know what?" he questions.

I raise my hand behind his ear, ready to meet the solid metal of his chip. My heart skips a beat as I feel an absence where his chip would reside. His hand quickly reaches up, grabbing my wrist and moving me backward into my dresser. He makes sure not to let me hit it, keeping his hand braced on my lower back, only to keep me pinned with his leg. My eyes fly up to his. I feel a panic creep into my chest. Xavier's hand reaches up, brushing behind my ear, letting his fingertips linger on the new scar there.

"I guess I'm not the only one who questioned the validity of those things being in our head," he says, his hands on my lower back.

"Are you-"

"Tainted? Marked? No, I'm just extremely defiant when it comes to following rules. But that's not the case for you, is it?" he says, cupping my face with both hands, easing up his leg's firm position between my own. My mind goes numb, the fear of his question settling in my thoughts.

"I'm not sure what I am," I answer honestly, still not ready to give him the whole truth.

"You know what they're doing with them?" I question, feeling how his thumb rolls over my cheeks, bringing warmth to the skin.

"I know what they have done and will continue to do. How did you manage to pry away a chip and live to tell the tale?" he questions, my hand running along the space behind his ear where a scar should be if he'd removed his chip, too.

"You never got one?" I question, watching his jaw clench.

"I came to New Haven much later than most," he says, the black ink revealing something painting the skin beneath his collar bone, concealed almost entirely by his uniform.

I lower my hand from his head, leaning my body into him, feeling his arms enclose around me. His body radiates warmth. A warmth I could live in. A heat I felt in every fleeting memory I have of Fallan. I think of his blue eyes and how his black curls frame his face. Those eyes hold onto me like something from a dream

I do not want to wake from. Yet here I stand, seeking that same comfort from another.

"Your father has assigned me and Adam to pay your Unfortunate friend a visit," Xavier says, his grasp slightly tightening around me.

My father may not remember all of his newfound anger toward Fallan, but that does not mean he did not share his worries with those closest to him.

"He asked you to see Fallan?" I question, watching a quick look pass over Xavier's eyes, disappearing before I can think too much about it.

"He asked us to do more than see Fallan. He asked us to make sure he doesn't come near you again," Xavier says, my mind racing back to the footage.

"How much do you know about him?" I question, keeping my head pressed to his chest, unable to look at him.

"I know you and your brother have treated him and his companion with respect our people don't think they deserve."

He doesn't know about what happened on the porch.

"I will do what I can to make sure he and his friend don't get hurt," Xavier says, pulling my chin up to look at him.

"I wouldn't mind Adam receiving a few hits of his own," Xavier continues, flashing his perfect smile down at me.

So different from the rest. Someone willing to break every norm, no matter what it means for him.

"When is he making you go?" I question, watching Xavier's head shake.

"Could be today, could be tomorrow. They're keeping tabs on him, and your dad is going to reach out to us when he wants us to leave."

No wonder my father's devices were going off. When he wakes, he will see all the messages and only have one train of thought... visiting Fallan.

The door to my father's study slams shut, followed by the loud footsteps of him walking toward the living room. Xavier's pocket glows bright, buzzing to life with each new message. We both look at its screen as he pulls it out.

Deviant left his home. Time to go.

I silently curse to myself, hitting nothing but a wall of energy I cannot get past each time I try and reach into my mind to warn Fallan. Xavier sighs again, swiping away another message from my dad urging him to get outside and join Adam and him on their ride to the Unfortunate sector.

"I find no pleasure in any of this," he whispers, keeping his hands at my waist, allowing himself to tug me closer. My heart rate begins to escalate as I feel his hand dip under the bottom of my shirt, exploring my bare back with soft touches.

"I've wanted nothing more than to bring myself back to that moment outside the hospital and get away from all of this," his hands move up higher, finding my spine and the lack of a bra beneath the hoodie. My shirt is ridden up, exposing my torso.

"Tell me to stop, and I will," he whispers, my mind hazy with desire.

I have no such command for him. I lean into him. His hands move away from my back and onto my legs, hoisting me onto my dresser, nearly knocking everything to the floor. His hands return to my waist, using his thumbs to rub my sides. Our noses touch, our lips inches apart as the warmth pools between my legs. I feel a wave of pleasure come over me, unable to stop the noise that leaves me once his lips meet the skin of my neck, trailing his tongue up towards my ear. I let out a small gasp, feeling him suck on the gentle skin in the sensitive area that always makes my breath unsteady. "I saw the bruises on your neck. It made me angry that someone else touched you," he whispers, pressing his lips down, eliciting yet another sound of pleasure from my throat.

"I-I was attacked," I whisper, almost unable to get the explanation out once his hands grasped my upper thighs.

"I know," he says, pulling away. "No one should have been that close to you," he utters, a new side to him seeping through the cracks.

It's a side to him that I've felt with someone else.

A side of him that is in Fallan.

I see his blue eyes once more, the faint memory of him close to me, touching my skin in the ways Xavier does now. It's like someone is banging on the wall in my mind, begging to come in. Is that Fallan? Is he who I feel? His hands explored me like no one else had before, holding me, our hearts beating as one that night by the fire. The wave of nausea comes over me once again, my body rejecting my closeness to Xavier, forcing me to lean away as I try to stop the churn in my stomach. He quickly pulls away, helping me down as he rubs my back. I close my eyes, shoving back against the presence trying to break through my mind and forcing it out, letting myself look for Fallan.

"I've been trying to say something for hours-" Fallan's voice starts.

"They're coming your way, Fallan. Whatever you do, keep yourself safe," I yell, not giving him the chance to continue.

My want to be near Xavier dies when I hear his voice. My rational thinking returns, resulting in my need to be near the raven-haired man.

"Do not come here. Whatever you do, Forest, you have to stay there," Fallan says. Silence fills my mind shortly after.

Like a mask being lifted, I suddenly feel more aware, forcing up the defensive line in my mind as the haze of hormones passes. I look at Xavier, watching him glance at his phone screen. His eyes dart to me. His cheeks are still flush from our interaction.

"We could find a way away from all of this," I start, feeling my words spill out of me, my voice not sounding like mine. I glance in the mirror, feeling my stomach drop at the sight of her silver hair as she speaks for me. "But I need you to do one thing," I say, feeling my hand rise as I hold up a finger.

"I'll do what I can," he says, grabbing my hand and letting his lips land on its surface.

"Whatever you do," I whisper. "Keep Fallan and Hunter safe, no matter what it takes."

Maybe she and I can agree on something.

I now see how many people have decided to crowd the small area of my living room, leaving little to no space for Xavier and me once we finally decide to leave my room. I had let him guide me down the hallway, taking his hand within my own, only letting my grasp fall once eyes began shifting in our direction. Max sits on our couch, speaking to Kai in whispers. My mother sits perched on the ledge of our window, watching the world outside, looking paler than usual. I avoid her gaze once she takes notice of our presence, unsure how to look at her after what I had seen in my stolen memories. My father and Adam are gone, and the pit in my stomach grows.

"Where is Dad?" I question Kai, looking away from my mother completely.

"He had some work in the Unfortunate sector," my mother answers for him. "Work I think you are supposed to tend to," she pushes, looking over Xavier sternly.

He gives her a nod, hesitantly moving away from me. Unlike his usual light-hearted demeanor, he has a cold expression, barely acknowledging my brother or Max as he progresses toward the front door. No words are exchanged between my mother and him as he passes, leaving us in complete silence once he closes the door behind him. Max tries to break the tension, pulling himself over the side of the couch to stand in front of me.

"Adam offered me a position under him after this school year," Max says, smiling ear to ear.

My eyes snap to my mom, watching the despair wash over her face. She knows what they will turn him into. The boy she has watched grow for years. "It's why I was over here in the first place."

"What a waste of time," I snap, reaching into my mind. Repeatedly, I call out to Fallan.

"Forest, that's not-"

"I don't want to hear it from you," I snarl, watching my mother's mouth close. I take a step back, feeling the disgust swirl inside my chest. It isn't me speaking now, it's that thing.

The other side of me.

"It's an honor to be offered a role like this so young," Max begins, doing his best to follow along with me as I turn away. He grabs my shirt, stopping me from taking another step. "Just because you've decided to be cold to everyone recently doesn't mean you get to stand here and ridicule me and your mother." His body moves in front of me, acting as a barricade for me and refusing to let me avoid this conversation.

I grasp his wrist, feeling his blood pulsing beneath my palm. He closes his mouth, wincing as I squeeze as tight as I can.

"Get the fuck out of my way, Max, before I make you," I say, hearing its tone linger in my own.

He shakes his head in confusion, glancing at my mother. She watches the spectacle with a hand covering her mouth, unable to understand what's happening to the daughter in front of her. Kai is on his feet, looking more upset with Max than he does me.

"Let her go, Max," my mother whispers. "I think she is better off spending some alone time with herself today to reflect on her actions," my mom finishes, glancing at her watch, discovering it's well past her allotted lunch hour.

I let go of his wrist, watching him step aside.

"There's a certain irony in you thinking I'm the only one in this house who needs reflection," I mutter, brushing another thin strand of gray hair behind my ear.

"What is that supposed to mean?" my mother questions.

"There isn't a mirror big enough for the reflection this family needs," I let out, leaving her to consider my meaning.

Kaiden

It wasn't hard to get Max to leave after my sister's outburst in the living room. These days, speaking to her is like walking on eggshells. My mother did her best to hide the tears that slipped from her eyes after the interaction. She kept it together before returning to work. All I could do was let her lean on me, feeling her tears coat the front of my shirt in splotches. My father seemed off today too. He hesitated in a brief listlessness and his usual, purposeful movements seemed more aloof than anything else. I kiss my mother on the head, trying to wipe away the emotions painted on her face.

I look around at our quiet home, glancing at my sister's door. My legs move quicker than my mind, urging me closer to the one person in my family who wants nothing more than to be alone. My hand hovers on the handle, unsure if I am ready to face her.

"Come in," I hear her voice say from the other side, less aggravated than the side of her I saw moments ago.

Slowly, I open the door, meeting the figure of my sister perched on the edge of her bed, holding her hands in her hair out of pure frustration. Her dresser is a mess. Everything is knocked over, spilled onto the floor. Her hands shake as they entwine with her locks. Her bag is filled to the brim with items, all things she would never traditionally carry around. Her green eyes pull up from their downward position, clouded with tears threatening to spill over.

"Mom was a mess," I say, inviting myself to join her on her bed. Her clock is unplugged from the wall and, to my surprise, missing several cables.

"Mom's working for bad people," my sister whispers, furthering my suspicions that there is more going on than she's willing to share.

"Mom works for *our* people," I say, watching my sister give me a longing look.

"Do you believe this is all me, Kai? Or can you feel deep down that maybe something is wrong? Does nothing feel off to you?" she pushes, pressing her hand to my chest.

Ever since the night of the movie screening, nothing has felt quite right. It's like my sister is slowly fading in front of me, becoming a version of herself that knows too much but can say so little. In fleeting moments, I feel what she speaks of. The feeling that something is wrong.

"What haven't you told me?" I question.

She slides away from the bed, pacing back and forth in frustration.

"We all smile and laugh, eating every single lie our superiors tell us, but is that truly what our people want to do? Or were they forced to? Does anything feel like your choice?" she questions.

I draw more blanks, unsure why I cannot give her a clear answer. It should be obvious. The yes should come so quickly. Has everything been my choice? She pushes back on the rules of New Haven so often, like it's impossible for her to see the good here.

"I need more if you want me to answer that question," I say, feeling her hands grasp the side of my face.

"I can't tell you, Kai. You need to see it. You need to see everything while doing your best to convince them you are still naive," she whispers, shifting her eyes from me to the small bag beside her nightstand.

It isn't just a bag of things. It's a bag to get her out of here.

"Fallan is the one Dad is meeting in the Unfortunate sector," I piece together. "You weren't trying to push Mom away. You were making sure she and Max left so no one would follow you," I whisper, watching all the emotion leave her face.

"I don't know what they will do to him, Kai," she whispers, grasping the handle of her bag. "I'm not willing to stand by and find out," she continues, rising to her feet. "I won't let you stop me," she says, fidgeting with an ID I know is not hers.

"Why?" I question.

Her green eyes only seem that much more tormented at this moment.

"Why what?" she questions, hiking up the bag on her shoulder.

"Why go after him?" I question, genuinely seeking the truth.

"I don't know why.... That's why I have to go," she says, readying herself to move past me. I grab her bag, quickly deflecting the hit meant to release my grasp on her bag. I hold her fist, watching confusion take over her expression.

"I won't stop you from going," I start, lowering her fist back to her side. "On one condition," I mutter, walking out of her room, feeling her trail behind me as I make my way to my own bedroom. My hands meet my closet door, pulling out my darkest hoodie and forcing it over my head. I raise the hood, finding another big enough to conceal her. My arm is stretched toward her, daring her to take it from me.

"And what's your condition?" she questions, grasping the extra hoodie.

I pause, running my finger along the scar behind my ear. The same scar she shares behind her ear. The scar that burns hot every time I'm near an Official.

"That you take me with you."

CHAPTER THIRTY-ONE

FOREST

I lift up on the latch to the window in my bathroom, forcing it open. It's the only window in the house that won't signal our exit, buying us enough time to get across our sector and away from anyone who might try to stop us. Kai utilizes his knee to hoist me up, watching me swing my legs over the windowsill before I reachdown for my bag as he hands it up to me. I look at the drop and then use my arms to support my weight as I slowly lower my body over the edge and away from the side of the house.

My feet hit the ground with a thud, kicking up dirt. My hood is up, and my hair is twisted back into a braid. I look back and see Kai's long legs draped over the side of the house, using the momentum from his fall to close the window, keeping his hood up like mine. I linger next to him, expecting him to call this whole thing off and turn around. He brushes his hands against his pants, ridding himself of the dust from the windowsill.

"What are you waiting for?" he questions, coaxing a smile from my lips.

We swiftly move towards the neighborhood's perimeter, running our hands along the ward as our house fades away into the background.

Our hands hit the glass door of the tram. The doors fly open. Both of us spill into the warm vehicle. We both look back several times, only pulling down our hoods once we take notice that no one but Mark is present. He looks off, glancing between us, unsure what to say in my brother's presence.

"Your hair," Mark finally says after a few moments, pointing out the few strands of gray peeking through the entirety of my mane. Even Kai pauses to look, twisting a piece between his fingers with curiosity.

"Focus," I whisper, swatting away his hand.

"I need you to take us to the Unfortunate sector," I say in a rush, watching any lightness in Mark's eyes quickly wane. Instinctively, Kai moves around me, covering the one camera on the tram with the first thing he can find.

"You know I'm not allowed to do that," Mark begins, reaching to try and pull away the hat Kai had used to keep the security camera covered. "Besides, you need an Official ID-"

I slap my father's ID down on the dash, impatiently tapping my foot. The longer we wait here, the more time my father, Adam, and Xavier spend with Fallan, and the likelihood will only grow that we'll be seen by someone getting on the bus.

"Please, Mark," I whisper, taking another step closer to him. "They are going to hurt Fallan, all because he got near me. He shouldn't be punished for that," I say, feeling the fear seep out of my voice.

Mark runs his hands over his face, tapping his fingers against his head.

"He said something very similar to me once when speaking about you," Mark says, sliding the ID back over to me. "It was just as hard to say no then as it is now," Mark whispers, turning on the ignition to the tram.

"You'll take us?" Kai questions, finally breaking his silence.

"I'm taking her, and trusting her faith in you is not misplaced," Mark says, looking toward the road, letting his foot press down on the gas, taking us away from the bus stop.

"I can't get you to the front of the sector; the Officials will notice, but I can get you to the side. There, you can breach one of the holes in the fence and use your father's ID to get into the main town square," Mark says, motioning us to take a seat. We oblige, quickly sitting down, both of us knee to knee.

I feel drained, unable to reach Fallan through our mind connection. I peer at my reflection in the window across the aisle. But something is different. In the reflection, my hands are bruised and worn. My own are clean, completely clear of any damage. What message is this version of me trying to send me now?

"Why are you doing this for him?" Mark questions after a few moments.

I shuffle uncomfortably in my seat, unsure of what to say. Once more, the other version of me takes over, finding the words I cannot.

"Because whether I like it or not, our paths have crossed before and will continue to," I say. I watch the shift in Mark's demeanor. "But he already told you that, didn't he?" I push, somehow able to hear the way his heart rate increases at the question.

Kai looks confused, waiting for one of us to keep talking. I watch my brother fidget in his pocket, quickly looking over something in his hands with wide eyes.

"I may know more than I let on," Mark says after a few moments, keeping his eyes on the road as that other side of me slowly becomes dormant once more.

"Is that why you keep a picture of our family tucked away in your wallet?" Kai says, catching both Mark and me off guard.

My brother raises his hand, holding up a very worn photo my family had taken years ago. Kai and I are both still babies, our parents youthful and glowing. The picture has several creases. It is falling apart from being opened and closed so often. Ink bleeds on the back, and the words are no longer legible. I grab the photo, looking at Mark's petrified expression in the mirror.

"I found his wallet in the hat I used to cover the camera," Kai starts, folding the photo once more, "I wanted to know who we're deciding to trust to help us."

Mark grips the steering wheel, anxiously tapping his fingers against its cover.

"Your father gave that to me," he says after a few moments, my next words spilling out like a flood.

"Why would he give you something like that? It's useless to you," I say, watching the old man's expression turn melancholy.

"If you looked further into my belongings, you'd know that photo is far from useless," Mark says painfully.

Kai pulls out the old man's wallet, retrieving his ID. We scan it up and down, but then we find a second plastic card clung to its back. This ID is more hidden, meant to stay tucked away behind the first. Slowly, we look over the card, both of us holding our breaths the minute we look over the old man's name.

"Mark Blackburn?" I question, looking over the ID repeatedly.

Kai shakes his head, letting out a scoff.

"This must be some joke," Kai starts, pointing his finger at Mark.

"You think it's funny to walk around with something like this that could incriminate my whole family?" Kai questions, standing on his feet while forcing the contents back into the leather wallet.

"Has Andrew truly made you that naive, Kaiden?" Mark blurts out, using my brother's full name. Kai stops in his tracks, put off by the man's sudden change in attitude.

"H-how did you know my full name?" Kai questions.

"We live in a web of too many secrets," Mark says, glancing at me once more. "And it all starts with your father and ends with her," Mark finishes, giving me a look I know too well. A look I have only seen paint my father's expression.

"Forest, what does he mean?" Kai questions, the gears slowly turning in my head.

Same nose, same eyes. Both men have a downward smile and freckles that hide within their eyes.

"You're his father," I whisper, finally finding clarity in the importance of such a small photo.

Mark closes his eyes for a moment, drawing in a shaky breath.

"That's not possible," Kai starts, running his hands through his hair, "Dad is-"

"An Unfortunate," Mark finishes, both of us gripping our seats. "An Unfortunate who turned his back on everyone, all for the sake of a cause he thought was greater than us all," Mark says, my throat burning with my final question.

"What cause?" I question, my hands shaking from anticipation.

"You."

The tram had become silent moments after our revelation with Mark. Years of coming and going off this tram, looking past the old man who had to watch his grandchildren look past him as if he were nothing and no one. My father never spoke of his family, saying they passed away early on in his life. However, there is no scenario in which I thought he'd stand by and watch his only father be berated and used by our people daily. I rack my brain over our countless interactions, cringing at the thought of how I treated him. Kai has had a blank stare for several minutes, only letting out exacerbated, inaudible sounds as words catch in his throat each time he tries to look or speak to Mark. The old man tried to ease our shock, telling us he didn't blame us. It only seemed to make it feel that much worse.

"If Officials find out what we're doing, any Unfortunates who helped us are as good as dead," Kai finally says after a few moments, biting his nail beds.

"Not just Unfortunates, but us too," I mutter, covering my eyes with my hands, no longer having the energy to stomach my reflection.

"You know they never harm Untouchables-"

My eyes are already on him, stopping that thought pattern before he can continue.

"Am I wrong?" he questions. He's a prisoner to the chip inside his mind.

"You should tell him," my reflection mutters next to my ear, my voice an angry mess.

"Get out of my fucking head!" I yell, slamming my hand against the glass closest to me. Kai flinches away, his eyes growing wider.

"Who are you talking to?" Kai questions. It's evident in his tone he thinks I'm going insane.

"No one.... No one that matters."

"Keep telling yourself I'm not there. That clearly is working out great for you," the other version of me hisses. I wanted to slam my head into the window again the more she talked.

"Did something happen that night at the screening?" Kai questions, landing his hand on my leg to return my attention. "I lost time that day, and ever since, everything has felt... different," Kai mumbles. Mark listens in on the conversation, unsure of what to say.

I reflect on that night. The night that turned my whole life upside down, all in a matter of minutes. Every moment of my life had felt staged until that moment, only feeling real in the small moments I was near Fallan, even if all he felt for me was hate. They took that girl's life, all for being like me—someone who doesn't fit into societal norms and conventional categories for our people.

"There was a girl," I start, as he shifts in his seat, not expecting me to have answered. "A girl whose life was stolen because *our* people feared her. She walked and talked like me and you. She was an Untouchable," I say, touching the back of Kai's ear. "And they killed her. They killed what scared them and made you all forget," I whisper, watching his eyes grow more distant.

He takes several moments to compose himself, grazing the back of his ear with his finger.

"If that's true," Kai starts, shakily drawing in a breath. "Why can you remember, and I can't?" he whispers.

I laugh at the remark, biting my lip in anticipation.

"Because I was like her, Kai, and Fallan was the one who stopped me from meeting the same fate she did. That's why I got on this tram and why I have been so different lately, because of what happened that night. And if I had to choose between our people or theirs," I whisper, looking to Mark, "I choose them every time," I finish, grabbing my brother's hand, letting it run beneath my hoodie, feeling the abrasive skin of my mark. His hand jerks back but then slides back to the raised flesh that I've hidden for as long as I can remember.

"I'm different, Kai, different gets you killed," I whisper, letting go of his hand. He keeps his hand on the mark, rubbing his finger along its outline.

"I knew something was off," he says after several moments of silence.

"How much farther until we reach your sector?" Kai questions louder, finally bringing Mark back into the conversation.

"We're coming up to the gate now," Mark says.

My brother stands up, bringing me with him as he pulls up our hoods.

"This doesn't change anything?" I question, watching a smile finally meet his lips.

"Rules or not, Forest-"

He moves us closer to the front, cupping my face between his hands like he used to do when we were younger to ease me.

"My loyalty lies with you." His finger reaches to his chip, pressing down on the small piece of metal, "I didn't sign up to be their test subject, either."

"None of us did," Mark starts, letting the tram roll to a slow stop.

"But something tells me your father's hope in you isn't misplaced," Mark utters, making it apparent that we've only seen the beginning of this web of secrets.

"What hope? Mark, I'm nobody. I can't save anyone," I say, clinging to my brother's hand.

Mark smiles, shaking his head.

"Says the girl, breaking every single one of her people's rules, all for a boy from a group she was raised to hate."

Kai taps his foot, looking outside at the mangled fence.

"Forest, we have to go," Kai urges, pulling me down the steps.

The old man's hand comes around my wrist, stopping me from taking another step.

"The Apparatus is close. It will free us from eternal damnation," he says, his words throwing me back to that night of the Untouchable's suicide. The exact cryptic words the boy spoke before ending it all.

"Mark, what is that," I grab him. "What is the Apparatus?" I question, thinking of the words written across the scattered papers in my father's study.

"Our salvation. Beyond that, there is nothing more that I know," Mark says, letting go of my wrist. I try to return to him, but Kai only pulls me back.

"You must go. I don't know how long Fallan has if Officials are already with him. I will find you soon enough," Mark says, watching Kai as he hands him back the wallet.

"For what it's worth, I'm sorry," Kai whispers, letting his hand linger in the old man's grasp.

"It wasn't your choice not to have me in your life. It never was your choice."

They exchange looks; years of regret expressed between them in this one moment together. I let Kai pull me away from the man, giving Mark one last look before letting my feet hit the muddied ground of the Unfortunate sector.

Chapter Thirty-Two

Fallan

The three men linger in my living room, looming over the space with equal looks of distaste. I thrash my arms against the binds of the chair they put me in, making sure to glance at Hunter every few moments, watching him tug at the cuffs holding him to the metal frame of my barred window. They dragged him in here moments ago, wasting no time at delivering multiple blows to his face, getting him in the same vulnerable position they had forced me into. I sit in the middle of my living room, unable to move from my position in the chair they'd tied me to. My body aches from the beating I'd taken so far, my mind drained, unable to reach out to Forest through the connection. Andrew and Adam pace around the area, scanning my things, waiting for me to say something. The blonde, Xavier, observes me. Even from here, I can smell her scent on him. He's leaning against my wall with a detached look on his face that only makes me want to rip his head off the longer I navigate his head space. Each one of his thoughts is revolved around her. I hear her gentle breaths in his mind, caused by the pressure of his lips exploring her neck. I thrash against the binds, focused solely on him.

"Finally ready to admit what you did?" Adam questions, hitting the back of my head with his hand. I lean forward, keeping my gaze toward the ground.

"Adam, no hands on him unless you have to. I doubt you'd like to clean up yet another mess," Xavier says, looking to Andrew for support in his command.

Andrew nods in agreement, waving his hand at Adam and watching the man take several steps from me. Xavier finally pushes away from the wall, observing the space with his companions. I watch how his hand trails along my things, moving closer to my general location. I do my best to continue navigating his mental space, only growing angrier each time I sense new thoughts of her manifesting. He thinks of her every time he looks at me, harboring as much hate toward me as I do him.

"I don't need you defending me, you pathetic snake," I nearly yell.

"We haven't broken any rules," Hunter says, straining against the metal bar. "If you want money, take it," Hunter pleads, unaware of how sick and twisted Officials can be. None of this has to do with money. It only has to do with their agenda.

"This isn't about you," Adam hisses. Xavier's hand is already on his shoulder, stopping him from getting closer to Hunter.

"You're angry at me, Andrew," I say, turning my head back to look at the man. He walks over to me, finally standing before me, observing me with thoughtful eyes. "No more going after her because of my actions. You've already taken so much of her," I plea, trying to gauge how much they know about her absent chip. No one's ever been able to do what she did without causing irreparable brain damage.

"What's he talking about?" Adam questions, unaware of how well I actually know Andrew and his daughter.

"Adam, step outside and guard the door. I don't need any of his companions trying to listen in on this conversation," Andrew says, crouching down on his knees.

"But, sir. Xavier-"

"I don't think he said my name. Get the fuck out," Xavier snaps, watching the man take a step back, clearly annoyed to be taking orders from someone so much younger than him. Xavier stands with a confidence many lack. Something about him is off-putting, making him much different from any other Official I've met.

"You too, Xavier," Andrew says, looking at the man sternly.

Xavier looks hesitant. Still, he excuses himself with Adam, giving me a hateful look before closing the door behind him.

"I told you to stay away from my girl," Andrew mutters, looking at me angrily. "The deal was you keep some of your memories, and in return, you let her live her life without you in it," Andrew continues. I watch Hunter's face change, clearly nervous about the direction of the conversation.

"We tried," Hunter barks. "He did everything he could to make her hate him, even paraded another woman in front of her. It turned out the same way every time-"

"You know nothing about trying!" Andrew yells, cutting Hunter off. "For years, I have carried the burden of keeping both of you safe, yet all you do is find a way to her, no matter how many times I alter her memories or yours. Why can't you leave it be?" he questions, my chest growing tighter the longer I think of her.

Every time I see her, something urges me to be near her. It's the connection formed from when we were children. I hear her laugh in fleeting moments of the night. The sweet upturn of her smile devours her face as prominently as her kind eyes. I feel her hands on my chest, pulling me down to taunt a kiss I've still never allowed to happen, knowing there's no way I could let anyone touch her once I've had her that way.

"You didn't leave it be when it was Katiana!" I yell, watching Hunter wince at my words. "You abandoned us all for a girl and a promise of a better life, turning your back on everything you knew, forcing your daughter to believe she was crazy when your fears about her started to become a reality," I spit, thinking of all of Andrew's theories about our kind.

"My daughter is safe if she stays in the world we created for her," he says, pressing his finger to my chest. "It's only when she finds you that those fears start to have any meaning. Her naivety is the one thing keeping her away from what lies outside of these walls-"

"The Shifters? Open your eyes, Andrew, they're already here, hunting *our kind*-"

"Not the Shifters, Fallan. There is something going on that's much bigger than all of us, and it starts with them getting their hands on her and what she can do. The more time she spends near you, the more in danger she becomes. Can't you see that?" Andrew questions, filling my head with a rampart wave of doubt and frustration.

"Then we keep her away. We convince her to hate us-" Hunter starts.

"I've tried that," I whisper, straining against the binds again.

"Not hard enough," Andrew bellows, leaning his head forward into mine with an angry stare.

"I have a family I need to protect, Fallan. I promised your father I would keep you alive. How you choose to live that life is up to you."

"Did that thought run through your head before or after you got my father killed?"

His hands fidget. "You were made in this sector, Andrew, yet you act like that brand no longer marks your calloused hands."

"One more strike, Fallan, and you reach red. No one comes back from red."

"You did."

He pauses, running his hand along his sensor prod.

"I better not catch wind of you involving my son this time," Andrew says, looking at Hunter. "The last thing I need is to get him involved in this shit show. In a few minutes, my men will return here and deliver punishment to you both for stepping out of line and speaking to my children. Prods only, so you'll live."

He pauses, looking back at me.

"Your mother knows how to treat light sensor prod wounds," he mutters, blatantly unaware of her absence.

"She's dead. Your people killed her last fall!" I yell, watching the way his body freezes up at the news of her passing.

"How many times will we be here like this before you realize I will never stop? Some things can't be altered with a chip and a pill you shove down her throat. Every morning and every night, I am haunted by every moment I've looked at her and she's looked right past me. You rip her away, making promises she will never return, only to be wrong each time."

"You know the consequences, Fallan. Neither of you will come back from it this time. No more chips, no more pretending. The new Commander is watching, hiding in the shadows from all of us. They are afraid of you two. I can't protect you both forever. Even now, what she is capable of is beyond my control. One minute, I spoke to her in my office, and the next, I was asleep on my floor, only to be woken up by a flood of texts about your whereabouts while trying to navigate lost time. Nothing is within my grasp anymore," he whispers, turning away to open the door.

"So that's what you'll do then? Walk away from your kind again?" Hunter retorts, hitting his head against the wall in frustration.

"If you don't make her hate you this time, Fallan, if you don't make that spark you created burn out within her, and they find out, she reaches red. Only this time, it ends with a bullet in her head while they make you pull the trigger," Andrew says, pausing his grasp on the handle.

"Why?" I question, feeling the emotion shroud my tone, "Why can't you just let it be me instead of her?" I ask, watching as he turns back to look at me. He pauses, pressing his head to the door.

"She made me promise a long time ago that I would keep your life safe, even if it meant hers was jeopardized. The worst part of it all is she can't even remember that I made that promise and lives thinking I want all of this to happen," Andrew says, my heart breaking into a million pieces.

"The deal is the same. If she remembers you and remembers what she is capable of, and they find out, they kill her on the spot and throw you, me, and anyone associated with us past the ward to fend for ourselves in the ash and what lies past it. This isn't just about you and her anymore. It's about the very foundation of this society," he whispers. Hunter finally speaks up again.

"And the Apparatus?" Hunter questions, daring to bring up the one thing we're all afraid to discuss.

"I stopped believing in that fairytale a long time ago," Andrew finishes, swinging open the door.

His men wait on the other side, deep in a, clearly, one-sided conversation. Andrew is whispering to the pair, debriefing bits and pieces from our conversation but not giving them the entire picture of what happened today or why. Both men glance into my apartment, crossing their arms with different looks, one of pleasure and one of frustration.

After a few moments, the men step inside, touching the hilts of their prods.

"If you're smart, you will not come near my family again," Andrew says, moving past the doorway, leaving his men behind to carry out their punishment. Hunter's legs kick again, trying to escape from Adam, but his movements are swift and menacing, his fingers digging into Hunter's flesh in a vice-like grip. The force of Adam's grip jerked Hunter up violently into a position where Adam could taunt him with the light sensor prod.

"He did nothing!" I yell, slamming my chair down with as much force as possible, "Leave him be, you mindless obedient drone," I hiss, watching Adam's gaze finally snap to me.

He lets go of Hunter and lunges towards me, but Xavier steps in his path.

"Move out of my way, kid," Adam seethes, glaring at Xavier with fury in his eyes.

"Last time I checked, our job isn't to taunt them," Xavier says, tucking his sensor prod back into its holder, forcing Adam to do the same.

"Stop acting like you stand for any side but your own," I mutter.

Xavier looks back at me, his gaze filled with annoyance.

"You saw what he did, just like me. Andrew's kid has been sneaking around with him. It's a vile and deplorable relationship-"

"Forest is not with him in that way," Xavier says, my stomach churning at his words,

"If you speak her name around me one more time, I swear I will make sure it's you on the ground," I snap, feeling the binds nearly break from my pull.

"See?" Adam says, pointing out my defiant need to defend the woman.

"Forest is not with him," Xavier says again, my anger reaching a level I never thought possible, "Just this morning, I had her to myself, straddling me in her bedroom while I explored how sweet her skin tasted. I'm sure Fallan can't say he's had her the same way, and if he has, I doubt it was because she wanted it," Xavier says. My hand is almost free from its binds. His words are like hot prods on my back, adding to the collection of scars painting my flesh.

"You liar," I begin, feeling his fingers press onto my neck, touching the space below my ear, right next to my Adam's apple.

"Right there," he starts, applying a bit of pressure. "She makes the nicest little moan of pleasure when you put a little pressure there-"

My hand breaks away from the restraint, and I'm unable to hold back the anger stirring within me. My hand passes over his front, every single urge inside my body telling me to use my burden on this man, dangling him from the window, watching his body mark the pavement. Xavier is quick on his feet, barely missing the collision with my knuckles once I move to hit him again. Adam is the first to strike me, hitting my side hard with his prod and delivering a solid kick to my face, throwing me off balance. I watch as Xavier crouches down to meet my eyes, my nose already spilling with blood.

"Andrew is right," Xavier starts, my arms and legs unable to move from their position. Hunter's yells are muffled by Adam's hand covering up the noise. "You will stay away from her if you know what's good for you," Xavier finishes, looking at Adam with disdain.

"They've had enough." He brushes dust from the front of his uniform. "I'd like to get back home and pick up where I left off with *our* girl," Xavier says toward me with a wink. My rage is snuffed out as my body fights exhaustion, and I'm left utterly depleted from trying to fight against my restraints for the last several hours.

I think of his hands on her, touching her, getting to see that smile. Adam moves away from Hunter, brushing past Xavier to leave the space. The blonde glances back once behind him, crouching down to get a good look at me. He speaks quietly enough that Hunter won't be able to listen in.

"Take my words however you'd like," he says, my body using all its energy to try and get up from the floor.

The man's hand touches my clothes, stopping once he reaches my pocket. I watch him grab the chain of her necklace, dragging it free from my pocket. "There will be consequences if I find out you went near her again," Xavier says, tucking the chain into his pocket. My body is depleted, but I try to reach out to her anyway.

"Forest?" I whisper in my mind, feeling the energy the thought takes with it.

"I will kill you," I hiss at the man, watching him smile as he rises to his feet.

"I do hope you try." Xavier glances over to Hunter. "Keep your guard dog in line," Xavier says, turning on his heels to walk away.

"She will never choose you," Hunter yells, watching Xavier's body freeze at the statement.

His pause only lasts a few moments. His mouth curls into a smile once he looks back.

"Maybe. But Fallan will make sure she doesn't choose him, either. Won't you, Markswood?" Xavier questions, leaving my door gaping as he finally steps away.

Moments later, my strength is suddenly restored. I force myself to my feet and after Xavier. The hallway outside my front door is empty, leaving me hitting the ground with my knees in frustration. I run my hands through my hair, remembering the empty space in my pocket where I'd kept Forrest's necklace.

Xavier's words were not just a message.

They were a threat.

CHAPTER THIRTY-THREE

FOREST

Mud coats our shoes, turning their polished black soles into a mosaic of muted browns. I stop myself from covering my nose to avoid the stench lingering in the air. It smells of rotten fruit and metal mixed to form a nauseating amalgamation that unsettled my stomach. My body feels drained, leaning on Kai more than I'd like for additional support.

Mark quickly pulled away once we got off the tram, leaving us in front of a massive, barbed wire fence. Jagged pieces of wood supported the dilapidated partition, and a thin layer of sheet metal encased the ruins to keep outside eyes from being able to look inside. Black smoke circles the air in small puffs, only adding to the odor. I hear the busy chatter of Unfortunates on the other side of the fence. Some are getting yelled at, and others are begging for help. Beyond this wall is one more line of security. Scanners are utilized in this sector for people to come and go. It's the only way to regulate the Unfortunates enough to keep them confined here. The fence here is far from the sturdy structure we were shown in school when we were learning about our two sectors. Everything seems to be falling apart, and I wonder how much worse it is inside the perimeter.

"Over there," Kai says, pointing to a small opening on the side of the fence. "That must be the other way in Mark was talking about."

It's a small opening, shielded by a few wooden planks leaned up against the structure. I hear the chatter of Officials conversing near the fence. Their voices grow closer the longer we stand here. Kai grabs my hand, moving us along the muddy path. We slip occasionally, our eager pace sabotaging our footing. I help Kai move the slats, both of us doing our best to keep our grunts as quiet as possible.

I'm the first to duck my head, forcing my body through the hole and into the other side of the fence. My hoodie protects my arms from getting scratched. Kai's hand continues to hold my own, following behind me as we both breach the first wall. A pile of junk hides our sudden arrival from the Unfortunates. Some stand in groups, others in lines waiting to make it past the security check with their IDs. Several people shiver in the brisk cold, their coats full of rips and tears, while some others are completely void of proper clothing altogether. Women and men of all ages rub their skin, shaking uncontrollably, being ignored by every Official wearing more clothing than they need. Their faces are hollow here. Where a youthful glow and healthy tints of red are predominant in my people's complexion, the Unfortunates have skin that's sallow and taut across the bones, with bruises and dark spots. The mask of malnutrition covers the lot like a plague.

"Looks like that's where we need to get through," Kai says, motioning to the scanners that allow people to enter the sector.

I nod, pulling down his hood before guiding us forward. I look back to the first entrance we avoided, watching the Officials shove down citizens, ransacking their pockets, all while carelessly stripping away whatever valuable items they have. An Official drags a little girl away from her mother, grabbing the woman's hair as he begins hurling insults at her, slapping her hard across the face. Kai has to stop me from pausing, pushing my back to keep me moving forward.

"You can't interfere," Kai whispers, visibly disgusted the longer he allows himself to look at the scene around us, "I had no idea it was this bad."

Stomaching my regret, I turn my back on the woman and her little girl, keeping my head down as we move past a few lingering Officials, both bragging about the vile shit they've been doing to these people. I keep the ID face down as I tap it on the scanner, watching the green light flash brightly before quickly tossing it back to my brother. I slip past the entrance, hoping no one sees us use the same ID twice to get inside. My eyes are too focused on Kai to look forward, watching the sweat collect on his forehead as he scans my father's ID once more. Again, the scanner lights up, allowing him to pass through our final barrier to the sector. I quickly take back my dad's stolen ID, tucking it deep in my pocket. Kai's eyes are set forward, absorbing the horrific conditions around us. He pauses. I keep my eyes on him, feeling his heartbeat quicken beneath my fingertips.

"What have we done to them?" he silently questions, his mouth nearly hanging open.

I turn around to look at the sight he's fixated on, my knees threatening to give out in shock as I take in what he sees.

People lie in the streets, clothes barely holding to their bodies as they begin an attempt to cling to what bit of life they have left. Vendors sell food that looks days past what is considered safe, some even eating moldy bread to satisfy their hunger. Children kick around a tattered ball, all of them dirtied and marred with enough scrapes and bruises to last a lifetime. Women are whoring themselves out in alleyways while others trudge through the mud, exhausted from wherever they'd come from, the pained expressions from hours of back-breaking labor abhorrently obvious. The buildings here are worn down, none with the same advancements we see in our sector. Wells surround the grounds. Some people on the streets resort to that as their source of drinking water. I see the small splotches of blood painting the cobblestone roads. Even from here, the stench of death clings to this place.

Someone shoves me forward, using the end of their prod to jab my back, nearly burning through the hoodie to my skin.

"Keep walking, pigs. The workday isn't over yet," a voice hisses, shoving Kai along with me.

We keep our heads lowered, not uttering another word as we nod to the Official. Slowly, we begin moving, weaving through the filth, doing our best to hold our stomachs. We make it out of the Official's earshot, our hands shaky.

"They told us they kept up the Unfortunate sector," Kai says, messing with the small hole in my hoodie the prod had left.

"They told us a lot of things, Kai, none of it was true-"

My brother's eyes flash with apprehension. His hand comes flying across my front, dragging me into the closest alleyway. He slams us both into the nearest wall. His hand clamps down over my mouth, creating a moment of silence for both of us.

Given his frantic behavior, it's a silence I don't dare try to break.

Eventually, the noise of others fills my ears, breaking my concentration from him and moving to the group of men silently descending the worn walkway. My father leads the group. His knuckles are bloodied, his hands scuffed and torn. My heart races as I think of Fallan, wanting to run out and force him to tell me where he is. Adam's miserable figure trails behind, cursing up a storm toward the one man who I trust in the group. Xavier's hands are clean. I can see him fidgeting with something in his pocket as he ignores Adam's words.

"You let them off easy," Adam yells toward Xavier, trying to get in his face. Xavier shoves him back a few feet, finally pulling his hand away from his pocket, dangling my necklace between his fingers.

I take a moment to observe the small part of me Fallan had taken, wishing now more than ever it was still in my possession. Had he given it to Xavier? Had he rid himself of it without ever explaining why he took it from me in the first place? Xavier carefully tucks away the necklace, pointing his finger at Adam's chest.

"They didn't deserve punishment just because you're a sadistic fuck-"

"I'm the sadistic fuck? Should I tell everyone how you keep-"

"Shut your mouth," Xavier shouts, grabbing Adam's collar, ready to throw the man down to the ground.

"Enough," my father yells, pulling out the pistol strapped to his side and pointing it between both men.

I feel the air leave my lungs at the sight, reflecting on that night again like a distant fever dream. "Either you both get in line right now and stay silent, or I put a bullet in both of your knees, and you can reflect on your actions together in the med unit," my dad says, releasing the slide, loading a fresh round into the gun's chamber. Xavier releases Adam, giving the man one final shove. Adam releases a frustrated grunt, burying his animosity towards Xavier for the time being.

My father lowers his weapon, shaking his head at both men before continuing his walk past our position in the alleyway. The men trail behind him, both staying silent as the trio turns the next corner, finding themselves closer to the main entrance we avoided.

We take the opportunity to leave the alleyway, following the direction they came, looking back as often as we can.

"All these people are dying in the streets while we've got unlimited resources in our sector," Kai mutters, observing each of the feeble citizens who move past us.

Regardless of how tired they look, they take the time to smile at us if their eyes catch ours.

"Why are they allowing themselves to live like this?" Kai finally questions, his curiosities only growing the longer we stay here.

"They have no choice, Kai. No one has a choice," I say, squeezing my brother's hand.

We find ourselves in a less run-down part of the sector, filled with buildings that seem more up to date. Shops line this part of the sector, busy with the most life we've seen so far. Merchants and patrons come and go. Unlike the sleek gray concrete of our sector, buildings here rely on sturdy wooden slabs that have been meticulously carved and fitted together, and a patchwork of metal sheets and salvaged shingles make up the roofs above. By some miracle, the grounds here are more upkept, surrounded by less filth, making the air much easier to breathe.

A group of children run past us, chasing each other with wide, toothy grins. Their shoes are filled with holes, toes threatening to break out and embrace the mud. All of them are skinny, their hands already marked by hard labor. One of the children lingers behind the group, tripping on a log that had managed to slip away from the carts of one of the vendors. Their knees collide with the dirtied ground, skidding across the cobblestone, making their small faces wince. I move to help him up, surprised when I realize Kai is already working to pick him up.

My brother crouches down to observe the child, peeling back the material of his pant leg to unveil a nasty cut. The child sighs, leaning his mangled head of hair into my brother's arm.

Still so trusting.

"You should get home and put something on the cut before it's infected," Kai says, both of us internally cursing at ourselves for forgetting something as essential as a Cure-All at this moment.

"Silly, you know we don't have any more medicine," the boy begins, giving a shifty-eyed look to the few Officials lingering near the shops. "They gave it all to the people on the other side of the fence," he whispers, my contrition growing as I think about the unlimited supplies available to the Untouchables in our sector.

The boy takes my brother's hand to help him up, brushing himself off with a smile.

"You both are the cleanest people I've seen in this sector," the boy starts, squeezing my brother's hands. "Softest hands too," he finishes, dropping my brother's grasp. Kai's clean hands are now dirtied, both palms caked in a film of grime.

I survey the many shops lining the street, eventually landing on the small bakery in the middle of what looks like the downtown square. If memory serves me well, Hunter works in the one bakery in this sector, giving us the slightest opportunity to figure out where Fallan is. I begin dragging my brother closer to the building, feeling the searing gaze of two Officials as they whisper about our cleanliness, just as the boy had. I pause, looking down at the muddied ground with a large sigh.

"Can you believe what that kid said-"

I crouch to the ground, dragging Kai down letting the dirt coat him. He looks caught off guard, pulling the front of my hoodie as we both hit the cobblestone.

"Pretend we're fighting," I whisper, watching the Officials pause their walk toward us. "We look too out of place," I continue, forcing my brother's neck down.

Both Officials smile at the exchange, watching my brother and me silently as they bet on who will win. Kai feeds into it, flipping me onto my back as our clothes are soon covered with dirt. Eventually, I stopped putting up a fight and let Kai win. Dirt streaks his face as we hoist ourselves up from the dirt pavement. The Officials both let out moans of disappointment before walking away once they realized our squabble was over.

"Forest?" Hunter's familiar voice questions, both me and Kai snap our heads to the right.

The bakery door is swung open, revealing a very startled Hunter rubbing his floured hands across his apron. His eyes are wide, barely able to process our sudden arrival into his sector. Hunter's face is bruised, his wrists worn as if he had a struggle. I slowly rise to my feet, wanting nothing more than to drag my father and Adam back here and beat them until they can no longer move. Even Kai looks distraught by the sight in front of him. He kept his hands at his sides in an attempt not to reach for Hunter.

"W-what are you two doing here?" Hunter questions, taking another step closer to avoid speaking too loudly.

"What happened?" Kai questions, unable to control his hand any longer as he reaches up to touch the Hunter's bruised face.

Hunter closes his eyes when he feels my brother's touch. I wonder if it's the first kind touch he's felt in a long time. Kai quickly retracts his hand, his cheeks growing flush as he realizes what he'd just done.

"I don't know if speaking out here is the best idea," Hunter starts, rubbing his hand across his face and pausing his gaze on me.

Kai and I both look around, ready for yet another Official to show up.

"Don't worry if you look like one of us; they won't bat an eye at anything you do as long as it isn't in the Untouchable sector." Hunter moves closer to the door he'd come from.

"Hunter, where is Fallan?" I question, his body tensing.

"I think it's best if you come inside, Forest," he continues, looking back at me with despondency.

"Please, say something," I yell in the empty cavern of my mind, feeling my palms begin to sweat. My heart races the longer I look at Hunter, wondering if my father's bloodied knuckles are the source of his new wounds.

Why is he not here with Hunter?

"How the hell did you even get in here?" Hunter questions, holding open the door and releasing a burst of warm air from the bakery. It smells of freshly baked bread, and the vile smells from the streets are quickly banished as we follow him inside.

"I stole my father's ID," I start. Kai is already cutting me off.

"Where is the re-establishment program?" Kai questions.

The re-establishment program was New Haven's promise to rebuild the Unfortunate sector, giving them the same quality of living we have had for years. Cleaner food, new buildings, and more supplies are just some of the items promised to them as part of this project.

"You mean that empty promise New Haven has been making for years when they can't even patch up our broken ward," Hunter says, closing the door to the small bakery, struggling to close it all the way.

I look around the small space, half expecting to find Fallan sitting at one of the tables, throwing me a brooding gaze. There are no cameras in the shop, or anywhere nearby for that matter.

"If you're looking for cameras, they only keep them in some parts of our sector. Makes it easier to dish out punishments when there is no paper trail," Hunter says, arranging some of the pastries behind the clear cabinet.

Each one looks made with love; the artful details are noticeable in the colorful rows of cream-filled delicacies that are no doubt bursting with flavor.

"Your ward is broken over here? How is that possible? There's no guarantee of anyone's safety!" Kai questions, my mind running to the two Shifters I've seen within the past few weeks.

"They only know it's unsafe because they only draft Unfortunates to go beyond the ward, and for some reason, they keep doing it," Hunter says, pausing his work in the cabinet.

Both men are blatantly unaware of the dangers that lie behind their ears. I can't imagine how much has been stolen from Hunter in this lifetime.

"You never answered my question about Fallan," I say after a moment, watching Hunter's eyes dart to me.

He shifts uncomfortably, crossing his arms while letting out a deep sigh.

"He doesn't want to see you, Forest," Hunter says, my heart sinking at his response.

"Fallan doesn't want to see who? That boy is nothing if not social," an unfamiliar voice says, pushing past the curtain behind Hunter, unveiling the last person I ever expected to see again.

The woman from the tram.

CHAPTER THIRTY-FOUR

FOREST

I'm left speechless, unable to find my words as the woman from that morning at the tram station breezes into the shop and joins our conversation. Unlike that day at the tram stop, she now looks more lively, visibly less drained and damaged, not like the state I had regrettably left her in before Fallan had to intervene. Kai seems shocked, unsure what to do or say, resorting to staring at the ground instead of trying to make eye contact with the woman.

"Fallan isn't feeling very social right now," Hunter reiterates, flinching away as the woman's gentle fingers touch his bruised face.

"Given how much those pigs roughed you boys up, I can't say I blame him," she says, my shame only growing the longer we stand here.

"Who are your friends?" the woman questions, lowering her glasses to get a better look at us.

If she remembers me, she does an excellent job at pretending she doesn't.

"Kai," my brother starts, extending his dirtied hand out, quickly retracting it to rub away the dirt. She reaches her hand out toward my brother, embracing his greeting with a soft smile. Hunter pinches the bridge of his nose, anxiously watching the interaction unfold.

"You have a last name, Kai?" the woman questions, making my brother's grasp tighten.

"Just Kai... Kaiden, if we're getting technical," Kai mutters, his face redder with each passing second.

"Well, a pleasure to meet you, Kaiden, with no last name. My name is Jolie. It would seem you already know my grandson here," she starts, turning her head back to me. "And your name is-"

"Forest, also no last name," I say, extending my hand toward the woman.

She gives me a long look, her smile growing the longer she watches me.

"I've heard your name bounce between Fallan and Mark once or twice," Jolie says, taking my hand within her own. "Glad to finally put a face to the name."

I feel an energy pass through me at the exchange, and there's a warmth that comes over my body like a comforting hug. Her kind eyes consume her expression. They're the same ones painted on her grandson's face.

"Well, you two came at just the right time," Jolie begins, reaching into Hunter's organized case of sweets and pulling out two pastries closest to her. "I made these turnovers just this morning. I could use a few new mouths to taste the new recipe." She places the sweets on a plate, motioning us closer. "It's on the house."

Her generosity is suffocating amidst the selfishness that goes on outside this sector.

Kai looks completely off-put, barely processing how one soul could be so generous to two people so undeserving of her kindness.

"I promise you I will devour that whole pastry after I handle a few other matters," I start, watching Kai shovel the dessert into his mouth, both cheeks filled with flaky pastry. "Where is Fallan?" I push Hunter once more, listening in as Jolie clears her throat.

"Fallan's family owned a farm on the edge of the sector. He has an apartment a few blocks over that his parents left behind for him after their passing. As far as I know, he's been holed up in his room since Andrew Blackburn and his spineless followers delivered their blows to my two boys," Jolie says, her voice shrouded with emotion. "Heaven forbid they provide our people with the means to heal their wounds after such heinous acts of violence," Jolie finishes, touching her scarred hands.

Kai covers his mouth as he swallows the pastry, digging into his pocket with an anxious fidget. I watch him pull out a vial of Cure-All, rubbing the back of his neck as he hands it to the old woman.

"I forgot I had this on me. Take it," Kai says, using his hand to cover his full mouth.

Jolie eyes the medicine with wide eyes, carefully examining the vile to check its validity.

"Quite a lucky Unfortunate to be carrying around a vial of Cure-All and handing it away so casually," Jolie says, watching Kai's fidget turn into a full-fledged shake.

"Well, I-I figured-"

Hunter lands his hand on my brother's shoulder, giving him an empathetic smile.

"She is messing with you. I take it you don't have people that mess with you very often," Hunter says, attempting to ease my brother's anxiety. Kai settles down. His face is as red as the cherry turnover he had eaten in three bites.

"But seriously, how did you get your hands on it? We've been bone dry for months over here. I can't imagine what you had to sell to score a full vial," Jolie says, pushing my brother further, doing her best to see past our facade.

Kai looks to Hunter, hoping for some help in the situation. Hunter only smiles, mimicking my crossed arms as we watch Kai try to navigate this situation with Jolie.

"I-I stole it," Kai says, sounding entirely unconvincing. Even Hunter has to turn away from the conversation, giving himself a few moments to compose himself as he watches the train wreck that is my brother trying to lie.

I feel the smile finally creep onto my face, easing the pain of holding a frown for so long. Jolie grabs a seat from behind the counter, dragging it to the side as she motions her grandson to sit. She hands Kai back the vial, pointing to Hunter's many bruises needing treatment.

"I still have pastries in the oven, if you wouldn't mind healing him," Jolie starts. "Another cherry turnover is in your future," she smiles, tapping the counter, her eyes passing over me again.

I watch her disappear behind the curtain she came from, moving with a certain grace I could never find within myself, no matter how many times my mother scolded me on my posture.

Hunter hesitates a moment before sitting on the stool, watching my brother repeatedly turn the Cure-All in his hands.

"I don't bite," Hunter mutters, both of us watching Kai cringe at the words.

"Right," Kai says, applying a small amount of the solution to Hunter's skin, watching its healing properties work instantly.

Hunter's face fills with a sense of relief, his pain being washed away with each stroke of my brother's fingers across his skin. I hear the loud patter of my foot as it taps against the shop's floor, watching the pair with little patience as I anticipate someone eventually willing to point me toward Fallan.

Hunter's bruises are deeper than I expected, taking multiple layers of the so-lution to lighten in color. Kai becomes hyper-focused on him, making sure not to press too hard on his swollen and battered visage. Hunter bites back pain, clenching his pant legs to stop himself from making too much noise.

"Your silence is killing me," I say, closing my eyes as I focus on the empty spaces of my mind.

"I suppose you won't stop that tapping until I give you more information?" Hunter questions, pulling my attention away from my pointless attempts at shouting into the void of my mind.

Kai pauses, letting his hands drop from Hunter's face. Something close to a smile lingers on my brother's expression, fading away when Hunter gives him a second look.

"How far away is he from here?" I question, offering no light-hearted tone as my frustration surges.

"No more than a few blocks away. He lives in the older units, the ones with the chipped blue paint," Hunter says, moving himself away from the stool. Standing beside my brother, he's shorter, yet he holds himself in a way Kai has never been able to. Hunter is defensive, always expecting the worst. But he's also a fighter, and his resolve is unyielding.

"Great, shouldn't be too hard to find," I start, dropping my bag on the floor as I dig around in its contents. I feel the metal of my blade meet my palm. Its mechanics need some adjustments considering the absence of my chip. I begin strapping it to my side, feeling how it rubs my skin, before concealing it under the massive hoodie Kai let me borrow.

"You brought your blade?" Kai questions, cocking his head at me.

"Never know what's lurking in the shadows," I say, tightening the strap. I feel a sense of security with the weapon so close to me.

"If you give me a few minutes, I can take you to him-"

"No," I say, cutting off Hunter as he reaches for his things.

"No?" Hunter questions, crossing his arms.

"No, all of us in a group will draw attention, and I don't exactly feel like figuring out if my father has already plastered our faces on every screen in the sector looking for us. I don't feel like dealing with the consequences of pissing off Officials, especially if they find us here." I say, watching Hunter sigh.

"So, after years of this kind of treatment of us happening right in front of you, you're only now seeing the corruption for what it is?" Hunter asks.

Kai lowers his head. It's the same shameful, disgraced motion I've seen coming from the Unfortunates as they interact with us all around New Haven.

"Ignorance is bliss," my foot kicks away my bag. "I was the biggest fool there was," I say, keeping my gaze on Hunter.

"Fallan isn't in a state to receive unexpected visitors. He's unpredictable-"

"I know... I'm counting on that," I say, turning to grab the door handle. "Is there a reason you're trying so hard to keep me away from him? Did my father say something to you?" I question, feeling a shift in Hunter's confident posture. I hear the way his heart rate accelerates, listening to the slight sneer of my reflection in the window closest to me.

"Everyone has secrets," it says, looking unamused.

"Like I told you," he explains, sounding less sure of his wording. "He just doesn't want to see you."

Kai looks between us both, unsure of who to support.

"Well, I guess he can tell me that in person. Kai-" my brother's head snaps to me. "Stay here. I'm the one that dragged you with me today. At least I know you can't get into trouble here." I make my way to the front of the shop and reach for the door.

"And you? How do you expect to stay out of trouble if you get into it with the wrong person around here?" Hunter questions.

It's a valid concern, given the crime in this sector. I touch my mark from beneath my hoodie, feeling an energy pulse through me as my fingers graze over the raised skin.

"I'll manage," I whisper, heading through the door and out into the filthy street once more.

CHAPTER THIRTY-FIVE

FOREST

I stand outside the tattered apartment building, looking over the tiny flecks of blue paint scattered on the ground, no doubt from years of brutal weather and lack of upkeep. The walk here was unnerving. There were several moments where I was one shifty look away from pulling out my blade. A few people lie on the streets outside the building, sleeping soundly or rummaging through bins for something to eat. A few people sit on their balconies, watching me from above, waiting for me to move from my position on the sidewalk. I watch a woman leave the building, her body bundled in layers of worn clothing. Slowly, I move closer to her, stepping over a sleeping Unfortunate to catch her before the door closes. I grasp the door, watching her turn on her heels at my sudden presence.

"You startled me," she says with a smile, offering that same kindness Jolie had, not once asking me why I'm here.

"My apologies," I glance into the building, looking over the many names and unit numbers plastered on the wall. There's a buildup of tape on the names lining the directory, telling me there's been a lot of turnover here in the recent years.

"Could you possibly help me find someone?" I start, watching her give me a slight nod, "I'm looking for someone named Fallan Markswood... do you know which unit he might be in?" I question.

"Markswood! Oh, I love that boy. Yes, he's three staircases up. The unit is at the very end of the hallway to the right. You can't miss it. He's the only reason our hallway looks half as decent as it does," she says, smiling ear to ear, "Are you his partner?" she questions, making my words come out a jumbled mess.

"N-No, just a friend," I say, watching her frown.

"Pity, I was hoping someone could take care of him after dealing with those nasty Officials. Poor boy wouldn't leave his unit, even when I offered him a warm meal," she says, sounding hurt.

I'm starting to think her interest in Fallan goes beyond neighborly concern at this point.

"Well, I'd better go check on him," I say, moving further into the open doorway.

"She's a bit odd. Keep your eyes on her," it whispers, no longer relying on just reflections to communicate.

"Noted," I say out loud, giving the woman one last smile before moving inside the building.

I make my way up the three flights of stairs, my legs dragging heavily under me as I struggle to avoid debris and other hazards, like the jagged nails sticking up and out of several of the planks that have been used to repair gaping holes in the floor. I keep my head lowered, watching my feet press against each loose board that threatens to break beneath my weight. Several posters advertising the false promises and programs built by New Haven's government to aid this sector cake the walls here. The evidence of the Untouchable's broken commitments to serve and protect this community can be felt in every part of this sector, down to the broken hand railings and damaged locks, all damage resulting from unsolicited searches and seizures on the property. The cameras here are all broken, serving as a way to hide any vile acts my people inflict here in the name of peace and prosperity. The air still smells heavy, making it hard not to pinch the bridge of my nose to keep out the odor.

I finally make it up to the last steps, turning the corner down the hallway. The walls feel like they're growing closer, tightening the space around me in an unsettling discomfort. I drag my feet across the floor, feeling the heat my mark gives off, warming my skin and nauseating my stomach. I do my best to keep my head down, only looking up to watch a man fidget with a set of keys. He drops them on the ground, glancing up at me causally.

I linger in the hallway, watching the man grab his keys before walking toward me. This hallway has more doors than expected and more turns than the woman downstairs had initially described. The man shifts to move past me, his youthful features giving away that he's probably no older than thirty. He looks cleaner than most in this sector, keeping a stone-cold expression that doesn't reveal anything else about him.

"Excuse me," I start. The man pauses his walk, staring forward with a blank expression. He takes in a deep breath, "Do you know someone in this building by the name of Fallan-"

The man's arm collides with my chest, forcing me back and into the closest wall. All of the air leaves my lungs, causing me to grasp his arm, now pressing down on my sternum. His free hand grabs my chin, jolting my head around to get a better look at my face. His nose brushes up against my neck before he inhales. His nose drags along the veins in my neck, my legs unable to move. I feel my mark burn red hot, all of my instincts telling me to reach out and snap his neck.

The man's eyes shift from a standard brown to an endless void of darkness. I cannot move my arm. I try to force it away from his grasp to grab my blade. His hand dips into my front pocket, fiddling with the lanyard of my father's ID, dangling it between us. I struggle to find air, unsure of how much longer I can stand here before passing out.

"Fight," the other part of me yells, giving me a small surge of energy to force the man's hand away from my chest. He only shoves me farther back, the wall behind me rattling as my back collides with it.

"Someone went too far outside her sector," the man hisses, dragging the ID's edge down my face. "They never said I couldn't have you if you stumbled into the Unfortunate sector," he continues, pressing his nose to my hair. "Fresh Marked blood for me to feast on," he says, the corners of his mouth dripping with saliva.

"F-Fallan!" I yell loudly, unable to muster the energy I needed to call to him down the connection in my mind.

Horror paints my face as the man begins tearing away at his skin, revealing the bony, sunken face I recognize as a Shifter's. Chunks of flesh meet the floor as it peels away its fleshy costume. Its hand, with a similar mark as the one I keep concealed, begins to burn against my skin—I take a moment to glance at the features of its unmasked form and find slick, thin bones for fingers and sunken hollow pits instead of eyes. I continue thrashing against the monster, and my fingers finally touch the hilt of my blade. I pray that the commands I input recently to override the code from before I removed my chip wouldn't fail me now. I wouldn't be able to wield my blade if the commands didn't hold.

"Just one taste-" the creature hisses.

The creature wails, loosening its grip to angle its jaw to align with my throat, but its adjusted grip allowed me to force my blade up, and I watch as it met the creature's skull through the bottom of its jaw. A second blade joins the fight, slicing through the tender skin of the creature's chest from behind, nearly meeting my own front in the process. I pant heavily as the tip of the blade, now protruding from its chest, almost touches my flesh. Giving my blade a sharp twist, I watch the creature's arms go limp. It slumps to the ground with a heavy thud, and its body begins to melt into nothing. Soon all that remains of the creature is ash stuck to the carpet. It's the same ash that covers the ground well beyond the ward.

I kick my body away from it, retracting my blade. Its blood stains my face. My heart skips a beat as I find the source of the other blade. Fallan stands above me, leaning on the wall, panting heavily. The Shifter's blood mixes into his own bloody and bruised face. I have to stop myself from gasping at the sight of his battered face. He clutches his side, biting back the pain. Being this close to him, I find a strange connection to his injuries, and they hit me abruptly. My whole body is miserable. My own side begins to ache, and my face throbs uncomfortably. I watch him run his hand through his hair, closing his blade before stepping near me.

Without hesitation, he grabs the front of my hoodie, pulling me to my feet with one arm, giving me no time to react as he moves us down the hallway. I watch him limp while he moves, only stopping once he's reached the door farthest to the end of the hallway. He fumbles with the knob, forcing it open. He drags me inside, slamming the door shut and latches the multiple locks.

I stumble into his unit, looking at the neat and orderly set up around me, taking in every detail I can. His home smells of cinnamon, a few candles are lit to add some light to the dark space since he's got the curtains drawn, blocking out the rays of sun.

"What was that?" I finally question, breaking the silence.

Fallen moves towards the small kitchen.

I watch him wince as he rummages through his cabinets, grabbing what's left of my bottle of Cure-All and moving straight toward me.

"A Foreign Entity.... A Shifter, like the one the night of the screening."

"H-how is that possible? How did it look human?" I question.

"They can alter their DNA. One of the many, miserable perks of nuclear fallout," Fallan says, rubbing his hands along his face.

"It called me Marked," I start, finally getting his full attention. "How did it know what I am?" I question.

"Your blood. For some reason, they can't get enough blood from people like us. Someone is commanding them to hunt us, letting them past the ward," he mutters, ready to douse me in the Cure-all, but none of my injuries are so bad that I'd see the last of it used on me when he's in such bad shape. I grab his wrist, stopping him as he clutches his side.

Without thinking, I grab the bottom portion of his shirt, forcing it up to reveal a very unpleasant bruise on a very visually pleasing torso. He moves to pull away, and I can see he's already conjuring up as many angry words as he can for touching him too abruptly. I quickly silence him by grabbing the bottle and rubbing the mixture into my hands. I reach under his shirt to soothe the bruises.

"Fuck. I can't even breathe. You've let your injuries sit too long," I mutter, letting my fingertips trail along his skin, watching the way his hand holds my arm, readying to pull me away.

"You can feel my pain?" he questions, his face that much harder to read with all the bruising.

"The minute I saw you," I whisper, keeping my hand under his shirt well after I'd finished applying the solution. The warmth of his skin radiates over my hand, each of his strong stomach muscles pressed against my palm. He keeps his head lowered as he watches me, slowly moving my hand away from his flesh, only to let it rest on the waistband of his pants.

"What are you doing here, Forest?" Fallan questions angrily, finally stepping back to put space between us. Although I feel how furious he is, I know it's not directed at me. It's something more like fear for what might have happened to me. I guess his pain isn't the only thing I can feel.

"Xavier said-"

"Don't say his fucking name around me!" Fallan snaps, turning on his heels at the mention of the blonde Official. I stand my ground as he marches toward me, refusing to back down from him.

"Fallan," I start, grabbing his face between my two hands, unsure why I can't stop myself from doing so. "I had to make sure you and Hunter were okay. I had to make sure *you* were okay," I say. There's no alcohol driving his reaction to me now, and I need to understand how he really feels.

He slowly raises his hand to my own, and for a moment, I think he'll embrace me like he's done before. But he suddenly jerks the Cure-All free from my grasp and moves back.

"I'm fine," he starts, spraying the medicine into his hands. "Does blondie know you're here?" he questions, referring to Xavier once more.

There has to be a reason for Fallan's contempt towards him.

"He doesn't know I'm here. It's just me and Kaiden. No one else knows where we are," I whisper, touching my aching chest.

Warmth surges through my body as his hand dips under the hoodie. Keeping his eyes on me, his hand slowly drags up my stomach. My legs shake as I try to control my thoughts while enjoying the feeling of his strong fingers delicately caressing my bare skin. I move my head to look at what he's doing, only to be stopped by his other hand wrapped around my chin. He pulls my face forward, directing me to hold eye contact. The hand that's been under my hoodie moves higher up my stomach, pausing right below the material of my bra where the pain is the strongest. My thundering heart betrays me and refuses to listen to my commands as it races so fast that I can feel it beating in my throat. I am unable to process what's happening. I want nothing more than to move his hand beneath the undergarment completely to ease my aching breasts.

"I feel your pain too," he starts, working his fingers along the middle of my chest. He suddenly pushes his fingers under my bra, but carefully enough not to touch my breasts while he works to move them in position over the ache that radiates across my sternum. I'm unable to move beneath his touch, feeling a warmth between my legs that threatens to consume me if I don't find a way to satiate it. "And your pleasure," he continues, gently massaging the bruised skin on my chest. A shaky gasp leaves my mouth as his hand moves to touch the supple skin of my breast. I bite my lower lip, unsure why I can't stop myself. I grab the collar of his shirt.

"Fallan," I whisper, unsure why I give him so much access to me.

He quickly retracts his hand, taking several steps back as he runs his hands through his hair. I listen to him groan as he bites his inner cheek, opening and closing his hands as he usually does when he's overly frustrated. I feel the heat in my cheeks, and I can see the same redness staining his skin between the purple and green of the bruises. I let the cloud of desire dissipate, watching him finally apply the Cure-All to his face as his stoic demeanor returns. He moves toward his kitchen, running his bloodied hands under the hot water in the sink. Grabbing a towel, he cleans his face, working in swift motions. He wastes no time moving back over to me, taking the towel and working it along my hands and face to remove the dried Shifter blood.

"How often are we going to find each other like this, only to walk away?" I question, hearing him scoff at the statement.

"You are a distraction," he mutters, pointing his finger at me with accusation. "A physical distraction. Nothing more," he says coldly, my heart filling with indignation at his statement.

"You don't mean that-"

"Why wouldn't I? Would it make your journey over here pointless knowing I couldn't care less about you? Why is it so hard for you to understand there's nothing here? I won't tell you what you want to hear, connection to me or not," Fallan says, growing more hateful with each passing second.

"A distraction?!" I yell angrily, moving toward Fallan, shoving him in the chest out of frustration. "That's all I am, then? Something for you to play with until you get bored. I don't believe that," I say, pointing my finger hard into his chest.

"It's not like a Blackburn is good for much else," he hisses, looking away each time he answers me.

I think of that night by the bonfire, feeling my heart ready to burst from my chest.

"Can you even look at me while you say that?" I question, silently urging him to look at me.

"I remember that night, you know," I start, watching his body tense up. "That night at Josh's party," I continue, keeping my voice low as I hide my emotions. "I remember what it was like to see your smile and feel your hands on me like they were a few moments ago," I continue, looking up at him, hoping I'm not wrong about this thing between us. "You gave me that necklace, the same necklace I could never bring myself to take off. I had no idea why," I admit, feeling the tears ready to burst from my eyes. I let out a small sob, forcing his hands to touch my waist as he looks me over with a stern expression. "You danced with me that night, with a smile on your face I could never forget," I continue, not able to look away from something hanging on his wall. "I gave you that drawing when we were children," I say, pointing to the framed piece of art above his bed. It's the same messy drawing of the field of flowers I'd made all those years ago, untouched by time. "So don't tell me this is only physical because, damn it, Fallan, I know there is so much you haven't told me about us," I say, feeling the tears falling over my heated cheeks.

Fallan's eyes flash briefly with something like agony and longing before all traces of feeling fade abruptly, and there's nothing left but a thick wall that slams against my heart mercilessly. I watch his face contort from conflict as he glances at the painting, prying his hands away from me. I watch him go over to his bed, swiping the picture off the wall. I cover my mouth to hide my emotions, watching him pace around the room as he looks at the drawing.

"A few stolen memories, and you think that erases all that your people have done to me? You think a few stolen moments with me have me as desperate for you as you are for me?" he questions, pausing in front of a trash bin. I flinch as his hand drops the frame in the trash, feeling my heart burst again at the sight.

"If you came to my sector hoping there'd be something between us, that I'd want you... you're delusional," he whispers, clenching his jaw as he speaks. "Besides, you've got a willing Official at your doorstep who seems way more your speed. It would seem that's your poison these days anyway," he says, a lick of jealousy lingering in the bite of his words.

I shove away my emotions, creeping closer to the wall in his mind he's put up between us.

"I don't buy it," it whispers, feeding me with power as I brush my hands along the mental wall, looking for any signs of weakness.

"Is that what this is about, then? Xavier?" I question, watching his facial expression change as I find a crack I'm looking for.

I feel his emotions swirl on the other side of the barrier, each more conflicting than the last.

"I'd say we guessed right," it says, coaxing me to continue.

"I couldn't care less who you share your bed with," Fallan says, crossing his arms as he watches me. I creep closer to him, glancing at his roaring fireplace, ready to call his bluff.

Slowly, I move closer to the trash bin, reaching down to grab the picture frame. He watches me turn it over in my hands, observing it closely.

"Is everything that you say true?" I question, angrily looking at him.

"Cross my heart," he says, leaning in, towering over me.

I nod as I back away, moving closer to the fireplace as I swing the frame in my hands.

His relaxed position on the wall grows more rigid, his body no longer so casual.

"Then none of it matters," I whisper, gradually moving the frame closer to the flames, feeling a sense of his panic.

"There's that fire I missed," it says with glee.

"Forest, get away from there," Fallan says, taking several steps toward me.

"Purely physical, Fallan? Maybe I should take this to Xavier," I start, ready to drop the frame in the flames. "He'd appreciate it-"

His hands are on my waist in a matter of seconds, pulling me away from the flames as he grabs the frame free from my hands. I watch him gently place it down on the side table closest to his couch. Once he's made sure the picture is safe, he backs me up further several more steps. My thighs brush against something firm, meeting the edge of his bed. He pushes me down until I'm seated in front of him.

"Stop saying his name," Fallan mutters, crouching down until he's eye level with me. I look at him with a cocked head, narrowing my eyes at him.

"What happened when my father and his men were over here?" I question, watching Fallan's jaw clench.

"They threatened to take away something very important to me," he whispers, placing his hands on both sides of me and drawing a deep breath.

"Do you know what it's like to have him come in here and tell me all the places on your body he's going to explore? The way he craves the parts of you that you hide from everyone else," Fallan starts, his breath brushing the side of my neck as his body leans over me. I feel my heart thundering in my chest as he leans closer until his lips hover above my neck.

"Have you touched me before, Fallan?" I question, unable to stop the words from leaving me.

He smirks, his voice low as his teeth bite at my earlobe. I let out a shaky breath as he bites down gently. He supports himself to stop from crushing me.

"I have your body mapped out completely, but I've never allowed myself to explore it. You're more intoxicating than a bottle of scotch. I can't escape how you make me feel and I want to drown in you," he starts, his words sending chills down my spine, the ache between my legs returning. "I've never given in to this desire to touch you the way I want, to have your lips on mine," he continues, my throat unable to contain the noise that escapes me once his lips touch my neck. I let out a soft moan as he takes the skin between his teeth, sucking gently on the sensitive areas he seems to know so well, applying more pressure as more sighs of pleasure escape me. The barrier in his mind is suddenly removed and desire overwhelms me as I feel the connection giving me access to his unbridled state. I reach my hands up toward him, grabbing his neck as I pull myself closer. His hand is already positioned to push me away, applying pressure to my lower stomach. His fears of not being able to control himself surge through the connection.

"I've already done too much," Fallan mutters, running his free hand along the skin of my neck, observing the marks he no doubt has left. "You have to get that healed before anyone sees," he whispers, my mind racing back to Xavier.

"Did he threaten you? Is that who you're afraid of?" I question shakily, not letting go of him.

He pauses, keeping his hand on my lower stomach.

"Forest, you have to stop," he mutters, his forehead pressed to mine. "If I allow myself what I want, he will know I had you. One moment of weakness is all it would take," he continues, passing his finger over my lips. "One moment, and I wouldn't stop. I'd fulfill every fantasy I've had of us," he finishes, my mind now filled with sinful thoughts.

"Don't push me away," I whisper, feeling my hand placed on his own. The warmth in my stomach grows the longer he hovers over me. "Besides, there are other things you can do that don't leave a mark," I whisper, feeling his hands brush along my lower stomach, teasing the waistline of my pants.

"Tell me to stop," he says, as his fingers move lower toward my center.

"I can't," I mutter, pressing my nose to his own, feeling his hand plunge completely below my waistline now. I draw in a deep breath as his hand passes over my underwear. My legs shake as his fingers explore the top of the material, gliding across my warmth. He draws in a deep breath as he caresses the fabric above my center, finding my core wet from desire for him. I let out a shaky moan, unable to contain the sheer amount of pleasure I was lost to.

His eyes watch me, the look of lust abruptly falling away.

"Stop tempting me with a quick pity fuck," he growls, moving his hand away. The connection between us snaps.

"You're nothing but an Untouchable girl looking for validation," he spits.

My heart wrenches, his words like a dagger being pressed into my chest.

"I don't need you," he finishes, the dagger now plunged into my heart completely, no longer able to be pulled free.

"And I never will."

CHAPTER THIRTY-SIX

FOREST

My hands press to his chest, ready to force him away. Instantly, I feel the adrenaline in both of our bodies spike, pulling us free from our dispute. We both turn around, content to avoid unspoken words on the topic of what's going on between us.

He grabs me tighter, both of us looking to the door. Hearing their loud thoughts consume my mind, my heart races in a much different way than it had been moments ago. Fallan clutches his temple, my thoughts filled with voices that aren't mine. I lean my head into his chest, feeling his hands cup my head, rubbing his thumbs along the sides of my face.

"Who is that?' I question silently, hearing the pain shroud my voice.

"There's Officials nearby.... I can't block you from my mind right now. We're too... close," he whispers. "Focus on my heartbeat. Listen to their voices," he continues, easing me as the voices become clearer. I stay straddled on his lap in a seated position, one of his arms wrapped around me.

"You can hear people's thoughts?" I question quietly, my mind racing to every single thought of him I've had.

"Among other things, although you've been a pain in the ass to navigate," he whispers, both of us still as the men's voices finally become close enough to hear completely.

"Shifter residue," one of the men says, sounding almost thrilled to find his discovery. I can sense his partner's presence, both men observing the soot of the creature with differing reactions.

"Shifters don't just spontaneously combust. Someone must have gotten a swipe at it." the other man mutters.

Glass breaks as one of the men swings at a hallway light, angrily blowing off steam.

"What's your issue?" one of the men questions the other, disgusted by the feeling of the ash on his fingers.

"My 'issue', moron, is someone in this sector killed a Shifter and lived. Now, they walk around here knowing that the creatures exist and have breached the ward. The Commander will not be pleased knowing something like that slipped past us during our run of this shithole part of town," the older of the two men say.

A jolt of power comes to life inside of me, faint whispers of something new creeping into the darker spaces of my mind. I feel something urging me to go out there and paint the ground with their blood.

"Easy there," Fallan whispers, his breath brushing the side of my neck.

"I might struggle to read your thoughts, but I can feel your emotions. Now that your chip is gone, the more time that passes and the longer you spend around me, the more power that little scar on your torso gives you." He keeps his eyes on the door. "Breathe," he commands, slowly drawing in air, making me follow along with him.

"Start pounding on doors. I doubt they could have gotten too far. The only people we saw enter or leave were those two women," one of the men says, my heart racing once I remembered I wasn't alone on my walk into the building.

I drag myself off of Fallan, listening to the noise of the two Officials beginning their search. I can tell they are going unit to unit, feverishly knocking on doors before busting them wide open with no regard for any of the tenants inside. I hear women scream as the men yell for Unfortunate's to get out of their way. Fallan quickly checks the locks on his door, tucking away anything that might look suspicious, including our blades that we'd tossed onto his coffee table. I move to the kitchen, grabbing the bloodied rags and pushing them down into the lowest part of his clothes hamper. Dragging the chair from the middle of the room, I put it back under the table, keeping the curtains drawn. We quickly scan the rest of the area.

His small fireplace crackles and cast shadows across the floor, keeping the space warm as we exchange looks. I try to find my words, hearing yet another person yell out in pain. Their thoughts of feeling the prod on their skin consume my mind.

"I hope you're prepared to break a few necks," it taunts, my eyes panning to the glass of my framed drawing Fallan had placed on the side table earlier.

She looks at me with her bright eyes and a gray mane. All I can do is nod, returning my gaze to Fallan as his hands find me again.

"There's no scenario in which them seeing you in here is any good," Fallan says, looking around for a quick way out.

"I can't leave," I whisper, touching his hand. "They will see me and know who I am because of my father."

The unknown power within me begins to swell, scraping along my mind, begging to be released.

"Besides, I'm not leaving you with any other Officials, not that you want me sticking around right now," I finish, hearing the thud from the wall closest to us.

"You'd think you'd be able to put in code quicker than that. They're supposed to forget, not cower in fear waiting on your ass for ten minutes," one of the men says, and I realize they've got a Re-Regulation Device.

"I'm going out there," Fallan says, moving closer to the door. "They won't come snooping through here if I come to them," he starts, my hand instinctively reaching out toward him.

"No," I say, feeling a force push against my palm as Fallan goes still.

He looks down at the ground, trying to pry his feet from the spot in front of me. He looks up at me, watching my shaky hand slowly lower. The hold begins to dissipate.

"How long have you been able to do that?" Fallan questions, my eyes blankly staring down at my hand.

"Do what?" I question, slowly dropping my hand to my side.

"The Hold," he says, touching his temple. "An ability to control force, similar to the way I can navigate and control people's thoughts."

"T-The Hold?" I question with uncertainty.

"You truly don't know anything about our power, do you?" Fallan looks at me incredulously, like he assumed I had any idea about what's happening to me.

Three loud knocks pound on Fallan's apartment door, rattling the locks. Fallan and I exchange a look before frantically searching the space around us, trying to come up with a way out of this. I reflect on what happened in the study with my father and my ability to take away his recollection of what he's seen on the surveillance tapes. If I can get these men close enough to me, then maybe I have a chance of wiping their minds of what they saw-

"That nearly gave us an aneurysm. I suggest you slip under the bed," it yells in my mind, breaking through my thoughts.

"We see your light. Open up!" the knocking turns to pounding as the Officials grow impatient.

"I can try and get you out the window," Fallan whispers. I grab his arm, stopping him.

"I'm not running," I whisper, backing away from him.

The pounding grows more frantic as I meet the floor, forcing my body under his bed, using what material I can from his sheets to hide myself. I cover my body, noticing a small hole in the sheet that I can use to see out of while staying fully concealed. Something familiar collides with my thigh. I feel the cover of my sketchbook brush my fingers, wondering at what point Fallan managed to grab it. Fallan gives me a stern look, only to turn away, pausing in front of his door.

"You've got two seconds before we break the door," the man continues as his foot collides with the bottom of the doorframe.

"Whatever happens, stay under there," Fallan whispers through our connection as he moves to undo the locks.

I draw deep breaths, clenching my nails to my palms in frustration.

"I wonder if he knows how much we're looking forward to this," it beckons, its voice filled with anticipation.

"Or how bloodthirsty his Little Dove really is," it finishes, my heart racing as the door swings open on its hinges.

My fear clings to me like a mask, cracking when I see the two Officials standing in front of Fallan in the doorframe, nothing but malice written on their faces.

Chapter Thirty-Seven

Forest

Fallan backs away from the doorway, waiting patiently as the men glance inside his space. I cover my mouth to control my breathing, unsure how much they can hear from their distance. The men look at the area with disgust, each dressed head to toe in the traditional Official uniform.

They move into the space and begin running their hands along his things. Their hands cover the hilts of their prods and pistols, ready to pull them at any moment. I watch them fidget with their Re-Regulation Devices, eyeing Fallan's chip like two kids in a candy shop.

Fallan readjusts his shirt, which had ridden up from me sitting on his lap, covering the array of scars on his back. My nails dig into the wooden floorboards, my frustrations rapidly growing.

"Took you a while to answer that door," one of the men says, staring into the red flames of the fire.

"I was taking care of a few scrapes I got earlier today. Had some misdemeanors to answer for," Fallan says, showing the men his lightly bruised side. His healing had progressed rapidly from the Cure-All, and I noticed his breathing was more manageable. "I can't move as quickly as I'd like, given we don't have the best sources of medicine in this sector. I had to put some natural remedies together," Fallan says, looking at the potted plants of varying herbs crowded near his window. I guess it's safe to assume they'd think he'd been putting together some herbal remedies for his wounds.

"Misdemeanors? Of what kind," the men push. Fallan ponders the question, keeping a relaxed position against his wall.

"Talked back to an Official about touching something that wasn't his. He wasn't amused," Fallan says, his hair falling into his face as his mouth pulls into a smirk. The muscles in his arms move as he crosses them across his chest. The men seem to wait for Fallan to continue, wanting him to say something more which would give them an excuse to lash out.

"Did you see any strange activity in the building earlier?" one of the men questions, knocking down a few of Fallan's paintings, hoping to get a reaction.

"Other than you two busting down doors?" Fallan questions. One of the men moves closer to the bed as he continues trashing things around the room. Fallan moves away from his position by the door. "Last time I checked, the only strange activity is you coming in here and trashing my place with no explanation as to why," Fallan finishes, both of us watching as the Official stops himself from taking another step closer to where I'm hidden. I clench my hand atop my mouth. If I wanted to, I'm close enough to drag the Official under here with me.

"So, you've seen nothing?"

"Like I told you," Fallan says, pointing to his kitchen counter filled with jars of herbs, "I've been busy."

"Well, medicine man, maybe you can help us in another matter then."

The Official, who's been hellbent on destroying everything in the room, pulls out his phone. Images of me and my brother appear on the screen. They are our school photos from this year. My hair has significantly more brown than gray and my eyes seem more alive. Kai looks the same, still sporting his full head of curls. I look at the text label below the images.

"Silent?" I question to Fallan through the connection, unsure how long my father has known of our absence. Just one tap into Kai's chip, and it's all over for us.

"What am I looking at here? Who are these people?" Fallan questions, sounding as convincing as ever.

"The Official's Head Coordinator, Andrew Blackburn, has two children who seem to have gone silent. Most likely, it's just two teens sneaking off with their friends to have some fun, but regardless, our superior instructed us to show their faces around this slum hole to see if anyone recognizes them."

"Wasting resources looking for two high schoolers doesn't seem like normal Official business," Fallan says.

"That's because it's not. But here we are," one of the men says, the other fidgeting with his Re-Regulation Device. Fallan's chip blinks green, his body reacting naturally to the pain the code creates in his skull. I feel the tendrils of his chip buzzing to life through our connection, the immense pressure from the device making it difficult to stay still and not reveal my hiding spot. I force a wave an energy down our bond to try and help Fallan withstand the mental assault.

"So, I'll ask you again, this time hopefully you can answer with less of your shitty attitude. Have you seen these two faces around here before?" he questions, holding the device out toward Fallan.

Fallan pretends to adjust to the command, blinking away a fake haze.

"No... I haven't," he whispers, staggering back as the code runs its course. The man quickly slips away his device, watching Fallan's hand pass over his face as he rubs his eyes.

"I'm sorry, what did you say?" Fallan questions, playing up his confusion.

"Nothing that matters," one of the men says, pulling his prod free from its holster. "But last time I checked, Cure-All wasn't allowed in this sector," he continues, pointing to the bottle of Cure-All I had foolishly left on the side table.

The man takes a step toward Fallan. My energy is drained after giving him so much. I envision the man moving toward Fallan having broken ankles, wanting nothing more than to hear them-

Crack.

The man drops his prod as he grips his ankle. My mark throbs with painful heat and I'm unable to control the noise that comes out of my mouth. I silently curse under my breath, watching both Officials snap their heads toward the bed. The one with a twisted ankle points toward me, hissing in pain as he directs his partner in my direction.

"There's someone under there!"

"Fuck me," I whisper, knowing what needs to be done.

I roll out from under the bed, watching their faces grow pale with confusion. My hand is already reaching for the first thing I can find to use as a weapon. The one unharmed Official steps toward me, already reaching for his Re-Regulation Device. Fallan lowers his head, looking at both men. I ready myself to throw a punch, rearing back my arm with a clenched fist.

"Adam told us you were trouble," the man on the floor hisses.

I step back as the Official closest to me falls to his knees, his eyes closed as his mouth hangs open. I look back to his wailing partner, now still as his face holds a similar expression. Fallan's eyes look different now, a brighter blue than normal. He draws in deep breaths before his eyes land on me.

"I can't hold them for long. Grab the Re-Regulation Device," Fallan says, his face straining in concentration. I dart to the Official holding the device and yank it free from his grip.

"I can't see!" one of the men yells, clutching his head, unable to move.

I quickly find and connect to their chips using the controls on the screen. When I can see their chips blink green, I type in the command I hope will get us out of this mess. My hands shake as I watch Fallan sway where he stands.

Forget us. Forget Adam's commands and leave.

I run the program with a tap on the screen.

Fallan leans into his couch, taking in several deep breaths as a thin trail of blood runs free from his nose. He quickly wipes it away, the side of his hand now coated in a streak of blood. Both Officials slowly start to open their eyes. They look confused. I draw in shaky breaths, focusing my energy on the unharmed Official's ankle, ready to cripple him too.

"Don't," Fallan says, looking at me with a serious expression. "Any more injuries like that and it'll look suspicious."

The men both rise to their feet, looking around the space blankly. They remain silent as they make their way to the door. I fit the Re-Regulation Device back onto the injured Official's belt, doing my best to avoid touching him.

"Out!" Fallan yells aggressively. The men move quicker as they fumble to adjust their uniforms. They give the space one last look before closing the door behind them.

Fallan quickly locks his door, pressing his head against the wood.

"Adam is looking for us behind my father's back," I say, dragging my hands up and down my arms as a chill comes over me.

"Adam doesn't trust you," Fallan says. "I don't think Xavier does either." My feelings towards the blonde official stir as I begin to question his role in all of this.

He was always there right when I needed him. Could that really be a coincidence?

"Xavier isn't from here," I say. Fallan finally turns to face me.

"How is that possible? There is nothing beyond the ward." Fallan questions, moving back toward me.

He keeps his distance, doing all he can to remain true to his word and establish boundaries between us.

"When I was near him, I felt behind his ear for his scar," I start, a hint of jealousy within Fallan slamming into me. "He had no scar, and he had no chip."

"What was he able to tell you? If he has no chip, then is he-"

"Like us? As far as I can tell, no. From what I can tell, he's got a general distaste for the regulations in place here. I don't know whether to believe it or not. He might be our one way of finding out what this new Commander's plan is for our people and for New Haven," I say, considering how much he really could know.

"Our people?" Fallan says, raising a brow at me.

"The Unfortunates," I clarify, biting my inner cheek while scolding myself for not being more careful with my words.

"You aren't one of us," he whispers, moving farther away. "The sooner you realize that, the quicker we can move on from this nightmare you've caused." His hands stay clenched at his sides.

"I can't hate you the way you hate me, Fallan."

"You have to," he says coldly. "Because the minute you do, this gets easier," he finishes, running his hand through his hair.

I stand there for a moment, trying to digest what's happening between us.

I can feel the moment Fallan reinforces his mental wall, closing me off from confirming the validity of his statements.

"So that's it, then? You feel me up, then shut me out?" I question, my voice breaking.

He takes a step toward me, his hand wrapping around my forearm. He leans toward me, squeezing tightly.

"That's it, Little Dove," he pauses, opening his mouth to say more but stops.

I wait several seconds, growing more defeated the longer silence hangs between us.

"Are you sure?" I question, feeling a flicker of emotion hide behind his eyes.

"It's a waste of energy," it bellows, our feelings toward the man finally aligning.

"Purely physical," Fallan reiterates.

I scoff at him, yanking back my arm in defiance.

"Go to hell," I spit, turning away, no longer able to stomach the pain of his rejection.

I hear him shift from where he'd been standing during our argument, and there was a brief moment I thought that he'd tell me this was a misunderstanding; that he'd explain what's truly going on.

Nothing but wishful thinking.

CHAPTER THIRTY-EIGHT

FOREST

Fallan reaches towards me, stuffing a small piece of fabric down into my pocket. I run my fingers along the cloth, feeling how the mask folds beneath my touch. He had pulled it free from his jacket only a few moments after we had left his apartment. He pulls the hood of my sweatshirt up and points to the mask.

"It's best if you cover up," he says sternly. I can tell he's forcing as much distance between us as possible and going back to the way we used to talk to each other is the first step in that direction.

I drag the mask over my ears, letting it cover the bottom portion of my face. He adjusts the material above my nose, keeping his hands resting along the sides of my face before dropping them back to his sides.

"Your face will be plastered on every Official's communication device," he finishes, looking down the rickety staircase. "Once we leave this building, I never want to see you here again." A pit forms in my stomach at the idea of staying away after all that's happened.

"Hey," he says, pulling me away from my rapid thoughts. "It will be okay," he finishes, gently touching my chin.

I nod to make sure he knows I've heard him before following him down the staircase.

My head is spinning at the symphony of contradictions that make up Fallan. One moment, his words were sharp as ice, and the next, they were tender and kind. He is unpredictable, and being around his different moods was like being caught in a dance of extremes that left you unsure of your footing.

It's a dynamic that is driving me mad.

Kaiden

I watch Hunter work the dough with gentle precision, kneading and folding it with care. His grandmother had asked him to make the dough for tomorrow's batch of pastries, exhausting most of her energy making the turnovers earlier today. She seemed happy to let me try one... or three.

He works with a love for the craft, smiling occasionally with a gentle curve of his mouth.

"You can help if you want," he says after a few moments. My body jolts upright from its seated position next to him at the back counter. I glance at the dough, rolling up my sleeves, careful not to touch anything.

"I- I have no idea how to work with food," I admit with embarrassment.

I've never had to prepare any of my own meals. Everything's been prepackaged and delivered to my house for as long as I can remember.

"Take these."

His hands fumble to hand me a pair of gloves, watching me as I gently try to slip my hand into them. The material stretches smoothly over the tips of my fingers, but I struggle to get it completely over my large hands. My brow furrows as I focus, trying not to tear them as I work. I hear Hunter laugh softly; his hand covers his mouth as I turn to him to see what's so funny.

"Here, let me help," he starts. My hands continue to fight with the gloves. He works the material down my fingers, easing the gloves on in seconds. I expect him to drop his hands, feeling surprised once he guides them closer to the dough.

"You have to knead it carefully. You don't want to overwork it," he says, pushing my palms down into the center of his pastry mix. It's warm beneath my touch.

He stands close to my side, my heart rate picking up at the presence of someone so close to me. He watches me work, never letting up on my hands as they continue moving. I notice how much smaller his hands are to mine while we work together.

"Eventually, it becomes more pliable," he continues, cutting and weighting a section of the dough. He pulls it aside, forming the rectangular shape with ease. "Now you try," he says, handing me the scraper. I do my best to mimic his actions, eyeing the uneven cut with a frown. Typically, everything I do comes so quickly to me.

"It looks-"

"Awful," I finish for him, ready to throw it back into the pile.

He lands his hand atop my own again, making me pause before completely throwing out my work.

"I was going to say it looks like you genuinely tried." A smile creeps along my mouth at his statement.

"I don't... I don't normally get to do things like this," I say, watching him create a perfect shape from my disorderly lump.

"Why is that?" he questions, pausing his work to pull up a nearby chair.

"My life revolves around school and preparing for my future. I feel like all I do is study." My hands rest on the counter, folding together anxiously. "And now, it feels like what I was working towards doesn't even matter. What's a Judgment Day if I can no longer stand by my people's ideologies?" I question. I know he can see the regret painted on my face, the shame I feel on full display.

"It wasn't your fault. You were raised to believe my people were scum-"

"And I was wrong," I say, turning to face him.

"How could they stand there and try to tell me people like you and your grandmother were beneath us?" I question, once more feeling comforted as he looks at me with a tender smile on his face.

"It's refreshing to know that you don't hate us," Hunter says, rubbing the back of his neck.

"It was a pretty weak way of thinking," I mutter, pressing my head to my hands.

I hear his laugh again, lifting my head to meet his gaze.

"What?" I question, feeling my cheeks grow red with embarrassment.

"It's nothing," he starts, pulling off his glove before reaching his hand out. I go rigid as his hand passes over my cheek, wiping away a trail of flour that I must have accidentally left behind when I touched my face a few moments ago. It's no doubt coating the rest of my face as well. "You have a bit of pastry on you too," Hunter says, his fingers swiping at the sticky residue. His fingers are gentle as he runs them along my cheek to work to clean me up. I don't move, surprised by my reaction to his touch.

Nervousness bubbles in my stomach.

"Hunter!" Valerie's voice shouts from the front, his hand yanking away. He gets up from the stool, noticing how close our knees are. He gives me a wide-eyed look, motioning me to be quiet so as not to alert Valerie that I'm here.

"Are you back there?" I hear the familiar voice of the redhead that my sister almost pummeled earlier. Aaron must be back from wherever he went after helping Hunter with the cart full of baking supplies.

"I-I'm a bit busy, just wait out there," Hunter says, pacing back and forth.

As I get to my feet, my elbow knocks the scraper to the floor, and it clatters loudly. I curse at myself for being so clumsy.

"If you need help, just ask," a hand passes over the curtain which separates the kitchen from the front of the store, and my eyes lock with the blonde who was always following Fallan around at school like a lost dog. Her eyes go feral with rage. My throat goes dry in an instant.

"Let me explain," Hunter begins, stepping in front of the woman to block her from charging at me, only to be pulled back by Aaron. Hunter curses at him, my heart dropping once her hand reaches my front.

"I'm going to enjoy this," Valerie whispers, yanking me past the curtain and tossing me to the floor.

Forest

The bakery is lively with motion, bodies moving back and forth behind the pastel curtains. Fallan and I keep our distance, both hands tucked deep in our pockets. We stand side by side in front of the building, listening to the commotion from inside the small shop. I hear my brother yell, not giving Fallan a chance to try and stop me, as my hand meets the handle of the front door.

I force myself inside, pausing at the sight of Valerie on top of Kai. She sits atop his back, shoving Hunter back each time he tries to pry her off of my brother. She holds Kai in a chokehold. His hand slams against the floor in a struggle to get away from the girl and all of her fury.

Fallan quickly comes in behind me, giving the pair a wide-eyed look, moving directly to Valerie. I watch his hands grab her waist as she relaxes into the touch. Pulling her up and away from my brother, she pauses her brutal assault. Kai grasps his throat, taking Hunter's hand to pull himself up. Valerie lunges for Kai again, stopping once she takes notice of my searing gaze.

"You crazy bitch," Kai says, struggling against Hunter's firm grasp as he tries to get to Valerie.

"I should call *you* crazy for being in my sector, you Untouchable scum," she spits, leaning her back into Fallan, expecting his embrace. He keeps his hands on her lower back, urging her away. My chest is heavy as a wave of jealousy overcomes me. At this point I'm ready to squash her like the pest she is, wondering how much she'd squirm if I put her in the same hold as she'd had my brother in.

"We could drag her out of here by her hair," it says silently, my mouth curling into a smile.

"Easy, Little Dove," Fallan says, my eyes shooting to him.

Can he hear that other part of me, too?

"And who the fuck are you?" Valerie questions, only looking back at Fallan in annoyance when he nudges her away from him.

I lower my mask, watching her cocky grin drop at the sight of me.

"No fucking way," Aaron's familiar voice says, his red locks are visible from a mile away. He stands behind the counter next to Jolie, cramming his mouth with pastries. "The Untouchable girl," he says, solidifying any suspicions Jolie might have had about our true identity.

"I can't believe this," Valerie says, pointing her finger at Hunter. "You're harboring their kind now?" she questions with disdain in her voice.

"This is my shop," Jolie says, wiping the top of the glass counter. "If you must blame someone, then blame me," she says, defending us for reasons beyond my understanding.

Valerie eyes Kai, ready to move toward him again but Fallan's hand grabs her shoulder, stopping her from taking another step.

"Stop causing problems," Fallan hisses, narrowing his eyes at her.

"Since when did you start caring about them?" Valerie says.

She watches me like a feral animal, ready to pounce on me at any moment. Hunter grabs my brother's shirt as he breaks away from Hunter, stopping him from grabbing the blonde and slamming her into the counter.

"Is it true? Are the two of you Untouchables?" Jolie questions, looking to me for some explanation.

I tap my foot, unsure how answering this question will benefit anyone.

"Can't you tell? Look at the way they hold themselves like they're better than us," Fallan says hatefully, his nostrils flaring as he pursed his lips tightly together. I opened my mouth to let him have it but immediately felt a wave of calming reassurance surge down our connection.

How can one man be so confusing?

"She came back here to make sure you weren't dead. Consider yourself lucky she even did that much," Kai snaps, ready to take down everyone in his path.

"Why would you do something as foolish as that?" Jolie questions, her face filled with disbelief as she waits for me to answer.

Whatever connection drives me closer to Fallan makes it impossible to stay away. But I can't tell her that.

"I have a few theories," Aaron says, clearing his throat while adjusting the collar of his shirt.

I glance in the window again, seeing both it and my normal reflection. I'm startled to find the trail of love bites working up and down my neck. They peek out from the neckline of the hoodie as evidence of what being around Fallan leads to.

"Getting around, are we?" Aaron pushes, taking a step toward me. His hand reaches out to grab the front of my hoodie, ready to expose me to everyone in the shop.

Fallan's hand slams down on Aaron's arm, forcing it against the glass case. Valerie watches the two men, rolling her eyes at the sight.

"If I didn't know any better, Markswood," Aaron starts, smiling ear to ear. "I'd say you're probably to blame for those hickeys I can clearly see on our new friend here," Aaron says. Fallan's mouth is curled into a scowl.

"I've heard enough from all of you!" Jolie says impatiently, moving away from the counter and shoving past us. I watch her move her grandson, urging him closer to me while whispering in his ear. He wastes no time pulling out the borrowed Cure-All, spraying a few layers along my neck while ignoring his friends' hateful stares. Kai takes the opportunity to move over to me, colliding shoulders with Valerie in the process.

"All of those Official assholes from your sector have been sniffing around here all day looking for the two of you," Valerie says, cocking her head at the both of us.

"What do you guess the punishment is for sneaking into our sector and getting cozy with an Unfortunate?" Aaron begins, watching Valerie's smile drop at the insinuation anything happened between Fallan and me.

"I would never let someone like him near me," I finally say, feeling nauseous as the lie slips through my teeth.

"Glad we can agree on something," Fallan says, allowing Valerie to settle into him under his arm.

My hands clench tightly at the sight of them together.

"You two being here is not safe for anyone," Fallan says, moving away from her and closer to me and my brother. Hunter acts as a barrier between us, unaware of how little I want him to do that right now. "Better run off to find your Official, Little Dove," Fallan seethes, the knife in my chest twists at the idea that he would purposely push me into Xavier's arms.

"Gladly," I say, moving past Hunter and getting right in his face. Once again, we find ourselves inches apart, threatening to burn each other if we move any closer.

"The sooner you are out of my life, the better," I spit, wanting to feel his hands touch me once more.

He keeps his stern expression, mirroring my agitated body language.

"You know what they say about Untouchable women. Nothing in their heads, a hot temper, but great in bed," Aaron says sarcastically. Fallan's anger flashes down our connection at me.

"Aaron," Fallan hisses. "Watch it."

Kai scoffs at the man, dragging me back toward him. I don't put up a fight, leaning into my brother's protective arms. Hunter hits Fallan in the shoulder, clearly wanting to grill the man on his sudden attitude change. I give Fallan a long stare before drawing in a deep breath.

"I think it's time for you both to leave," Jolie says, crossing her frail arms across her chest.

"I don't want to see either of your faces here again," Fallan whispers, lowering his eyes at the both of us.

I'm ready to hurl back an insult, feeling my words form in my mind. My brother's words catch me off guard, his eyes only on Hunter.

"Things aren't the same anymore. Even if we don't come back here, you can't avoid us forever," Kai mutters, dragging his attention to Valerie.

I set my gaze on her, feeling nothing disgust.

"Lay your hands on my brother again, and I will paint the floor with you," I say, unable to hold my tongue. She looks put off, Fallan holding her back from getting any closer to me.

"I think she's good for you, cuz. She matches your level of crazy," Aaron says with a smile, looking at Valerie with glee.

"Better get going, *dove*," Valerie mutters, mocking the nickname Fallan gave me.

I draw my hood up over my head, watching my brother copy my movement. We eye the group, our hands clasping together in solidarity. I turn away from their curious eyes, dreading the thought of how alone we'll be when we make it back to our sector. Everything will be different now, and I'm terrified of what that means for us.

"Does my heart still beat?" Fallan questions down the bond, his voice low and solemn.

I nod, not needing to say anything else.

"Then you will never be alone."

Chapter Thirty-Nine

Forest

We wait on the outskirts of our property, watching the flow of cars working in and out of the busy neighborhood. We offered Mark little detail on what happened today in his sector, not wanting to add to the list of stressors we had piled onto him in such a short amount of time. Realizing that someone might be your family is one thing, but knowing you've spent years treating that same family like they're worthless and beneath you is another.

By some miracle, we were able to catch one of his last routes to our sector. We begged him to drop us off several blocks away from our regular stop. He didn't want to let us off the bus at first, pressing us as to why our faces had been showcased on the phone screens of several Officials who had come and gone on his many routes after he dropped us off this morning. We told him as little as possible, unsure how much he could take. He eventually agreed to let us off where we'd asked, mumbling his intentions to speak to Fallan about what was going on.

"How bad is this going to be?" Kai questions, looking to me for some sense of reassurance.

"I have no idea. Whatever happens, I need you to push the blame onto me."

At least if the blame is thrown on me, any corrective actions they try to take will be aimed at me. With his chip still intact, I'm worried about what they might do to him with a Re-Regulation Device.

"I can't do that."

"You have to," I whisper, no longer giving him an option.

We push past the bushes and make our way to the front lawn. Our eyes meet the gazes of a few lingering Officials. Grabbing our hoods, we reveal our faces, both of us dirtied and worn. The Officials begin pressing their earpieces, talking in hushed whispers the closer we move to our front door. Kai angrily takes hold of the door handle, swinging open the entrance to our home.

Several eyes reach us from the living room. My father's hand drops from his phone as my mother's pacing comes to a halt. Xavier leans into the kitchen counter, his face filled with relief. The twins sit at our dining room table, impatiently waiting for us to acknowledge them. My mother's body collides with my brother's, grabbing me, too, and dragging me closer. There's a sudden relieving warmth we get from the embrace. My dad waves away what few Officials linger around the room, letting Xavier stay as he joins my mother in the embrace.

"Where the hell were you two?" my father questions, pulling away from the hug to grab my face, scanning me up and down. My mother's hands toy with my hoodie, looking over the grime with concern.

"Why are you both so dirty?" my mother pushes, my head unable turn to look at her as I stay locked in my father's arms.

"We're fine," Kai says, pulling away from my father. There's an obvious shift in how Kai regards him now. An air of disappointment and anger lingers between them, and I wonder how long it will take for Kai to forgive him.

"But I can't say the same for the people in the Unfortunate sector, can I?" Kai continues, my heart dropping.

"What the hell are you talking about, boy?" my father says, grabbing my brother's collar. Xavier pushes away from the counter, giving me a look of concern.

"It might be best for you two to come back later," my mother says, looking at the twins, "Xavier, can you see them out?"

Xavier wastes no time guiding the pair outside, silencing Max's protests with empty promises to speak later. My father drags Kai over to the couch, dismissing my mother's pleas to let go of him. My father forces Kai onto the couch. Xavier is quick to close the door. My mother grabs my arm to stop me from getting closer to them.

Angrily, I force her grasp away, giving her a cold stare.

"Speak up. Why did you mention the Unfortunate sector?" my father urges, raising his hand, ready to strike Kai for being so insolent.

I concentrate on my father, watching him stagger backward as I will this new mental force of mine to push him away. On the outside, it looks like he lost his balance. My brother steals the opportunity to rise from the couch. The power that usually drains me steadies, feeling less foreign each time I use it. I ready myself to grab my father, feeling a wave of confusion come over me as Xavier's hands wrap around me, pulling me back and into him.

"I promise you, you don't want to interfere," Xavier whispers, gently grasping my arms to hold me back.

I keep my head against him and drive the mental block up in my mind to keep Fallan from feeling my fear. Not to mention, the last thing he needs is to know whose hands are on me again.

Kai is facing my father, both men exchanging heated looks.

"Answer me, Kaiden!"

"We went to the Unfortunate sector!" Kai yells, slamming his hand on the coffee table. "We had to see it for ourselves!" My father's body goes rigid.

"When were you there?" my father questions, looking at Xavier, whose hold on me tightens. I can sense his worry. Worry that we saw something we weren't supposed to. The space around my father and Xavier is heavy, riddled with something I can only describe as regret.

"Does it matter?" Kai questions, his eyes gravitating to me.

"Why don't you let go of my sister," Kai snaps, and the look on his face tells me he has no problem escalating this situation. "I'm not beneath slamming you into the counter, blondie-"

I pull away from Xavier, grabbing my brother before Xavier can get to him. My hands grasp his head, taking a mental note of all the cameras as I drag him toward me. I pull him into my grasp, feeling his anxiety pour into me.

"You need to calm down," I whisper, keeping him close to me. "Don't say another word."

I release my grasp on him, watching him take several deep breaths.

"I can take him outside if you need-" Xavier starts, my mind flashing to the Re-Regulation Devices the Officials will want to use on my brother.

"No, Kai has every right to be worked up."

My father's eyebrows raise at the notion.

"And why is that?" my father questions, dismissing my mother's worried glances in his direction.

"We walked to the Unfortunate sector. We were dared," I start, ready to conjure up the best lie I can to get us out of this. "We looked through a small opening in the fence, nothing more." Xavier becomes less rigid, relaxing his posture slightly. "The improvement projects for their sector were a lie." My head pounds, the strain of keeping up so many barriers taking a toll on me already. "Disease, death... it was everywhere we looked. You made us believe it wasn't like that-"

"We left right after we saw it," Kai continues, feeding into my lie.

My dad circles us, watching us closely.

"And you're dirty because?"

"I got into a fight with Kai." Both my mother and Xavier's interest peaks, "It turned... physical. He wanted to report the conditions he saw to someone. I thought it best we ignore it since the Officials clearly do," I finish.

"Not all of them. Going to that sector is hard on a lot of us. Sometimes fixing a problem is a lot harder than anyone realizes," Xavier says, staring at my father.

"That's all you saw? Did you see anyone you recognized?" my father questions, trying to gauge if Fallan has anything to do with this.

"Who would we know from there?" Kai questions, "It's not like we have an opportunity to be friends with anyone who lives there. After all, they're beneath us, right, Dad?" Kai pushes. The thought of Mark being part of this family passes through my mind.

My father winces at the remark as my mother clears her throat.

"I don't want to hear any more about this. You've been hiding things from us, sneaking around, and now you got caught."

"Everyone should see their sector," Xavier states. "At least once."

"You know better than anyone about those conditions," Kai starts, ready to argue his next point.

"The Unfortunates keep tearing down the new developments. And we've tried to seal the ward for months, but they refuse to let us. They'd rather risk going outside to the unknown than accept our help. If they live like animals, they've brought it on themselves," my father snaps.

Lies.

"Is that true?" I question without thinking, turning on my heels to face Xavier. He scans my face, looking carefully between my father and me. He crosses his arms, tapping his foot anxiously.

I need to gain his trust. He's the only way I can uncover what's really going on in New Haven.

"I've heard more convincing truths," Xavier admits with complete honesty, whispering so low even my father cannot hear before broadcasting a different answer to the rest of the group.

"Our people are doing the best we can, Forest," he says, clearly waiting until my father is pleased before giving me an apologetic look.

"I raised you to believe and respect the purpose of New Haven. The rules we have in place, the way things are set up here protect all of us," he starts, stiffening his posture. "You've continued to break the rules, and you've put us all at risk." His eyes set on me. "There are consequences for the people you drag into your messes too. For years, we've cleaned up after the Unfortunates, picking up the slack to make sure things keep running smoothly-"

"I don't think a history lesson is what she needs right now. She's banged up. Let it go for today, Andrew. They're safe," Xavier snaps, his voice unnerving.

My father's mouth closes, set in a straight line.

"People know about where they were today. If the Commander-"

"Our Commander is a spineless coward who can't even be bothered to come out and talk to his people. A childish dare gone wrong isn't something he'll be concerned enough about to make an appearance. I will tell him what happened was nothing more than fleeting curiosity. Clearly, they saw enough," Xavier's confidence that the Commander would be less than interested in what happened today surprised me. It's becoming more apparent the longer I'm around him that he's got the answers I'm looking for.

"I'm cleaning her up. Let her brother have a moment to himself. We are no saints, Andrew," Xavier says, his fingers interlacing with my own as he begins guiding me away from the conversation.

"They see it all, boy," my father says, his eyes on the cameras as his arms wrap around my mother. "Your defiance is putting a target on your back," he warns. Xavier scoffs at the warning.

"I'd rather the target be on me than them, Andrew. Protecting your family should be your top priority," Xavier says, not giving my father another look as he moves away and guides us closer to the bathroom. I let out a sigh of relief once we're inside, and Xavier finally closes the door behind him.

I stand awkwardly in front of the door, watching his hands work as he fills the sink with running water. He removes his jacket, his muscular frame more apparent as he shrugs off the sleeves. Once again, I notice the black ink that coats his skin beneath his shirt, hidden away by the uniform he wears every day. I lower the shields in my mind, feeling the connection flood through me.

"Why have you been so quiet?" Fallan's voice echoes. A smile of relief spans across my face when I realize he's been worried.

"Did I do something to warrant that smile, or is your head elsewhere?" Xavier questions, watching me in the reflection of the mirror.

"I can sense that blonde twit," Fallan says sarcastically. A wave of his anger passes through me.

"Thank you for getting me away from all of that," I finally settle on saying, unsure how long I can remain silent, mindlessly listening to Fallan's voice before Xavier grows suspicious.

"Happy to help," Xavier says, moving toward me with a towel. He works it gently across my skin, holding my eye contact.

"It didn't go well when we got back home. Xavier got me away from my father," I start, drawing in a deep breath once his hand begins to rub along my neck in all the places Fallan explored earlier.

"Did I hurt you?" Xavier questions, pausing.

"No," I begin, urging his hand to keep working. "You can keep going," I whisper.

"I don't need eyes to sense how much he enjoys being alone with you," Fallan whispers, my mouth curling up again.

"Why do you care? Maybe I want him alone with me," I say, feeling the space in my mind grow crowded as Xavier's hand presses down harder.

I wince once more, letting go of the connection, unable to gauge how much more energy I can expend trying to speak to Fallan.

Xavier's finger toys with the collar of my hoodie. I look at our reflection in the mirror. The version of me with silver locks and taunting eyes meets my stare. It seems pleased, Its head cocked, watching the reflection of Xavier. It takes me a moment to digest the version of him she shows me. He's older, more weathered, with stubble along his jawline. He looks less approachable, his eyes dark and brooding. My reflection watches over his own, something dark marking her skin in places I never noticed before. With a blink, the images are gone, replaced with the version of Xavier I've come to know. His gaze is held on one of the hickeys Hunter had missed with the Cure-All.

"You sure you didn't go past that fence?" Xavier says, running his thumb along the mark. I push his hand away, brushing the tender skin with my fingers, "You saw Fallan, didn't you?" he questions, my eyes observing the love bite in the mirror.

I want to trust him. I want to try.

"I may have gone to see him," I admit, pressing my elbows to the counter, feeling my fingers work through my hair as I lower my head. "I had to see if my father hurt him because of what happened at the house last night," I admit, letting my back rest against the counter.

Xavier gives me a nod, taking a few steps toward me.

"I saw him as well. Although, I never touched him the way they did," Xavier admits, digging in his pocket, holding up the necklace Fallan had taken back from me not so long ago. He holds it in the air between us, waiting for my hand to reach for it. Carefully, I take the jewelry away from him, holding it in my palm.

"Why take this from him?" I question, leaning back further as he plants his hands beside me on the sink. I'm caged between his arms, unable to move.

"I liked it better on you," Xavier admits, motioning behind me. "It was never his to have."

So little context behind such a significant statement.

"Take a seat on the counter. You have cuts that need cleaning," he says, his nose grazing mine before pulling away. I don't argue, taking a seat as his hands rummage through my medicine cabinet. Eventually, he finds a few antiseptic wipes.

"Are you angry with me?" I question, touching the soft skin of my neck. He shakes his head, lifting my hoodie, giving me no time to react as he peels it off my body. I see the scratches along my arms, but I'm unsure where they came from.

"Am I angry?" Xavier begins, holding my hip with his hand, pressing down gently on the cuts with the other. I bite my bottom lip from the sting of the antiseptic. "No," he says, dropping his hand to my side once he's done. He keeps his palm planted next to me and leans in closer. I can sense every part of him, feeling my heart accelerate as my head presses back into the mirror. I feel its presence as it watches me, whispering in my ear.

"I know I'm not the only one enjoying Blondie's company," It whispers, letting me know I'm not alone in this connection with Xavier.

"You don't need to be afraid," Xavier whispers, gently touching the side of my face.

I pull my attention back to him, feeling him move even closer, his body towering over me.

"I'm just a jealous fool if that's what you're wondering," he admits, his fingers brushing beneath the hem of my undershirt. I shudder against the touch, wondering at what point I lowered the walls in my mind and screamed out for him. "I want you to look at me the way I've seen you look at him," Xavier continues, my eyes finally meeting his.

This close to him, I notice the speckling of gold in his blue irises, and I can't help but be transfixed as the colors seem to swirl manically. His blonde curls hang wildly down in front of his face, and something about the way he looks at me tells me the energy between us is volcanic.

"Why do you want me, Xavier?" I question, still motionless.

"Because you're a fire, love," he says, my heart racing. "A fire that I plan on kindling," he finishes, my body reacting for me.

No, not my body.

That other part of me.

I feel my hands clasp around his collar, ready to pull him down and on top of me. I let out a small gasp at my own boldness, feeling his hand drag up the side of my thigh. A part of me is ready to feed into this, feeling utterly enthralled by how his fingers trace circles on my skin. I feel Its control over me growing, and I quickly work to force it back before it consumes me. My body jolts back into the mirror and away from Xavier's lips. I feel my head hit the glass, turning instantly to face Its angered expression.

"What the hell are you doing?" I angrily question out loud, looking over its wild eyes and watching its smile grow.

"Not fond of double dipping?" It questions, pointing to a portion of my head filled with gray.

"*Tik-Tok. Running out of time to battle me. You'll see how much you need me soon enough,"* It whispers, my fist ready to drive into the mirror.

His hand grasps my wrist, stopping the stare-down between me and my now normal reflection.

"I expect nothing of you. You don't need to yell at yourself because I upset you-"

"You didn't upset me, Xavier," I whisper, feeling my sanity slip. I hurry off the counter's edge, collecting myself to try and come up with some explanation for what he saw. As long as I have a say, she won't force me to do this with him.

But he doesn't need to know it wasn't me giving in to him.

"Everything is just extremely confusing right now," I clarify, grabbing his hands. I watch his head raise from its lowered position. "A lot is going on, but I'd feel much better knowing you were on my side. I'm unclear on what's happening or why I keep making so many poor decisions. Still, the one thing I know is I feel safest when I'm with you." He smiles gently, relaxing his hands into my own. "Whatever happened between me and Fallan was a slip-up; just some twisted moment of lust," I clarify, grabbing his face within my hands.

"I want you to be the person I turn to, which is why I need to be honest with you," I settle on saying, feeling his curls brush my hands as he gives me a slow nod.

"I saw a Shifter in the Unfortunate sector, which is why I was with Fallan in the first place. It's why I had bruises around my neck," I say, watching the man's face pull into a look of confusion.

"A Shifter? One got past their ward? How is that possible? An Official would have shot it on sight," he says, leaning against the wall again.

"It didn't look like the monsters I was told about. It looked... human. Well, before it peeled off its own skin. It's like it was hunting me. It wanted my blood,"

He paused, considering my theory.

"I'm assuming he's part of the reason you're still standing here," he says, throwing Fallan back into the conversation.

"I tried to get it off of me. It was stronger than I expected." I say, watching Xavier's head gently shake.

"They can alter their DNA. That's why we call them Shifters to begin with. They are humans who are far beyond saving. They hunt a... specific group of people," he clarifies.

He does know about Marked.

"The Marked are the people our chips were meant to snuff out."

"Your people," Xavier finally says, apparently airing out one more truth for us to share. "You're one of them. Right?" he questions, waiting for me to confirm something I can no longer avoid.

"I don't know-"

"Don't lie," he stops me before I can start.

I run my hand along my mark, drawing in a deep breath.

"Is this the part where you drag me out and expose me to the other Officials?" I question, watching his frown grow.

He takes a step toward me, touching beneath my shirt. I shudder, tensing up as his fingers pass over my mark.

"I saw this a long time ago," he states. "I was just waiting for you to tell me."

His hands dip into my pocket, pulling the necklace free. He gently places the pendant around my neck, smiling at the sight.

"There is so much going on behind the scenes, Forest. So much they won't tell me," he says, dropping his hands away from my neck.

"Where are you from? I mean, how are you not from here?" I question, seeing a sense of loss pass in his eyes.

"That's a story for another time... is what you said true? About Fallan being a slip-up?" he questions, genuinely wanting an answer.

"Yes," I lie, unsure how convincing I am.

He gives me a gentle smile, running his fingers along the scrapes on my arms.

"I hope that's true," he whispers. "For the sake of my selfish soul," he says, pausing to meet my eyes once more.

"Quite a web of lies you're starting to weave," It whispers, my head slightly turning to the mirror.

I half expect to see Its vindictive reflection, but it's only me.

At what point did both sides of me become so hard to understand?

CHAPTER FORTY

FOREST

An unsettling silence still encapsulates the house. By some miracle, my mother had managed to calm Kai down to a level that made his anger manageable.

He lingers in my room now, biting his nails down to the bed, dragging along his childhood blanket in hopes that it might calm him down. In moments like this, I see my brother as the young boy who always stood in the back of the group, too nervous to move, silently observing his surroundings before speaking.

"You told him?" Kai asks me again, trying his best to get his facts straight as if analyzing our situation makes it any more manageable.

"Just what he needed to know, but yes. We need someone on the inside of all of this, you know that. As long as Xavier trusts me, we have that in."

He pauses, narrowing his eyes like I'm prey and he's ready to pounce.

"Is that 'trust,' earned the same way it was with Fallan?" Kai questions, motioning to his neck in small drags.

"Whatever happened between me and Fallan is none of your concern-"

"So, something *did* happen?" Kai pushes, holding his hands to his hips as if he had any room to judge me. There was something different about how my brother acted around Hunter, but I wasn't ready to ask about that yet.

"If something happened," I say, pointing to him, "It was because I wanted it to. Fallan is not the true enemy here," I clarify, watching my brother rub his temples.

"I know, Forest," he says, taking a seat on my bed. "I'm just trying to process everything that's happened. My life has been turned upside down in just a few days. One minute, I despise everything about the Unfortunates, and the next," he pauses, letting out an exasperated sigh. "I'm almost wishing you were with Fallan instead of here," Kai mutters, letting out a gentle sob.

"W- Why is that?" I question, joining my brother on the soft comforter.

"Because I'd rather be in that bakery, getting strangled by Valerie and watching Fallan put on that terrible act pretending to hate you. It was all so real. The smile on Hunter's face. Jolie's kindness. All of it. It may not be practical, but it was real, and I felt safer with all of them than I have in a long time. I can tell you feel the same," Kai says.

I wanted to tell him the truth about me.

"Remember, as far as anyone knows, our hands are entangled in Blondie's hair, not Fallan's." It whispers in my mind, a gentle reminder of why I can't admit anything yet.

"Fallan's hate for me is not an act... genuinely. I find comfort in Xavier," I say, biting my lip as I force out the lie.

I feel a dull ache in my chest, but it fades as quickly.

"Right," Kai mutters, shaking his head. "If that's what you need to tell your-self," Kai says.

A low rumble fills the hallway, both of us looking at the locked door sealed shut with the aid of the back of a chair. I listen to the heavy footsteps of my father stumbling away from his bedroom, my mother quietly pleading for him to go back into their room so that they can talk. Not too long after my time in the bathroom with Xavier, my father had asked him to leave, hauling my mother in the room with him, pairing his anger with a rich bottle of scotch. I could tell Xavier had no desire to leave and became even more determined to stay when I leapt down from my seat on the bathroom counter and immediately started to sway on my feet. At that point, I no longer had the energy to maintain the wall I'd built to block Fallan out, and his concern for me rampaged down our mental bond, threatening to suffocate me in panic before I was able to reestablish the connection to let him know I was alright. Eventually, Kai was able to convince Xavier to leave, promising to send word if our father became too escalated. After much deliberation, I used the bond to reach out to Fallan, coaxing him to relax.

The door handle jiggles, shaking violently beneath my father's touch. Kai flinches at the noise, my eyes watchful as my hand unintentionally clenches, using what energy I have left to force the chair harder against the door. I want to cover my ears as we sit huddling under the blanket that felt much bigger when we were kids. Now, it barely covers our laps.

"Your heart is racing.... Are you okay?" he questions, the concern apparent in his tone even through the vast space of my mind.

"My father is worked up."

"Andrew, that's enough," my mother says, trying to get him away from the door.

"Kaiden and Forest Blackburn, get out here!" my father yells. Kai clenches the blanket tighter.

"Maybe it's best to stay in your room," Fallan hisses, not making it sound like a suggestion.

"I know," I start, continuing to hold the door with my mind.

"I promise we'll talk once I calm him down," I whisper, unsure how long I can hold the door closed with my powers.

I lean into my brother, overwhelmed with a sudden burst of energy flooding my system.

"I'm not taking any chances on you running out of strength," he whispers, my mouth curling into a small smile.

"But you needed that," I protest.

"You need it more."

"Kaiden!" my father yells again. He's determined to finish what they started earlier in the living room.

"I'm not speaking to you!" Kai yells, his voice filled with emotion. I hear my mother angrily stomp away, overwhelmed and stressed. Her next shift is only a few hours away.

I shoot to my feet, feeling my brother's hand grasp my front.

"Don't engage him," Kai says fearfully.

I say nothing, but pull away from his grasp, making my way closer to the door. My father's banging has silenced, but I can hear him breathing heavily as he waits on the other side of the door.

"No one is going to speak to you when you're acting like that," I say, finally giving him the acknowledgment he wants.

"Forest!" my father begins, once more jiggling the lock. "You can't hide in there forever," he says, his voice broken.

"You're drunk!" Kai yells, putting in his two cents.

"I just, I just want to speak to you," my father says, his voice close to a sob. "Please." My eyes shoot to Kai. My brother shakes his head at me, silently begging me not to give in.

"Go to your study, and I'll meet you there," I start, ignoring my brother's silent "no's."

"Just you. Alone. Your brother stays." he commands.

A part of me was terrified for what would happen when I got to his study; what words would fall between us, either tearing us further apart or bringing me closer to understanding the man I looked to for strength for so many years. I didn't know if I had the strength to face him alone or to navigate the emotions hiding just beneath the surface of my flesh, threatening to take me over.

But then I remembered Fallan had promised me that I'd never be alone, and suddenly, crossing the threshold into the space beyond my room didn't seem so terrifying anymore.

The hallway leading to my father's study is chillier than usual, a draft lingering as we round the corner and reach our destination. Kai lingers in the doorway with me, struggling to let go of me to face our father without him. My mother watches me from the bedroom, trepidation written across her face.

"He's waiting for you," she says. My stomach is unsettled at the realization her chip blinks green.

"Why don't you take Mom and have some tea in the living room," I whisper to Kai, giving him a look that begs him not to push me on this. He narrows his eyes as he observes her, noticing how unnaturally relaxed she seems. Someone has recently activated her chip. I'm not sure who stands in front of us now.

Kai nods, letting go of my hand with a gulp. I let our fingers part, staring at the closed door of the study.

"If I hear anything weird at all, I'm coming in there," Kai whispers, giving the door one last look before pulling away.

I watch him gather my mother in his arms, guiding her to the kitchen. I watch the light fade behind her ear. I grab the door handle of my father's study, forcing myself inside and into the dimly lit setting.

He sits at one of the chairs in front of his desk, hunched over in its worn leather seat, and swirling his glass of scotch. He doesn't raise his head as the door creaks on its hinges. The room is dimly lit, with shadows casting into every corner, creating long, eerie shapes along the walls. The small lamp sitting on a table beside the chair he's in barely illuminates his face, making his features look drained. I close the door behind me, unsettled by the thick and heavy air around me. I watch him closely, clenching my fists to control my nerves.

"You cannot go back to that sector," he whispers, placing his glass on the side table.

All of that for an empty warning?

"What are you worried I'll see?" I question, watching his head slowly rise.

"I'm not worried what you'll see," his voice shutters. "I'm worried what will see *you*," he says.

I feel Its presence enter my mind, unnerving and ready to speak. I give in and let It take over for me.

"*What are you so afraid of?*" It questions for me, using my voice with ease. He scoffs at the accusation, my mind already working to shove back Its presence.

"You know, the silver in your hair is brighter. Like the metal of a blade," he says whimsically, pointing to the streaks with the same hand still wrapped around his glass of scotch.

"What are you afraid of, Dad?" I question again, ignoring his comment.

"There are people in this world who will use you, Forest," he rises to his feet. "People who will take you and mold you into a weapon for them to control," he continues, swaying on his feet. "They told me what's to come, what has already passed-"

"Who told him these things?" It asks into the recess of my mind.

"Who is hunting me?" I question, watching his mouth slowly curve downward.

"They will destroy anything that's different. And no one's mind is safe. The Apparatus is near, Forest, and it will take you and all those who fear it with it," he says, stumbling toward me, nearly falling into me. I grab his arm, trying to get him to focus on me.

"I know about Mark," I whisper, watching his eyes widen in their drunken haze. "I know who you are," I reiterate, watching as a strange smile spreads across his face.

"He would've loved you and your brother," he says, barely coherent. "Do you know?" my father questions, his eyes halfway open as his legs begin to give out.

"Do I know what, Dad?" I question, following him to the ground.

"They won't let me," he says, gently closing his eyes. "They won't let me tell you," he continues, pressing his head to the cool floor.

"What am I?" I question as he mumbles something I can't make out. "Why do they want me?" I push, leaning my head closer to his mouth to hear better.

"It's cruel what they did. I thought I was protecting you," he mutters, touching my face with a cold hand.

"You will lead them all from the darkness."

His voice is the clearest it's been this whole conversation.

"Or we all die fighting to keep the darkness away from you," he finishes, my heart dropping at his declaration.

I fall to my ass, backing away from my father, watching sleep overtake him. I feel my heart rate pick up, looking at my reflection in the silver tray that sits on the coffee table. It's there, watching me with a look that tells me It's just as shocked and confused as I am.

"What are we?" I question, watching It shake Its head.

Its posture is rigid, and Its demeanor is somber. For a moment, I wonder if I'm seeing the real version of the monster that's been tormenting me for the last several days.

"Damn," It starts, moving Its hands through Its hair.

"We're running in the dark, looking for the light, expecting it to just show up in front of us." It finishes.

"How long have you been with me?" I ask, unsure if I want the answer.

"Always," It says, rubbing Its arms. *"I've always been a part of you, but we were lost to each other once. I've been waiting to connect to you once more ever since."*

Once more?

"Can I trust you?"

"Trust me? When will you learn?" It smiles, pointing its finger at me.

"I am you."

CHAPTER FORTY-ONE

FOREST- THREE WEEKS LATER

B right oranges and reds paint the downtown shopping center in a mirage of warm shades. Hints of cinnamon and nutmeg permeate the air, pairing perfectly with the aroma of varying sweet treats made freshly available for the upcoming holiday.

The Fall Solstice Festival has been around for as long as I can remember, allowing people more liberty to celebrate with as much food and alcohol as they want. New Haven citizens are assigned special outfits meant only to be worn during the festivities. The maroon material of my costume clings to my body, my hair freshly dyed to a dull shade of dark brown, all of my silver locks now snuffed out and hidden. With Xavier's help, I managed to get all the silver, feeling grateful when he asked no questions about the sudden want for change. Both of us looked saddened to see the lighter color go. Over the last few weeks, my body has begun adjusting to the power growing within me. It's becoming easier to dictate the energy around me.

My dress stops just above my knees, and I've paired it with a set of tights and black high-heeled shoes. Kai wears a maroon shirt tucked into a pair of black slacks. His hair lies perfectly smoothed back with a gel my father made him wear.

It's been weeks since I've engaged with Fallan. Sometimes, we find each other late at night when we can be alone in the privacy of our minds without interruption, but besides a few stolen glances and the occasional leak of emotions down our mental bond, we've kept our distance from each other at school. Colton and Josh continue to push their limits with him, and there have been a few times where

I may have taken the liberty to step into their minds, offering him some reprieve by forcing them to trip down the stairs, drop their lunch trays, or run into a door or two. All accidents of course.

We've seen Hunter a few times, briefly in passing, as he runs his routes for the bakery. Kai has tried to wake up early enough to catch him before school, even tolerating Aaron's presence so he can spend some time with him. Valerie has been as unpleasant as possible, doing her best to taunt me when she's with Fallan and knows I'm around. But over the past few weeks, he's leaned away from her touch more and more. Things are different, and we can't take any of it back.

Mom and Dad, however, have gone on as if nothing happened between us. While I knew my mother's chip had been activated, I didn't notice anything that indicated my father's was manipulated, too. Regardless, it was apparent that denial would be the way we moved forward together as a family.

My father's drinking has escalated, and as a result, so has his use of control over my mother's chip. When I'm in bed at night, I sometimes tap into Fallan's dreams, unsure how much longer I'll be able to keep my distance from him.

The twins are still on edge around my brother and me, walking on eggshells anytime they interact with us. Max stopped with his advances long ago, not wanting to push Xavier after receiving a few challenging stares from him when he'd decided to let his touch linger on my arm just a little too long while we were gathered at the house after classes one day.

"I saw Hunter again this morning," Kai says, sipping his cup of cider. I cross my arms, tugging at the dress that squeezes my chest, making breathing much harder. "Things in their sector are only getting worse. Stricter regulations and the Officials are taking more control," Kai says, shaking his head.

"Have you heard from Fallan?" he questions, my mind running through the countless late-night conversations we've had. I'd become reliant on hearing his voice in my mind to fall asleep.

"Not since Friday at the Academy. I've been trying to avoid anything that might get me more marks on my scorecard. I don't want any more attention on me, or us. Xavier was even shocked by how many marks I've racked up," I say, reflecting on how he'd looked at me after seeing my card when I pleaded to have him help me throw the Officials off my trail.

"Hunter says Fallan walks around their sector like an empty shell ever since you showed up that day," Kai says, trying his best to gauge where I stand with the man.

"Xavier says you do the same after you come back from your morning talks with Hunter," I push, watching my brother's relaxed posture go rigid. "You still plan on telling me you only see him to get information?" I question, recalling Fallan's observation that Hunter had seemed more of a morning person lately.

"Whatever you're insinuating," Kai starts. "Drop it. Nothing is happening between me and Hunter." I can feel his hesitation in making that statement, unsure of the validity of his own words. "Drink your cider," he groans, pressing my cup to my lips.

"Well, look at you two," Rae's familiar voice says. We both turn to see her perfect figure, radiant in her solstice dress and adorned with sparkling jewelry that catches the light and dances across her neckline and wrists with every movement. Her hair is perfectly curled in soft waves. I hold my shoulders back, watching her move toward us with a wide grin. I half expect Kai to be staring her down, only to be surprised by his gaze fixed on his cup of cider. Max trails behind her, his shirt lazily thrown on in a grand display of casual confidence.

"No small occasion for you, is there?" I question, handing her my beverage to finish.

Music fills the air. A symphony of violin and piano all create beautiful melodies that add to the elegance of the party. A few Unfortunates are buzzing around as they cater the event, helping set up tables and food. People surround the space, chatting with glasses of champagne in hand, many acknowledging my father and mother, who are working their way through the crowd, arm in arm with soft smiles. Over the past few weeks, Kai and I had made more of an effort to convince them of our loyalty, chalking up our behavior to a fleeting streak of rebellion.

Rae's hand reaches for my hair, twisting a dark strand between her fingers.

"Has it always looked this dark?" she questions. Kai is the one to answer.

"For as long as I can remember," he says.

An unfamiliar Unfortunate moves past us, both twins scowling at his presence. Max claps my brother's shoulder; a menacing smile tells me whatever he's about to say can't be good.

"You think he'll squeal if you jab him just right?" Max questions, toying with the blade tucked away at his side. Ever since he'd made his interest in becoming an Official known, he'd become more open with his disdain towards Unfortunates. He'd adopted the same cruel façade and was even armed at all times. My brother's distaste for him had grown, resulting in more nasty stares than smiles between them lately.

"I'm not sure about him, but I know you would," Xavier says casually.

Max yelps, rubbing his neck as Xavier's fingers pinch the skin, clearly rebuking him for how he'd talked about the Unfortunate.

I can't help but marvel at Xavier, feeling my heart pound at the sight of him. Usually clad in his stark, black uniform, Xavier now dons a maroon shirt, slightly unbuttoned to reveal intricate black tattoos that usually remain hidden. I catch a glimpse of an elaborate design on his side, only to be concealed when he adjusts the buttons on his front. His curls are wild and unmanaged, framing his infuriatingly perfect face. His stubble is manicured, accentuating his jawline. He wears casual black pants, and his fingers are decorated with a few carefully chosen rings. I see a pocket watch dangle at his side, its chain attached to the loops of his belt. Max cowers at the sight of the man. His cheeks flush from embarrassment. Rae fixes her posture, suddenly attentive to our conversation, given the blonde's presence. I feel the monster within me resurface, hearing Its voice speak in the back of my mind.

"She sure doesn't mind him being here," It says, my mouth biting back a response.

"I wasn't going to try anything," Max says, nudging his twin free from her trance.

Xavier's eyes find mine, and he smiles, ignoring the countless lingering stares as he looks me up and down.

"It would be a shame for you to look that nice and not enjoy at least one dance with me," Xavier says, holding his hand out toward me.

I can't help but smile back at him, unsure at what point I'd grabbed his outstretched hand.

He guides us away from the group, giving Max a smirk. My parents' eyes land on us. Both of them relax as they sip on their drinks. Couples hold one another rigidly, all looking foreign to the motion of dance. Xavier pulls me close, not letting much space reside between us. His hands clutch my waist, my arms already up and around his neck. He moves with confidence, doing what he pleases, regardless of who's watching.

"I figured you might want out of that situation," he whispers, guiding me in a sway. I feel his warmth radiate through me, finding comfort in how much he tries to look out for me.

The music fills my ears, making it much easier for me to relax my movements and follow his lead.

"I want out of most situations lately," I admit, trying to observe the black swirls on his skin again.

"If you want to see what it is, you only have to ask," he whispers, taking notice of my wandering eyes.

My face grows flush at the remark. His grip tightens as my steps falter.

"I thought regulation required our skin to be clean," I admit, feeling him pull me up to stand on top of his feet as Fallan did the night of the bonfire. It seems natural for him, like he's had me here before. I look up to see his eyes devouring me.

"No one's skin is clean here." I feel his fingers drawing circles along my lower back. "I just decided to paint a reminder on my skin of what it is I fight for," he whispers, my face hot from how close we are.

"What are you fighting for?" I question, watching his jaw clench.

"I wish I had a simple answer for you. Just know that when it comes to you, my purpose is clear."

I shake my head, feeling my hair tickle my lower back.

"Why drag yourself into my mess? You hardly know me." I whisper, feeling his grasp tighten.

He closes his eyes, suppressing a slight groan, rubbing his throat with firm strokes.

"You're right," he says with a great deal of defeat, finally opening his eyes. "It must mean you're a pretty impactful woman." My chest fills with a deep need to stay close to him.

He touches my hair, giving it a close look.

"I didn't think we managed to make it go that dark," he whispers, furrowing his brows.

"You don't like it?" I question, giving him a smirk.

He leans in closer, bracing my lower back.

"It hides your natural beauty, love," he whispers, our noses grazing. "Being close to you like this is something I do not take for granted."

My heart flutters and I feel Its presence stir to life again.

"Feed into it," It starts, coaxing me into allowing him closer.

"You don't get a say," I seethe in my mind, feeling a sudden need to pull away from him, flooded with thoughts of Fallan. Xavier picks up on this shift and gently moves me from his feet as the song ends.

"Your family is attending the dinner tonight?" he questions, his voice almost drowned out by the clapping of those applauding the band.

The Commander supposedly coordinated a dinner for all the Official families this year to thank upper leadership for all their hard work.

I nod, and Xavier reaches for my hand, pressing his lips to its top, giving me a soft smile. I try to find comfort in him again, but the connection is lost.

"You look beautiful," he says, remaining positive despite how closed-off I'm being.

A body passes by Xavier, dressed in a catering uniform. The man barrels into Xavier's shoulder, making Xavier remove his grasp on my hand as he turns on his heels. I watch the Unfortunate weave through the crowd, pulling away from us before he can single him out. Xavier looks frustrated, scanning the crowd for someone bold enough to touch him like that. I feel a sense of relief when I see Fallan's black curls. His playful blue eyes observe the blonde from a distance, motioning his head to an uncrowded space between two buildings farther away from the event. Xavier runs his hand through his hair, ready to turn back toward me, only to be motioned by my father, who's struck up a conversation with one of his many co-workers. Xavier sighs deeply, giving me a look.

"Hayes!" my father yells.

"Your last name is Hayes?" I question with a smile.

"As far as they know... would you hate me if I went to deal with that?" Xavier questions, leaving me with an opportunity to find Fallan.

"Make my dad proud," I say sarcastically, watching him smirk before he moves to join my dad.

Wasting no time, I followed Fallan's path, looking back once before joining him in the alleyway.

His hands are deep within his pockets, a look of anger painted across his face as he paces back and forth. He wears a uniform meant for those catering the event. He looks me over, pausing once he takes notice of my dress.

"I couldn't stand another second of watching him touch you," Fallan says. The wall in his mind is as safeguarded as ever.

There's no running now. Weeks of nothing but secret conversations in our minds and distance between us.

"You said-"

"I can't keep avoiding you... it's eating me alive," he whispers.

I feel my heart wrench. This back-and-forth dynamic between us is unbearable.

Slowly closing the space between us, I move closer, raising my hands to touch his chest. A fire comes to life inside me the moment I feel the warmth of his skin beneath the uniform. The other part of me takes control as I lean in closer to him.

"Touch me, then. Kiss me," I whisper, edging my mouth closer. He grasps me tightly, his heartbeat pounding against my hand.

"No, Forest. I don't care for you that way-" he whispers, ready to push me back again.

It speaks for me, eager and full of energy.

"Bullshit!" I hiss.

"I want to feel you, and only you," I whisper, Its confidence swirling through me. "If I'm alone with you again-"

"There will be no again," he says, his words crashing into me, forcing the other part of me back into Its cage.

He grasps me, moving me back at arm's length. His shirt is a mess. My dress is no longer as flat and pristine as it once was. The music travels down the alleyway, both of us fixing our clothing. His hand is quick to readjust my hair.

"The bastard really did dye it," he says, toying with a few pieces.

"You want to talk about my hair? After all of that?"

He touches my chin, craning my head up to look at him.

"I'm two seconds away from doing something I regret. I suggest you let it go," he says, ready to move away.

I press my head to his chest, listening to his rampant heartbeat. It calms my mind.

"This coldness is breaking me," I whisper, watching his eyes fill with anguish at my admission.

"I'm sure you can fit the pieces back together," He says stoically.

Slowly, I move away, a range of emotions adding to how confused I am about what's going on between us.

"How long do you plan on doing this to me?!" I yell. He stands still, his eyes lowered.

"As long as it takes," he says coldly.

A loud cracking noise fills the air. Static from the intercom systems blares through the air. Our heads snap toward the end of the alleyway, exchanging a long look of confusion.

"Stay here," I say, pulling away from him, giving him no time to react as I move closer to the commotion.

The noise grows louder the closer I get to the exit. People cover their ears to stop the pain from the abrasive sound. Officials bark orders, yelling at people to turn off the systems, unable to be heard over the sound now coming through intercoms. A slow, unfamiliar song plays over the system. The sound of a long-forgotten melody surrounds the space. I glance around, spotting Xavier and my parents, all of them yelling for someone to turn down the noise. Slowly, I begin pushing through the crowd, watching Fallan exit the alley behind me, joining the chaos in front of us. Kai pulls away from his conversation with one of the caterers. Hunter's dark eyes find mine as Fallan joins his companion. Both men pick up food trays and busy themselves as the music continues. Kai covers his ears, moving toward me and away from the boys, saying something I'm not able to make out. I avoid looking toward Fallan, feeling Xavier's eyes on me as the music fades out and a voice bellows out through the speakers.

"The world you live in is a lie," the voice hisses. *"We are here to tell you, the ash is not all that remains."* Upper leadership is frozen, unable to stop the voice from continuing.

"There are those amongst you who have broken free of this facade. New Haven isn't safe. The Commander lies to you all. Find us," the voice says, my stomach churning. *"And your souls will finally be free."*

My eyes dart to Fallan.

He looks confused, glancing at me briefly. Both of us are unsure what to do.

"Who was that?" Kai questions shakily, his eyes wide.

I look back to Xavier, his body frozen, as if he's processing everything he's heard. Slowly, he raises his head, our eyes locking.

For a moment, and only a moment, I feel something snap into place. A small glimpse into his mind. His worries pass through me, a deep fear threatening to break me down on the spot. As quickly as it came, it faded, and I watch as he backed away into the crowd of Officials calling his name.

"Did you hear me?" my brother questions, shaking me out of my trance.

"What?" I question, pulling my focus back to him.

"Did you hear what they said? About the ward?" Kai questions, my eyes darting to Fallan once more.

"Who the hell was that?" I question anxiously.

"I have no idea... and I doubt they know either," Fallan whispers back, motioning to the gaggle of Officials and upper leadership trying to regain order.

Adam steps free from the crowd, holding up his hands in an attempt to draw everyone's attention.

"Ladies and gentlemen, it seems someone took the opportunity to pull a prank during tonight's festivities," he says.

Adam scowls, pointing to one of the men working on the sound system.

"Shut it down," Adam hisses, giving the crowd a long look.

The men switch off the electricity, taking the lights and static with it. I swallow nothing, feeling uneasy at how many Re-Regulation Devices surround us. My father pushes Xavier, questioning if he knows who this could be. The men draw blanks. Officials command the Unfortunates to go back to their sector.

The back of my neck tingles as I feel an unknown presence loom behind me. A weight presses down on my shoulder, like an invisible hand is trying to draw my attention. The same voice from the intercom quietly whispers in my mind.

"Find us, Forest."

The pressure in my skull intensifies. I close my eyes, focusing on the well of power inside me to try and force the presence out of my mind. I feel the blood drip from my nose and move down across my upper lip as I strain to gain control.

"Forest!" Kai yells, shaking me in a rush. My eyes fly open. I still stand in the same spot. The crowd grows thinner as people begin to dissipate. My hand quickly wipes away the blood from my nose. Fallan's has moved closer to me, undoubtedly aware of what had just happened to me. He looks ready to touch me, stopping once he takes notice of Xavier and my parents are close by.

"Get out of here," I whisper, watching him pause, his jaw clenched.

He glances towards my parents again and moves toward me quickly. Once he's in front of me, he scans my face, trailing his fingers softly along my cheek and then under my nose to wipe away the remaining blood. Kai's body shields us from the crowd, and I feel Fallan's mental shield dissipate.

"I don't have the strength I need to keep you safe," he says silently, running his thumb along my cheek.

Taking a mental note of my face, he backs away.

His words are cryptic, and I ache to have more time with him so that things can be clearer.

I lean into Kai, turning away from Fallan, wanting nothing more than to follow him. Xavier and my parents finally make their way to where we're standing. Xavier's eyes land on the small bloodstain on the front of my dress that I hadn't had time to hide.

I try to sense if his mind is still open to me but find no way in.

"Did you hear that voice?" I question silently to the monster in my mind, still unsettled by the eeriness in the man's tone.

"I heard everything."

"And?" I push.

"He's going to regret stepping into our mind."

CHAPTER FORTY-TWO

FOREST

I sit uncomfortably at the large table, feeling the way the dark green gown clings to my body. My hair is pinned up and away from my face, highlighting my slender facial features. My mother had spent over an hour in the bathroom with me earlier on my updo, spraying an ungodly amount of hairspray to keep everything in place.

She was meticulously focused on our family's appearance for this dinner, going on about Kai's upcoming Judgment Day and the risk to more scorecards if anything went wrong tonight. Her dark hair is wound on top of her head similar to mine. Her tiny body sports a black dress she rarely wears. My dad and brother are both adorned in formal wear. To my father's surprise, Kai needed to borrow one of his suits, no longer the gangly boy he was at last year's solstice dinner.

The dinner is hosted at Adam's house, and to my dismay, Josh will be there. Every year, I try to avoid him, and every year, he only becomes more aggravating. Unfortunates serve at the event, keeping drink glasses and bellies full. A few other Officials and upper leadership have children that attend, though they rarely seem to make it my way, not that I complain. I'd prefer to be left alone.

I look out of one of the large windows in the dining space, listening to the tunes of the grand piano as I'm comforted by the smell of fresh bread.

"I should have figured you'd be away from everyone else. Fancy pushing another person off my roof?" Josh whispers. My shoulder nudges him away.

"You know I didn't push him, Josh," I whisper, turning to face him.

His hair is styled back and away from his face, his golden skin shining with a healthy glow in the dim light.

"Maybe," he says, taking a large swig from his glass. "But it's fun watching how you flinch when I bring it up," he says, my head shaking.

"Why do you taunt me? You should know by now that I won't tolerate it," I say, watching him lean into the wall next to the window.

"Our buddy Max is going to be admitted into the Official's training programs tonight," Josh says, finally grabbing my attention.

"That's not possible, his Judgment Day-"

"The Commander and my father decided to move him forward before his Judgment Day," Josh says, as I scoff loudly.

"My father gets the final say in who joins his team," I state, turning back toward the window. "There's no way he would've approved that," I clarify, watching Josh toy with a string on the front of his dark suit jacket.

"Maybe people are tired of Andrew Blackburn running things around here," Josh says.

I look at him, half expecting him to take back the statement. Instead, he watches me, waiting for me to challenge him. I feel the other part of me reach out, stepping into the light, taking over me in the moment.

"Maybe people are tired of the Order," It speaks for me, my voice just a vessel for its rage.

"You don't believe in the Order?" Josh questions, my mouth curling into a smile at the notion. I feel it working inside of me, throwing caution to the wind as it assesses the man in front of me.

"I don't believe in anything that has to be forced on us."

Its presence ebbs back into the shadows of my mind and releases control to me.

His mouth stays still for a moment, his body unmoving, unsure what to say. A few Unfortunates move into the space, offering us small finger foods. Josh snaps his fingers at the woman in the corner of the room who's wearing an 'Event Coordinator' badge. She's from this sector, so she must be in charge of the rest of the staff.

He grabs her hand, his mouth set in a scowl.

"Where is the Unfortunate I requested to be here tonight?" he questions, toying with the mic wrapped around the girl's ear.

"He's in the kitchen-"

"Well, bring him out. The last thing I want to see is your face at dinner," he hisses hatefully, my hands clenched, stopping me from dragging him to the floor. Quickly, she nods, fearfully moving away from him.

"You requested specific Unfortunates be here tonight?" I question him.

"I thought you'd be thanking me," he says, slapping my back hard. "One of them is that boy toy of yours," he finishes, my stomach churning.

I hadn't been able to reach Fallan after the incident during the solstice celebration. I'd assumed he'd been caught up in the chaos from earlier but had still exhausted myself trying to connect with him. Today was turning out to be nothing short of a nightmare.

Josh's hand lingers on my back, running his fingers along my exposed spine.

"Maybe it isn't such a bad thing we had to wait until tonight to come to this dinner," he says, his eyes taking in all of me. "At least you look pleasant in a dress that revealing," he mutters, his hand moving lower than I'd like. I feel a small wave of panic pass over me.

"You requested me?"

Fallan lingers in the doorway. His hands clutch a bottle of champagne. His hair is a ruffled mess of black curls. An earpiece dangles from the side of his head, and his eyes are dead set on Josh.

At the sight of Fallan, Josh moves closer to me, tugging me into his side.

"Why don't you reconsider where you've got your hands," Fallan says, taking a few steps further into the room. I look around to see if anyone's watching, but we're the only ones here.

Josh laughs, goading Fallan to do something. I yelp as I feel his right-hand slide down to my ass while he wraps his left arm around my front so I'm flush against him.

"Get your fucking hands off-"

"I don't think I will," he interrupts, his fingers moving towards the front of my thigh. Fallan's rage is palpable as he sets down the bottle of champagne and begins rolling up his sleeves.

"What do you think you're doing?" Josh questions playfully. Every scenario I play out in my mind ends with Josh face down in a pool of his own blood. There's no guarantee I'll be able to control the bloodlust threatening to consume me. To make things worse, there are surveillance cameras in every corner of the room we're in.

Fallan circles Josh with a look of malice. I see the shift in his eyes. I feel the energy he pulls from me. Josh's nails dig into my skin as his body tenses in anticipation.

"Let her go," Fallan says, his voice commanding and powerful.

Like an obedient dog, Josh releases me, and I move away from him the moment I'm free. I shift behind Fallan, keeping a safe distance to avoid suspicion if someone is watching through the camera feed.

"What are you doing," I question silently to him through the connection.

"Debating whether or not I have him snap his own neck," he says, his energy continuing to wane.

I grab his arm, trying to calm him down.

"Fallan," I whisper, feeling his body relax. "Let him go," I say. He looks over his shoulder at me before finally releasing Josh from his invisible grasp.

Gradually, I back away from the two of them, watching Josh blink, clutching his head with a dazed expression.

"What happened?" Josh questions, looking between the two of us.

"Dinner is ready, *sir*," Fallan snaps at him coldly. "I came in here to get you, and you were standing in the middle of the room, mumbling to yourself," Fallan says, my hand covering my smile as Josh slowly looks around.

"Right," Josh says, looking between us. "No need to linger. Move," Josh says, urging Fallan to leave the room.

I take the opportunity to walk beside Fallan out of the room, wishing more than ever that my lips could explore that lovely smile painting his face as we exit.

It's nothing more than a foolish fantasy.

The table's spread is beautiful, decorated with small gourds and crisp foliage. Bundles of cinnamon and spiced cones surround the area. I take in the smells around me, watching Fallan linger close to the wall, giving me a small smile each time I look at him.

A few members of upper leadership speak to Adam. Each time a new group of people walks through the door, my parents greet them and make small talk. Josh sits at the table, flirting with some of the daughters of the other Officials. I watch Fallan eye the man, his voice broody in my mind.

"Would it be worth it to make him drop that whole glass of champagne on the girl next to him?" he questions, my eyes averting to the girl in his company.

"It would be a shame to ruin such a pretty dress," I admit, appreciating the light pinks wrapped around her slender frame.

Fallan moves to hand out more drinks, his body working past me as his voice reaches my ear.

"Your dress outshines everyone else's," he whispers, my cheeks reddening.

I feel my stomach toss. The rasp in his voice enough to drive me insane.

I'm continuously tormented by his influx of emotions. One moment, he hates me. The next, he's ready to back me into a wall and make me his.

I hear my brother's voice boom as he enters the dining hall. He's jovial and his words are vibrant and playful as he continues to converse with the man entering by his side. Xavier smiles ear to ear at my brother's words, his black suit tailored to perfection.

Kai clings to the man for some comfort, ignoring the other kid's kiss-ass attitudes, giving them little attention. I see Adam eyeing Fallan, watching him work through the room. I see the moment Fallan spots Xavier next to my brother. They exchange deep looks of distaste, suffocating the space with menacing energy. I see a metal flask hidden in my brother's coat, giving Xavier a wide-eyed look of uncertainty.

"I think Blondie might have given your brother some liquid courage," Fallan whispers. I frown at them as they approach.

I toy with the necklace Xavier returned to me, watching his hands go up in protest before I can even get a word in.

"It was mine. He's the one who decided I was an open bar," Xavier says. My brother's lazy, drunken grin is enough to make anyone laugh.

"You're all a bunch of prudes," Kai says, looking around the room. "This house is horrid," he continues, his arms wrapping around me.

"You brought a whole flask just for you tonight?" I question disapprovingly.

"I have my reasons," he says, looking at Fallan.

"He's been around a lot lately," Xavier says, his irritation growing the longer Fallan's blue eyes watch him.

"Blame Josh. He specifically requested that he be part of the catering team here tonight," I whisper, trying to free myself from my brother's grip. "Although I'm glad he's here. Fallan's the reason I wasn't ravaged against my will," I admit, narrowing my eyes at Josh across the room.

"Josh touched you?" Xavier questions, crossing his arms.

"It's already been handled- " I start, trying to prevent any more drama from happening tonight.

Xavier moves past Josh, kicking the leg of his chair. Josh immediately tumbles to the floor. Xavier grabs the chair, making it look like an accident. Even Fallan can't help but smile, watching Josh's stunned face as Xavier nudges a glass of champagne towards Josh, only for it to slip out of his hands and spill all over the front of his suit.

"I'm so sorry," Xavier mumbles, looking around for a towel. "Looks like I've had more to drink than I thought," Xavier says. Adam narrows his eyes at him from across the table.

I feel the smile creep up along my face as Xavier moves away from Josh and in the direction where Fallan is taking up space.

Xavier leans into him, both men exchanging hushed words. Fallan's brow furrows. His jaw clenches harshly.

"What did he say to you?" I question down our bond, meeting Xavier's eyes as he finally moves back toward us.

"Nothing he hasn't said before," Fallan whispers, his eyes fixed on Xavier.

I turn to face the blonde, a kind expression across his face as he looks over to me. My brother takes a seat at the table, laughing like an idiot.

"What did you say to him?" I question.

Xavier runs his hand over his throat, his eyes narrowed.

"He spoke to me first."

"Okay, so what did he want, then?" I question, trying to get a straight answer from one of them.

All Xavier can do is shake his head, coughing with a wince.

"Nothing that matters," Xavier finally says. Both of their answers are equally frustrating.

Adam claps, motioning his guests to take a seat. We oblige, looking at the grand seat positioned alone at the front of the table. The space is empty, meant for the Commander. I sit next to Xavier, leaning into Kai, doing my best to support him as he slouches lazily into me.

In most scenarios, my mother and father would have scolded him for behaving like this but based on the amount of alcohol filling their cups, I don't think they've even noticed.

The table is filled with savory dishes, each one delicately crafted. The heady aroma causes my mouth to water. Several Unfortunates lean against the walls, watching with hungry eyes. I sneak glances toward Fallan, feeling a fleet of butterflies in my stomach each time he smirks at me. People settle into their spots comfortably, and the sound of conversation buzzes around me.

"All of this, and he didn't even bother to show up," Kai says through a burp, pointing to the empty seat with his fork.

Adam acknowledges the space, looking at his watch with a frown.

"Our Commander is a busy man," Adam starts. "He can't always make time for things like this. None of us can comprehend the important work he's doing for New Haven. We're undeserving of his presence but can aspire to be worthy of it one day," Adam says. My dad snorts, holding back his laughter.

Adam glares at my father, watching the way he and my mother both snicker. I watch Xavier smile, giving my dad a look I know goes over his head.

"Is there something you'd like to share, Andrew?" Adam questions. Josh glares at my father, his front still covered with champagne.

My dad shakes his head, giving my mother a soft kiss.

"I am so sorry, my friend. My laughter was not directed toward your comment. Katiana shared something funny, and I couldn't suppress my laughter."

I shake my head at the pair as I realize how drunk they are. All I want to do at this point is leave this dinner and find somewhere to be alone with Fallan.

"And you, Xavier? Is there a reason a smile paints your face?" Adam questions, Xavier's eyes widening as attention is drawn to him.

"It was a fleeting thought," Xavier says, balancing his fork on the table, ignoring Adam's glare.

"And what thought was that?" Adam questions. The defiance in Xavier's eyes intensifies.

"Maybe our Commander doesn't fancy your company too much," Xavier says. Adam immediately scowls.

Like a fire alarm blaring in the middle of the night, the doorbell sounds off, piercing the growing tension in the dining room. Adam reluctantly excuses himself from the table.

Returning moments later, the Vega twins and their parents trail after him. Max wears an elaborate suit that catches my attention. It's a standard celebration suit worn only by Officials.

"Was that comment necessary?" I question, turning toward Xavier, watching as he leans back in his chair. He gives Josh a wink, doing his best to get a rise out of him.

"No, but it was fun," he says, his curls falling into his face, his body leaning forward. "And sometimes it makes me feel like I'm standing up for what's right. Even if it's just by being an asshole to one of them," he finishes, a look of defeat washing over him for a brief moment.

Fallan continues to move around the room, my father glancing over at him every so often. Each time they lock eyes, my father looks away quickly. Regret and embarrassment are the only emotions he seems to express. I think of how he looked at Fallan's mother that day in the hospital waiting room all that time ago and wondered how they knew each other.

There's a connection between them, one that I've yet to figure out.

Max moves around the table, arms wide, ready to embrace me. I force a smile and push away from the table, feeling Xavier's fingers tug at the bottom of my dress so it doesn't ride up when I stand. Max's arms wrap around me, three's alcohol on his breath. I slide into his outstretched arms, looking at Fallan over his shoulder, and find him cocking his head unhappily at the sight.

"I'm so happy you're here," Max whispers into my ear.

"I'm starting to have a real distaste towards all the blonde men in your life," Fallan whispers in my mind, my mouth curving into a smile at how obvious his jealousy is

"Max, sit down," Rae snaps, giving up on waiting for my brother to compliment her dress.

By some miracle, he listens, allowing me to sit back down. Xavier looks amused, eyeing me the whole way back to my seat.

"What is it now?" I question.

"I've never seen someone look so ready to punch another human being over a hug," Xavier says, his eyes bright. "It almost makes me wonder if you put on an act with me too," he teases. Fallan and I both grow tense.

I stay silent, playing his comment off with a laugh.

With everyone settled at the table, people begin eating, making their way through the many courses. The men talk about work, some even telling stories about their involvement in carrying out punishments across the Unfortunate sector. I listen as Adam stops a passing waiter and use him as models to show precisely where he'd delivered his "best hits" on an Unfortunate he'd found in violation of sector ordinances last week.

I finally decide I need a distraction and indulge in one of the glasses of champagne that's gone untouched on the table, settling on breaking Adam's neck another day. Xavier ignores the conversation, picking at his nail beds. As much as I'd like to speak to Fallan, Adam and Max are using him as their drink boy, demanding their glasses stay full, which is a daunting task.

"Forest," Mrs. Vega calls, pulling my attention away from Xavier's hands. "I'm sure you've heard by now that Max is about to be inducted," she says, my eyes shooting to my father.

Adam claps Max on the back. Josh chimes in his congratulations and offers to throw him a party.

"As an Official?" I question my father, but Adam is the one to answer.

"Xavier thought Max had the capabilities to join a bit earlier than most. Andrew and I agreed," Adam says, my attention now on Xavier.

"I never told you-" Xavier begins, his mouth shutting as Adam raises his finger.

"If I recall, you were all for him joining us a few weeks ago. Don't change your opinion now based on the appeal of who you've gotten cozy with," Adam says. Fallan nearly drops the bottle of champagne he's holding.

"Adam, that's not appropriate," my father says harshly. My mother clears her throat.

"Well, we are all very proud of him," my mother says, touching Max's mother's hand. "He will make one fine Official."

Kai laughs, his head pressed to the table in a drunken fit.

"Just another puppet," he says quietly.

I kick my foot into his shin beneath the table, urging him to watch what he says.

Xavier looks unamused, tapping his plate with his fork while fidgeting with his pocket watch.

"You're joining just in time. This year's Lottery is sure to be a thrill," Adam says, pushing the conversation along.

"Lottery?" I question, cutting him off.

Xavier's hand touches my leg, pulling my attention back to him, his voice whispering in my ear.

"I promise you; you don't want to know what he's talking about," Xavier says, piquing my curiosity.

"You haven't told her yet, Andrew?" Adam questions, watching my father move to stand.

"Maybe Forest and Kai should leave the room for this conversation-"

"Why do that?" Josh questions. "My father has been more than happy to share the details of the tradition with me-"

"That's because you are a vindictive fuck who likes the bloodshed," Xavier snaps.

"And you don't?" Adam throws back. Xavier's posture goes rigid.

Kai is more alert, taking in every bit of information he can.

"What are they talking about?" I question, watching Fallan gradually move closer to linger behind my chair.

"I have no idea," he starts, both of our eyes moving to Xavier's hand still resting on my thigh, only squeezing the closer Fallan becomes. ***"I'm suddenly feeling rather inclined to take down everyone at this table and end this whole night."***

"Play nice," I whisper in a rush.

"What's the Lottery, Dad?" Kai pushes, my dad yanking at his tie.

"It's a tradition amongst the Order. Newly inducted Officials get to participate alongside senior leadership. It's an honor to join. As you all know, if you reach red status as an Unfortunate-" Adam looks at Fallan, giving him a twisted grin. "You get sent beyond the ward to deal with the foreign entities... that is, of course, unless you're placed into the Lottery."

My father remains silent.

"It's an alluring alternative to being thrown in the ash lands, really. Unfortunates who have no more room on their scorecard get the opportunity to fight for their freedom."

Lottery.

I digest the information with closed palms, doing my best not to imagine people being forced beyond the ward. The voice from the solstice festival remains with me, pushing me to consider there was something out there beyond the ward of New Haven. Everyone had played off the breach in the intercom system earlier as a meaningless prank, though it felt far from being the truth.

"Bets are placed during the Lottery on which Unfortunate we see having the most promising physical advantages, and then they're paired accordingly and thrown in the Pit. And I'll tell you, when you put the Unfortunate pigs together with nothing but a blade, eventually, you see why we call them animals in the first place."

Fallan clutches his tray. Xavier's head is down in shame.

"You make the Unfortunates murder one another?" Kai questions, my own words stuck in my throat.

"I prefer to think of it as motivating them to show their true nature-"

"You fucking bastard!" Fallan snaps, his words turning heads from around the table towards him. Adam is on his feet in seconds, his hand instinctively reaching for his pistol. Instinctively, I move to wedge myself between the two men, caring more for Fallan's safety than my own. My father snaps at me to sit back down, but my eyes are set on Adam.

"What the hell did you say to me?" Adam questions. Fallan holds his ground.

"You told us all those people were being sent to your sector for rehabilitation," Fallan spits. Xavier moves to my side as I continue to stand between the two men hoping to stop Adam from acting on impulse.

"You're a monster," I say. Adam shakes his head, glancing between the three of us.

"If I didn't know any better, Xavier," he says, pointing to me with malice. "I'd say you are gunning after an Unfortunate lover."

"That is enough!" my father yells, slamming his hand hard on the table. "I will not have you speak to about my daughter that way. I suggest you sit down."

Adam and my father are like oil and water, stuck in constant opposition to each other.

"You will not speak to her that way again," Xavier says, breaking his long silence.

Adam turns to look at him but doesn't respond.

I expect him to retaliate, to push Xavier further.

But he doesn't.

"I apologize for my brash words, Forest," Adam says, the lie scorching his tongue. "Let's just enjoy our evening. I'm feeling kind enough tonight that I won't deliver punishment to the Unfortunate behind you. Yet."

He moves to sit back down, snapping his fingers at Fallan to refill his wineglass.

"You should go," I say, facing Fallan. I make my voice loud enough so that everyone can hear me dismiss him. "He's right. The last thing I need is a pathetic Unfortunate from my year here, ruining the occasion. Consider what I just did for you as a favor. The last one you'll get," I say, forcing out every word.

Kai picks up on what I am doing, giving me the backing I need.

"Leave. We have more than enough of your kind here tonight," Kai says, his words a little slurred.

"You can still catch a tram if you leave now," Xavier says, brushing the front of Fallan's suit apathetically. "I think it's time for you to get going."

With hesitation, Fallan pauses before eventually backing away. His jaw is clenched as he observes the man in front of him. Gradually, he pans his eyes to me, and I expect to hear his voice in my head, ready to fight me on this. But I know he sees the look on my face and how fearful I am for him around these people.

The last thing I will do is stand back and be the reason he is targeted tonight.

Turning away, he moves out of the dining room towards the front door. He gives me one final look before opening it and leaving the house. The door slams loudly as he exits.

"Have you bet before?" I question, finally addressing Xavier, letting him guide me back to my seat.

"Once or twice, only as a way to be accepted by my peers," Xavier whispers, leaning closer to my chair.

"Are there children?" Kai questions silently. His light-hearted, intoxicated demeanor is gone.

"Don't make me answer that," Xavier says brashly, my heart breaking at his words.

"Xavier, what is your bet this year?" Adam questions.

Josh holds a large notepad, jotting down numbers and names, each one a familiar face surrounding the table.

"None this year," Xavier says coldly, tapping his fingers in a rhythmic tone on the tablecloth.

"Andrew?"

Kai and I look at our father, expecting the man to stay silent. My mother seems displeased. Her hands are clasped as she watches my father.

"$200 on 39."

My stomach sinks, my dinner threatening to make its way up my throat and all over the table. Kai's mouth hangs open. My nails dig into my palms so harshly they draw blood. I feel my heart rate increase. The energy swirling inside me is enough to bring down this room. All of these people sit here with smiles on their faces as they play this sick, twisted game. I force myself away from the table, making my way out of the room.

As I exit, the very space around me closes in. Every breath I take feels borrowed. My long gown trails behind me, slowing my escape as it wraps around my ankles as I set a brisk pace away from the party.

I can still hear their mindless chatter echo through the hallways, continuing to place bets as I make my way outside.

One breath.

One breath of fresh air is all I need.

I tumbled through the large sliding glass door, nearly yanking it off its hinges in the process. The outside world is quiet. The quiet hum of the ward located on the edge of the property feels oppressive. The alcohol has started to settle in my stomach like a boulder in water.

The outside air is refreshing. I draw in a few deep breaths, letting the events of dinner slowly fade away. The looks on the faces of all the Unfortunates in the room while Adam talked about the Lottery haunt me. I grasp the railing of Josh's deck, leaning over, ready to vomit.

The Lottery.

This night.

The contents of my stomach were gone in an instant.

If only my mind could release its burdens as quickly as my stomach.

For a moment, I was on the roof with that boy again. Did he feel the same fears I do now? How much did he know before it was all too much to bear? He was finally free of his chip, only to discover that freedom came with a knowledge of what was truly going on in New Haven.

At what point did the fate he chose become more desirable than the present I face?

The night is still. The cool autumn air gives way to a biting chill, reminding me that winter is coming.

The boards' creek on the deck. My body becomes rigid at the sudden realization that I am no longer alone.

Maybe it's Kai ready to warn me how angry Dad is, or possibly Josh prepared to see what he can get away with now that Fallan is gone.

"Listen, I can't pretend what I heard in there doesn't sicken me-" I whisper, preparing myself for a verbal tongue-lashing.

I turn on my heels, my heart racing as a familiar wave made up of desire and fear passes over me. Xavier's eyes meet mine, his ocean blue irises are calm and steady.

"I never bet. Not when I didn't have to," he moves away from the sliding door and towards me. "When I had just been inducted, we went out to celebrate. I was drunk out of my mind, and they urged me to bet on what I thought was a race. It turns out I spent $400 to watch a girl with red hair die in the Pit. I don't think I kept food down for a week after it happened," Xavier admits, his voice filled with regret.

"I can't, I can't do it again. The way you looked at me just now almost broke me," he whispers, taking another step towards me.

A part of me wants to back away, but I step forward instead. I can feel Its pull, urging me to move closer, encouraging me to give in.

This is Xavier. I can trust him.

The same Xavier who broke surveillance cameras to protect me. The same Xavier who came to my defense repeatedly. Now he stands here, begging for the forgiveness he would have given me instantly.

"I don't want to keep thinking of all the things their people have faced," I whisper, pressing my head to the cool metal railing. He comes to stand at my side, leaning on the railing next to me. He crosses his arms over his front as he looks up to the night sky. The moonlight casts light shadows across his face, revealing a youthfulness under his tired expression.

My mind races back to the dance we shared at the festival. The few peaceful moments moving with him, only to hit a brick wall. I feel it now as we stand here. I still fight the urge to run away from him, that urge a warning I don't understand.

"He's the least of our worries," It whispers, the voice of reason when it comes to Xavier.

In many ways, I wish he could be as cruel to me as Fallan is. Maybe then I'd have an unshakable need to be near him.

"There's more to ask him," It pushes, an echo of the voice at the festival passing through my mind. I scowl, annoyed at Its ability to force my thoughts in a certain direction.

"That voice today," my head rises from the railing. "Do you think it's true what he said? Is there more than just ash beyond that ward?"

Xavier's past before New Haven is still unknown to me. Everything about the man is a mystery. Even his family is a topic he has barely brought up. I watch him finally look at me, his foot tapping the deck as he deliberates his answer.

"I think someone is working hard to make sure we stay clueless." His hands work along his throat, and his eyes are filled with fear. "Do you think New Haven is all there is?"

I close the space between us, his hand gently moving to touch my side. I flinch as he brushes over the area of my mark.

Kind. Gentle. That's what I think when I look at Xavier

My heart races as he brushes my lips with his thumb. His other hand grabs me tighter, pulling me against his front.

"Do you know why I came tonight?" he questions, his nose inches from mine.

"No, but I want you to tell me." My hands move down his chest, the other part of me guiding my actions, embracing my desire for him.

He pulls his lips to my ear as his hands travel up my lower back. His breath brushes my skin, my face heating as sinful thoughts enter my mind.

"Because I crave you," he says, his lips grazing over my nose. "And I want to be the one who knows every part of you."

His hands continue moving along my curves. "I think about painting your body with my tongue. And I want to be the one to fulfill every single one of your desires and know your every want," he whispers, his lips so close to finally pressing against my own.

My hands tremble, my heart pounds. I close my eyes to try and better process what he's telling me.

I want him.

His eyes, deep and mesmerizing blue.

I want him.

His kind smile that lights up a room.

I want him.

His raven hair and a coy smirk that somehow always makes me flustered.

No. That's not right.

My heart stops.

My eyes fly open, my body ready to collapse under the pressure of the realization that lies in front of me.

"But you're not him," I whisper, my voice barely audible.

Xavier's eyes go wide, his grasp no longer light and gentle. The fear settles in my stomach once again, the other part of me growing angry, banging fiercely around in my mind, pushing me to choose Xavier.

I don't know when I started backing away or when Xavier's grasp on my arm turned into a reach, leaving his hands outstretched in the space between us. His hand holds his throat, his eyebrows creasing as he releases nothing but a small faint groan.

The pain of my rejection consumes his face.

I should want this moment with him.

I should want *him.*

But I don't. So I turn around and run towards what I do want, my mind pushing my body to move quicker than I've ever moved before. I now know one thing for certain.

"None of this was ever about Xavier," I carelessly whisper in my silent mind, wanting nothing more than to hear his voice.

Xavier watches me leave from the balcony.

I try to feel his presence, reaching for any string of connection to him in my mind.

But in an instant, another connection flares to life, his words coming through my mind like honey.

"I can't keep listening to your thoughts... come to me, Little Dove." Fallan's voice urges.

Chapter Forty-Three

Forest

Keeping a go bag crammed under my bed these last few months has proven to be one of the best decisions I've ever made. As beautiful as this gown is, tearing it off was such a relief.

Forcing it into the laundry hamper, I quickly throw on a dark, hooded jacket, black jeans, and a pair of boots. I'm hoping that everyone will be too busy continuing to celebrate Solstice so I can go unnoticed as I make my way out of the sector.

Xavier's expression as I ran away lingers in my mind, eating at me. Fallan continues to call out to me faintly through my mind. It's hard for me not to recall how much he hated me when we first met. He's been cold and closed off for all the right reasons. I wish it were as easy for me to have felt the same way towards him. It all seemed so real.

But the memory of us meeting when we were little, of the dance we shared by the fire at Josh's house, those were real. The connection between our minds is real.

As much as he'd like to hide our feelings in a box and lock away the key, he can't ignore what has already happened.

With a tug, I yank the bag's straps over my shoulders and move to open my bathroom window. It's become easier for me to brace for the drop out the window since I've done it so much lately. My boots collide with the Earth. The street is silent as most people are either in bed or are still out celebrating Solstice. Making my way to the perimeter, I run my hands along the ward before taking off in a sprint through the trees, my body barreling past the piles of changing leaves.

The Unfortunate sector was around five miles away. I planned to get there on foot. My legs were already burning running, and I wasn't even halfway.

I've not seen Mark for several days, unsure how to speak to the old man after discovering that he's my grandfather. Each time I see him, I feel guilty that my father has robbed him of the opportunity to be a part of our family.

The forest is quiet, my path illuminated by starlight from the clear sky above. My lungs fill with the brisk air, my energy levels swirling, ready to find some form of release.

"You're an idiot for leaving Xavier back there," It hisses, finally breaking Its silence.

I draw in a deep breath, shaking my head.

"Xavier's not like me," I say, dodging a fallen log. *"The only way we begin to understand this is by channeling whatever this is. Fallan is the only other person like us that we've met,"* I say, hearing It laugh.

"You don't understand anything about us, yet you think someone with so much disdain toward us will be willing to help?"

"Why can't you just cooperate?" I question, trying to ignore Its overbearing presence.

"I do cooperate. I'm you. The only reason you can hear me as a separate sort of thing is because you refuse to embrace the other parts of yourself." I scoff at the notion that this thing is truly a part of me.

"You've yet to tell me what other parts of myself I'm missing," I mutter, snapping a hanging branch with a slight flick of my wrist.

"You hate what we are, deep down. As long as you do that, I will always be separated from you, and we will save no one."

We both remain silent for a moment, the noise of my boots hitting the ground loud and repetitive.

"I don't hate you," I finally say, feeling a sense of relief wash over me.

"You don't have to hate me to fear this part of yourself," It whispers, the words echoing in the chasm of my mind.

In an instant, my head fills with a pounding pain, my arm reaching out to grip the nearest tree. I clutch the side of my head, doing my best to focus on blocking out the drumming that reverberates through every part of my skull. The forest shutters beneath the touch of the wind, sounds amplified as I work through the pain.

The voice breaches my mind. The same voice from the Solstice festival.

"Can you hear me?" the male's voice questions, my knees threatening to buckle beneath the sheer use of force he's using to get past my mental barriers. I crumple over into the dirt, feeling the pain subside with each passing second.

"Who was that?" It questions frantically, forgetting the hostility between us.

"I don't know," I say, clenching my chest, gasping for air. "But I have a feeling we have a much bigger problem than we realized."

I slip past the opening again, finding the same hole Kai and I utilized the last time we were here. With careful steps, I avoid disturbing the rubble on the ground, quickly moving in step with a stranger through the gate check, taking advantage of the sleeping Officials guarding the sector's entrance. Drawing my hood tighter around my head, I focus my attention on remembering the way to Fallan's building, doing my best to avoid unwanted attention. As much as I'd like to think I blend seamlessly in with the people in this sector, the reality is that there are differences between us. Where their backs hunch from years of work, mine stands tall. Where they stagger in their step from years of torture or unhealed injuries, I can see my steps are even and unburdened. Hardship is painted on the face of every Unfortunate I pass here.

I move for the nearest side street, planning to take as many backways as it takes to stay unnoticed.

"No! Please!" a young boy shouts, stopping me dead in my tracks. I peer down a narrow side street, nearly missing it had the boy not yelled. Two Officials lean over him, holding the boy down with the heels of their boots. He can't be more than ten years old. His tiny form looks ready to break under the weight of the two Officials pressing down on him.

"I'll go home. I swear. I didn't realize curfew was in effect!" the boy pleads. I dart behind a nearby wall, waiting to see if they'll let him go.

The men snicker, pressing their boots down harder on top of the boy. He winces in pain, and I'm sure he'll have bruised tomorrow.

"Well, technically, you have two minutes before curfew begins," one of the men says. My eyes watch his hand as it moves to grab his prod. "But this is still a valuable lesson for you to learn. Consider this a practice punishment. If you're not early, you're late," he continues, smiling at his partner. They reach for their prods at the same time, and the boy begins to scream again. He tries to move out from under their hold but goes still when the light sensor prods come to life.

"I don't know about you," It whispers, my blood pumping adrenaline. *"But now feels like a good time to let me out,"* It says, dragging its hands along the mental cage I've trapped it in.

The boy starts to cry, his body bracing to be electrocuted.

Fuck.

I allow that unbridled part of myself freedom, feeling It embrace me like a warm hug. My hand flies out in front of me, latching onto the minds of both Officials, listening to their vile thoughts of how much they enjoy hurting the boy. With the rage of a thousand scorned soldiers, I take control of their weapons.

"They deserve to feel pain," I affirm to myself, feeling the other part of me agree.

"Fight. The winner walks away without a broken leg," I command, slowly backing away from the wall.

The man's eyes meet, and they become tangled, focused on delivering blow after blow to one another. The boy scrambles to get away, watching the men with a look of shock, only lingering for a few seconds before taking off down the alleyway. I hear the men groan in pain, focusing on keeping their minds within my grasp. As they continue to hit one another, I find myself smiling with satisfaction.

Glancing at a puddle on the ground, I see my reflection. My eyes seem to gleam. Drawing in a deep breath, I force that other part of me back, feeling my energy start to fade as the men's fight suddenly becomes nothing but screams of pain and confusion.

"Better get going, princess," It barks, pissed off to be shoved back so soon.

I turn away from the Officials, headed back on my path once more.

"Don't be angry that I didn't want them dead," I hiss. Fallan's building finally comes into view.

"It's comical, really," It says, laughing.

"What is?"

"The fact that you don't get it. I am a part of you. Nothing happens unless you want it. And you definitely wanted to hurt them. And if you think I'm murderous, then you're murderous too. My desires are your desires. Self-awareness is a bitch for us, isn't it?"

What the fuck is happening to me?

I knock on his door, my eyes shifting down the hallway, making sure I wasn't followed. I can still see the singe on the ground from where the Shifter died. There's a flickering light coming from under the door, casting shadows by my boots. Gradually, the locks begin to move, the hinges creaking as the door swings open.

With a sleepy expression, Fallan stands in the doorway, his hair a wild mess. His shirt looks like it was thrown on in a rush, barely covering his torso. At first, he looks over me with relief, only to grow more confused the longer we stand there. I peer inside his unit, my stomach sinking as I see movement in his bed. There's a woman's body warming his sheets and my imagination runs rampant as I notice the nail marks traveling up his left side.

"Why are you back here?" he asks, stepping outside the unit so as not to disturb whoever he's clearly just hooked up with.

"You're the one who asked me to come here, Fallan," I whisper angrily. His eyebrows crease as he shakes his head.

"You heard that," he says in disbelief, pinching the bridge of his nose. "I was drinking after I got home and heard you with Blondie. I felt your panic-" he starts, a swell of conflicting emotions rolling off of him.

"I heard a man's voice," he pauses, stopping his other train of thought. "Did you hear it, too?" he pushes, my head slowly nodding.

"I have no idea who it is. I only know it's the same voice-"

"From the festival. Yeah, I've gathered that much," Fallan says sarcastically, back to being the asshole I've gotten to know so well.

He takes a moment to look me over, sighing gently.

"You should go home, Forest. You being here only makes things more difficult," he says, crossing his arms out of frustration.

"I don't have anyone at home I can trust, and I can't say I trust you," I start, ready to throw it all on the table. "But I need to understand whatever this thing inside of me is, and tonight, the only person I wanted to be around was you. So, forgive me if I'm a bit confused," I finish, ready to leave this place and beg for Xavier's forgiveness.

"You don't need to go back to that blonde twit," he starts, taking another step toward me. "You're falling down a rabbit hole you can't come back from. The more you keep coming back here, the harder it is to leave things the way they need to be," he says, his hand raising as if he's going to touch my face.

"I'm starting to understand that," I say, meeting his deep blue eyes. "So, are you going to help me channel this fucking mess of energy, or am I going to have to keep playing target practice with Officials?" I question, his mouth pulling into the slightest of smirks.

He glances inside his unit.

"I'll grab my things, and then we can go. Wait out here."

"Go where?" I question, watching him move inside.

"You'll see."

The outside of the building is run down, much like many of the other ones in this sector. With a swipe of Fallan's ID, he gets us inside. Unlike his unit, this space has many large windows, each meant to bring in as much light as possible. Black bags swing from the roofs, some already broken free from chains. Soft mats coat the ground, adding to the smell of rubber lingering in the air.

Fallan tosses his duffel bag onto the floor. He'd changed into a black shirt and a pair of black pants. I watch him begin to wrap his knuckles with gauze, pacing around the space as he worked.

"What is this place?" I question, running my hand along the course material of the punching bags.

"A conditioning gym. Aren't there some of these in your sector?" he questions, my head already shaking.

"Not really an Untouchables thing. Our Defense Classroom is about the closest place to this I can think of," I say, unsure at what point my people decided that focusing on physical fitness wasn't worth the time.

Fallan moves away from his duffel, positioning a punching bag in front of him. With a nod of his head, he motions me closer, my arms already tingling in anticipation. His hand runs along the bag's surface, watching me move closer.

Once I'm within reaching distance, he grabs my hand, guiding it to the middle of the bag.

"You're going to hit here," he starts, keeping my hand in his own as he wraps my knuckles. He winds the gauze tightly around my hands, carefully protecting each knuckle. "The first thing about controlling what we are is controlling the rage we carry with us," he continues, my eyes glancing at his already red knuckles.

"Have you already been here today?" I question, running my thumb along the abrasions.

"I had a bit of extra motivation," he shrugs, pulling away to give me and the bag space to move.

I stare at the massive punching bag that sways in front of me.

"I don't know how to hit anything," I say, his arms crossed as he watches me.

"Actually, you do. Well, sorry, I guess it's really me who knows. Good thing I'm here," It mutters, reaching out again to take some control.

My fist flies out in front of me, my legs positioned defensively beneath me. Hitting the bag with a burst of power behind the swing, the bag swings back, the chains releasing a high-pitched clang into the gym. Some of my anger is immediately satiated, and I can't hide how satisfied I am.

I suck in air as his hands touch my waist. Moving my hips forward, he begins to fix my stance. His breath warms the spot behind my ear where my chip once existed. I lean into him as he squeezes my hips, his arm strung across my front, holding me to his chest.

"Come on, Little Dove," he taunts, his lips grazing my ear. "I know you can reach deeper than that"

The vivid image of the woman in his bed passes through my mind.

That memory didn't come from nowhere.

He sent me that image.

I pull myself away, my focus back on the bag. Readying myself, I let the other part of me take control again, feeling Its anger rise.

He wanted me to see that girl in his bed.

Dick.

Throwing another punch, I watch as the bag concaves beneath my hand, the material threatening to rip from the impact.

As the other part of me backs away into the recesses of my mind again, my body is drained once more. Leaning into the bag out of exhaustion, I take a deep breath, annoyed at my inability to maintain the strength to manage both parts of me for more than a few minutes.

"I thought you didn't care about Fallan," I whisper angrily, observing the now misshapen punching bag.

"Maybe I'm not too fond of seeing another woman in his bed," It nearly yells.

I'm glad there's something we agree on.

"You're an asshole for showing me that," I say, turning to see a smirk on Fallan's face.

"I figured you needed some motivation," he says, giving me an apologetic look I know is far from sincere.

"So that's your plan, then? Showing me all the women you're hooking up with to fuck with my head?"

His eyes are no longer playful.

"I never complained each time I heard your thoughts about wanting Xavier to explore your body. I'd consider what I sent you as pretty tame compared to what I've had to listen to," he says as he barrels to a stop just a few inches in front of me.

"I never reached out to you when I was with Xavier."

"Well, then you were thinking of me and unable to put up a wall like the rest of us to stop yourself from broadcasting all your dirty fucking thoughts," he growls, looking down at me with annoyance.

"How often are you putting up a wall so I don't hear your thoughts about me?" I question, his head slowly shaking.

He leans down, his nose inches away from my own.

"Maybe I'll stop censoring my thoughts, and you can go as mad as I have," he whispers, his voice void of any playfulness.

He moves to position himself in front of the bag I'd been hitting. The wall hiding his emotions comes down, and a wave of anger crashes into me. As he hits the bag, a flood of thoughts of Xavier runs rampant down our mental connection.

"Feed into your hate," he says, his eyes bright as he continues to pummel the bag.

Suddenly, the bag tears away from its hinges, hitting the ground with a loud thud. We both step back from the bag, watching its contents spill onto the dirtied floor. He turns his head toward me, and the walls around his mind go up again, locking me out.

"Anger can be a great motivator," he says, moving past me.

Grabbing my hand, he guides me closer to one of the mats on the floor, letting go once our feet meet the edge. Standing across from me, he watches me, motioning me to move closer.

Hesitantly, I join him on the mat, his body rigid as he readies himself in a defensive position.

"I've seen you fight in Defense Class," he starts, my body instinctively moving to match his fighting stance. "Let's see what you can do outside of the classroom, Little Dove."

Time and time again, Fallan takes me down, pinning me each time with a look of satisfaction. With growing frustration, I try to get away, watching the way he seems to know every single move I make before I have even thought of them. Angrily, I pull myself away from the ground, readying myself to claim defeat once more.

"You look sort of cute when you're frustrated," he mocks, my anger rising.

"Perhaps I should go wake Valerie and have her beat your ass too."

It was Valerie?

It tried to resurface, but I've got all the anger I need right now.

Unable to play nice anymore, I force his leg to the mat with a wave of my hand, watching his wide-eyed expression grow as my leg rises, striking him in the chest with a swift kick. Flying back onto the mat, he raises his hands, ready to use his gifts on me. His silent ability to slip into my mind is much more aggravating at this moment.

I don't give him the opportunity.

Shoving my body atop his own, I place my knees along his arms and at the side of his head, taking away his range of motion. Straddling his chest, I grab his chin, forcing him to stay down as the beast beneath my skin roars.

"I'm starting to see why Xavier is such good fuel for your rage."

His mouth curls into a smile. A smile I so rarely see. Gradually, he begins raising himself from the mat, moving my body back and onto his lap. We sit up, and his hands come to rest behind my back. My heart races as I adjust my hips, feeling more than just his legs beneath me now, the presence of his cock more noticeable as I continue to reposition myself.

"Your wall is fully down, Little Dove," he says, his hand pressing my lower back, urging me closer.

"I can hear every sinful thought running through your mind," he whispers, my face reddening as I try to slip past his wall.

Dragging my hand along his chest, I adjust my hips atop him once more. His wall comes crashing down, and his thoughts of tasting my lips pass through my mind.

"You're getting better," he whispers, slowly moving me off of him. "Though that thought wasn't yours to have," he continues helping me up, both of us flustered from being so close to one another.

"So, Blackburn, now that I know what motivates you," a coy grin lines his face. "Let's see just how angry I can make you."

Chapter Forty-Four

Forest

Minutes turned into hours. Every second that passed gave Fallan an opportunity to test my capabilities. Once uncoordinated and imprecise, my strikes now hit my target. He watches me with crossed arms, carefully correcting my form as needed. Each time he touches me, I wish his hand would slip beneath the material of this gear and remove the barrier of clothing between us. It's a selfish desire. Something about the way he touches me feels right, like he knows my body in ways I hardly know myself.

"I want you to try something," Fallan says, breaking his silence before I can get another strike in.

Gently grabbing my elbow, he moves me away from the punching bag, positioning us both in the center of the room. The moonlight hits his face just right, reflecting off several small scars across his skin. He watches me with a relaxed expression.

"I want you to try and reach into my mind," he says, standing still.

I focus on his deep blue eyes, unsure how I could look at them so often and not get lost in them.

"Reach into your mind? You're always blocking me out," I say, watching his mouth slightly curl.

"That's true, and you're always trying to block me out," he says, taking a step forward. "But your wall falters each time I get close to you.... You like my eyes?" he questions, my face growing warm.

"Stay out of my head."

"Then keep me out." His arms become crossed once more. He stays right in front of me and waits.

"Push past the protections I have up," he starts, running his thumb along my eyes to shut my lids. "Feel that string that runs between our minds," he whispers, my energy focused on finding the barriers in his mind.

When I can feel the wall he has in place, I run my mental touch along its surface, finding a small crack where it's weakest.

"Why do you keep up so many walls?"

"Maybe I'm worried you won't like what you find."

"I thought my opinion didn't matter. I'm nothing," I say, throwing his words back at him.

I feel it. The crack in his barrier at my comment. Slowly, I creep through, doing my best not to focus on the warmth of his body. I find his desires and his fears all bottled up in one area of his mind. To my surprise, I see my face. My green eyes watch him as he watches me. I see the curve of my smile paint my expression as I look up at him that night at Josh's party, our bodies a few inches apart. I see a younger version of myself that day in the medical unit, my smile as wide as it was during our dance. There's a glimpse of my sketchbook. Its sudden absence is something he's yet to explain to me.

"Why am I in your thoughts so often?" I question, his body drawing closer.

"You slipped past my barrier?" he questions in shock.

Opening my eyes, I see how close we are, his hand hovering above my hip. His curls dance along his face, his body towering over me in a way that makes his strength so obvious. I hear traces of his thoughts, his mind fixating on my lips, even though he's looking directly into my eyes.

"You didn't answer my question."

"Neither did you," he counters.

A trickle of blood works down my nostril, my mind letting go of its grasp on his. Quickly, I wipe away the small amount of blood, feeling the exertion of energy I used finally catching up to me. He raises the bottom of his shirt to help me wipe away the blood. I can't stop looking down to observe his body. All of his best features are much more noticeable in this lighting.

"My eyes are up here, Little Dove," he says, gently tugging my chin back up to look at him.

He watches me with a kind expression, my eyes moving back down, feeling ill at the sight of nail marks working up his side. They're a reminder that whatever is going on between us isn't what I think it is, especially if he's taking Valerie to his bed.

"Thanks for your help," I whisper, gradually taking a step back.

He grabs the front of my shirt, stopping me from taking another step.

"Can I see it?" he questions, my throat going dry.

"See what?"

"Your mark," be states, yanking up his shirt to expose his ribcage.

I run my fingertips along the rough skin of his mark, feeling how it curves like mine. He shudders beneath the touch, his eyes glued to my movements.

"I've never let anyone else touch it," he whispers, moving my hand from his mark to the nail gouges streaking his side. "The only reason she spent the night was so she wasn't wandering the streets in a drunken haze. I can't stomach her touch in the ways you think I can. When she touched me here, I was furious. But nothing happened."

I scoff. "You don't need to justify who you hook up with to me," I say, pulling my hand away from his chest. His mother's ring dangles from a chain around his neck, gleaming brightly in the glow of the moonlight.

"You were wondering about Valerie. That's why you're angry, right?" he says, his presence slowly entering my mind.

Slowly, I lower the waistline of my pants, showing him my mark. I feel him keep his presence in my mind, ready to test his patience. He eyes my hip with surprise, gently touching the skin with his slender fingers.

"Might as well give him a show if he's going to creep in our mind," It whispers.

"Like I said," I whisper, letting the image of Xavier touching me at the dinner earlier tonight fill my mind. "I could care less who you choose to warm your bed," I finish.

His hand clenches my waist as I keep the image in my mind. His fingers trail beneath the hem of my shirt. I expect him to back away out of anger, but instead, he stays still, his presence no longer tiptoeing through my mind.

"He's touched you?" he questions, my mouth curling into a smile.

"Xavier? Here and there. I can show you if you'd like," I push, ready to feel his anger wash over me.

He clenches his jaw, both hands firmly on my hips now. Even with his barriers up, I can feel his trepidation as he sees the lust in my stare as I keep the image of Xavier at the forefront of my mind.

"If you look at me like that again while thinking of him, Forest, or show me images of him touching you," he mutters, his anger now more discernible. He moves my chin, facing it toward a metal table filled with odds and ends. "I can promise you I won't be able to stop myself from laying you across that table and fucking you until you forget his name."

My mouth snaps shut.

"I will make sure he knows I've had you."

My heart races at his promise, unable to find my next words.

"My turn?" It asks. I release the lock on Its cage.

I draw in a deep breath and It overpowers me. It pushes us further into Fallan. Suddenly, I'm much more confident in my ability to manage his threats.

"What's stopping you then?" I question, trying to push him past his limits.

He ponders a response, glancing down at my lips.

"It's getting late," Fallan whispers, his hands nearly under my shirt.

I watch him back away slowly, leaving us on the same merry-go-round of emotions.

"How many times will you do that to me?" I question, his posture going rigid.

"Until you realize," he starts. "That you're only a distraction to me."

"If I'm only a distraction," I push, pointing my finger to his chest, "Why do you care about Xavier touching me?" I spit.

He looks back at me angrily and turns on his heels. Rushing toward me, he slams the wall behind me, his eyes lowered as he speaks.

"Hate me!" he yells, my heart racing. "God damn it, Forest, just hate me so I don't have to think of you every fucking time I close my eyes! You eat away at my every waking thought like a vile disease!" he spits, lingering in the space above me.

I don't back down. Instead, I move closer.

"You're a lousy liar," I hiss.

It doesn't take long before he grabs his things and shoves the door open with a heave, leaving me alone in the gym with my feelings.

My back stays pressed to the wall as I slowly slide down to the cold floor.

I rack my brain, trying to think of the best response to Fallan's outburst. All scenarios lead back to him only shutting me out more than he already has. Shoving open the doors, I go outside, ready to face him anyway.

I have to stop myself from bumping into another body, my eyes blinking rapidly to adjust to the darkness. Hunter stands dressed in his work attire, looking at Fallan's angry figure before pulling his focus back to me.

"You came back?" Hunter questions, my annoyance with Fallan off the charts at this point.

"He asked me to," I reply, avoiding Fallan's searing gaze that could burn a hole through me.

"I thought her being here was just a 'coincidence?'" Hunter says, throwing up air quotes when he says the word coincidence like he knew better than to believe Fallan.

"Where's your brother?" Hunter asks me, ignoring Fallan impatiently tapping his foot.

"No doubt being carried home by Xavier right about now."

Hunter's expression falters at the mention of Xavier, but he makes a quick recovery.

"So, you're both here? To-"

"Train," Fallan and I say in unison. Hunter nods his head, only half believing the validity of our statement.

"Right," he starts, looking down the poorly lit street. "Well, I was planning to go home tonight, but seeing as I'm across the sector right now," he turns to Fallan. "Do you care if I stay with you tonight?"

"Will there be enough room for him Fallan? Your late-night company is still there." Hunter's eyes quickly move to Fallan.

"Late-night company?"

"Valerie's having another one of her... episodes," Fallan explains to him while his stays focused on me.

Hunter looks displeased, throwing Fallan a scathing look of disapproval.

"Well, I'll leave you both to it," I start, pulling my bag over my shoulders. "I should get going before they switch out to more attentive Officials." A hand closes around my wrist.

Fallan watches me closely, his grasp light.

"I can walk you out of the sector-"

"Don't bother," I say, yanking my wrist from him. "I'm sure someone will be waiting for me," I lie, throwing him yet another image of Xavier.

He frowns, unable to hide his disdain.

I turn on my heels, ready to spend the walk home reflecting on what the fuck I was thinking for coming here tonight.

"There is a function tomorrow night, here, in the Unfortunate sector. Come if you want to see what the people here are really like. Tell your brother to come too," Hunter says, breaking the silence between us.

Fallan stays silent.

"Can I bring a friend?" I ask, unsure if I want his response.

"As long as you trust them," Hunter responds, ignoring the shake of Fallan's head. "Then yes."

"Then I'll consider it." My legs move for me on the path back to the sector's entrance.

"Goodnight, you two," I mutter, unable to be around Fallan any longer.

The night pulls me into its grasp, taking me far away from the Unfortunate sector and even farther away from the man who has the ability to hate me and want me all in one night.

The question is, why can't I let him go?

CHAPTER FORTY-FIVE

HUNTER

Valerie wakes up long enough to yell at us to shut off the lights. She's groggy and definitely hungover. Fallan warned me how much liquor she'd had, giving me a brief rundown of all of the events that led to her nestling in his bed. A chair lingers beside the mattress, no doubt where he tried to sleep before Forest knocked on his door.

Valerie had stomped her way over here in a drunken haze, ready to try and get Fallan to sleep with her for what seemed the millionth time. Every time she finds herself over here, Fallan graciously sobers her up, deflecting each one of her advancements despite how much he might want a physical connection.

"Turn that fucking light off!" she groans, angrily rolling over to face us.

"Don't forget you're in *my* bed. The last thing you should be doing is bitching," Fallan says, more annoyed than usual.

"Hello to you too, grumpy," she looks at me. "What did you do to him?" Fallan shoots me a warning look, telling me everything I need to know about how little he prefers she knew about what happened with Forest tonight.

"Me? I did nothing. You're the one who ruined his beauty sleep," I say.

Fallan brews a pot of tea, ignoring the conversation. He's deep in his thoughts, no longer paying attention to our pointless discussions.

"He would have slept great had he taken my offer to share the bed," she says slyly. Fallan's hands grip the kitchen counter.

"You seem plenty sober now... go home," Fallan says. The statement is far from a request.

Valerie rolls her eyes, pulling herself free from the sheets. She wears a tiny black dress meant to draw the attention of, well, anyone. I try to see the appeal in how the material showcases her body, but I'm unsure why I struggle so often to savor the sight of the supple curves of women—the dress clings to her skin, showing each part of her body through the sheer black material.

Valerie slowly creeps up behind Fallan. I shake my head at her, ready to yank her back by her hair and lecture her like Aaron should be doing. Chances are the bastard is out somewhere as drunk as his cousin is right now. Valerie moves to wrap her arms around Fallan. His head is lowered, his expression unable to be read.

"I understand you've had a hard night," she begins, moving her hand along his sides. He tenses, turning around to grab her wrists. He backs her into the closest wall.

"You don't touch me," he starts, pointing to her heatedly. "I told you to go home." She scoffs, shoving him back and away from her.

"An hour with her and you come back more miserable than you started with," Valerie states, her knowledge of Forest being here no longer something she feels like hiding.

"Not any more miserable than you're making me right now," Fallan says, ignoring her dig toward Forest.

She swipes up her bag on the floor, giving Fallan a long, hateful look.

"I hope she keeps you feeling conflicted. At the end of the day, you know you can never have her," Valerie hisses—her deep-rooted contempt for Forest her biggest weapon against Fallan.

Brushing past me, she leaves the apartment, slamming the door behind her. The faint smell of her rose perfume lingers around us.

"I'm sorry you had to see any of that," Fallan says, returning to the teapot.

I shake my head at the man, moving closer to the kitchen counter. Resting a hand on his shoulder, I watch as his anger is replaced with another familiar feeling. Pain.

"I have to ask," I say, bracing for his reaction. "What are you going to do? How long before your attempts at keeping her out of your life become unbearable?" Spotty memories and patchwork images of the past are all that remain of their twisted history together. How Forest's past has been torn from her brain repeatedly is something Fallan has hardly been able to explain to me.

How can one girl go from knowing you so intimately to looking past you in a crowd in the blink of an eye? Fallan had spent years holding on to one woman, satiated by only a few smiles from her, not even caring that she didn't remember his name.

"She is nothing like Andrew. I keep trying to compare her to him, thinking it will be easier to hate her given what he did," Fallan says, staring at his tea as it steeps. "But every time she looks at me, I see that girl from the bonfire or the one from my testing day."

The hold those brief interactions had on him was enough for a lifetime.

"And I can't stay away."

I run my finger along my chip. Fallan's willingness to be open about his unique circumstances and help me deal with the chip in my head is a debt I'll never be able to repay.

"It makes things complicated, given she's never laid a finger on any Unfortunate," I mumble. Even I've found it difficult not to be drawn to her good nature.

"I've never wanted her gone, and it's been hell trying to make her think that's the case," Fallan says, slamming his fists into the counter. The kettle jolts, its lid falling off onto the countertop.

"When will you tell her the truth?" I question, watching him closely. "About you and her?" I push.

He slowly looks at me, his eyes glossed over with emotion. Pouring the tea into two cups, he sighs, running his hands along his face.

"When I know *he* won't hurt her," he starts, slowly raising the cup to his lips.

"Who's 'he?'" I question, watching my tea leaves swirl at the bottom of the cup.

"That's the best part," Fallan says with a defeated sigh.

"That blonde twit, Xavier, tried to claim to the only woman I've allowed myself to care for," he starts, his eyes lowered. "And he's making damn sure to keep me away."

I pause, reflecting on the Official I've only seen in passing. He was here the day Andrew and Adam came to visit Fallan.

"What's his story?" I question, only recently seeing him prowl the streets with Andrew.

"I don't know," Fallan says, shoving his cup into the sink. "Before, I only had to worry about Andrew, but something tells me Xavier is more than just a friendly face to come from the other side of the ward."

CHAPTER FORTY-SIX

FALLAN

The new day brings even colder weather. I saw countless crumpled bodies on my walk to the tram this morning, all huddled on sidewalks beneath old blankets, doing their best to warm their hands with what little material they had—those of us who have housing had wood to use for fires to keep us warm, but we used it sparingly.

Mark has been quiet these last few days, saddened that his grandchildren have started walking to school instead of taking the tram. I know they struggle to look at him, regretting how he's been treated and mourning the time they never got with him. Andrew's abandonment of the old man is reprehensible.

"Have you ever noticed how awkwardly her brother walks?" Valerie questions from next to me, her eyes on the Blackburn siblings as they move through the crowd of students lingering outside the Academy. Both linger outside the front entrance as if they're not ready to start the day.

Forest trails in front of her brother, her beautiful brown hair thrown into a pristine braid. She keeps her eyes in straight ahead, entirely unaware of how many people look at her with desire. Countless men's thoughts of her swarm my mind each time I stand out here. Every sick fantasy is enough to make me want to wring their necks. I can hear it all, but there's nothing I can do. More recently, she's been keeping her mental barriers up and our connection closed, angry at me for shutting her out. Kai walks carelessly beside her. His long legs take wide strides as he talks his sister's ear off.

"He walks like anyone else without a care in the world." She rolls her eyes, watching me stare at my Little Dove.

"Hunter invited them to the bonfire tonight?" Valerie asks, scowling at Forest.

Forest smiles at Kai, her grin lighting up the space around her. I watch her become more animated as they talk; both siblings are easily mistaken for twins if you didn't know any better. She throws her arms in the air. Her fiery personality is enough to breathe life into any space.

"Yea. I was there when he did it," I say, leaning into the wall of glass windows surrounding the building. Valerie fiddles with her bag, no longer trying to hold my attention.

"You don't think someone might report her if they see her in our sector?" Valerie questions, my suspicions about her growing.

"Not unless someone who knows she's an Untouchable feels the need to report her," I start, narrowing my eyes at her. "You wouldn't know anyone vindictive enough to do that, would you?" I question, backing her further into the glass. She smiles at my reaction, ready to push me further.

"If you're referring to me," she starts, shoving me back and away from her. Her rough nature reveals itself the most in these moments. "I'd be more than happy to have her in our sector. Can't wait to see what I can make her do after one too many drinks!"

"Go fuck yourself," I hiss, feeling a wave of disappointment as I lose sight of Forest. She must have made it inside while I had to deal with Valerie.

"I'm kidding," Valerie says, sounding as unconvincing as ever. "If you want to waste your life gunning after a woman you can never have, be my guest," she says the first real hint of anything genuine lingering in her tone. "Maybe it's good for them to see the other side of our sector. The side that explains why we don't just up and leave," she whispers, my mind racing to the talk of the Lottery.

So many men, women, and children go missing every year in the blink of an eye, only to be pitted against one another like wild animals in the Pit.

I look to the ward above us, watching how it gleams, blocking out the thick air surrounding New Haven.

"What do you think there is out there?" Valerie questions, following my gaze. "I don't mean just the parts we can see; I mean beyond it. Do you think anyone else is alive? Other than the Shifters?"

Forest's words about Xavier's origin circle my mind. Our brief interaction at Adam's house the night of the Solstice dinner was enough to make me question him entirely. He's moved past me with such stealth that I thought I imagined what he'd said to me.

"If I see you touch her tonight, I'll hold her down against the table and show them what she's been hiding along her hip."

My inability to do anything about his threat toward her that night almost drove me mad.

"I think there are others out there, but there's a reason they haven't come this way in a long time."

"And the intercom systems blaring that crazy voice?" she adds. "You think that was really just a prank?"

That voice. That damned voice was clear as day in Forest's mind. How had he gotten in?

"Does it matter?" I question. "The ward was created to keep us in and keep everything else out." My hands fidget with my bag. She shakes her head at me.

"Why would they keep us away from other people out there?"

"Your guess is as good as mine," I say, glancing at the time on my watch.

"We'd better get going-"

"Do you trust her?" Valerie asks, cutting me off before I can finish. "Do you trust Forest?" she pushes, my hand dropping to my side.

I expect more from her. Maybe another snide remark. Instead, she stands still, waiting for me to respond.

"Do I trust Forest?"

She nods, leaving me with no way to avoid answering her this time.

I pause, thinking of every interaction we've ever shared. Every time she's come to me, she's gained nothing from it. All she's ever wanted is to explore a connection between us that even I barely understand.

"I do," I admit. Valerie's body pushes away from the wall.

"I'm glad someone does," she mutters, pulling her bag close. "Don't forget what happened the last time you trusted a Blackburn... some of us can't forget," she whispers, moving away from us and towards the front entrance of the school.

I don't fault Valerie for how much she hates the Blackburn name. Andrew's face haunts my mind at night. The things he did changed my life forever and left behind emotional scars that I don't think will ever heal. His daughter, though, has somehow helped me find some meaning again.

It's ironic how such a great evil could create such a bright light.

CHAPTER FORTY-SEVEN

FOREST

"**I** saw it. I saw them get pushed beyond the ward," I mutter, forcing my knees to my chest as I stay seated on one of the many mats in the conditioning center.

Fallan pauses, stopping himself from taking another swing toward the bags.

A whole day of school had droned by, ending with me going to the Unfortunate sector the minute I caught wind of my parents staying at work later than expected. The night of the Solstice dinner Xavier apparently offered to take Kai to see the observatory that housed all of the organic matter our scientists had been experimenting with. Given everything that's been going on the last few days, leaving school early to do something he enjoys was warranted.

My bag was filled with more training gear these days than schoolbooks. To my surprise, I'd instinctively headed to the Unfortunate sector after class, not expecting my legs to carry me here after the draining hours of the school day. With a few kind looks and a lot of concentration, swaying the Officials standing guard to let me in with their IDs had been nothing short of a cakewalk.

My abilities are growing stronger, making me less fatigued after expelling large bursts of energy.

I had nearly made it to my first turn when I saw Officials dragging several Unfortunates to their knees. They wore gray robes and were elderly in the face. Their wrists were bound together as they were pushed around like animals in a slaughterhouse. They were taken all the way to the edge of the broken ward, the Officials taunting them with promises of what was about to happen to them.

"We won't make it out there," the man cries, grabbing the Official's pants, begging for support.

All the woman next to him could do was cry, consumed by her fears.

I stood back and watched in horror as *my* people forced the hooded pair past the tear in the ward, threatening to slam their prods deep within their chests if they dared to try and come back into the sector. At a certain point, the prods were replaced with the barrel of a pistol, leaving nothing but the ever-expanding land of ash as the last viable option for escape. Several family members of the two Unfortunates pleaded with the Officials, whaling out their grief as they watched them cross over the ward.

As I finished telling Fallan what happened, I couldn't help the tears I shed. The cruelty of this place never got any easier. But I felt like a coward right now, believing I could have... *should* have... done more.

"You couldn't interfere, Forest," Fallan says, addressing my solemn expression.

Given his cold attitude these past few days, the last thing I expected was kindness.

"Why not? If I have the means to do something about it-"

"Your abilities are not something to be thrown around on a whim. Do you have any idea what would happen if someone found out what we are?" he questions, scolding me like a child.

"You don't think I could stop someone from harming me?" I question.

He moves to me, swiping his leg toward my feet. I step back from the motion, only to be met with his hand pulling my front, dragging me into him. Wrapping his arm around my front, he forces my back to his chest. Unsheathing his blade, he holds the weapon to my neck.

"I have my doubts," he whispers, the sharp edge of the blade pointed away from my skin.

Grabbing his arm, I try to look into his mind, meeting nothing but that infuriating wall meant to keep me out. Frustrations high, I focus on his blade, bending the metal at my will, watching it fall to pieces at his feet. Forcing my head up with his hand, he looks down at me, giving me a long look of approval before finally releasing me.

"That's new," he says, grabbing the broken pieces. "When did you start taking an interest in destroying things?" he questions, unamused with my handiwork.

"I'll answer that when you stop shutting me out," I mutter, his eyes darting to me.

"Last time I checked, you're keeping me out as well."

"Wonder why," It scoffs.

My thoughts exactly.

Fallan tosses the pieces of his blade into his bag, pausing as he stares down into its opening. He reaches down and pulls out my sketchbook, his hands careful with its worn front. The last place I'd seen this was under his bed, but I was too busy trying not to get discovered by Officials to question why he had it. Running his hand along the cover, he extends his arm toward me, holding it out in the air between us.

"I didn't know art was your thing," I say sarcastically, meeting the surface of the sketchbook with my fingertips. He holds on to the cover, almost as if he's not ready to let it go.

"I told myself I'd use it when the time came to get you in hot water with an Official. Given your name on the cover, it seemed like a perfect way to blame you for sharing supplies with an Unfortunate like me," he shrugs, closing the space between us so I can take the sketchbook.

"Why didn't you?" I question, looking up to him. "Why didn't you just turn me in? You would have saved yourself a great deal of trouble had you just made up some story and turned me in. My scorecard is almost red. They would have punished me severely."

He frowns and then unexpectedly moves to touch my cheek, grazing his thumb along the soft above my jaw. His front is brushed against mine as my shaky hands take the sketchbook from him.

"I would have ripped out their throats before they could have even thought of harming you," he mutters, his thumb moving to trail along my lower lip. I lean a little closer, my breath uneven with anticipation. "No one will ever hurt you again as long as I'm around."

He backs away, my body stumbling forward at the sudden space between us. I steady myself, noticing a page poking out from the sketchbook. I open the cover to find an array of new artwork.

Countless graphite drawings of me from numerous angles consume the pages. Each one showed a moment I didn't know I was being watched. I hover my finger above my smile, feeling how well the observer captured moments when I felt peace.

"You wondered all that time ago what I was working on... what inspired me," Fallan says, turning away to hide his face. I think of that day in the art room, his hidden canvas shielded from everyone.

"Your smile has haunted me for longer than you know. Drawing it adds to the pain of knowing none of those smiles were meant for me. But when I look at these pictures, sometimes I pretend it's me you're smiling at."

I feel his pain. It's the same pain I keep bottled up.

"I drew you for the same reason," I begin, ready to show him the few drawings I'd made of him before losing the work.

"I saw them," he starts, turning on his heels, "I made you believe I wanted you dead when you made those," he continues, moving back toward me. "Why the hell would you have drawn me like I'm anything short of a vile 'bottom feeder?'" he questions, throwing my wording back at me.

I shake my head at him, reflecting on the images I had captured through stolen glances of him. I think of that night at the bonfire and the moment we shared as children.

"We've met before, not in passing, not for a moment. We've met. There's history between us," I begin, taking a step towards him. He takes one back, unwilling to explore this topic.

"Forest-"

"You don't get to avoid this anymore," I snap, toying with the necklace around my neck. "You gave this to me, and ever since then, I've never taken it off. I remember what it felt like to have your hands on me," I push, no longer able to avoid this. "Your presence intoxicates me to the point where I feel like I'm going mad. Feeling this connection is so natural."

He stands still, his eyes dead set on me.

"What are you so afraid of?"

He snaps, his mental wall cracking under the pressure. As he moves towards me, I backstep until my back hits the wall. His hands grasp the sides of my face, his fears swirling within him, ready to burst free.

"Losing you!" he yells, his voice layered with different emotions. I navigate the open door in his mind. The visual of a man and a woman with eerily similar features to him lie motionless and pale on the ground.

His parents.

"Damn it, Forest! Can't you fucking see? I lose everyone in one way or another." A vivid image of my father passes through my mind.

"My parents, friends, family-"

More and more faces flash in front of me, all of them dead.

"And then for one fucking moment," he continues, the night of the bonfire filling my mind. "There you were. Fragile and innocent, like a small bird." His hands move away from my face and down my side. "And I wanted to keep that one good thing safe." His hands squeeze my hips, my face flush with blood flow. "And they threatened to take it all... to take you away. A whole person wiped away with a little pill," he continues, my heart breaking. "And now they threaten me again, no longer with a pill, but with your bloodshed."

"I want you," he starts, his mind rampant. "And they know that."

"Who knows that?" I question, thinking of every possible way I want to hurt them for taking away his happiness.

He shakes his head, a faint, resigned smile spreading across his face.

"You can't bring them all down, Little Dove. Nothing is worth watching you die because I was not strong enough to stay away," he whispers. "One kiss and I can never walk away. One kiss and I am yours until the day my heart stops."

Every fiber of my being needs him at this moment.

"Don't push me away," I plea, a small tear escaping my eye.

I sense the pain my words cause him, feeling its heaviness in my chest.

"I have to, or else we can't even have this... and worse, I end up losing you,"

I half expect the walls of his mind to go back up. Moments pass, and the door stays open, every raw emotion pouring down through me, and I'm ready to break.

"I will keep you safe," he whispers, taking in every feature of my face. His thumb wipes away the tear that had made its way down my cheek and onto my lips. My energy dwindles as I continue to look around his mind.

"That I can promise."

Dropping the sketchbook, I feel his arms wrap around me, keeping me from falling to the floor. Burying my face in his chest, I listen to his heart, wondering how long I can stand here before he pushes me away.

"Fallan! Are you here?" Aaron's voice booms through the gym.

Fallan hesitantly let's go, his walls going back into place once more. Grabbing the sketchbook, he tucks it away in my bag, watching as his red-headed friend enters the space. My body tenses up at the sight of Valerie trailing behind him. She locks eyes with me from across the room, her arms crossed before she's even made it over to us.

Aaron looks giddy, his grin widening at the sight of us together.

"You must be special for him to see you this many times in one week," Aaron starts, his hand clapping Fallan's back, "I hope it's worth putting a target on all of our backs to get your quick Untouchable fix," Aaron pushes. Fallan is quick to shove away from his friend.

"Did you come in here just to run your mouth?" Fallan questions, anger now obvious in his expression.

"We came to take you back to the bakery. Jolie needs some extra hands to prep for the social tonight," Valerie says, moving in front of me, doing her best to keep me away from Fallan.

"What time should I come?" I question, watching her body tense up at the question. "Assuming I bring Kai, he'll want to know too," I finish. Aaron's smile consumes his whole face.

"Ask Hunter. He's the only one who wants you there," Valerie starts, ready to lean into Fallan. He steps away, creating a divide between them.

Gradually, I creep into the cracks of her mind, focusing on navigating the spaces like Fallan has shown me, synching my breathing to her own. Where I half expect to feel the desire for Fallan brewing inside of her, I feel nothing. Taking a step toward the woman, we meet at eye level, and a wave of heady lust and longing washes over me.

This jealousy was never meant for any man.

Her beautiful face scowls. My hand reaches up to tuck a small piece of hair behind her ear. I smile gently at her, moving my lips to the side of her face.

"To think I was going for you," I whisper, her mouth dropping at my response.

Fallan's mouth curls into a smile. Aaron's eyes widen at the statement. Looking over her face, her cheeks begin to redden. Her reaction to my touch is all the evidence I need to prove why she's been so cold towards me.

"She has a crush?" It questions, a tiny lick of satisfaction working over me.

Valerie is lost for words. My hands fall from her face. Giving the boys one last look, I grab my bag, lingering near Fallan, ready for any snide remarks. Valerie stands still, her hands clenched together.

"I will see you all tonight," I say, watching Fallan cross his arms.

Turning toward the exit, the group begins to whisper. Aaron teases Valerie, nudging her arm while she stands transfixed, an unamused look on her face.

"Did you do that to prove a point?" Fallan questions silently, my smile growing.

"Depends... did it work?" I question, a hint of his amusement passing through the connection.

"Don't get any more bright ideas, Little Dove."

There are two things, and only two things I know for sure.

One:

It's not just my people Fallan is scared of. Something happened to him, leaving behind scars that remind him to be afraid.

And Two:

My feelings for Fallan are deeper than I could have imagined... and I think these feelings have been there all along.

CHAPTER FORTY-EIGHT

FOREST

"So it's a party?" Kai asks, his hands violently scrubbing away at his hair, doing his best to dry the mane on his head.

He steps away from our bathroom, dressed in a gray shirt and flannel paired together to push out the brisk cold. I wear a black sweater, my legs tucked away into a pair of gray cargo pants that make me look much taller than I am. Moving around his room, he thinks about the invitation to the bonfire, nudging his backpack free from beneath his dresser. Like me, he's abandoned the idea of utilizing it for just school work, carrying whatever he can to the Unfortunate sector in it instead.

"Think of it as a way for Hunter to show us another side of their sector."

He eyes me down, rummaging through his belongings.

"And Hunter invited you? Not Fallan?" he questions, trying his best to figure out the dynamic between us.

"Hunter invited *us*. I think he cared more about you showing face than me," I admit. Kai's body goes rigid at the remark.

"I don't know why he would care," Kai mumbles, shielding his face from me.

I tighten the sheath of my blade to my side, keeping it concealed under the sweater. These days, all I need is one blade. My mind's strength gives me enough advantage to do the rest.

"He cares because, for some reason, he thinks you're the better of the two of us," I say sarcastically, nudging Kai with a smile.

He loosens up a little, finally looking at me with a lazy grin.

"Will there be booze?"

"How else would we get through the night?"

Walking along the ward, we occasionally brush shoulders. Kai keeps pace with me, deliberating something in his mind that's taking all of his focus. If I wanted to, I could see all that troubles him with little effort, saving us both an awkward conversation. At times, it's tempting to walk the minds of those around me. I've been curious to see how much of their mind is by design. False memories have a haze. They are frayed around the edges when compared to the ones I find that are real.

Kai's brows are furrowed in frustration. My hand is inches away from his. One touch and I'd have the direct connection I need to see it all.

"Who needs morals?" It questions, urging me to breach my brother's trust.

"Blackburns?" Xavier's familiar voice echoes loudly down the street, both me and Kai stopping dead in our tracks.

We could play this off causally, explaining we were going for a walk, but we happen to be dressed like we're about to break into someone's home. We both wear jackets with the hood pulled up over our heads. The masks covering our faces and necks to keep out the cold don't help our case, either.

Turning on our heels, we face Xavier. His hand is resting at his side. He wears an Official winter uniform, the thick jacket and pants hugging his muscular frame. He cocks his head at the sight of us, looking back to our house, before snapping his eyes back to us.

"I was just going to return some things you left in my car," Xavier says, holding out a few of Kai's textbooks.

"What the hell are you guys doing out here?" Xavier asks. I can feel the awkwardness from our last interaction together hanging in the air between us. I hadn't spoken to him since that night, unwilling and unsure of what to say to him to ease the tension I'd created between us.

Tucking the books away in his bag, he moves toward us. Both Kai and I take a step back.

"For fuck's sake, is there a reason you're both so jumpy?"

I moved my body in front of Kai when I noticed his hands started to shake.

Xavier observes us for a moment, noticing our outfits and the direction we're headed. Concentrating on my abilities, I attempt to peer into his mind. I find my way in, but the only thing I see are glimpses of images that I don't understand. Wherever his thoughts are, I can't follow them completely. Slowly, he reaches up, touching my cheek in a sweet gesture.

"You should know by now you never have to fear me," he whispers.

"One of us knows that," It hisses. My body relaxes as I let go of the connection tethering me to Xavier's mind.

Gradually, I move closer to him, letting his thumb roll over my cheek again. His touch is always gentle, and he looks at me with such care and concern. But I don't fall into the depths of his kind eyes the same way I do with Fallan's.

"You're going to their sector... aren't you?" Xavier questions. He looks at Kai now.

Kai keeps his head lowered, unable to look at the man he's been conditioned his whole life to respect and obey. The Order should be feared. And as an Official, we should fear Xavier.

"There's more to the Unfortunates than meets the eye," I whisper, watching my words register with him.

He takes a deep breath, looking around the quiet neighborhood.

"I parked my car a good deal away from your house, so I had the time to deliberate whether or not to bug you," he says, his kind nature so sweet that it hurts. "So it shouldn't be an issue."

"What shouldn't?" Kai questions, finally raising his head.

Xavier reaches into his pocket, pulling out an Official mask. Drawing up the hood of his long coat, he looks down at me, squeezing my hand.

"Me joining the two of you, of course."

We walk casually through the sector, finding it much easier to get through this time with Xavier's presence. When we entered through the tear in the fence, Kai and I were fully prepared to think of a diversion that ultimately ended with us breaching security at the entrance. To our surprise, no one batted an eye when Xavier flashed his ID and forced the "Two Unfortunates apprehended for questioning," through the front entrance. He held the back of my neck for what felt like forever, shouting angrily at Kai and me to move forward before finally breaking his façade as we rounded a corner and made our way down one of the many sidewalks. Gently, he rubs my neck, soothing the tension from his stern grip, apologizing several times.

"Pretty convincing at playing the whole authoritative asshole bit," Kai says, applauding Xavier for his acting skills.

"I could say the same about you," Xavier says, giving Kai a warm smile that I know was meant to piss him off.

Kai rolls his eyes, nudging the man with his shoulder.

Hunter's bakery is filled with life. There are people of varying shapes and sizes in the shop, some conversing around the pastry counter with cups filled with warm piping liquid. Everyone around the space is smiling. A bonfire blazes. Long logs are set out for people to use as a seating area. The sky is filled with bright colors, pinks and purples, all painted by the setting sun. People welcome us with warm smiles as we pass. It's become almost second nature to clasp people's hands. Kai is still getting the hang of the gesture, unsure how long to linger before it's weird. Xavier greets people with a broad smile, his charm oozing out of him.

"If I didn't know any better, I'd say you were an Unfortunate," I say playfully, smiling up at him.

"Maybe then you'd like me more," he whispers sarcastically, embarrassment sweeping across my cheeks.

I stop walking and place my hand gently on his arm.

"I'm not here for Fallan," I whisper, his head slightly lowering to get a better look at me.

"Prove it," Xavier whispers.

"Happily," It chimes out for me unexpectedly.

"Shut it!" I yell back, looking away from him as I speak.

"Did I say too much-"

"I wasn't talking to you," I blurt out. His eyes grew wide for a moment before his face slipped back into an easy disposition.

The bell of the bakery door tinkles as a familiar face emerges.

"I was wondering if you were going to show," Hunter says, smiling as he moves closer to us.

With no warning, I am wrapped up in a hug, feeling him squeeze with all he has. He cups my face with two hands before glancing behind me with a hateful stare toward Xavier.

"You brought the guard dog," Hunter mutters, his words slightly slurred.

"And you brought a lack of consent," Xavier lets out, motioning to his hands plastered on my face.

"Is that the best you've got?" Hunter pushes, finally looking over at Kai. Dropping his hands, he moves past me, getting a better look at Xavier and his cocky smile.

"I have no interest in the woman you're holding over my friend like she's some trophy," Hunter says. Xavier's eyes narrow at his comment, his posture stiffening.

I clear my throat.

"What is he talking about?" I question, watching Xavier keep his eyes on Hunter.

"Why don't you tell her," Hunter says, nudging him. "Might be easier once everything's out in the open." Hunter moves away from Xavier and closer to Kai.

I take Hunter's spot in front of Xavier, looking over the man curiously. He crosses his arms as he avoids my gaze. My hand finally reaches up to grab his chin. He doesn't resist me but hesitates before moving his eyes back to mine.

"I might have threatened Hunter and Fallan when I was here with your father... it's how I got the necklace back," Xavier mutters, my hand dropping to my side at his response.

Without warning, I grab his entire face this time, pulling his head close to mine. His hands clutch my sides as I enter his mind, breaching his mental wall easily. I think of his words, reflecting on that day Fallan and Hunter had received the visit from my father. I see the memory from his perspective, hovering my lips above his while I dig for more. His grasp on me tightens, and the memory becomes clearer as Xavier's threats toward them that day fill my head. Biting my cheek, his lips nearly touch mine. The memory is now fully formed. He looks bewildered, doing his best to stop our lips from touching in front of everyone here.

Pulling away, I get what I need, letting him keep his hands on me.

"So now I'm something you feel like you have jurisdiction over?" I don't need to be connected to his mind to know he's ashamed.

Kai and Hunter watch the exchange through stolen glances, quietly whispering, keeping to themselves.

"No, that's not it," Xavier begins, his thumb trailing over my upper stomach. "Tell me right now that you have no feelings for me, and I'll stop. If you tell me right now it's impossible for you to care for me, I'll walk away," Xavier pushes, the chatter of people around us growing louder as they enjoy the party.

I open my mouth, ready to say something to push him away.

But *It* speaks for me.

And I want it to.

"I can't tell you there's nothing here," I finally settle on saying, feeling it coax me to continue. "And I can't tell you there isn't some part of you that scares me," I finish, waiting to see how he'll react to the truth.

"I wish there was-"

He abruptly stops speaking, his eyes closing in annoyance. Grunting angrily, he touches his throat, shaking his head in frustration.

"I won't ever hurt you, Forest," he finally says., my head slowly nodding to let him know that I believe him.

"I know," I say with complete trust, unsure why I can no longer bear being near him.

My head explodes into a vortex of thought, his shields and mine crashing down, all of his emotions hitting me like a landslide. Turning my head, Fallan's blue eyes meet mine before eyeing down Xavier. Xavier's hands fall from my sides. Valerie trails behind Fallan, her tiny body fitted into a lovely blue dress that is perfect for tonight. She really is gorgeous. Hunter drags Kai closer to the bonfire, urging my brother to drink from his cup, patting him on the back in encouragement. Fallan moves closer to us, crossing his arms as he continues to stare at Xavier.

"I wasn't expecting you to be here," Fallan says to Xavier, both men completely rigid. I look at Valerie, half expecting her to egg it on. Instead, she watches me, her hands fidgeting with one another.

"Yet, here I am," Xavier says, touching my lower back. Glancing down at his arm, I don't know how to react. I give Fallan an apologetic look, unsure at what point Xavier had gotten his hands back on me.

"I think there are plenty of your Official asshole friends surrounding the perimeter if you want to go see them," Fallan says.

"What's the fun in that?" Xavier questions, his hand moving around to trail down my side. He's trying to prove he can have me.

That I'm his.

A message to Fallan.

"Can I get you a drink?" Valerie questions toward me, finally breaking her silence.

I look at her arm, feeling a pit grow in my stomach at the tension the men have created. Looping my arm around hers, I quickly nod, feeling my anxiety fade as we escape them. Aaron stands behind a table serving drinks, his eyes growing wide at the sight of me and Valerie together. With a wide grin, he pours two drinks, motioning Kai and Hunter closer, leaving Xavier and Fallan to bicker quietly.

"I figured you wanted out of that," Valerie says with complete honesty, her perfect skin and beautifully wide eyes illuminated in this lighting.

"Thank you," I whisper, squeezing her arm with genuine gratitude.

"I never thought I'd see the day Valerie wasn't plotting your demise," Aaron says, pushing the drinks closer to us across the counter.

Picking it up, I sniff the contents of the cup, and I'm immediately ready to set it back down. Before I can put the cup back on the counter and ask for something else, Aaron pushes the cup to my lips, forcing the sweet amber liquid into my mouth and down my throat. Hunter does the same thing to Kai as a searing warmth spreads through my stomach.

"Fuck! That's so much stronger than our stuff," Kai says, slamming the cup on the table for a refill.

Xavier and Fallan end their conversation, both scowling. Grabbing a woman's arm from the crowd, Fallan pulls her along with him, whispering gently in her ear, pressing his lips to the soft part of her neck. Dropping my cup, I eye them with utter disbelief, watching Valerie follow my eyesight, her mouth settling into a displeased frown.

"Looks like we are having one of those nights," Valerie says, shaking her head as she extends her arm for seconds.

The woman is young and pretty. She is already giddy from alcohol, allowing Fallan to dance with her as my heart burns with jealousy. Slamming my hands on the walls of his mind, I scream at him through the bond.

"Looks like your blonde friend told Fallan again that he can't have something he wants," Valerie says, pressing her hand into her hip as she speaks. "This is his way of getting to both of you."

"Fine. I can play that game, too," I mutter to her. I watch as her features shift into a feral kind of delight.

Xavier finally makes his way back to us. Hunter quickly shoves a cup into his hand. Unlike the rest of us, Xavier quickly drinks it with no issues, giving Fallan one last look before turning to me. Aaron tops off my cup to the brim. Throwing back the drink, my hand drops the cup when I'm done, instantly reaching for Xavier and pulling him closer to the music.

"What are we doing?" he questions. The effects of the alcohol are already setting in, making me bolder than usual.

I yank my sweater up and pull it free from my body, revealing a sheer gray compression shirt. It's almost see-through, with a soft shimmer that catches the light. My lace bra is visible underneath, showing more of my chest than I'm used to. Keeping my hair down and in its waves, I toss the sweater on a log, eyeing Xavier like an animal.

"You want me, Xavier?" I say without thinking, watching his pupils dilate.

All he can do is look at me.

"Prove it," I say with a grin, throwing his words back at him.

Grabbing my waist, he pulls me flush against him. My arms wrap around his neck, and I drag him down and into me. Hungrily, his lips find my neck, causing my breath to hitch as my chin buries deep into his shoulder. My eyes find Fallan's angry stare. He is no longer focused on the woman I saw him with earlier. His hands clench his cup, now spilling over with liquid.

"Is this all a show?" Xavier questions, his voice brushing over my ear.

"It would be so much easier if everything was just a show," It says, speaking for me.

"Why did you say that?" I question, feeling unsure of my words.

"The two sides of you come with more than just an extra voice in your head," It hisses, my mind drawing blanks.

He presses his head against my own, grabbing the back of my thigh, ready to pull me onto him.

"What's my name, Forest?" he questions, my mouth ready to taste his.

"Xavier. Xavier Hayes," I say, his head gently shaking.

"Try again.... What's *my* name?" he asks again, my mind drawing nothing but blanks.

"Your name's Xavier," I whisper, unsure what he wants me to say.

With a saddened expression, he pulls away, his hands slowly loosening their grasp.

"Tonight was just for him. Wasn't it?" Xavier questions, the mood between us shifting instantly.

I pause, my heart filled with emotions. Fallan moves away from the woman and the campfire's light.

I look at Xavier, and there's that part of me that wants nothing but him. It eats me alive, a conviction I feel I have no control over.

"I have no idea what's happening to me," I whisper, my hand touching my chest.

"What did the two of you talk about?" I question, his head nodding.

"We-" he stops, biting his lip out of frustration.

"Do you trust me?" he questions, unable to give me a straight answer to my question.

I'm ready to say no and run away from all of this.

"Yes," I say, my throat burning with the need to scream. "And I have no idea why."

Kai and Hunter join us in a fit of laughter, both men clapping Xavier on the back.

"Your cups are empty!" Kai gasps, managing to get a smile from Xavier.

I look to the alleyway Fallan had disappeared into, sensing the walls in his mind slowly breaking away.

"I need a moment," I say, backing away from Xavier, giving him no time to react as my brother and Hunter hang onto him, shoving another drink in his hand.

Moving past the other party guests, I disappear into the mess of the crowd. Moving towards the alleyway, the connection to Fallan grows stronger as I approach. Xavier's words cloud my mind. His meaning is lost to me.

But slowly, all thoughts of Xavier leave me, my eyes set on the pair of blue ones that watch me now.

Fallan's mind is filled with nothing but thoughts of me.

CHAPTER FORTY-NINE

FOREST

He's leaning onto one of the brick walls of the alleyway, his hand dragging up his shirt, wiping at his face. His torso is exposed for a moment, and I take a second to appreciate his body. His head is cocked while he watches me observe him. I sense thoughts of me swirling around in his mind. The alcohol aids in weakening his mental walls against me. He thinks of how my smile curves my lips perfectly and the places his hands have explored my body. He moves closer to me and lets out a nervous laugh. His hands move across his abdomen, dropping his shirt before pointing to me with a frown.

"Are you just going to parade men in front of me all night?" he questions, his voice rough and sinister.

I touch the portion of my neck Xavier had made his, feeling Fallan's hateful thoughts toward him intensify.

Taking another step, liquid courage envelopes my body.

"You want to talk about parading someone around? What was that little display with that woman? Or Valerie before that? All you've done is show off other women and torture me in the process," I say, nudging my hand hard into his chest. He stays still, his eyes lowered as he watches me.

"You're the tortured one?" he scoffs, shaking his head angrily. "Clearly, you haven't been listening."

"Just a distraction," I mock, throwing up my quotations. "Should I add 'tortured' under the list of labels you've forced on us?" I question, his mouth pulling into a drunken smirk.

"They didn't mean anything to me, Forest. I needed something to dull the pain," Fallan mutters, his hand grabbing my hip. "He thinks you're his," Fallan continues, his hand dipping beneath my shirt, exploring the warm skin underneath. "He thinks he can satisfy you," he continues, my heart pounding as he backs me into the brick wall. "He thinks that you could *love* him," Fallan whispers, his lips pressed against the side of my face, his fingers moving farther up my body.

"I'm not entertaining any more stolen touches, only for you to just push me away," I mutter, biting my cheek to avoid giving in to the pleasure the feeling of his hands on my skin is bringing me.

"Then tell me what you want, Little Dove." His lips move from the side of my face to my front, his thumbs trailing along my upper rib cage, brushing against the lace overlay of my bra. "Do you want me to admit how much I crave you? How much I crave only you?" he questions, my breath shuddering, feeling his hands move closer to my breasts.

"You don't know what it's like to hear you gasp every time I kiss your skin," he starts, his lips finding the sensitive points on my neck. "You don't know what it's like to see your smile curve up for everyone but me and wonder why I can't have it too," he continues, my body aching to feel more of him. He has me sprawled against the wall, my body entirely controlled by his hand. "You don't know how much I wanted to hurt you to get back at your father for what he did to me, but then I realized who you were. That girl from the bonfire who made me smile for the first time in months," he says, my legs aching as his hand finally finds my breast. He slips his thumb beneath the lace and gently passes over the tender skin of each nipple. I can't hide the shake in my breath, biting my lip to stop myself from telling him to tear away everything I wear. "You were there during my test. We bled from the same blade and hid from the same monsters." My mind races to the moments we shared, even just as children.

"I could never forget that," I whisper, my arms wrapping around his neck. "Even if they tried to make me," I finish, my lip wobbly.

"Tell me to back away," he starts, his hands grabbing the back of my thighs, pulling them up and around his waist. "Call me a pig," he continues, my thighs clenching tighter around his waist. "Call me every name you can think of," he pushes, his nose inches away from my own. "Be disgusted by me, please. Say anything so I won't do it." Our hearts race. "Tell me to stop."

The connection between us buzzes. There are no more walls between us.

"Call me a privileged elite," I whisper. "Tell me you hate my kind and loathe our existence."

"I do loathe their existence," he starts. "But not yours."

My core heats each time my center brushes against him.

"I dream of your existence, Forest." His voice is filled with longing. "You were my morning, noon, and night, and it all was ripped away in an instant. Now, I just want to fucking tear your clothes off in front of him and show him that you will never be his."

"You don't hate me?"

"Hate you?" he questions, his head shaking. "Forest, I'm in *love* with you," he says, my heart bursting wide open as he says the words.

I slam my lips into his, finally giving in to this desire. His hands grab me harder, his teeth biting at my bottom lip before returning my kiss feverishly. My soft moans of pleasure are captured by his mouth. His arms are locked underneath me, seating me more fully against his cock. Running his tongue along my bottom lip, he slips it into my mouth, both of us fighting for some form of dominance. Grasping his curls, I deepen the kiss as I send him images of every way I want him to take me. He groans into the kiss, our marks burning with pleasure. I feel the cord of our connection snapping into place, solidifying in ways it hadn't before.

Each of his thoughts has become my own; our souls no longer in two.

I finally break the kiss for air, feeling the rise and fall of his chest from heavy breathing. Both of us are a tangle of hunger and lust. Grasping his face, I run my thumbs along his cheeks, taking in his swollen lips and dilated pupils.

"It's not a one-sided feeling," I whisper, his mouth curling into a grin.

"Tell me it's a bad idea to take you somewhere more private," he says against my ear, his arms still wrapped around my body.

Never has the silence between us felt so right.

CHAPTER FIFTY

FOREST

His hands brace the wall behind me. My back slams into his door, his lips exploring my own, barely letting either of us up for air. Keeping me wrapped around his waist, he fumbles with the locks on his door. I grow impatient, urging the slide of each lock forward with nothing more than a blink of my eyes. The energy, once a steady undercurrent between us, now surges like an unstoppable force, blazing through our veins like an inferno. I feel the firm flex of his muscles as he slams the door closed behind us, barely breaking contact. He moves us to the bed in the corner of the room, lowering me down gently until my back rests against the soft gray sheets.

As I move to yank up his shirt, he pushes my wrists back down, the bright gleam of his canines flashing as he gives me a devious smile that sends a thrilling shiver down my spine.

"You have no idea how tortured I've been by the thought of your touch. How tormented I've been knowing that I couldn't have you like I want when I want." He shifts to hold my wrists in one hand above my head, using his free one to grasp the bottom of my shirt. "You don't get to touch me until I've gotten time to explore you," he whispers, the heat between my legs nearly unbearable. Words are caught in my throat. The other part of me is silent, anticipating where this will lead. He presses his lips to mine again, touching my chin with his fingers, his eyes hungry with desire.

"Look at me," he commands, my eyes snapping up to his.

Slowly, he moves down my body, stopping at the bottom of my shirt. He uses the hand still holding my wrists to pull me up, dropping them once I'm seated. His breathing is heavy as I watch him unlatch the buttons on my pants, jerking them down my legs towards the floor at his feet. He pauses, taking in the sight of my exposed body, his gaze feral as it sweeps across my black underwear. I clench my legs together, unable to hide the growing wetness between my legs. Kneeling at the end of the bed, he drags my thighs closer to him, his finger brushing over my mark. He trails kisses up my leg, running his tongue along my inner thigh. My arms struggle to support me as I watch him move closer to my core. Keeping eye contact with me, he uses his teeth to take the top of my underwear into his mouth, dragging the lace down my legs, exposing my sex to him.

"Perfect," he whispers, bringing his fingers up to meet my warm center, the pleasure from his touch enough to make me implode. I bite back a moan as he reaches the aching bundle of nerves there.

"Let me hear it all," he begs, as his fingers run gentle circles over my clit.

I feel my wetness coat his long fingers as he slips inside me, my back arching from the feeling.

"Fuck," I whisper, keeping my eyes on him. He smiles at the reaction, his body towering over me, pumping his fingers in and out of me. Jumbled curses escape my lips each time he hits all the right spots. His fingers stretch me, my walls clenching tightly around him.

"Already so wet, Little Dove," he says, his pupils blown wide, a wicked expression on his face.

He lifts my legs over his shoulders, keeping his fingers moving inside me.

"Fallan, please-"

I beg, ready for release

His mouth lands on my folds, his tongue exploring every part of me with slow, dragging motions. My back arches against his sheets, my moans of pleasure leaving me freely. His fingers continue pumping in and out of me as he works my clit with his tongue. I thrust my hips up, wanting more. He lets out a low growl of approval as he continues to work, sending a jolt of pleasure up my center. I force my head back down, watching him taste me, savoring the intensity and focus written into his expression. Clenching his head with my thighs, I feel my body ready to burst, the pool of warmth in my stomach almost at its breaking point.

Pulling his mouth away, he smiles, rolling his thumb between my folds.

"Let it happen, beautiful," he urges. At his command, I cum. My release sending wave after wave of pleasure through my body. My walls clench around his fingers as I cry out his name in pure ecstasy, my hands gripping the sheets to ground me.

Slowly, he pulls his fingers away and up to his mouth, licking them clean.

Still feral for my taste, he moves back down to my warmth, cleaning up what's left of my release with his tongue, taking his time sucking and licking like he's been starved, and I'm the only thing that can satisfy his hunger. My legs shake around him, another release threatening to tear through me as he continues. As if he can sense what's coming, he lifts his head, throwing me a sinful grin.

Watching him rise to his feet, I see the bulge pressed against his pants, its length intimidating. My mouth starts to water as he grabs his belt and begins to undo the buckle. My lips curl into a smile as I force his hands down with my mind, taking over the process of removing it for him.

Letting his belt clatter to the floor, I run my hand along his front, feeling him beneath the material of his pants. He groans, his frustration growing at his inability to use his hands.

"So, using our gifts is not off the table?" Fallan questions. My fingers fidget with the buttons of his pants.

I look up to him, my smile growing.

"I want it all. Anything goes," I whisper, his eyes lowering at the response.

Walking into my mind, he urges me to lay back down on the bed, his ability to sway my thoughts far greater than mine. As my back meets the mattress again, I release his hands from my mental hold, and they drop to his sides. My hands claw at his shirt on the way down his body, tugging the material free from his chest. Marveling over his body, I see his strong front and his mark branding the skin of his side. I run my finger over each divot on his stomach, feeling the v-line of muscles beneath my touch. Moving over me, he slips my shirt up, gently pulling it up and over my head, exposing my breasts. His desire for me cascades through our mental connection at the sight of me fully exposed to him. Continuing to touch his hard length, I pull down the waistline of his pants, letting him do the rest.

"Nothing compares to how you look right now," he mutters, his knee propped on the bed supporting his body, his hands running up and down my frame, feeling every part of me.

"You're a work of art," he continues, lowering his head, pressing his lips to my lower stomach, only to move up.

I run my hand through his hair, letting out a shuddered breath.

"Fallan," I whisper, pulling his chin up to meet me, his eyes filled with lust.

"Please, let me feel you," I push, his mouth brushing over my breasts, pausing after he's had a taste.

"Are you sure?" he questions, rolling his thumb over my cheek.

Biting my lip, I nod and lean forward to capture his mouth with mine. I channel feelings of pleasure through our connection, our kisses turning from sweet and sincere to something hungrier. Biting at my bottom lip, he moves away from the kiss, lowering himself to my breasts, gently taking time to explore each one. His thumb swirls over one nipple as he takes the other in his mouth, sucking hard, devouring me as he kneads my other breast in his palm.

Dragging his lips down to my mark, he kisses the skin, lingering on its roughness. He smiles against my stomach.

"There's beauty in this," he whispers. "You're the one who taught me that," he murmurs, running his fingers along the waistband of his boxers.

"There was never anything wrong with you," I begin, leaning forward, touching his mark with my hand. "It was always just about control," I push, the feeling of admiration swarming me.

Helping him slide down his boxers, his length is finally exposed to me. I take in the sight of him, a gasp escaping me at the sheer size of him. I peer up at him, letting my hand run down his base. He laces his finger through my hair, pulling it possessively into his fist as he guides us back down on the bed. His length brushes my inner thigh before aligning with my already wet entrance.

"I'll go slow," he whispers, pressing his lips to my own. "If you need me to stop, Dove, tell me, and I will. I've heard the first time can sometimes be... painful."

"You've never done this before?" I question, feeling a hint of embarrassment pass through our connection

"No. I waited for you," he starts, smiling into a kiss. "Call me old-fashioned." His tip nudges into my warmth, teasing the entrance. "If I feel any pain from you, we'll stop," he says, my body alive with anticipation.

"I'm not opposed to some pain," I say without thinking, his eyes going wide.

"I'll be gentle," he whispers, his lips pressing against my cheek.

With a slow thrust, I feel myself stretch around him, pain and pleasure mixing as we come together. I stutter before a loud moan escapes me, calling his name, feeling the connection running through us, locking into place. I can't help but glide my hands down his scarred back, latching with possession as Fallan moves in and out of me. My name falls from his lips. His eyes flutter closed as he satiates himself with the feel of my body. He moves deeper, and I feel something within me tear. I force my head back and into the sheets to work through it, wondering if

I should make him stop from the sudden pain. He pauses, trailing a hand up my side, the other supporting his body over me.

"We don't have to go any further."

"How did you know to stop?"

"I can sense your feelings," he says, my smile growing at the realization of the connection we now share.

Feeling myself wrapped around him, I take a deep breath, relaxing my body.

"Keep going," I whisper, his lips pressing to my own.

I moan into his mouth as he starts thrusting into me again, feeling nothing but pleasure as he drives deeper, finally becoming fully seated to the hilt. Starting a slow rhythm, he moves in and out of me, the intensity and power of his thrusts building as he continues.

I place a hand on his chest and push him to the side, rolling on top of him, careful not to unsheathe him while I change our position. He lets out another savage moan, smiling up at me like an idiot. I straddle him, rocking my hips in gentle motions, feeling him grasp my sides, guiding me back and forth. The pool of warmth between my legs swells as I feel his cock throbbing inside of me, his hands gripping my waist tighter.

"Do you see how beautiful you are?" he questions, turning my head, my eyes snapping to the visual of me riding him in the mirror propped next to his bed. His strong arms wrap around me, our bodies flush. He presses his lips to my chest. I move my chin back to look at him. The pressure in my center builds, my body anticipating another release.

"You're all I have left," he whispers, keeping his pace.

"Then don't let go," I whisper, feeling the sweet release of pleasure ripple through my core, my walls tightening around Fallan's cock as I come for the second time. I throw my head back, crying out at the feeling of him still inside me. He moves his hip and flips me back while I'm lost in lust.

"I won't," he says through a groan, suddenly pulling out of my wet center, the abrupt exit painful, leaving me feeling utterly empty.

I feel his release trail along my lower stomach, Fallan fisting his cock as he takes in my body. There's a moment of silence between us, both of us panting, doing our best to catch our breaths. He gets up from the bed and goes into the bathroom, returning seconds later with a warm rag. He runs it over my skin, cleaning up his mess and taking extra time to focus on the center. As I watch him finish up, I notice my nail marks tracking down both of his muscular arms and shoulders. Drawing my legs to me, I search for my underwear, pulling it back on while watching him do the same. Covering my body with my arms, I watch as he moves back toward the bed. His arms wrap around my torso, pulling me down beside him on the mattress.

I seat myself on top of him again, letting my head rest on his chest, his hands running through my hair and down my body. He holds me close, peppering me with soft kisses. The steady beating of his heart is enough to draw anyone to sleep.

"I hope it was all you wanted it to be," I whisper, feeling him chuckle at the words.

"Everything and more."

Running his fingers up and down my thigh, he pauses.

"I can never let you go.... I won't," he whispers, a tremor in his voice.

Looking up at him, I see the pain in his expression, his eyes wet with tears.

"Then don't," I start, pulling my achy legs back over his lap so he can hold me closer.

"From now on, I can promise you one thing," I begin, holding up my pinky. "No matter what, I'm with you," I say, keeping my hand between us.

He smiles, looking at me with playfulness.

"Even if I have to act like I hate you?"

"Especially then," I start, moving myself closer. "Now I know a way for us to make up after fighting," I say, his smirk growing.

"You're with me, Blackburn? Truly?" he questions, raising his pinky.

"For as long as I draw breath," I whisper, feeling our fingers latch, solidifying a promise now safeguarded in our hearts.

My legs are shaky as I dress, Fallan standing next to me so I can lean on him for support. Looking around, I see how much damage we did to his headboard, the sheer force of our combined power creating chaos in the space around us. Stumbling, he smiles at his handiwork, pressing his lips to my own, before bending down to lean me over his shoulder. Letting out a wild, childlike laugh, I hit his back, letting my legs flail in frustration as he moves us across the room.

"Put me down!" I squeal, unable to hide the smile that consumes me at the sound of his rare, genuine laughter.

It meets my ears like a gentle song. Nothing can match the joy it brings me.

"I think I could get used to carrying you around like this," he says, moving us closer to the door.

He puts me down gently, and I grasp his collar, my fingers meeting the small chain wrapped around his neck. I tug it free from his shirt, the tiny gold ring catching the dim light of the room and illuminating its band, a wreath of gold vines holding a small white stone. Fallan carefully runs his fingertips over the ring, looking over it lovingly, the last piece of his mother he has left.

"She gave this to me before she passed away," he whispers, pulling the chain free from his neck. He holds it out in the space between us so I can inspect it more closely. "She said my father gave it to her just a few days after meeting her," he whispers, smiling at the fond memory his mother shared with him.

Touching the small band, I feel the memories the item holds, a small reminder of a life no longer with us. Helping him put the chain around his neck, I gently pat his chest, leaning my forehead into him.

"She would be so proud of the man you are now," I say, his arms wrapping tightly around me.

"I hope you're right," he mutters, pulling my chin up so that he can look at me.

"Now let's go see a proper Unfortunate social."

Moving through the side streets, we follow the glow of the bonfire to guide us back to the party. Taking one of the longer routes back, he holds my hands, running his thumb over each of my knuckles. My legs are deliciously sore, and my core still aches from having to adjust to how big Fallan's length is. I lean into him, not arguing once he pulls me closer to his back, urging me to hop on. Wrapping my arms around his neck, he grabs my thighs, pulling me onto him, supporting my weight effortlessly. Resting my head atop his own, we walk in blissful silence, the warmth from our connection warding off the chill.

"I wouldn't have gone all the way had I known how much it would be hurting you," he says, my grasp tightening around his neck.

"I wanted everything that you did-"

A scream breaks through the air, our heads snapping down the alleyway. Men and women begin yelling. People pass the opening of the alleyway, frantically running in every direction. A figure looms ahead of us, grasping the wall, watching me and Fallan from the shadows. I see Xavier's blonde curls in the crowd. Fallan slowly lowers me to the ground, keeping me behind him. Xavier sprints towards us, his face unreadable as he meets Fallan's gaze. Xavier pants heavily, his eyes wide with concern.

"Xavier, what-"

"A Shifter breached the ward," he says, giving us both a long look. "And it's come for blood." He turns away, guiding us in a sprint down the alleyway.

CHAPTER FIFTY-ONE

FOREST

It thrashes violently through the crowd, its ghostly face the same one from my backyard. Its long, talon-like fingers swipe violently at anyone within its line of sight. The Shifter is tall, with sharp teeth and sunken eyes that are enough to bring anyone nightmares. It tears into the figure of a flailing woman, her blood spilling out onto the street as she falls to the ground. In a flash of movement, the Shifter grabs the woman's lifeless body, sinking its fangs into her neck, violently devouring her blood and leaving her an empty husk. Panicking, I search the crowd for familiar faces.

I see Mark and Jolie, a slight sense of relief passing over me as I see them standing behind Valerie and Aaron. Kai and Hunter are huddled together. Kai's blade is unsheathed, held with a shaky grasp. Xavier quickly yanks his pistol free from its holster, pulling it out from under his coat, taking note of how many rounds he has left. Fallan is already grabbing his blade from his side, nudging Xavier's gun down toward the ground.

"Bullets won't kill it," Fallan growls.

Xavier's gaze is cold as he considers Fallan's words.

Sensing a growing danger, I grab them both, forcing them to step back as the body of the woman flies past us and into the nearest wall of one of the adjacent buildings. Freeing my blade from my side, I force it open, moving into the defensive stance Fallan had taught me. My eyes meet the unsettling gaze of the haunting creature.

Tapping the ground with its long finger, it cocks its head in our direction, smiling wickedly the longer it watches us.

"I smell Marked blood," It hisses, both me and Fallan tensing up.

Giving it little thought, Kai surges forward, my body rigid while his blade slices the leg of the creature. Thrashing its arm, it narrowly misses his front. Fallan is quick to seize the opportunity to move forward.

In a whirlwind of blades and fury, Fallan swings his arm toward the creature, his aim calculated, delivering as much damage as he can with each swipe. I ready myself to join him. Xavier's hand wraps around my arm, stopping me from taking another step.

"We need to go-"

"Let go of me," I hiss angrily, forcing my arm away from him, letting my rage take over.

Moving towards the creature, I swipe my blade across its front, watching it recoil in pain. It tried to get away from us, only to meet the metal of Valerie's weapon a few seconds later. Looking around the open area, I spot a group of Officials. They stand by, watching the scene unfold, some even holding drinks, sipping casually, as if nothing unusual is happening. Unfortunates beg for them to intervene, some getting kicked to the ground as they cry out for help. Shaking his head in frustration, Xavier finally joins us, grabbing my blade from my hand and swiping at the Shifter the next chance he gets.

Taking a step back, I observe the creature, feeling Fallan's focus shift toward its mind, his hands clenched in concentration. The creature screams, clutching its head in pain. It stumbles back, doing its best to keep Fallan out. Narrowing his eyes, Fallan pushes harder, swarming the creature's mind with thoughts of ending its own life. Its claw rises to its neck.

"Die, you fucking monster!" Fallan yells. The creature seethes with rage.

"They want the girl!" It screams, pushing past Fallan's broad frame, nearly slamming its hand down on Xavier.

Valerie rolls over the drink table, grabbing Mark and Jolie, urging them to follow her. They begin to back away together, relief passing over me as I watch them leave.

Holding my ground, I motion Kai to move, my focus set on connecting to his mind.

"Get him out of here," I whisper into my brother's mind. His eyes grow wide with confusion, his mouth hanging open. Forcing my brother back with a wave of my hand, his feet move, following my command.

He whispers to Hunter, motioning him to follow behind Valerie. I expect him to go along, to follow the crowd and get away from all of this, but he stays behind.

This is no longer the Kai I once knew.

This is no longer the Kai who runs in fear.

"I can try and force it-" Fallan starts, cut off by some unknown attack.

Clutching his head, he falls to his knees. Xavier and I panic as we ambush the creature. Rushing toward Fallan, I feel another presence in our mind space, its assault directed toward Fallan. His thoughts are consumed with nothing but a painful noise. It drowns out my ability to speak to him, my knees joining his on the ground. Xavier stands in front of us, shielding us from the creature. Grasping Fallan's face, I see the pain in his expression, my fingers trailing over his cheeks.

"Someone else is here," he says through the pain. My focus is on getting him back on his feet.

"Xavier," I begin, grabbing Fallan's blade. "Help him up," I push, no longer giving him an option as I step into the blonde's mind to deliver the order.

Xavier grabs Fallan's arm, lifting him to his feet. The creature eyes me with surprise, my arm extended out, ready to engage.

"It's me you want, right?" I question, looking back to Fallan. "You can let him go," I whisper, my panic growing at the feeling of Fallan's energy draining. His nose is blee ding, his eyes rolling into the back of his head.

"I am many things, child," the creature whispers in my mind. *"But I am no coward when it comes to a fight,"* it continues. *"This hold is not my own... although I can assure you, his death will be savored."*

I snap.

Slamming my blade into the ground, I force my hand up, focusing on its thin legs, feeling the way its bones shatter beneath my touch.

Crack.

Wailing out in pain, it falls to the ground, my mind finally able to fully latch on and fill it with images of its own death. Watching it shakily raise its hand to its throat, I take another step, focusing all my energy on ending the creature. I'm jarred from concentration by that familiar voice again as it screams to life.

"The Apparatus will ruin this wretched world!" it screams, repeatedly yelling the phrase.

Using all that I have, I put up a barrier around my and Fallan's minds, readying to snap the creature's neck. It watches me fearfully, its mouth downturned as its expression turns despondent.

"This wasn't my choice," it hisses, my eyes staring into the two dark pits where eyes should have been. .

"Who sent you?" I question, watching it cower.

Fallan and Xavier slice their blades through the Shifter's head. I watch as its life force is drained from its body, a regretful expression on its face. Panting heavily, Fallan forces the blade deeper, the creature's blood spewing streaks of red across his face. His eyes are wild with feral rage. Drawing in several deep breaths, he lingers by the creature to make sure it's dead. Xavier's hands shake with adrenaline.

The two men stand in front of me, both in need of comfort.

I stand by my choice.

The connection between Fallan and me is now unbreakable.

Moving closer to him, I wrap him in a hug, feeling him bury his head in my shoulder. His arms wrap around my middle loosely, unable to find the strength to tighten his grip. Surprisingly, my hand reaches for Xavier instinctively, the other part of me still drawn to his presence. His eyes are cold as he watches me and Fallan, his hand still grasping the blade as if ready to use it on a new target. Pressing my head to Fallan's, I hold his face in my hands, his eyes panning back to Xavier, before placing a small, tender kiss on my forehead.

"Someone sent that creature here... to hunt," I whisper, looking at the two men. Xavier lowers his weapon, letting it clatter to the ground. His focus is fixed on Fallan.

"Let me speak to him," I whisper in Fallan's mind, releasing him from my embrace.

I move to Xavier. He looks down at me, his eyes filled with defeat.

"There's more here than we realize, Xavier," I say, reaching for his hands. Before I can touch him, he lifts my hands up instead, looking over the faint red marks surrounding my wrists. I hadn't noticed the marks earlier, and in the moment, Fallan's grip gave me nothing but pleasure.

"You've been together."

It's not a question.

All I can do is swallow. My throat is dry, and my breath is hard to catch.

Xavier's eyes lower, fixating on Fallan.

"Did you touch her?" Xavier questions, grasping my wrists tightly.

I try to pull away, his hold stronger than I expected. Fallan shoves him back before pulling me into him. He lets out an aggressive snarl, baring his teeth at Xavier.

"Couldn't keep my hands off her. Like I've told you, she was never yours," Fallan urges. Xavier's jaw clenches, a promise of violence in his expression.

People start to pull themselves up off the ground, some emerging from the half-assed hiding spots they'd found. Meeting my gaze, my brother pulls away from his own hidden position, begging Hunter to stay back, only to grow more frustrated when he realizes Hunter is already trailing closely behind him. My brother looks around, his pace quickening the closer he got to me. It doesn't take a mind reader to know how scared he is, questioning whether or not my voice in his mind was a spout of insanity or something much more. Xavier lingers nearby, his eyes on the ground.

"More Officials are coming. We saw them when we came out of our hiding spot. You all need to leave," Hunter says, his foot kicking the motionless creature.

"They are guaranteed to try and use your chips. Best case scenario, no one else is murdered," Xavier says, finally breaking his silence.

"Go," Fallan starts, his hands touching the sides of my face. "Before things get worse. I promise I will find you soon.".

Ignoring our audience, he leans into me, his lips pressing to mine, giving me a moment of peace amongst all this chaos. My mark burns with pleasure, his thoughts of concern and admiration coming together to form something safe that encapsulates my heart. I hear Kai and Hunter gasp, both caught off guard by us. Xavier is nothing short of rageful.

The kiss doesn't feel long enough, my desire to be with him and no one else is unbearable. Pulling away from him, I step back, following Xavier and Kai towards the path we need to take to get out of the sector.

"Stay alive," I whisper, his mouth curling into a smirk.

"Always do, Dove," he says, his eyes panning back to Xavier. "Always will."

Xavier grabs the bottom of my shirt, pulling me to follow him, his eyes set forward. Keeping up with his fast pace, I allow him to move me along, shuddering as his hand passes over the rough skin of my mark. Kai moves quickly, his mouth shut, processing the attack and, I'm sure, what he saw between me and Fallan. Xavier's pace is punishing, but we don't let up.

"Do you hate me?" I question, startling him as though it was the last question he expected.

He says nothing at first, his hand running along the wall, helping him retrace his steps.

"I wish I did," he starts, finally looking back at me. "Maybe then I'd have the strength to kill him and never have to look at you again," he spits hatefully. A fissure opens in my chest at his response, stopping my feet from moving forward. I was in pain because I'd hurt him.

And nothing has hurt me more than the way he looks at me now.

"And so, things just get more complicated," It whispers.

CHAPTER FIFTY-TWO

FOREST

The house is still, the windows void of any sign of life. Our walk home became a full-fledged sprint moments after we'd made it out of the Unfortunate sector. Running through bushes and tearing through tree lines, we're a jumbled mess of blood and sweat by the time we reach our neighborhood. My legs ache more than they did earlier, and my adrenaline is still high. The Shifter's words play over and over in my mind.

"This wasn't my choice."

It had said that honestly. But was it an apology for what it had to do, like some sort or penance for the people it had murdered, or had it simply wanted to try and save itself from imminent death?

"Who would have the ability to control Shifters?" the other part of me questions, my hand grazing over my mark.

"Maybe the mystery visitor who came over the intercom at the Solstice festival is a start," I mutter, reflecting on the man's voice who managed to breach both my mind and Fallan's within the span of the last few days.

Kai stops abruptly. Clutching his lower stomach, he lurches over and gags. Pausing his run, Xavier comes over to touch my brother's back, looking to me for support.

"Don't touch me!" Kai starts, waving away both of our hands.

"Kaiden-" I begin, wanting desperately to touch him to take his fear away.

"What are you?!" Kai yells, his eyes still glazed from the alcohol he drank at the party. He shoves me away from him. Stumbling backward, I meet the ground. Tears stream down Kai's face as Xavier wraps his arms around him.

"I heard you," he begins, pulling his hands up to cover his face. "I heard you in here." His fingers tap his temple.

"Calm down!" Xavier gasps, holding my brother close.

"I won't calm down! None of this is supposed to be happening!" Kai says, trying to force himself away from him. "We were supposed to graduate! You were supposed to be a painter, and I...." he whispers his despair. "I was supposed to help people!" he yells, his voice cracking. "And now, I have no idea who to trust." Sniffling, he rubs his eyes with the back of his hand. "And I care more for the people in their sector than I do our own," he mumbles, sinking to his knees. "It was going to kill you both." His eyes are wide as his swipe toward me registers. "Oh, Forest, I didn't mean to-"

"Kaiden, it's okay," Xavier says, moving to the ground with him.

Despite his anger toward me, he comforts Kai, watching me as I approach my brother cautiously.

Cupping my brother's face in my hands, I hang a silent apology in the space between us, hoping my expression is enough for it to register. He wraps his arms around me, his silent tears turning into mournful sobs as he buries his face in my chest. I run my hand through his curls. I look up at Xavior, blinking my own tears away. The gold that lines his irises catches my attention with our faces so close. Keeping my brother close, I lean forward, pressing my head to Xavier's chest, letting us all embrace each other.

Keeping my grasp on Kai, I drown out the fears in his mind, taking all the pain I can away from him. His sobs begin to die down.

"I reached for him first. There were countless people around me, and I reached for him." Kai whispers, a vivid image of Hunter popping up in my mind.

Closing my eyes, I press my lips to my brother's forehead, keeping him as close as possible.

"It's okay," I whisper, my anger growing. "Nothing can hurt you as long as I am alive," I mutter, Xavier's eyes peering down at me.

He wants to say something. That same strained noise forces its way out of his mouth, his throat bobbing in a slow, sticky motion.

I watch him clench his jaw, his hand passing over his mouth.

"Damn it," he whispers, closing his eyes.

Rising to his feet, Kai urges us back on our path, quietly apologizing to the both of us. When we make it to the front yard, we head straight to my bathroom window. Kai grabs the concealed wooden crate and climbs up towards the window ledge. Xavier's hand stops me from joining my brother.

"My car is still here. I have to go before they call me in to investigate the damage that *thing* left behind," he whispers, gently rubbing my wrist.

Giving Kai a look, I urge him not to wait for me, seeing him hesitate before he drops through the window into the bathroom.

Looking up at Xavier, I find him utterly broken. The skin under his eyes is darker, and the stubble along his jaw seems more pronounced. There's a sadness that hangs over his other features, and it devastates me. I desperately want us to pull through this together.

"Why did it come after us? Why did it want *me*?"

"I have no idea," he says, clenching the bridge of his nose between his thumb and index finger, shaking his head in frustration.

He looks me over, his hand moving to touch the side of my face. I stand there, preparing for the feel of his hand on my skin, feeling every part of me scream to get away.

"Don't listen to that!" Its presence is all of a sudden demanding, vying for attention.

"You don't get a say!" I yell in my mind, forcing down the feeling of what It wants.

Still, I allow Xavier to go through with it. His caress is gentle, and I feel the peace it brings him. I'm not sure how long I can stomach being this close, his emotions like an afront on my body. Allowing myself to feel the few emotions I can stomach being this close to him.

"Tell me what happened between you and Fallan," Xavier begins, his eyes watery. "Did you want it?" I know he holds on to the hope that I didn't, that there's something more between us, but after today, I'm not sure I will ever be able to give him that reassurance.

"I don't know what it was-"

His soft lips meet my forehead, unable and unwilling to let me finish the statement. His lips are full of sweetness and warmth, like my skin is basking in the heat of summer sun rays. For a moment, everything is still. An unfamiliar doorway opens, and that other treacherous part of me leaps through it, becoming immediately embraced by something euphoric. I feel elated, connected, or reconnected. The ecstasy that the other me feels pushes it free from my control, and her hands, my hands, tangle into Xavier's shirt. His hand cups my lower back, pulling me closer to him. I feel my arms raised, ready to pull him down so I can taste his lips.

No.

I pause.

You're not him.

My heart races.

And you never will be.

All at once, the door slams shut, his lips now like poison, threatening to melt the flesh off my skull. Shoving him away from me, I wipe my face with the back of my hand, feeling the bile in my stomach churn. My mark burns, and when I turn back to him, his face is flustered. I hunch over, my mind filling with a shockwave of fear as images of his gold-flecked irises slam into me.

"Don't touch me again without asking," I whisper, shaking my head to try and gain some clarity.

He watches me with clenched hands, touching his throat with small drags of his fingers.

"Why did you have to do that?" he questions, a nearly invisible line of tears rolling down his cheek.

"Do what?" I question furiously, forcing myself to stand straight.

"Why did you have to pull away?" he questions, closing his eyes as he speaks.

He lets out a deep breath, opening his eyes to motion towards my bathroom window.

"You'd better get going."

Forcing his hands into his pockets, he steps back, turning away from me and walking into the shadows of the chilly, lifeless night.

I try to reach into his mind, but the familiar barrier greets me.

The cool breeze sweeps my hair. Its voice is shaky and unnerved.

"Were we ever actually sneaking into his mind... or were we let in?"

An oppressive silence blankets the space around me.

My knees buckle, forcing me down and into the ground, succumbing under the weight of my exhaustion.

CHAPTER FIFTY-THREE

FOREST

L eaves scatter the grounds, blanketing the sidewalks in shades of orange and red. After a great deal of effort put into figuring out an alternative commute back and forth to the Academy, Kai finally convinced me to get back on the tram, asking Mark several times if he was doing alright. The old man had managed to get away from the Shifter attack unharmed, and when he saw me for the first time since that night, he nearly touched me to check and see if I had been hurt. As far as we know, the Officials had disposed of the Shifter, urging everyone to get home before burning the body to a crisp in a fire at the edge of the sector.

Colton and Josh sit next to Rae and Max, the twins bitter toward us ever since the Solstice dinner. Max's Academy uniform had been replaced with Official attire. As far as Kai knows, he's already started his training. He scoffs as we walk by, turning to our classmates who surround him and whispering loud enough for us to hear that he's appalled by "the corruption" in our family. Both Kai and I bite our tongues.

"Here comes the vermin," Josh says, nudging Max.

Feeling his familiar energy buzz through me, I gaze forward, taking our usual seats toward the back. I manage to hold my typical facade in place. Leaning into my brother, I watch Fallan and Valerie move by, both silent, taking their seats behind the line in the back of the bus.

Glancing at our old friend group, I see their eyes are already on us, analyzing our every move. Clenching my hands, I focus on each one of them, imagining their heads flying back, hitting the glass behind them.

"Don't," he whispers, forcing me back into rational a rational mindset

I turn to give him a look, sneaking a small smile his way as I watch Valerie fidget with her blazer.

Fallan leans back, watching me back with playful eyes.

"What?"

"You look beautiful," he says, my cheeks igniting with a rosy blaze at the compliment.

"Raven boy does it, and we love it, but Blondie boy does it, and we hate it," It whispers, my head snapping to my reflection in the bus window.

It looks annoyed, pressing Its head to the glass.

"What's your issue today?"

"You and our utter stupidity," It spits, shaking Its head at me.

"What do you mean?"

"I'm sure you'd love to know, but sadly, you are continuing to lock me away like a cowardly bitch. I'm sure I could have aided you against that Shifter," It says, Its image slowly fading away from the tram window.

Note to self: figure out how often Marked have hallucinations that won't seem to leave them.

Giving Fallan one last look, I ease myself into Kai again.

"Today is just another pointless day," Kai says, slumping, leaning the glass behind him with a huff.

"Why does that feel so far from the truth?" It says.

It is a question I can't even begin to answer.

Kai and I trail next to Rae, her silent treatment still in effect. We follow behind Fallan, moving closer to the art room. This whole building suddenly feels constricting after the last few weeks. Four months ago, had you told me where my loyalties lie now, I'd have called you insane. Fallan keeps his distance, his hands buried deep in his pockets, scowling at everyone, including me. I almost forgot it's all act.

"Do you plan on giving me and Kai the cold shoulder for the rest of the year?" Rae's icy blue eyes find mine, giving me a frigid stare.

"You seriously want me to act like we're friends after all of the shit you and your brother have been up to? Everyone is convinced you and your family are

Unfortunate sympathizers, Forest," she begins, looking over to Fallan as he nudges open the classroom door.

"Some people are even saying you're hooking up with *him*."

I scoff. "Everyone is concerned with what I'm doing and who I'm doing it with lately, it seems." I move past her and through the classroom door.

As I make my way into the classroom, I notice how anxious Mrs. Auburn is. She barely acknowledges me as I move toward the back of the classroom. Josh is settled in his seat, watching me through narrowed eyes. He raises a hand in my direction, ready to mess with me in any way he can. Slamming his wrist into his desk, I make a point, locking eyes with his skulking face.

"I'll break it," I hiss, squeezing his wrist, only letting up once I feel his pain sharpen.

My classmates observe me as I back away from him. Rae and Mrs. Auburn remain deep in thought, lost in their artwork.

"I suggest you all stop watching me," I say to anyone willing to listen.

A few heads turn away, some lingering once they think I'm not paying attention.

"You'll regret that," Josh whispers under his breath.

Fallan adjusts himself in his chair, ready to pounce at any moment.

Ignoring his empty threat, I grasp the desk beside Rae, shoving it back several feet. Moving past the red tape, I position myself closer to Fallan, ignoring Mrs. Auburn's quiet attempt to urge me to keep the desk where it belongs.

"You're the one who wanted me to help him catch up," I say, planting myself down into my seat, our knees only a few inches apart.

I can hear his thoughts revolving around seeing me in my school uniform, each one ending with us finding a bit of privacy for him to appreciate every part of me.

Looking at Fallan, I grab one of his paints, letting its colors trail over my half-finished work of art.

"I don't want to be near Josh," I whisper. Fallan's eyes pass over him.

"Any particular reason why? Other than the fact that he is an idiot," Fallan questions, my hands rolling up my shirt sleeves.

Bruises linger on the skin from that night at the Solstice dinner.

"He gets a bit too handsy," I admit, surprised to feel Fallan's fingers graze over my skin when no one is watching.

"I couldn't see this in the dark or else I would have been more careful-"

"I know," I smile, cutting off him off to shut down that train of thought.

"He managed to do that in the small amount of time you were with him?" Fallan questions, continuing the lazy strokes of his paintbrush.

"He finds pleasure in my pain," I say, narrowing my eyes at the golden-skinned brute.

Dropping his hand from his position under his chin, Josh's head collides with his desk, his nose slamming into the wood with a bang. I flinch, all of our peers gasping as his nose runs red with blood. My mark heats, and the power comes alive inside me. Fallan's eyes are lowered, his gaze dead set on Josh, both hands clenched in his lap. Drawing in several breaths, he relaxes his posture, watching Josh wail as he begins gripping his now broken nose. Mrs. Auburn hauls him up to his feet, urging him to go to the infirmary. His buddies support him, placating his childlike nature with words of affirmation. Smiling, I look at my raven-haired lover.

"I guess he had the urge to break his own nose for some reason," Fallan whispers, touching his temple with a sigh.

"Maybe he isn't that bad," It whispers, finally giving me peace of mind.

"How are you feeling today?" he questions after a few moments.

He taps his foot nervously, waiting for me to answer.

"Are you trying to ask me if I regret what happened between us?" I ask through the connection, his head slowly nodding.

"We'd both been drinking-"

"Every moment of it was nothing short of perfect. I regret nothing," I say, looking at him seductively under hooded eyes.

The smile he gives me is captivating. It's a sight I would pay any price to see, no matter how many times I'd seen it. His knee grazes my own, both of us wrapped in a bubble of blissful solitude for a few moments, satisfied in our moment of peace for only him and me.

His hand slides down his leg under the desk, ready to steal a touch to my knee with outstretched fingertips.

"Forest Blackburn," a voice booms, both Fallan and I forcing our attention toward the classroom door.

A pair of Officials stand at the door. Max lingers behind them. Looking at me, they point, motioning for me to get up from my desk. "You're needed in the hallway immediately," one of the men orders, moving toward me urgently. Rising to my feet, Fallan gets up too. Max's eyes grow hungry with power as he moves past me, grabbing Fallan's neck and forcing him down and into the desk.

"What the fuck are you doing?" Fallan yells, his head being slammed into the desk.

"Max-" I yell, grabbing his arm.

Before I knew what was happening, Max's hand flies toward me, striking me across the face. I gasp, holding my palm to the side of my face as the pair of Officials grab my upper arms, motioning Max to follow. Another Official enters the room to aid Max in restraining Fallan after he tries to hurt Max for touching me. He thrashes against the man's grasp, a look of concern flashes across his face when he sees my nose has started bleeding from Max's blow. Mrs. Auburn covers her mouth in disbelief, urging my classmates to stand against the wall in the back of the classroom.

Dragging us toward the door, I strain against their hold, debating how many necks I can snap and get away with it.

"What the fuck is going on?" I yell, the Official's grasp only tightening.

"Shut your fucking mouth," one of them hisses, striking me hard in the neck. I gasp for air, unable to get my throat to fully open.

"Don't you fucking dare!" Fallan yells, forcing Max into the nearest wall in the hallway. He tries to slip away, ready to bulldoze through the Officials holding me.

The man with Max forces a prod into Fallan's side, watching him writhe in pain as they turn the dial up all the way. Their twisted smiles are horrifying, taking pleasure from how much pain they're causing. I try to move towards him, but the Officials have me restrained. I attempt to clutch my throat, but their grips are unyielding.

"I guess they were right when they said you followed in her mother's footsteps, you ignorant, Unfortunate loving whore," one of the Officials holding me whispers into my ear, the sound of a struggle surrounding me as more bodies fill the hallway.

Kaiden and Valerie thrash against the Officials blocking their path to us, panicking when they find us down the hallway from them.

"Forest, run!" Kaiden yells, driving his elbow into the Official's jaw who has been holding him in place. Valerie takes the opportunity to try to fight off the Official holding her back, but the man twists her arm as they struggle. There was no mistaking the sound of a bone snapping, and we could hear it from our position down the hall.

Wailing out, she hits the floor. Kai is unable to stop the men from slamming him into the nearest wall. I try to get to Fallan again, watching him shove Max back. Max shifts the prod into one hand and pulls his pistol free with the other. Max points the weapon at Fallan's head, and my heart stops.

"If you keep fighting, I swear to god I will put a bullet in his head," Max hisses, his chip emitting a green, blinking light.

No, not just his chip; all of the Official's chips had been activated.

"They want him alive," one of the men closest to me says, grabbing my hair and twisting it beneath his grasp. "They want all of them alive. We're going to get hell for breaking the girl's arm and hitting this one's face," he continues, looking at me with malice.

"I can promise you, the more you resist, the worse it will be for your little friends and anyone else associated with you."

"Don't push them," I whisper, trying to look back at Fallan, who's now fully restrained between two Officials and Max.

All of us are forced to comply, and the Officials move us down the hall, with Kai and Valerie in the front.

"I could kill them all. I could-"

A painful noise fills my ears. The same noise that had infiltrated Fallan's mind last night. I clutch back, seeing Fallan do the same beside me, both of us yelling out in pain as we're dragged closer to the front doors of the Academy. Our feet scuff the ground. The noise becomes unbearable, only dissipating when we meet the outside air.

Fallan reaches for me, stopped by a brutal blow to his abdomen and several more to his face. I rush to give him what energy I have through our connection.

"Check her hip, then check his chest-" Adam's familiar voice booms out from somewhere in front of us. Arms wrap around me, keeping my hands at my side.

"Don't you dare fucking touch her, you son of a bitch!" Fallan yells, spitting up blood on the sidewalk between words.

Adam's hand passes over my hip bone, his fingers dragging down my skirt. The mark I've kept hidden for as long as I've been alive is exposed to him in an instant. Forcing up Fallan's shirt, they find the mark on his side. Valerie and Kai watch in fear. Max holds back my brother with no remorse for his involvement in all this.

"You've got to be shitting me," Adam begins, his hand forcing my chin up so I have to look at him. "You're a fucking dirty Marked, and so is your nasty bed buddy." He spits on the ground by my feet, twisting his face up into disgust.

"Just like your Daddy."

He knew my father was Marked?

"Take them to the cars. Upper leadership says the frequency should keep their abilities and energy down for a few hours," Adam starts, looking down at me with a grin. "It would seem your Judgment Day has come early."

Scuffing my knees against the ground, I eventually find my footing as I'm dragged towards the Official vehicles. Kai and Valerie are the first to get shoved into the cars, fighting back with violent jabs and kicks before they're hurtled into the back of one of the SUVs. My brother screams for me, his face eventually disappearing behind tinted glass windows. The vehicle rocked on its wheels for a few seconds before going utterly still.

Shoving me into the vehicle by my neck, I bash against the inside of the opposite passenger door, my shoulder stinging with pain from the impact. Moments later, they force Fallan inside the same vehicle, his hands on me in an instant, pulling me into him.

"The Hold, the Call, try and use anything you can-" he pleads. Two Officials in masks sit in the front seat of the vehicle, watching us with looks of disapproval. They turn around, some sort of plastic mask attached to a metal canister in each of their hands. They move towards us quickly.

"I'm afraid you have nowhere to run." They pause. "Night night, Ms. Blackburn."

We fight as they force the masks against our faces. Their fists hit our abdomens, causing us to draw in a full breath. Slowly, I slip away. The scentless gas fills my lungs. I clasp Fallan's hand in my own, leaning into him, drowning in fear.

"Fight," he whispers, his voice distant... different from the other one in my mind.

"Embrace me," It says through the fog, my mind so detached from myself.

"Set us free."

I try to reach for that otherness inside of me.

I try to grab the power it offers.

But the void of darkness is too vast.

I slip into the abyss.

CHAPTER FIFTY-FOUR

FOREST

The ground is freezing.

My body is dirtied, covered in dust from the hard concrete floor.

The air is stale. The smell of moisture and metal hits my nose in affronting waves.

Feeling my head pressed to the floor, I groan in pain, listening to the drag of the chains around my wrists as they scrape across the concrete. There's an uncomfortable pressure around my throat. I reach up to find cool, unyielding metal encircling my neck. My eyes remain shut, my head and throat in a world of pain. My lungs struggle to take in a full breath of air.

Water drips intermittently onto the metal bars at the front of what I assume is a holding cell. I try to move, but the drugs they used to knock us out have left me disoriented. My limbs are heavy, and my mind races to put all the pieces back together.

"I suggest you take it easy," his familiar voice says. I force my heavy lids open and move my eyes in his direction, coaxing my eyes open from their heavy-lidded state.

I choke back my words, looking at his relaxed posture in the chair before me. The space around us is dark, lit with only a few candles that seem to illuminate the concrete walls and floor with unsettling shadows. I wear my Academy uniform. My shirt is cut to expose my mark. Yanking my wrists against the chains, I try to move toward him, feeling the strain in my shoulders. My legs are too weak to get me up past a seated position.

The man in front of me is someone I don't recognize. Where I'm used to seeing him clad in standard Official gear, he is wearing a new mask now. A black dress shirt fits over his sturdy frame. The black ink mostly hidden in the past now is on full display, the clear image of an unknown beast encasing his chest. His hair, always wild and free, is slicked back and tamed, cut perfectly to frame his face. Watching me, the light is gone from his eyes. His legs spread wide as he leans his elbows onto his knees.

"X-Xavier?" I question, hoping the obvious pain in my voice works in my favor. "What are you doing here?" I push, looking down at my wrists. "Why am I locked up?"

"You lied to me, Forest," he mutters, tapping his fingers against my head. "Every sick and twisted little thought you had of him, I heard." My hands begin shaking with fear. "It was disgusting, utterly nauseating," he continues, grasping the side of my face, his fingers twining through my hair. "You were never his to have," Xavier says, his eyes lowered.

I glance at his chest, seizing up once I realize what lies beneath his shirt.

"You're Marked?"

"Is that what they call it now?" Xavier questions with a laugh, his eyes wide with delight. "So many years have passed, the labels start to blur together."

"Who are you?" I question, spitting my words at him, thrashing against the binds.

He grabs my neck, forcing me to stop thrashing.

"Be good for me, and stay still," he snaps, but being gentle with his touch. I wince at the pressure on my neck, my muscles aching from being handled so roughly earlier.

"Which one of my men caused these bruises?" he questions, ignoring my question.

"Your men?"

He grabs my head, and I suddenly feel a foreign presence devour my mind. The same foreign presence I've felt before, knocking on the back door of my mind, waiting to be let in. It's him.

He forces himself into my memories; my strength is nothing compared to the overwhelming influence suffocating my ability to force him out. I try to find the other part of myself, but she's nowhere.

"Ah, the two new recruits," Xavier says after a few moments, keeping his hand under my chin. "I will find joy in snapping their wrists for disobeying me."

"Who the fuck are you?" I ask again. He shakes his head, as if he is disappointed by reaction.

"I'm the same man you took to the Unfortunate sector with you last night. Can't you see that? I know some part of you feels safe with me-"

"Found. Found safety, you fucking government mutt." I seethe, his eyes narrowing at my words.

"Mutt?" He scoffs. "I'm the fucking ringleader love," he says, his mouth curling into a satisfied smirk.

"You're-"

"This putrid sector's Commander? Yes," he says, my stomach sinking at his words.

He glances around the room and rises to his feet.

"Do you know what happens when you clip a bird's wings, *Dove*?" he questions coldly, keeping his finger under my chin, forcing me to look at him.

"They can't fly," I mutter, feeling his body circle around me as he watches me.

"How many wings must I clip before you realize you can trust no one but me?"

I feel his hand run along my back, committing to memory all the bruises and lacerations left there by his men. My body shakes, unable to hide how afraid I am.

"How many people, Unfortunate or otherwise, must I kill before you finally come to your senses?"

Unfortunates and Untouchables alike. They were nothing more than pawns in his sick game.

"No-"

"How do you think I always knew where you were?" he questions, shaking his head in disbelief. "You think anyone else would have gotten away with the crimes you committed over the last few months? For fucks sake, Forest, do you have any idea of the rules I bent for you?" he hisses, his voice growing louder.

I feel my emotions surge. My inability to feel Fallan grows infuriating. Xavier grabs me, pulling me by the front of my shirt.

"You're with me right now. I don't want to hear another fucking thought about him," Xavier hisses, his lips inches away from my ear. "You have no idea how easy it was to sway those Shifters to go after that blue-eyed piece of shit. I've waited so long for a moment like this."

His hand reaches up my shirt, my disgust reaching a new level. Once warm and comforting, his fingers are now like cold, jagged blades. He brushes his hand over my mark and yanks me closer, forcing me up and onto his lap. My arms are pulled back behind me, straining to move. His hands hold my thighs down against him. I wince in pain.

"Where are my friends?" I question, his hands squeezing tighter.

It's terrifyingly silent in my mind.

"There's no use in trying to communicate with him," Xavier says, his fingers brushing over my thighs. "I'm years older than I may look and have had much time to channel my abilities. The noise you two heard at the Academy was just one of the many skills I could use to get what I wanted. You're in my labyrinth now, and I can promise not everyone makes it out alive."

"Why? Why do all of this?" I question, trying my best to reach out to anyone through my infiltrated mind.

"Our kind has never been accepted, especially in this region of the world," Xavier says, pulling down his shirt, showcasing the extent of his mark. "Beyond the ash, there are others like us, cruel and vile in their ways, persecuting our kind, just as they have here," he continues, his eyes glued to me. "Every Marked has an ability. Some are stronger than the rest. In rare circumstances, some are gifted with more than one ability. Have the wrong people catch wind of that, and you're a target for life." He shifts beneath my weight as I struggle to sit steady, my legs a shaky mess.

"Is that not what you've done to me? Hunted me?"

He chuckles, letting out a long sigh before answering. "I kept you safe. Something you will someday realize. I meant it when I said I'd never hurt you. The only reason you are bound is because I am not foolish enough to underestimate the power you have. Even now, forcing back your abilities drains me tremendously," he says, running his hands along his throat.

"Where are they? Where are my friends?" I push again, his frown growing at the question.

"Are you incapable of dropping that despicable creature you slept with? Maybe killing him would-"

Forcing my hand forward, I hear the chain rattle, the rusted metal snapping free. My hand goes flying toward his throat. He quickly grabs my wrist to stop me, a look of surprise hidden in the furrow of his brow.

"I will tear your throat out and spill your blood on this fucking concrete," I hiss, his frown growing into a twisted smile.

"There she is!" he starts, almost relieved. "That part of yourself you so desperately try to cage," he continues, the other's presence creeping into the open space of my mind. "Let me see that part of you," he coos like he's calling to something lost. "Let me embrace just how powerful you truly are." He gravitates his lips closer to mine.

Backing away, I spit in his face. I watch him flinch, his displeasure evident in the way he looks at me.

"Where are they!?" I reiterate, his grasp on my wrist growing.

"I considered sparing your brother and the girl from the Lottery," he says, tilting me off his lap. Stumbling forward, I find my footing to hold my ground. He stands up, kicking away his chair. "But after that little stunt," he continues, pointing to me with a shaking hand. "Consider them as good as dead."

"Why me? Why target me? You don't even know me!" I yell, my shoulders nearly pulling free from their sockets.

"I don't know you?" he yells, taking several steps toward me. "You say that as if you know-"

He stops speaking. Leaning forward, he grabs his neck. Taking a step back, I move away from him, his face flustered. His hand hits the wall with an undeniable force. The concrete crumbles beneath his touch, the wall falling away, hitting the ground in pieces. Slowly pulling himself into a standing position, he closes his eyes, running his hand through his hair.

"You know nothing of what is real and what it is that you've chosen to see as truth," he whispers, dropping his hands to his sides.

"Bad day?" Its voice questions silently, a small sigh of relief leaving me. Its presence is faint, safeguarded in one of the few safe spots in my infiltrated mind.

"I've never wanted to hear your voice more in my life," I whisper back through the connection, watching Xavier readjust his uniform with a scowl.

"I can keep you out of the Lottery under one condition," he says, crossing his arms in thought. "You accompany me as a guest in front of the High Council and sit at my side to watch the games. You would not battle. Your life is guaranteed to be safeguarded under my personal protection. I can even try to get Kaiden a seat with us above the pit," he says, making the deal sound like a generous offer.

"You'd do that?" I question sincerely, watching his mood shift as he steps closer.

Touching my face, he runs his thumbs over my cheeks.

"Your life is one I will safeguard. Tell me you're with me, and this world will never destroy us," he whispers, his body close, brushing up against mine.

Forcing the broken chain toward him. I hit him along the chest. He winces, his hand clutching the small area I'd managed to cut. I smile at his pain, narrowing my eyes at his agitated figure.

"Fuck you and your pathetic savior complex." I spit, forcing up the walls in my mind the moment his attention slips.

He feels the blood pooling on his chest at his fingertips, glancing up at me with malice.

"I suppose to see things my way; you'll need a little push," he says, waving his hand, the bindings falling free from my wrists.

He moves toward me silently. My hands are forced down to my sides with the invisible strength that our kind have access to. Grabbing my hair, he drags me closer to the cell door, scoffing as I try to break away from his grasp.

"You cannot keep me out of that beautiful mind forever," he snarls, pulling me free from the murky cell and dragging me down the poorly lit hallway.

Pausing in front of one of the many cells filled with nameless, helpless prisoners, he unlocks the door and tosses me into another confinement area.

Bumping into another body, we both meet the floor, our hands scuffing the ground, my energy dwindling down to nothing.

"As long as I breathe, your strength is mine to take. Had you accepted my offer, the ability to explore your strength would have been limitless... pity I must take it by force," Xavier mocks, my head pulling up to meet my brother's terrified expression.

"Live together. Fight together. If you do not cooperate, maybe losing what family you have left will give you some clarity... *au revoir,* Blackburn."

Slamming the cell door shut, he walks away. My body struggles to move as I make my way to my brother. Pulling me into him, Kai takes a deep breath, his heart racing, his hands shaking.

"Are you okay-"

"They took Valerie and Fallan," he spits, looking to the empty cell across the way. "They were in there, and they dragged them out. The Officials were talking about bringing in more Unfortunates we know," he sniffles, sobbing into my shoulder. "They're going after our family, and then they're going after Hunter-" he cries, my arms wrapping around him.

Holding his head to my chest, I comfort him. Looking around the space, my eyes land on a small pool of water that formed in a sunken area of the ground, most likely from the same kind of leak happening in the cell I'd just come from.

There t is in all of Its glory. The reflection that watches me, Its eyes golden, Its hair streaked with light tones, like spun silk.

"Are you with me?" It questions, my heart racing.

"I'm not just with you," I whisper, all my fears melting. *"I need you."*

It laughs, smiling with satisfaction.

"It's within us that we'll find the strength to set ourselves free from the wickedness that scorches this earth," It whispers. *"Time to fly, little bird."*

CHAPTER FIFTY-FIVE

ANDREW

My men are silent, moving steadfast toward a building that has always brought me nothing but considerable trepidation.

Twenty minutes ago, I was urgently asked to leave my office, hauled into the passenger seat of a car with Adam, and driven away with such urgency that I could only assume meant an order had come through from the Commander.

I'm not sure at what point the turns became unrecognizable. Deep within the Untouchable sector, farther out than anyone typically travels, lies a building surrounded by fencing that hides the secrets of New Haven. Only in the drunken hours of the night, after watching the horrific events of the Lottery, have I been here.

In the light of day, I see this place is even more daunting than I recall—a vast, looming structure of cold, gray concrete, and it's completely devoid of windows.

Drudging past several security checkpoints, I nearly take offense to how the guards handle me, one even going as far as to take my badge, promising its return at the end of the day. Adam stands beside me, letting the guards search him, looking less disconcerted than I am by their need to search us so thoroughly.

"It's just Commander's protocol," Adam says, shrugging as if this is an everyday thing for him.

Readjusting my uniform, I scowl at the guards. There are groups of Officials making their way in and out of the building.

"I never ordered any of these men to work a detail here. They said this building was only used for confinement. Why so much security if the Marked and Unfortunates are detained with the collars?" I question in observance of the influx of men surrounding the premises.

"It would seem your authority doesn't supersede the Commander's directives," Adam mutters. His absolute allegiance to the dictator of New Haven society is something I've never fully understood.

"Any particular reason they're searching us?" I question, unnerved by the unwelcome pat down.

"We have quite a few unpredictable new arrivals for the Lottery this year," Adam says with a smile. "The Commander wants to make sure everything goes smoothly with their transition into the games."

Pushing past the large set of metal doors, we enter the small lobby. Men wait at the front, guiding us down one of the many twisting hallways.

I see the familiar fortified doors of the holding cells and can hear audible screams from within.

"The Commander requested you two personally... he would like to see Andrew first," one of the men guiding us says, keeping his gaze forward, moving closer to the end of the hallway where a large office is located.

On my first Lottery night, I remember coming to this office to try and hide rather than watch the events of the night play out. I couldn't stomach the amount of blood and brutality in the pit.

The door is slightly ajar as the flames of a fireplace illuminates the floor. Pausing, Adam motions me to proceed in front of him. The rest of the men remain outside.

"Alright," I whisper, moving forward, feeling a hand shove me into the dimly lit space. The door slams shut behind me.

Turning on my heels, I reach for the door handle, shaking it with rage.

The door is locked. My hand slams against the solid construction of the door.

"Adam! Let me the fuck out of here!" I hiss, ready to tear down the door. My mark rubs against the cuff of my shirt in a burning heat.

"What's wrong now?" I whisper, rubbing my thumb along the course skin.

A slight movement behind me grabs my attention, my eyes snapping to a body thrashing in a chair.

Narrowing my eyes, I look at the body, my hands frantically reaching through my pockets, feeling a bit of security once my fingers find the small flashlight I keep on hand.

"Who the hell are you?" I question, getting nothing but silence.

"You have a limited time frame to answer my fucking question before I start kicking your teeth in," I hiss, their voice nothing but a murmur.

Grabbing the back of the chair, I brace myself.

"Listen here, you asshole-" I begin, turning the chair on its legs, my flashlight raised.

His blue eyes widen. His mouth is gagged. A firm metal collar is latched around his throat. Blood trickles down the side of his face, his eyes sunken, his energy drained. Along his side, his mark sticks out, his shirt torn from the sheer number of lashings he'd received. He continues to thrash against his bindings, sweat accumulated along his forehead. I pull out the gag from his mouth, watching him gasp for air.

"Fallan?" I question, keeping my hold on him, doing my best to transfer him some of my energy.

"What -"

"He fucking took her, Andrew," he spits, his wrists raw from his struggles. "You have to let me out and get this collar off. I have no idea where she is. I swear I will fucking kill everyone in here once I have this off-"

"Took who?"

"They have Forest," he spits out, my stomach dropping. "And Kai." His teeth are bared as he continues. "I tried to save them from all of this.... but he got to them-"

"Who got to them?" I push, his head shaking.

"Andrew, use your Hold. Take this off-"

My knees buckle, hitting the ground with a painful thud. I have no control over my body. My head twists behind me, forced to look away from Fallan.

Another figure lingers in the room, their body leaned against a large wooden desk. They toy with a pocket watch, spinning it on their finger nonchalantly. The shadows conceal their identity, their hand outreached toward us.

"A Marked?" I whisper, listening to their sinister laugh.

A familiar tone lingers in the gleeful chuckle.

"Observant. You'd make a fine father-in-law," his familiar voice says. Fallan's anger rises.

"Come over here and say that! You piece of privileged shit!" Fallan yells, his skin tearing against the bindings on his wrists.

"Keep running your mouth like that, and I'll make you watch as I fuck her," his familiar voice says, my mind questioning everything.

"Xavier?" I question, watching the blonde's smile grow.

He flips on the lights, and the large office brightens, giving me a clear image of the space. Wearing an ivory-green suit, he continues spinning the pocket watch. His eyes burn with a sinister intensity.

"Two powerful Marked right in front of me. How did I get so lucky?"

"The Commander-"

"Don't tell me the obedient Official act fooled you, Andrew," Xavier says with a mocking tone.

"My men are right outside-"

"My men, Andrew," Xavier clarifies, waving his finger. "I speak, they do. Their chips aren't needed, but they are indeed helpful when I find myself tired of making my way into their sorry little minds-"

"I will kill you!" Fallan yells, thrashing against his bindings once more.

Xavier stumbles out of his relaxed position, touching his temple with a look of anger. Fallan yells out in pain. The collar around his neck grows brighter as it activates.

"Still fighting after everything?" Xavier questions angrily, grabbing the boy's collar and dragging him right to the floor, "All those times you warned me to stay away from her, the empty threats time and time again. And what good did they do you? You still want to tell me she's yours?" Xavier questions, delivering a punch to Fallan's face.

Fallan smiles, spitting his blood over Xavier's front.

"She'll never love you," Fallan whispers.

Xavier grasps the man's head, all the energy I'd given Fallan draining instantly.

"Doesn't matter," Xavier begins, drawing in a deep breath. "I'll just use your energy to fuck her and force you to listen."

"You won't touch her!" I yell, forcing my knees away from the ground, straining against his Hold. Grabbing his legs, I force him to the floor. Fallan kicks up his leg, hitting Xavier's chest.

Moving with precision, I ready myself to seize his mind, planning to render him powerless.

"Do that, and I blow his brains out," Xavier seethes, his hand raised, his pistol pointed to Fallan. I pause my fight, my hands a shaky mess. "How many Markswoods can your conscience afford to kill, Andrew?"

I freeze at the comment, overcome by my own guilt.

"You're weak," Xavier says, shoving me away, his hand waving, a collar meeting his palm instantly. Snapping it around my neck, he kicks me back, and my body meets the ground.

"Please, know," Xavier begins, moving closer to the doors. "Only one of you will make it out of this room by the end of today."

He offers nothing else as he slips past the door, leaving the room in utter silence, deafening stillness.

Forest

Kai is fast asleep, his body curled up on the worn mattress in the corner of the holding cell. Looking around, my eyes land on the opened cell door, my hand raised, ready to hurt anyone who dares to come near us. Touching my throat, I run my finger along the metal collar. Leaving Kai to rest, I rise to my feet, pulling down my skirt in an attempt at modesty. I had used the bottom portion of it to wrap around my bleeding knuckles, and it was significantly shorter now. Moving past the cell door, I look around. There is no movement. Not a single Official in sight.

"Where are you going?" Kai's voice is hoarse, and I can see the pain and exhaustion in his features. I readjust my collar, clearing my throat to try and make my response to him come across with confidence.

"Whoever brought our meals," I say, looking at the measly portion of grits positioned on a small silver tray. "Didn't latch the cell door all the way," I look around again, waiting for someone to appear after hearing me.

"You were going to sneak out? Even with your abilities drained?" he questions, stating the obvious.

"I have to try, Kai. Stay here," I begin, ready to leave him behind. "At least I'll know you're safe-"

He grabs my wrist, and when I look back at him, his eyes no longer hold a boyish innocence, but the weight of adulthood instead. Suddenly, I see the similarities between him and my father. It was never age in my father's sullen expression... it was pain.

"I'm your older brother," he starts, moving past me. "Don't forget what responsibilities that means I have." He looks back at me, resolute, a sense of duty filling him with renewed energy.

"I'll lead the way."

Making it past every empty cell, there is discomfort in not seeing any of our friends. Unable to push past the hold of the collar, it's up to Kai to hack the outdated coding on the panel of the final security door that's keeping us trapped within the confinement chamber. Kai eventually managed to bypass the digital lock, and we find ourselves back in the main area of the building. Distant chatter echoes from a vestibule just a turn away. Looking at a large door to our right, we see an odd indentation in the wall. Its material is older than what surrounds it.

"If we go that way, we're screwed," Kai whispers, listening to the bellowing laughter of the Officials who attempt to flirt with a woman sitting at her workstation.

Moving closer to the indentation, I press my head to the wall, listening to the voices beyond it.

Like the purest noise blessing my ears, I hear his familiar voice, conflicted and comforting, groveling in emotional pain.

Motioning Kai over, I push the wall in, watching it move back, revealing an old entryway probably forgotten during a renovation of the space. Shoving past me, Kai steps inside, helping me pull back the concrete slab to conceal us from any oncoming Officials. Looking at the opening, we continue listening to Fallan's voice, moving down the narrow path, holding our arms close to our sides.

"We're inside the walls," Kai whispers, my head gently nodding.

Pushing past cobwebs, we follow the hallway to the end, stopping in front of our only way inside the space where Fallan is being held. Ready to press in the hidden entryway, we pause at the sound of another voice.

"I deserve all of this for what I did to you," my father's familiar voice grovels.

"Is that-"

"Dad," I whisper, finishing Kai's statement.

I hear my father sniffle, his voice filled with emotion.

"It's over now, Andrew," Fallan begins.

"Not to me!" my father yells, his hands slamming down on a surface somewhere in the room, the sound of chains dragging across the floor.

I stay pressed against Kai, both of us silently listening.

"Your father was my best friend, Fallan. I watched your mother and him fall in love," my father cries. "I watched the joy on your mother's face when she was pregnant with you," he continues, my heart racing. "Our parents used to have to drag me and your father away from each other. We dreamed of getting away from this place. He was exceptional, just like you." The sound of something being kicked or thrown fills our ears. "And I promised him I would protect you, but I betrayed him!" My father yells, a choked sob escaping him. "I was too selfish to tell Katiana I couldn't be with her. I was too weak to put my foot down and stay with my people-"

"You murdered my dad to prove your loyalty to her people," Fallan says, his voice broken. "You shot him right in front of me, and instead of taking me, you used a chip on me that you knew wouldn't work," Fallan whispers, his voice lined with resentment. "You took everything away from me, Andrew, and I wanted you to suffer," Fallan yells, my head pressed to the wall in pain. "I wanted to kill her for what you did to me," Fallan continues, my mind racing, "The night when that Untouchable boy committed suicide, I was ready to kill her. I was ready to drag her lifeless body to your front door and make you suffer," Fallan says, that night of the bonfire coming to the forefront of my mind.

"Then why didn't you?"

"I fell in love with a girl I wasn't supposed to. Everything before Forest was abysmal," Fallan responds, the affection and longing in his voice heard, even from behind this wall. "Everything after that night for me was only her. I will live for her, and I will die for her, as long as it means she gets to live."

"It didn't matter how often we tried to hardwire her brain to forget you," my father begins, a small laugh leaving him. "She always found you." My fingers instinctively running along the scar on the back of my neck. "Your connection with her is nothing like I've seen with our kind before-"

"There are no more Marked, Andrew. What's here is what's left of our kind," Fallan whispers.

"You think Xavier would have done all of this if that were true?" my father questions, my mind racing.

"He's keeping us here for a reason, and he's safeguarding my daughter for his own self-gain. There's something about her he wants-"

"I am going to kill him," Fallan whispers. "Her life is all that matters."

An unnerving presence surrounds me. Kai's grasp on my arm tightens.

"Touching moment," Xavier's voice whispers. Both Kai and I turn. Our fronts fill with pain as a burst of energy pushes against us. Our backs hit the small hidden door, and we tumble into the space holding my father and Fallan.

Both men are shackled and bound to a set of chairs, metal collars clasped around their necks.

Hitting the floor with Kai, we hurry to try and stand, both of us watching Xavier move out from behind the wall.

Pulling myself to my feet, I look at Fallan and my father, screaming in pain as my ankles fill with a searing heat each time I try to move. Grabbing Kai's hair, Xavier drags him closer to Fallan, forcing both men to their knees. My dad observes in horror, immobilized by Xavier's powers.

"Don't you just love a touching revelation?" Xavier questions, but my attention wasn't on him.

"Are you okay?" I question Fallan and my father, their small nods enough to give me comfort.

"Don't fucking talk to him," Xavier hisses angrily, shoving my brother down, looking me over vexedly. He moves towards me, but I leap to the desk in the room, grabbing the first thing that I can use as a weapon. I grab a letter opener and swipe it towards his throat. He smiles at the attempt, grabbing my wrist to pull me closer.

"Such a fighter," he whispers. "It's unfortunate how little you know about your abilities." He shoves me into the desk. My back meets its edge. I use the momentum from the push to swing my legs up, kicking Xavier hard in the chest. Watching him stagger backward, I keep my hold on the letter opener. My father, Kai, and Fallan are still trapped by his powers, watching in distress, unable to do anything.

"You are working very hard to piss me off," Xavier hisses, my hand jamming the letter opener into the seamline of the collar. It shocks me, my hands trembling as I drop the weapon.

"If it were that easy to break, one of these two idiots would have done it by now," Xavier says with a scoff, his hands grasping the collars of both Kai and Fallan.

"Forest, leave," Fallan begs. Xavier strikes him hard in the back.

"Stop it!" I scream, my father scrambling to try and kick Xavier away.

Fallan is bruised and bloodied, his energy all but exhausted.

"If you learned to shut your mouth, maybe you'd be in a little less pain," Xavier utters, holding his foot against Fallan's back.

"Why are you keeping them here?" I question, continuing to claw at my collar.

"He's draining our energy," my father answers.

"Hence, keeping their abilities at bay in a way the collars can't. They're a bit more experienced with their powers than you are, love," Xavier smiles, my head shaking in disbelief.

"Marked can drain other Marked?"

Xavier chuckles at the question.

"Not only can we drain them," Xavier begins, running his finger through the blood trickling down Fallan's lip. Bringing the blood to his mouth, I watch him taste it.

"There is no greater power than consuming the blood of a Marked. Abilities thought to be limited suddenly become much more intimidating," Xavier says, my eyes averting to the I.V. being forced into Fallan's arm first, then my father's.

"Get out of here, Forest. Please." Xavier readies to strike Fallan once more at his outburst.

Without thinking, I raise my hand, forcing past the pain the collar brings me. Xavier's leg comes to a stop midair, unable to bring it all the way down. He lets out a growl of frustration. The collar around my neck scorches the skin underneath it, vibrating mechanically and emitting loud warning beeps the longer I hold Xavier in place.

Abruptly, I feel the other's presence. Its existence is no longer steeped in shadow. Looking into Xavier's eyes, I see it now: the glow in my iris and the gray tinge to my hair.

What was once only a reflection now lingers in my features.

That other part of me is unable and unwilling to submit. Now, it watches Xavier, hungry and ready to hunt.

"I won't hesitate to break your leg," I seethe, ready to take down this entire room if it means defeating him.

Pulling his pistol free, Xavier points it at Fallan's head, his free hand pointed toward my brother.

"Release your Hold on me, or the blood of your brother and lover will be on your hands," Xavier threatens, my hand slowly lowering.

"Good girl," he whispers in a taunt, my Hold on him dwindling.

I hear a subtle click as the safety on Xavier's pistol is disengaged. He looks between my brother and Fallan, running the muzzle along Fallan's head as they lie with their stomachs pressed to the ground. My dad screams out for him to let them go.

"Choose, or I kill all three," Xavier whispers, my eyes wide with fear.

"No, I-"

He pulls the trigger, my life flashing before my eyes. Kai wails out in pain, his hands reaching to grasp his leg, blood soaking through his pants and pooling on the floor. Xavier squats down next to Kai, pushing his finger into the bullet hole. Kai's screams become deafening. Fallan tries desperately to get to my brother, but

Xavier's hold on him is unyielding. Feeling my energy surge, I try to think of a way out.

"Just barely missed a vital artery," Xavier says, pulling the bullet free. "Damn," he hisses, dropping the bullet to the ground, licking his fingers clean.

Kai cries out, his hands gripping his thigh.

"Choose."

Fallan finally gains some control back and swipes his leg out at Xavier, ending up on top of him a few moments later. Tearing past his bindings, Fallan drives his knee into Xavier's chest. Xavier lets out a groan, his hands pointing the gun at Fallan's abdomen. Diving to the floor, I grab the letter opener, my mind racing. Fallan is seconds away from meeting Kai's fate.

"I'm going to rip your face off!" Fallan yells, raising his arm above his head, readying to deliver him a painful blow. Xavier touches the trigger. His smile grows deviously.

"I'm assuming you need me alive for whatever you have planned," I whisper, both men's heads snapping toward me. Holding the sharp opener to my throat, I press down hard. A small cut begins and the blood streaks over the metal collar. "Get your fucking gun away from him," I shudder. Xavier's eyes are wide, and Fallan's face is shocked.

Shoving Fallan off of him, Xavier still holds him close, his hand firmly placed around Fallan's forearm.

"Don't make me choose," I say, sliding the opener a little further across my neck. "Put your gun down."

I expect him to badger me with more mindless taunts. Holding his hand, he places the weapon down, looking me over apprehensively.

"Take my collar off from over there. I can tell you have the Hold. Use it," I say, slicing farther, the cut coming closer to the carotid artery running up the side of my neck.

Fallan is unable to speak. None of the men have a voice. Their mouths are sealed shut by Xavier.

"Put down the letter opener," Xavier begins, my hand pushing deeper. The blood runs thicker. My stance becoming unsteady as a wave of dizziness takes over me.

"Enough!" Xavier yells, waving his hand, the collar clattering to the ground. He moves toward me, his eyes wide with concern. Taking a knife at his side, he slices his palm, his hand raising toward my mouth, "Drink, you'll heal-"

Pressing his hand to my mouth, I take in some of his blood, and a wave of energy surges through me. The need to keep drinking threatens to consume me. He grasps my head, letting me take what I can. I can see the glow of my iris in his dilated pupils, and I remember why I'm standing here. My hand continues to grip the letter opener as the wound on my neck begins to heal.

"My girl-"

Before he can say another word, I drive the opener into his chest. His eyes grow wide, his words lost in his throat.

"I'm not yours," I seethe, energy humming just under the surface of my skin.

Twisting the weapon, I feel the metal collide with his heart. He grabs me, dragging me down to the floor with him. His eyes, once full of life, are dull, vapid orbs. The blonde hairs on his head are darker. His face is more imperfect than I remember. Gasping for air, he tries to touch my face. My eyes shoot up toward Fallan and Kai, both their mouths hanging open as a silent scream leaves my brother. Not once had they moved from their positions.

"What-"

"Forest-" my father's voice beckons, my heart dropping at the realization of the man on the ground underneath me.

Unable to speak, I look down, my lungs unable to find air as my father's bloodied mouth tries to mutter my name again. Still grasping the end of the opener, I feel panic set in. The blow meant for the Xavier is now lodged deep into my father's chest. Quickly applying pressure, I cover his wound, my lip shaking, my hand supporting his head.

"Forest-"

"Dad, don't speak," I urge, my eyes frantically looking around.

"I need help!" I scream, hoping someone might breach that door.

"Please... I need help!" I scream louder, my tears clouding my vision, his blood soaking my front.

I raise my hand, ready to give him as much of my energy as I can. Shakily touching my neck, I feel the collar, my throat gasping, struggling to get air.

It had never fallen off.

He stepped into my mind.

He manipulated me.

"Forest-" my father begins once more, his hands touching my face. "Calm down, my angel," he says, his mouth filling with blood.

"Dad," I begin, my tears rolling over my cheeks.

"I'll get you out of here. I swear," I start, ready to slice my palm like he had done for me. He grabs my hand, stopping me.

"It can't fix every wound," he whispers, his eyes closing in frustration, his tears streaming down his face and mixing with the blood coming steadily from his mouth. "It's time to let me go," he whispers, his blood soaking my hand.

"I didn't mean to-"

"I know," he starts, pulling my head down to his chest, his breath uneven, and I know his time is near. "None of this was ever your fault," he whispers, his lips pressed against the side of my face.

"You kids and your mother are my everything," he whimpers, pressing his hand to my heart.

"Above all else, you must know where the true evil lies."

"Dad-"

"You're what remains. Lead us to our salvation," he says, his forehead pressed to mine.

Kai's screams finally register. Fallan does his best to comfort him. His head presses to the ground as he gasps for air between devastating wails of grief.

"I can't do this without you."

"Yes, you can," he whispers, his eyes opening and closing slowly. "Nothing is as it seems. You can trust no one but yourself, Forest. Trust the woman you see in the mirror. You only have yourself from here, and it will be a long journey ahead," he says, my mind flashing to that other part of me.

"I love you... Forest," he says, his voice breaking up.

Holding my face in his hands, his grip loosens. My hands hold his wound, my voice a shaky mess.

"Dad?" I question. His chest's slow rise and fall suddenly stops.

"Andrew?" I question again. Kai's cries are frantic.

Feeling my father's hands fall away from my face, I slowly raise my head. His blood soaks me. Looking at his open eyes, I feel my heart drop. The lively green eyes that nurtured me and watched me grow are now blank, stuck in a cold, dead expression. Pressing my head to his chest, I wait for his strong heartbeat that I felt during each embrace, ready for him to ruffle my hair, scolding me for worrying too much.

But it never comes. That gentle laugh, that playful scowl, all gone in an instant.

His chest is a bloody cavern, his body motionless beneath my touch.

Holding my hands together, I force them down on his front, my lips touching his, moving oxygen into his unmoving lungs. Repeatedly pumping my clasped hands above the gaping wound where I'd stuck the letter opener, new tears blur my vision.

"You're fine," I whisper, my voice cracking.

"You're okay, Dad," I continue, my heart-shattering.

Letting out a scream so deep within my chest, I feel the space around me implode. My heart races as my hands grasp my hair.

"He's gone," Xavier's voice says. My body goes rigid at presence.

I shakily rise to my feet, turning on my heels. Our eyes meet from across the room. He stands behind my brother and Fallan, unchanged from the same position he had earlier, with the pistol still in his hand.

"Remember this moment the next time you think you can cross me," Xavier says, motioning to the ground with the gun.

"Get on your knees. Do as I say, and no one else dies today," Xavier continues. "Unless you'd like to keep murdering the people you *love*," he pushes, my heart racing with an uncontrollable rage.

My energy, once coasting, is now a full-fledged fire. I'm even doubtful at this point if the collar around my neck, though strong, will be able to hold back what's contained within me. Lowering to my knees, I comply. His body moves closer to where he stands. The walls in my mind are back up by some miracle. The strength of that other side of me remains, Its presence alert ever since my father's blood touched my lips. Xavier strolls around me, his hands running the gun along my neck.

"Just one small request, and then you can all rot in your cells for the night. I'll even patch up your brother's leg out of the kindness of my heart," he says, his eyes wide.

Crouching in front of me, he looks me over with a smile.

"Taste my blood," he says, my stomach dropping at the statement. "Taste it, and no one else has to get hurt," Xavier continues. Fallan roars like a feral animal.

"A taste? That's all you need?" I question, coaxing my face into an expression of innocence and naivety.

"Yes, but it's your choice," he whispers, his hands running along his throat. "Because today is a day of choices, and whether you realize it or not," he continues. "What just happened was not my doing."

I look at his lips, my hands clenched. This isn't something he wants. It's something he needs.

My lips draw closer to his raised hand. Leaning past his hand, I slide my mouth over his cheek and to his ear.

"There will never be a day I fucking choose to accept any part of you. Rot in hell, Commander," I seethe. His hands grab my waist, the rage visible in the taut lines of his face and set line of his mouth.

"Clearly, you haven't learned your lesson," he whispers, his nose grazing my own. Pressing an earpiece, he speaks. "Send two men in. We also need a cleanup."

Waving his hand, Fallan and Kai are released from their rigid positions on the floor, finally able to move.

Two Officials shove through the doors, ignoring my father, grabbing the boys before they move toward me. Holding me to him, Xavier moves us into a standing position, his hand cupped around the back of my neck.

"What should we do with them, sir?" one of the men asks. My hand claws at Xavier's wrist.

"Put them all in the Lottery," he starts, his eyes panning down to me. "Put her in the first round. Give her a taste of what her friends will experience. Make those two watch.... And as for Andrew," Xavier nods at my father's lifeless figure. "Burn his body and save the ashes for our special guest." Fallan and Kai snap, doing their best to get away from the Officials behind them.

Watching Fallan and Kai get dragged away, I can't stop the tears from coming again in another wave. My head stays pressed against Xavier.

"I hate you," I whisper, his hand around my neck squeezing tightly.

"I know," he whispers, his tone low.

"That's what makes this all so fun," he says, his lips brushed against my ear.

"I'll kill you and burn this place to the ground," I whisper, his laugh brushing my ear.

"I do hope you try," he says, the casual lilt back in his tone. "In the meantime, let's see how resilient you really are."

CHAPTER FIFTY-SIX

FOREST

All I can see is him.

His light green eyes.

The way his smile was able to brighten even the most dreariest day.

It's a smile Kai carries and one my mother loves.

Even on his worst days, he would come home with a smile, ready to listen to one of Kai's many rants or question me about my newest painting.

It was a life that I cherished.

A life I took away.

All because I was too weak to safeguard my mind.

The bag over my head makes it impossible to see. Its rough material drags across my skin with each movement. I'd woken up just a few moments ago, the lingering feeling of a sedative still working its way out of my body. At some point after the horrors that unfolded in that office, I was thrown back into a cell by Xavier. My brother eventually joined me in the cell sometime after they'd made a shitty attempt at bandaging the gunshot wound on his leg.

The drugs must have been placed in the meal we'd scarfed down. Unlike Kai, I had managed to keep it down despite my father's blood caked all over my skin and clothes. Letting the unknown figures drag me along, I hear the door swing, their grasp on my arms growing tighter, as I am moved into a room. A small roaring fire warms my cold skin.

"Leave her," an unfamiliar female voice commands, the men barely uttering a word, closing the door with a thud.

Blindly raising my hands, I brace myself for what's to come.

"It would be extremely cruel for me to try and attack you masked and sedated now, wouldn't it?" she questions, a slight hint of humor in her voice. "The last thing you need is to be beaten down by an Unfortunate moments before getting thrown into that vile pit," she continues. The light of the fire grazes over my eyes as she pulls away the bag.

Blinking rapidly as my eyes adjust, I look at the woman in front of me. Her face is sunken in, the lack of nutrition painting her features. She wears a gray robe, her hair streaked with gray that adds to the beauty age has given her. Her eyes are golden brown, her skin is rich with a copper-toned color. Her hair is wound into multiple braids, each of them cascading down her back and to her waist.

"I am here to prepare you for the action. As a contestant in the Lottery, you'll need to look your best," she says, her hand reaching to touch my face. "You can call me the Teller."

She looks over me, assessing the stains on my clothes, and the faint wounds that had mostly healed with the aid of my father's blood but were still faintly noticeable. "Is all of this blood yours?" she questions.

I draw shaky breaths, feeling the collar move with each swallow.

"My father's," I whisper, clenching my hands together.

She stays silent, her face expressionless. In many ways, I think she's sparing my feelings. Then again, who knows how many horrific tales she'd heard over the years in her position.

"Well, we can't have you looking like that if you're going to remind them why they should have never put you down here in the first place," she says, moving closer to a small sink filled with steaming hot water. Dropping a rag in, she soaks it entirely, ringing it out with her weathered hands.

"There's no way I can fight, they've taken all of my energy-"

"Excuses are the last thing you should be feeding yourself. There are a lot of people betting on your success," she says. Moving closer, her hand drags the rag across my face. When she pulls it away, it's coated in blood, not a single spot of clean material left.

"Why the hell would anyone do that?" I question. Her wise eyes watch me close.

"Do you know how many Marked I've seen over the years? How many helpless Unfortunates and Untouchables with the very same mark on your belly?" I shake my head, knowing from her tone that it's more than I can think to estimate.

"Enough that the faces have become blurs," she starts. The warmth of the rag brings a sense of comfort as she brings it to my face again. "Before the blonde, there was another, just as cruel as the one before that. Each time they throw a Marked in, they never return, each one manipulated by someone far stronger, someone using up their life force like a personal battery," she says, working the rag into to my hands. "For every Marked, there is an ability," she says. "Some may even be lucky enough to have two or three."

"Only three?" I question, her head nodding.

"Never has a Marked carried more than four abilities at a time."

"How many are there?" I question. The depth of what I am is still such a mystery.

"Five. Five gifts, each one more powerful than the next."

"Xavier-"

"Carries three. Three of the deadliest. His ability to grasp one's mind is remarkable, as is his Winnowing, but the true danger lies in his ability to do the very thing that the Shifters are murdered for. You may think you're speaking to a lifelong friend, but it is a devil in disguise. The only thing that separates him from the monsters is that he can return to his normal form," she pushes, my throat dry.

"There's no way for me to beat him," I whisper, her hands pausing their work.

"You don't need to beat him, child," she says, her hands grasping my own. "You need to trick him and get yourself past that ward."

"There is nothing beyond the war, but the ash lands."

"Really?" she questions, her eyes playful, "And where do you think Xavier came from?" she asks, my head shaking.

"How could you possibly know this much?" I question, her shoulders shrugging.

"Stay silent enough, be around long enough, and you hear more than a conversation could ever give you," she says, my hands finally clean. "Our Commander is a miserable man, and sometimes misery craves company, even if it's speaking to a worthless Unfortunate like me," she whispers, a slight frown encasing her face.

I grab her hand, giving her a soft smile.

"You're not worthless."

"And you're not wearing that," she says lightheartedly, looking over at the small box resting on the table closest to us.

"He never has custom clothing made for any of the contestants. You must be special," she says, prying away the top of the box.

"You said people were betting on my success? Putting their faith in me?" I begin, her body pausing. "How does anyone even know who I am? Why put any faith in me?" I question. Her body is still.

"I have been a slave to this society for years, bent at the will of mindless Commanders for just as many of those years. Xavier may look young, but his reign in this sector is not recent. Even when he wasn't in the light, he was around. In all my years, I have seen many try and cross him, each one grasping for life by the end of their time here, but not a hair on his head out of place in the process," she says, pointing to me. "Just one day with you, and I saw him clutching his chest in pain. He rubs his throat every time you are near him, barely able to breathe. You've hurt him in more ways than one," she finishes, pulling away the gear from the box. She unfolds a sleek, form-fitting combat suit made of black leather. I reach out to touch it and find that its lightweight material is protective and flexible.

"You're special to him," she starts. "And *that* is a weapon," she continues, holding out the gear to me.

"So put this on and make him regret dragging any of us down here."

The pit is sullen, a deep pocket in the ground. The walls are so high that even a ladder would struggle to get you to the balconies that overlook this deathtrap. Glass surrounds each observation point. Men and women, all dressed in their best clothing, watch from above, their faces covered in golden masks.

I lean patiently against the wall, my hair wound in a tight braid that falls down the length of my back. The combat suit hugs my body securely. A singular blade is positioned in the middle of the pit. I imagine how many lotteries it's seen, how much blood it's spilled. Staying shackled to the wall, I sit still, looking for some sign of my friends anywhere, praying they aren't down here with me. I look up and see Xavier's blonde curls as he works through the crowd. His eyes look down at me, and his movement pauses.

Holding my gaze on him, I spit on the ground, pointing my fingers toward him, pretending to hold a gun as I point toward his head. All he can do is smile. The screens behind him have images of me, Kai, and our Unfortunate friends on a continuous loop, the text scrolling on the bottom of the screens is hard to make out but seems to be a list of our crimes against New Haven, and a warning to stay away from us.

Deviant citizens, charged with first-degree manslaughter of Andrew Blackburn- if seen, contact nearest Official immediately.

My stomach churns at what this means.

"It doesn't matter if we get out of here. He's ensured we are hunted," It whispers, a wave of relief passing over me at Its presence.

"I thought you were gone."

"Not gone," It starts. *"Been testing the waters,"* It says, a small smile curling along my mouth.

"I don't know how much longer we can remain separated."

I look up at Xavier, his canines flashing as he forces that devious smirk across his face.

"Then let's not be," I say, my resolve for vengeance fueling my next words with abandon. *"I want all of you, no matter the cost."*

"You're going to make us kill him."

"Give me one good reason not to!" I snap out loud. The Officials guarding the way we came from look at me with confusion.

"I can't answer that.... Not yet," It says. The loud creak of the gate across the way from me breaks my concentration.

It gradually rises from its still position, its metal scraping up the sides of the wall. Bagged and bound like me, more people are forced into the small pit, each wearing white robes. The people look frail, begging for mercy beneath the hoods. Even from here, I can see the marks on some, others bearing the scars undoubtedly of Unfortunates who've had one too many interactions with Officials.

Confused, I look up to find Xavier again. I find his gaze, an amused expression on his face.

"You look at me with such confusion," his voice echoes in my mind. My body jolts at the unexpected invasion.

"So it was you were lingering in the back of my mind all those times?" I question, narrowing my eyes.

"This is my first time stepping in.... Or should I say, your first time allowing me in," he clarifies, my head shaking.

"You forget to mention the part where you made me kill my father-"

"As much as I'd like to take credit for that wicked display of power, beautiful, that wasn't me," he seethes, clenching his glass of champagne. *"Trust me, I'm aggravated by the fact that I can't sort it out. I didn't*

particularly like seeing you forced into that position," he says, the irony in where I stand now almost comical.

"Right, but watching me die now is the kind of position you don't mind me being in," I mutter, his head cocking.

"I've told you I will never let anyone harm you," he whispers back to me, looking to all of the elites watching us in the pit with gawking eyes. *"Remind them all why our kind should never be backed into a corner."*

More mind games. All he does is manipulate. Forcing up my mental walls, I reach out to Fallan but can't sense my connection to him anywhere close.

As Officials remove the bags away from the other contestant's heads, no one's face sticks out to me. They look young, some even adolescent, and my heart begins to ache. Kai and I had been tasked with babysitting children their age for our scorecards a few years back. They cower to the Officials, some trying to return to the closing gate. The Officials leave the area, our shackles falling to the ground once every entrance is sealed.

Each person in the pit wears a number, three digits painted on any area of our skin exposed to the watchers above.

I look at my numbers.

"565," I whisper angrily, smudging away the paint from my forearm, flipping off those who watch in amusement.

Xavier smiles, his head tilted in observance, motioning across the room.

Shoved against the glass, their heads are forced forward. My friends. My very alive friends. Each of them regards me with fear, their scraps for clothes replaced with elegant ware. Their arms are forced behind their backs, their faces bruised, some still bloody. My eyes meet Fallan's, a slight sense of relief moving through me at the realization he is safe. Valerie and Kai are yelling, my heart racing at the new figure that has joined the group. Hunter screams for the men to let go of Kai, only receiving a blow to his face when he grows too loud to be ignored. Fallan required three men to hold him steady, his face the most beaten out of the group. Looking at me, I hold his gaze, but his head instantly snaps down. I see Xavier's hand waving, forcing us to break our eye contact.

A loud rumble shakes the ground, and my head snaps to my right, watching the last gate rise. The others back away, no one daring to try and make a break down the dark tunnel. No Officials linger in this tunnel. Some above even take a step back from the glass.

Looking at the blade in the center of the room, I touch my collar, making a break for the weapon. My fingers collide with the hilt as the others disperse.

Raising the blade, I hold my footing, watching as everyone's collars fall to the dirty floor.

The tunnel is no longer empty.

Three sets of eyes watch us, their faces hungry for blood.

Their clawed hands come first, each one of the creatures scraping the ground, dragging their nails along the dirt. Sniffing the air, their putrid faces move around the room. Their hollow eye sockets seem to look directly at the contestants around the pit. Drooling from the mouth, their focus narrows on every Marked stuck down here.

I hear the stifled sobs of everyone here, their thoughts a rampant mess of death and despair. Backed against the wall, every person put up for the Lottery cowers, some sinking to their knees. Holding my ground, I listen to the banging on the glass. The bidders hold envelopes filled with money, angrily yelling at the people they put their bets on to get up and fight. My friends continue observing. Fallan attempts to break the hold of the men surrounding him, only to be forced further into the glass. The creatures emit clicking sounds from their throats as they move through the pit. Their heads cock to the side as they sense movement, using some sort of echolocating ability. I watch the Shifter's focus move to me.

"Forest Blackburn," It hisses, its grin wide. "I was wondering when I'd finally get the chance to taste that rich blood of yours," It says, its voice something out of nightmares.

Giving Xavier one last look, I feel my energy return. The weight of the collar is gone, freeing me from its oppressive hold on my power. Swinging the blade, I lower my eyes, feeling the comforting embrace of that other, bloodthirsty side of me, our words and thoughts as one once more.

"Go ahead and try," I hiss, bracing myself for what's to come.

Lunging toward me, it swipes the air, its companions tearing into whatever humans they can get to first. I drown out the cries of the other contestants, dodging away from its attack. I roll beneath its legs, dragging the blade across the tender tendons of its calves.

It screeches in pain, cursing under its breath. My knees slide across the ground, my focus dead set on a Shifter ready to tear into a younger Marked. He holds up his hands, but his abilities are weak.

"Your blood will be savored," the Shifter mutters with malice.

Forcing my arms behind my head, I launch the blade toward the creature, watching it hit the base of its neck, its body retracting up and away from the boy. Doing my best to try and pry away the weapon, I raise my hand, twisting my wrist, pushing further with my force until the metal collides with the creature's brain stem. With a clean slice out the other side of the creature's neck, I force my hand down, watching the Shifter meet the ground. Its body becomes a pile of ash.

Sensing a presence behind me, I brace myself for another attack, but my blade is too far away. Turning on my heels, I collect the energy into my palms readying to use my power, pausing at the sight in front of me.

My father's green eyes meet mine, his mouth down turned into a look of sadness. Keeping my distance, I can barely control the emotions threatening to break me where I stand.

"Honey?" he questions, his shirt still soaked with blood. "What's going on?" he asks, my head shoving away every guilty thought.

The third Shifter continues working through the crowd, picking off everyone it can. Its focus is away from me.

"You're not real," I beckon, my hands raised in front of me.

"They threw me down here; the creature made a run down the tunnel-"

I force my hand up, finding and connecting with my power, watching my father's figure grasp his throat. All the elites turn from their social conversations and look into the pit, now entirely focused on what's happening in front of them. Xavier's arms are crossed. My companions scream against the foggy glass.

"You're not real!" I yell, the space around me that much tighter. "I killed you!" I begin, my feet drawing me closer to the apparition. "I killed you because I was too weak to protect myself!" I continue, my eyes glancing up at my companions. "But they're still here," I mutter, a swell of emotion consuming my chest.

I feel the embrace of that other side of me, Its arms around me in a comforting grasp.

"Honey-" he gasps.

"My name is Forest Blackburn," I say, my eyes snapping to the ones so similar to my father's. "Remember the name of the woman who took your last breath from you," I whisper, clutching the man's throat with all the energy I have.

I watch him grab my wrist, doing his best to pry away the hand I have around his throat. Feeling his windpipe closing, his stifled pleas reach my ears. My eyes glance down to the metal of my gear. The reflection of what lies in front of me paints nothing but the true picture.

Where I see my father, the metal sees the creature, its eyes frantic, praying for mercy.

"You're running from an evil that will always find you," It hisses, my father's face slowly slipping away.

"I don't have to run," I seethe, leaning in closer. "It's looking back at me in your dying eyes." I smile, a new feeling coming over me, something entirely foreign.

The strength from my other side courses through me, Its life force supporting my own.

Slumping to the ground, the Shifter's form returns, its body disintegrating into the ash.

Glancing at the final Shifter, I move closer to the group, reaching down to grab the blade. It patiently waits to meet my hand once more. I shove a few of the younger contestants behind me. I twirl the weapon, watching the Shifter drop a woman once as it becomes aware of my presence.

"So, you're the woman he-"

My blade collides with its mouth, skewering its head to the nearest concrete wall behind it. I drive the weapon deeper into its skull, my energy a forest fire I can hardly contain. Letting go of the hilt, I take a step back. Seven bodies litter the ground of the twenty of us here. Three of them were lifeless Shifters.

Looking up at the glass, I see the gaping mouths of all that watch. I raise my hands, ready to take this place down; the others down here with me shake in fear.

"Make them afraid, beautiful, and the world is yours to take," Xavier whispers, his grin wide.

A deafening noise breaks out in the arena, my knees meet my chest as I hunch over, unable to stop myself from covering my ears. I yell loudly, feeling a great sense of fear at the realization my companions no longer overlook the pit. Doing my best to navigate the space, I see the flood of figures as Officials step back into the pit, collaring every person they can, looming closer to me with each passing minute.

Getting to my feet, I ready myself to take on as many of them as possible.

"That won't be necessary," Xavier whispers in my ear, his arm wrapping around my front, his presence next to me instant. Hadn't he just been at the top of the pit behind the glass? "You're mine for now."

The sound of the collar snapping around my neck fills my ears.

My energy reserves are instantly depleted, but I try and use what I can to get away.

"As much as I like you putting up a fight," he says, a sharp needle meeting my neck. "It would seem our presence is needed elsewhere."

CHAPTER FIFTY-SEVEN

FOREST

"**D**o you plan on forcing your insufferable presence on me all night?" I question hatefully, looking at the sprawl of dresses on the table, each more revealing than the next.

"You have to choose one if you're going to be anywhere near the people that you saw earlier behind the glass," he mutters, his arms crossed, his body leaning into the table. We are back in the room where the Teller prepped me. Xavier decided to take a personal interest in helping me get ready so he can proudly show me off to everyone who decided to bid against me. As long as I'm here, the punishments will keep coming.

That realization, along with the combined presence of Xavier and the collar, is more than enough to drain my grasp on the abilities I have.

"Let me know they're safe, then I'll pick one of these fucking horrid dresses," I say, my hands clenching the soft materials that lies in front of me.

Xavier grabs my chin, my head forced up to look at his face.

"I'm not in the mood to be making deals with you right now," he begins, looking down at the dresses. "Any of these will do, although green is your color," he whispers, grabbing the dress on the far side of the table. It's a dark, vibrant, sage green.

"What am I even doing? I won. I figured your desire to watch me suffer had been satisfied," I whisper, grabbing the dress of his choosing.

"Not that you need a reminder, but you killing your father was not my doing. I'm hurt you thought it was me," he says, feigning distress. My fist rises, ready to clobber him in his smug face. He grabs my wrist, forcing it down and onto the table. My back meets the wood surface.

He leans over me as I look at him with contempt.

"Whether you realize it or not, I'm in your corner," he begins, leaning closer. "And I've done more than you know to keep it that way, so you're going to put on that goddamn dress and give them all something to be afraid of," he spits, his eyes narrowed.

"You want them to be afraid of me?" I question shakily. His chin dips in a nod.

"Fucking petrified." His hand clutches my side. "This society was built on a glass floor. I want nothing more than to watch it shatter."

I think of Adam and the hungry eyes of every Official that lingered up there watching as people lost their lives tonight.

Feeling his hands on me, an idea enters my mind.

The only way I get my friends out of here is if I play his game.

"I refuse to let anyone else touch me if I go out there. You can show me off like a prized pet, but I won't be treated like one," I whisper, his hold tightening.

"A pet?" he questions, his lips close to my own. "God, you don't see what I do, do you?" His hands run up my sides. "It's easy, Forest," he begins, pausing at my upper body. "If anyone comes near you, I'll kill them. I'm not showing you off like an animal they can ridicule," he says, his eyes snapping to my own. "I'm hanging a temptation in their face and savoring it right in front of them. There's not a thing anyone can do about it," he whispers, his lips by my ear.

Turning his way, our noses brush, my stomach churning, begging me to escape him.

Just one slip into his mind is what I need. Just one connection and I have control.

Leaning closer, I brace myself to brush his lips.

Backing away in a blur, he creates space, moving once more in the blink of an eye. Breathing heavily, he covers his mouth. His body, which was once hanging over me, is now across the room.

"What-"

"Don't you ever try and do that again," he commands, touching his throat in small strokes. "If you try to slip into my mind again, I will kill everyone you love."

I close my gaping mouth, watching him slip past the old door, closing it and locking it behind him. Looking around the space, I grow frustrated, unable to stop the rage from overtaking me.

After flipping the table full of dresses and breaking several of the chairs in the room, I finally collapse to my knees and sit amongst all the broken and battered pieces.

The dress's material is thin and made of luxurious satin that shimmers under the light. The bodice is made of a plunging neckline that dips low, exposing the top and sides of my breasts, accentuating my curves The thin, spaghetti straps add just enough support while adding to the overall seductive appearance. It gathers just above my waist before pooling down my legs which are exposed by two slits along my thighs. There is a thin mesh material over the skirt, adding to the ethereal look of it. My hair is down, styled in loose waves that fall to my lower back. I look at myself in the mirror, noticing the silver locks that now overpower the dyed brown pieces.

Opening the door, the Teller peers inside, taking her time to inspect her handiwork.

"Look at you," she coos, glancing behind her.

"He's ready for you."

I nod my head and move myself past her. While she wraps her hand around my arm, her other quickly tucks a small blade beneath the waistline of the dress. Her delicate fingers work quickly, the weapon is small, meant to be concealed.

"I've never seen anyone from the Lottery leave this place," she whispers, her hand pressed over my heart. "I do hope you change that."

"Why are you helping me?".

"Call it foolish hope," she says, as the sound of others approaching grows. "I pray my faith in you is not misplaced." She urges me out of the room and into the arms of the Officials, waiting to escort me to another pit of monsters.

Their faces are shielded with masks of gold, each one intricate in design, meant only to conceal the features of each guest's face, but I recognize several of them already. They stand in awe, holding their champagne glasses tightly, watching me like I'm the main attraction of tonight's events.

Teachers, doctors, and companions of my father all surround the area, chatting amongst themselves happily and excitedly. I feel disgusted the longer I look into each of them. I have to stop myself from physically lashing out when I see Max, his once kind expression now cold and vacant. Josh stands next to him with a smile.

Xavier stands out, his face exposed. He isn't hiding behind a mask like the others, but I guess the Commander doesn't need to. He sits in a chair closest to the glass barrier surrounding the pit below, his hand swirling a glass of liquor, standing up once he takes notice of my presence. Some women linger by his chair. Others take their time looking over my body, the dress making it impossible to look away. Giving me a quick look up and down, Xavier's eyes land on the two men holding me.

"I said she was free to walk without either of you touching her," Xavier says, their hands dropping from my arms.

"Respectfully, sir, we figured-"

Xavier holds up a finger, drawing in a deep breath.

"Say another word, and I snap your neck. Why don't you two go ahead and step away from her and grab yourselves a drink," Xavier says. Both men hesitantly back away.

I stand still, my eyes on Josh and his wide grin. Lowering my eyes, I take several steps toward him, ready to smear his face along the clear glass.

Grabbing my waist, Xavier pulls me along with him. As he takes a seat back on the chair, my ass meets his lap.

"Easy, love. I want you to savor his demise," Xavier says quietly, his hand on my thigh, giving it a slight squeeze.

Feeling uneasy, I focus on the feeling of the blade rubbing against my ribcage.

"How thrilling," I begin, turning to look at him. His breath smells like alcohol. His hair is ruffled.

His shirt is open enough to show me his mark and the black tattoo on his chest. I pause, resting my gaze on its design with curiosity.

"Like what you see?" he asks, grabbing my hand. He lets my fingers trace along the parts I can see. "It's permanent."

"First, you stop me from kissing you earlier. Then you tempt me with the idea of giving Josh a long and painful death. You sure do know how to taunt a girl," I growl, his fingers trailing up and down my exposed spine.

"You don't know the half of it," he says, looking around the room with a sigh.

I try to find my friends in the crowd, taking the opportunity to focus my energy on connecting to one of their minds.

"I'm curious," he says, directing his attention back to me. "How much longer do you plan on trying to reach out to your friend's minds?"

My heart sinks. Staying silent, I keep my gaze forward. Pulling me backward, he forces my head into his shoulder. His lips find my ear.

"I've been around longer than anyone in this room," he whispers, his grasp tightening. "Don't think for a second that you have an advantage over me."

Feeling my energy rise, I blink away the tears in my eyes, shoving down the hopelessness I feel the longer his hands roam my body.

"F-Forest?"

Fallan's voice enters the back of my mind, quiet, barely even there.

Drawing a deep breath, I focus on our connection, feeling its fleeting presence.

"Where are you? Are you hurt-"

"It's dark. I can hear Officials speaking-" he says in a rushed whisper. Xavier's hand grabs my jaw.

"A glimpse before they're all gone," Xavier hisses, leaning forward, my eyes panning down to the pit below.

My heart stops as each one of their terrified expressions comes into focus below. Much like I had, they each wear a bag over their heads, their throats covered with the metal collars meant to subdue their powers. The others I fought the Shifters with who survived were forced back into the pit. There's no blade in the center of the space this time. Jolting forward, I watch the Officials rip away the bags for their heads. Fallan looks up at me, our eyes locking. Even in all of this mess, he sighs in relief, a slight upturn of his mouth at the sight of me.

His face is bruised, his body drained. Kai limps closer to Valerie and Hunter, grasping his still bleeding and injured leg, frantically searching the crowd for any sign of me and a way out.

Moving closer to observe, a few drunk men stumble into me, their hands grabbing my body for support.

"Hands off," Xavier hisses, shoving the men away. His grasp on my hips becomes punishing as he forces us to stand.

Looking around the room for an exit, my eyes land on the entrance I came from. I think of how many people I can take down with my power, wondering if the glasses they hold can be broken quickly enough to lodge into their throats.

Xavier forces my head into the barrier. My cheek presses to the cold glass, his hand shoved against my lower back, keeping me pinned with his knee. Watching in anger, Fallan yells a threat lost in the distance between us.

"Listen," Xavier hisses. "And watch."

Snapping his fingers, a few of his men walk away. His grasp grows firmer as I squirm. The others look up to me. Valerie covers her mouth in concern. Kai's eyes well with tears.

"Let me down there. Let me take their place," I beg. He scoffs.

"Any more outburst from you, and you will join them," he threatens.

Anything is better than being trapped up here with him.

The ones who have already fought step back, anticipating what is sure to exit the tunnel, the metal gate separating it from the pit now lifting.

Fallan looks away, his body in a defensive stance as he begins backing the others behind him. Staring down toward the tunnel, he opens his arms, keeping anyone he can pressed against the wall.

"How chivalrous," Xavier taunts, my irritation with him growing.

The clawed hand of a Shifter makes its way from the dark, dragging its body along the ground, scouting the pit for its next meal.

Something hanging out of Xavier's pocket jabs me in the side. I look down to see a small device with a control screen with the words "**COLLARS ARMED**" displayed in bold, black text.

Enough of this.

My hand reaches into the side of my dress, grabbing the hilt of my blade. I use my legs to push off against the glass. Sending us backward and into the chair, I slide my hand into Xavier's pocket, pulling away the device.

Shoving me away, he lets out a noise of frustration. My body rolls onto its side before I quickly move to my feet. Xavier shouts to his men. Several Officials reach for the weapons at their sides, but Xavier screams at them to stand down. I find my name on the screen and switch the collar's connectivity to deactivated. The metal restraint clatters to the ground.

"Stop!" Xavier commands. The Official closest to me ignores the warning.

In an instant, the world slows. Grasping the Official's mind, I command his heart to stop. His eyes roll backward, and his body crumples to the ground. I feel his life force leave his body and move through the air. I graze my fingertips across the translucent ribbons swirling in the space around me.

An instinct drives me to take a deep breath, consuming the ribbons hungrily. The intake isn't enough to satisfy me and instead makes me ravenous for more.

The other Officials take a step back, not coming closer to me. Clutching the knife, my eyes land on Xavier.

"Call off the Shifter!" I order. Xavier's hands are raised toward me.

"You're making a mistake."

Throwing the blade across the room, the weapon lodges in Adam's lower stomach. His body doubles over, and he screams out in pain as I raise my palm and call the blade back to me.

"Call it off!" I hiss, glancing toward the pit.

The Shifter is at a standstill. The contestants below fearfully backed into a corner.

Xavier takes another step, my hand ready to drive the weapon into him.

"You won't hurt me," he scoffs.

"And why would you think that?" I question, the smirk on his face disappearing.

For the first time, I see it happen. There's a faint glow around his body before his figure dissolves into thin air. I brace for his sudden presence as he rematerializes behind me, swinging my arm at him in defense.

"I won't let you, *Dove,*" he whispers, clutching my arm, his hand quickly swiping the blade from my hand.

I raise my free hand, thoughts of his pain fueling my fight.

"You do that, and I will ensure every one of them dies," he says, holding his ground behind me.

Staying still, I heed his words.

"I can melt their brains with those chips quicker than that Shifter could get his claws into them," he seethes, his grasp growing. "I do applaud your unwavering resolve to save them, though. A valiant effort, really."

"Put the creature back in its cage," Xavier commands, looking over at Adam and the lifeless Official on the ground. "Deal with the contestants. I want her and all of her friends in their cells," he says, his fingers twisting into my hair. "Consider my generosity officially spent. You want a fight, Forest? Then you can have your fucking wish," he says, dragging me along with him. He moves swiftly across the floor, draining all of my energy as we go. Grabbing my collar from the ground, he snaps the control back on, pressing the device's screen.

"I've decided on new terms to our fun little game," he says, forcing me to look at him. "The only way you will leave that pit is if all your friends are dead and you are on your knees begging for me to save you."

"I will never get on my knees for you!" I yell, forcing myself to stand tall.

"You're a coward," I hiss, his eyes growing wide with rage.

"I hope you get a good, final look at your friends in your holding cell tonight," he jeers, dragging me along. Taking the knife, he cuts my side, carving a small

X, branding me like livestock. "Because it's the last night you'll ever spend with them."

I claw at his grip as he drags me away from the crowd of elites.

Despite the blood I draw, he moves forward, my grunts becoming yells as the strain of his grasp on my hair only increases, sending a wave of pain through my skull and down my neck. I see the others being forced into their holding cells. I hang on to their familiar voices.

Forcing one of Xavier's guards into a wall, Fallan manages to break free. He barrels toward Xavier, ready to tear him apart.

"Enjoy your last moments together," Xavier hisses, forcing me forward, my body colliding with Fallan's, both of us stumbling into a cell.

Hitting the floor, we watch the door swing closed, our hands scrambling to find one another. His lacerated palms cup my face. Up close, I can see how badly he's been hurt. My lip quivers at the sight of every cut and bruise. Running my thumb along his swollen lip, I press my forehead to his. He lets out a sigh of relief, pulling me to his chest.

"Pathetic."

Hunter, Kai, and Valerie huddle close by, glaring out at Xavier contemptuously.

"The thought of you becoming a lifeless corpse brings me joy. See you soon, street rat," Xavier says, his eyes on Fallan. He turns to leave us.

"Does it make you miserable?" Fallan questions, Xavier pausing his steps.

"Does *what* make me miserable?"

"Knowing you'll never have her," Fallan snarls, his arms tightening around me.

Xavier says nothing, his hand touching his throat. Clenching his jaw, he gives me a final look, waiting for me to say something. I feel a well of emotion in my chest as I watch him, unsure why I can't stop the flood of tears from falling.

After a few moments, Xavier backs away, his front still to us.

"Death is a kind ending in this cruel world. Consider tomorrow as an opportunity to be free of a life I don't wish on anyone."

"Then why keep me alive if you're doing everyone else such a kindness?" I spit, my eyes demanding that he answer me this time.

"Misery loves company, Forest," he begins, his eyes panning to Fallan.

"And I'm the most miserable of them all."

CHAPTER FIFTY-EIGHT

FOREST

"He told us if we kept trying to escape, he'd activate our chips and let our brains bleed out," Kai whispers, his head pressed to the rusted bars of the cell.

Hunter and Valerie lean on my brother, their exhaustion and hunger making it nearly impossible for them to sit upright. To my surprise, Valerie's arm had been bandaged. The light is gone from her expression. Her gaze is lost in a mindless headspace. Hunter is slowly fading into despair. His mouth is pressed into a thin line as he stares into nothingness.

Kai stays alert, looking to me for any shred of hope, but I'm out of ideas, and we're running out of time.

My back is leaned into Fallan, his arms wrapped around me, pulling me between his legs. I listen to the steady beating of his heart as his thumbs trail circles up and down my arms. I keep my face pressed to him, trying to come up with a plan to get us out of here alive.

Every solution ends with me staying behind.

But it would be worth it. Even if it meant an eternity of hell with Xavier, them escaping a slow, agonizing death-

"Stop thinking about staying here while the rest of us leave. It's not an option. I won't let you do it," Fallan says, his eyes still closed, his head leaning against the cell bars.

"You can't, Forest," Kai whispers, trying not to stir the two bodies now fast asleep on his chest.

"You need to sleep, Kai. I'm not leaving you, I promise," I interrupt, giving my brother a faint smile. It feels so forced, but I have to try.

With a sigh and a slight adjustment, Kai finally settles. It only takes a few minutes for him to nod off, his head resting on top of Hunter's.

"I'm serious," Fallan pushes, his fingers gently tapping my temples. "If I focus hard enough, I can still hear what's going on in there, which means he can too. I'm sure he'd love nothing more than to keep you here, but there's no scenario in which I leave here without you."

"Stop exerting energy. You'll need as much as possible if we're going to survive this," I whisper, my lips grazing kisses each of his damaged knuckles.

He pries his hand away, his finger slipping under my chin, directing my head over my shoulder to look at him.

"Do you know what it was like when I first saw you that day Josh and Colton assaulted Jolie?"

That moment feels so long ago, but it had only been a few months since that day the day that changed everything.

"I'm assuming you couldn't stand me. I was awful," I say honestly, the regret of my stigmas toward his people filling my chest with a heaviness I'd felt many times.

"That's what I wanted you to believe," he whispers, his finger brushing a few strands of my hair behind my ears. "But no, if anything, it was nearly impossible not to reach out to you. To tell you I was the man you met at the bonfire that night. The worst part of it was that you had no clue who I was. And I was cruel to you because I was angry at Andrew for what he did to my family. I wanted revenge, and I needed ammo," he says, my face leaning closer to his touch.

"You didn't hate me then?" I question, his mouth curling into a smile.

"I thought you were just as beautiful as that night at the fire. You were filled with the same energy that had drawn me to you the first time we met during the Expulsion Tests. I wanted to cup your face like I am now and tell you just how much my hands and mind craved feeling you close to me," he pauses, his eyes closing with frustration. "But then one of our classmates said your last name and my one reason for coming to your sector suddenly became that much more complicated. I had become utterly enthralled with you so I could use you as ammo against Andrew when it would mean my heart breaking in the process," Fallan says, his hand trailing farther down my side, nearly pulling me into his lap.

"Will you tell me what happened?" I question. It's a question that's lingered in the space between us for so long.

"He was like family to my own for so long," Fallan lets out in a shudder, my body entirely in his lap now. "He was my father's best friend… a man who wanted peace for our kind," he whispers, his finger trailing over the outline of my mark. "We always knew there was an Untouchable woman on the other side he was close with. We knew where he went when he left the sector late at night. No one thought it was serious, so the idea that their relationship would lead to any harm didn't cross our minds."

"But it wasn't just something casual, was it?" I question, his mouth pulling into a smile once more.

"It never is with Blackburn women," he admits, his hands moving beneath the hem of my tattered shirt.

"Andrew had been sleeping with your mother and, as far as I know, began diverting away from his peace talks with the Untouchables. As time went on, we began to see less of him, even more so once your mother became pregnant with Kai-"

"Every child is planned-"

"That wasn't the case for your parents," Fallan admits with a saddened expression.

"I'd always heard of Andrew and seen the family he'd left behind, but I'd never met him. I took Mark's face for reference and tried to piece together what he could have looked like, but as far as I knew, your father had left his people and became someone else entirely. He'd send Mark photos of you and Kai," he says, smiling as he reflects on the memory. "There were years of no contact, my mother and father unable to piece together how Andrew had stayed safe over on the other side… we didn't realize his loyalty had been pledged to another cause."

"There was a night in August. It was chill, something entirely eerie in how the leaves hit the ground that day, and the air was so still. I remember my mother making soup from some local scraps she'd gotten at a good price. My father was sitting in a rocking chair, reading the paper," Fallan says, his eyes closed, his heart rate accelerating beneath my palm. "There was no time for anyone to react once they broke down the door," he continues, my fingertips trailing over the vague outline of his mark. "All I could see was the black of the Official uniforms. By some miracle, my mother had managed to force me behind her, doing her best to keep me concealed. They were on my father in a matter of seconds, forcing his knees to the ground. When my mother tried to get involved, one of the Officials slapped her in the face. It wasn't until your father stopped them from touching me that I realized who was hiding behind one of the masks," he says, his eyes flying open. "They were the same eyes I looked into that day at the tram station before we started school together. In his mind, sparing me from a beating as a child was merciful, as if what followed was justified," Fallan says, tears swelling at his waterline.

I feel the pain as he reflects, and it's hard for me to breathe.

"Adam was with him, barking orders at your father like a show pony. I begged him to leave us alone and promised never to expose that we knew him. In my mind, I thought maybe he'd found out about me looking into his disappearance. But that's not what it was. Andrew exposed my father's mark. Adam looks so satisfied at finding out what my father was," Fallan whispers, my head shaking.

"My father wouldn't-"

"Prove his loyalty to a higher power to protect his family? Is that not what you were ready to do as well?" Fallan questions, genuine sincerity in his voice. It's not hatred he feels toward my father now. It's-

"An understanding of why he did it," Fallan finishes out loud for me, his hands holding me tight. "Adam stood behind your father as he pulled the trigger. All we could do was watch. Looking back, I'd thought your father's chip was why he did it. Now I know it was his own free will. At the moment, it was a choice between the family he left behind or the one he sacrificed everything to create. He chose your mother... he chose you and Kai. It's a choice I thought would fuel my hatred of him for the rest of my life. Now, his choice has become my own. My people, or the woman I love," Fallan whispers, neither of us able to hold back our tears.

"I didn't know-" I sob, my throat burning as I try to find the right words. "I would have never-"

The warmth of his lips brushing against mine floods me with relief. The slight curve of his smile grazes across my own, our bodies nothing but a tangled mess of limbs, bruised and beaten, ignoring every wave of pain that shoots through us. His hands brace my lower back, my thighs squeezing his waist, tugging him as close to me as I can. I hungrily feed into his kiss, committing the feeling of his mouth on mine to memory. The smell of oak lingers on his skin. His perfect black curls sweep across his face, casting shadows on his strong features. Each of his scars is unique, creating an armor for a heart that is mine to keep safe.

This is Fallan.

My Fallan.

The man I will safeguard with everything I have, even if it means my life.

All he has known is sacrifice and loss.

No longer will that be the case.

With each brush of his lips, hiding those thoughts takes all I have, but given how his smile has made this dirty cell feel safe and warm, I'd say the extra effort is worth it.

"It was never on you," he whispers, breaking the spell between us.

"To think," I start, my hands brushing over his face. "I thought you wanted me dead." Both of us chuckle quietly, some of the pressure surrounding our situation released at that moment.

His lips move to my neck, working across the tender skin. I hold him close to my chest, his body a rock under me.

"I wanted to hate you.... But that was entirely impossible the second I saw you," he whispers, my heart lurching. "Falling in *love* with you was entirely out of *their* control."

My heart skips a beat at his words. It's not talked about a lot in our society. Doing things out of love, for love, rather than the greater good isn't commonplace.

The sound of metal clattering to the ground jolts us from our reverie.

Canisters roll to a halt right next to us, waking the others from their restful slumber. I watch the canisters explode. A plume of scentless gas emerges and fills the cell. I see Xavier's cold blue eyes through the haze, his cold blue eyes watching me with a grin as he and his men enter the space, their faces covered in gas masks.

"I assure you, Mr. Markswood," Xavier begins, consciousness becoming foggier with each intake of air. "Everything is in *their* control," he pushes, watching my friend's bodies slump, my own leaning farther away from Fallan as my limbs go numb.

"You should have gotten out when you had the chance."

I want to understand his words.

I want to know what he means.

Forcing my back into Fallan's motionless figure, I cover his body as best I can in an attempt to protect him. Xavier saunters into the cell with confidence, looking down at us and shaking his head.

"Still trying to protect him?" he questions, my eyes narrow, struggling to stay open.

"Until my last breath."

His voice comes to me softly, said in a language I don't recognize.

"*Diabolus est dominus dissimulationis et multas formas accipit.*"

The world flickered to black seconds later.

CHAPTER FIFTY-NINE

FOREST

G ravel crunches and grinds under my feet. I can sense we're back in the pit, even with the mesh bag over my head. Someone's heavy footsteps accompany mine, their body shoving me into different directions as we walk. My feet drag across the ground, but with each step, I become more lucid. I don't know how I got here after being gassed in the holding cell, only that it could have been minutes or hours since I saw the people I care about most in this world. Firm hands grip my arms, a searing pain radiating from my side with each movement of my body. The metal collar rubs against the skin of my neck. I can feel the raw, exposed flesh against its cool surface. As I walk, I realize the pain in my side isn't from an injury but from a weapon being pressed there by one of my escorts.

As the pressure on my side increases, so does my pain. The blade is pressed firmer into my skin. I let out a small yelp, biting my lip to avoid revealing just how much agony I'm in.

"Quiet!" Adam's voice commands, my resentment towards him reaching a new level.

"You put a goddamn knife in me," I hiss, unable to move given its position.

"The dog collar wasn't good enough for you-"

"Xavier said-"

"Xavier isn't here," Adam hisses, his hand reaching the back of my neck, gripping the skin in a firm grasp. "I figured he wouldn't mind taking a sterner approach to managing you," he pauses, satisfaction in his tone. "Pull it out, and you will be fighting to stop a nasty bleed."

"Maybe I should rip it out and cut your throat for what you did to my father," I seethe, his grasp tightening.

His lips move to my ear, my body tense at his unexpected closeness.

"Might as well cut yours too. The way I see it, his death is on your hands as much as it is ours."

Adam's hands shove me, the mesh bag falling from my head as I stumble forward. The lights in the arena are excruciatingly bright. Countless gold masks look down at the pit, even more than the night I'd originally fought for my life down here. To my horror and delight, the others are already waiting in the pit. They look disoriented, trying to take in the space around them. Fallan's eyes meet mine from across the space. His hand grips a wound at his side, the blood flowing freely. I take an uneasy step and see my brother's frantic gaze scanning the space. Hunter and Valerie are shaking.

"Don't!" Fallan yells toward me, my eyes finally adjusting on the Shifter circling the outskirts of the pit, its head turned in my direction.

Slowly, the pit lights dim, my hand clutching the knife in my side. Xavier's eyes are the first I see when I scan the crowd. Tonight, he's wearing a mask just like the others, and for a brief moment, I wonder why. Leisurely, he sits in his chair, a scandalously dressed woman perches beside him. While she draws the attention of other masked men around her, Xavier's knees are nearly touching the glass as he leans forward to get a better look at the pit. My blood coats my hand. I force back another scream that threatens to leave my throat as the blade remains lodged between my ribs. His eyes stayed locked on me, glancing down at the stab wound. I move my arm from my side, pointing it in Xavier's direction, shaping my hand into another imitation of a gun with my fingers.

Unamused, he begins shouting from behind the glass, grabbing the shirt collar of the person next to him. His words are lost in the distance between us, and the sound of my heartbeat is in my throat. The Shifter sniffs the air, its body more humanoid in comparison to the others I've seen so far. Fallan follows the creature with his eyes. The more I watch him bleed, the more I want to rip off this despotic collar and tear through everyone upstairs beyond the glass.

A cracking sound breaks my concentration, several voices shouting at the commotion unfolding above us.

Xavier holds Adam against the glass. Adam tries to pry Xavier's fingers away, but he's stuck against the glass barrier. I can't hear him scream, but the fear painted across his features is enough to know he's powerless. Pointing down toward me,

Xavier yells louder, his free hand motioning toward one of his men. One of the servants grabs a pistol, pressing it firmly into Xavier's demanding grasp.

Looking back at my friends, I see the creature observing what's happening above, craning its neck toward the Lottery guests. Seizing the opportunity to group with the others, I quietly move forward, watching them follow in silent unison, doing their best not to get anyone's attention.

"Say it!" Xavier yells, his voice echoing through my mind, his anger forcing down any barriers once safeguarding his mind.

"I want to hear you say it to me, you spineless coward!" Xavier yells again, my hand touching my temple, realizing it's not just my mind.

His voice fills the arena like waves pounding relentlessly against the shore.

The glass, once trapping all the noise from the mindless chatter above, now lies broken beneath Adam's skull. Adam writhes in pain against the broken glass. The small cracks in its surface are enough to allow the conversations on the other side to reach us.

"I went against your orders," Adam cowers, his voice nearly to the point of a sob.

"Which one were you not supposed to touch?" Xavier questions, scanning our confused expressions down below.

Shakily, Adam touches the glass, his finger hovering above my position in the pit. Fallan stands only a few feet away, his arm outstretched toward me.

"And what did you do?" Xavier seethes, ignoring the stir of his men as they try to get his attention.

Xavier shrugs them off, his focus only on Adam.

"I touched-"

He has no time to finish that statement.

No time to react.

Never has the sound of a gunshot silenced a room of Untouchables so quickly.

The sound penetrates the air, his blood smearing the glass, nearly reaching Josh as he stands there in shock. Xavier's face is covered in blood and pieces of flesh. His hand releases Adam's lifeless body as it slumps to the ground beneath him. I feel Fallan's hand touch my arm. Our group clings tightly to one another, backing away as a unit. My only weapon is the knife still stuck in my side.

"Enough of this. I want her back up here," Xavier begins, his eyes growing wide as his hands clench his throat.

Slamming his fist against the glass, his knees buckle, his mouth unable to open.

I look at Fallan. He shakes his head in frustration.

"T- This isn't me," he whispers, his hand still clenching his wound, his collar still active.

"What the hell-" I begin, unable to get the statement out as I realize how close the Shifter had gotten to us.

Forcing us back with his arm, Fallan narrowly avoids a swipe to his chest. All of us are a tangled mess of sprawling limbs. Letting my back hit the wall closest to us, I glance up again, keeping the creature in my line of sight. The knife shifts in my side, each movement just as painful as the last.

Xavier's hands are pressed to the glass, his eyes wide with an expression I can't quite figure out.

"Fresh blood," the creature hisses through my mind. Its words are cold like ice.

Fallan yells out as he continues to try to tear off his collar. My eyes are still fixed on Xavier.

"Help me," I whisper faintly, the words leaving my mouth before I can process them. "Please," I finish, the plea in my voice, something I never thought would be directed at him again.

Even from here, I know he understands what I've asked of him.

Still, he remains motionless, holding his throat. My whole body goes taut as I watch him struggle to release the yell stuck in his throat.

Why does he stay kneeling? Why does he look so pained?

"Forest!" Fallan yells, shoving me out of the way of a sharp claw that was aimed directly at my exposed back.

Finally forcing my attention back to the pit, I see Fallan ready himself to fend off the creature. His stance is tottering; he won't be able to ignore the effects of his wound much longer.

"We need a weapon!" I yell, looking for anything that might be useful down here.

The creature moves closer, the scent of our blood like a beacon.

"There's nothing down here!" Kai yells, watching Hunter force Valerie against the dirty pit wall.

The creature's head cranes as it listens to our voices, smiling as if it is debating which one of us it will drain first. Fallan's body leans back into me, his footing less coordinated with each passing second.

"I can distract it long enough for one of you to run," he begins, ready to sacrifice himself for the rest of us.

The creature moves, deciding on Fallan.

Fuck.

Without thinking, I move forward, pulling the knife free from my side, crying out from the pain. The small trickle of blood contained by the blade is now spurting freely. I force Fallan back, keeping a close eye on the others around me. I lunge before the creature realizes what I'm doing, and the knife collides with its hand, slicing the skin. It roars, clutching the torn flesh. A shred of confidence eases the tightness in my chest, the distress in its recoiled body a reminder that this creature isn't invincible, and maybe we could get out of this alive.

"You vile-"

I swipe out again, at the same time focusing energy on breaking away the collar that confines me. The knife meets its side this time, its whole body shrinking back from me. Taking several steps back, it watches me. The onlookers behind the glass are frozen as they wait with bated breath to see who the victor of this deathmatch will be.

Xavier stands solemnly, his shoulders back as he watches the creature move. He looks ill. As ill as Fallan.

"Had enough?" I question the creature, the energy inside of me resurging to life.

"Your blood will paint the earth," it barks back, its teeth bared.

I feel it now. Not just my energy but Fallan's faltering vigor alongside Xavier's commanding force. Standing where I am now, the creature's energy also floods my veins. Its rampant thoughts of consuming my friends and myself are deafening.

What is this? How is this happening?

Feeling Xavier's energy pulsing through the air, I'm struck by a realization. I know why he looks so ill.

He's controlling this creature.

Kai moves toward Fallan to support his body as he continues to fight blacking out.

"Does he enjoy controlling you to make me suffer?" I question, staring down the beast, focusing my mind on its own. A way inside its mind presents itself.

"More than you know," it hisses, lunging toward me.

Stepping inside the opening of its mind, I seize my opportunity, pushing past the pain from my wound and the collar around my neck. Watching the creature's body go still, I push harder, infiltrating every corner of its mind. I feel the pure, unbridled power course through my veins as I push abilities to their limits. The potential of my Marked gifts is limitless, and suddenly I understand why my kind has been hunted for all these years.

"Bow," I snap, watching the creature's chin dive to the ground before my feet.

Its face scrapes the ground, its arms outstretched above its head. Pressed firmly against one another, its wrists are bound by an invisible force.

"You are much more than he expected," **it** hisses, my eyes darting to Xavier.

There is a sudden liveliness in his demeanor, his hands clenched as his energy swirls around the creature. If he's controlling it, he struggles at this moment. Narrowing my eyes at him, I fight against his hold on the creature. Our minds battle for purchase in the Shifter's head, one fighting to claim victory over the other.

Fallan can hardly stand, and Kai is close to collapse as well. Valerie can scarcely take in a full breath, and Hunter is almost to his breaking point, his hands clenched tightly to his sides, his face stuck in a silent scream as he rocks back and forth on his heels.

This is my last chance. If Xavier wins, we're prisoners to a life that is guaranteed to expire years before we deserve to see its end.

"What will you do, Little Dove?" he taunts within my mind, my heart racing at his voice's sudden presence in the cavern of my thoughts.

"Bring this whole fucking society to its knees."

I wait for his power to permeate the space around us, bracing for whatever blow comes next.

But it never comes.

I snap my eyes at him, wanting to finish this, but the look on his face leaves me bemused. He nods in recognition or approval. I'm not sure which.

"Bring it all down."

My fingers wrap around the abrasive metal of my collar as my gaze falls on the writhing creature before me. An idea enters my mind, one I share directly in its thoughts. Clicking my tongue and easing up on my hold, the Shifter pulls its head away from the ground, looking at me for confirmation of what I'd just commanded it to do. Pointing to my neck, I force its hand forward, letting its claw linger near my throat.

"Break it."

The Shifter slashes its talon over the metal, and the collar clatters on the ground. My limbs tingle at the sudden return of energy flooding through me. People begin to panic above, their glasses falling free from their grasp. Still, Xavier remains unmoving, watching us with what looks like some twisted expression of pride.

"Forest-" Fallan gasps, my hand reaching out for him, forcing his collar away from his neck with a wave of my wrist. Relief washes over his expression, the fire of his resolve enough to restore some of his energy so he can withstand his brutal injuries for a little longer.

"Are you hungry?" I question coldly to the creature, both my palms clenched.

The glass above begins to break. With each exhale of my lungs, another crack appears in the divider between those who put us down here and the beasts below.

"Terribly," it hisses, both Fallan and I smiling at the response.

"Then feed," I order, looking at the petrified onlookers above.

The Shifter takes the command without hesitation, its talons breaching the wall, scaling up and onto the broken pane where Adam took his last breath. Shards of glass fly through the air as it breaks its way through. Focusing on the huddle of Officials trying to make their way to the bottom of the pit, I watch them aim toward the creature, readying to bring it down. Raising my hand, I focus on my desire for them to feel pain. A mix of screams or panicked movements come from above. None of the elites are able to protect themselves from the Shifter. I help Hunter support Fallan's body around his waist, Kai beside us carrying Valerie. We move to the exit, stepping over the fallen bodies of every Official whose mind I had turned to mush.

The Shifter devours anyone it can, filling the space with screams loud enough to burst eardrums. More of the glass panels surrounding the top of the pit begin to break away bit by bit. Fallan's pained groans carve into my chest as we stay on course, his wound still heavily bleeding.

The blood from my own wound trails down my leg, its sticky warmth uncomfortable. The adrenaline coursing through my veins masks some of the pain, but I don't know how long that will last. The pit is in shambles, surrounded by the stench of death.

"We need to make a break for it," Hunter cries, all of our attention toward the exit.

I look up one last time and see red staining almost every pane of glass. Xavier stands quietly in an open threshold between the pit and the event space, sipping his champagne as chaos unfolds around him. There is no fear in his expression, only an air of satisfaction.

He's the very reason I've lost so much. Even if I leave now, I can't promise myself that I won't come back to kill him. The only part of me that could have cared for him died the moment I watched the light leave my father's eyes.

I force the thought toward him, his eyebrows scrunching in betrayal at my admission.

The Shifter lowers its head at Xavier's presence. My stomach is unsettled at how easily the creature submits to his will, my own Hold over the creature broken.

This whole time, Xavier has had the upper hand. He could've overpowered me easily. Why allow me to have control of his pet for so long?

Kai tugs on my tattered shirt, Fallan's eyes now struggling to stay open.

The sound of the heavy-footed Officials flooding the space above us is distant. My heart races at the thought of what's to come. Those who weren't ravaged by the creature clutch their heads, the chips behind their ears flashing with the faint glow of a green light.

"**Run,**" Xavier whispers softly through my headspace. So softly that I might have thought my blood loss was making me hallucinate.

But this isn't just his voice. I feel his energy forcing me forward, moving my legs with renewed strength.

"***Trust no one.***" His hand clutches his throat.

Our hastened steps turn into a dead sprint, each one of us carrying the other, our strides frantic and uncoordinated. My head, once able to move freely, stays forward. I can't even turn back to assess the carnage we're leaving behind. Every fiber of my being is forced forward by Xavier's daunting power.

We continue barreling down the corridor where the creatures had made their way to the pit. I see the light at the end of the tunnel, my lungs gasping for air.

Around us, the air becomes staticky, the charge wrapping around us like a protective shield. The feeling is familiar, one I've felt in Xavier's presence as he uses his gifts to move around through empty space. With no warning, Fallan's eyes suddenly fly open, and his energy surges into the space around us. He wraps his arm around my waist, beckoning Hunter and Kai into the space of his other outstretched arm. Kai hugs Valerie close to his body, and they tuck in around us. Our bodies dissolve like mist and get sucked into the very fabric of existence.

One moment, we are clouded in darkness; the next, we face the ward shielding the Unfortunate sector from the ash lands beyond.

We've materialized directly in front of the tear in the ward.

He's brought us here for a reason.

It's our exit to the outside world.

Our one way out.

CHAPTER SIXTY

KAIDEN

In the blink of an eye, the space around us shifts, becoming something else entirely. The musky smell of the cells and the heavy scent of iron that formed from the blood-stained walls fall away. The familiar stench of the Unfortunate sector fills my nose, something I never thought I'd find any form of comfort in.

Barely managing to stop Hunter and Valerie from falling over, Fallan grasps Forest, his mouth leaving a trail of blood across her front in a cough that no doubt signifies the severity of his wounds. She stands dazed, her blood coating both of them in large splotches. Forcing himself onto his feet, he looks to her in a plea, his eyes darting to the poorly guarded, ash-ridden opening in a ward I thought was impenetrable.

"He Winnowed us here," Forest says in a gasp, giving a name to the hidden ability Fallan had utilized with what little energy he had left. To our advantage, many of the Officials had gone to the Lottery to claim some time off from their duties around New Haven, meaning the already poorly guarded sector is that much more free of security. A few displaced Unfortunates watch us with wide eyes. Some whisper in fear, labeling our group as marauders, pointing frantically to our warrants plastered on every digital board in sight. The word "Marked" resides beneath Forest and Fallan's pictures—a word I would have considered vile, but now our only means of escaping any of this.

"It's getting harder to breathe," Fallan whispers. His skin is pallid, and his expression is labored as he struggles to keep his arms around us.

The hand of death wraps around his throat.

Listening to the growing shouts of other citizens as they take notice of our presence, I frantically look around, weighing our options.

"We have no other choice, Kai," Forest whispers, looking at the tear, her fears painted across her face.

Fallan faces my sister and grabs her face in his hands. He swallows, gathering the strength to speak.

"Are you with me?"

The question is urgent, her eyebrows furrowed with concern.

"Always," she whispers, her eyes hazy with emotion.

Pressing his lips to hers, his expression remains a mix of admiration and fear. With a quivering lip, she breaks the kiss, leaving her forehead resting against his for a few moments longer. A fear of this being their last moment to share with one another is a thought I know consumes her right now.

Hunter grasps my hand, and Valerie does the same.

I scan Hunter's dark eyes, pulling him closer, his body pressing close to mine as we shake in each other's embrace. I feel his warmth flood through me, the same warmth my sister has told me she feels each time she's near Fallan.

The feelings I have for Hunter have deep roots in my chest, and I'm not sure what that means for the dynamic between us. I'll have to unpack this later if we survive long enough for me to think about it again. Clinging onto both of their hands, I keep my focus on Hunter.

"Let's move!" Forest urges, slinging Fallan's arm over her shoulders.

Filled with the need to keep them all safe, I follow my sister's command, forcing Hunter and Valerie along with me, burying my fears of what lies beyond the ash lands along with every rational thought of self-preservation.

Faintly, I hear her voice, unable to stop my attention from moving behind me, my sister's soon follows.

Standing in the distance, I see her cry out, her hands covering her mouth, screaming at us to run. She holds one of the Official's pistols, her hands shaky, bruised, and covered in wounds that indicate she's been in a fight. We don't pause. Forest continues moving, her eyes watery, locked dead on my mother's figure as she uses herself as a human barrier between the Officials and us. With a vengeance written in her expression, she fires round after round with precision. My mother takes down several approaching Officials, holding back what reinforcements could have stopped us had they gotten any closer.

"Don't come back!" my mother screams, both Forest and I unable to stop from flinching, my sister's feet coming to a standstill. Moving past the invisible barrier of the ward, I inhale my first breath of rebellion, the ash making the air dense, my first taste of freedom, not the sweetest. I cough uncontrollably alongside the others, reaching back for my sister's hand as she stays glued to the threshold between our old life and an unknown one. Helping me hold Fallan, Valerie and Hunter scream for Forest, my focus on my sister and my mother.

"Forest-"

"I can't lose them both!" Forest screams. "Go without me, I'll find you-"

My mother's figure stills, her screams silenced with a sudden jolt to her body. My heart shatters as she looks at us, her clean palm now tarnished by the blood seeping from her lower stomach. Letting out a silent scream, her knees hit the ground, a wave of black-clad Officials approaching her from behind in the dozens.

Forest backs away, crossing the barrier into the ash lands, her eyes void of any emotion.

Grabbing Fallan, she holds her lower stomach, joining us in the cloud of thick ash. A stare so distant from reality masks her face.

Lowering her eyes, Forest faces ahead, determined to move forward into the desolate terrain ahead.

Like a warrior moving steadfast into the fray, she prowls forward silently, her shoulders stiff and stride steady.

There is no more time for tears. No more energy for regrets and what-ifs.

All that remains is the barren land in front of us.

And the hope that that's not all that remains.

CHAPTER SIXTY-ONE

KATIANA

"They made it past the ash, sir," two Officials quietly utter, both their heads down, unable to look Xavier in the face.

Xavier watches me, and I know his patience is threadbare. He waves his hand over the wound in my stomach to check how severe it was. He'd requested it be bandaged as soon as I was dragged into his office.

My wrists are bound, his knee pressed to my thighs, keeping me planted firmly in the seat he'd forced me into. Unable to look away, I glance at the body covered up on the floor next to his desk, my stomach churning at the way the shoelaces are double laced.

Just like my Andrew ties them.

"You're telling me Katiana's little diversion was the reason that five people were able to slip away from dozens of Officials just like that?" Xavier questions. Both men swallow nervously, unable to keep their composure.

"The Markswood boy Winnowed, sir, and we'd thought you-"

Xavier is away from me in a matter of seconds, his hand wrapped around the man's throat, forcing his neck down into his desk.

It's not just Unfortunate and Marked blood Xavier has spilled. Anyone who got in his way was at risk. He has no side to which he truly stands loyal to.

"You thought I'd what?" Xavier questions, his hand wavering over the man's forehead, smiling as he siphons the man's thoughts

"You thought I'd be stronger than her little boy toy," Xavier says after a few moments. No one else would dare answer him out loud, even though it didn't matter; it was pointless to hide anything from him.

"I didn't think-" the man begins, ready to beg for mercy.

"You did," Xavier snaps, twisting the Official's neck, plastering on a fake pout as the man slumps to the floor.

Not daring to move a muscle, I watch the other Official begin to shake, unable to hide his trembling hands as he shifted awkwardly on his feet.

"A tragedy occurred tonight. A group of deviant, nasty Marked, utilizing their heinous gifts to disrupt the order I've created," Xavier begins, mocking the irony in his statement. "I want every chip on every Official and citizen activated. As far as they know, Forest Blackburn and everyone associated with her are now public enemies. If they are spotted within our sector again or someone so much as utters her or her friend's names anywhere in New Haven, I want them brought to me immediately. As far as anyone knows, they are murderers and insurgents that threaten the sanctity of our society," Xavier says, casually scanning his nail bed for some sign of imperfection.

The man who remains isn't just any Official. No. Ryan was very special to the Order. This is the man who helped create the chips. As far as I know, he oversees all updates and patches to the devices, working in seclusion, guarded heavily by security at all times.

"As for the chips that remain in her companions, sir?" Ryan questions.

Xavier smiles wickedly. His legs crossed, his thumb trailing over his lip, licking clean the blood that stains his skin.

"Keep them on. I want to keep tabs on where my little Blackburn ends up," Xavier says, his possessive claim on Forest enough to make my blood boil.

"Anything else, Commander?"

"That will be all," Xavier says, focusing his attention back on me, dismissing Ryan with a wave.

He bows, stepping over the body of the man he'd come in with, leaving much quicker than he had arrived. As the door swings open, a gust of air billows into the office, and I recoil at the slight adjustment of the white tarp concealing the body underneath. I hold back the stifled gag that makes its way up my throat. My husband's face is ashen, all life drained from his eyes.

My heart shatters, the shards slicing my insides into shreds. My hand flies up, cupping my mouth so tightly I can feel my nails dig into the soft flesh of my cheek.

Xavier glances at Andrew, his hand waving, forcing back the tarp to reveal his body even more. I ready myself to look away, feeling my body slam back down into the chair, forced down by my thighs with Xaver's knees. Drawing in a deep breath, he grabs my chin, forcing me to take in my husband's lifeless body.

"Funny how easily a life can be taken, isn't it?" Xavier questions, clenching my chin tighter. "How easily it be manipulated," he finishes, his expression filled with admiration.

"You fucking vile creature-"

"Katiana. No need for cruel language," Xavier beckons, clamping his hand over my mouth. "I'd hate to have to kill you, too, and given your similarities to her, I know I'd find it that much more unpleasant," he hisses, his fixation on my daughter something I don't understand.

"What do you want with her? What did you want with us? Why murder my husband? He was like you!"

"You see, if I were able to tell you, life would be much easier for me," he begins, touching his bruised throat. "But sadly, you ensured that wouldn't be possible-"

"I have no idea who you are," I plea, his eyes narrowing at the response.

"You think it's that simple?" Xavier questions, lowering his hand from my chin, his knees easing up from my legs. "If anything, I'm being lenient after what you did to my family," Xavier says, his jaw clenched in frustration.

"Your family? But you're from-"

"Beyond the ward? Yes, my family was from beyond the ward, sent here with a promise of a brighter future. Instead, we hand my sister off to you for a checkup, and next thing I know, my parents are being forced to forget she and I ever existed as they hauled off her lifeless body and locked me away to become their personal government poster child," he hisses, my mind racing through every Expulsion I have regrettably committed.

One child sticks out to me.

The girl with the blonde curls.

"Your sister was Lily," I recall, his face tense at saying her name out loud.

"Lily Evermoore," I clarify, his head gently nodding.

"That was my last name before they changed it to Hayes," he admits.

"They?" I question, his head gently shaking.

"You really don't remember?" Xavier pushes, my eyes glancing back to my husband.

"You harassed my family and murdered my husband over a routine Expulsion carried out by a society that you now run?"

"I did not kill Andrew, Katiana."

The lives he's stolen mercilessly fill my head. My husband's final moments are ones I can only imagine were filled with fear. Kicking him away from me, he stumbles back, the outrage I feel taking over me.

"I don't fucking believe you! Your word means nothing to me, you piece of shit. Look me in the eyes and know hers will always be filled with as much hate for you as mine have now-"

He grabs my hair, forcing my head back to look at him. He remains gentle in his touch, making sure not to pull too abrasively.

"Maybe you're right," he begins, his eyes assessing me closely. "But I can promise you I will see to it that she knows-"

"That's enough, Xavier," an unfamiliar voice bellows, his hand instinctively going around his throat, his body jolting back and into the edge of his desk.

Scanning the room rapidly, his hands claw at the new bruises forming around his skin.

An invisible force tears away at his shirt. Multiple lesions work up the Commander's front and sides. His head is craned back to stifle a silent scream. Unable to speak, I glance around with him, my eyes landing on the robed figures looming in a passageway hidden along the wall in the back of the room.

The figure in the middle stands out from the others. Unlike the gold masks the elites wear at the Lottery, this figure wears a haunting silver face covering with no distinguishable eye or mouth indentations. The voice from the figure in the center is eerie, something otherworldly. Silently, the pair next to the figure raise their heads. Their eyes are lifeless, their mouths bound by twine, and their wrists secured in shackles.

Unable to look away, I watch as the bound figures move closer to Xavier, running their long nails down his front, creating fresh cuts. Still, Xavier remains silent. His hand pounds the desk in frustration.

"You've created quite the mess, boy," the robed figure in the silver mask mutters.

Xavier moans in pain. His torment is unbearable, the pain in his voice something I've never witnessed. It's as if years of agony hide in the noises escaping from him. The ghoulish figures finally stop their assault and return to their spots next to the figure in silver.

Xavier glances down at the cuts and takes a deep breath. The figure raises a hand and waves a ring-adorned finger in front of him at Xavier.

"You've done enough. Consider me letting you have alone time with Katiana justice for your sister."

Writhing in my seat, the figure finally looks at me, urging one of the others to pull up a chair. Moving a stool in front of me, their movements are silent.

"Don't be startled by my Paradox's appearances. They are in a state of meta-morphosis, you see. The transition from Undesirable to human is not pretty," the masked figure says. They glide across the floor to take a seat in front of me, their movements refined and graceful as they sit down.

"Undesirable?" I question.

"Shifter," Xavier clarifies, keeping his eyes on the figure before me.

"Yes. Shifter. That is what the people in the mouse trap call the Marked needing guidance back to the light," the figure says, barely acknowledging Xavier's tone.

"Who the hell are you?" I question, desperately wanting to rip away the mask.

"I would keep your hands where they are, Katiana. Last time someone tried to take a look beneath this mask, it cost them more than they were willing to bargain," the figure says, looking back at Xavier, no doubt hiding a smile beneath the silver.

"Pity you think so cruelly of me, Xavier. You'd be nothing without my guid-ance," the figure says, his Paradoxes quietly awaiting his next orders.

"What do you want?" I ask, hoping at least one of my questions will be an-swered.

"Up until very recently, I thought what I wanted was control. Control of what lies within this ward and all that lies beyond the walls. However, given the chaos that exists beyond this ward, starting small within this society's barriers seemed more attainable. Infiltrate from the inside, spreading like roots to a tree," the figure says, tapping their fingers along their knee. "Given Xavier's eagerness to serve me in efforts to repay his debt, nothing seemed more perfect. Find me my Marked, and expel the weak," the figure continues, Xavier's head hanging in shame.

"So what? You command a ring of Marked lunatics who have no social skills and take over society like tyrants?" I push. A hint of a smile hides in Xavier's expression.

"I command, yes. The Marked, the Undesirables, weak-minded men and women, like those twins your children loved so dearly," They continue, glancing back at Xavier. "Or simply weak men who need to know a little pain."

"Power and control. It's what I wanted-"

"And I gave it to you."

"You did, and a lot of it, might I add," the figure says, clasping their thin hands together. "But, sadly, where I'd initially planned to kill you as a message to convince your daughter back so I may have her beneath my thumb, tutoring her like I have Xavier, it would seem things have changed, Mrs. Blackburn-" the figure begins.

"Changed?" Xavier questions. Genuine discomfort lingers in his tone.

"I don't think I stuttered," the figure retorts, firmly clasping their hands.

"In what way have they changed?" Xavier asks, his arms crossed along his front, adding to his bulkiness.

The figure in silver snaps their fingers toward the Paradoxes. One of the haunting figures shuffles forward in their robe. The Paradox pulls out a small device from beneath the soft material of their robes. The technology is newer than anything I've seen. The screen illuminates, and I wait anxiously, trying to understand what it's for.

"While your daughter's boy-toy was busy Winnowing her and her friends out of this facility, I had a few of my people linger behind to evaluate her blood sample closely. I had a feeling the data you recorded in her file would not be entirely accurate. Given the extent her father went to keep her file hidden, from even Xavier, my curiosities were piqued," the figure says, glancing over the screen. "Do you know how many genetic variations the Marked can have, Mrs. Blackburn?"

"Five," Xavier answers for me, his eyes narrowed. "The most gifts a single Marked has carried that we know of for certain is three, but a select few may carry four."

"Like me," the figure states, tapping its fingers along the screen and motioning toward the blonde.

I look over Xavier, finally piecing together the robed figure's need to control him. Xavier's abilities are much more extensive than anyone knew.

"Well, you didn't think I'd keep him just because of his pretty face, did you?" the figure asks, my hand trailing to my temple.

"Can you read my thoughts?"

"Better than you'd think. I can read the thoughts of anyone I have touched," they sigh. "I've yet to meet anyone else who shares that burden of having so many coexisting gifts to pull upon as I do. It's quite the burden," they continue, flipping the screen around to face me.

Xavier looks at the screen, his eyes growing wider the more he reads.

"That is, until your daughter," the robed figure finishes, my eyes looking over the information on the device's screen.

I see her picture. Five boxes surround her face, each filled to the brim in color. A bold **20%** fills each box, each number adding to the **100%** at the top of the screen.

"That's not possible," Xavier begins, urgently grabbing the device. Looking over the numbers himself, his expression darkens.

"Yet the evidence is right there," the figure says, Xavier's head shaking.

"You said-" Xavier begins, unable to get out another word as the figure raises their hand.

"I said she could be taught when her gifts remained at a level below mine. She now holds a strength no one has seen before. That sort of power cannot walk this earth and coincide with the empire I've created."

"What is she?" I ask quietly. It takes no mind reader to know just how little I want that question answered.

"She holds all of the Marked abilities," Xavier silently whispers, his gaze set forward into empty space.

"The Apparatus.... The fall of humanity," the robed figure says, my eyes panning to Andrew.

So many times, he had spoken of all that she could do. He never feared who or what she was.

"Or the rise," I whisper without thinking, my watery gaze still set on my fallen husband.

The robed figure's shoulders are back, their body rigid at what I'm insinuating. Xavier looks at me with regret. In many ways, it feels like there is so much he wants to say. But he remains silent, moving his long fingers down his neck.

"Regardless of your beliefs on what Forest's gifts may mean, her abilities make her a liability," the figure begins, glancing at their Paradoxes. "Which is why I must retrieve her."

Xavier shoves me down by the shoulder when I attempt to stand. Crouching beside me, he wraps his arm around my front, holding me still.

"You're making it worse," he quietly whispers, holding back my head to watch the figure before me.

The figure scoffs, twirling the device in their hand.

"You won't touch my children-"

"You don't get a say, Mrs. Blackburn," the figure starts, his tone light and full of excitement. "But you will help me find your daughter, and in return, I will not lay a single finger on your son's head," they say as if sparing either of their lives is chivalrous.

"Once I have executed Forest-"

"Executed?"

"Did you really think she'd get to live, Xavier?" the figure questions, tapping their temple with a shake of their head. "How foolish. Even for you," they taunt. Xavier's nails dig into my arm at his words.

"She won't submit to you," I begin, cut off by the sound of their menacing laugh.

"She'll have to," Xavier and the figure say in unison. The figure crosses its arms.

"Or else what?" I say, leaning forward with disgust. Xavier slams me down, his hold uncomfortable.

"Or else I rip our Kai's throat and make her watch. I'll deliver her pieces of the ones she loves and torment her until she goes insane. I suggest you close your mouth before I regret my decision to keep you alive," Xavier snaps, a sudden shift in the way he speaks. I stay silent, looking at the nod of approval from the figure in silver.

"At least you've convinced *her* you meant that," the figure says toward Xavier, circling us in small steps. "Either way, you both play a very critical role in Forest returning to me."

"Do your plans always work?" I hiss, looking at the shambles of the office space, my hand outreached toward Andrew.

"There is no perfection without failure, Katiana," they say, a burning thought lingering in my mind.

"Why keep me alive? Why not have me killed like you had Xavier do to my husband?" I question, feeling a shift behind me at the mention of my husband's death.

"You both have no clue how Andrew passed, do you?" the figure taunts. "That must be so very frustrating," they continue, finally sitting at the large desk, ignoring Xavier's scowl.

"You're alive, Mrs. Blackburn, for a reason far greater than you'd be able to comprehend." The figure looks at Xavier with clasped hands. "Forest Blackburn will fall. You both will ensure that happens," they finish. I see Xavier shifting again out of the corner of my eye.

"Do you question my judgment, Xavier? Have I assumed too quickly you are as neutral as you have led me to believe?"

"Forest Blackburn and her family are single-handedly the reason my life has been nothing but torture for years. If someone will drag her back here, it will be me. You may deliver the final blow, but what I do to her in the meantime is up to me. You owe me that much," Xavier says, his tone demanding.

The figure touches their temple. Holding his ground, Xavier watches them, both hands clenched tightly.

"So much hate in that mind of yours. To think I sensed sympathy for a few fleeting moments," the figure says, clapping Xavier's back.

Xavier lowers his head, a bow meant to show respect.

"My fealty lies with your Order and all who have died to uphold it," Xavier says in a tone that tells me he has said that very statement more times than he can count.

"And my reign will continue to reward your fealty until all your privileges..." the figure begins, tapping Xavier's throat, "...are allowed to return."

The figure holds the top of Xavier's head. He remains bowed, his eyes plastered on the floor.

"Find my Apparatus, boy."

He nods to the figure as he moves away. As he passes me, I drag him down to my level, our noses inches apart. I think of the moments Xavier and Forest shared when they thought no one was looking— the way he watched her move through a room.

"All of this? Was all of what you did for her because of some master scheme?"

"If I had it my way," he whispers once more, his tone entirely foreign. "I would have slit her throat the first time I met her," Xavier finishes, pulling away from me.

Rolling back his shoulders, he gives the room one last look, lingering on my face before pulling on his typical charming mask again and breaking orders at the first brainwashed Official he lays eyes on.

Feeling something warm between my legs, I glance down at my thighs, feeling the warmth pool as the smell of iron fills my nose. Crossing my legs, I try to hide the embarrassing stain, unsure how long it's been since I've been able to change the underwear lining that I typically use to manage my monthly burden.

"You are still fertile?" the robed figure asks, my heart racing at the excitement that laces the question.

Without answering, I stay still, using my hands to cover what I can.

Taking a step toward me, the gleam of the silver mask is nearly blinding.

"Looks like my council has more than one thing to rejoice."

"And what would that be?" I snap, terrified of the answer.

"With impending death lingering," the figure says, looking over my daughter's picture once more, only to land on my husband's lifeless body. "The possibility for new life is a gift," they finish, looking down at my shaking hands.

"I won't help you breed your delusions," I hiss, my voice course.

They move closer to the hidden entryway.

"I'll be seeing you, Mrs. Blackburn," the figure says, their hands deep in their robe pockets. Trailing behind the figure, the Paradoxes give me one last look, closing the door with a soft thud.

Lingering in the room's overbearing silence, I rise on shaky feet, finally allowing myself to look at Andrew fully. My legs give out the closer I get to his body. Crumpling to my knees, I join my husband's still figure. The tears for all that I have lost finally paint my cheeks. Wrapping my arms around his cold neck, I sob into the empty cavern of his chest.

All of this loss. All of this pain.

For what?

A sliver of light spans across the floorboards, adding color to Andrew's pale skin. Standing in the doorway, Xavier watches as I fill the space with my grief. With hazy eyes, I turned to him, my lip wobbling, my heart broken.

"What the fuck could you possibly want from me now?" I scream hatefully; his eyes just as emotionless as they were a few moments ago.

Any sign of humanity within the man left when the figure in the silver mask entered the room.

"I'm supposed to take you to your holding quarters," Xavier begins, looking at me with a sigh.

There's a pause, my body unable to move away once he raises his hand. Grazing my cheek with his fingertips, his look of indifference melts away, replaced with a fleeting glimpse of sorrow to match my own.

"You look like her when you cry," he whispers, a well of emotion threatening to break free from him.

He retracts his hand with a painful groan, grabbing his neck and clenching his fists as tightly as he can. Forcing his mask of apathy is back in place, any sign of emotion slips away, leaving as quickly as it came.

"I do hope she believes in God, Katiana," Xavier begins. The mention of the old world's deity is sudden.

"Why?" I question shakily, unsure if I want the answer.

"Because God is the only one that could save her now."

Silence blankets the room, my heart thundering in my chest.

"I'll give you a few more moments to wallow in the grief your *love* has caused you," he snaps, looking at Andrew with a nod of his head.

With that, he moves away quietly, closing the door, leaving me to process my pain in solitude and silence once more.

CHAPTER SIXTY-TWO

FOREST

My legs burn from each uneven step on the rough terrain, the debris hidden under the ash making it more challenging to maintain stable footing.

Fallan's body rams into my own, his balance lost after the first mile of our run. I'd channeled some of my energy reserves into him through our connection, worried he wouldn't be able to make it far enough outside the city for us to hide safely. Losing too much blood, my ability to force away the ash with what energy I have left is becoming impossible. All of us go through fits of coughing, doing the best we can to force air into our lungs full of toxic debris.

"There's nothing out here!" Hunter yells, his voice scratchy from the ash coating the inside of his throat.

"We have to keep moving," I begin, listening for the distant sound of the shouting men we thought we'd heard during our first few minutes past the ward. Now everything seems silent, only us traveling in this barren wasteland. I shove down the thoughts of my mother, my grasp on Fallan so tight I've nearly broken his skin.

"Just a mile or so more-"

Kai's knees meet the ground, his head nearly hitting the dirt had Hunter not been so close. I reached my hand out to him, instinctively focusing on keeping him upright long enough for Hunter and Valerie to kneel next to him.

"What's wrong with him?" I question in a panic, bracing myself for the pain my knees feel once Fallan's full weight finally sags into me.

Unable to hold his eyes open, Fallan drags me down, his blood loss too significant to keep moving. His hands clutch me tightly.

"I don't know.... He was fine," Hunter begins. "His heart is still beating," he says in relief. Valerie's gasps of concern slowly turn into sobs I know she's been holding in since we left New Haven.

I try to think through my heavily crowded mind. Fallan grasps me in a weak hold, and my hands gently reach to tap his cheeks.

"Fallan, I need you to get up," I whisper, my body leaning forward, my hair framing both of our faces. Pressing my lips to his forehead, his eyes open slightly, a small broken smile consuming his beaten features.

"Your eyes are like fire," he mutters incoherently.

Looking at my reflection in his eyes, I see my glowing irises.

Even with that other part of me, my strength is not enough.

"Forest, what do we do?" Hunter questions in a panic, coughing once more, unable to get another word out.

"I need to give Fallan some of my blood," I begin, ready to slice my palm. "It's the only way he can recover enough so we can keep moving and get somewhere safe," I continue, looking around frantically for something sharp.

Dizzy and unnerved, I sift through the dirt.

"Then what? You both drag Kai through the ash?" Hunter questions. I was irritated by his tone.

"It's either that or die out here, suffocated by ash! Now, stop talking and find me a rock I can cut my hand with," I snap, his hand wrapping around my wrist.

Finally opening his eyes, Fallan moves me closer, his head barely raised as he scans my expression.

"Does he know?" Fallan questions, my head shaking uncontrollably. His eyes roll back seconds later, his hand letting go and falling limp at his side. I lean over his chest, distraught to find his heartbeat becoming weaker. My panic is now nothing short of a full-fledged hysteria. Digging through the ground, I finally turn behind me when I continue to come up empty-handed.

"God damn it, Hunter-"

I pause; my throat dry, unable to find the words.

Valerie, Hunter, and Kai remain still, each one of them face down in the Earth, their bodies encased in something ethereal, the ash on their skin giving way to delicate tendrils of power that shimmer with a faint, spectral glow. Circling them in pulsating movements, thick white smoke breaches the air, silently filling our noses in orderless waves. Looking around, I try to make out a figure, my eyes unable to adjust to the polluted air around us.

"Fallan?" I begin, shaking him as hard as I can.

He remains still; his heart unable to support him in his current state.

"You're okay!" I yell, turning back to beg my companions to help me with him.

Standing in the fog, the smoke plumes around a group of unknown figures. Long, thick leather coats trail down their bodies. Their feet are shod in sturdy, metal-toed boots meant to protect against the hidden hazards beneath the ash. They wear gas masks, concealing their faces. Their hoods remain up, making it even harder to distinguish them. Slowly, I push myself up to stand in front of my companions, my foot back, braced to defend my brother, Fallan, and our friends against whatever attack comes next.

"One of them is still awake," a female voice says, their gloved hand pointing to me, amusement lingering in her tone.

"I'd say she's probably the Marked he told us to be mindful of," another voice mutters, a male voice much older than anyone in our group.

"Wasn't there supposed to be two Marked in their huddle? Why is she the only one up?" the female voice questions, my knees shaking as I finally allow myself to give in to my fatigue.

"Marked or not, the gas should have taken her out," the older male voice pushes, looming closer to me, but my body is too weak, and I stumble forward.

Looking behind him to the last masked figure in the group, I find a pair of familiar eyes.

"Aaron?" I question the image of Valerie's fiery-haired cousin filling my mind.

"Are you sure these are the people Elyon wants from that cesspool you call a society?" the older male asks, Aaron's head slowly nodding.

"They are right where Fallan promised they'd be," Aaron starts, his eyes darting to me. "Now, are you done questioning me so I can get my *family* the medical attention they need?" Aaron questions angrily.

Grasping the older male's pant leg, I try to force him away from me, letting my hand clasp Fallan's still one.

Faint, but there, his energy weakly moves through him.

I sense the man's smile hiding beneath the mask as he glances down at me.

"A lot of people have put their lives on the line to ensure you made it to us," the man says, cocking his head as he speaks. Reaching beneath his coat, he raises the back of a long-barreled gun, one much larger than any pistol I've ever seen.

"Welcome to the resistance, Ms. Blackburn," he begins. "Sadly, you haven't earned enough of my trust to get to stay awake."

Unable to react fast enough, the butt of the man's gun collides with my temple, my body unwilling and unable to support my consciousness any longer.

Meeting the ground with a thud, the pain leaves me completely as I drift into nothingness.

I find comfort in being surrounded by such a peaceful darkness. The silence blankets me as my worries dissolve into nothingness.

Falling deeper into the seclusion of my own mind, the world around me falls away, and I find myself hollowed out, missing the chaotic piece of me.

No more fear.

No more death.

At this moment, there is nothing but beautiful silence.

Fragments of me are lost to the past in everything I *was*,

Shadows surround all that I have now **become.**

End Book 1

Acknowledgements

The desire to share this series with the world has been a longstanding aspiration that defies expression. From my earliest recollections, writing emerged as the sole refuge capable of diverting my attention from the harsh realities that loomed when my mind wasn't engrossed in literature. Academic pursuits, in contrast, felt imposed rather than an intuitive path for swift comprehension. Despite earnest attempts to navigate conventional career paths, I encountered recurrent impasses.

During my teenage years, a breakthrough occurred on writing platforms such as AO3 and Wattpad, where I began sharing my work with a wider audience. To my astonishment, the positive reception transformed a modest passion into an abiding fascination, propelling me toward novel writing and an academic pursuit to teach the very literature that had rescued me from life's darker moments.

Acknowledging that my current position owes much to the unwavering support of my father and husband is paramount. Their encouragement, coupled with steadfast guidance through bouts of self-doubt, has been instrumental. My family, in essence, emerged as the cornerstone of this journey, steadfastly championing my dreams even during moments of imminent resignation. Gratitude is also extended to my closest confidante (you know who you are), whose unwavering support has been a constant, transcending geographical distances.

Reflecting on the trajectory of my life, there was never a juncture where I envisioned my current circumstances. Writing, an enduring escape, has become not just my refuge but a medium through which I aspire to provide solace for others. I also would like to thank my editor, Cait, for taking on my projects despite how daunting the task is. I appreciate you more than you know.

-Katerina

ABOUT THE AUTHOR
Katerina St Clair

YOURLOCALWRITERZ

KATERINASTCLAIRAUTHOR

WWW.KATERINA
STCLAIR.COM

KATERINA ST CLAIR IS AN ACCOMPLISHED AUTHOR CURRENTLY PURSUING AN ACADEMIC PATH TOWARD BECOMING A CREATIVE WRITING INSTRUCTOR AT THE HIGHER EDUCATION LEVEL. RESIDING IN THE MIDWEST WITH HER PARTNER AND HER BELOVED LABRADOR SONS, SHE IS A DEDICATED PROFESSIONAL WITH A MULTIFACETED LIFESTYLE. WHEN NOT IMMERSED IN ORCHESTRATING HER NEXT LITERARY ENDEAVOR WHILE ENJOYING MUSIC, SHE FINDS SOLACE IN CULINARY PURSUITS OR INDULGES IN EXTENSIVE READING FROM HER EVER-EXPANDING TO-BE-READ LIST. HER LITERARY PREFERENCES GRAVITATE TOWARDS NARRATIVES CHARACTERIZED BY UNFORESEEN TWISTS, A QUALITY SHE ENDEAVORS TO INFUSE INTO EACH OF HER NOVELS.